MW00528116

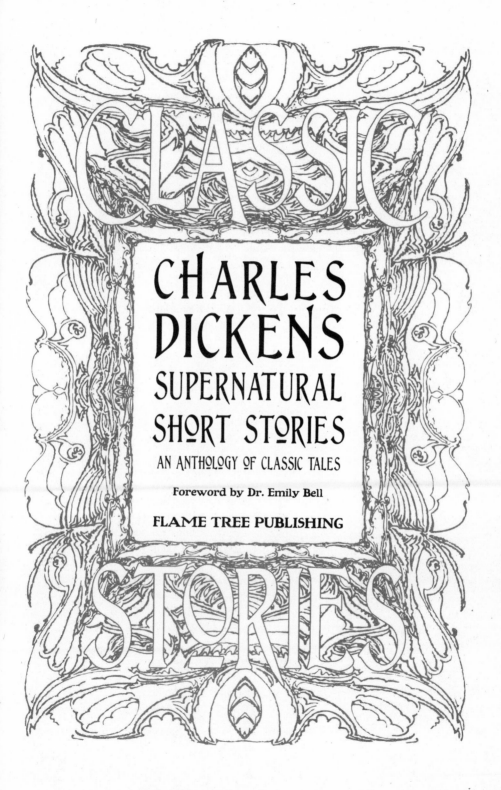

# CLASSIC

# CHARLES DICKENS

## SUPERNATURAL SHORT STORIES

### AN ANTHOLOGY OF CLASSIC TALES

Foreword by Dr. Emily Bell

**FLAME TREE PUBLISHING**

# STORIES

This is a FLAME TREE Book

Publisher & Creative Director: Nick Wells
Senior Project Editor: Josie Karani

Publisher's Note: Due to the historical nature of classic fiction, we're aware that there
may be some language used which has the potential to cause offence to the modern
reader. However, wishing overall to preserve the integrity of the text, rather than
imposing contemporary sensibilities, we have left it unaltered.

FLAME TREE PUBLISHING
6 Melbray Mews, Fulham,
London SW6 3NS, United Kingdom
www.flametreepublishing.com

First published 2020

ISBN: 978-1-83964-193-0

The cover image is created by Flame Tree Studio
based on artwork by Slava Gerj and Gabor Ruszkai.

A copy of the CIP data for this book is available from the British Library.

Printed and bound in China

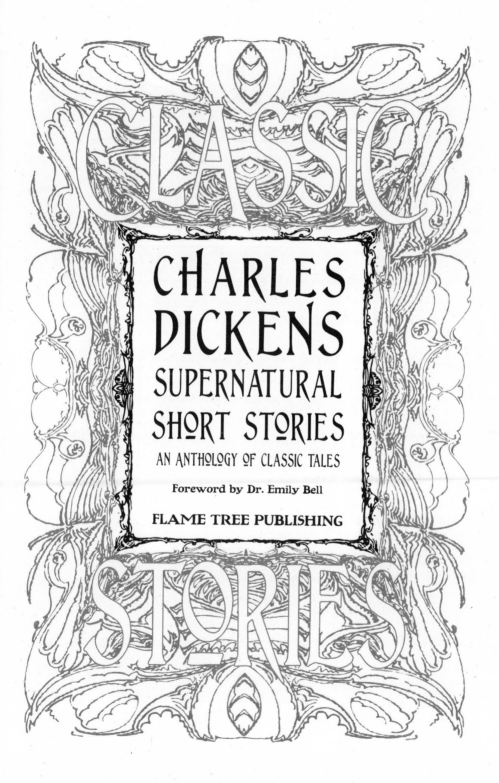

# CHARLES DICKENS
## SUPERNATURAL
## SHORT STORIES
### AN ANTHOLOGY OF CLASSIC TALES

Foreword by Dr. Emily Bell

**FLAME TREE PUBLISHING**

# Contents

## Ghostly Tales

# Murder & Revenge

# Fantasy & Adventure

*Charles Dickens and Wilkie Collins*

# Foreword: Charles Dickens Supernatural Short Stories

**CHARLES DICKENS,** though best known today for his novels, was a master of the short story. He wrote short-form pieces, both fiction and non-fiction, before he ever attempted a novel, submitting his first short story anonymously, 'with fear and trembling', to a Fleet Street publisher in 1833. That first foray into literary creation heralded the start of his writing career. Yet even after he became famous around the world as a novelist, Dickens continued to write short stories that allowed him to experiment with ideas of fancy, fantasy, revenge and the supernatural.

The short story was still an embryonic form when Dickens slipped his first story into an editor's letterbox in the 1830s; his own journals, *Household Words* and *All the Year Round*, would play an important part in solidifying its importance in the literary culture of the Victorian period. Dickens wrote short stories throughout the rest of his life, producing around one hundred pieces – including social observation, tales of revenge, stories-within-stories, Christmas stories, and ghost stories. These last two categories are often intertwined; as Mamilius says in Shakespeare's *The Winter's Tale*, '[a] sad tale's best for winter'. Dickens's Christmas books formed part of, and shaped, the tradition of telling ghost stories at Christmas, blending the religious with the supernatural. Like Shakespeare's character, he offers stories '[o]f sprites and goblins', of friendly spirits and terrifying ones, and most often of a past that returns to haunt the present and shape the future. Readers of this collection will see familiar strands in *The Haunted Man and the Ghost's Bargain* and *The Chimes*, both of which laid the foundations for the *It's A Wonderful Life*-esque redemption story and both of which still resonate today, encouraging the reader to reflect on their own life and relationships and change for the better, or face the worst.

The powerful contrast of comedy and tragedy, evident in all Dickens's works, is distilled in the short stories: 'It is the custom on the stage', he wrote in *Oliver Twist*, 'to present the tragic and the comic scenes, in as regular alternation, as the layers of red and white in a side of streaky, well-cured bacon'. The wonderful description of the joys of childhood in 'A Christmas Tree', punctuated with the horror of the death mask, formless nightmares and the ghost of a drowned girl, all in the branches of the Christmas tree, is an evocative example. The author began to develop clearer ideas of what short stories should – and should not – be, coming to dislike the moralising he saw in the works of other writers. 'The world is too much with us, early and late', he wrote in 1853, 'Leave this precious old escape from it, alone'. This changing approach makes his later short fiction distinct from earlier attempts.

Dickens's short stories fall broadly into chronological categories as well as thematic ones: in his early career he tried his hand at a range of topics, while from the 1840s he restricted himself to Christmas stories for a decade in the same vein, producing some form of Christmas publication for twenty-five years. From 1850 to 1868, a wider range of short stories appeared in the pages of his journals. As this collection shows, he had an ongoing fascination with the supernatural and the macabre which, when combined with his sincere wish to do good, resulted in some of the most celebrated stories of all time.

Within this collection are several stories-within-stories from *The Pickwick Papers*, a technique employed by Dickens to include a polyphony of different voices. Later in his career he involved collaborators to create this diversity of perspective, such as Elizabeth Gaskell and Wilkie Collins, as in 'The Haunted House' and 'A Message from the Sea', included here. That his journals and collaborations were 'conducted by' himself was crucial to Dickens, as are the musical connotations of his role as conductor: Dickens is an author who wrote to be heard, as highlighted by the 'staves' of *A Christmas Carol* and the 'quarters' of *The Chimes*. In 1868, he once again took on the challenge of writing these voices alone, penning a series of short stories from the point of view of four children to capture the innocence and humour of childhood without patronising young readers; 'The Magic Fishbone', one of the last stories Dickens completed and a fitting end to this collection, is the most successful of these attempts, offering a Victorian fairy tale that owes much to Dickens's own childhood reading and experience – Dickens too was menaced by a snapping pug-dog next door, and escaped from his world by reading the tales of Ali Baba in *The Arabian Nights*, as Scrooge also does.

The short stories are often overlooked by readers today, and the range brought together in this collection cast Dickens in a new light: more intimate, more strikingly interested in the psychological, the supernatural and the unexplained, and still relevant in their ability to surprise us, and push us to revisit the past to transform the future.

*Dr. Emily Bell*
*Editor, Dickens Letters Project*

# Publisher's Note

**CHARLES DICKENS** is an iconic figure in Victorian literature and has produced some of the most-loved and best-known fictional characters. He is known primarily for his novels, including the most famous *Oliver Twist, David Copperfield, Bleak House* and *A Tale of Two Cities*. However, his short stories were much more plentiful than his novels, and are often slightly overlooked in favour of them. In this collection we bring together the very best of his supernatural stories, which explore apparitions, spirits, goblins and the very terrifying human mind. Some are chilling in nature, while others are much more lighthearted. Although, of course similar themes do abound throughout Dickens' works, and so we have grouped them in a way we hope proves both interesting and satisfying. We also offer two recommended reads at the end of each story to direct the reader to similar stories.

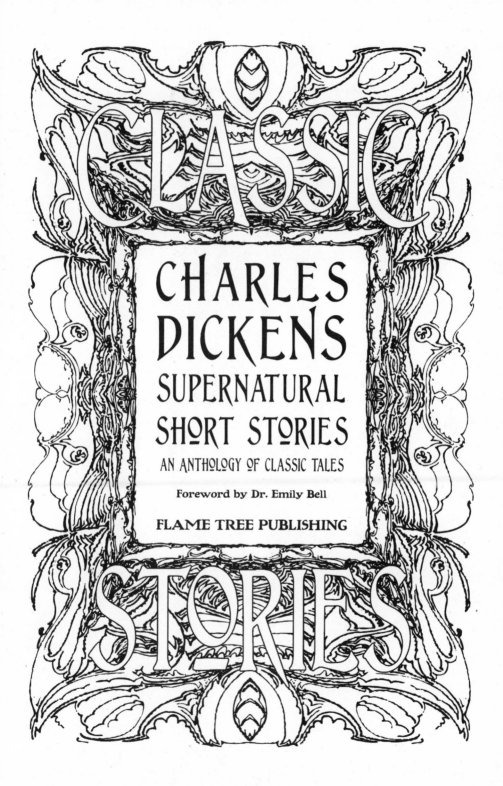

CLASSIC

# CHARLES DICKENS

## SUPERNATURAL SHORT STORIES

### AN ANTHOLOGY OF CLASSIC TALES

Foreword by Dr. Emily Bell

**FLAME TREE PUBLISHING**

STORIES

# Ghostly Tales

# The Ghosts of the Mail

**MY UNCLE** was one of the merriest, pleasantest, cleverest fellows, that ever lived. I wish you had known him, gentlemen. On second thoughts, gentlemen, I don't wish you had known him, for if you had, you would have been all, by this time, in the ordinary course of nature, if not dead, at all events so near it, as to have taken to stopping at home and giving up company, which would have deprived me of the inestimable pleasure of addressing you at this moment. Gentlemen, I wish your fathers and mothers had known my uncle. They would have been amazingly fond of him, especially your respectable mothers; I know they would. If any two of his numerous virtues predominated over the many that adorned his character, I should say they were his mixed punch and his after-supper song. Excuse my dwelling on these melancholy recollections of departed worth; you won't see a man like my uncle every day in the week.

I have always considered it a great point in my uncle's character, gentlemen, that he was the intimate friend and companion of Tom Smart, of the great house of Bilson and Slum, Cateaton Street, City. My uncle collected for Tiggin and Welps, but for a long time he went pretty near the same journey as Tom; and the very first night they met, my uncle took a fancy for Tom, and Tom took a fancy for my uncle. They made a bet of a new hat before they had known each other half an hour, who should brew the best quart of punch and drink it the quickest. My uncle was judged to have won the making, but Tom Smart beat him in the drinking by about half a salt-spoonful. They took another quart apiece to drink each other's health in, and were staunch friends ever afterwards. There's a destiny in these things, gentlemen; we can't help it.

In personal appearance, my uncle was a trifle shorter than the middle size; he was a thought stouter too, than the ordinary run of people, and perhaps his face might be a shade redder. He had the jolliest face you ever saw, gentleman: something like Punch, with a handsome nose and chin; his eyes were always twinkling and sparkling with good-humour; and a smile – not one of your unmeaning wooden grins, but a real, merry, hearty, good-tempered smile – was perpetually on his countenance. He was pitched out of his gig once, and knocked, head first, against a milestone. There he lay, stunned, and so cut about the face with some gravel which had been heaped up alongside it, that, to use my uncle's own strong expression, if his mother could have revisited the earth, she wouldn't have known him. Indeed, when I come to think of the matter, gentlemen, I feel pretty sure she wouldn't, for she died when my uncle was two years and seven months old, and I think it's very likely that, even without the gravel, his top-boots would have puzzled the good lady not a little; to say nothing of his jolly red face. However, there he lay, and I have heard my uncle say, many a time, that the man said who picked him up that he was smiling as merrily as if he had tumbled out for a treat, and that after they had bled him, the first faint glimmerings of returning animation, were his jumping up in bed, bursting out into a loud laugh, kissing the young woman who held the basin, and demanding a mutton chop and a pickled walnut. He was very fond of pickled walnuts, gentlemen. He said he always found that, taken without vinegar, they relished the beer.

My uncle's great journey was in the fall of the leaf, at which time he collected debts, and took orders, in the north; going from London to Edinburgh, from Edinburgh to Glasgow, from Glasgow back to Edinburgh, and thence to London by the smack. You are to understand that his second visit to Edinburgh was for his own pleasure. He used to go back for a week, just to look up his old friends; and what with breakfasting with this one, lunching with that, dining with the third, and supping with another, a pretty tight week he used to make of it. I don't know whether any of you, gentlemen, ever partook of a real substantial hospitable Scotch breakfast, and then went out to a slight lunch of a bushel of oysters, a dozen or so of bottled ale, and a noggin or two of whiskey to close up with. If you ever did, you will agree with me that it requires a pretty strong head to go out to dinner and supper afterwards.

But bless your hearts and eyebrows, all this sort of thing was nothing to my uncle! He was so well seasoned, that it was mere child's play. I have heard him say that he could see the Dundee people out, any day, and walk home afterwards without staggering; and yet the Dundee people have as strong heads and as strong punch, gentlemen, as you are likely to meet with, between the poles. I have heard of a Glasgow man and a Dundee man drinking against each other for fifteen hours at a sitting. They were both suffocated, as nearly as could be ascertained, at the same moment, but with this trifling exception, gentlemen, they were not a bit the worse for it.

One night, within four-and-twenty hours of the time when he had settled to take shipping for London, my uncle supped at the house of a very old friend of his, a Bailie Mac something and four syllables after it, who lived in the old town of Edinburgh. There were the bailie's wife, and the bailie's three daughters, and the bailie's grown-up son, and three or four stout, bushy eye-browed, canny, old Scotch fellows, that the bailie had got together to do honour to my uncle, and help to make merry. It was a glorious supper. There was kippered salmon, and Finnan haddocks, and a lamb's head, and a haggis – a celebrated Scotch dish, gentlemen, which my uncle used to say always looked to him, when it came to table, very much like a Cupid's stomach – and a great many other things besides, that I forget the names of, but very good things, notwithstanding. The lassies were pretty and agreeable; the bailie's wife was one of the best creatures that ever lived; and my uncle was in thoroughly good cue. The consequence of which was, that the young ladies tittered and giggled, and the old lady laughed out loud, and the bailie and the other old fellows roared till they were red in the face, the whole mortal time. I don't quite recollect how many tumblers of whiskey-toddy each man drank after supper; but this I know, that about one o'clock in the morning, the bailie's grown-up son became insensible while attempting the first verse of 'Willie brewed a peck o' maut'; and he having been, for half an hour before, the only other man visible above the mahogany, it occurred to my uncle that it was almost time to think about going, especially as drinking had set in at seven o'clock, in order that he might get home at a decent hour. But, thinking it might not be quite polite to go just then, my uncle voted himself into the chair, mixed another glass, rose to propose his own health, addressed himself in a neat and complimentary speech, and drank the toast with great enthusiasm. Still nobody woke; so my uncle took a little drop more – neat this time, to prevent the toddy from disagreeing with him – and, laying violent hands on his hat, sallied forth into the street.

It was a wild, gusty night when my uncle closed the bailie's door, and settling his hat firmly on his head to prevent the wind from taking it, thrust his hands into his pockets, and looking upward, took a short survey of the state of the weather. The clouds were drifting over the moon at their giddiest speed; at one time wholly obscuring her; at another, suffering her to burst forth in full splendour and shed her light on all the objects around; anon, driving over her again, with increased velocity, and shrouding everything in darkness. "Really, this won't do," said my uncle, addressing himself to the weather, as if he felt himself personally offended. "This is not at all the kind of thing for my voyage. It will not do at any price," said my uncle, very impressively. Having repeated this, several times, he recovered his balance with some difficulty – for he was rather giddy with looking up into the sky so long – and walked merrily on.

The bailie's house was in the Canongate, and my uncle was going to the other end of Leith Walk, rather better than a mile's journey. On either side of him, there shot up against the dark sky, tall, gaunt, straggling houses, with time-stained fronts, and windows that seemed to have shared the lot of eyes in mortals, and to have grown dim and sunken with age. Six, seven, eight storey high, were the houses; storey piled upon storey, as children build with cards – throwing their dark shadows over the roughly paved road, and making the dark night darker. A few oil lamps were scattered at long distances, but they only served to mark the dirty entrance to some narrow close, or to show where a common stair communicated, by steep and intricate windings, with the various flats above. Glancing at all these things with the air of a man who had seen them too often before, to think them worthy of much notice now, my uncle walked up the middle of the street, with a thumb in each waistcoat pocket, indulging from time to time in various snatches of song, chanted forth with such good-will and spirit, that the quiet honest folk started from their first sleep and lay trembling in bed till the sound died away in the distance; when, satisfying themselves that it was only some drunken ne'er-do-weel finding his way home, they covered themselves up warm and fell asleep again.

I am particular in describing how my uncle walked up the middle of the street, with his thumbs in his waistcoat pockets, gentlemen, because, as he often used to say (and with great reason too) there is nothing at all extraordinary in this story, unless you distinctly understand at the beginning, that he was not by any means of a marvellous or romantic turn.

Gentlemen, my uncle walked on with his thumbs in his waistcoat pockets, taking the middle of the street to himself, and singing, now a verse of a love song, and then a verse of a drinking one, and when he was tired of both, whistling melodiously, until he reached the North Bridge, which, at this point, connects the old and new towns of Edinburgh. Here he stopped for a minute, to look at the strange, irregular clusters of lights piled one above the other, and twinkling afar off so high, that they looked like stars, gleaming from the castle walls on the one side and the Calton Hill on the other, as if they illuminated veritable castles in the air; while the old picturesque town slept heavily on, in gloom and darkness below: its palace and chapel of Holyrood, guarded day and night, as a friend of my uncle's used to say, by old Arthur's Seat, towering, surly and dark, like some gruff genius, over the ancient city he has watched so long. I say, gentlemen, my uncle stopped here, for a minute, to look about him; and then, paying a compliment to the weather, which had a little cleared up, though the moon was sinking, walked on again, as royally as before; keeping the middle of the road with great dignity, and looking as if he would very much like to meet with somebody who would dispute possession of it with him. There was nobody at all disposed to contest the point, as it happened; and so, on he went, with his thumbs in his waistcoat pockets, like a lamb.

When my uncle reached the end of Leith Walk, he had to cross a pretty large piece of waste ground which separated him from a short street which he had to turn down to go direct to his lodging. Now, in this piece of waste ground, there was, at that time, an enclosure belonging to some wheelwright who contracted with the Post Office for the purchase of old, worn-out mail coaches; and my uncle, being very fond of coaches, old, young, or middle-aged, all at once took it into his head to step out of his road for no other purpose than to peep between the palings at these mails – about a dozen of which he remembered to have seen, crowded together in a very forlorn and dismantled state, inside. My uncle was a very enthusiastic, emphatic sort of person, gentlemen; so, finding that he could not obtain a good peep between the palings he got over them, and sitting himself quietly down on an old axle-tree, began to contemplate the mail coaches with a deal of gravity.

There might be a dozen of them, or there might be more – my uncle was never quite certain on this point, and being a man of very scrupulous veracity about numbers, didn't like to say – but there they stood, all huddled together in the most desolate condition imaginable. The doors had been torn from their hinges and removed; the linings had been stripped off, only a shred hanging here and there by a rusty nail; the lamps were gone, the poles had long since vanished, the ironwork was rusty, the paint was worn away; the wind whistled through the chinks in the bare woodwork; and the rain, which had collected on the roofs, fell, drop by drop, into the insides with a hollow and melancholy sound. They were the decaying skeletons of departed mails, and in that lonely place, at that time of night, they looked chill and dismal.

My uncle rested his head upon his hands, and thought of the busy, bustling people who had rattled about, years before, in the old coaches, and were now as silent and changed; he thought of the numbers of people to whom one of these crazy, mouldering vehicles had borne, night after night, for many years, and through all weathers, the anxiously expected intelligence, the eagerly looked-for remittance, the promised assurance of health and safety, the sudden announcement of sickness and death. The merchant, the lover, the wife, the widow, the mother, the school-boy, the very child who tottered to the door at the postman's knock – how had they all looked forward to the arrival of the old coach. And where were they all now?

Gentlemen, my uncle used to *say* that he thought all this at the time, but I rather suspect he learned it out of some book afterwards, for he distinctly stated that he fell into a kind of doze, as he sat on the old axle-tree looking at the decayed mail coaches, and that he was suddenly awakened by some deep church bell striking two. Now, my uncle was never a fast thinker, and if he had thought all these things, I am quite certain it would have taken him till full half-past two o'clock at the very least. I am, therefore, decidedly of opinion, gentlemen, that my uncle fell into a kind of doze, without having thought about anything at all.

Be this as it may, a church bell struck two. My uncle woke, rubbed his eyes, and jumped up in astonishment.

In one instant, after the clock struck two, the whole of this deserted and quiet spot had become a scene of most extraordinary life and animation. The mail coach doors were on their hinges, the lining was replaced, the ironwork was as good as new, the paint was restored, the lamps were alight; cushions and greatcoats were on every coach-box, porters were thrusting parcels into every boot, guards were stowing away letter-bags, hostlers were dashing pails of water against the renovated wheels; numbers of men were pushing about, fixing poles into every coach; passengers arrived, portmanteaus were handed up, horses were put to; in short, it was perfectly clear that every mail there, was to be off directly. Gentlemen, my uncle opened his eyes so wide at all this, that, to the very last moment of his life, he used to wonder how it fell out that he had ever been able to shut 'em again.

"Now then!" said a voice, as my uncle felt a hand on his shoulder, "you're booked for one inside. You'd better get in."

"I booked!" said my uncle, turning round.

"Yes, certainly."

My uncle, gentlemen, could say nothing, he was so very much astonished. The queerest thing of all was that although there was such a crowd of persons, and although fresh faces were pouring in, every moment, there was no telling where they came from. They seemed to start up, in some strange manner, from the ground, or the air, and disappear in the same way. When a porter had put his luggage in the coach, and received his fare, he turned round and was gone; and before my uncle had well begun to wonder what had become of him, half a dozen fresh ones started up, and staggered along under the weight of parcels, which seemed big enough to crush them. The passengers were all dressed so oddly too! Large, broad-skirted laced coats, with great cuffs and no collars; and wigs, gentlemen – great formal wigs with a tie behind. My uncle could make nothing of it.

"Now, are you going to get in?" said the person who had addressed my uncle before. He was dressed as a mail guard, with a wig on his head and most enormous cuffs to his coat, and had a lantern in one hand, and a huge blunderbuss in the other, which he was going to stow away in his little arm-chest. "*Are* you going to get in, Jack Martin?" said the guard, holding the lantern to my uncle's face.

"Hollo!" said my uncle, falling back a step or two. "That's familiar!"

"It's so on the way-bill," said the guard.

"Isn't there a 'Mister' before it?" said my uncle. For he felt, gentlemen, that for a guard he didn't know, to call him Jack Martin, was a liberty which the Post Office wouldn't have sanctioned if they had known it.

"No, there is not," rejoined the guard coolly.

"Is the fare paid?" inquired my uncle.

"Of course it is," rejoined the guard.

"It is, is it?" said my uncle. "Then here goes! Which coach?"

"This," said the guard, pointing to an old-fashioned Edinburgh and London mail, which had the steps down and the door open. "Stop! Here are the other passengers. Let them get in first."

As the guard spoke, there all at once appeared, right in front of my uncle, a young gentleman in a powdered wig, and a sky-blue coat trimmed with silver, made very full and broad in the skirts, which were lined with buckram. Tiggin and Welps were in the printed calico and waistcoat piece line, gentlemen, so my uncle knew all the materials at once. He wore knee breeches, and a kind of leggings rolled up over his silk stockings, and shoes with buckles; he had ruffles at his wrists, a three-cornered hat on his head, and a long taper sword by his side. The flaps of his waist-coat came half-way down his thighs, and the ends of his cravat reached to his waist. He stalked gravely to the coach door, pulled off his hat, and held it above his head at arm's length, cocking his little finger in the air at the same time, as some affected people do, when they take a cup of tea. Then he drew his feet together, and made a low, grave bow, and then put out his left hand. My uncle was just going to step forward, and shake it heartily, when he perceived that these attentions were directed, not towards him, but to a young lady who just then appeared at the foot of the steps, attired in an old-fashioned green velvet dress with a long waist and stomacher. She had no bonnet on her head, gentlemen, which was muffled in a black silk hood, but she looked round for an instant as she prepared to get into the coach, and such a beautiful face as she disclosed, my uncle had never seen – not even in a picture. She got into the coach, holding up her dress with one hand; and as my uncle always said with a round oath, when he told the story, he wouldn't have believed it possible that legs and feet could have been brought to such a state of perfection unless he had seen them with his own eyes.

But, in this one glimpse of the beautiful face, my uncle saw that the young lady cast an imploring look upon him, and that she appeared terrified and distressed. He noticed, too, that the young fellow in the powdered wig, notwithstanding his show of gallantry, which was all very fine and grand, clasped her tight by the wrist when she got in, and followed himself immediately afterwards. An uncommonly ill-looking fellow, in a close brown wig, and a plum-coloured suit, wearing a very large sword, and boots up to his hips, belonged to the party; and when he sat himself down next to the young lady, who shrank into a corner at his approach, my uncle was confirmed in his original impression that something dark and mysterious was going forward, or, as he always said himself, that "there was a screw loose somewhere." It's quite surprising how quickly he made up his mind to help the lady at any peril, if she needed any help.

"Death and lightning!" exclaimed the young gentleman, laying his hand upon his sword as my uncle entered the coach.

"Blood and thunder!" roared the other gentleman. With this, he whipped his sword out, and made a lunge at my uncle without further ceremony. My uncle had no weapon about him, but with great dexterity he snatched the ill-looking gentleman's three-cornered hat from his head, and, receiving the point of his sword right through the crown, squeezed the sides together, and held it tight.

"Pink him behind!" cried the ill-looking gentleman to his companion, as he struggled to regain his sword.

"He had better not," cried my uncle, displaying the heel of one of his shoes, in a threatening manner. "I'll kick his brains out, if he has any, or fracture his skull if he hasn't." Exerting all his strength, at this moment, my uncle wrenched the ill-looking man's sword from his grasp, and flung it clean out of the coach window, upon which the younger gentleman vociferated, "Death and lightning!" again, and laid his hand upon the hilt of his sword, in a very fierce manner, but didn't draw it. Perhaps, gentlemen, as my uncle used to say with a smile, perhaps he was afraid of alarming the lady.

"Now, gentlemen," said my uncle, taking his seat deliberately, "I don't want to have any death, with or without lightning, in a lady's presence, and we have had quite blood and thundering enough for one journey; so, if you please, we'll sit in our places like quiet insides. Here, guard, pick up that gentleman's carving-knife."

As quickly as my uncle said the words, the guard appeared at the coach window, with the gentleman's sword in his hand. He held up his lantern, and looked earnestly in my uncle's face, as he handed it in, when, by its light, my uncle saw, to his great surprise, that an immense crowd of mail-coach guards swarmed round the window, every one of whom had his eyes earnestly fixed upon him too. He had never seen such a sea of white faces, red bodies, and earnest eyes, in all his born days.

"This is the strangest sort of thing I ever had anything to do with," thought my uncle; "allow me to return you your hat, sir."

The ill-looking gentleman received his three-cornered hat in silence, looked at the hole in the middle with an inquiring air, and finally stuck it on the top of his wig with a solemnity the effect of which was a trifle impaired by his sneezing violently at the moment, and jerking it off again.

"All right!" cried the guard with the lantern, mounting into his little seat behind. Away they went. My uncle peeped out of the coach window as they emerged from the yard, and observed that the other mails, with coachmen, guards, horses, and passengers, complete, were driving round and round in circles, at a slow trot of about five miles an hour. My uncle burned with indignation, gentlemen. As a commercial man, he felt that the mail-bags were not to be trifled with, and he resolved to memorialise the Post Office on the subject, the very instant he reached London.

At present, however, his thoughts were occupied with the young lady who sat in the farthest corner of the coach, with her face muffled closely in her hood; the gentleman with the sky-blue coat sitting opposite to her; the other man in the plum-coloured suit, by her side; and both watching her intently. If she so much as rustled the folds of her hood, he could hear the ill-looking man clap his hand upon his sword, and could tell by the other's breathing (it was so dark he couldn't see his face) that he was looking as big as if he were going to devour her at a mouthful. This roused my uncle more and more, and he resolved, come what might, to see the end of it. He had a great admiration for bright eyes, and sweet faces, and pretty legs and feet; in short, he was fond of the whole sex. It runs in our family, gentleman – so am I.

Many were the devices which my uncle practised, to attract the lady's attention, or at all events, to engage the mysterious gentlemen in conversation. They were all in vain; the gentlemen wouldn't talk, and the lady didn't dare. He thrust his head out of the coach window at intervals, and bawled out to know why they didn't go faster. But he called till he was hoarse; nobody paid the least attention to him. He leaned back in the coach, and thought of the beautiful face, and the feet and legs. This answered better; it whiled away the time, and kept him from wondering where he was going, and how it was that he found himself in such an odd situation. Not that this would have worried him much, anyway – he was a mighty free and easy, roving, devil-may-care sort of person, was my uncle, gentlemen.

All of a sudden the coach stopped. "Hollo!" said my uncle, "what's in the wind now?"

"Alight here," said the guard, letting down the steps.

"Here!" cried my uncle.

"Here," rejoined the guard.

"I'll do nothing of the sort," said my uncle.

"Very well, then stop where you are," said the guard.

"I will," said my uncle.

"Do," said the guard.

The passengers had regarded this colloquy with great attention, and, finding that my uncle was determined not to alight, the younger man squeezed past him, to hand the lady out. At this moment, the ill-looking man was inspecting the hole in the crown of his three-cornered hat. As the young lady brushed past, she dropped one of her gloves into my uncle's hand, and softly whispered, with her lips so close to his face that he felt her warm breath on his nose, the single word "Help!" Gentlemen, my uncle leaped out of the coach at once, with such violence that it rocked on the springs again.

"Oh! you've thought better of it, have you?" said the guard, when he saw my uncle standing on the ground.

My uncle looked at the guard for a few seconds, in some doubt whether it wouldn't be better to wrench his blunderbuss from him, fire it in the face of the man with the big sword, knock the rest of the company over the head with the stock, snatch up the young lady, and go off in the smoke. On second thoughts, however, he abandoned this plan, as being a shade too melodramatic in the execution, and followed the two mysterious men, who, keeping the lady between them, were now entering an old house in front of which the coach had stopped. They turned into the passage, and my uncle followed.

Of all the ruinous and desolate places my uncle had ever beheld, this was the most so. It looked as if it had once been a large house of entertainment; but the roof had fallen in, in many places, and the stairs were steep, rugged, and broken. There was a huge fireplace in the room into which they walked, and the chimney was blackened with smoke; but no warm blaze lighted it up now. The white feathery dust of burned wood was still strewed over the hearth, but the stove was cold, and all was dark and gloomy.

"Well," said my uncle, as he looked about him, "a mail travelling at the rate of six miles and a half an hour, and stopping for an indefinite time at such a hole as this, is rather an irregular sort of proceeding, I fancy. This shall be made known. I'll write to the papers."

My uncle said this in a pretty loud voice, and in an open, unreserved sort of manner, with the view of engaging the two strangers in conversation if he could. But, neither of them took any more notice of him than whispering to each other, and scowling at him as they did so. The lady was at the farther end of the room, and once she ventured to wave her hand, as if beseeching my uncle's assistance.

At length the two strangers advanced a little, and the conversation began in earnest.

"You don't know this is a private room, I suppose, fellow?" said the gentleman in sky-blue.

"No, I do not, fellow," rejoined my uncle. "Only, if this is a private room specially ordered for the occasion, I should think the public room must be a *very* comfortable one;" with this, my uncle sat himself down in a high-backed chair, and took such an accurate measure of the gentleman, with his eyes, that Tiggin and Welps could have supplied him with printed calico for a suit, and not an inch too much or too little, from that estimate alone.

"Quit this room," said both men together, grasping their swords.

"Eh?" said my uncle, not at all appearing to comprehend their meaning.

"Quit the room, or you are a dead man," said the ill-looking fellow with the large sword, drawing it at the same time and flourishing it in the air.

"Down with him!" cried the gentleman in sky-blue, drawing his sword also, and falling back two or three yards. "Down with him!" The lady gave a loud scream.

Now, my uncle was always remarkable for great boldness, and great presence of mind. All the time that he had appeared so indifferent to what was going on, he had been looking slyly about for some missile or weapon of defence, and at the very instant when the swords were drawn, he espied, standing in the chimney-corner, an old basket-hilted rapier in a rusty scabbard. At one bound, my uncle caught it in his hand, drew it, flourished it gallantly above his head, called aloud to the lady to keep out of the way, hurled the chair at the man in sky-blue, and the scabbard at the man in plum-colour, and taking advantage of the confusion, fell upon them both, pell-mell.

Gentlemen, there is an old story – none the worse for being true – regarding a fine young Irish gentleman, who being asked if he could play the fiddle, replied he had no doubt he could, but he couldn't exactly say, for certain, because he had never tried. This is not inapplicable to my uncle and his fencing. He had never had a sword in his hand before, except once when he played Richard the Third at a private theatre, upon which occasion it was arranged with Richmond that he was to be run through, from behind, without showing fight at all. But here he was, cutting and slashing with two experienced swordsman, thrusting, and guarding, and poking, and slicing, and acquitting himself in the most manful and dexterous manner possible, although up to that time he had never been aware that he had the least notion of the science. It only shows how true the old saying is, that a man never knows what he can do till he tries, gentlemen.

The noise of the combat was terrific; each of the three combatants swearing like troopers, and their swords clashing with as much noise as if all the knives and steels in Newport market were rattling together, at the same time. When it was at its very height, the lady (to encourage my uncle most probably) withdrew her hood entirely from her face, and disclosed a countenance of such dazzling beauty, that he would have fought against fifty men, to win one smile from it and die. He had done wonders before, but now he began to powder away like a raving mad giant.

At this very moment, the gentleman in sky-blue turning round, and seeing the young lady with her face uncovered, vented an exclamation of rage and jealousy, and, turning his weapon against her beautiful bosom, pointed a thrust at her heart, which caused my uncle to utter a cry of apprehension that made the building ring. The lady stepped lightly aside, and snatching the young man's sword from his hand, before he had recovered his balance, drove him to the wall, and running it through him, and the panelling, up to the very hilt, pinned him there, hard and fast. It was a splendid example. My uncle, with a loud shout of triumph, and a strength that was irresistible, made his adversary retreat in the same direction, and plunging the old rapier into the very centre of a large red flower in the pattern of his waistcoat, nailed him beside his friend; there they both stood, gentlemen, jerking their arms and legs about in agony, like the toy-shop figures that are moved by a piece of pack-thread. My uncle always said, afterwards, that this was one of the surest means he knew of, for disposing of an enemy; but it was liable to one objection on the ground of expense, inasmuch as it involved the loss of a sword for every man disabled.

"The mail, the mail!" cried the lady, running up to my uncle and throwing her beautiful arms round his neck; "we may yet escape."

"May!" cried my uncle; "why, my dear, there's nobody else to kill, is there?" My uncle was rather disappointed, gentlemen, for he thought a little quiet bit of love-making would be agreeable after the slaughtering, if it were only to change the subject.

"We have not an instant to lose here," said the young lady. "He (pointing to the young gentleman in sky-blue) is the only son of the powerful Marquess of Filletoville."

"Well then, my dear, I'm afraid he'll never come to the title," said my uncle, looking coolly at the young gentleman as he stood fixed up against the wall, in the cockchafer fashion that I have described. "You have cut off the entail, my love."

"I have been torn from my home and my friends by these villains," said the young lady, her features glowing with indignation. "That wretch would have married me by violence in another hour."

"Confound his impudence!" said my uncle, bestowing a very contemptuous look on the dying heir of Filletoville.

"As you may guess from what you have seen," said the young lady, "the party were prepared to murder me if I appealed to any one for assistance. If their accomplices find us here, we are lost. Two minutes hence may be too late. The mail!" With these words, overpowered by her feelings, and the exertion of sticking the young Marquess of Filletoville, she sank into my uncle's arms. My uncle caught her up, and bore her to the house door. There stood the mail, with four long-tailed, flowing-maned, black horses, ready harnessed; but no coachman, no guard, no hostler even, at the horses' heads.

Gentlemen, I hope I do no injustice to my uncle's memory, when I express my opinion, that although he was a bachelor, he had held some ladies in his arms before this time; I believe, indeed, that he had rather a habit of kissing barmaids; and I know, that in one or two instances, he had been seen by credible witnesses, to hug a landlady in a very perceptible manner. I mention the circumstance, to show what a very uncommon sort of person this beautiful young lady must have been, to have affected my uncle in the way she did; he used to say, that as her long dark hair trailed over his arm, and her beautiful dark eyes fixed themselves upon his face when she recovered, he felt so strange and nervous that his legs trembled beneath him. But who can look in a sweet, soft pair of dark eyes, without feeling queer? I can't, gentlemen. I am afraid to look at some eyes I know, and that's the truth of it.

"You will never leave me," murmured the young lady.

"Never," said my uncle. And he meant it too.

"My dear preserver!" exclaimed the young lady. "My dear, kind, brave preserver!"

"Don't," said my uncle, interrupting her.

"Why?" inquired the young lady.

"Because your mouth looks so beautiful when you speak," rejoined my uncle, "that I'm afraid I shall be rude enough to kiss it."

The young lady put up her hand as if to caution my uncle not to do so, and said – No, she didn't say anything – she smiled. When you are looking at a pair of the most delicious lips in the world, and see them gently break into a roguish smile – if you are very near them, and nobody else by – you cannot better testify your admiration of their beautiful form and colour than by kissing them at once. My uncle did so, and I honour him for it.

"Hark!" cried the young lady, starting. "The noise of wheels, and horses!"

"So it is," said my uncle, listening. He had a good ear for wheels, and the trampling of hoofs; but there appeared to be so many horses and carriages rattling towards them, from a distance, that it was impossible to form a guess at their number. The sound was like that of fifty brakes, with six blood cattle in each.

"We are pursued!" cried the young lady, clasping her hands. "We are pursued. I have no hope but in you!"

There was such an expression of terror in her beautiful face, that my uncle made up his mind at once. He lifted her into the coach, told her not to be frightened, pressed his lips to hers once more, and then advising her to draw up the window to keep the cold air out, mounted to the box.

"Stay, love," cried the young lady.

"What's the matter?" said my uncle, from the coach-box.

"I want to speak to you," said the young lady; "only a word. Only one word, dearest."

"Must I get down?" inquired my uncle. The lady made no answer, but she smiled again. Such a smile, gentlemen! It beat the other one, all to nothing. My uncle descended from his perch in a twinkling.

"What is it, my dear?" said my uncle, looking in at the coach window. The lady happened to bend forward at the same time, and my uncle thought she looked more beautiful than she had done yet. He was very close to her just then, gentlemen, so he really ought to know.

"What is it, my dear?" said my uncle.

"Will you never love any one but me – never marry any one beside?" said the young lady.

My uncle swore a great oath that he never would marry anybody else, and the young lady drew in her head, and pulled up the window. He jumped upon the box, squared his elbows, adjusted the ribands, seized the whip which lay on the roof, gave one flick to the off leader, and away went the four long-tailed, flowing-maned black horses, at fifteen good English miles an hour, with the old mail-coach behind them. Whew! How they tore along!

The noise behind grew louder. The faster the old mail went, the faster came the pursuers – men, horses, dogs, were leagued in the pursuit. The noise was frightful, but, above all, rose the voice of the young lady, urging my uncle on, and shrieking, "Faster! Faster!"

They whirled past the dark trees, as feathers would be swept before a hurricane. Houses, gates, churches, haystacks, objects of every kind they shot by, with a velocity and noise like roaring waters suddenly let loose. But still the noise of pursuit grew louder, and still my uncle could hear the young lady wildly screaming, "Faster! Faster!"

My uncle plied whip and rein, and the horses flew onward till they were white with foam; and yet the noise behind increased; and yet the young lady cried, "Faster! Faster!" My uncle gave a loud stamp on the boot in the energy of the moment, and – found that it was gray morning, and he was sitting in the wheelwright's yard, on the box of an old Edinburgh mail, shivering with the cold and wet and stamping his feet to warm them! He got down, and looked eagerly inside for the beautiful young lady. Alas! There was neither door nor seat to the coach. It was a mere shell.

Of course, my uncle knew very well that there was some mystery in the matter, and that everything had passed exactly as he used to relate it. He remained staunch to the great oath he had sworn to the beautiful young lady, refusing several eligible landladies on her account, and dying a bachelor at last. He always said what a curious thing it was that he should have found out, by such a mere accident as his clambering over the palings, that the ghosts of mail-coaches and horses, guards, coachmen, and passengers, were in the habit of making journeys regularly every night. He used to add, that he believed he was the only living person who had ever been taken as a passenger on one of these excursions. And I think he was right, gentlemen – at least I never heard of any other.

**If you enjoyed this, you might also like...**
The Ghost in the Bride's Chamber, see page 267
To Be Read at Dusk, see page 132

# The Lawyer and the Ghost

**I KNEW** a man – let me see – forty years ago now – who took an old, damp, rotten set of chambers, in one of the most ancient inns, that had been shut up and empty for years and years before. There were lots of old women's stories about the place, and it certainly was very far from being a cheerful one; but he was poor, and the rooms were cheap, and that would have been quite a sufficient reason for him, if they had been ten times worse than they really were.

He was obliged to take some mouldering fixtures that were on the place, and, among the rest, was a great lumbering wooden press for papers, with large glass doors, and a green curtain inside; a pretty useless thing for him, for he had no papers to put in it; and as to his clothes, he carried them about with him, and that wasn't very hard work, either.

Well, he had moved in all his furniture – it wasn't quite a truck-full – and had sprinkled it about the room, so as to make the four chairs look as much like a dozen as possible, and was sitting down before the fire at night, drinking the first glass of two gallons of whisky he had ordered on credit, wondering whether it would ever be paid for, and if so, in how many years' time, when his eyes encountered the glass doors of the wooden press.

"Ah," says he, "if I hadn't been obliged to take that ugly article at the old broker's valuation, I might have got something comfortable for the money. I'll tell you what it is, old fellow," he said, speaking aloud to the press, having nothing else to speak to, "if it wouldn't cost more to break up your old carcass, than it would ever be worth afterward, I'd have a fire out of you in less than no time."

He had hardly spoken the words, when a sound resembling a faint groan, appeared to issue from the interior of the case. It startled him at first, but thinking, on a moment's reflection, that it must be some young fellow in the next chamber, who had been dining out, he put his feet on the fender, and raised the poker to stir the fire.

At that moment, the sound was repeated; and one of the glass doors slowly opening, disclosed a pale and emaciated figure in soiled and worn apparel, standing erect in the press. The figure was tall and thin, and the countenance expressive of care and anxiety; but there was something in the hue of the skin, and gaunt and unearthly appearance of the whole form, which no being of this world was ever seen to wear.

"Who are you?" said the new tenant, turning very pale; poising the poker in his hand, however, and taking a very decent aim at the countenance of the figure. "Who are you?"

"Don't throw that poker at me," replied the form; "if you hurled it with ever so sure an aim, it would pass through me, without resistance, and expend its force on the wood behind. I am a spirit."

"And pray, what do you want here?" faltered the tenant.

"In this room," replied the apparition, "my worldly ruin was worked, and I and my children beggared. In this press, the papers in a long, long suit, which accumulated for years, were deposited. In this room, when I had died of grief, and long-deferred hope, two wily harpies divided the wealth for which I had contested during a wretched existence, and of which, at last, not one farthing was left for my unhappy descendants. I terrified them from the spot, and since that day have prowled by night – the only period at which I can revisit the earth – about the scenes of my long-protracted misery. This apartment is mine: leave it to me."

"If you insist upon making your appearance here," said the tenant, who had had time to collect his presence of mind during this prosy statement of the ghost's, "I shall give up possession with the greatest pleasure; but I should like to ask you one question, if you will allow me."

"Say on," said the apparition sternly.

"Well," said the tenant, "I don't apply the observation personally to you, because it is equally applicable to most of the ghosts I ever heard of; but it does appear to me somewhat inconsistent, that when you have an opportunity of visiting the fairest spots of earth – for I suppose space is nothing to you – you should always return exactly to the very places where you have been most miserable."

"Egad, that's very true; I never thought of that before," said the ghost.

"You see, Sir," pursued the tenant, "this is a very uncomfortable room. From the appearance of that press, I should be disposed to say that it is not wholly free from bugs; and I really think you might find much more comfortable quarters: to say nothing of the climate of London, which is extremely disagreeable."

"You are very right, Sir," said the ghost politely, "it never struck me till now; I'll try change of air directly."

In fact, he began to vanish as he spoke; his legs, indeed, had quite disappeared.

"And if, Sir," said the tenant, calling after him, "if you would have the goodness to suggest to the other ladies and gentlemen who are now engaged in haunting old empty houses, that they might be much more comfortable elsewhere, you will confer a very great benefit on society."

"I will," replied the ghost; "we must be dull fellows – very dull fellows, indeed; I can't imagine how we can have been so stupid."

With these words, the spirit disappeared; and what is rather remarkable, he never came back again.

**If you enjoyed this, you might also like...**
The Baron of Grogzwig, see page 24
A Christmas Tree, see page 140

# The Baron of Grogzwig

**THE BARON VON KOELDWETHOUT**, of Grogzwig in Germany, was as likely a young baron as you would wish to see. I needn't say that he lived in a castle, because that's of course; neither need I say that he lived in an old castle; for what German baron ever lived in a new one? There were many strange circumstances connected with this venerable building, among which, not the least startling and mysterious were, that when the wind blew, it rumbled in the chimneys, or even howled among the trees in the neighbouring forest; and that when the moon shone, she found her way through certain small loopholes in the wall, and actually made some parts of the wide halls and galleries quite light, while she left others in gloomy shadow. I believe that one of the baron's ancestors, being short of money, had inserted a dagger in a gentleman who called one night to ask his way, and it *was sup*posed that these miraculous occurrences took place in consequence. And yet I hardly know how that could have been, either, because the baron's ancestor, who was an amiable man, felt very sorry afterwards for having been so rash, and laying violent hands upon a quantity of stone and timber which belonged to a weaker baron, built a chapel as an apology, and so took a receipt from Heaven, in full of all demands.

Talking of the baron's ancestor puts me in mind of the baron's great claims to respect, on the score of his pedigree. I am afraid to say, I am sure, how many ancestors the baron had; but I know that he had a great many more than any other man of his time; and I only wish that he had lived in these latter days, that he might have had more. It is a very hard thing upon the great men of past centuries, that they should have come into the world so soon, because a man who was born three or four hundred years ago, cannot reasonably be expected to have had as many relations before him, as a man who is born now. The last man, whoever he is – and he may be a cobbler or some low vulgar dog for aught we know – will have a longer pedigree than the greatest nobleman now alive; and I contend that this is not fair.

Well, but the Baron Von Koeldwethout of Grogzwig! He was a fine swarthy fellow, with dark hair and large moustachios, who rode a-hunting in clothes of Lincoln green, with russet boots on his feet, and a bugle slung over his shoulder like the guard of a long stage. When he blew this bugle, four-and-twenty other gentlemen of inferior rank, in Lincoln green a little coarser, and russet boots with a little thicker soles, turned out directly: and away galloped the whole train, with spears in their hands like lacquered area railings, to hunt down the boars, or perhaps encounter a bear: in which latter case the baron killed him first, and greased his whiskers with him afterwards.

This was a merry life for the Baron of Grogzwig, and a merrier still for the baron's retainers, who drank Rhine wine every night till they fell under the table, and then had the bottles on the floor, and called for pipes. Never were such jolly, roystering, rollicking, merry-making blades, as the jovial crew of Grogzwig.

But the pleasures of the table, or the pleasures of under the table, require a little variety; especially when the same five-and-twenty people sit daily down to the same board, to discuss the same subjects, and tell the same stories. The baron grew weary, and wanted excitement. He took to quarrelling with his gentlemen, and tried kicking two or three of them every day after dinner. This was a pleasant change at first; but it became monotonous after a week or so, and the baron felt quite out of sorts, and cast about, in despair, for some new amusement.

One night, after a day's sport in which he had outdone Nimrod or Gillingwater, and slaughtered "another fine bear," and brought him home in triumph, the Baron Von Koeldwethout sat moodily at the head of his table, eyeing the smoky roof of the hall with a discontented aspect. He swallowed huge bumpers of wine, but the more he swallowed, the more he frowned. The gentlemen who had been honoured with the dangerous distinction of sitting on his right and left, imitated him to a miracle in the drinking, and frowned at each other.

"I will!" cried the baron suddenly, smiting the table with his right hand, and twirling his moustache with his left. "Fill to the Lady of Grogzwig!"

The four-and-twenty Lincoln greens turned pale, with the exception of their four-and-twenty noses, which were unchangeable.

"I said to the Lady of Grogzwig," repeated the baron, looking round the board.

"To the Lady of Grogzwig!" shouted the Lincoln greens; and down their four-and-twenty throats went four-and-twenty imperial pints of such rare old hock, that they smacked their eight-and-forty lips, and winked again.

"The fair daughter of the Baron Von Swillenhausen," said Koeldwethout, condescending to explain. "We will demand her in marriage of her father, ere the sun goes down tomorrow. If he refuse our suit, we will cut off his nose."

A hoarse murmur arose from the company; every man touched, first the hilt of his sword, and then the tip of his nose, with appalling significance.

What a pleasant thing filial piety is to contemplate! If the daughter of the Baron Von Swillenhausen had pleaded a preoccupied heart, or fallen at her father's feet and corned them in salt tears, or only fainted away, and complimented the old gentleman in frantic ejaculations, the odds are a hundred to one but Swillenhausen Castle would have been turned out at window, or rather the baron turned out at window, and the castle demolished. The damsel held her peace, however, when an early messenger bore the request of Von Koeldwethout next morning, and modestly retired to her chamber, from the casement of which she watched the coming of the suitor and his retinue. She was no sooner assured that the horseman with the large moustachios was her proffered husband, than she hastened to her father's presence, and expressed her readiness to sacrifice herself to secure his peace. The venerable baron caught his child to his arms, and shed a wink of joy.

There was great feasting at the castle, that day. The four-and-twenty Lincoln greens of Von Koeldwethout exchanged vows of eternal friendship with twelve Lincoln greens of Von Swillenhausen, and promised the old baron that they would drink his wine "Till all was blue" – meaning probably until their whole countenances had acquired the same tint as their noses. Everybody slapped everybody else's back, when the time for parting came; and the Baron Von Koeldwethout and his followers rode gaily home.

For six mortal weeks, the bears and boars had a holiday. The houses of Koeldwethout and Swillenhausen were united; the spears rusted; and the baron's bugle grew hoarse for lack of blowing.

Those were great times for the four-and-twenty; but, alas! their high and palmy days had taken boots to themselves, and were already walking off.

"My dear," said the baroness.

"My love," said the baron.

"Those coarse, noisy men—"

"Which, ma'am?" said the baron, starting.

The baroness pointed, from the window at which they stood, to the courtyard beneath, where the unconscious Lincoln greens were taking a copious stirrup-cup, preparatory to issuing forth after a boar or two.

"My hunting train, ma'am," said the baron.

"Disband them, love," murmured the baroness.

"Disband them!" cried the baron, in amazement.

"To please me, love," replied the baroness.

"To please the devil, ma'am," answered the baron.

Whereupon the baroness uttered a great cry, and swooned away at the baron's feet.

What could the baron do? He called for the lady's maid, and roared for the doctor; and then, rushing into the yard, kicked the two Lincoln greens who were the most used to it, and cursing the others all round, bade them go – but never mind where. I don't know the German for it, or I would put it delicately that way.

It is not for me to say by what means, or by what degrees, some wives manage to keep down some husbands as they do, although I may have my private opinion on the subject, and may think that no Member of Parliament ought to be married, inasmuch as three married members out of every four, must vote according to their wives' consciences (if there be such things), and not according to their own. All I need say, just now, is, that the Baroness Von Koeldwethout somehow or other acquired great control over the Baron Von Koeldwethout, and that, little by little, and bit by bit, and day by day, and year by year, the baron got the worst of some disputed question, or was slyly unhorsed from some old hobby; and that by the time he was a fat hearty fellow of forty-eight or thereabouts, he had no feasting, no revelry, no hunting train, and no hunting – nothing in short that he liked, or used to have; and that, although he was as fierce as a lion, and as bold as brass, he was decidedly snubbed and put down, by his own lady, in his own castle of Grogzwig.

Nor was this the whole extent of the baron's misfortunes. About a year after his nuptials, there came into the world a lusty young baron, in whose honour a great many fireworks were let off, and a great many dozens of wine drunk; but next year there came a young baroness, and next year another young baron, and so on, every year, either a baron or baroness (and one year both together), until the baron found himself the father of a small family of twelve. Upon every one of these anniversaries, the venerable Baroness Von Swillenhausen was nervously sensitive for the well-being of her child the Baroness Von Koeldwethout; and although it was not found that the good lady ever did anything material towards contributing to her child's recovery, still she made it a point of duty to be as nervous as possible at the castle of Grogzwig, and to divide her time between moral observations on the baron's housekeeping, and bewailing the hard lot of her unhappy daughter. And if the Baron of Grogzwig, a little hurt and irritated at this, took heart, and ventured to suggest that his wife was at least no worse off than the wives of other barons, the Baroness Von Swillenhausen begged all persons to take notice, that nobody but she, sympathised with her dear daughter's sufferings; upon which, her relations and friends remarked, that to be sure she did cry a great deal more than her son-in-law, and that if there were a hard-hearted brute alive, it was that Baron of Grogzwig.

The poor baron bore it all as long as he could, and when he could bear it no longer lost his appetite and his spirits, and sat himself gloomily and dejectedly down. But there were worse troubles yet in store for him, and as they came on, his melancholy and sadness increased. Times changed. He got into debt. The Grogzwig coffers ran low, though the Swillenhausen family had looked upon them as inexhaustible; and just when the baroness was on the point of making a thirteenth addition to the family pedigree, Von Koeldwethout discovered that he had no means of replenishing them.

"I don't see what is to be done," said the baron. "I think I'll kill myself."

This was a bright idea. The baron took an old hunting-knife from a cupboard hard by, and having sharpened it on his boot, made what boys call 'an offer' at his throat.

"Hem!" said the baron, stopping short. "Perhaps it's not sharp enough."

The baron sharpened it again, and made another offer, when his hand was arrested by a loud screaming among the young barons and baronesses, who had a nursery in an upstairs tower with iron bars outside the window, to prevent their tumbling out into the moat.

"If I had been a bachelor," said the baron sighing, "I might have done it fifty times over, without being interrupted. Hallo! Put a flask of wine and the largest pipe in the little vaulted room behind the hall."

One of the domestics, in a very kind manner, executed the baron's order in the course of half an hour or so, and Von Koeldwethout being apprised thereof, strode to the vaulted room, the walls of which, being of dark shining wood, gleamed in the light of the blazing logs which were piled upon the hearth. The bottle and pipe were ready, and, upon the whole, the place looked very comfortable.

"Leave the lamp," said the baron.

"Anything else, my lord?" inquired the domestic.

"The room," replied the baron. The domestic obeyed, and the baron locked the door.

"I'll smoke a last pipe," said the baron, "and then I'll be off." So, putting the knife upon the table till he wanted it, and tossing off a goodly measure of wine, the Lord of Grogzwig threw himself back in his chair, stretched his legs out before the fire, and puffed away.

He thought about a great many things – about his present troubles and past days of bachelorship, and about the Lincoln greens, long since dispersed up and down the country, no one knew whither: with the exception of two who had been unfortunately beheaded, and four who had killed themselves with drinking. His mind was running upon bears and boars, when, in the process of draining his glass to the bottom, he raised his eyes, and saw, for the first time and with unbounded astonishment, that he was not alone.

No, he was not; for, on the opposite side of the fire, there sat with folded arms a wrinkled hideous figure, with deeply sunk and bloodshot eyes, and an immensely long cadaverous face, shadowed by jagged and matted locks of coarse black hair. He wore a kind of tunic of a dull bluish colour, which, the baron observed, on regarding it attentively, was clasped or ornamented down the front with coffin handles. His legs, too, were encased in coffin plates as though in armour; and over his left shoulder he wore a short dusky cloak, which seemed made of a remnant of some pall. He took no notice of the baron, but was intently eyeing the fire.

"Halloa!" said the baron, stamping his foot to attract attention.

"Halloa!" replied the stranger, moving his eyes towards the baron, but not his face or himself "What now?"

"What now!" replied the baron, nothing daunted by his hollow voice and lustreless eyes. "I should ask that question. How did you get here?"

"Through the door," replied the figure.

"What are you?" says the baron.

"A man," replied the figure.

"I don't believe it," says the baron.

"Disbelieve it then," says the figure.

"I will," rejoined the baron.

The figure looked at the bold Baron of Grogzwig for some time, and then said familiarly, "There's no coming over you, I see. I'm not a man!"

"What are you then?" asked the baron.

"A genius," replied the figure.

"You don't look much like one," returned the baron scornfully.

"I am the Genius of Despair and Suicide," said the apparition. "Now you know me."

With these words the apparition turned towards the baron, as if composing himself for a talk – and, what was very remarkable, was that he threw his cloak aside, and displaying a stake, which was run through the centre of his body, pulled it out with a jerk, and laid it on the table, as composedly as if it had been a walking-stick.

"Now," said the figure, glancing at the hunting-knife, "are you ready for me?"

"Not quite," rejoined the baron; "I must finish this pipe first."

"Look sharp then," said the figure.

"You seem in a hurry," said the baron.

"Why, yes, I am," answered the figure; "they're doing a pretty brisk business in my way, over in England and France just now, and my time is a good deal taken up."

"Do you drink?" said the baron, touching the bottle with the bowl of his pipe.

"Nine times out of ten, and then very hard," rejoined the figure, drily.

"Never in moderation?" asked the baron.

"Never," replied the figure, with a shudder, "that breeds cheerfulness."

The baron took another look at his new friend, whom he thought an uncommonly queer customer, and at length inquired whether he took any active part in such little proceedings as that which he had in contemplation.

"No," replied the figure evasively; "but I am always present."

"Just to see fair, I suppose?" said the baron.

"Just that," replied the figure, playing with his stake, and examining the ferule. "Be as quick as you can, will you, for there's a young gentleman who is afflicted with too much money and leisure wanting me now, I find."

"Going to kill himself because he has too much money!" exclaimed the baron, quite tickled. "Ha! ha! that's a good one." (This was the first time the baron had laughed for many a long day.)

"I say," expostulated the figure, looking very much scared; "don't do that again."

"Why not?" demanded the baron.

"Because it gives me pain all over," replied the figure. "Sigh as much as you please: that does me good."

The baron sighed mechanically at the mention of the word; the figure, brightening up again, handed him the hunting-knife with most winning politeness.

"It's not a bad idea though," said the baron, feeling the edge of the weapon; "a man killing himself because he has too much money."

"Pooh!" said the apparition, petulantly, "no better than a man's killing himself because he has none or little."

Whether the genius unintentionally committed himself in saying this, or whether he thought the baron's mind was so thoroughly made up that it didn't matter what he said, I have no means of knowing. I only know that the baron stopped his hand, all of a sudden, opened his eyes wide, and looked as if quite a new light had come upon him for the first time.

"Why, certainly," said Von Koeldwethout, "nothing is too bad to be retrieved."

"Except empty coffers," cried the genius.

"Well; but they may be one day filled again," said the baron.

"Scolding wives," snarled the genius.

"Oh! They may be made quiet," said the baron.

"Thirteen children," shouted the genius.

"Can't all go wrong, surely," said the baron.

The genius was evidently growing very savage with the baron, for holding these opinions all at once; but he tried to laugh it off, and said if he would let him know when he had left off joking he should feel obliged to him.

"But I am not joking; I was never farther from it," remonstrated the baron.

"Well, I am glad to hear that," said the genius, looking very grim, "because a joke, without any figure of speech, *is the* death of me. Come! Quit this dreary world at once."

"I don't know," said the baron, playing with the knife; "it's a dreary one certainly, but I don't think yours is much better, for you have not the appearance of being particularly comfortable. That puts me in mind – what security have I, that I shall be any the better for going out of the world after all!" he cried, starting up; "I never thought of that."

"Dispatch," cried the figure, gnashing his teeth.

"Keep off!" said the baron. "I'll brood over miseries no longer, but put a good face on the matter, and try the fresh air and the bears again; and if that don't do, I'll talk to the baroness soundly, and cut the Von Swillenhausens dead." With this the baron fell into his chair, and laughed so loud and boisterously, that the room rang with it.

The figure fell back a pace or two, regarding the baron meanwhile with a look of intense terror, and when he had ceased, caught up the stake, plunged it violently into its body, uttered a frightful howl, and disappeared.

Von Koeldwethout never saw it again. Having once made up his mind to action, he soon brought the baroness and the Von Swillenhausens to reason, and died many years afterwards: not a rich man that I am aware of, but certainly a happy one: leaving behind him a numerous family, who had been carefully educated in bear and boar-hunting under his own personal eye. And my advice to all men is, that if ever they become hipped and melancholy from similar causes (as very many men do), they look at both sides of the question, applying a magnifying-glass to the best one; and if they still feel tempted to retire without leave, that they smoke a large pipe and drink a full bottle first, and profit by the laudable example of the Baron of Grogzwig.

**If you enjoyed this, you might also like...**

The Portrait Painter's Story, see page 240
The Trial for Murder, see page 251

# A Christmas Carol

## Stave One
## Marley's Ghost

**MARLEY WAS DEAD,** to begin with. There is no doubt whatever about that. The register of his burial was signed by the clergyman, the clerk, the undertaker, and the chief mourner. Scrooge signed it. And Scrooge's name was good upon 'Change for anything he chose to put his hand to. Old Marley was as dead as a door-nail.

Mind! I don't mean to say that I know, of my own knowledge, what there is particularly dead about a door-nail. I might have been inclined, myself, to regard a coffin-nail as the deadest piece of ironmongery in the trade. But the wisdom of our ancestors is in the simile; and my unhallowed hands shall not disturb it, or the Country's done for. You will, therefore, permit me to repeat, emphatically, that Marley was as dead as a door-nail.

Scrooge knew he was dead? Of course he did. How could it be otherwise? Scrooge and he were partners for I don't know how many years. Scrooge was his sole executor, his sole administrator, his sole assign, his sole residuary legatee, his sole friend, and sole mourner. And even Scrooge was not so dreadfully cut up by the sad event, but that he was an excellent man of business on the very day of the funeral, and solemnised it with an undoubted bargain.

The mention of Marley's funeral brings me back to the point I started from. There is no doubt that Marley was dead. This must be distinctly understood, or nothing wonderful can come of the story I am going to relate. If we were not perfectly convinced that Hamlet's Father died before the play began, there would be nothing more remarkable in his taking a stroll at night, in an easterly wind, upon his own ramparts, than there would be in any other middle-aged gentleman rashly turning out after dark in a breezy spot – say St. Paul's Church-yard, for instance – literally to astonish his son's weak mind.

Scrooge never painted out Old Marley's name. There it stood, years afterwards, above the warehouse door: Scrooge and Marley. The firm was known as Scrooge and Marley. Sometimes people new to the business called Scrooge Scrooge, and sometimes Marley, but he answered to both names. It was all the same to him.

Oh! but he was a tight-fisted hand at the grindstone, Scrooge! a squeezing, wrenching, grasping, scraping, clutching, covetous, old sinner! Hard and sharp as flint, from which no steel had ever struck out generous fire; secret, and self-contained, and solitary as an oyster. The cold within him froze his old features, nipped his pointed nose, shrivelled his cheek, stiffened his gait; made his eyes red, his thin lips blue; and spoke out shrewdly in his grating voice. A frosty rime was on his head, and on his eyebrows, and his wiry chin. He carried his own low temperature always about with him; he iced his office in the dog-days; and didn't thaw it one degree at Christmas.

External heat and cold had little influence on Scrooge. No warmth could warm, no wintry weather chill him. No wind that blew was bitterer than he, no falling snow was more intent upon its purpose, no pelting rain less open to entreaty. Foul weather didn't know where to have him. The heaviest rain, and snow, and hail, and sleet could boast of the advantage over him in only one respect. They often "came down" handsomely and Scrooge never did.

Nobody ever stopped him in the street to say, with gladsome looks, "My dear Scrooge, how are you? When will you come to see me?" No beggars implored him to bestow a trifle, no children asked him what it was o'clock, no man or woman ever once in all his life inquired the way to such and such a place, of Scrooge. Even the blind men's dogs appeared to know him; and, when they saw him coming on, would tug their owners into doorways and up courts; and then would wag their tails as though they said, "No eye at all is better than an evil eye, dark master!"

But what did Scrooge care? It was the very thing he liked. To edge his way along the crowded paths of life, warning all human sympathy to keep its distance, was what the knowing ones call "nuts" to Scrooge.

Once upon a time – of all the good days in the year, on Christmas Eve – old Scrooge sat busy in his counting-house. It was cold, bleak, biting weather: foggy withal: and he could hear the people in the court outside go wheezing up and down, beating their hands upon their breasts, and stamping their feet upon the pavement stones to warm them. The City clocks had only just gone three, but it was quite dark already – it had not been light all day – and candles were flaring in the windows of the neighbouring offices, like ruddy smears upon the palpable brown air. The fog came pouring in at every chink and keyhole, and was so dense without, that, although the court was of the narrowest, the houses opposite were mere phantoms. To see the dingy cloud come drooping down, obscuring everything, one might have thought that nature lived hard by and was brewing on a large scale.

The door of Scrooge's counting-house was open, that he might keep his eye upon his clerk, who in a dismal little cell beyond, a sort of tank, was copying letters. Scrooge had a very small fire, but the clerk's fire was so very much smaller that it looked like one coal. But he couldn't replenish it, for Scrooge kept the coal-box in his own room; and so surely as the clerk came in with the shovel, the master predicted that it would be necessary for them to part. Wherefore the clerk put on his white comforter, and tried to warm himself at the candle; in which effort, not being a man of strong imagination, he failed.

"A merry Christmas, uncle! God save you!" cried a cheerful voice. It was the voice of Scrooge's nephew, who came upon him so quickly that this was the first intimation he had of his approach.

"Bah!" said Scrooge. "Humbug!"

He had so heated himself with rapid walking in the fog and frost, this nephew of Scrooge's, that he was all in a glow; his face was ruddy and handsome; his eyes sparkled, and his breath smoked again.

"Christmas a humbug, uncle!" said Scrooge's nephew. "You don't mean that, I am sure?"

"I do," said Scrooge. "Merry Christmas! What right have you to be merry? What reason have you to be merry? You're poor enough."

"Come, then," returned the nephew gaily. "What right have you to be dismal? What reason have you to be morose? You're rich enough."

Scrooge, having no better answer ready on the spur of the moment, said, "Bah!" again; and followed it up with "Humbug!"

"Don't be cross, uncle!" said the nephew.

"A Merry Christmas, uncle! God save you!" cried a cheerful voice.

"What else can I be," returned the uncle, "when I live in such a world of fools as this? Merry Christmas! Out upon merry Christmas! What's Christmas-time to you but a time for paying bills without money; a time for finding yourself a year older, and not an hour richer; a time for balancing your books, and having every item in 'em through a round dozen of months presented dead against you? If I could work my will," said Scrooge indignantly, "every idiot who goes about with 'Merry Christmas' on his lips should be boiled with his own pudding, and buried with a stake of holly through his heart. He should!"

"Uncle!" pleaded the nephew.

"Nephew!" returned the uncle sternly, "keep Christmas in your own way, and let me keep it in mine."

"Keep it!" repeated Scrooge's nephew. "But you don't keep it."

"Let me leave it alone, then," said Scrooge. "Much good may it do you! Much good it has ever done you!"

"There are many things from which I might have derived good, by which I have not profited, I dare say," returned the nephew; "Christmas among the rest. But I am sure I have always thought of Christmas-time, when it has come round – apart from the veneration due to its sacred name and origin, if anything belonging to it can be apart from that – as a good time; a kind, forgiving, charitable, pleasant time; the only time I know of, in the long calendar of the year, when men and women seem by one consent to open their shut-up hearts freely, and to think of people below them as if they really were fellow-passengers to the grave, and not another race of creatures bound on other journeys. And therefore, uncle, though it has never put a scrap of gold or silver in my pocket, I believe that it *has* done me good, and *will* do me good; and I say, God bless it!"

The clerk in the tank involuntarily applauded. Becoming immediately sensible of the impropriety, he poked the fire, and extinguished the last frail spark for ever.

"Let me hear another sound from *you*," said Scrooge, "and you'll keep your Christmas by losing your situation! You're quite a powerful speaker, sir," he added, turning to his nephew. "I wonder you don't go into Parliament."

"Don't be angry, uncle. Come! Dine with us tomorrow."

Scrooge said that he would see him— Yes, indeed he did. He went the whole length of the expression, and said that he would see him in that extremity first.

"But why?" cried Scrooge's nephew. "Why?"

"Why did you get married?" said Scrooge.

"Because I fell in love."

"Because you fell in love!" growled Scrooge, as if that were the only one thing in the world more ridiculous than a merry Christmas. "Good afternoon!"

"Nay, uncle, but you never came to see me before that happened. Why give it as a reason for not coming now?"

"Good afternoon," said Scrooge.

"I want nothing from you; I ask nothing of you; why cannot we be friends?"

"Good afternoon!" said Scrooge.

"I am sorry, with all my heart, to find you so resolute. We have never had any quarrel to which I have been a party. But I have made the trial in homage to Christmas, and I'll keep my Christmas humour to the last. So A Merry Christmas, uncle!"

"Good afternoon," said Scrooge.

"And A Happy New Year!"

"Good afternoon!" said Scrooge.

His nephew left the room without an angry word, notwithstanding. He stopped at the outer door to bestow the greetings of the season on the clerk, who, cold as he was, was warmer than Scrooge; for he returned them cordially.

"There's another fellow," muttered Scrooge, who overheard him: "my clerk, with fifteen shillings a week, and a wife and family, talking about a merry Christmas. I'll retire to Bedlam."

This lunatic, in letting Scrooge's nephew out, had let two other people in. They were portly gentlemen, pleasant to behold, and now stood, with their hats off, in Scrooge's office. They had books and papers in their hands, and bowed to him.

"Scrooge and Marley's, I believe," said one of the gentlemen, referring to his list. "Have I the pleasure of addressing Mr. Scrooge, or Mr. Marley?"

"Mr. Marley has been dead these seven years," Scrooge replied. "He died seven years ago, this very night."

"We have no doubt his liberality is well represented by his surviving partner," said the gentleman, presenting his credentials.

It certainly was; for they had been two kindred spirits. At the ominous word "liberality" Scrooge frowned, and shook his head, and handed the credentials back.

"At this festive season of the year, Mr. Scrooge," said the gentleman, taking up a pen, "it is more than usually desirable that we should make some slight provision for the poor and destitute, who suffer greatly at the present time. Many thousands are in want of common necessaries; hundreds of thousands are in want of common comforts, sir."

"Are there no prisons?" asked Scrooge.

"Plenty of prisons," said the gentleman, laying down the pen again.

"And the Union workhouses?" demanded Scrooge. "Are they still in operation?"

"They are. Still," returned the gentleman, "I wish I could say they were not."

"The Treadmill and the Poor Law are in full vigour, then?" said Scrooge.

"Both very busy, sir."

"Oh! I was afraid, from what you said at first, that something had occurred to stop them in their useful course," said Scrooge. "I am very glad to hear it."

"Under the impression that they scarcely furnish Christian cheer of mind or body to the multitude," returned the gentleman, "a few of us are endeavouring to raise a fund to buy the Poor some meat and drink, and means of warmth. We choose this time, because it is a time, of all others, when Want is keenly felt, and Abundance rejoices. What shall I put you down for?"

"Nothing!" Scrooge replied.

"You wish to be anonymous?"

"I wish to be left alone," said Scrooge. "Since you ask me what I wish, gentlemen, that is my answer. I don't make merry myself at Christmas, and I can't afford to make idle people merry. I help to support the establishments I have mentioned – they cost enough; and those who are badly off must go there."

"Many can't go there; and many would rather die."

"If they would rather die," said Scrooge, "they had better do it, and decrease the surplus population. Besides – excuse me – I don't know that."

"But you might know it," observed the gentleman.

"It's not my business," Scrooge returned. "It's enough for a man to understand his own business, and not to interfere with other people's. Mine occupies me constantly. Good afternoon, gentlemen!"

Seeing clearly that it would be useless to pursue their point, the gentlemen withdrew. Scrooge resumed his labours with an improved opinion of himself, and in a more facetious temper than was usual with him.

Meanwhile the fog and darkness thickened so, that people ran about with flaring links, proffering their services to go before horses in carriages, and conduct them on their way. The ancient tower of a church, whose gruff old bell was always peeping slily down at Scrooge out of a Gothic window in the wall, became invisible, and struck the hours and quarters in the clouds, with tremulous vibrations afterwards, as if its teeth were chattering in its frozen head up there. The cold became intense. In the main street, at the corner of the court, some labourers were repairing the gas-pipes, and had lighted a great fire in a brazier, round which a party of ragged men and boys were gathered: warming their hands and winking their eyes before the blaze in rapture. The water-plug being left in solitude, its overflowings suddenly congealed, and turned to misanthropic ice. The brightness of the shops, where holly sprigs and berries crackled in the lamp heat of the windows, made pale faces ruddy as they passed. Poulterers' and grocers' trades became a splendid joke: a glorious pageant, with which it was next to impossible to believe that such dull principles as bargain and sale had anything to do. The Lord Mayor, in the stronghold of the mighty Mansion House, gave orders to his fifty cooks and butlers to keep Christmas as a Lord Mayor's household should; and even the little tailor, whom he had fined five shillings on the previous Monday for being drunk and blood-thirsty in the streets, stirred up tomorrow's pudding in his garret, while his lean wife and the baby sallied out to buy the beef.

Foggier yet, and colder! Piercing, searching, biting cold. If the good St. Dunstan had but nipped the Evil Spirit's nose with a touch of such weather as that, instead of using his familiar weapons, then indeed he would have roared to lusty purpose. The owner of one scant young nose, gnawed and mumbled by the hungry cold as bones are gnawed by dogs, stooped down at Scrooge's keyhole to regale him with a Christmas carol; but, at the first sound of

"God bless you, merry gentleman, May nothing you dismay!"

Scrooge seized the ruler with such energy of action, that the singer fled in terror, leaving the keyhole to the fog, and even more congenial frost.

At length the hour of shutting up the counting-house arrived. With an ill-will Scrooge dismounted from his stool, and tacitly admitted the fact to the expectant clerk in the tank, who instantly snuffed his candle out, and put on his hat.

"You'll want all day tomorrow, I suppose?" said Scrooge.

"If quite convenient, sir."

"It's not convenient," said Scrooge, "and it's not fair. If I was to stop half-a-crown for it, you'd think yourself ill used, I'll be bound?"

The clerk smiled faintly.

"And yet," said Scrooge, "you don't think *me* ill used when I pay a day's wages for no work."

The clerk observed that it was only once a year.

"A poor excuse for picking a man's pocket every twenty-fifth of December!" said Scrooge, buttoning his great-coat to the chin. "But I suppose you must have the whole day. Be here all the earlier next morning."

The clerk promised that he would; and Scrooge walked out with a growl. The office was closed in a twinkling, and the clerk, with the long ends of his white comforter dangling below his waist (for he boasted no great-coat), went down a slide on Cornhill, at the end of a lane of boys, twenty times, in honour of its being Christmas-eve, and then ran home to Camden Town as hard as he could pelt, to play at blindman's buff.

Scrooge took his melancholy dinner in his usual melancholy tavern; and having read all the newspapers, and beguiled the rest of the evening with his banker's book, went home to bed. He lived in chambers which had once belonged to his deceased partner. They were a gloomy suite of rooms, in a lowering pile of building up a yard, where it had so little business to be, that one could scarcely help fancying it must have run there when it was a young house, playing at hide-and-seek with other houses, and have forgotten the way out again. It was old enough now, and dreary enough; for nobody lived in it but Scrooge, the other rooms being all let out as offices. The yard was so dark that even Scrooge, who knew its every stone, was fain to grope with his hands. The fog and frost so hung about the black old gateway of the house, that it seemed as if the Genius of the Weather sat in mournful meditation on the threshold.

Now, it is a fact that there was nothing at all particular about the knocker on the door, except that it was very large. It is also a fact that Scrooge had seen it, night and morning, during his whole residence in that place; also that Scrooge had as little of what is called fancy about him as any man in the City of London, even including – which is a bold word – the corporation, aldermen, and livery. Let it also be borne in mind that Scrooge had not bestowed one thought on Marley since his last mention of his seven-years'-dead partner that afternoon. And then let any man explain to me, if he can, how it happened that Scrooge, having his key in the lock of the door, saw in the knocker, without its undergoing any intermediate process of change – not a knocker, but Marley's face.

Marley's face. It was not in impenetrable shadow, as the other objects in the yard were, but had a dismal light about it, like a bad lobster in a dark cellar. It was not angry or ferocious, but looked at Scrooge as Marley used to look: with ghostly spectacles turned up on its ghostly forehead. The hair was curiously stirred, as if by breath of hot air; and, though the eyes were wide open, they were perfectly motionless. That, and its livid colour, made it horrible; but its horror seemed to be in spite of the face, and beyond its control, rather than a part of its own expression.

As Scrooge looked fixedly at this phenomenon, it was a knocker again.

To say that he was not startled, or that his blood was not conscious of a terrible sensation to which it had been a stranger from infancy, would be untrue. But he put his hand upon the key he had relinquished, turned it sturdily, walked in, and lighted his candle.

He *did* pause, with a moment's irresolution, before he shut the door; and he *did* look cautiously behind it first, as if he half expected to be terrified with the sight of Marley's pigtail sticking out into the hall. But there was nothing on the back of the door, except the screws and nuts that held the knocker on, so he said, "Pooh, pooh!" and closed it with a bang.

The sound resounded through the house like thunder. Every room above, and every cask in the wine merchant's cellars below, appeared to have a separate peal of echoes of its own. Scrooge was not a man to be frightened by echoes. He fastened the door, and walked across the hall, and up the stairs: slowly, too: trimming his candle as he went.

You may talk vaguely about driving a coach and six up a good old flight of stairs, or through a bad young Act of Parliament; but I mean to say you might have got a hearse up that staircase, and taken it broadwise, with the splinter-bar towards the wall, and the door towards the balustrades: and done it easy. There was plenty of width for that, and room to spare; which is perhaps the reason why Scrooge thought he saw a locomotive hearse going on before him in the gloom. Half-a-dozen gas-lamps out of the street wouldn't have lighted the entry too well, so you may suppose that it was pretty dark with Scrooge's dip.

Up Scrooge went, not caring a button for that. Darkness is cheap, and Scrooge liked it. But, before he shut his heavy door, he walked through his rooms to see that all was right. He had just enough recollection of the face to desire to do that.

Sitting-room, bedroom, lumber-room. All as they should be. Nobody under the table, nobody under the sofa; a small fire in the grate; spoon and basin ready; and the little saucepan of gruel (Scrooge had a cold in his head) upon the hob. Nobody under the bed; nobody in the closet; nobody in his dressing-gown, which was hanging up in a suspicious attitude against the wall. Lumber-room as usual. Old fire-guard, old shoes, two fish baskets, washing-stand on three legs, and a poker.

Quite satisfied, he closed his door, and locked himself in; double locked himself in, which was not his custom. Thus secured against surprise, he took off his cravat; put on his dressing-gown and slippers, and his nightcap; and sat down before the fire to take his gruel.

It was a very low fire indeed; nothing on such a bitter night. He was obliged to sit close to it, and brood over it, before he could extract the least sensation of warmth from such a handful of fuel. The fire-place was an old one, built by some Dutch merchant long ago, and paved all round with quaint Dutch tiles, designed to illustrate the Scriptures. There were Cains and Abels, Pharaoh's daughters, Queens of Sheba, Angelic messengers descending through the air on clouds like feather beds, Abrahams, Belshazzars, Apostles putting off to sea in butter-boats, hundreds of figures to attract his thoughts; and yet that face of Marley, seven years dead, came like the ancient Prophet's rod, and swallowed up the whole. If each smooth tile had been a blank at first, with power to shape some picture on its surface from the disjointed fragments of his thoughts, there would have been a copy of old Marley's head on every one.

"Humbug!" said Scrooge; and walked across the room.

After several turns he sat down again. As he threw his head back in the chair, his glance happened to rest upon a bell, a disused bell, that hung in the room, and communicated, for some purpose now forgotten, with a chamber in the highest story of the building. It was with great astonishment, and with a strange, inexplicable dread, that, as he looked, he saw this bell begin to swing. It swung so softly in the outset that it scarcely made a sound; but soon it rang out loudly, and so did every bell in the house.

This might have lasted half a minute, or a minute, but it seemed an hour. The bells ceased, as they had begun, together. They were succeeded by a clanking noise, deep down below, as if some person were dragging a heavy chain over the casks in the wine merchant's cellar. Scrooge then remembered to have heard that ghosts in haunted houses were described as dragging chains.

The cellar door flew open with a booming sound, and then he heard the noise much louder on the floors below; then coming up the stairs; then coming straight towards his door.

"It's humbug still!" said Scrooge. "I won't believe it."

His colour changed, though, when, without a pause, it came on through the heavy door, and passed into the room before his eyes. Upon its coming in, the dying flame leaped up, as though it cried, "I know him! Marley's Ghost!" and fell again.

The same face: the very same. Marley in his pigtail, usual waistcoat, tights, and boots; the tassels on the latter bristling, like his pigtail, and his coat-skirts, and the hair upon his head. The chain he drew was clasped about his middle. It was long, and wound about him like a tail; and it was made (for Scrooge observed it closely) of cash-boxes, keys, padlocks, ledgers, deeds, and heavy purses wrought in steel. His body was transparent; so that Scrooge, observing him, and looking through his waistcoat, could see the two buttons on his coat behind.

Scrooge had often heard it said that Marley had no bowels, but he had never believed it until now.

No, nor did he believe it even now. Though he looked the phantom through and through, and saw it standing before him; though he felt the chilling influence of its death-cold eyes; and marked the very texture of the folded kerchief bound about its head and chin, which wrapper he had not observed before; he was still incredulous, and fought against his senses.

"How now!" said Scrooge, caustic and cold as ever. "What do you want with me?"

"Much!" – Marley's voice, no doubt about it.

"Who are you?"

"Ask me who I *was*."

"Who *were* you, then?" said Scrooge, raising his voice. "You're particular, for a shade." He was going to say "*to* a shade," but substituted this, as more appropriate.

"In life I was your partner, Jacob Marley."

"Can you – can you sit down?" asked Scrooge, looking doubtfully at him.

"I can."

"Do it, then."

Scrooge asked the question, because he didn't know whether a ghost so transparent might find himself in a condition to take a chair; and felt that, in the event of its being impossible, it might involve the necessity of an embarrassing explanation. But the Ghost sat down on the opposite side of the fire-place, as if he were quite used to it.

"You don't believe in me," observed the Ghost.

"I don't," said Scrooge.

"What evidence would you have of my reality beyond that of your own senses?"

"I don't know," said Scrooge.

"Why do you doubt your senses?"

"Because," said Scrooge, "a little thing affects them. A slight disorder of the stomach makes them cheats. You may be an undigested bit of beef, a blot of mustard, a crumb of cheese, a fragment of an underdone potato. There's more of gravy than of grave about you, whatever you are!"

Scrooge was not much in the habit of cracking jokes, nor did he feel in his heart by any means waggish then. The truth is, that he tried to be smart, as a means of distracting his own attention, and keeping down his terror; for the spectre's voice disturbed the very marrow in his bones.

To sit staring at those fixed glazed eyes in silence, for a moment, would play, Scrooge felt, the very deuce with him. There was something very awful, too, in the spectre's being provided with an infernal atmosphere of his own. Scrooge could not feel it himself, but this was clearly the case; for though the Ghost sat perfectly motionless, its hair, and skirts, and tassels were still agitated as by the hot vapour from an oven.

"You see this toothpick?" said Scrooge, returning quickly to the charge, for the reason just assigned; and wishing, though it were only for a second, to divert the vision's stony gaze from himself.

"I do," replied the Ghost.

"You are not looking at it," said Scrooge.

"But I see it," said the Ghost, "notwithstanding."

"Well!" returned Scrooge, "I have but to swallow this, and be for the rest of my days persecuted by a legion of goblins, all of my own creation. Humbug, I tell you; humbug!"

At this the spirit raised a frightful cry, and shook its chain with such a dismal and appalling noise, that Scrooge held on tight to his chair, to save himself from falling in a swoon. But how much greater was his horror when the phantom, taking off the bandage round his head, as if it were too warm to wear indoors, its lower jaw dropped down upon its breast!

Scrooge fell upon his knees, and clasped his hands before his face.

"Mercy!" he said. "Dreadful apparition, why do you trouble me?"

"Man of the worldly mind!" replied the Ghost, "do you believe in me or not?"

"I do," said Scrooge. "I must. But why do spirits walk the earth, and why do they come to me?"

To sit staring at those fixed glazed eyes in silence, for a moment, would play, Scrooge felt, the very deuce with him.

"It is required of every man," the Ghost returned, "that the spirit within him should walk abroad among his fellow-men, and travel far and wide; and, if that spirit goes not forth in life, it is condemned to do so after death. It is doomed to wander through the world – oh, woe is me! – and witness what it cannot share, but might have shared on earth, and turned to happiness!"

Again the spectre raised a cry, and shook its chain and wrung its shadowy hands.

"You are fettered," said Scrooge, trembling. "Tell me why?"

"I wear the chain I forged in life," replied the Ghost. "I made it link by link, and yard by yard; I girded it on of my own free-will, and of my own free-will I wore it. Is its pattern strange to *you*?"

Scrooge trembled more and more.

"Or would you know," pursued the Ghost, "the weight and length of the strong coil you bear yourself? It was full as heavy and as long as this, seven Christmas-eves ago. You have laboured on it since. It is a ponderous chain!"

Scrooge glanced about him on the floor, in the expectation of finding himself surrounded by some fifty or sixty fathoms of iron cable, but he could see nothing.

"Jacob!" he said imploringly. "Old Jacob Marley, tell me more! Speak comfort to me, Jacob!"

"I have none to give," the Ghost replied. "It comes from other regions, Ebenezer Scrooge, and is conveyed by other ministers, to other kinds of men. Nor can I tell you what I would. A very little more is all permitted to me. I cannot rest, I cannot stay, I cannot linger anywhere. My spirit never walked beyond our counting-house – mark me; – in life my spirit never roved beyond the narrow limits of our money-changing hole; and weary journeys lie before me!"

It was a habit with Scrooge, whenever he became thoughtful, to put his hands in his breeches pockets. Pondering on what the Ghost had said, he did so now, but without lifting up his eyes, or getting off his knees.

"You must have been very slow about it, Jacob," Scrooge observed in a business-like manner, though with humility and deference.

"Slow!" the Ghost repeated.

"Seven years dead," mused Scrooge. "And travelling all the time?"

"The whole time," said the Ghost. "No rest, no peace. Incessant torture of remorse."

"You travel fast?" said Scrooge.

"On the wings of the wind," replied the Ghost.

"You might have got over a great quantity of ground in seven years," said Scrooge.

The Ghost, on hearing this, set up another cry, and clanked its chain so hideously in the dead silence of the night, that the Ward would have been justified in indicting it for a nuisance.

"Oh! captive, bound, and double-ironed," cried the phantom, "not to know that ages of incessant labour, by immortal creatures, for this earth must pass into eternity before the good of which it is susceptible is all developed! Not to know that any Christian spirit working kindly in its little sphere, whatever it may be, will find its mortal life too short for its vast means of usefulness! Not to know that no space of regret can make amends for one life's opportunities misused! Yet such was I! Oh, such was I!"

"But you were always a good man of business, Jacob," faltered Scrooge, who now began to apply this to himself.

"Business!" cried the Ghost, wringing its hands again. "Mankind was my business. The common welfare was my business; charity, mercy, forbearance, and benevolence were, all, my business. The dealings of my trade were but a drop of water in the comprehensive ocean of my business!"

It held up its chain at arm's length, as if that were the cause of all its unavailing grief, and flung it heavily upon the ground again.

"At this time of the rolling year," the spectre said, "I suffer most. Why did I walk through crowds of fellow-beings with my eyes turned down, and never raise them to that blessed Star which led the Wise Men to a poor abode? Were there no poor homes to which its light would have conducted *me*?"

Scrooge was very much dismayed to hear the spectre going on at this rate, and began to quake exceedingly.

"Hear me!" cried the Ghost. "My time is nearly gone."

"I will," said Scrooge. "But don't be hard upon me! Don't be flowery, Jacob! Pray!"

"How it is that I appear before you in a shape that you can see, I may not tell. I have sat invisible beside you many and many a day."

It was not an agreeable idea. Scrooge shivered, and wiped the perspiration from his brow.

"That is no light part of my penance," pursued the Ghost. "I am here to-night to warn you that you have yet a chance and hope of escaping my fate. A chance and hope of my procuring, Ebenezer."

"You were always a good friend to me," said Scrooge. "Thankee!"

"You will be haunted," resumed the Ghost, "by Three Spirits."

Scrooge's countenance fell almost as low as the Ghost's had done.

"Is that the chance and hope you mentioned, Jacob?" he demanded in a faltering voice.

"It is."

"I—I think I'd rather not," said Scrooge.

"Without their visits," said the Ghost, "you cannot hope to shun the path I tread. Expect the first tomorrow when the bell tolls One."

"Couldn't I take 'em all at once, and have it over, Jacob?" hinted Scrooge.

"Expect the second on the next night at the same hour. The third, upon the next night when the last stroke of Twelve has ceased to vibrate. Look to see me no more; and look that, for your own sake, you remember what has passed between us!"

When it had said these words, the spectre took its wrapper from the table, and bound it round its head as before. Scrooge knew this by the smart sound its teeth made when the jaws were brought together by the bandage. He ventured to raise his eyes again, and found his supernatural visitor confronting him in an erect attitude, with its chain wound over and about its arm.

The apparition walked backward from him; and, at every step it took, the window raised itself a little, so that, when the spectre reached it, it was wide open. It beckoned Scrooge to approach, which he did. When they were within two paces of each other, Marley's Ghost held up its hand, warning him to come no nearer. Scrooge stopped.

Not so much in obedience as in surprise and fear; for, on the raising of the hand, he became sensible of confused noises in the air; incoherent sounds of lamentation and regret; wailings inexpressibly sorrowful and self-accusatory. The spectre, after listening for a moment, joined in the mournful dirge; and floated out upon the bleak, dark night.

Scrooge followed to the window: desperate in his curiosity. He looked out.

The air was filled with phantoms, wandering hither and thither in restless haste, and moaning as they went. Every one of them wore chains like Marley's Ghost; some few (they might be guilty governments) were linked together; none were free. Many had been personally known to Scrooge in their lives. He had been quite familiar with one old ghost in a white waistcoat, with a monstrous iron safe attached to its ankle, who cried piteously at being unable to assist a wretched woman with an infant, whom it saw below upon a doorstep. The misery with them all was, clearly, that they sought to interfere, for good, in human matters, and had lost the power for ever.

Whether these creatures faded into mist, or mist enshrouded them, he could not tell. But they and their spirit voices faded together; and the night became as it had been when he walked home.

Scrooge closed the window, and examined the door by which the Ghost had entered. It was double locked, as he had locked it with his own hands, and the bolts were undisturbed. He tried to say "Humbug!" but stopped at the first syllable. And being, from the emotion he had undergone, or the fatigues of the day, or his glimpse of the Invisible World, or the dull conversation of the Ghost, or the lateness of the hour, much in need of repose, went straight to bed without undressing, and fell asleep upon the instant.

## Stave Two
### The First of the Three Spirits

**WHEN SCROOGE** awoke it was so dark, that, looking out of bed, he could scarcely distinguish the transparent window from the opaque walls of his chamber. He was endeavouring to pierce the darkness with his ferret eyes, when the chimes of a neighbouring church struck the four quarters. So he listened for the hour.

To his great astonishment, the heavy bell went on from six to seven, and from seven to eight, and regularly up to twelve; then stopped. Twelve! It was past two when he went to bed. The clock was wrong. An icicle must have got into the works. Twelve!

He touched the spring of his repeater, to correct this most preposterous clock. Its rapid little pulse beat twelve, and stopped.

"Why, it isn't possible," said Scrooge, "that I can have slept through a whole day and far into another night. It isn't possible that anything has happened to the sun, and this is twelve at noon!"

The idea being an alarming one, he scrambled out of bed, and groped his way to the window. He was obliged to rub the frost off with the sleeve of his dressing-gown before he could see anything; and could see very little then. All he could make out was, that it was still very foggy and extremely cold, and that there was no noise of people running to and fro, and making a great stir, as there unquestionably would have been if night had beaten off bright day, and taken possession of the world. This was a great relief, because "Three days after sight of this First of Exchange pay to Mr. Ebenezer Scrooge or his order," and so forth, would have become a mere United States security if there were no days to count by.

Scrooge went to bed again, and thought, and thought, and thought it over and over, and could make nothing of it. The more he thought, the more perplexed he was; and, the more he endeavoured not to think, the more he thought.

Marley's Ghost bothered him exceedingly. Every time he resolved within himself, after mature inquiry, that it was all a dream, his mind flew back again, like a strong spring released, to its first position, and presented the same problem to be worked all through, "Was it a dream or not?"

Scrooge lay in this state until the chime had gone three quarters more, when he remembered, on a sudden, that the Ghost had warned him of a visitation when the bell tolled one. He resolved to lie awake until the hour was passed; and, considering that he could no more go to sleep than go to Heaven, this was, perhaps, the wisest resolution in his power.

The quarter was so long, that he was more than once convinced he must have sunk into a doze unconsciously, and missed the clock. At length it broke upon his listening ear.

"Ding, dong!"

"A quarter past," said Scrooge, counting.

"Ding, dong!"

"Half past," said Scrooge.

"Ding, dong!"

"A quarter to it," said Scrooge.

"Ding, dong!"

"The hour itself," said Scrooge triumphantly, "and nothing else!"

He spoke before the hour bell sounded, which it now did with a deep, dull, hollow, melancholy One. Light flashed up in the room upon the instant, and the curtains of his bed were drawn.

The curtains of his bed were drawn aside, I tell you, by a hand. Not the curtains at his feet, nor the curtains at his back, but those to which his face was addressed. The curtains of his bed were drawn aside; and Scrooge, starting up into a half-recumbent attitude, found himself face to face with the unearthly visitor who drew them: as close to it as I am now to you, and I am standing in the spirit at your elbow.

It was a strange figure – like a child: yet not so like a child as like an old man, viewed through some supernatural medium, which gave him the appearance of having receded from the view, and being diminished to a child's proportions. Its hair, which hung about its neck and down its back, was white, as if with age; and yet the face had not a wrinkle in it, and the tenderest bloom was on the skin. The arms were very long and muscular; the hands the same, as if its hold were of uncommon strength. Its legs and feet, most delicately formed, were, like those upper members, bare. It wore a tunic of the purest white; and round its waist was bound a lustrous belt, the sheen of which was beautiful. It held a branch of fresh green holly in its hand: and, in singular contradiction of that wintry emblem, had its dress trimmed with summer flowers. But the strangest thing about it was, that from the crown of its head there sprung a bright clear jet of light, by which all this was visible; and which was doubtless the occasion of its using, in its duller moments, a great extinguisher for a cap, which it now held under its arm.

Even this, though, when Scrooge looked at it with increasing steadiness, was *not* its strangest quality. For, as its belt sparkled and glittered, now in one part and now in another, and what was light one instant at another time was dark, so the figure itself fluctuated in its distinctness: being now a thing with one arm, now with one leg, now with twenty legs, now a pair of legs without a head, now a head without a body: of which dissolving parts no outline would be visible in the dense gloom wherein they melted away. And, in the very wonder of this, it would be itself again; distinct and clear as ever.

"Are you the Spirit, sir, whose coming was foretold to me?" asked Scrooge.

"I am!"

The voice was soft and gentle. Singularly low, as if, instead of being so close beside him, it were at a distance.

"Who and what are you?" Scrooge demanded.

"I am the Ghost of Christmas Past."

"Long Past?" inquired Scrooge; observant of its dwarfish stature.

"No. Your past."

Perhaps Scrooge could not have told anybody why, if anybody could have asked him; but he had a special desire to see the Spirit in his cap; and begged him to be covered.

"What!" exclaimed the Ghost, "would you so soon put out, with worldly hands, the light I give? Is it not enough that you are one of those whose passions made this cap, and force me through whole trains of years to wear it low upon my brow?"

Scrooge reverently disclaimed all intention to offend or any knowledge of having wilfully "bonneted" the Spirit at any period of his life. He then made bold to inquire what business brought him there.

"Your welfare!" said the Ghost.

Scrooge expressed himself much obliged, but could not help thinking that a night of unbroken rest would have been more conducive to that end. The Spirit must have heard him thinking, for it said immediately:

"Your reclamation, then. Take heed!"

It put out its strong hand as it spoke, and clasped him gently by the arm.

"Rise! and walk with me!"

It would have been in vain for Scrooge to plead that the weather and the hour were not adapted to pedestrian purposes; that bed was warm, and the thermometer a long way below freezing; that he was clad but lightly in his slippers, dressing-gown, and nightcap; and that he had a cold upon him at that time. The grasp, though gentle as a woman's hand, was not to be resisted. He rose: but, finding that the Spirit made towards the window, clasped its robe in supplication.

"I am a mortal," Scrooge remonstrated, "and liable to fall."

"Bear but a touch of my hand *there*," said the Spirit, laying it upon his heart, "and you shall be upheld in more than this!"

As the words were spoken, they passed through the wall, and stood upon an open country road, with fields on either hand. The city had entirely vanished. Not a vestige of it was to be seen. The darkness and the mist had vanished with it, for it was a clear, cold, winter day, with the snow upon the ground.

"Good Heaven!" said Scrooge, clasping his hands together as he looked about him. "I was bred in this place. I was a boy here!"

The Spirit gazed upon him mildly. Its gentle touch, though it had been light and instantaneous, appeared still present to the old man's sense of feeling. He was conscious of a thousand odours floating in the air, each one connected with a thousand thoughts, and hopes, and joys, and cares long, long forgotten!

"Your lip is trembling," said the Ghost. "And what is that upon your cheek?"

Scrooge muttered, with an unusual catching in his voice, that it was a pimple; and begged the Ghost to lead him where he would.

"You recollect the way?" inquired the Spirit.

"Remember it!" cried Scrooge with fervour; "I could walk it blindfold."

"Strange to have forgotten it for so many years!" observed the Ghost. "Let us go on."

"You recollect the way?" inquired the spirit. "Remember it!" cried Scrooge with fervour; "I could walk it blindfold."

They walked along the road, Scrooge recognising every gate, and post, and tree, until a little market-town appeared in the distance, with its bridge, its church, and winding river. Some shaggy ponies now were seen trotting towards them with boys upon their backs, who called to other boys in country gigs and carts, driven by farmers. All these boys were in great spirits, and shouted to each other, until the broad fields were so full of merry music, that the crisp air laughed to hear it.

"These are but shadows of the things that have been," said the Ghost. "They have no consciousness of us."

The jocund travellers came on; and as they came, Scrooge knew and named them every one. Why was he rejoiced beyond all bounds to see them? Why did his cold eye glisten, and his heart leap up as they went past? Why was he filled with gladness when he heard them give each other Merry Christmas, as they parted at cross-roads and by-ways for their several homes? What was merry Christmas to Scrooge? Out upon merry Christmas! What good had it ever done to him?

"The school is not quite deserted," said the Ghost. "A solitary child, neglected by his friends, is left there still."

Scrooge said he knew it. And he sobbed.

They left the high-road by a well-remembered lane, and soon approached a mansion of dull red brick, with a little weather-cock surmounted cupola on the roof and a bell hanging in it. It was a large house, but one of broken fortunes: for the spacious offices were little used, their walls were damp and mossy, their windows broken, and their gates decayed. Fowls clucked and strutted in the stables; and the coach-houses and sheds were overrun with grass. Nor was it more retentive of its ancient state within; for, entering the dreary hall, and glancing through the open doors of many rooms, they found them poorly furnished, cold, and vast. There was an earthly savour in the air, a chilly bareness in the place, which associated itself somehow with too much getting up by candle-light, and not too much to eat.

They went, the Ghost and Scrooge, across the hall, to a door at the back of the house. It opened before them, and disclosed a long, bare, melancholy room, made barer still by lines of plain deal forms and desks. At one of these a lonely boy was reading near a feeble fire; and Scrooge sat down upon a form, and wept to see his poor forgotten self as he had used to be.

Not a latent echo in the house, not a squeak and scuffle from the mice behind the panelling, not a drip from the half-thawed water-spout in the dull yard behind, not a sigh among the leafless boughs of one despondent poplar, not the idle swinging of an empty storehouse door, no, not a clicking in the fire, but fell upon the heart of Scrooge with softening influence, and gave a freer passage to his tears.

The Spirit touched him on the arm, and pointed to his younger self, intent upon his reading. Suddenly a man in foreign garments: wonderfully real and distinct to look at: stood outside the window, with an axe stuck in his belt, and leading by the bridle an ass laden with wood.

"Why, it's Ali Baba!" Scrooge exclaimed in ecstasy. "It's dear old honest Ali Baba! Yes, yes, I know. One Christmas-time when yonder solitary child was left here all alone, he *did* come, for the first time, just like that. Poor boy! And Valentine," said Scrooge, "and his wild brother, Orson; there they go! And what's his name, who was put down in his drawers, asleep, at the gate of Damascus; don't you see him? And the Sultan's Groom turned upside down by the Genii: there he is upon his head! Serve him right! I'm glad of it. What business had *he* to be married to the Princess?"

To hear Scrooge expending all the earnestness of his nature on such subjects, in a most extraordinary voice between laughing and crying; and to see his heightened and excited face; would have been a surprise to his business friends in the City, indeed.

"Why, it's Ali Baba!" Scrooge exclaimed in ecstasy. "It's dear old honest Ali Baba."

"There's the Parrot!" cried Scrooge. "Green body and yellow tail, with a thing like a lettuce growing out of the top of his head; there he is! Poor Robin Crusoe he called him, when he came home again after sailing round the island. 'Poor Robin Crusoe, where have you been, Robin Crusoe?' The man thought he was dreaming, but he wasn't. It was the Parrot, you know. There goes Friday, running for his life to the little creek! Halloa! Hoop! Halloo!"

Then, with a rapidity of transition very foreign to his usual character, he said, in pity for his former self, "Poor boy!" and cried again.

"I wish," Scrooge muttered, putting his hand in his pocket, and looking about him, after drying his eyes with his cuff: "but it's too late now."

"What is the matter?" asked the Spirit.

"Nothing," said Scrooge. "Nothing. There was a boy singing a Christmas Carol at my door last night. I should like to have given him something: that's all."

The Ghost smiled thoughtfully, and waved its hand: saying, as it did so, "Let us see another Christmas!"

Scrooge's former self grew larger at the words, and the room became a little darker and more dirty. The panels shrunk, the windows cracked; fragments of plaster fell out of the ceiling, and the naked laths were shown instead; but how all this was brought about Scrooge knew no more than you do. He only knew that it was quite correct: that everything had happened so; that there he was, alone again, when all the other boys had gone home for the jolly holidays.

He was not reading now, but walking up and down despairingly. Scrooge looked at the Ghost, and, with a mournful shaking of his head, glanced anxiously towards the door.

It opened; and a little girl, much younger than the boy, came darting in, and, putting her arms about his neck, and often kissing him, addressed him as her "dear, dear brother."

"I have come to bring you home, dear brother!" said the child, clapping her tiny hands, and bending down to laugh. "To bring you home, home, home!"

"Home, little Fan?" returned the boy.

"Yes!" said the child, brimful of glee. "Home for good and all. Home for ever and ever. Father is so much kinder than he used to be, that home's like Heaven! He spoke so gently to me one dear night when I was going to bed, that I was not afraid to ask him once more if you might come home; and he said Yes, you should; and sent me in a coach to bring you. And you're to be a man!" said the child, opening her eyes; "and are never to come back here; but first we're to be together all the Christmas long, and have the merriest time in all the world."

"You are quite a woman, little Fan!" exclaimed the boy.

She clapped her hands and laughed, and tried to touch his head; but, being too little, laughed again, and stood on tiptoe to embrace him. Then she began to drag him, in her childish eagerness, towards the door; and he, nothing loath to go, accompanied her.

A terrible voice in the hall cried, "Bring down Master Scrooge's box, there!" and in the hall appeared the schoolmaster himself, who glared on Master Scrooge with a ferocious condescension, and threw him into a dreadful state of mind by shaking hands with him. He then conveyed him and his sister into the veriest old well of a shivering best parlour that ever was seen, where the maps upon the wall, and the celestial and terrestrial globes in the windows, were waxy with cold. Here he produced a decanter of curiously light wine, and a block of curiously heavy cake, and administered instalments of those dainties to the young people: at the same time sending out a meagre servant to offer a glass of "something" to the postboy who answered that he thanked the gentleman, but, if it was the same tap as he had tasted before, he had rather not. Master Scrooge's trunk being by this time tied on to the top of the chaise, the children bade the schoolmaster good-bye right willingly; and, getting into it, drove gaily down the garden sweep; the quick wheels dashing the hoar frost and snow from off the dark leaves of the evergreens like spray.

"Always a delicate creature, whom a breath might have withered," said the Ghost. "But she had a large heart!"

"So she had," cried Scrooge. "You're right. I will not gainsay it, Spirit. God forbid!"

"She died a woman," said the Ghost, "and had, as I think, children."

"One child," Scrooge returned.

"True," said the Ghost. "Your nephew!"

Scrooge seemed uneasy in his mind; and answered briefly, "Yes."

Although they had but that moment left the school behind them, they were now in the busy thoroughfares of a city, where shadowy passengers passed and repassed; where shadowy carts and coaches battled for the way, and all the strife and tumult of a real city were. It was made plain enough, by the dressing of the shops, that here, too, it was Christmas-time again; but it was evening, and the streets were lighted up.

The Ghost stopped at a certain warehouse door, and asked Scrooge if he knew it.

"Know it!" said Scrooge. "Was I apprenticed here?"

They went in. At sight of an old gentleman in a Welsh wig, sitting behind such a high desk, that if he had been two inches taller, he must have knocked his head against the ceiling, Scrooge cried in great excitement:

"Why, it's old Fezziwig! Bless his heart, it's Fezziwig alive again!"

Old Fezziwig laid down his pen, and looked up at the clock, which pointed to the hour of seven. He rubbed his hands; adjusted his capacious waistcoat; laughed all over himself, from his shoes to his organ of benevolence; and called out, in a comfortable, oily, rich, fat, jovial voice:

"Yo ho, there! Ebenezer! Dick!"

Scrooge's former self, now grown a young man, came briskly in, accompanied by his fellow-'prentice.

"Dick Wilkins, to be sure!" said Scrooge to the Ghost. "Bless me, yes. There he is. He was very much attached to me, was Dick. Poor Dick! Dear, dear!"

"Yo ho, my boys!" said Fezziwig. "No more work to-night. Christmas-eve, Dick. Christmas, Ebenezer! Let's have the shutters up," cried old Fezziwig with a sharp clap of his hands, "before a man can say Jack Robinson!"

You wouldn't believe how those two fellows went at it! They charged into the street with the shutters – one, two, three – had 'em up in their places – four, five, six – barred 'em and pinned 'em – seven, eight, nine – and came back before you could have got to twelve, panting like race-horses.

"Hilli-ho!" cried old Fezziwig, skipping down from the high desk with wonderful agility. "Clear away, my lads, and let's have lots of room here! Hilli-ho, Dick! Chirrup, Ebenezer!"

Clear away! There was nothing they wouldn't have cleared away, or couldn't have cleared away, with old Fezziwig looking on. It was done in a minute. Every movable was packed off, as if it were dismissed from public life for evermore; the floor was swept and watered, the lamps were trimmed, fuel was heaped upon the fire; and the warehouse was as snug, and warm, and dry, and bright a ball-room as you would desire to see upon a winter's night.

In came a fiddler with a music-book, and went up to the lofty desk, and made an orchestra of it, and tuned like fifty stomachaches. In came Mrs. Fezziwig, one vast substantial smile. In came the three Miss Fezziwigs, beaming and lovable. In came the six young followers whose hearts they broke. In came all the young men and women employed in the business. In came the housemaid, with her cousin the baker. In came the cook, with her brother's particular friend the milkman. In came the boy from over the way, who was suspected of not having board enough from his master; trying to hide himself behind the girl from next door but one, who was proved to have had her ears pulled by her mistress. In they all came, one after another; some shyly, some boldly, some gracefully, some awkwardly, some pushing, some pulling; in they all came, any how and every how. Away they all went, twenty couple at once; hands half round and back again the other way; down the middle and up again; round and round in various stages of affectionate grouping; old top couple always turning up in the wrong place; new top couple starting off again as soon as they got there; all top couples at last, and not a bottom one to help them! When this result was brought about, old Fezziwig, clapping his hands to stop the dance, cried out, "Well done!" and the fiddler plunged his hot face into a pot of porter, especially provided for that purpose. But, scorning rest upon his reappearance, he instantly began again, though there were no dancers yet, as if the other fiddler had been carried home, exhausted, on a shutter, and he were a bran-new man resolved to beat him out of sight, or perish.

There were more dances, and there were forfeits, and more dances, and there was cake, and there was negus, and there was a great piece of Cold Roast, and there was a great piece of Cold Boiled, and there were mince-pies, and plenty of beer. But the great effect of the evening came after the Roast and Boiled, when the fiddler (an artful dog, mind! The sort of man who knew his business better than you or I could have told it him!) struck up "Sir Roger de Coverley." Then old Fezziwig stood out to dance with Mrs. Fezziwig. Top couple, too; with a good stiff piece of work cut out for them; three or four and twenty pair of partners; people who were not to be trifled with; people who *would* dance, and had no notion of walking.

But if they had been twice as many – ah! four times – old Fezziwig would have been a match for them, and so would Mrs. Fezziwig. As to *her*, she was worthy to be his partner in every sense of the term. If that's not high praise, tell me higher, and I'll use it. A positive light appeared to issue from Fezziwig's calves. They shone in every part of the dance like moons. You couldn't have predicted, at any given time, what would become of them next. And when old Fezziwig and Mrs. Fezziwig had gone all through the dance; advance and retire, both hands to your partner, bow and curtsy, cork-screw, thread-the-needle, and back again to your place; Fezziwig "cut" – cut so deftly, that he appeared to wink with his legs, and came upon his feet again without a stagger.

When the clock struck eleven, this domestic ball broke up. Mr. and Mrs. Fezziwig took their stations, one on either side the door, and, shaking hands with every person individually as he or she went out, wished him or her a Merry Christmas. When everybody had retired but the two 'prentices, they did the same to them; and thus the cheerful voices died away, and the lads were left to their beds; which were under a counter in the back-shop.

During the whole of this time Scrooge had acted like a man out of his wits. His heart and soul were in the scene, and with his former self. He corroborated everything, remembered everything, enjoyed everything, and underwent the strangest agitation. It was not until now, when the bright faces of his former self and Dick were turned from them, that he remembered the Ghost, and became conscious that it was looking full upon him, while the light upon its head burnt very clear.

"A small matter," said the Ghost, "to make these silly folks so full of gratitude."

"Small!" echoed Scrooge.

The Spirit signed to him to listen to the two apprentices, who were pouring out their hearts in praise of Fezziwig; and, when he had done so, said:

"Why! Is it not? He has spent but a few pounds of your mortal money: three or four, perhaps. Is that so much that he deserves this praise?"

"It isn't that," said Scrooge, heated by the remark, and speaking unconsciously like his former, not his latter self. "It isn't that, Spirit. He has the power to render us happy or unhappy; to make our service light or burdensome; a pleasure or a toil. Say that his power lies in words and looks; in things so slight and insignificant that it is impossible to add and count 'em up: what then? The happiness he gives is quite as great as if it cost a fortune."

He felt the Spirit's glance, and stopped.

"What is the matter?" asked the Ghost.

"Nothing particular," said Scrooge.

"Something, I think?" the Ghost insisted.

"No," said Scrooge, "no. I should like to be able to say a word or two to my clerk just now. That's all."

His former self turned down the lamps as he gave utterance to the wish; and Scrooge and the Ghost again stood side by side in the open air.

"My time grows short," observed the Spirit. "Quick!"

This was not addressed to Scrooge, or to any one whom he could see, but it produced an immediate effect. For again Scrooge saw himself. He was older now; a man in the prime of life. His face had not the harsh and rigid lines of later years; but it had begun to wear the signs of care and avarice. There was an eager, greedy, restless motion in the eye, which showed the passion that had taken root, and where the shadow of the growing tree would fall.

He was not alone, but sat by the side of a fair young girl in a mourning dress: in whose eyes there were tears, which sparkled in the light that shone out of the Ghost of Christmas Past.

"It matters little," she said softly. "To you, very little. Another idol has displaced me; and, if it can cheer and comfort you in time to come as I would have tried to do, I have no just cause to grieve."

"What Idol has displaced you?" he rejoined.

"A golden one."

"This is the even-handed dealing of the world!" he said. "There is nothing on which it is so hard as poverty; and there is nothing it professes to condemn with such severity as the pursuit of wealth!"

"You fear the world too much," she answered gently. "All your other hopes have merged into the hope of being beyond the chance of its sordid reproach. I have seen your nobler aspirations fall off one by one, until the master passion, Gain, engrosses you. Have I not?"

"What then?" he retorted. "Even if I have grown so much wiser, what then? I am not changed towards you."

She shook her head.

"Am I?"

"Our contract is an old one. It was made when we were both poor, and content to be so, until, in good season, we could improve our worldly fortune by our patient industry. You *are* changed. When it was made you were another man."

"I was a boy," he said impatiently.

"Your own feeling tells you that you were not what you are," she returned. "I am. That which promised happiness when we were one in heart is fraught with misery now that we are two. How often and how keenly I have thought of this I will not say. It is enough that I *have* thought of it, and can release you."

"Have I ever sought release?"

"In words. No. Never."

"In what, then?"

"In a changed nature; in an altered spirit; in another atmosphere of life; another Hope as its great end. In everything that made my love of any worth or value in your sight. If this had never been between us," said the girl, looking mildly, but with steadiness, upon him, "tell me, would you seek me out and try to win me now? Ah, no!"

He seemed to yield to the justice of this supposition in spite of himself. But he said, with a struggle, "You think not."

"I would gladly think otherwise if I could," she answered. "Heaven knows! When *I* have learned a Truth like this, I know how strong and irresistible it must be. But if you were free today, tomorrow, yesterday, can even I believe that you would choose a dowerless girl – you who, in your very confidence with her, weigh everything by Gain: or, choosing her, if for a moment you were false enough to your one guiding principle to do so, do I not know that your repentance and regret would surely follow? I do; and I release you. With a full heart, for the love of him you once were."

He was about to speak; but, with her head turned from him, she resumed.

"You may – the memory of what is past half makes me hope you will – have pain in this. A very, very brief time, and you will dismiss the recollection of it gladly, as an unprofitable dream, from which it happened well that you awoke. May you be happy in the life you have chosen!"

She left him, and they parted.

"Spirit!" said Scrooge, "show me no more! Conduct me home. Why do you delight to torture me?"

"One shadow more!" exclaimed the Ghost.

"No more!" cried Scrooge. "No more! I don't wish to see it. Show me no more!"

But the relentless Ghost pinioned him in both his arms, and forced him to observe what happened next.

They were in another scene and place; a room, not very large or handsome, but full of comfort. Near to the winter fire sat a beautiful young girl, so like that last that Scrooge believed it was the same, until he saw *her*, now a comely matron, sitting opposite her daughter. The noise in this room was perfectly tumultuous, for there were more children there than Scrooge in his agitated state of mind could count; and, unlike the celebrated herd in the poem, they were not forty children conducting themselves like one, but every child was conducting itself like forty. The consequences were uproarious beyond belief; but no one seemed to care; on the contrary, the mother and daughter laughed heartily, and enjoyed it very much; and the latter, soon beginning to mingle in the sports, got pillaged by the young brigands most ruthlessly. What would I not have given to be one of them! Though I never could have been so rude, no, no! I wouldn't for the wealth of all the world have crushed that braided hair, and torn it down; and, for the precious little shoe, I wouldn't have plucked it off, God bless my soul! to save my life. As to measuring her waist in sport, as they did, bold young brood, I couldn't have done it; I should have expected my arm to have grown round it for a punishment, and never come straight again. And yet I should have dearly liked, I own, to have touched her lips; to have questioned her, that she might have opened them; to have looked upon the lashes of her downcast eyes, and never raised a blush; to have let loose waves of hair, an inch of which would be a keepsake beyond price: in short, I should have liked, I do confess, to have had the lightest licence of a child, and yet to have been man enough to know its value.

But now a knocking at the door was heard, and such a rush immediately ensued that she, with laughing face and plundered dress, was borne towards it in the centre of a flushed and boisterous group, just in time to greet the father, who came home attended by a man laden with Christmas toys and presents. Then the shouting and the struggling, and the onslaught that was made on the defenceless porter! The scaling him, with chairs for ladders, to dive into his pockets, despoil him of brown-paper parcels, hold on tight by his cravat, hug him round the neck, pummel his back, and kick his legs in irrepressible affection! The shouts of wonder and delight with which the development of every package was received! The terrible announcement that the baby had been taken in the act of putting a doll's frying-pan into his mouth, and was more than suspected of having swallowed a fictitious turkey, glued on a wooden platter! The immense relief of finding this a false alarm! The joy, and gratitude, and ecstasy! They are all indescribable alike. It is enough that by degrees, the children and their emotions got out of the parlour, and, by one stair at a time, up to the top of the house, where they went to bed, and so subsided.

And now Scrooge looked on more attentively than ever, when the master of the house, having his daughter leaning fondly on him, sat down with her and her mother at his own fireside; and when he thought that such another creature, quite as graceful and as full of promise, might have called him father, and been a spring-time in the haggard winter of his life, his sight grew very dim indeed.

"Belle," said the husband, turning to his wife with a smile, "I saw an old friend of yours this afternoon."

"Who was it?"

"Guess!"

"How can I? Tut, don't I know?" she added in the same breath, laughing as he laughed. "Mr. Scrooge."

"Mr. Scrooge it was. I passed his office window; and as it was not shut up, and he had a candle inside, I could scarcely help seeing him. His partner lies upon the point of death, I hear; and there he sat alone. Quite alone in the world, I do believe."

"Spirit!" said Scrooge in a broken voice, "remove me from this place."

"I told you these were shadows of the things that have been," said the Ghost. "That they are what they are, do not blame me!"

"Remove me!" Scrooge exclaimed. "I cannot bear it!"

He turned upon the Ghost, and seeing that it looked upon him with a face in which in some strange way there were fragments of all the faces it had shown him, wrestled with it.

"Leave me! Take me back! Haunt me no longer!"

In the struggle – if that can be called a struggle in which the Ghost, with no visible resistance on its own part, was undisturbed by any effort of its adversary – Scrooge observed that its light was burning high and bright; and dimly connecting that with its influence over him, he seized the extinguisher cap, and by a sudden action pressed it down upon its head.

The Spirit dropped beneath it, so that the extinguisher covered its whole form; but, though Scrooge pressed it down with all his force, he could not hide the light, which streamed from under it in an unbroken flood upon the ground.

He was conscious of being exhausted, and overcome by an irresistible drowsiness; and, further, of being in his own bedroom. He gave the cap a parting squeeze, in which his hand relaxed; and had barely time to reel to bed before he sank into a heavy sleep.

## Stave Three
### The Second of the Three Spirits

**AWAKING IN THE MIDDLE** of a prodigiously tough snore, and sitting up in bed to get his thoughts together, Scrooge had no occasion to be told that the bell was again upon the stroke of One. He felt that he was restored to consciousness in the right nick of time, for the especial purpose of holding a conference with the second messenger dispatched to him through Jacob Marley's intervention. But, finding that he turned uncomfortably cold when he began to wonder which of his curtains this new spectre would draw back, he put them every one aside with his own hands, and, lying down again, established a sharp look-out all round the bed. For he wished to challenge the Spirit on the moment of its appearance, and did not wish to be taken by surprise and made nervous.

Gentlemen of the free-and-easy sort, who plume themselves on being acquainted with a move or two, and being usually equal to the time of day, express the wide range of their capacity for adventure by observing that they are good for anything from pitch-and-toss to manslaughter; between which opposite extremes, no doubt, there lies a tolerably wide and comprehensive range of subjects. Without venturing for Scrooge quite as hardily as this, I don't mind calling on you to believe that he was ready for a good broad field of strange appearances, and that nothing between a baby and a rhinoceros would have astonished him very much.

Now, being prepared for almost anything, he was not by any means prepared for nothing; and consequently, when the bell struck One, and no shape appeared, he was taken with a violent fit of trembling. Five minutes, ten minutes, a quarter of an hour went by, yet nothing came. All this time he lay upon his bed, the very core and centre of a blaze of ruddy light, which streamed upon it when the clock proclaimed the hour; and which, being only light, was more alarming than a dozen ghosts, as he was powerless to make out what it meant, or would be at; and was sometimes apprehensive that he might be at that very moment an interesting case of spontaneous combustion, without having the consolation of knowing it. At last, however, he began to think – as you or I would have thought at first; for it is always the person not in the predicament who knows what ought to have been done in it, and would unquestionably have done it too – at last, I say, he began to think that the source and secret of this ghostly light might be in the adjoining room, from whence, on further tracing it, it seemed to shine. This idea taking full possession of his mind, he got up softly, and shuffled in his slippers to the door.

The moment Scrooge's hand was on the lock, a strange voice called him by his name, and bade him enter. He obeyed.

It was his own room. There was no doubt about that. But it had undergone a surprising transformation. The walls and ceiling were so hung with living green, that it looked a perfect grove; from every part of which bright gleaming berries glistened. The crisp leaves of holly, mistletoe, and ivy reflected back the light, as if so many little mirrors had been scattered there; and such a mighty blaze went roaring up the chimney as that dull petrifaction of a hearth had never known in Scrooge's time, or Marley's, or for many and many a winter season gone. Heaped up on the floor, to form a kind of throne, were turkeys, geese, game, poultry, brawn, great joints of meat, sucking-pigs, long wreaths of sausages, mince-pies, plum-puddings, barrels of oysters, red-hot chestnuts, cherry-cheeked apples, juicy oranges, luscious pears, immense twelfth-cakes, and seething bowls of punch, that made the chamber dim with their delicious steam. In easy state upon this couch there sat a jolly Giant, glorious to see; who bore a glowing torch, in shape not unlike Plenty's horn, and held it up, high up, to shed its light on Scrooge as he came peeping round the door.

"Come in!" exclaimed the Ghost. "Come in! and know me better, man!"

Scrooge entered timidly, and hung his head before this Spirit. He was not the dogged Scrooge he had been; and, though the Spirit's eyes were clear and kind, he did not like to meet them.

"I am the Ghost of Christmas Present," said the Spirit. "Look upon me!"

Scrooge reverently did so. It was clothed in one simple deep green robe, or mantle, bordered with white fur. This garment hung so loosely on the figure, that its capacious breast was bare, as if disdaining to be warded or concealed by any artifice. Its feet, observable beneath the ample folds of the garment, were also bare; and on its head it wore no other covering than a holly wreath, set here and there with shining icicles. Its dark brown curls were long and free; free as its genial face, its sparkling eye, its open hand, its cheery voice, its unconstrained demeanour, and its joyful air. Girded round its middle was an antique scabbard; but no sword was in it, and the ancient sheath was eaten up with rust.

"You have never seen the like of me before!" exclaimed the Spirit.

"Never," Scrooge made answer to it.

"Have never walked forth with the younger members of my family; meaning (for I am very young) my elder brothers born in these later years?" pursued the Phantom.

"I don't think I have," said Scrooge. "I am afraid I have not. Have you had many brothers, Spirit?"

"More than eighteen hundred," said the Ghost.

"A tremendous family to provide for," muttered Scrooge.

The Ghost of Christmas Present rose.

"Spirit," said Scrooge submissively, "conduct me where you will. I went forth last night on compulsion, and I learnt a lesson which is working now. To-night, if you have aught to teach me, let me profit by it."

"Touch my robe!"

Scrooge did as he was told, and held it fast.

Holly, mistletoe, red berries, ivy, turkeys, geese, game, poultry, brawn, meat, pigs, sausages, oysters, pies, puddings, fruit, and punch, all vanished instantly. So did the room, the fire, the ruddy glow, the hour of night, and they stood in the city streets on Christmas morning, where (for the weather was severe) the people made a rough, but brisk and not unpleasant kind of music, in scraping the snow from the pavement in front of their dwellings, and from the tops of their houses, whence it was mad delight to the boys to see it come plumping down into the road below, and splitting into artificial little snow-storms.

The house-fronts looked black enough, and the windows blacker, contrasting with the smooth white sheet of snow upon the roofs, and with the dirtier snow upon the ground; which last deposit had been ploughed up in deep furrows by the heavy wheels of carts and waggons; furrows that crossed and recrossed each other hundreds of times where the great streets branched off; and made intricate channels, hard to trace, in the thick yellow mud and icy water. The sky was gloomy, and the shortest streets were choked up with a dingy mist, half thawed, half frozen, whose heavier particles descended in a shower of sooty atoms, as if all the chimneys in Great Britain had, by one consent, caught fire, and were blazing away to their dear hearts' content. There was nothing very cheerful in the climate or the town, and yet was there an air of cheerfulness abroad that the clearest summer air and brightest summer sun might have endeavoured to diffuse in vain.

For, the people who were shovelling away on the housetops were jovial and full of glee; calling out to one another from the parapets, and now and then exchanging a facetious snowball – better-natured missile far than many a wordy jest – laughing heartily if it went right, and not less heartily if it went wrong. The poulterers' shops were still half open, and the fruiterers' were radiant in their glory. There were great, round, pot-bellied baskets of chestnuts, shaped like the waistcoats of jolly old gentlemen, lolling at the doors, and tumbling out into the street in their apoplectic opulence. There were ruddy, brown-faced, broad-girthed Spanish onions, shining in the fatness of their growth like Spanish Friars, and winking from their shelves in wanton slyness at the girls as they went by, and glanced demurely at the hung-up mistletoe. There were pears and apples clustered high in blooming pyramids; there were bunches of grapes, made, in the shopkeepers' benevolence, to dangle from conspicuous hooks that people's mouths might water gratis as they passed; there were piles of filberts, mossy and brown, recalling, in their fragrance, ancient walks among the woods, and pleasant shufflings ankle deep through withered leaves; there were Norfolk Biffins, squab and swarthy, setting off the yellow of the oranges and lemons, and, in the great compactness of their juicy persons, urgently entreating and beseeching to be carried home in paper bags, and eaten after dinner. The very gold and silver fish, set forth among these choice fruits in a bowl, though members of a dull and stagnant-blooded race, appeared to know that there was something going on; and, to a fish, went gasping round and round their little world in slow and passionless excitement.

The Grocers'! oh, the Grocers'! nearly closed, with perhaps two shutters down, or one; but through those gaps such glimpses! It was not alone that the scales descending on the counter made a merry sound, or that the twine and roller parted company so briskly, or that the canisters were rattled up and down like juggling tricks, or even that the blended scents of tea and coffee were so grateful to the nose, or even that the raisins were so plentiful and rare, the almonds so extremely white, the sticks of cinnamon so long and straight, the other spices so delicious, the candied fruits so caked and spotted with molten sugar as to make the coldest lookers-on feel faint, and subsequently bilious. Nor was it that the figs were moist and pulpy, or that the French plums blushed in modest tartness from their highly-decorated boxes, or that everything was good to eat and in its Christmas dress; but the customers were all so hurried and so eager in the hopeful promise of the day, that they tumbled up against each other at the door, crashing their wicker baskets wildly, and left their purchases upon the counter, and came running back to fetch them, and committed hundreds of the like mistakes, in the best humour possible; while the Grocer and his people were so frank and fresh, that the polished hearts with which they fastened their aprons behind might have been their own, worn outside for general inspection, and for Christmas daws to peck at if they chose.

But soon the steeples called good people all to church and chapel, and away they came, flocking through the streets in their best clothes, and with their gayest faces. And at the same time there emerged, from scores of by-streets, lanes, and nameless turnings, innumerable people, carrying their dinners to the bakers' shops. The sight of these poor revellers appeared to interest the Spirit very much, for he stood with Scrooge beside him in a baker's doorway, and, taking off the covers as their bearers passed, sprinkled incense on their dinners from his torch. And it was a very uncommon kind of torch, for once or twice, when there were angry words between some dinner-carriers who had jostled each other, he shed a few drops of water on them from it, and their good-humour was restored directly. For they said, it was a shame to quarrel upon Christmas-day. And so it was! God love it, so it was!

In time the bells ceased, and the bakers were shut up; and yet there was a genial shadowing forth of all these dinners, and the progress of their cooking, in the thawed blotch of wet above each baker's oven; where the pavement smoked as if its stones were cooking too.

"Is there a peculiar flavour in what you sprinkle from your torch?" asked Scrooge.

"There is. My own."

"Would it apply to any kind of dinner on this day?" asked Scrooge.

"To any kindly given. To a poor one most."

"Why to a poor one most?" asked Scrooge.

"Because it needs it most."

"Spirit!" said Scrooge after a moment's thought. "I wonder you, of all the beings in the many worlds about us, should desire to cramp these people's opportunities of innocent enjoyment."

"I!" cried the Spirit.

"You would deprive them of their means of dining every seventh day, often the only day on which they can be said to dine at all," said Scrooge; "wouldn't you?"

"I!" cried the Spirit.

"You seek to close these places on the Seventh Day," said Scrooge. "And it comes to the same thing."

"*I* seek!" exclaimed the Spirit.

"Forgive me if I am wrong. It has been done in your name, or at least in that of your family," said Scrooge.

"There are some upon this earth of yours," returned the Spirit, "who lay claim to know us, and who do their deeds of passion, pride, ill-will, hatred, envy, bigotry, and selfishness in our name, who are as strange to us, and all our kith and kin, as if they had never lived. Remember that, and charge their doings on themselves, not us."

Scrooge promised that he would; and they went on, invisible, as they had been before, into the suburbs of the town. It was a remarkable quality of the Ghost (which Scrooge had observed at the baker's), that, notwithstanding his gigantic size, he could accommodate himself to any place with ease; and that he stood beneath a low roof quite as gracefully and like a supernatural creature as it was possible he could have done in any lofty hall.

And perhaps it was the pleasure the good Spirit had in showing off this power of his, or else it was his own kind, generous, hearty nature, and his sympathy with all poor men, that led him straight to Scrooge's clerk's; for there he went, and took Scrooge with him, holding to his robe; and, on the threshold of the door, the Spirit smiled, and stopped to bless Bob Cratchit's dwelling with the sprinklings of his torch. Think of that! Bob had but fifteen "Bob" a week himself; he pocketed on Saturdays but fifteen copies of his Christian name; and yet the Ghost of Christmas Present blessed his four-roomed house!

Then up rose Mrs. Cratchit, Cratchit's wife, dressed out but poorly in a twice-turned gown, but brave in ribbons, which are cheap, and make a goodly show for sixpence; and she laid the cloth, assisted by Belinda Cratchit, second of her daughters, also brave in ribbons; while Master Peter Cratchit plunged a fork into the saucepan of potatoes, and, getting the corners of his monstrous shirt collar (Bob's private property, conferred upon his son and heir in honour of the day) into his mouth, rejoiced to find himself so gallantly attired, and yearned to show his linen in the fashionable Parks. And now two smaller Cratchits, boy and girl, came tearing in, screaming that outside the baker's they had smelt the goose, and known it for their own; and, basking in luxurious thoughts of sage and onion, these young Cratchits danced about the table, and exalted Master Peter Cratchit to the skies, while he (not proud, although his collars nearly choked him) blew the fire, until the slow potatoes, bubbling up, knocked loudly at the saucepan lid to be let out and peeled.

"What has ever got your precious father, then?" said Mrs. Cratchit. "And your brother, Tiny Tim? And Martha warn't as late last Christmas-day by half an hour!"

"Here's Martha, mother!" said a girl, appearing as she spoke.

"Here's Martha, mother!" cried the two young Cratchits. "Hurrah! There's *such* a goose, Martha!"

"Why, bless your heart alive, my dear, how late you are!" said Mrs. Cratchit, kissing her a dozen times, and taking off her shawl and bonnet for her with officious zeal.

"We'd a deal of work to finish up last night," replied the girl, "and had to clear away this morning, mother!"

"Well! never mind so long as you are come," said Mrs. Cratchit. "Sit ye down before the fire, my dear, and have a warm, Lord bless ye!"

"No, no! There's father coming," cried the two young Cratchits, who were everywhere at once. "Hide, Martha, hide!"

So Martha hid herself, and in came little Bob, the father, with at least three feet of comforter, exclusive of the fringe, hanging down before him; and his threadbare clothes darned up and brushed to look seasonable; and Tiny Tim upon his shoulder. Alas for Tiny Tim, he bore a little crutch, and had his limbs supported by an iron frame!

"Why, where's our Martha?" cried Bob Cratchit, looking round.

"Not coming," said Mrs. Cratchit.

"Not coming!" said Bob with a sudden declension in his high spirits; for he had been Tim's blood horse all the way from church, and had come home rampant. "Not coming upon Christmas-day!"

Martha didn't like to see him disappointed, if it were only in joke; so she came out prematurely from behind the closet door, and ran into his arms, while the two young Cratchits hustled Tiny Tim, and bore him off into the wash-house, that he might hear the pudding singing in the copper.

"And how did little Tim behave?" asked Mrs. Cratchit when she had rallied Bob on his credulity, and Bob had hugged his daughter to his heart's content.

"As good as gold," said Bob, "and better. Somehow, he gets thoughtful, sitting by himself so much, and thinks the strangest things you ever heard. He told me, coming home, that he hoped the people saw him in the church, because he was a cripple, and it might be pleasant to them to remember upon Christmas-day who made lame beggars walk and blind men see."

Bob's voice was tremulous when he told them this, and trembled more when he said that Tiny Tim was growing strong and hearty.

His active little crutch was heard upon the floor, and back came Tiny Tim before another word was spoken, escorted by his brother and sister to his stool beside the fire; and while Bob, turning up his cuffs – as if, poor fellow, they were capable of being made more shabby – compounded some hot mixture in a jug with gin and lemons, and stirred it round and round, and put it on the hob to simmer, Master Peter and the two ubiquitous young Cratchits went to fetch the goose, with which they soon returned in high procession.

Such a bustle ensued that you might have thought a goose the rarest of all birds; a feathered phenomenon, to which a black swan was a matter of course – and, in truth, it was something very like it in that house. Mrs. Cratchit made the gravy (ready beforehand in a little saucepan) hissing hot; Master Peter mashed the potatoes with incredible vigour; Miss Belinda sweetened up the apple sauce; Martha dusted the hot plates; Bob took Tiny Tim beside him in a tiny corner at the table; the two young Cratchits set chairs for everybody, not forgetting themselves, and, mounting guard upon their posts, crammed spoons into their mouths, lest they should shriek for goose before their turn came to be helped. At last the dishes were set on, and grace was said. It was succeeded by a breathless pause, as Mrs. Cratchit, looking slowly all along the carving-knife, prepared to plunge it in the breast; but when she did, and when the long-expected gush of stuffing issued forth, one murmur of delight arose all round the board, and even Tiny Tim, excited by the two young Cratchits, beat on the table with the handle of his knife, and feebly cried Hurrah!

There never was such a goose. Bob said he didn't believe there ever was such a goose cooked. Its tenderness and flavour, size and cheapness, were the themes of universal admiration. Eked out by apple sauce and mashed potatoes, it was a sufficient dinner for the whole family; indeed, as Mrs. Cratchit said with great delight (surveying one small atom of a bone upon the dish), they hadn't ate it all at last! Yet every one had had enough, and the youngest Cratchits, in particular, were steeped in sage and onion to the eyebrows! But now, the plates being changed by Miss Belinda, Mrs. Cratchit left the room alone – too nervous to bear witnesses – to take the pudding up, and bring it in.

Suppose it should not be done enough! Suppose it should break in turning out! Suppose somebody should have got over the wall of the back-yard and stolen it, while they were merry with the goose – a supposition at which the two young Cratchits became livid! All sorts of horrors were supposed.

Hallo! A great deal of steam! The pudding was out of the copper. A smell like a washing-day! That was the cloth. A smell like an eating-house and a pastrycook's next door to each other, with a laundress's next door to that! That was the pudding! In half a minute Mrs. Cratchit entered – flushed, but smiling proudly – with the pudding, like a speckled cannon-ball, so hard and firm, blazing in half of half-a-quartern of ignited brandy, and bedight with Christmas holly stuck into the top.

Oh, a wonderful pudding! Bob Cratchit said, and calmly too, that he regarded it as the greatest success achieved by Mrs. Cratchit since their marriage. Mrs. Cratchit said that, now the weight was off her mind, she would confess she had her doubts about the quantity of flour. Everybody had something to say about it, but nobody said or thought it was at all a small pudding for a large family. It would have been flat heresy to do so. Any Cratchit would have blushed to hint at such a thing.

At last the dinner was all done, the cloth was cleared, the hearth swept, and the fire made up. The compound in the jug being tasted, and considered perfect, apples and oranges were put upon the table, and a shovel full of chestnuts on the fire. Then all the Cratchit family drew round the hearth in what Bob Cratchit called a circle, meaning half a one; and at Bob Cratchit's elbow stood the family display of glass. Two tumblers and a custard cup without a handle.

These held the hot stuff from the jug, however, as well as golden goblets would have done; and Bob served it out with beaming looks, while the chestnuts on the fire sputtered and cracked noisily. Then Bob proposed:

"A merry Christmas to us all, my dears. God bless us!"

Which all the family re-echoed.

"God bless us every one!" said Tiny Tim, the last of all.

He sat very close to his father's side, upon his little stool. Bob held his withered little hand in his, as if he loved the child, and wished to keep him by his side, and dreaded that he might be taken from him.

"Spirit," said Scrooge with an interest he had never felt before, "tell me if Tiny Tim will live."

"I see a vacant seat," replied the Ghost, "in the poor chimney-corner, and a crutch without an owner, carefully preserved. If these shadows remain unaltered by the Future, the child will die."

"No, no," said Scrooge. "Oh, no, kind Spirit! say he will be spared."

"If these shadows remain unaltered by the Future, none other of my race," returned the Ghost, "will find him here. What then? If he be like to die, he had better do it, and decrease the surplus population."

Scrooge hung his head to hear his own words quoted by the Spirit, and was overcome with penitence and grief.

"Man," said the Ghost, "if man you be in heart, not adamant, forbear that wicked cant until you have discovered What the surplus is, and Where it is. Will you decide what men shall live, what men shall die? It may be that, in the sight of Heaven, you are more worthless and less fit to live than millions like this poor man's child. Oh God! to hear the Insect on the leaf pronouncing on the too much life among his hungry brothers in the dust!"

Scrooge bent before the Ghost's rebuke, and, trembling, cast his eyes upon the ground. But he raised them speedily on hearing his own name.

"Mr. Scrooge!" said Bob. "I'll give you Mr. Scrooge, the Founder of the Feast!"

"The Founder of the Feast, indeed!" cried Mrs. Cratchit, reddening. "I wish I had him here. I'd give him a piece of my mind to feast upon, and I hope he'd have a good appetite for it."

"My dear," said Bob, "the children! Christmas-day."

"It should be Christmas-day, I am sure," said she, "on which one drinks the health of such an odious, stingy, hard, unfeeling man as Mr. Scrooge. You know he is, Robert! Nobody knows it better than you do, poor fellow!"

"My dear!" was Bob's mild answer. "Christmas-day."

"I'll drink his health for your sake and the Day's," said Mrs. Cratchit, "not for his. Long life to him! A merry Christmas and a happy New Year! He'll be very merry and very happy, I have no doubt!"

The children drank the toast after her. It was the first of their proceedings which had no heartiness in it. Tiny Tim drank it last of all, but he didn't care twopence for it. Scrooge was the Ogre of the family. The mention of his name cast a dark shadow on the party, which was not dispelled for full five minutes.

After it had passed away they were ten times merrier than before, from the mere relief of Scrooge the Baleful being done with. Bob Cratchit told them how he had a situation in his eye for Master Peter, which would bring in, if obtained, full five-and-sixpence weekly. The two young Cratchits laughed tremendously at the idea of Peter's being a man of business; and Peter himself looked thoughtfully at the fire from between his collars, as if he were deliberating what particular investments he should favour when he came into the receipt of that bewildering income. Martha, who was a poor apprentice at a milliner's, then told them what kind of work she had to do, and how many hours she worked at a stretch, and how she meant to lie abed tomorrow morning for a good long rest; tomorrow being a holiday she passed at home. Also how she had seen a countess and a lord some days before, and how the lord "was much about as tall as Peter"; at which Peter pulled up his collars so high, that you couldn't have seen his head if you had been there. All this time the chestnuts and the jug went round and round; and by-and-by they had a song, about a lost child travelling in the snow, from Tiny Tim, who had a plaintive little voice, and sang it very well indeed.

There was nothing of high mark in this. They were not a handsome family; they were not well dressed; their shoes were far from being waterproof; their clothes were scanty; and Peter might have known, and very likely did, the inside of a pawn-broker's. But they were happy, grateful, pleased with one another, and contented with the time; and when they faded, and looked happier yet in the bright sprinklings of the Spirit's torch at parting, Scrooge had his eye upon them, and especially on Tiny Tim, until the last.

By this time it was getting dark, and snowing pretty heavily; and as Scrooge and the Spirit went along the streets, the brightness of the roaring fires in kitchens, parlours, and all sorts of rooms was wonderful. Here, the flickering of the blaze showed preparations for a cosy dinner, with hot plates baking through and through before the fire, and deep red curtains, ready to be drawn to shut out cold and darkness. There, all the children of the house were running out into the snow to meet their married sisters, brothers, cousins, uncles, aunts, and be the first to greet them. Here, again, were shadows on the window blinds of guests assembling; and there a group of handsome girls, all hooded and fur-booted, and all chattering at once, tripped lightly off to some near neighbour's house; where, woe upon the single man who saw them enter – artful witches, well they knew it – in a glow!

But, if you had judged from the numbers of people on their way to friendly gatherings, you might have thought that no one was at home to give them welcome when they got there, instead of every house expecting company, and piling up its fires half-chimney high. Blessings on it, how the Ghost exulted! How it bared its breadth of breast, and opened its capacious palm, and floated on, outpouring, with a generous hand, its bright and harmless mirth on everything within its reach! The very lamp-lighter, who ran on before, dotting the dusky street with specks of light, and who was dressed to spend the evening somewhere, laughed out loudly as the Spirit passed, though little kenned the lamp-lighter that he had any company but Christmas.

And now, without a word of warning from the Ghost, they stood upon a bleak and desert moor, where monstrous masses of rude stone were cast about, as though it were the burial-place or giants; and water spread itself wheresoever it listed; or would have done so, but for the frost that held it prisoner; and nothing grew but moss and furze, and coarse, rank grass. Down in the west the setting sun had left a streak of fiery red, which glared upon the desolation for an instant, like a sullen eye, and, frowning lower, lower, lower yet, was lost in the thick gloom of darkest night.

"What place is this?" asked Scrooge.

"A place where Miners live, who labour in the bowels of the earth," returned the Spirit. "But they know me. See!"

A light shone from the window of a hut, and swiftly they advanced towards it. Passing through the wall of mud and stone, they found a cheerful company assembled round a glowing fire. An old, old man and woman, with their children and their children's children, and another generation beyond that, all decked out gaily in their holiday attire. The old man, in a voice that seldom rose above the howling of the wind upon the barren waste, was singing them a Christmas song; it had been a very old song when he was a boy; and from time to time they all joined in the chorus. So surely as they raised their voices, the old man got quite blithe and loud; and, so surely as they stopped, his vigour sank again.

The Spirit did not tarry here, but bade Scrooge hold his robe, and, passing on above the moor, sped whither? Not to sea? To sea. To Scrooge's horror, looking back, he saw the last of the land, a frightful range of rocks, behind them; and his ears were deafened by the thundering of water, as it rolled and roared, and raged among the dreadful caverns it had worn, and fiercely tried to undermine the earth.

Built upon a dismal reef of sunken rocks, some league or so from shore, on which the waters chafed and dashed, the wild year through, there stood a solitary lighthouse. Great heaps of seaweed clung to its base, and storm-birds – born of the wind, one might suppose, as seaweed of the water – rose and fell about it, like the waves they skimmed.

But, even here, two men who watched the light had made a fire that through the loophole in the thick stone wall shed out a ray of brightness on the awful sea. Joining their horny hands over the rough table at which they sat, they wished each other Merry Christmas in their can of grog; and one of them, the elder too, with his face all damaged and scarred with hard weather, as the figure-head of an old ship might be, struck up a sturdy song that was like a gale in itself.

Again the Ghost sped on, above the black and heaving sea – on, on – until, being far away, as he told Scrooge, from any shore, they lighted on a ship. They stood beside the helmsman at the wheel, the look-out in the bow, the officers who had the watch; dark, ghostly figures in their several stations; but every man among them hummed a Christmas tune, or had a Christmas thought, or spoke below his breath to his companion of some bygone Christmas-day, with homeward hopes belonging to it. And every man on board, waking or sleeping, good or bad, had had a kinder word for one another on that day than on any day in the year; and had shared to some extent in its festivities; and had remembered those he cared for at a distance, and had known that they delighted to remember him.

It was a great surprise to Scrooge, while listening to the moaning of the wind, and thinking what a solemn thing it was to move on through the lonely darkness over an unknown abyss, whose depths were secrets as profound as death: it was a great surprise to Scrooge, while thus engaged, to hear a hearty laugh. It was a much greater surprise to Scrooge to recognise it as his own nephew's, and to find himself in a bright, dry, gleaming room, with the Spirit standing smiling by his side, and looking at that same nephew with approving affability!

"Ha, ha!" laughed Scrooge's nephew. "Ha, ha, ha!"

If you should happen, by any unlikely chance, to know a man more blessed in a laugh than Scrooge's nephew, all I can say is, I should like to know him too. Introduce him to me, and I'll cultivate his acquaintance.

It is a fair, even-handed, noble adjustment of things, that, while there is infection in disease and sorrow, there is nothing in the world so irresistibly contagious as laughter and good-humour. When Scrooge's nephew laughed in this way, holding his sides, rolling his head, and twisting his face into the most extravagant contortions, Scrooge's niece, by marriage, laughed as heartily as he. And their assembled friends, being not a bit behindhand, roared out lustily.

"Ha, ha! Ha, ha, ha, ha!"

"He said that Christmas was a humbug, as I live!" cried Scrooge's nephew. "He believed it, too!"

"More shame for him, Fred!" said Scrooge's niece indignantly. Bless those women! they never do anything by halves. They are always in earnest.

She was very pretty; exceedingly pretty. With a dimpled, surprised-looking, capital face; a ripe little mouth, that seemed made to be kissed – as no doubt it was; all kinds of good little dots about her chin, that melted into one another when she laughed; and the sunniest pair of eyes you ever saw in any little creature's head. Altogether she was what you would have called provoking, you know; but satisfactory, too. Oh, perfectly satisfactory!

"He's a comical old fellow," said Scrooge's nephew, "that's the truth; and not so pleasant as he might be. However, his offences carry their own punishment, and I have nothing to say against him."

"I'm sure he is very rich, Fred," hinted Scrooge's niece. "At least, you always tell *me* so."

"What of that, my dear?" said Scrooge's nephew. "His wealth is of no use to him. He don't do any good with it. He don't make himself comfortable with it. He hasn't the satisfaction of thinking – ha, ha, ha! – that he is ever going to benefit Us with it."

"I have no patience with him," observed Scrooge's niece. Scrooge's niece's sisters, and all the other ladies, expressed the same opinion.

"Oh, I have!" said Scrooge's nephew. "I am sorry for him; I couldn't be angry with him if I tried. Who suffers by his ill whims? Himself always. Here he takes it into his head to dislike us, and he won't come and dine with us. What's the consequence? He don't lose much of a dinner."

"Indeed, I think he loses a very good dinner," interrupted Scrooge's niece. Everybody else said the same, and they must be allowed to have been competent judges, because they had just had dinner; and, with the dessert upon the table, were clustered round the fire, by lamp-light.

"Well! I am very glad to hear it," said Scrooge's nephew, "because I haven't any great faith in these young housekeepers. What do *you* say, Topper?"

Topper had clearly got his eye upon one of Scrooge's niece's sisters, for he answered that a bachelor was a wretched outcast, who had no right to express an opinion on the subject. Whereat Scrooge's niece's sister – the plump one with the lace tucker, not the one with the roses – blushed.

"Do go on, Fred," said Scrooge's niece, clapping her hands. "He never finishes what he begins to say! He is such a ridiculous fellow!"

Scrooge's nephew revelled in another laugh, and, as it was impossible to keep the infection off, though the plump sister tried hard to do it with aromatic vinegar, his example was unanimously followed.

"I was only going to say," said Scrooge's nephew, "that the consequence of his taking a dislike to us, and not making merry with us, is, as I think, that he loses some pleasant moments, which could do him no harm. I am sure he loses pleasanter companions than he can find in his own thoughts, either in his mouldy old office or his dusty chambers. I mean to give him the same chance every year, whether he likes it or not, for I pity him. He may rail at Christmas till he dies, but he can't help thinking better of it – I defy him – if he finds me going there in good temper, year after year, and saying, 'Uncle Scrooge, how are you?' If it only puts him in the vein to leave his poor clerk fifty pounds, *that's* something; and I think I shook him yesterday."

It was their turn to laugh, now, at the notion of his shaking Scrooge. But, being thoroughly good-natured, and not much caring what they laughed at, so that they laughed at any rate, he encouraged them in their merriment, and passed the bottle, joyously.

After tea they had some music. For they were a musical family, and knew what they were about when they sung a Glee or Catch, I can assure you: especially Topper, who could growl away in the bass like a good one, and never swell the large veins in his forehead, or get red in the face over it. Scrooge's niece played well upon the harp; and played, among other tunes, a simple little air (a mere nothing: you might learn to whistle it in two minutes), which had been familiar to the child who fetched Scrooge from the boarding-school, as he had been reminded by the Ghost of Christmas Past. When this strain of music sounded, all the things that Ghost had shown him came upon his mind; he softened more and more; and thought that if he could have listened to it often, years ago, he might have cultivated the kindnesses of life for his own happiness with his own hands, without resorting to the sexton's spade that buried Jacob Marley.

But they didn't devote the whole evening to music. After awhile they played at forfeits; for it is good to be children sometimes, and never better than at Christmas, when its mighty Founder was a child himself. Stop! There was first a game at blindman's buff. Of course there was. And I no more believe Topper was really blind than I believe he had eyes in his boots. My opinion is, that it was a done thing between him and Scrooge's nephew; and that the Ghost of Christmas Present knew it. The way he went after that plump sister in the lace tucker was an outrage on the credulity of human nature. Knocking down the fire-irons, tumbling over the chairs, bumping up against the piano, smothering himself amongst the curtains, wherever she went, there went he! He always knew where the plump sister was. He wouldn't catch anybody else. If you had fallen up against him (as some of them did) on purpose, he would have made a feint of endeavouring to seize you, which would have been an affront to your understanding, and would instantly have sidled off in the direction of the plump sister. She often cried out that it wasn't fair; and it really was not. But when, at last, he caught her; when, in spite of all her silken rustlings, and her rapid flutterings past him, he got her into a corner whence there was no escape, then his conduct was the most execrable. For his pretending not to know her; his pretending that it was necessary to touch her head-dress, and further to assure himself of her identity by pressing a certain ring upon her finger, and a certain chain about her neck, was vile, monstrous! No doubt she told him her opinion of it when, another blind man being in office, they were so very confidential together behind the curtains.

Scrooge's niece was not one of the blindman's buff party, but was made comfortable with a large chair and a footstool, in a snug corner where the Ghost and Scrooge were close behind her. But she joined in the forfeits, and loved her love to admiration with all the letters of the alphabet. Likewise at the game of How, When, and Where, she was very great, and, to the secret joy of Scrooge's nephew, beat her sisters hollow: though they were sharp girls too, as Topper could have told you. There might have been twenty people there, young and old, but they all played, and so did Scrooge; for, wholly forgetting, in the interest he had in what was going on, that his voice made no sound in their ears, he sometimes came out with his guess quite loud, and very often guessed right, too, for the sharpest needle, best Whitechapel, warranted not to cut in the eye, was not sharper than Scrooge; blunt as he took it in his head to be.

The Ghost was greatly pleased to find him in this mood, and looked upon him with such favour, that he begged like a boy to be allowed to stay until the guests departed. But this the Spirit said could not be done.

"Here is a new game," said Scrooge. "One half-hour, Spirit, only one!"

It was a game called Yes and No, where Scrooge's nephew had to think of something, and the rest must find out what; he only answering to their questions yes or no, as the case was. The brisk fire of questioning to which he was exposed elicited from him that he was thinking of an animal, a live animal, rather a disagreeable animal, a savage animal, an animal that growled and grunted sometimes, and talked sometimes, and lived in London, and walked about the streets, and wasn't made a show of, and wasn't led by anybody, and didn't live in a menagerie, and was never killed in a market, and was not a horse, or an ass, or a cow, or a bull, or a tiger, or a dog, or a pig, or a cat, or a bear. At every fresh question that was put to him, this nephew burst into a fresh roar of laughter; and was so inexpressibly tickled, that he was obliged to get up off the sofa, and stamp. At last the plump sister, falling into a similar state, cried out:

"I have found it out! I know what it is, Fred! I know what it is!"

"What is it?" cried Fred.

"It's your uncle Scro-o-o-o-oge!"

Which it certainly was. Admiration was the universal sentiment, though some objected that the reply to "Is it a bear?" ought to have been "Yes": inasmuch as an answer in the negative was sufficient to have diverted their thoughts from Mr. Scrooge, supposing they had ever had any tendency that way.

"He has given us plenty of merriment, I am sure," said Fred, "and it would be ungrateful not to drink his health. Here is a glass of mulled wine ready to our hand at the moment; and I say, 'Uncle Scrooge!'"

"Well! Uncle Scrooge!" they cried.

"A merry Christmas and a happy New Year to the old man, whatever he is!" said Scrooge's nephew. "He wouldn't take it from me, but may he have it nevertheless. Uncle Scrooge!"

Uncle Scrooge had imperceptibly become so gay and light of heart, that he would have pledged the unconscious company in return, and thanked them in an inaudible speech, if the Ghost had given him time. But the whole scene passed off in the breath of the last word spoken by his nephew; and he and the Spirit were again upon their travels.

Much they saw, and far they went, and many homes they visited, but always with a happy end. The Spirit stood beside sick-beds, and they were cheerful; on foreign lands, and they were close at home; by struggling men, and they were patient in their greater hope; by poverty, and it was rich. In almshouse, hospital, and gaol, in misery's every refuge, where vain man in his little brief authority had not made fast the door, and barred the Spirit out, he left his blessing, and taught Scrooge his precepts.

It was a long night, if it were only a night; but Scrooge had his doubts of this, because the Christmas holidays appeared to be condensed into the space of time they passed together. It was strange, too, that, while Scrooge remained unaltered in his outward form, the Ghost grew older, clearly older. Scrooge had observed this change, but never spoke of it, until they left a children's Twelfth-Night party, when, looking at the Spirit as they stood together in an open place, he noticed that its hair was grey.

"Are spirits' lives so short?" asked Scrooge.

"My life upon this globe is very brief," replied the Ghost. "It ends to-night."

"To-night!" cried Scrooge.

"To-night at midnight. Hark! The time is drawing near."

The chimes were ringing the three-quarters past eleven at that moment.

"Forgive me if I am not justified in what I ask," said Scrooge, looking intently at the Spirit's robe, "but I see something strange, and not belonging to yourself, protruding from your skirts. Is it a foot or a claw?"

"It might be a claw, for the flesh there is upon it," was the Spirit's sorrowful reply. "Look here."

From the foldings of its robe it brought two children; wretched, abject, frightful, hideous, miserable. They knelt down at its feet, and clung upon the outside of its garment.

"Oh, Man! look here! Look, look, down here!" exclaimed the Ghost.

They were a boy and girl. Yellow, meagre, ragged, scowling, wolfish; but prostrate, too, in their humility. Where graceful youth should have filled their features out, and touched them with its freshest tints, a stale and shrivelled hand, like that of age, had pinched, and twisted them, and pulled them into shreds. Where angels might have sat enthroned, devils lurked, and glared out menacing. No change, no degradation, no perversion of humanity, in any grade, through all the mysteries of wonderful creation, has monsters half so horrible and dread.

Scrooge started back, appalled. Having them shown to him in this way, he tried to say they were fine children, but the words choked themselves, rather than be parties to a lie of such enormous magnitude.

"Spirit! are they yours?" Scrooge could say no more.

"They are Man's," said the Spirit, looking down upon them. "And they cling to me, appealing from their fathers. This boy is Ignorance. This girl is Want. Beware of them both, and all of their degree, but most of all beware this boy, for on his brow I see that written which is Doom, unless the writing be erased. Deny it!" cried the Spirit, stretching out its hand towards the city. "Slander those who tell it ye! Admit it for your factious purposes, and make it worse! And bide the end!"

"Have they no refuge or resource?" cried Scrooge.

"Are there no prisons?" said the Spirit, turning on him for the last time with his own words. "Are there no workhouses?"

The bell struck Twelve.

Scrooge looked about him for the Ghost, and saw it not. As the last stroke ceased to vibrate, he remembered the prediction of old Jacob Marley, and, lifting up his eyes, beheld a solemn Phantom, draped and hooded, coming like a mist along the ground towards him.

## Stave Four
### The Last of the Spirits

**THE PHANTOM** slowly, gravely, silently approached. When it came near him, Scrooge bent down upon his knee; for in the very air through which this Spirit moved it seemed to scatter gloom and mystery.

It was shrouded in a deep black garment, which concealed its head, its face, its form, and left nothing of it visible, save one outstretched hand. But for this, it would have been difficult to detach its figure from the night, and separate it from the darkness by which it was surrounded.

He felt that it was tall and stately when it came beside him, and that its mysterious presence filled him with a solemn dread. He knew no more, for the Spirit neither spoke nor moved.

"I am in the presence of the Ghost of Christmas Yet to Come?" said Scrooge.

The Spirit answered not, but pointed onward with its hand.

"You are about to show me shadows of the things that have not happened, but will happen in the time before us," Scrooge pursued. "Is that so, Spirit?"

The upper portion of the garment was contracted for an instant in its folds, as if the Spirit had inclined its head. That was the only answer he received.

Although well used to ghostly company by this time, Scrooge feared the silent shape so much that his legs trembled beneath him, and he found that he could hardly stand when he prepared to follow it. The Spirit paused a moment, as observing his condition, and giving him time to recover.

But Scrooge was all the worse for this. It thrilled him with a vague uncertain horror to know that, behind the dusky shroud, there were ghostly eyes intently fixed upon him, while he, though he stretched his own to the utmost, could see nothing but a spectral hand and one great heap of black.

"Ghost of the Future!" he exclaimed, "I fear you more than any spectre I have seen. But, as I know your purpose is to do me good, and as I hope to live to be another man from what I was, I am prepared to bear you company, and do it with a thankful heart. Will you not speak to me?"

It gave him no reply. The hand was pointed straight before them.

"Lead on!" said Scrooge. "Lead on! The night is waning fast, and it is precious time to me, I know. Lead on, Spirit!"

The phantom moved away as it had come towards him. Scrooge followed in the shadow of its dress, which bore him up, he thought, and carried him along.

They scarcely seemed to enter the City; for the City rather seemed to spring up about them, and encompass them of its own act. But there they were in the heart of it; on 'Change, amongst the merchants; who hurried up and down, and chinked the money in their pockets, and conversed in groups, and looked at their watches, and trifled thoughtfully with their great gold seals; and so forth, as Scrooge had seen them often.

The Spirit stopped beside one little knot of business men. Observing that the hand was pointed to them, Scrooge advanced to listen to their talk.

"No," said a great fat man with a monstrous chin, "I don't know much about it either way. I only know he's dead."

"When did he die?" inquired another.

"Last night, I believe."

"Why, what was the matter with him?" asked a third, taking a vast quantity of snuff out of a very large snuff-box. "I thought he'd never die."

"God knows," said the first with a yawn.

"What has he done with his money?" asked a red-faced gentleman with a pendulous excrescence on the end of his nose, that shook like the gills of a turkey-cock.

"I haven't heard," said the man with the large chin, yawning again. "Left it to his company, perhaps. He hasn't left it to *me*. That's all I know."

This pleasantry was received with a general laugh.

"It's likely to be a very cheap funeral," said the same speaker; "for, upon my life, I don't know of anybody to go to it. Suppose we make up a party, and volunteer?"

"I don't mind going if a lunch is provided," observed the gentleman with the excrescence on his nose. "But I must be fed if I make one."

Another laugh.

"Well, I am the most disinterested among you, after all," said the first speaker, "for I never wear black gloves, and I never eat lunch. But I'll offer to go if anybody else will. When I come to think of it, I'm not at all sure that I wasn't his most particular friend; for we used to stop and speak whenever we met. Bye, bye!"

Speakers and listeners strolled away, and mixed with other groups. Scrooge knew the men, and looked towards the Spirit for an explanation.

The Phantom glided on into a street. Its finger pointed to two persons meeting. Scrooge listened again, thinking that the explanation might lie here.

He knew these men, also, perfectly. They were men of business: very wealthy, and of great importance. He had made a point always of standing well in their esteem: in a business point of view, that is; strictly in a business point of view.

"How are you?" said one.

"How are you?" returned the other.

"Well!" said the first. "Old Scratch has got his own at last, hey?"

"So I am told," returned the second. "Cold, isn't it?"

"Seasonable for Christmas-time. You are not a skater, I suppose?"

"No. No. Something else to think of. Good morning!"

Not another word. That was their meeting, their conversation, and their parting.

Scrooge was at first inclined to be surprised that the Spirit should attach importance to conversations apparently so trivial; but, feeling assured that they must have some hidden purpose, he set himself to consider what it was likely to be. They could scarcely be supposed to have any bearing on the death of Jacob, his old partner, for that was Past, and this Ghost's province was the Future. Nor could he think of any one immediately connected with himself, to whom he could apply them. But nothing doubting that, to whomsoever they applied, they had some latent moral for his own improvement, he resolved to treasure up every word he heard, and everything he saw; and especially to observe the shadow of himself when it appeared. For he had an expectation that the conduct of his future self would give him the clue he missed, and would render the solution of these riddles easy.

He looked about in that very place for his own image, but another man stood in his accustomed corner, and, though the clock pointed to his usual time of day for being there, he saw no likeness of himself among the multitudes that poured in through the Porch. It gave him little surprise, however; for he had been revolving in his mind a change of life, and thought and hoped he saw his new-born resolutions carried out in this.

Quiet and dark, beside him stood the Phantom, with its outstretched hand. When he roused himself from his thoughtful quest, he fancied, from the turn of the hand, and its situation in reference to himself, that the Unseen Eyes were looking at him keenly. It made him shudder, and feel very cold.

They left the busy scene, and went into an obscure part of the town, where Scrooge had never penetrated before, although he recognised its situation and its bad repute. The ways were foul and narrow; the shops and houses wretched; the people half naked, drunken, slipshod, ugly. Alleys and archways, like so many cesspools, disgorged their offences of smell, and dirt, and life upon the straggling streets; and the whole quarter reeked with crime, with filth and misery.

Far in this den of infamous resort, there was a low-browed, beetling shop, below a pent-house roof, where iron, old rags, bottles, bones, and greasy offal were bought. Upon the floor within were piled up heaps of rusty keys, nails, chains, hinges, files, scales, weights, and refuse iron of all kinds. Secrets that few would like to scrutinise were bred and hidden in mountains of unseemly rags, masses of corrupted fat, and sepulchres of bones. Sitting in among the wares he dealt in, by a charcoal stove made of old bricks, was a grey-haired rascal, nearly seventy years of age, who had screened himself from the cold air without by a frouzy curtaining of miscellaneous tatters hung upon a line, and smoked his pipe in all the luxury of calm retirement.

Scrooge and the Phantom came into the presence of this man, just as a woman with a heavy bundle slunk into the shop. But she had scarcely entered, when another woman, similarly laden, came in too, and she was closely followed by a man in faded black, who was no less startled by the sight of them than they had been upon the recognition of each other. After a short period of blank astonishment, in which the old man with the pipe had joined them, they all three burst into a laugh.

"Let the charwoman alone to be the first!" cried she who had entered first. "Let the laundress alone to be the second; and let the undertaker's man alone to be the third. Look here, old Joe, here's a chance! If we haven't all three met here without meaning it!"

"You couldn't have met in a better place," said old Joe, removing his pipe from his mouth. "Come into the parlour. You were made free of it long ago, you know; and the other two an't strangers. Stop till I shut the door of the shop. Ah! How it skreeks! There an't such a rusty bit of metal in the place as its own hinges, I believe; and I'm sure there's no such old bones here as mine. Ha! ha! We're all suitable to our calling, we're well matched. Come into the parlour. Come into the parlour."

The parlour was the space behind the screen of rags. The old man raked the fire together with an old stair-rod, and, having trimmed his smoky lamp (for it was night) with the stem of his pipe, put it into his mouth again.

While he did this, the woman who had already spoken threw her bundle on the floor, and sat down in a flaunting manner on a stool; crossing her elbows on her knees, and looking with a bold defiance at the other two.

"What odds, then? What odds, Mrs. Dilber?" said the woman. "Every person has a right to take care of themselves. *He* always did!"

"That's true, indeed!" said the laundress. "No man more so."

"Why, then, don't stand staring as if you was afraid, woman! Who's the wiser? We're not going to pick holes in each other's coats, I suppose?"

"No, indeed!" said Mrs. Dilber and the man together. "We should hope not."

"Very well, then!" cried the woman. "That's enough. Who's the worse for the loss of a few things like these? Not a dead man, I suppose?"

"No, indeed," said Mrs. Dilber, laughing.

"If he wanted to keep 'em after he was dead, a wicked old screw," pursued the woman, "why wasn't he natural in his lifetime? If he had been, he'd have had somebody to look after him when he was struck with Death, instead of lying gasping out his last there, alone by himself."

"It's the truest word that ever was spoke," said Mrs. Dilber, "It's a judgment on him."

"I wish it was a little heavier judgment," replied the woman; "and it should have been, you may depend upon it, if I could have laid my hands on anything else. Open that bundle, old Joe, and let me know the value of it. Speak out plain. I'm not afraid to be the first, nor afraid for them to see it. We knew pretty well that we were helping ourselves before we met here, I believe. It's no sin. Open the bundle, Joe."

But the gallantry of her friends would not allow of this; and the man in faded black, mounting the breach first, produced *his* plunder. It was not extensive. A seal or two, a pencil-case, a pair of sleeve-buttons, and a brooch of no great value, were all. They were severally examined and appraised by old Joe, who chalked the sums he was disposed to give for each upon the wall, and added them up into a total when he found that there was nothing more to come.

"That's your account," said Joe, "and I wouldn't give another sixpence, if I was to be boiled for not doing it. Who's next?"

Mrs. Dilber was next. Sheets and towels, a little wearing apparel, two old-fashioned silver tea-spoons, a pair of sugar-tongs, and a few boots. Her account was stated on the wall in the same manner.

"I always give too much to ladies. It's a weakness of mine, and that's the way I ruin myself," said old Joe. "That's your account. If you asked me for another penny, and made it an open question, I'd repent of being so liberal, and knock off half-a-crown."

"And now undo *my* bundle, Joe," said the first woman.

Joe went down on his knees for the greater convenience of opening it, and, having unfastened a great many knots, dragged out a large heavy roll of some dark stuff.

"What do you call this?" said Joe. "Bed-curtains?"

"Ah!" returned the woman, laughing and leaning forward on her crossed arms. "Bed-curtains!"

"You don't mean to say you took 'em down, rings and all, with him lying there?" said Joe.

"Yes, I do," replied the woman. "Why not?"

"You were born to make your fortune," said Joe, "and you'll certainly do it."

"I certainly shan't hold my hand, when I can get anything in it by reaching it out, for the sake of such a man as He was, I promise you, Joe," returned the woman coolly. "Don't drop that oil upon the blankets, now."

"His blankets?" asked Joe.

"Whose else's do you think?" replied the woman. "He isn't likely to take cold without 'em, I dare say."

"I hope he didn't die of anything catching? Eh?" said old Joe, stopping in his work, and looking up.

"Don't you be afraid of that," returned the woman. "I an't so fond of his company that I'd loiter about him for such things, if he did. Ah! You may look through that shirt till your eyes ache; but you won't find a hole in it, nor a threadbare place. It's the best he had, and a fine one too. They'd have wasted it, if it hadn't been for me."

"What do you call wasting of it?" asked old Joe.

"Putting it on him to be buried in, to be sure," replied the woman with a laugh. "Somebody was fool enough to do it, but I took it off again. If calico an't good enough for such a purpose, it isn't good enough for anything. It's quite as becoming to the body. He can't look uglier than he did in that one."

Scrooge listened to this dialogue in horror. As they sat grouped about their spoil, in the scanty light afforded by the old man's lamp, he viewed them with a detestation and disgust which could hardly have been greater, though they had been obscene demons, marketing the corpse itself.

"Ha, ha!" laughed the same woman when old Joe, producing a flannel bag with money in it, told out their several gains upon the ground. "This is the end of it, you see! He frightened every one away from him when he was alive, to profit us when he was dead! Ha, ha, ha!"

"Spirit!" said Scrooge, shuddering from head to foot. "I see, I see. The case of this unhappy man might be my own. My life tends that way now. Merciful Heaven, what is this?"

He recoiled in terror, for the scene had changed, and now he almost touched a bed: a bare, uncurtained bed: on which, beneath a ragged sheet, there lay a something covered up, which, though it was dumb, announced itself in awful language.

The room was very dark, too dark to be observed with any accuracy, though Scrooge glanced round it in obedience to a secret impulse, anxious to know what kind of room it was. A pale light, rising in the outer air, fell straight upon the bed: and on it, plundered and bereft, unwatched, unwept, uncared for, was the body of this man.

Scrooge glanced towards the Phantom. Its steady hand was pointed to the head. The cover was so carelessly adjusted that the slightest raising of it, the motion of a finger upon Scrooge's part, would have disclosed the face. He thought of it, felt how easy it would be to do, and longed to do it; but had no more power to withdraw the veil than to dismiss the spectre at his side.

Oh, cold, cold, rigid, dreadful Death, set up thine altar here, and dress it with such terrors as thou hast at thy command: for this is thy dominion! But of the loved, revered, and honoured head thou canst not turn one hair to thy dread purposes, or make one feature odious. It is not that the hand is heavy, and will fall down when released; it is not that the heart and pulse are still; but that the hand WAS open, generous, and true; the heart brave, warm, and tender; and the pulse a man's. Strike, Shadow, strike! And see his good deeds springing from the wound, to sow the world with life immortal!

No voice pronounced these words in Scrooge's ears, and yet he heard them when he looked upon the bed. He thought, if this man could be raised up now, what would be his foremost thoughts? Avarice, hard dealing, griping cares? They have brought him to a rich end, truly!

He lay, in the dark, empty house, with not a man, a woman, or a child to say he was kind to me in this or that, and for the memory of one kind word I will be kind to him. A cat was tearing at the door, and there was a sound of gnawing rats beneath the hearth-stone. What *they* wanted in the room of death, and why they were so restless and disturbed, Scrooge did not dare to think.

"Spirit!" he said, "this is a fearful place. In leaving it, I shall not leave its lesson, trust me. Let us go!"

Still the Ghost pointed with an unmoved finger to the head.

"I understand you," Scrooge returned, "and I would do it if I could. But I have not the power, Spirit. I have not the power."

Again it seemed to look upon him.

"If there is any person in the town who feels emotion caused by this man's death," said Scrooge, quite agonised, "show that person to me, Spirit! I beseech you."

The Phantom spread its dark robe before him for a moment, like a wing; and, withdrawing it, revealed a room by daylight, where a mother and her children were.

She was expecting some one, and with anxious eagerness; for she walked up and down the room; started at every sound; looked out from the window; glanced at the clock; tried, but in vain, to work with her needle; and could hardly bear the voices of her children in their play.

At length the long-expected knock was heard. She hurried to the door, and met her husband; a man whose face was careworn and depressed, though he was young. There was a remarkable expression in it now; a kind of serious delight of which he felt ashamed, and which he struggled to repress.

He sat down to the dinner that had been hoarding for him by the fire, and, when she asked him faintly what news (which was not until after a long silence), he appeared embarrassed how to answer.

"Is it good," she said, "or bad?" to help him.

"Bad," he answered.

"We are quite ruined?"

"No. There is hope yet, Caroline."

"If _be_ relents," she said, amazed, "there is! Nothing is past hope, if such a miracle has happened."

"He is past relenting," said her husband. "He is dead."

She was a mild and patient creature, if her face spoke truth; but she was thankful in her soul to hear it, and she said so with clasped hands. She prayed forgiveness the next moment, and was sorry; but the first was the emotion of her heart.

"What the half-drunken woman, whom I told you of last night, said to me when I tried to see him and obtain a week's delay, and what I thought was a mere excuse to avoid me, turns out to have been quite true. He was not only very ill, but dying, then."

"To whom will our debt be transferred?"

"I don't know. But, before that time, we shall be ready with the money; and, even though we were not, it would be bad fortune indeed to find so merciless a creditor in his successor. We may sleep to-night with light hearts, Caroline!"

Yes. Soften it as they would, their hearts were lighter. The children's faces, hushed and clustered round to hear what they so little understood, were brighter; and it was a happier house for this man's death! The only emotion that the Ghost could show him, caused by the event, was one of pleasure.

"Let me see some tenderness connected with a death," said Scrooge; "or that dark chamber, Spirit, which we left just now, will be for ever present to me."

The Ghost conducted him through several streets familiar to his feet; and, as they went along, Scrooge looked here and there to find himself, but nowhere was he to be seen. They entered poor Bob Cratchit's house, – the dwelling he had visited before, – and found the mother and the children seated round the fire.

Quiet. Very quiet. The noisy little Cratchits were as still as statues in one corner, and sat looking up at Peter, who had a book before him. The mother and her daughters were engaged in sewing. But surely they were very quiet!

"'And he took a child, and set him in the midst of them.'"

Where had Scrooge heard those words? He had not dreamed them. The boy must have read them out, as he and the Spirit crossed the threshold. Why did he not go on?

The mother laid her work upon the table, and put her hand up to her face.

"The colour hurts my eyes," she said.

The colour? Ah, poor Tiny Tim!

"They're better now again," said Cratchit's wife. "It makes them weak by candle-light; and I wouldn't show weak eyes to your father, when he comes home, for the world. It must be near his time."

"Past it rather," Peter answered, shutting up his book. "But I think he has walked a little slower than he used, these few last evenings, mother."

They were very quiet again. At last she said, and in a steady, cheerful voice, that only faltered once:

"I have known him walk with – I have known him walk with Tiny Tim upon his shoulder very fast indeed."

"And so have I," cried Peter. "Often."

"And so have I," exclaimed another. So had all.

"But he was very light to carry," she resumed, intent upon her work, "and his father loved him so, that it was no trouble: no trouble. And there is your father at the door!"

She hurried out to meet him; and little Bob in his comforter – he had need of it, poor fellow – came in. His tea was ready for him on the hob, and they all tried who should help him to it most. Then the two young Cratchits got upon his knees, and laid, each child, a little cheek against his face, as if they said, "Don't mind it, father. Don't be grieved!"

Bob was very cheerful with them, and spoke pleasantly to all the family. He looked at the work upon the table, and praised the industry and speed of Mrs. Cratchit and the girls. They would be done long before Sunday, he said.

"Sunday! You went today, then, Robert?" said his wife.

"Yes, my dear," returned Bob. "I wish you could have gone. It would have done you good to see how green a place it is. But you'll see it often. I promised him that I would walk there on a Sunday. My little, little child!" cried Bob. "My little child!"

He broke down all at once. He couldn't help it. If he could have helped it, he and his child would have been farther apart, perhaps, than they were.

He left the room, and went up-stairs into the room above, which was lighted cheerfully, and hung with Christmas. There was a chair set close beside the child, and there were signs of some one having been there lately. Poor Bob sat down in it, and, when he had thought a little and composed himself, he kissed the little face. He was reconciled to what had happened, and went down again quite happy.

They drew about the fire, and talked; the girls and mother working still. Bob told them of the extraordinary kindness of Mr. Scrooge's nephew, whom he had scarcely seen but once, and who, meeting him in the street that day, and seeing that he looked a little – "just a little down, you know," said Bob, inquired what had happened to distress him. "On which," said Bob, "for he is the pleasantest-spoken gentleman you ever heard, I told him. 'I am heartily sorry for it, Mr. Cratchit,' he said, 'and heartily sorry for your good wife.' By-the-bye, how he ever knew *that* I don't know."

"Knew what, my dear?"

"Why, that you were a good wife," replied Bob.

"Everybody knows that," said Peter.

"Very well observed, my boy!" cried Bob. "I hope they do. 'Heartily sorry,' he said, 'for your good wife. If I can be of service to you in any way,' he said, giving me his card, 'that's where I live. Pray come to me.' Now, it wasn't," cried Bob, "for the sake of anything he might be able to do for us, so much as for his kind way, that this was quite delightful. It really seemed as if he had known our Tiny Tim, and felt with us."

"I'm sure he's a good soul!" said Mrs. Cratchit.

"You would be sure of it, my dear," returned Bob, "if you saw and spoke to him. I shouldn't be at all surprised – mark what I say! – if he got Peter a better situation."

"Only hear that, Peter," said Mrs. Cratchit.

"And then," cried one of the girls, "Peter will be keeping company with some one, and setting up for himself."

"Get along with you!" retorted Peter, grinning.

"It's just as likely as not," said Bob, "one of these days; though there's plenty of time for that, my dear. But, however and whenever we part from one another, I am sure we shall none of us forget poor Tiny Tim – shall we – or this first parting that there was among us?"

"Never, father!" cried they all.

"And I know," said Bob, "I know, my dears, that when we recollect how patient and how mild he was, although he was a little, little child, we shall not quarrel easily among ourselves, and forget poor Tiny Tim in doing it."

"No, never, father!" they all cried again.

"I am very happy," said little Bob, "I am very happy!"

Mrs. Cratchit kissed him, his daughters kissed him, the two young Cratchits kissed him, and Peter and himself shook hands. Spirit of Tiny Tim, thy childish essence was from God!

"Spectre," said Scrooge, "something informs me that our parting moment is at hand. I know it, but I know not how. Tell me what man that was whom we saw lying dead?"

The Ghost of Christmas Yet To Come conveyed him, as before – though at a different time, he thought: indeed, there seemed no order in these latter visions, save that they were in the Future – into the resorts of business men, but showed him not himself. Indeed, the Spirit did not stay for anything, but went straight on, as to the end just now desired, until besought by Scrooge to tarry for a moment.

"This court," said Scrooge, "through which we hurry now, is where my place of occupation is, and has been for a length of time. I see the house. Let me behold what I shall be in days to come."

The Spirit stopped; the hand was pointed elsewhere.

"The house is yonder," Scrooge exclaimed. "Why do you point away?"

The inexorable finger underwent no change.

Scrooge hastened to the window of his office, and looked in. It was an office still, but not his. The furniture was not the same, and the figure in the chair was not himself. The Phantom pointed as before.

He joined it once again, and, wondering why and whither he had gone, accompanied it until they reached an iron gate. He paused to look round before entering.

A churchyard. Here, then, the wretched man, whose name he had now to learn, lay underneath the ground. It was a worthy place. Walled in by houses; overrun by grass and weeds, the growth of vegetation's death, not life; choked up with too much burying; fat with repleted appetite. A worthy place!

The Spirit stood among the graves, and pointed down to One. He advanced towards it trembling. The Phantom was exactly as it had been, but he dreaded that he saw new meaning in its solemn shape.

"Before I draw nearer to that stone to which you point," said Scrooge, "answer me one question. Are these the shadows of the things that Will be, or are they shadows of the things that May be only?"

Still the Ghost pointed downward to the grave by which it stood.

"Men's courses will foreshadow certain ends, to which, if persevered in, they must lead," said Scrooge. "But if the courses be departed from, the ends will change. Say it is thus with what you show me!"

The Spirit was immovable as ever.

Scrooge crept towards it, trembling as he went; and, following the finger, read upon the stone of the neglected grave his own name, Ebenezer Scrooge.

"Am *I* that man who lay upon the bed?" he cried upon his knees.

The finger pointed from the grave to him, and back again.

"No, Spirit! Oh no, no!"

The finger still was there.

"Spirit!" he cried, tight clutching at its robe, "hear me! I am not the man I was. I will not be the man I must have been but for this intercourse. Why show me this, if I am past all hope?"

For the first time the hand appeared to shake.

"Good Spirit," he pursued, as down upon the ground he fell before it: "your nature intercedes for me, and pities me. Assure me that I yet may change these shadows you have shown me by an altered life?"

The kind hand trembled.

"I will honour Christmas in my heart, and try to keep it all the year. I will live in the Past, the Present, and the Future. The Spirits of all Three shall strive within me. I will not shut out the lessons that they teach. Oh, tell me I may sponge away the writing on this stone!"

In his agony, he caught the spectral hand. It sought to free itself, but he was strong in his entreaty, and detained it. The Spirit, stronger yet, repulsed him.

Holding up his hands in a last prayer to have his fate reversed, he saw an alteration in the Phantom's hood and dress. It shrunk, collapsed, and dwindled down into a bedpost.

## Stave Five
## The End of It

**YES!** and the bedpost was his own. The bed was his own, the room was his own. Best and happiest of all, the Time before him was his own, to make amends in!

"I will live in the Past, the Present, and the Future!" Scrooge repeated as he scrambled out of bed. "The Spirits of all Three shall strive within me. Oh, Jacob Marley! Heaven and the Christmas Time be praised for this! I say it on my knees, old Jacob; on my knees!"

He was so fluttered and so glowing with his good intentions, that his broken voice would scarcely answer to his call. He had been sobbing violently in his conflict with the Spirit, and his face was wet with tears.

"They are not torn down," cried Scrooge, folding one of his bed-curtains in his arms, "they are not torn down, rings and all. They are here – I am here – the shadows of the things that would have been may be dispelled. They will be. I know they will!"

His hands were busy with his garments all this time; turning them inside out, putting them on upside down, tearing them, mislaying them, making them parties to every kind of extravagance.

"I don't know what to do!" cried Scrooge, laughing and crying in the same breath; and making a perfect Laocoön of himself with his stockings. "I am as light as a feather, I am as happy as an angel, I am as merry as a school-boy. I am as giddy as a drunken man. A merry Christmas to everybody! A happy New Year to all the world! Hallo here! Whoop! Hallo!"

He had frisked into the sitting-room, and was now standing there: perfectly winded.

"There's the saucepan that the gruel was in!" cried Scrooge, starting off again, and going round the fire-place. "There's the door by which the Ghost of Jacob Marley entered!

There's the corner where the Ghost of Christmas Present sat! There's the window where I saw the wandering Spirits! It's all right, it's all true, it all happened. Ha, ha, ha!"

Really, for a man who had been out of practice for so many years, it was a splendid laugh, a most illustrious laugh. The father of a long, long line of brilliant laughs!

"I don't know what day of the month it is," said Scrooge. "I don't know how long I have been among the Spirits. I don't know anything. I'm quite a baby. Never mind. I don't care. I'd rather be a baby. Hallo! Whoop! Hallo here!"

He was checked in his transports by the churches ringing out the lustiest peals he had ever heard. Clash, clash, hammer; ding, dong, bell! Bell, dong, ding; hammer, clang, clash! Oh, glorious, glorious!

Running to the window, he opened it, and put out his head. No fog, no mist; clear, bright, jovial, stirring, cold; cold, piping for the blood to dance to; Golden sun-light; Heavenly sky; sweet fresh air; merry bells. Oh, glorious! Glorious!

"What's today?" cried Scrooge, calling downward to a boy in Sunday clothes, who perhaps had loitered in to look about him.

"Eh?" returned the boy with all his might of wonder.

"What's today, my fine fellow?" said Scrooge.

"Today!" replied the boy. "Why, Christmas Day."

"It's Christmas Day!" said Scrooge to himself. "I haven't missed it. The Spirits have done it all in one night. They can do anything they like. Of course they can. Of course they can. Hallo, my fine fellow!"

"Hallo!" returned the boy.

"Do you know the Poulterer's in the next street but one, at the corner?" Scrooge inquired.

"I should hope I did," replied the lad.

"An intelligent boy!" said Scrooge. "A remarkable boy! Do you know whether they've sold the prize Turkey that was hanging up there? – Not the little prize Turkey: the big one?"

"What! the one as big as me?" returned the boy.

"What a delightful boy!" said Scrooge. "It's a pleasure to talk to him. Yes, my buck!"

"It's hanging there now," replied the boy.

"Is it?" said Scrooge. "Go and buy it."

"Walk-ER!" exclaimed the boy.

"No, no," said Scrooge, "I am in earnest. Go and buy it, and tell 'em to bring it here, that I may give them the directions where to take it. Come back with the man, and I'll give you a shilling. Come back with him in less than five minutes, and I'll give you half-a-crown!"

The boy was off like a shot. He must have had a steady hand at a trigger who could have got a shot off half so fast.

"I'll send it to Bob Cratchit's," whispered Scrooge, rubbing his hands, and splitting with a laugh. "He shan't know who sends it. It's twice the size of Tiny Tim. Joe Miller never made such a joke as sending it to Bob's will be!"

The hand in which he wrote the address was not a steady one; but write it he did, somehow, and went down-stairs to open the street-door, ready for the coming of the poulterer's man. As he stood there, waiting his arrival, the knocker caught his eye.

"I shall love it as long as I live!" cried Scrooge, patting it with his hand. "I scarcely ever looked at it before. What an honest expression it has in its face! It's a wonderful knocker! – Here's the Turkey. Hallo! Whoop! How are you? Merry Christmas!"

It *was* a Turkey! He never could have stood upon his legs, that bird. He would have snapped 'em short off in a minute, like sticks of sealing-wax.

"Why, it's impossible to carry that to Camden Town," said Scrooge. "You must have a cab."

The chuckle with which he said this, and the chuckle with which he paid for the Turkey, and the chuckle with which he paid for the cab, and the chuckle with which he recompensed the boy, were only to be exceeded by the chuckle with which he sat down breathless in his chair again, and chuckled till he cried.

Shaving was not an easy task, for his hand continued to shake very much; and shaving requires attention, even when you don't dance while you are at it. But, if he had cut the end of his nose off, he would have put a piece of sticking-plaster over it, and been quite satisfied.

He dressed himself "all in his best," and at last got out into the streets. The people were by this time pouring forth, as he had seen them with the Ghost of Christmas Present; and, walking with his hands behind him, Scrooge regarded every one with a delighted smile. He looked so irresistibly pleasant, in a word, that three or four good-humoured fellows said, "Good morning, sir! A merry Christmas to you!" And Scrooge said often afterwards that, of all the blithe sounds he had ever heard, those were the blithest in his ears.

He had not gone far when, coming on towards him, he beheld the portly gentleman who had walked into his counting-house the day before, and said, "Scrooge and Marley's, I believe?" It sent a pang across his heart to think how this old gentleman would look upon him when they met; but he knew what path lay straight before him, and he took it.

"My dear sir," said Scrooge, quickening his pace, and taking the old gentleman by both his hands, "how do you do? I hope you succeeded yesterday. It was very kind of you. A merry Christmas to you, sir!"

"Mr. Scrooge?"

"Yes," said Scrooge. "That is my name, and I fear it may not be pleasant to you. Allow me to ask your pardon. And will you have the goodness—" Here Scrooge whispered in his ear.

"Lord bless me!" cried the gentleman, as if his breath were taken away. "My dear Mr. Scrooge, are you serious?"

"If you please," said Scrooge. "Not a farthing less. A great many back-payments are included in it, I assure you. Will you do me that favour?"

"My dear sir," said the other, shaking hands with him, "I don't know what to say to such munifi—"

"Don't say anything, please," retorted Scrooge. "Come and see me. Will you come and see me?"

"I will!" cried the old gentleman. And it was clear he meant to do it.

"Thankee," said Scrooge. "I am much obliged to you. I thank you fifty times. Bless you!"

He went to church, and walked about the streets, and watched the people hurrying to and fro, and patted the children on the head, and questioned beggars, and looked down into the kitchens of houses, and up to the windows; and found that everything could yield him pleasure. He had never dreamed that any walk – that anything – could give him so much happiness. In the afternoon he turned his steps towards his nephew's house.

He passed the door a dozen times before he had the courage to go up and knock. But he made a dash, and did it.

"Is your master at home, my dear?" said Scrooge to the girl. Nice girl! Very.

"Yes sir."

"Where is he, my love?" said Scrooge.

"He's in the dining-room, sir, along with mistress. I'll show you up-stairs, if you please."

"Thankee. He knows me," said Scrooge, with his hand already on the dining-room lock. "I'll go in here, my dear."

He turned it gently, and sidled his face in round the door. They were looking at the table (which was spread out in great array); for these young housekeepers are always nervous on such points, and like to see that everything is right.

"Fred!" said Scrooge.

Dear heart alive, how his niece by marriage started! Scrooge had forgotten, for the moment, about her sitting in the corner with the footstool, or he wouldn't have done it on any account.

"Why, bless my soul!" cried Fred, "who's that?"

"It's I. Your uncle Scrooge. I have come to dinner. Will you let me in, Fred?"

Let him in! It is a mercy he didn't shake his arm off. He was at home in five minutes. Nothing could be heartier. His niece looked just the same. So did Topper when *he* came. So did the plump sister when *she* came. So did every one when *they* came. Wonderful party, wonderful games, wonderful unanimity, won-der-ful happiness!

But he was early at the office next morning. Oh, he was early there! If he could only be there first, and catch Bob Cratchit coming late! That was the thing he had set his heart upon.

And he did it; yes, he did! The clock struck nine. No Bob. A quarter past. No Bob. He was full eighteen minutes and a half behind his time. Scrooge sat with his door wide open, that he might see him come into the tank.

His hat was off before he opened the door; his comforter too. He was on his stool in a jiffy; driving away with his pen, as if he were trying to overtake nine o'clock.

"Hallo!" growled Scrooge in his accustomed voice as near as he could feign it. "What do you mean by coming here at this time of day?"

"I am very sorry, sir," said Bob. "I *am* behind my time."

"You are!" repeated Scrooge. "Yes. I think you are. Step this way, sir, if you please."

"It's only once a year, sir," pleaded Bob, appearing from the tank. "It shall not be repeated. I was making rather merry yesterday, sir."

"Now, I'll tell you what, my friend," said Scrooge. "I am not going to stand this sort of thing any longer. And therefore," he continued, leaping from his stool, and giving Bob such a dig in the waistcoat that he staggered back into the tank again: "and therefore I am about to raise your salary!"

Bob trembled, and got a little nearer to the ruler. He had a momentary idea of knocking Scrooge down with it, holding him, and calling to the people in the court for help and a strait-waistcoat.

"A merry Christmas, Bob!" said Scrooge with an earnestness that could not be mistaken, as he clapped him on the back. "A merrier Christmas, Bob, my good fellow, than I have given you for many a year! I'll raise your salary, and endeavour to assist your struggling family, and we will discuss your affairs this very afternoon, over a Christmas bowl of smoking bishop, Bob! Make up the fires and buy another coal-scuttle before you dot another i, Bob Cratchit!"

* * *

Scrooge was better than his word. He did it all, and infinitely more; and to Tiny Tim, who did NOT die, he was a second father. He became as good a friend, as good a master, and as good a man as the good old City knew, or any other good old city, town, or borough in the good old world. Some people laughed to see the alteration in him, but he let them laugh, and little heeded them; for he was wise enough to know that nothing ever happened on this globe, for good, at which some people did not have their fill of laughter in the outset; and, knowing that such as these would be blind anyway, he thought it quite as well that they should wrinkle up their eyes in grins as have the malady in less attractive forms. His own heart laughed: and that was quite enough for him.

He had no further intercourse with Spirits, but lived upon the Total-Abstinence Principle ever afterwards; and it was always said of him that he knew how to keep Christmas well, if any man alive possessed the knowledge. May that be truly said of us, and all of us! And so, as Tiny Tim observed, God bless Us, Every One!

**If you enjoyed this, you might also like...**
A Christmas Tree, see page 140
The Ghosts of the Mail, see page 11

# The Haunted Man and the Ghost's Bargain

## Chapter I
## The Gift Bestowed

**EVERYBODY SAID SO.**

Far be it from me to assert that what everybody says must be true. Everybody is, often, as likely to be wrong as right. In the general experience, everybody has been wrong so often, and it has taken, in most instances, such a weary while to find out how wrong, that the authority is proved to be fallible. Everybody may sometimes be right; "but *that's* no rule," as the ghost of Giles Scroggins says in the ballad.

The dread word, Ghost, recalls me.

Everybody said he looked like a haunted man. The extent of my present claim for everybody is, that they were so far right. He did.

Who could have seen his hollow cheek; his sunken brilliant eye; his black-attired figure, indefinably grim, although well-knit and well-proportioned; his grizzled hair hanging, like tangled sea-weed, about his face, – as if he had been, through his whole life, a lonely mark for the chafing and beating of the great deep of humanity, – but might have said he looked like a haunted man?

Who could have observed his manner, taciturn, thoughtful, gloomy, shadowed by habitual reserve, retiring always and jocund never, with a distraught air of reverting to a bygone place and time, or of listening to some old echoes in his mind, but might have said it was the manner of a haunted man?

Who could have heard his voice, slow-speaking, deep, and grave, with a natural fulness and melody in it which he seemed to set himself against and stop, but might have said it was the voice of a haunted man?

Who that had seen him in his inner chamber, part library and part laboratory, – for he was, as the world knew, far and wide, a learned man in chemistry, and a teacher on whose lips and hands a crowd of aspiring ears and eyes hung daily, – who that had seen him there, upon a winter night, alone, surrounded by his drugs and instruments and books; the shadow of his shaded lamp a monstrous beetle on the wall, motionless among a crowd of spectral shapes raised there by the flickering of the fire upon the quaint objects around him; some of these phantoms (the reflection of glass vessels that held liquids), trembling at heart like things that knew his power to uncombine them, and to give back their component parts to fire and vapour; – who that had seen him then, his work done, and he pondering in his chair before the rusted grate and red flame, moving his thin mouth as if in speech, but silent as the dead, would not have said that the man seemed haunted and the chamber too?

Who might not, by a very easy flight of fancy, have believed that everything about him took this haunted tone, and that he lived on haunted ground?

His dwelling was so solitary and vault-like, – an old, retired part of an ancient endowment for students, once a brave edifice, planted in an open place, but now the obsolete whim of forgotten architects; smoke-age-and-weather-darkened, squeezed on every side by the overgrowing of the great city, and choked, like an old well, with stones and bricks; its small quadrangles, lying down in very pits formed by the streets and buildings, which, in course of time, had been constructed above its heavy chimney stalks; its old trees, insulted by the neighbouring smoke, which deigned to droop so low when it was very feeble and the weather very moody; its grass-plots, struggling with the mildewed earth to be grass, or to win any show of compromise; its silent pavements, unaccustomed to the tread of feet, and even to the observation of eyes, except when a stray face looked down from the upper world, wondering what nook it was; its sun-dial in a little bricked-up corner, where no sun had straggled for a hundred years, but where, in compensation for the sun's neglect, the snow would lie for weeks when it lay nowhere else, and the black east wind would spin like a huge humming-top, when in all other places it was silent and still.

His dwelling, at its heart and core – within doors – at his fireside – was so lowering and old, so crazy, yet so strong, with its worn-eaten beams of wood in the ceiling, and its sturdy floor shelving downward to the great oak chimney-piece; so environed and hemmed in by the pressure of the town yet so remote in fashion, age, and custom; so quiet, yet so thundering with echoes when a distant voice was raised or a door was shut, – echoes, not confined to the many low passages and empty rooms, but rumbling and grumbling till they were stifled in the heavy air of the forgotten Crypt where the Norman arches were half-buried in the earth.

You should have seen him in his dwelling about twilight, in the dead winter time.

When the wind was blowing, shrill and shrewd, with the going down of the blurred sun. When it was just so dark, as that the forms of things were indistinct and big – but not wholly lost. When sitters by the fire began to see wild faces and figures, mountains and abysses, ambuscades and armies, in the coals. When people in the streets bent down their heads and ran before the weather. When those who were obliged to meet it, were stopped at angry corners, stung by wandering snow-flakes alighting on the lashes of their eyes, – which fell too sparingly, and were blown away too quickly, to leave a trace upon the frozen ground. When windows of private houses closed up tight and warm. When lighted gas began to burst forth in the busy and the quiet streets, fast blackening otherwise. When stray pedestrians, shivering along the latter, looked down at the glowing fires in kitchens, and sharpened their sharp appetites by sniffing up the fragrance of whole miles of dinners.

When travellers by land were bitter cold, and looked wearily on gloomy landscapes, rustling and shuddering in the blast. When mariners at sea, outlying upon icy yards, were tossed and swung above the howling ocean dreadfully. When lighthouses, on rocks and headlands, showed solitary and watchful; and benighted sea-birds breasted on against their ponderous lanterns, and fell dead. When little readers of story-books, by the firelight, trembled to think of Cassim Baba cut into quarters, hanging in the Robbers' Cave, or had some small misgivings that the fierce little old woman, with the crutch, who used to start out of the box in the merchant Abudah's bedroom, might, one of these nights, be found upon the stairs, in the long, cold, dusky journey up to bed.

When, in rustic places, the last glimmering of daylight died away from the ends of avenues; and the trees, arching overhead, were sullen and black. When, in parks and woods, the high wet fern and sodden moss, and beds of fallen leaves, and trunks of trees, were lost to view, in masses of impenetrable shade. When mists arose from dyke, and fen, and river. When lights in old halls and in cottage windows, were a cheerful sight. When the mill stopped, the wheelwright and the blacksmith shut their workshops, the turnpike-gate closed, the plough and harrow were left lonely in the fields, the labourer and team went home, and the striking of the church clock had a deeper sound than at noon, and the churchyard wicket would be swung no more that night.

When twilight everywhere released the shadows, prisoned up all day, that now closed in and gathered like mustering swarms of ghosts. When they stood lowering, in corners of rooms, and frowned out from behind half-opened doors. When they had full possession of unoccupied apartments. When they danced upon the floors, and walls, and ceilings of inhabited chambers, while the fire was low, and withdrew like ebbing waters when it sprang into a blaze. When they fantastically mocked the shapes of household objects, making the nurse an ogress, the rocking-horse a monster, the wondering child, half-scared and half-amused, a stranger to itself, – the very tongs upon the hearth, a straddling giant with his arms a-kimbo, evidently smelling the blood of Englishmen, and wanting to grind people's bones to make his bread.

When these shadows brought into the minds of older people, other thoughts, and showed them different images. When they stole from their retreats, in the likenesses of forms and faces from the past, from the grave, from the deep, deep gulf, where the things that might have been, and never were, are always wandering.

When he sat, as already mentioned, gazing at the fire. When, as it rose and fell, the shadows went and came. When he took no heed of them, with his bodily eyes; but, let them come or let them go, looked fixedly at the fire. You should have seen him, then.

When the sounds that had arisen with the shadows, and come out of their lurking-places at the twilight summons, seemed to make a deeper stillness all about him. When the wind was rumbling in the chimney, and sometimes crooning, sometimes howling, in the house. When the old trees outside were so shaken and beaten, that one querulous old rook, unable to sleep, protested now and then, in a feeble, dozy, high-up "Caw!" When, at intervals, the window trembled, the rusty vane upon the turret-top complained, the clock beneath it recorded that another quarter of an hour was gone, or the fire collapsed and fell in with a rattle.

When a knock came at his door, in short, as he was sitting so, and roused him.

"Who's that?" said he. "Come in!"

Surely there had been no figure leaning on the back of his chair; no face looking over it. It is certain that no gliding footstep touched the floor, as he lifted up his head, with a start, and spoke. And yet there was no mirror in the room on whose surface his own form could have cast its shadow for a moment; and, Something had passed darkly and gone!

"I'm humbly fearful, sir," said a fresh-coloured busy man, holding the door open with his foot for the admission of himself and a wooden tray he carried, and letting it go again by very gentle and careful degrees, when he and the tray had got in, lest it should close noisily, "that it's a good bit past the time to-night. But Mrs. William has been taken off her legs so often—"

"By the wind? Ay! I have heard it rising."

"By the wind, sir – that it's a mercy she got home at all. Oh dear, yes. Yes. It was by the wind, Mr. Redlaw. By the wind."

He had, by this time, put down the tray for dinner, and was employed in lighting the lamp, and spreading a cloth on the table. From this employment he desisted in a hurry, to stir and feed the fire, and then resumed it; the lamp he had lighted, and the blaze that rose under his hand, so quickly changing the appearance of the room, that it seemed as if the mere coming in of his fresh red face and active manner had made the pleasant alteration.

"Mrs. William is of course subject at any time, sir, to be taken off her balance by the elements. She is not formed superior to *that*."

"No," returned Mr. Redlaw good-naturedly, though abruptly.

"No, sir. Mrs. William may be taken off her balance by Earth; as for example, last Sunday week, when sloppy and greasy, and she going out to tea with her newest sister-in-law, and having a pride in herself, and wishing to appear perfectly spotless though pedestrian. Mrs. William may be taken off her balance by Air; as being once over-persuaded by a friend to try a swing at Peckham Fair, which acted on her constitution instantly like a steam-boat. Mrs. William may be taken off her balance by Fire; as on a false alarm of engines at her mother's, when she went two miles in her nightcap. Mrs. William may be taken off her balance by Water; as at Battersea, when rowed into the piers by her young nephew, Charley Swidger junior, aged twelve, which had no idea of boats whatever. But these are elements. Mrs. William must be taken out of elements for the strength of *her* character to come into play."

As he stopped for a reply, the reply was "Yes," in the same tone as before.

"Yes, sir. Oh dear, yes!" said Mr. Swidger, still proceeding with his preparations, and checking them off as he made them. "That's where it is, sir. That's what I always say myself, sir. Such a many of us Swidgers! – Pepper. Why there's my father, sir, superannuated keeper and custodian of this Institution, eighty-seven year old. He's a Swidger! – Spoon."

"True, William," was the patient and abstracted answer, when he stopped again.

"Yes, sir," said Mr. Swidger. "That's what I always say, sir. You may call him the trunk of the tree! – Bread. Then you come to his successor, my unworthy self – Salt – and Mrs. William, Swidgers both. – Knife and fork. Then you come to all my brothers and their families, Swidgers, man and woman, boy and girl. Why, what with cousins, uncles, aunts, and relationships of this, that, and t'other degree, and whatnot degree, and marriages, and lyings-in, the Swidgers – Tumbler – might take hold of hands, and make a ring round England!"

Receiving no reply at all here, from the thoughtful man whom he addressed, Mr. William approached, him nearer, and made a feint of accidentally knocking the table with a decanter, to rouse him. The moment he succeeded, he went on, as if in great alacrity of acquiescence.

"Yes, sir! That's just what I say myself, sir. Mrs. William and me have often said so. 'There's Swidgers enough,' we say, 'without *our* voluntary contributions,' – Butter. In fact, sir, my father is a family in himself – Castors – to take care of; and it happens all for the best that we have no child of our own, though it's made Mrs. William rather quiet-like, too. Quite ready for the fowl and mashed potatoes, sir? Mrs. William said she'd dish in ten minutes when I left the Lodge."

"I am quite ready," said the other, waking as from a dream, and walking slowly to and fro.

"Mrs. William has been at it again, sir!" said the keeper, as he stood warming a plate at the fire, and pleasantly shading his face with it. Mr. Redlaw stopped in his walking, and an expression of interest appeared in him.

"What I always say myself, sir. She *will* do it! There's a motherly feeling in Mrs. William's breast that must and will have went."

"What has she done?"

"Why, sir, not satisfied with being a sort of mother to all the young gentlemen that come up from a variety of parts, to attend your courses of lectures at this ancient foundation – its surprising how stone-chaney catches the heat this frosty weather, to be sure!" Here he turned the plate, and cooled his fingers.

"Well?" said Mr. Redlaw.

"That's just what I say myself, sir," returned Mr. William, speaking over his shoulder, as if in ready and delighted assent. "That's exactly where it is, sir! There ain't one of our students but appears to regard Mrs. William in that light. Every day, right through the course, they puts their heads into the Lodge, one after another, and have all got something to tell her, or something to ask her. 'Swidge' is the appellation by which they speak of Mrs. William in general, among themselves, I'm told; but that's what I say, sir. Better be called ever so far out of your name, if it's done in real liking, than have it made ever so much of, and not cared about! What's a name for? To know a person by. If Mrs. William is known by something better than her name – I allude to Mrs. William's qualities and disposition – never mind her name, though it *is* Swidger, by rights. Let 'em call her Swidge, Widge, Bridge – Lord! London Bridge, Blackfriars, Chelsea, Putney, Waterloo, or Hammersmith Suspension – if they like."

The close of this triumphant oration brought him and the plate to the table, upon which he half laid and half dropped it, with a lively sense of its being thoroughly heated, just as the subject of his praises entered the room, bearing another tray and a lantern, and followed by a venerable old man with long grey hair.

Mrs. William, like Mr. William, was a simple, innocent-looking person, in whose smooth cheeks the cheerful red of her husband's official waistcoat was very pleasantly repeated. But whereas Mr. William's light hair stood on end all over his head, and seemed to draw his eyes up with it in an excess of bustling readiness for anything, the dark brown hair of Mrs. William was carefully smoothed down, and waved away under a trim tidy cap, in the most exact and quiet manner imaginable. Whereas Mr. William's very trousers hitched themselves up at the ankles, as if it were not in their iron-grey nature to rest without looking about them, Mrs. William's neatly-flowered skirts – red and white, like her own pretty face – were as composed and orderly, as if the very wind that blew so hard out of doors could not disturb one of their folds. Whereas his coat had something of a fly-away and half-off appearance about the collar and breast, her little bodice was so placid and neat, that there should have been protection for her, in it, had she needed any, with the roughest people. Who could have had the heart to make so calm a bosom swell with grief, or throb with fear, or flutter with a thought of shame! To whom would its repose and peace have not appealed against disturbance, like the innocent slumber of a child!

"Punctual, of course, Milly," said her husband, relieving her of the tray, "or it wouldn't be you. Here's Mrs. William, sir! – He looks lonelier than ever to-night," whispering to his wife, as he was taking the tray, "and ghostlier altogether."

Without any show of hurry or noise, or any show of herself even, she was so calm and quiet, Milly set the dishes she had brought upon the table, – Mr. William, after much clattering and running about, having only gained possession of a butter-boat of gravy, which he stood ready to serve.

"What is that the old man has in his arms?" asked Mr. Redlaw, as he sat down to his solitary meal.

"Holly, sir," replied the quiet voice of Milly.

"That's what I say myself, sir," interposed Mr. William, striking in with the butter-boat. "Berries is so seasonable to the time of year! – Brown gravy!"

"Another Christmas come, another year gone!" murmured the Chemist, with a gloomy sigh. "More figures in the lengthening sum of recollection that we work and work at to our torment, till Death idly jumbles all together, and rubs all out. So, Philip!" breaking off, and raising his voice as he addressed the old man, standing apart, with his glistening burden in his arms, from which the quiet Mrs. William took small branches, which she noiselessly trimmed with her scissors, and decorated the room with, while her aged father-in-law looked on much interested in the ceremony.

"My duty to you, sir," returned the old man. "Should have spoke before, sir, but know your ways, Mr. Redlaw – proud to say – and wait till spoke to! Merry Christmas, sir, and Happy New Year, and many of 'em. Have had a pretty many of 'em myself – ha, ha! – and may take the liberty of wishing 'em. I'm eighty-seven!"

"Have you had so many that were merry and happy?" asked the other.

"Ay, sir, ever so many," returned the old man.

"Is his memory impaired with age? It is to be expected now," said Mr. Redlaw, turning to the son, and speaking lower.

"Not a morsel of it, sir," replied Mr. William. "That's exactly what I say myself, sir. There never was such a memory as my father's. He's the most wonderful man in the world. He don't know what forgetting means. It's the very observation I'm always making to Mrs. William, sir, if you'll believe me!"

Mr. Swidger, in his polite desire to seem to acquiesce at all events, delivered this as if there were no iota of contradiction in it, and it were all said in unbounded and unqualified assent.

The Chemist pushed his plate away, and, rising from the table, walked across the room to where the old man stood looking at a little sprig of holly in his hand.

"It recalls the time when many of those years were old and new, then?" he said, observing him attentively, and touching him on the shoulder. "Does it?"

"Oh many, many!" said Philip, half awaking from his reverie. "I'm eighty-seven!"

"Merry and happy, was it?" asked the Chemist in a low voice. "Merry and happy, old man?"

"Maybe as high as that, no higher," said the old man, holding out his hand a little way above the level of his knee, and looking retrospectively at his questioner, "when I first remember 'em! Cold, sunshiny day it was, out a-walking, when some one – it was my mother as sure as you stand there, though I don't know what her blessed face was like, for she took ill and died that Christmas-time – told me they were food for birds. The pretty little fellow thought – that's me, you understand – that birds' eyes were so bright, perhaps, because the berries that they lived on in the winter were so bright. I recollect that. And I'm eighty-seven!"

"Merry and happy!" mused the other, bending his dark eyes upon the stooping figure, with a smile of compassion. "Merry and happy – and remember well?"

"Ay, ay, ay!" resumed the old man, catching the last words. "I remember 'em well in my school time, year after year, and all the merry-making that used to come along with them. I was a strong chap then, Mr. Redlaw; and, if you'll believe me, hadn't my match at football within ten mile. Where's my son William? Hadn't my match at football, William, within ten mile!"

"That's what I always say, father!" returned the son promptly, and with great respect. "You ARE a Swidger, if ever there was one of the family!"

"Dear!" said the old man, shaking his head as he again looked at the holly. "His mother – my son William's my youngest son – and I, have sat among 'em all, boys and girls, little children and babies, many a year, when the berries like these were not shining half so bright all round us, as their bright faces. Many of 'em are gone; she's gone; and my son George (our eldest, who was her pride more than all the rest!) is fallen very low: but I can see them, when I look here, alive and healthy, as they used to be in those days; and I can see him, thank God, in his innocence. It's a blessed thing to me, at eighty-seven."

The keen look that had been fixed upon him with so much earnestness, had gradually sought the ground.

"When my circumstances got to be not so good as formerly, through not being honestly dealt by, and I first come here to be custodian," said the old man, "—which was upwards of fifty years ago – where's my son William? More than half a century ago, William!"

"That's what I say, father," replied the son, as promptly and dutifully as before, "that's exactly where it is. Two times ought's an ought, and twice five ten, and there's a hundred of 'em."

"It was quite a pleasure to know that one of our founders – or more correctly speaking," said the old man, with a great glory in his subject and his knowledge of it, "one of the learned gentlemen that helped endow us in Queen Elizabeth's time, for we were founded afore her day – left in his will, among the other bequests he made us, so much to buy holly, for garnishing the walls and windows, come Christmas. There was something homely and friendly in it. Being but strange here, then, and coming at Christmas time, we took a liking for his very picter that hangs in what used to be, anciently, afore our ten poor gentlemen commuted for an annual stipend in money, our great Dinner Hall. A sedate gentleman in a peaked beard, with a ruff round his neck, and a scroll below him, in old English letters, 'Lord! keep my memory green!' You know all about him, Mr. Redlaw?"

"I know the portrait hangs there, Philip."

"Yes, sure, it's the second on the right, above the panelling. I was going to say – he has helped to keep *my* memory green, I thank him; for going round the building every year, as I'm a doing now, and freshening up the bare rooms with these branches and berries, freshens up my bare old brain. One year brings back another, and that year another, and those others numbers! At last, it seems to me as if the birth-time of our Lord was the birth-time of all I have ever had affection for, or mourned for, or delighted in, – and they're a pretty many, for I'm eighty-seven!"

"Merry and happy," murmured Redlaw to himself.

The room began to darken strangely.

"So you see, sir," pursued old Philip, whose hale wintry cheek had warmed into a ruddier glow, and whose blue eyes had brightened while he spoke, "I have plenty to keep, when I keep this present season. Now, where's my quiet Mouse? Chattering's the sin of my time of life, and there's half the building to do yet, if the cold don't freeze us first, or the wind don't blow us away, or the darkness don't swallow us up."

The quiet Mouse had brought her calm face to his side, and silently taken his arm, before he finished speaking.

"Come away, my dear," said the old man. "Mr. Redlaw won't settle to his dinner, otherwise, till it's cold as the winter. I hope you'll excuse me rambling on, sir, and I wish you good night, and, once again, a merry—"

"Stay!" said Mr. Redlaw, resuming his place at the table, more, it would have seemed from his manner, to reassure the old keeper, than in any remembrance of his own appetite. "Spare me another moment, Philip. William, you were going to tell me something to your excellent wife's honour. It will not be disagreeable to her to hear you praise her. What was it?"

"Why, that's where it is, you see, sir," returned Mr. William Swidger, looking towards his wife in considerable embarrassment. "Mrs. William's got her eye upon me."

"But you're not afraid of Mrs. William's eye?"

"Why, no, sir," returned Mr. Swidger, "that's what I say myself. It wasn't made to be afraid of. It wouldn't have been made so mild, if that was the intention. But I wouldn't like to – Milly! – him, you know. Down in the Buildings."

Mr. William, standing behind the table, and rummaging disconcertedly among the objects upon it, directed persuasive glances at Mrs. William, and secret jerks of his head and thumb at Mr. Redlaw, as alluring her towards him.

"Him, you know, my love," said Mr. William. "Down in the Buildings. Tell, my dear! You're the works of Shakespeare in comparison with myself. Down in the Buildings, you know, my love. – Student."

"Student?" repeated Mr. Redlaw, raising his head.

"That's what I say, sir!" cried Mr. William, in the utmost animation of assent. "If it wasn't the poor student down in the Buildings, why should you wish to hear it from Mrs. William's lips? Mrs. William, my dear – Buildings."

"I didn't know," said Milly, with a quiet frankness, free from any haste or confusion, "that William had said anything about it, or I wouldn't have come. I asked him not to. It's a sick young gentleman, sir – and very poor, I am afraid – who is too ill to go home this holiday-time, and lives, unknown to any one, in but a common kind of lodging for a gentleman, down in Jerusalem Buildings. That's all, sir."

"Why have I never heard of him?" said the Chemist, rising hurriedly. "Why has he not made his situation known to me? Sick! – give me my hat and cloak. Poor! – what house? – what number?"

"Oh, you mustn't go there, sir," said Milly, leaving her father-in-law, and calmly confronting him with her collected little face and folded hands.

"Not go there?"

"Oh dear, no!" said Milly, shaking her head as at a most manifest and self-evident impossibility. "It couldn't be thought of!"

"What do you mean? Why not?"

"Why, you see, sir," said Mr. William Swidger, persuasively and confidentially, "that's what I say. Depend upon it, the young gentleman would never have made his situation known to one of his own sex. Mrs. Williams has got into his confidence, but that's quite different. They all confide in Mrs. William; they all trust *her*. A man, sir, couldn't have got a whisper out of him; but woman, sir, and Mrs. William combined!"

"There is good sense and delicacy in what you say, William," returned Mr. Redlaw, observant of the gentle and composed face at his shoulder. And laying his finger on his lip, he secretly put his purse into her hand.

"Oh dear no, sir!" cried Milly, giving it back again. "Worse and worse! Couldn't be dreamed of!"

Such a staid matter-of-fact housewife she was, and so unruffled by the momentary haste of this rejection, that, an instant afterwards, she was tidily picking up a few leaves which had strayed from between her scissors and her apron, when she had arranged the holly.

Finding, when she rose from her stooping posture, that Mr. Redlaw was still regarding her with doubt and astonishment, she quietly repeated – looking about, the while, for any other fragments that might have escaped her observation:

"Oh dear no, sir! He said that of all the world he would not be known to you, or receive help from you – though he is a student in your class. I have made no terms of secrecy with you, but I trust to your honour completely."

"Why did he say so?"

"Indeed I can't tell, sir," said Milly, after thinking a little, "because I am not at all clever, you know; and I wanted to be useful to him in making things neat and comfortable about him, and employed myself that way. But I know he is poor, and lonely, and I think he is somehow neglected too. – How dark it is!"

The room had darkened more and more. There was a very heavy gloom and shadow gathering behind the Chemist's chair.

"What more about him?" he asked.

"He is engaged to be married when he can afford it," said Milly, "and is studying, I think, to qualify himself to earn a living. I have seen, a long time, that he has studied hard and denied himself much. – How very dark it is!"

"It's turned colder, too," said the old man, rubbing his hands. "There's a chill and dismal feeling in the room. Where's my son William? William, my boy, turn the lamp, and rouse the fire!"

Milly's voice resumed, like quiet music very softly played:

"He muttered in his broken sleep yesterday afternoon, after talking to me" (this was to herself) "about some one dead, and some great wrong done that could never be forgotten; but whether to him or to another person, I don't know. Not *by* him, I am sure."

"And, in short, Mrs. William, you see – which she wouldn't say herself, Mr. Redlaw, if she was to stop here till the new year after this next one—" said Mr. William, coming up to him to speak in his ear, "has done him worlds of good! Bless you, worlds of good! All at home just the same as ever – my father made as snug and comfortable – not a crumb of litter to be found in the house, if you were to offer fifty pound ready money for it – Mrs. William apparently never out of the way – yet Mrs. William backwards and forwards, backwards and forwards, up and down, up and down, a mother to him!"

The room turned darker and colder, and the gloom and shadow gathering behind the chair was heavier.

"Not content with this, sir, Mrs. William goes and finds, this very night, when she was coming home (why it's not above a couple of hours ago), a creature more like a young wild beast than a young child, shivering upon a door-step. What does Mrs. William do, but brings it home to dry it, and feed it, and keep it till our old Bounty of food and flannel is given away, on Christmas morning! If it ever felt a fire before, it's as much as ever it did; for it's sitting in the old Lodge chimney, staring at ours as if its ravenous eyes would never shut again. It's sitting there, at least," said Mr. William, correcting himself, on reflection, "unless it's bolted!"

"Heaven keep her happy!" said the Chemist aloud, "and you too, Philip! and you, William! I must consider what to do in this. I may desire to see this student, I'll not detain you any longer now. Good-night!"

"I thank'ee, sir, I thank'ee!" said the old man, "for Mouse, and for my son William, and for myself. Where's my son William? William, you take the lantern and go on first, through them long dark passages, as you did last year and the year afore. Ha ha! *I* remember – though I'm eighty-seven! 'Lord, keep my memory green!' It's a very good prayer, Mr. Redlaw, that of the learned gentleman in the peaked beard, with a ruff round his neck – hangs up, second on the right above the panelling, in what used to be, afore our ten poor gentlemen commuted, our great Dinner Hall. 'Lord, keep my memory green!' It's very good and pious, sir. Amen! Amen!"

As they passed out and shut the heavy door, which, however carefully withheld, fired a long train of thundering reverberations when it shut at last, the room turned darker.

As he fell a musing in his chair alone, the healthy holly withered on the wall, and dropped – dead branches.

As the gloom and shadow thickened behind him, in that place where it had been gathering so darkly, it took, by slow degrees, – or out of it there came, by some unreal, unsubstantial process – not to be traced by any human sense, – an awful likeness of himself!

Ghastly and cold, colourless in its leaden face and hands, but with his features, and his bright eyes, and his grizzled hair, and dressed in the gloomy shadow of his dress, it came into his terrible appearance of existence, motionless, without a sound. As *he* leaned his arm upon the elbow of his chair, ruminating before the fire, *it* leaned upon the chair-back, close above him, with its appalling copy of his face looking where his face looked, and bearing the expression his face bore.

This, then, was the Something that had passed and gone already. This was the dread companion of the haunted man!

It took, for some moments, no more apparent heed of him, than he of it. The Christmas Waits were playing somewhere in the distance, and, through his thoughtfulness, he seemed to listen to the music. It seemed to listen too.

At length he spoke; without moving or lifting up his face.

"Here again!" he said.

"Here again," replied the Phantom.

"I see you in the fire," said the haunted man; "I hear you in music, in the wind, in the dead stillness of the night."

The Phantom moved its head, assenting.

"Why do you come, to haunt me thus?"

"I come as I am called," replied the Ghost.

"No. Unbidden," exclaimed the Chemist.

"Unbidden be it," said the Spectre. "It is enough. I am here."

Hitherto the light of the fire had shone on the two faces – if the dread lineaments behind the chair might be called a face – both addressed towards it, as at first, and neither looking at the other. But, now, the haunted man turned, suddenly, and stared upon the Ghost. The Ghost, as sudden in its motion, passed to before the chair, and stared on him.

The living man, and the animated image of himself dead, might so have looked, the one upon the other. An awful survey, in a lonely and remote part of an empty old pile of building, on a winter night, with the loud wind going by upon its journey of mystery – whence or whither, no man knowing since the world began – and the stars, in unimaginable millions, glittering through it, from eternal space, where the world's bulk is as a grain, and its hoary age is infancy.

"Look upon me!" said the Spectre. "I am he, neglected in my youth, and miserably poor, who strove and suffered, and still strove and suffered, until I hewed out knowledge from the mine where it was buried, and made rugged steps thereof, for my worn feet to rest and rise on."

"I *am* that man," returned the Chemist.

"No mother's self-denying love," pursued the Phantom, "no father's counsel, aided *me*. A stranger came into my father's place when I was but a child, and I was easily an alien from my mother's heart. My parents, at the best, were of that sort whose care soon ends, and whose duty is soon done; who cast their offspring loose, early, as birds do theirs; and, if they do well, claim the merit; and, if ill, the pity."

It paused, and seemed to tempt and goad him with its look, and with the manner of its speech, and with its smile.

"I am he," pursued the Phantom, "who, in this struggle upward, found a friend. I made him – won him – bound him to me! We worked together, side by side. All the love and confidence that in my earlier youth had had no outlet, and found no expression, I bestowed on him."

"Not all," said Redlaw, hoarsely.

"No, not all," returned the Phantom. "I had a sister."

The haunted man, with his head resting on his hands, replied "I had!" The Phantom, with an evil smile, drew closer to the chair, and resting its chin upon its folded hands, its folded hands upon the back, and looking down into his face with searching eyes, that seemed instinct with fire, went on:

"Such glimpses of the light of home as I had ever known, had streamed from her. How young she was, how fair, how loving! I took her to the first poor roof that I was master of, and made it rich. She came into the darkness of my life, and made it bright. – She is before me!"

"I saw her, in the fire, but now. I hear her in music, in the wind, in the dead stillness of the night," returned the haunted man.

"*Did* he love her?" said the Phantom, echoing his contemplative tone. "I think he did, once. I am sure he did. Better had she loved him less – less secretly, less dearly, from the shallower depths of a more divided heart!"

"Let me forget it!" said the Chemist, with an angry motion of his hand. "Let me blot it from my memory!"

The Spectre, without stirring, and with its unwinking, cruel eyes still fixed upon his face, went on:

"A dream, like hers, stole upon my own life."

"It did," said Redlaw.

"A love, as like hers," pursued the Phantom, "as my inferior nature might cherish, arose in my own heart. I was too poor to bind its object to my fortune then, by any thread of promise or entreaty. I loved her far too well, to seek to do it. But, more than ever I had striven in my life, I strove to climb! Only an inch gained, brought me something nearer to the height. I toiled up! In the late pauses of my labour at that time, – my sister (sweet companion!) still sharing with me the expiring embers and the cooling hearth, – when day was breaking, what pictures of the future did I see!"

"I saw them, in the fire, but now," he murmured. "They come back to me in music, in the wind, in the dead stillness of the night, in the revolving years."

" – Pictures of my own domestic life, in aftertime, with her who was the inspiration of my toil. Pictures of my sister, made the wife of my dear friend, on equal terms – for he had some inheritance, we none – pictures of our sobered age and mellowed happiness, and of the golden links, extending back so far, that should bind us, and our children, in a radiant garland," said the Phantom.

"Pictures," said the haunted man, "that were delusions. Why is it my doom to remember them too well!"

"Delusions," echoed the Phantom in its changeless voice, and glaring on him with its changeless eyes. "For my friend (in whose breast my confidence was locked as in my own), passing between me and the centre of the system of my hopes and struggles, won her to himself, and shattered my frail universe. My sister, doubly dear, doubly devoted, doubly cheerful in my home, lived on to see me famous, and my old ambition so rewarded when its spring was broken, and then—"

"Then died," he interposed. "Died, gentle as ever; happy; and with no concern but for her brother. Peace!"

The Phantom watched him silently.

"Remembered!" said the haunted man, after a pause. "Yes. So well remembered, that even now, when years have passed, and nothing is more idle or more visionary to me than the boyish love so long outlived, I think of it with sympathy, as if it were a younger brother's or a son's. Sometimes I even wonder when her heart first inclined to him, and how it had been affected towards me. – Not lightly, once, I think. – But that is nothing. Early unhappiness, a wound from a hand I loved and trusted, and a loss that nothing can replace, outlive such fancies."

"Thus," said the Phantom, "I bear within me a Sorrow and a Wrong. Thus I prey upon myself. Thus, memory is my curse; and, if I could forget my sorrow and my wrong, I would!"

"Mocker!" said the Chemist, leaping up, and making, with a wrathful hand, at the throat of his other self. "Why have I always that taunt in my ears?"

"Forbear!" exclaimed the Spectre in an awful voice. "Lay a hand on Me, and die!"

He stopped midway, as if its words had paralysed him, and stood looking on it. It had glided from him; it had its arm raised high in warning; and a smile passed over its unearthly features, as it reared its dark figure in triumph.

"If I could forget my sorrow and wrong, I would," the Ghost repeated. "If I could forget my sorrow and my wrong, I would!"

"Evil spirit of myself," returned the haunted man, in a low, trembling tone, "my life is darkened by that incessant whisper."

"It is an echo," said the Phantom.

"If it be an echo of my thoughts – as now, indeed, I know it is," rejoined the haunted man, "why should I, therefore, be tormented? It is not a selfish thought. I suffer it to range beyond myself. All men and women have their sorrows, – most of them their wrongs; ingratitude, and sordid jealousy, and interest, besetting all degrees of life. Who would not forget their sorrows and their wrongs?"

"Who would not, truly, and be happier and better for it?" said the Phantom.

"These revolutions of years, which we commemorate," proceeded Redlaw, "what do *they* recall! Are there any minds in which they do not re-awaken some sorrow, or some trouble? What is the remembrance of the old man who was here to-night? A tissue of sorrow and trouble."

"But common natures," said the Phantom, with its evil smile upon its glassy face, "unenlightened minds and ordinary spirits, do not feel or reason on these things like men of higher cultivation and profounder thought."

"Tempter," answered Redlaw, "whose hollow look and voice I dread more than words can express, and from whom some dim foreshadowing of greater fear is stealing over me while I speak, I hear again an echo of my own mind."

"Receive it as a proof that I am powerful," returned the Ghost. "Hear what I offer! Forget the sorrow, wrong, and trouble you have known!"

"Forget them!" he repeated.

"I have the power to cancel their remembrance – to leave but very faint, confused traces of them, that will die out soon," returned the Spectre. "Say! Is it done?"

"Stay!" cried the haunted man, arresting by a terrified gesture the uplifted hand. "I tremble with distrust and doubt of you; and the dim fear you cast upon me deepens into a nameless horror I can hardly bear. – I would not deprive myself of any kindly recollection, or any sympathy that is good for me, or others. What shall I lose, if I assent to this? What else will pass from my remembrance?"

"No knowledge; no result of study; nothing but the intertwisted chain of feelings and associations, each in its turn dependent on, and nourished by, the banished recollections. Those will go."

"Are they so many?" said the haunted man, reflecting in alarm.

"They have been wont to show themselves in the fire, in music, in the wind, in the dead stillness of the night, in the revolving years," returned the Phantom scornfully.

"In nothing else?"

The Phantom held its peace.

But having stood before him, silent, for a little while, it moved towards the fire; then stopped.

"Decide!" it said, "before the opportunity is lost!"

"A moment! I call Heaven to witness," said the agitated man, "that I have never been a hater of any kind, – never morose, indifferent, or hard, to anything around me. If, living here alone, I have made too much of all that was and might have been, and too little of what is, the evil, I believe, has fallen on me, and not on others. But, if there were poison in my body, should I not, possessed of antidotes and knowledge how to use them, use them? If there be poison in my mind, and through this fearful shadow I can cast it out, shall I not cast it out?"

"Say," said the Spectre, "is it done?"

"A moment longer!" he answered hurriedly. "*I would forget it if I could*! Have *I* thought that, alone, or has it been the thought of thousands upon thousands, generation after generation? All human memory is fraught with sorrow and trouble. My memory is as the memory of other men, but other men have not this choice. Yes, I close the bargain. Yes! I WILL forget my sorrow, wrong, and trouble!"

"Say," said the Spectre, "is it done?"

"It is!"

"It is. And take this with you, man whom I here renounce! The gift that I have given, you shall give again, go where you will. Without recovering yourself the power that you have yielded up, you shall henceforth destroy its like in all whom you approach. Your wisdom has discovered that the memory of sorrow, wrong, and trouble is the lot of all mankind, and that mankind would be the happier, in its other memories, without it. Go! Be its benefactor! Freed from such remembrance, from this hour, carry involuntarily the blessing of such freedom with you. Its diffusion is inseparable and inalienable from you. Go! Be happy in the good you have won, and in the good you do!"

The Phantom, which had held its bloodless hand above him while it spoke, as if in some unholy invocation, or some ban; and which had gradually advanced its eyes so close to his, that he could see how they did not participate in the terrible smile upon its face, but were a fixed, unalterable, steady horror melted before him and was gone.

As he stood rooted to the spot, possessed by fear and wonder, and imagining he heard repeated in melancholy echoes, dying away fainter and fainter, the words, "Destroy its like in all whom you approach!" a shrill cry reached his ears. It came, not from the passages beyond the door, but from another part of the old building, and sounded like the cry of some one in the dark who had lost the way.

He looked confusedly upon his hands and limbs, as if to be assured of his identity, and then shouted in reply, loudly and wildly; for there was a strangeness and terror upon him, as if he too were lost.

The cry responding, and being nearer, he caught up the lamp, and raised a heavy curtain in the wall, by which he was accustomed to pass into and out of the theatre where he lectured, – which adjoined his room. Associated with youth and animation, and a high amphitheatre of faces which his entrance charmed to interest in a moment, it was a ghostly place when all this life was faded out of it, and stared upon him like an emblem of Death.

"Halloa!" he cried. "Halloa! This way! Come to the light!" When, as he held the curtain with one hand, and with the other raised the lamp and tried to pierce the gloom that filled the place, something rushed past him into the room like a wild-cat, and crouched down in a corner.

"What is it?" he said, hastily.

He might have asked "What is it?" even had he seen it well, as presently he did when he stood looking at it gathered up in its corner.

A bundle of tatters, held together by a hand, in size and form almost an infant's, but in its greedy, desperate little clutch, a bad old man's. A face rounded and smoothed by some half-dozen years, but pinched and twisted by the experiences of a life. Bright eyes, but not youthful. Naked feet, beautiful in their childish delicacy, – ugly in the blood and dirt that cracked upon them. A baby savage, a young monster, a child who had never been a child, a creature who might live to take the outward form of man, but who, within, would live and perish a mere beast.

Used, already, to be worried and hunted like a beast, the boy crouched down as he was looked at, and looked back again, and interposed his arm to ward off the expected blow.

"I'll bite," he said, "if you hit me!"

The time had been, and not many minutes since, when such a sight as this would have wrung the Chemist's heart. He looked upon it now, coldly; but with a heavy effort to remember something – he did not know what – he asked the boy what he did there, and whence he came.

"Where's the woman?" he replied. "I want to find the woman."

"Who?"

"The woman. Her that brought me here, and set me by the large fire. She was so long gone, that I went to look for her, and lost myself. I don't want you. I want the woman."

He made a spring, so suddenly, to get away, that the dull sound of his naked feet upon the floor was near the curtain, when Redlaw caught him by his rags.

"Come! you let me go!" muttered the boy, struggling, and clenching his teeth. "I've done nothing to you. Let me go, will you, to the woman!"

"That is not the way. There is a nearer one," said Redlaw, detaining him, in the same blank effort to remember some association that ought, of right, to bear upon this monstrous object. "What is your name?"

"Got none."

"Where do you live?

"Live! What's that?"

The boy shook his hair from his eyes to look at him for a moment, and then, twisting round his legs and wrestling with him, broke again into his repetition of "You let me go, will you? I want to find the woman."

The Chemist led him to the door. "This way," he said, looking at him still confusedly, but with repugnance and avoidance, growing out of his coldness. "I'll take you to her."

The sharp eyes in the child's head, wandering round the room, lighted on the table where the remnants of the dinner were.

"Give me some of that!" he said, covetously.

"Has she not fed you?"

"I shall be hungry again tomorrow, sha'n't I? Ain't I hungry every day?"

Finding himself released, he bounded at the table like some small animal of prey, and hugging to his breast bread and meat, and his own rags, all together, said:

"There! Now take me to the woman!"

As the Chemist, with a new-born dislike to touch him, sternly motioned him to follow, and was going out of the door, he trembled and stopped.

"The gift that I have given, you shall give again, go where you will!"

The Phantom's words were blowing in the wind, and the wind blew chill upon him.

"I'll not go there, to-night," he murmured faintly. "I'll go nowhere to-night. Boy! straight down this long-arched passage, and past the great dark door into the yard, – you see the fire shining on the window there."

"The woman's fire?" inquired the boy.

He nodded, and the naked feet had sprung away. He came back with his lamp, locked his door hastily, and sat down in his chair, covering his face like one who was frightened at himself.

For now he was, indeed, alone. Alone, alone.

## Chapter II
## The Gift Diffused

**A SMALL MAN** sat in a small parlour, partitioned off from a small shop by a small screen, pasted all over with small scraps of newspapers. In company with the small man, was almost any amount of small children you may please to name – at least it seemed so; they made, in that very limited sphere of action, such an imposing effect, in point of numbers.

Of these small fry, two had, by some strong machinery, been got into bed in a corner, where they might have reposed snugly enough in the sleep of innocence, but for a constitutional propensity to keep awake, and also to scuffle in and out of bed. The immediate occasion of these predatory dashes at the waking world, was the construction of an oyster-shell wall in a corner, by two other youths of tender age; on which fortification the two in bed made harassing descents (like those accursed Picts and Scots who beleaguer the early historical studies of most young Britons), and then withdrew to their own territory.

In addition to the stir attendant on these inroads, and the retorts of the invaded, who pursued hotly, and made lunges at the bed-clothes under which the marauders took refuge, another little boy, in another little bed, contributed his mite of confusion to the family stock, by casting his boots upon the waters; in other words, by launching these and several small objects, inoffensive in themselves, though of a hard substance considered as missiles, at the disturbers of his repose, – who were not slow to return these compliments.

Besides which, another little boy – the biggest there, but still little – was tottering to and fro, bent on one side, and considerably affected in his knees by the weight of a large baby, which he was supposed by a fiction that obtains sometimes in sanguine families, to be hushing to sleep. But oh! the inexhaustible regions of contemplation and watchfulness into which this baby's eyes were then only beginning to compose themselves to stare, over his unconscious shoulder!

It was a very Moloch of a baby, on whose insatiate altar the whole existence of this particular young brother was offered up a daily sacrifice. Its personality may be said to have consisted in its never being quiet, in any one place, for five consecutive minutes, and never going to sleep when required. "Tetterby's baby" was as well known in the neighbourhood as the postman or the pot-boy. It roved from door-step to door-step, in the arms of little Johnny Tetterby, and lagged heavily at the rear of troops of juveniles who followed the Tumblers or the Monkey, and came up, all on one side, a little too late for everything that was attractive, from Monday morning until Saturday night. Wherever childhood congregated to play, there was little Moloch making Johnny fag and toil. Wherever Johnny desired to stay, little Moloch became fractious, and would not remain. Whenever Johnny wanted to go out, Moloch was asleep, and must be watched. Whenever Johnny wanted to stay at home, Moloch was awake, and must be taken out. Yet Johnny was verily persuaded that it was a faultless baby, without its peer in the realm of England, and was quite content to catch meek glimpses of things in general from behind its skirts, or over its limp flapping bonnet, and to go staggering about with it like a very little porter with a very large parcel, which was not directed to anybody, and could never be delivered anywhere.

The small man who sat in the small parlour, making fruitless attempts to read his newspaper peaceably in the midst of this disturbance, was the father of the family, and the chief of the firm described in the inscription over the little shop front, by the name and title of A. Tetterby and Co., Newsmen. Indeed, strictly speaking, he was the only personage answering to that designation, as Co. was a mere poetical abstraction, altogether baseless and impersonal.

Tetterby's was the corner shop in Jerusalem Buildings. There was a good show of literature in the window, chiefly consisting of picture-newspapers out of date, and serial pirates, and footpads. Walking-sticks, likewise, and marbles, were included in the stock in trade. It had once extended into the light confectionery line; but it would seem that those elegancies of life were not in demand about Jerusalem Buildings, for nothing connected with that branch of commerce remained in the window, except a sort of small glass lantern containing a languishing mass of bull's-eyes, which had melted in the summer and congealed in the winter until all hope of ever getting them out, or of eating them without eating the lantern too, was gone for ever. Tetterby's had tried its hand at several things. It had once made a feeble little dart at the toy business; for, in another lantern, there was a heap of minute wax dolls, all sticking together upside down, in the direst confusion, with their feet on one another's heads, and a precipitate of broken arms and legs at the bottom. It had made a move in the millinery direction, which a few dry, wiry bonnet-shapes remained in a corner of the window to attest. It had fancied that a living might lie hidden in the tobacco trade, and had stuck up a representation of a native of each of the three integral portions of the British Empire, in the act of consuming that fragrant weed; with a poetic legend attached, importing that united in one cause they sat and joked, one chewed tobacco, one took snuff, one smoked: but nothing seemed to have come of it – except flies. Time had been when it had put a forlorn trust in imitative jewellery, for in one pane of glass there was a card of cheap seals, and another of pencil-cases, and a mysterious black amulet of inscrutable intention, labelled ninepence. But, to that hour, Jerusalem Buildings had bought none of them. In short, Tetterby's had tried so hard to get a livelihood out of Jerusalem Buildings in one way or other, and appeared to have done so indifferently in all, that the best position in the firm was too evidently Co.'s; Co., as a bodiless creation, being untroubled with the vulgar inconveniences of hunger and thirst, being chargeable neither to the poor's-rates nor the assessed taxes, and having no young family to provide for.

Tetterby himself, however, in his little parlour, as already mentioned, having the presence of a young family impressed upon his mind in a manner too clamorous to be disregarded, or to comport with the quiet perusal of a newspaper, laid down his paper, wheeled, in his distraction, a few times round the parlour, like an undecided carrier-pigeon, made an ineffectual rush at one or two flying little figures in bed-gowns that skimmed past him, and then, bearing suddenly down upon the only unoffending member of the family, boxed the ears of little Moloch's nurse.

"You bad boy!" said Mr. Tetterby, "haven't you any feeling for your poor father after the fatigues and anxieties of a hard winter's day, since five o'clock in the morning, but must you wither his rest, and corrode his latest intelligence, with *your* wicious tricks? Isn't it enough, sir, that your brother 'Dolphus is toiling and moiling in the fog and cold, and you rolling in the lap of luxury with a – with a baby, and everything you can wish for," said Mr. Tetterby, heaping this up as a great climax of blessings, "but must you make a wilderness of home, and maniacs of your parents? Must you, Johnny? Hey?" At each interrogation, Mr. Tetterby made a feint of boxing his ears again, but thought better of it, and held his hand.

"Oh, father!" whimpered Johnny, "when I wasn't doing anything, I'm sure, but taking such care of Sally, and getting her to sleep. Oh, father!"

"I wish my little woman would come home!" said Mr. Tetterby, relenting and repenting, "I only wish my little woman would come home! I ain't fit to deal with 'em. They make my head go round, and get the better of me. Oh, Johnny! Isn't it enough that your dear mother has provided you with that sweet sister?" indicating Moloch; "isn't it enough that you were seven boys before without a ray of gal, and that your dear mother went through what she *did* go through, on purpose that you might all of you have a little sister, but must you so behave yourself as to make my head swim?"

Softening more and more, as his own tender feelings and those of his injured son were worked on, Mr. Tetterby concluded by embracing him, and immediately breaking away to catch one of the real delinquents. A reasonably good start occurring, he succeeded, after a short but smart run, and some rather severe cross-country work under and over the bedsteads, and in and out among the intricacies of the chairs, in capturing this infant, whom he condignly punished, and bore to bed. This example had a powerful, and apparently, mesmeric influence on him of the boots, who instantly fell into a deep sleep, though he had been, but a moment before, broad awake, and in the highest possible feather. Nor was it lost upon the two young architects, who retired to bed, in an adjoining closet, with great privacy and speed. The comrade of the Intercepted One also shrinking into his nest with similar discretion, Mr. Tetterby, when he paused for breath, found himself unexpectedly in a scene of peace.

"My little woman herself," said Mr. Tetterby, wiping his flushed face, "could hardly have done it better! I only wish my little woman had had it to do, I do indeed!"

Mr. Tetterby sought upon his screen for a passage appropriate to be impressed upon his children's minds on the occasion, and read the following.

"'It is an undoubted fact that all remarkable men have had remarkable mothers, and have respected them in after life as their best friends.' Think of your own remarkable mother, my boys," said Mr. Tetterby, "and know her value while she is still among you!"

He sat down again in his chair by the fire, and composed himself, cross-legged, over his newspaper.

"Let anybody, I don't care who it is, get out of bed again," said Tetterby, as a general proclamation, delivered in a very soft-hearted manner, "and astonishment will be the portion of that respected contemporary!" – which expression Mr. Tetterby selected from his screen. "Johnny, my child, take care of your only sister, Sally; for she's the brightest gem that ever sparkled on your early brow."

Johnny sat down on a little stool, and devotedly crushed himself beneath the weight of Moloch.

"Ah, what a gift that baby is to you, Johnny!" said his father, "and how thankful you ought to be! 'It is not generally known, Johnny,'" he was now referring to the screen again, "'but it is a fact ascertained, by accurate calculations, that the following immense percentage of babies never attain to two years old; that is to say—'"

"Oh, don't, father, please!" cried Johnny. "I can't bear it, when I think of Sally."

Mr. Tetterby desisting, Johnny, with a profound sense of his trust, wiped his eyes, and hushed his sister.

"Your brother 'Dolphus," said his father, poking the fire, "is late to-night, Johnny, and will come home like a lump of ice. What's got your precious mother?"

"Here's mother, and 'Dolphus too, father!" exclaimed Johnny, "I think."

"You're right!" returned his father, listening. "Yes, that's the footstep of my little woman."

The process of induction, by which Mr. Tetterby had come to the conclusion that his wife was a little woman, was his own secret. She would have made two editions of himself, very easily. Considered as an individual, she was rather remarkable for being robust and portly; but considered with reference to her husband, her dimensions became magnificent. Nor did they assume a less imposing proportion, when studied with reference to the size of her seven sons, who were but diminutive. In the case of Sally, however, Mrs. Tetterby had asserted herself, at last; as nobody knew better than the victim Johnny, who weighed and measured that exacting idol every hour in the day.

Mrs. Tetterby, who had been marketing, and carried a basket, threw back her bonnet and shawl, and sitting down, fatigued, commanded Johnny to bring his sweet charge to her straightway, for a kiss. Johnny having complied, and gone back to his stool, and again crushed himself, Master Adolphus Tetterby, who had by this time unwound his torso out of a prismatic comforter, apparently interminable, requested the same favour. Johnny having again complied, and again gone back to his stool, and again crushed himself, Mr. Tetterby, struck by a sudden thought, preferred the same claim on his own parental part.

The satisfaction of this third desire completely exhausted the sacrifice, who had hardly breath enough left to get back to his stool, crush himself again, and pant at his relations.

"Whatever you do, Johnny," said Mrs. Tetterby, shaking her head, "take care of her, or never look your mother in the face again."

"Nor your brother," said Adolphus.

"Nor your father, Johnny," added Mr. Tetterby.

Johnny, much affected by this conditional renunciation of him, looked down at Moloch's eyes to see that they were all right, so far, and skilfully patted her back (which was uppermost), and rocked her with his foot.

"Are you wet, 'Dolphus, my boy?" said his father. "Come and take my chair, and dry yourself."

"No, father, thank'ee," said Adolphus, smoothing himself down with his hands. "I an't very wet, I don't think. Does my face shine much, father?"

"Well, it *does* look waxy, my boy," returned Mr. Tetterby.

"It's the weather, father," said Adolphus, polishing his cheeks on the worn sleeve of his jacket. "What with rain, and sleet, and wind, and snow, and fog, my face gets quite brought out into a rash sometimes. And shines, it does – oh, don't it, though!"

Master Adolphus was also in the newspaper line of life, being employed, by a more thriving firm than his father and Co., to vend newspapers at a railway station, where his chubby little person, like a shabbily-disguised Cupid, and his shrill little voice (he was not much more than ten years old), were as well known as the hoarse panting of the locomotives, running in and out. His juvenility might have been at some loss for a harmless outlet, in this early application to traffic, but for a fortunate discovery he made of a means of entertaining himself, and of dividing the long day into stages of interest, without neglecting business. This ingenious invention, remarkable, like many great discoveries, for its simplicity, consisted in varying the first vowel in the word "paper," and substituting, in its stead, at different periods of the day, all the other vowels in grammatical succession. Thus, before daylight in the winter-time, he went to and fro, in his little oilskin cap and cape, and his big comforter, piercing the heavy air with his cry of "Morn-ing Pa-per!" which, about an hour before noon, changed to "Morn-ing Pepper!" which, at about two, changed to "Morn-ing Pip-per!" which in a couple of hours changed to "Morn-ing Pop-per!" and so declined with the sun into "Eve-ning Pup-per!" to the great relief and comfort of this young gentleman's spirits.

Mrs. Tetterby, his lady-mother, who had been sitting with her bonnet and shawl thrown back, as aforesaid, thoughtfully turning her wedding-ring round and round upon her finger, now rose, and divesting herself of her out-of-door attire, began to lay the cloth for supper.

"Ah, dear me, dear me, dear me!" said Mrs. Tetterby. "That's the way the world goes!"

"Which is the way the world goes, my dear?" asked Mr. Tetterby, looking round.

"Oh, nothing," said Mrs. Tetterby.

Mr. Tetterby elevated his eyebrows, folded his newspaper afresh, and carried his eyes up it, and down it, and across it, but was wandering in his attention, and not reading it.

Mrs. Tetterby, at the same time, laid the cloth, but rather as if she were punishing the table than preparing the family supper; hitting it unnecessarily hard with the knives and forks, slapping it with the plates, dinting it with the salt-cellar, and coming heavily down upon it with the loaf.

"Ah, dear me, dear me, dear me!" said Mrs. Tetterby. "That's the way the world goes!"

"My duck," returned her husband, looking round again, "you said that before. Which is the way the world goes?"

"Oh, nothing!" said Mrs. Tetterby.

"Sophia!" remonstrated her husband, "you said *that* before, too."

"Well, I'll say it again if you like," returned Mrs. Tetterby. "Oh nothing – there! And again if you like, oh nothing – there! And again if you like, oh nothing – now then!"

Mr. Tetterby brought his eye to bear upon the partner of his bosom, and said, in mild astonishment:

"My little woman, what has put you out?"

"I'm sure *I* don't know," she retorted. "Don't ask me. Who said I was put out at all? *I* never did."

Mr. Tetterby gave up the perusal of his newspaper as a bad job, and, taking a slow walk across the room, with his hands behind him, and his shoulders raised – his gait according perfectly with the resignation of his manner – addressed himself to his two eldest offspring.

"Your supper will be ready in a minute, 'Dolphus," said Mr. Tetterby. "Your mother has been out in the wet, to the cook's shop, to buy it. It was very good of your mother so to do. *You* shall get some supper too, very soon, Johnny. Your mother's pleased with you, my man, for being so attentive to your precious sister."

Mrs. Tetterby, without any remark, but with a decided subsidence of her animosity towards the table, finished her preparations, and took, from her ample basket, a substantial slab of hot pease pudding wrapped in paper, and a basin covered with a saucer, which, on being uncovered, sent forth an odour so agreeable, that the three pair of eyes in the two beds opened wide and fixed themselves upon the banquet. Mr. Tetterby, without regarding this tacit invitation to be seated, stood repeating slowly, "Yes, yes, your supper will be ready in a minute, 'Dolphus – your mother went out in the wet, to the cook's shop, to buy it. It was very good of your mother so to do" – until Mrs. Tetterby, who had been exhibiting sundry tokens of contrition behind him, caught him round the neck, and wept.

"Oh, Dolphus!" said Mrs. Tetterby, "how could I go and behave so?"

This reconciliation affected Adolphus the younger and Johnny to that degree, that they both, as with one accord, raised a dismal cry, which had the effect of immediately shutting up the round eyes in the beds, and utterly routing the two remaining little Tetterbys, just then stealing in from the adjoining closet to see what was going on in the eating way.

"I am sure, 'Dolphus," sobbed Mrs. Tetterby, "coming home, I had no more idea than a child unborn—"

Mr. Tetterby seemed to dislike this figure of speech, and observed, "Say than the baby, my dear."

"—Had no more idea than the baby," said Mrs. Tetterby. "Johnny, don't look at me, but look at her, or she'll fall out of your lap and be killed, and then you'll die in agonies of a broken heart, and serve you right. – No more idea I hadn't than that darling, of being cross when I came home; but somehow, 'Dolphus—" Mrs. Tetterby paused, and again turned her wedding-ring round and round upon her finger.

"I see!" said Mr. Tetterby. "I understand! My little woman was put out. Hard times, and hard weather, and hard work, make it trying now and then. I see, bless your soul! No wonder! Dolf, my man," continued Mr. Tetterby, exploring the basin with a fork, "here's your mother been and bought, at the cook's shop, besides pease pudding, a whole knuckle of a lovely roast leg of pork, with lots of crackling left upon it, and with seasoning gravy and mustard quite unlimited. Hand in your plate, my boy, and begin while it's simmering."

Master Adolphus, needing no second summons, received his portion with eyes rendered moist by appetite, and withdrawing to his particular stool, fell upon his supper tooth and nail. Johnny was not forgotten, but received his rations on bread, lest he should, in a flush of gravy, trickle any on the baby. He was required, for similar reasons, to keep his pudding, when not on active service, in his pocket.

There might have been more pork on the knucklebone, – which knucklebone the carver at the cook's shop had assuredly not forgotten in carving for previous customers – but there was no stint of seasoning, and that is an accessory dreamily suggesting pork, and pleasantly cheating the sense of taste. The pease pudding, too, the gravy and mustard, like the Eastern rose in respect of the nightingale, if they were not absolutely pork, had lived near it; so, upon the whole, there was the flavour of a middle-sized pig. It was irresistible to the Tetterbys in bed, who, though professing to slumber peacefully, crawled out when unseen by their parents, and silently appealed to their brothers for any gastronomic token of fraternal affection. They, not hard of heart, presenting scraps in return, it resulted that a party of light skirmishers in nightgowns were careering about the parlour all through supper, which harassed Mr. Tetterby exceedingly, and once or twice imposed upon him the necessity of a charge, before which these guerilla troops retired in all directions and in great confusion.

Mrs. Tetterby did not enjoy her supper. There seemed to be something on Mrs. Tetterby's mind. At one time she laughed without reason, and at another time she cried without reason, and at last she laughed and cried together in a manner so very unreasonable that her husband was confounded.

"My little woman," said Mr. Tetterby, "if the world goes that way, it appears to go the wrong way, and to choke you."

"Give me a drop of water," said Mrs. Tetterby, struggling with herself, "and don't speak to me for the present, or take any notice of me. Don't do it!"

Mr. Tetterby having administered the water, turned suddenly on the unlucky Johnny (who was full of sympathy), and demanded why he was wallowing there, in gluttony and idleness, instead of coming forward with the baby, that the sight of her might revive his mother. Johnny immediately approached, borne down by its weight; but Mrs. Tetterby holding out her hand to signify that she was not in a condition to bear that trying appeal to her feelings, he was interdicted from advancing another inch, on pain of perpetual hatred from all his dearest connections; and accordingly retired to his stool again, and crushed himself as before.

After a pause, Mrs. Tetterby said she was better now, and began to laugh.

"My little woman," said her husband, dubiously, "are you quite sure you're better? Or are you, Sophia, about to break out in a fresh direction?"

"No, 'Dolphus, no," replied his wife. "I'm quite myself." With that, settling her hair, and pressing the palms of her hands upon her eyes, she laughed again.

"What a wicked fool I was, to think so for a moment!" said Mrs. Tetterby. "Come nearer, 'Dolphus, and let me ease my mind, and tell you what I mean. Let me tell you all about it."

Mr. Tetterby bringing his chair closer, Mrs. Tetterby laughed again, gave him a hug, and wiped her eyes.

"You know, Dolphus, my dear," said Mrs. Tetterby, "that when I was single, I might have given myself away in several directions. At one time, four after me at once; two of them were sons of Mars."

"We're all sons of Ma's, my dear," said Mr. Tetterby, "jointly with Pa's."

"I don't mean that," replied his wife, "I mean soldiers – serjeants."

"Oh!" said Mr. Tetterby.

"Well, 'Dolphus, I'm sure I never think of such things now, to regret them; and I'm sure I've got as good a husband, and would do as much to prove that I was fond of him, as—"

"As any little woman in the world," said Mr. Tetterby. "Very good. *Very* good."

If Mr. Tetterby had been ten feet high, he could not have expressed a gentler consideration for Mrs. Tetterby's fairy-like stature; and if Mrs. Tetterby had been two feet high, she could not have felt it more appropriately her due.

"But you see, 'Dolphus," said Mrs. Tetterby, "this being Christmas-time, when all people who can, make holiday, and when all people who have got money, like to spend some, I did, somehow, get a little out of sorts when I was in the streets just now. There were so many things to be sold – such delicious things to eat, such fine things to look at, such delightful things to have – and there was so much calculating and calculating necessary, before I durst lay out a sixpence for the commonest thing; and the basket was so large, and wanted so much in it; and my stock of money was so small, and would go such a little way; – you hate me, don't you, 'Dolphus?"

"Not quite," said Mr. Tetterby, "as yet."

"Well! I'll tell you the whole truth," pursued his wife, penitently, "and then perhaps you will. I felt all this, so much, when I was trudging about in the cold, and when I saw a lot of other calculating faces and large baskets trudging about, too, that I began to think whether I mightn't have done better, and been happier, if – I – hadn't—" the wedding-ring went round again, and Mrs. Tetterby shook her downcast head as she turned it.

"I see," said her husband quietly; "if you hadn't married at all, or if you had married somebody else?"

"Yes," sobbed Mrs. Tetterby. "That's really what I thought. Do you hate me now, 'Dolphus?"

"Why no," said Mr. Tetterby. "I don't find that I do, as yet."

Mrs. Tetterby gave him a thankful kiss, and went on.

"I begin to hope you won't, now, 'Dolphus, though I'm afraid I haven't told you the worst. I can't think what came over me. I don't know whether I was ill, or mad, or what I was, but I couldn't call up anything that seemed to bind us to each other, or to reconcile me to my fortune. All the pleasures and enjoyments we had ever had – *they* seemed so poor and insignificant, I hated them. I could have trodden on them. And I could think of nothing else, except our being poor, and the number of mouths there were at home."

"Well, well, my dear," said Mr. Tetterby, shaking her hand encouragingly, "that's truth, after all. We *are* poor, and there *are* a number of mouths at home here."

"Ah! but, Dolf, Dolf!" cried his wife, laying her hands upon his neck, "my good, kind, patient fellow, when I had been at home a very little while – how different! Oh, Dolf, dear, how different it was! I felt as if there was a rush of recollection on me, all at once, that softened my hard heart, and filled it up till it was bursting. All our struggles for a livelihood, all our cares and wants since we have been married, all the times of sickness, all the hours of watching, we have ever had, by one another, or by the children, seemed to speak to me, and say that they had made us one, and that I never might have been, or could have been, or would have been, any other than the wife and mother I am. Then, the cheap enjoyments that I could have trodden on so cruelly, got to be so precious to me – Oh so priceless, and dear! – that I couldn't bear to think how much I had wronged them; and I said, and say again a hundred times, how could I ever behave so, 'Dolphus, how could I ever have the heart to do it!"

The good woman, quite carried away by her honest tenderness and remorse, was weeping with all her heart, when she started up with a scream, and ran behind her husband. Her cry was so terrified, that the children started from their sleep and from their beds, and clung about her. Nor did her gaze belie her voice, as she pointed to a pale man in a black cloak who had come into the room.

"Look at that man! Look there! What does he want?"

"My dear," returned her husband, "I'll ask him if you'll let me go. What's the matter! How you shake!"

"I saw him in the street, when I was out just now. He looked at me, and stood near me. I am afraid of him."

"Afraid of him! Why?"

"I don't know why – I – stop! husband!" for he was going towards the stranger.

She had one hand pressed upon her forehead, and one upon her breast; and there was a peculiar fluttering all over her, and a hurried unsteady motion of her eyes, as if she had lost something.

"Are you ill, my dear?"

"What is it that is going from me again?" she muttered, in a low voice. "What *is* this that is going away?"

Then she abruptly answered: "Ill? No, I am quite well," and stood looking vacantly at the floor.

Her husband, who had not been altogether free from the infection of her fear at first, and whom the present strangeness of her manner did not tend to reassure, addressed himself to the pale visitor in the black cloak, who stood still, and whose eyes were bent upon the ground.

"What may be your pleasure, sir," he asked, "with us?"

"I fear that my coming in unperceived," returned the visitor, "has alarmed you; but you were talking and did not hear me."

"My little woman says – perhaps you heard her say it," returned Mr. Tetterby, "that it's not the first time you have alarmed her to-night."

"I am sorry for it. I remember to have observed her, for a few moments only, in the street. I had no intention of frightening her."

As he raised his eyes in speaking, she raised hers. It was extraordinary to see what dread she had of him, and with what dread he observed it – and yet how narrowly and closely.

"My name," he said, "is Redlaw. I come from the old college hard by. A young gentleman who is a student there, lodges in your house, does he not?"

"Mr. Denham?" said Tetterby.

"Yes."

It was a natural action, and so slight as to be hardly noticeable; but the little man, before speaking again, passed his hand across his forehead, and looked quickly round the room, as though he were sensible of some change in its atmosphere. The Chemist, instantly transferring to him the look of dread he had directed towards the wife, stepped back, and his face turned paler.

"The gentleman's room," said Tetterby, "is upstairs, sir. There's a more convenient private entrance; but as you have come in here, it will save your going out into the cold, if you'll take this little staircase," showing one communicating directly with the parlour, "and go up to him that way, if you wish to see him."

"Yes, I wish to see him," said the Chemist. "Can you spare a light?"

The watchfulness of his haggard look, and the inexplicable distrust that darkened it, seemed to trouble Mr. Tetterby. He paused; and looking fixedly at him in return, stood for a minute or so, like a man stupefied, or fascinated.

At length he said, "I'll light you, sir, if you'll follow me."

"No," replied the Chemist, "I don't wish to be attended, or announced to him. He does not expect me. I would rather go alone. Please to give me the light, if you can spare it, and I'll find the way."

In the quickness of his expression of this desire, and in taking the candle from the newsman, he touched him on the breast. Withdrawing his hand hastily, almost as though he had wounded him by accident (for he did not know in what part of himself his new power resided, or how it was communicated, or how the manner of its reception varied in different persons), he turned and ascended the stair.

But when he reached the top, he stopped and looked down. The wife was standing in the same place, twisting her ring round and round upon her finger. The husband, with his head bent forward on his breast, was musing heavily and sullenly. The children, still clustering about the mother, gazed timidly after the visitor, and nestled together when they saw him looking down.

"Come!" said the father, roughly. "There's enough of this. Get to bed here!"

"The place is inconvenient and small enough," the mother added, "without you. Get to bed!"

The whole brood, scared and sad, crept away; little Johnny and the baby lagging last. The mother, glancing contemptuously round the sordid room, and tossing from her the fragments of their meal, stopped on the threshold of her task of clearing the table, and sat down, pondering idly and dejectedly. The father betook himself to the chimney-corner, and impatiently raking the small fire together, bent over it as if he would monopolise it all. They did not interchange a word.

The Chemist, paler than before, stole upward like a thief; looking back upon the change below, and dreading equally to go on or return.

"What have I done!" he said, confusedly. "What am I going to do!"

"To be the benefactor of mankind," he thought he heard a voice reply.

He looked round, but there was nothing there; and a passage now shutting out the little parlour from his view, he went on, directing his eyes before him at the way he went.

"It is only since last night," he muttered gloomily, "that I have remained shut up, and yet all things are strange to me. I am strange to myself. I am here, as in a dream. What interest have I in this place, or in any place that I can bring to my remembrance? My mind is going blind!"

There was a door before him, and he knocked at it. Being invited, by a voice within, to enter, he complied.

"Is that my kind nurse?" said the voice. "But I need not ask her. There is no one else to come here."

It spoke cheerfully, though in a languid tone, and attracted his attention to a young man lying on a couch, drawn before the chimney-piece, with the back towards the door. A meagre scanty stove, pinched and hollowed like a sick man's cheeks, and bricked into the centre of a hearth that it could scarcely warm, contained the fire, to which his face was turned. Being so near the windy house-top, it wasted quickly, and with a busy sound, and the burning ashes dropped down fast.

"They chink when they shoot out here," said the student, smiling, "so, according to the gossips, they are not coffins, but purses. I shall be well and rich yet, some day, if it please God, and shall live perhaps to love a daughter Milly, in remembrance of the kindest nature and the gentlest heart in the world."

He put up his hand as if expecting her to take it, but, being weakened, he lay still, with his face resting on his other hand, and did not turn round.

The Chemist glanced about the room; – at the student's books and papers, piled upon a table in a corner, where they, and his extinguished reading-lamp, now prohibited and put away, told of the attentive hours that had gone before this illness, and perhaps caused it; – at such signs of his old health and freedom, as the out-of-door attire that hung idle on the wall; – at those remembrances of other and less solitary scenes, the little miniatures upon the chimney-piece, and the drawing of home; – at that token of his emulation, perhaps, in some sort, of his personal attachment too, the framed engraving of himself, the looker-on. The time had been, only yesterday, when not one of these objects, in its remotest association of interest with the living figure before him, would have been lost on Redlaw. Now, they were but objects; or, if any gleam of such connexion shot upon him, it perplexed, and not enlightened him, as he stood looking round with a dull wonder.

The student, recalling the thin hand which had remained so long untouched, raised himself on the couch, and turned his head.

"Mr. Redlaw!" he exclaimed, and started up.

Redlaw put out his arm.

"Don't come nearer to me. I will sit here. Remain you, where you are!"

He sat down on a chair near the door, and having glanced at the young man standing leaning with his hand upon the couch, spoke with his eyes averted towards the ground.

"I heard, by an accident, by what accident is no matter, that one of my class was ill and solitary. I received no other description of him, than that he lived in this street. Beginning my inquiries at the first house in it, I have found him."

"I have been ill, sir," returned the student, not merely with a modest hesitation, but with a kind of awe of him, "but am greatly better. An attack of fever – of the brain, I believe – has weakened me, but I am much better. I cannot say I have been solitary, in my illness, or I should forget the ministering hand that has been near me."

"You are speaking of the keeper's wife," said Redlaw.

"Yes." The student bent his head, as if he rendered her some silent homage.

The Chemist, in whom there was a cold, monotonous apathy, which rendered him more like a marble image on the tomb of the man who had started from his dinner yesterday at the first mention of this student's case, than the breathing man himself, glanced again at the student leaning with his hand upon the couch, and looked upon the ground, and in the air, as if for light for his blinded mind.

"I remembered your name," he said, "when it was mentioned to me down stairs, just now; and I recollect your face. We have held but very little personal communication together?"

"Very little."

"You have retired and withdrawn from me, more than any of the rest, I think?"

The student signified assent.

"And why?" said the Chemist; not with the least expression of interest, but with a moody, wayward kind of curiosity. "Why? How comes it that you have sought to keep especially from me, the knowledge of your remaining here, at this season, when all the rest have dispersed, and of your being ill? I want to know why this is?"

The young man, who had heard him with increasing agitation, raised his downcast eyes to his face, and clasping his hands together, cried with sudden earnestness and with trembling lips:

"Mr. Redlaw! You have discovered me. You know my secret!"

"Secret?" said the Chemist, harshly. "I know?"

"Yes! Your manner, so different from the interest and sympathy which endear you to so many hearts, your altered voice, the constraint there is in everything you say, and in your looks," replied the student, "warn me that you know me. That you would conceal it, even now, is but a proof to me (God knows I need none!) of your natural kindness and of the bar there is between us."

A vacant and contemptuous laugh, was all his answer.

"But, Mr. Redlaw," said the student, "as a just man, and a good man, think how innocent I am, except in name and descent, of participation in any wrong inflicted on you or in any sorrow you have borne."

"Sorrow!" said Redlaw, laughing. "Wrong! What are those to me?"

"For Heaven's sake," entreated the shrinking student, "do not let the mere interchange of a few words with me change you like this, sir! Let me pass again from your knowledge and notice. Let me occupy my old reserved and distant place among those whom you instruct. Know me only by the name I have assumed, and not by that of Longford—"

"Longford!" exclaimed the other.

He clasped his head with both his hands, and for a moment turned upon the young man his own intelligent and thoughtful face. But the light passed from it, like the sunbeam of an instant, and it clouded as before.

"The name my mother bears, sir," faltered the young man, "the name she took, when she might, perhaps, have taken one more honoured. Mr. Redlaw," hesitating, "I believe I know that history. Where my information halts, my guesses at what is wanting may supply something not remote from the truth. I am the child of a marriage that has not proved itself a well-assorted or a happy one. From infancy, I have heard you spoken of with honour and respect – with something that was almost reverence. I have heard of such devotion, of such fortitude and tenderness, of such rising up against the obstacles which press men down, that my fancy, since I learnt my little lesson from my mother, has shed a lustre on your name. At last, a poor student myself, from whom could I learn but you?"

Redlaw, unmoved, unchanged, and looking at him with a staring frown, answered by no word or sign.

"I cannot say," pursued the other, "I should try in vain to say, how much it has impressed me, and affected me, to find the gracious traces of the past, in that certain power of winning gratitude and confidence which is associated among us students (among the humblest of us, most) with Mr. Redlaw's generous name. Our ages and positions are so different, sir, and I am so accustomed to regard you from a distance, that I wonder at my own presumption when I touch, however lightly, on that theme. But to one who – I may say, who felt no common interest in my mother once – it may be something to hear, now that all is past, with what indescribable feelings of affection I have, in my obscurity, regarded him; with what pain and reluctance I have kept aloof from his encouragement, when a word of it would have made me rich; yet how I have felt it fit that I should hold my course, content to know him, and to be unknown. Mr. Redlaw," said the student, faintly, "what I would have said, I have said ill, for my strength is strange to me as yet; but for anything unworthy in this fraud of mine, forgive me, and for all the rest forget me!"

The staring frown remained on Redlaw's face, and yielded to no other expression until the student, with these words, advanced towards him, as if to touch his hand, when he drew back and cried to him:

"Don't come nearer to me!"

The young man stopped, shocked by the eagerness of his recoil, and by the sternness of his repulsion; and he passed his hand, thoughtfully, across his forehead.

"The past is past," said the Chemist. "It dies like the brutes. Who talks to me of its traces in my life? He raves or lies! What have I to do with your distempered dreams? If you want money, here it is. I came to offer it; and that is all I came for. There can be nothing else that brings me here," he muttered, holding his head again, with both his hands. "There *can* be nothing else, and yet—"

He had tossed his purse upon the table. As he fell into this dim cogitation with himself, the student took it up, and held it out to him.

"Take it back, sir," he said proudly, though not angrily. "I wish you could take from me, with it, the remembrance of your words and offer."

"You do?" he retorted, with a wild light in his eyes. "You do?"

"I do!"

The Chemist went close to him, for the first time, and took the purse, and turned him by the arm, and looked him in the face.

"There is sorrow and trouble in sickness, is there not?" he demanded, with a laugh.

The wondering student answered, "Yes."

"In its unrest, in its anxiety, in its suspense, in all its train of physical and mental miseries?" said the Chemist, with a wild unearthly exultation. "All best forgotten, are they not?"

The student did not answer, but again passed his hand, confusedly, across his forehead. Redlaw still held him by the sleeve, when Milly's voice was heard outside.

"I can see very well now," she said, "thank you, Dolf. Don't cry, dear. Father and mother will be comfortable again, tomorrow, and home will be comfortable too. A gentleman with him, is there!"

Redlaw released his hold, as he listened.

"I have feared, from the first moment," he murmured to himself, "to meet her. There is a steady quality of goodness in her, that I dread to influence. I may be the murderer of what is tenderest and best within her bosom."

She was knocking at the door.

"Shall I dismiss it as an idle foreboding, or still avoid her?" he muttered, looking uneasily around.

She was knocking at the door again.

"Of all the visitors who could come here," he said, in a hoarse alarmed voice, turning to his companion, "this is the one I should desire most to avoid. Hide me!"

The student opened a frail door in the wall, communicating where the garret-roof began to slope towards the floor, with a small inner room. Redlaw passed in hastily, and shut it after him.

The student then resumed his place upon the couch, and called to her to enter.

"Dear Mr. Edmund," said Milly, looking round, "they told me there was a gentleman here."

"There is no one here but I."

"There has been some one?"

"Yes, yes, there has been some one."

She put her little basket on the table, and went up to the back of the couch, as if to take the extended hand – but it was not there. A little surprised, in her quiet way, she leaned over to look at his face, and gently touched him on the brow.

"Are you quite as well to-night? Your head is not so cool as in the afternoon."

"Tut!" said the student, petulantly, "very little ails me."

A little more surprise, but no reproach, was expressed in her face, as she withdrew to the other side of the table, and took a small packet of needlework from her basket. But she laid it down again, on second thoughts, and going noiselessly about the room, set everything exactly in its place, and in the neatest order; even to the cushions on the couch, which she touched with so light a hand, that he hardly seemed to know it, as he lay looking at the fire. When all this was done, and she had swept the hearth, she sat down, in her modest little bonnet, to her work, and was quietly busy on it directly.

"It's the new muslin curtain for the window, Mr. Edmund," said Milly, stitching away as she talked. "It will look very clean and nice, though it costs very little, and will save your eyes, too, from the light. My William says the room should not be too light just now, when you are recovering so well, or the glare might make you giddy."

He said nothing; but there was something so fretful and impatient in his change of position, that her quick fingers stopped, and she looked at him anxiously.

"The pillows are not comfortable," she said, laying down her work and rising. "I will soon put them right."

"They are very well," he answered. "Leave them alone, pray. You make so much of everything."

He raised his head to say this, and looked at her so thanklessly, that, after he had thrown himself down again, she stood timidly pausing. However, she resumed her seat, and her needle, without having directed even a murmuring look towards him, and was soon as busy as before.

"I have been thinking, Mr. Edmund, that *you* have been often thinking of late, when I have been sitting by, how true the saying is, that adversity is a good teacher. Health will be more precious to you, after this illness, than it has ever been. And years hence, when this time of year comes round, and you remember the days when you lay here sick, alone, that the knowledge of your illness might not afflict those who are dearest to you, your home will be doubly dear and doubly blest. Now, isn't that a good, true thing?"

She was too intent upon her work, and too earnest in what she said, and too composed and quiet altogether, to be on the watch for any look he might direct towards her in reply; so the shaft of his ungrateful glance fell harmless, and did not wound her.

"Ah!" said Milly, with her pretty head inclining thoughtfully on one side, as she looked down, following her busy fingers with her eyes. "Even on me – and I am very different from you, Mr. Edmund, for I have no learning, and don't know how to think properly – this view of such things has made a great impression, since you have been lying ill. When I have seen you so touched by the kindness and attention of the poor people down stairs, I have felt that you thought even that experience some repayment for the loss of health, and I have read in your face, as plain as if it was a book, that but for some trouble and sorrow we should never know half the good there is about us."

His getting up from the couch, interrupted her, or she was going on to say more.

"We needn't magnify the merit, Mrs. William," he rejoined slightingly. "The people down stairs will be paid in good time I dare say, for any little extra service they may have rendered me; and perhaps they anticipate no less. I am much obliged to you, too."

Her fingers stopped, and she looked at him.

"I can't be made to feel the more obliged by your exaggerating the case," he said. "I am sensible that you have been interested in me, and I say I am much obliged to you. What more would you have?"

Her work fell on her lap, as she still looked at him walking to and fro with an intolerant air, and stopping now and then.

"I say again, I am much obliged to you. Why weaken my sense of what is your due in obligation, by preferring enormous claims upon me? Trouble, sorrow, affliction, adversity! One might suppose I had been dying a score of deaths here!"

"Do you believe, Mr. Edmund," she asked, rising and going nearer to him, "that I spoke of the poor people of the house, with any reference to myself? To me?" laying her hand upon her bosom with a simple and innocent smile of astonishment.

"Oh! I think nothing about it, my good creature," he returned. "I have had an indisposition, which your solicitude – observe! I say solicitude – makes a great deal more of, than it merits; and it's over, and we can't perpetuate it."

He coldly took a book, and sat down at the table.

She watched him for a little while, until her smile was quite gone, and then, returning to where her basket was, said gently:

"Mr. Edmund, would you rather be alone?"

"There is no reason why I should detain you here," he replied.

"Except—" said Milly, hesitating, and showing her work.

"Oh! the curtain," he answered, with a supercilious laugh. "That's not worth staying for."

She made up the little packet again, and put it in her basket. Then, standing before him with such an air of patient entreaty that he could not choose but look at her, she said:

"If you should want me, I will come back willingly. When you did want me, I was quite happy to come; there was no merit in it. I think you must be afraid, that, now you are getting well, I may be troublesome to you; but I should not have been, indeed. I should have come no longer than your weakness and confinement lasted. You owe me nothing; but it is right that you should deal as justly by me as if I was a lady – even the very lady that you love; and if you suspect me of meanly making much of the little I have tried to do to comfort your sick room, you do yourself more wrong than ever you can do me. That is why I am sorry. That is why I am very sorry."

If she had been as passionate as she was quiet, as indignant as she was calm, as angry in her look as she was gentle, as loud of tone as she was low and clear, she might have left no sense of her departure in the room, compared with that which fell upon the lonely student when she went away.

He was gazing drearily upon the place where she had been, when Redlaw came out of his concealment, and came to the door.

"When sickness lays its hand on you again," he said, looking fiercely back at him, "— may it be soon! – Die here! Rot here!"

"What have you done?" returned the other, catching at his cloak. "What change have you wrought in me? What curse have you brought upon me? Give me back *my*self!"

"Give me back myself!" exclaimed Redlaw like a madman. "I am infected! I am infectious! I am charged with poison for my own mind, and the minds of all mankind. Where I felt interest, compassion, sympathy, I am turning into stone. Selfishness and ingratitude spring up in my blighting footsteps. I am only so much less base than the wretches whom I make so, that in the moment of their transformation I can hate them."

As he spoke – the young man still holding to his cloak – he cast him off, and struck him: then, wildly hurried out into the night air where the wind was blowing, the snow falling, the cloud-drift sweeping on, the moon dimly shining; and where, blowing in the wind, falling with the snow, drifting with the clouds, shining in the moonlight, and heavily looming in the darkness, were the Phantom's words, "The gift that I have given, you shall give again, go where you will!"

Whither he went, he neither knew nor cared, so that he avoided company. The change he felt within him made the busy streets a desert, and himself a desert, and the multitude around him, in their manifold endurances and ways of life, a mighty waste of sand, which the winds tossed into unintelligible heaps and made a ruinous confusion of. Those traces in his breast which the Phantom had told him would "die out soon," were not, as yet, so far upon their way to death, but that he understood enough of what he was, and what he made of others, to desire to be alone.

This put it in his mind – he suddenly bethought himself, as he was going along, of the boy who had rushed into his room. And then he recollected, that of those with whom he had communicated since the Phantom's disappearance, that boy alone had shown no sign of being changed.

Monstrous and odious as the wild thing was to him, he determined to seek it out, and prove if this were really so; and also to seek it with another intention, which came into his thoughts at the same time.

So, resolving with some difficulty where he was, he directed his steps back to the old college, and to that part of it where the general porch was, and where, alone, the pavement was worn by the tread of the students' feet.

The keeper's house stood just within the iron gates, forming a part of the chief quadrangle. There was a little cloister outside, and from that sheltered place he knew he could look in at the window of their ordinary room, and see who was within. The iron gates were shut, but his hand was familiar with the fastening, and drawing it back by thrusting in his wrist between the bars, he passed through softly, shut it again, and crept up to the window, crumbling the thin crust of snow with his feet.

The fire, to which he had directed the boy last night, shining brightly through the glass, made an illuminated place upon the ground. Instinctively avoiding this, and going round it, he looked in at the window. At first, he thought that there was no one there, and that the blaze was reddening only the old beams in the ceiling and the dark walls; but peering in more narrowly, he saw the object of his search coiled asleep before it on the floor. He passed quickly to the door, opened it, and went in.

The creature lay in such a fiery heat, that, as the Chemist stooped to rouse him, it scorched his head. So soon as he was touched, the boy, not half awake, clutching his rags together with the instinct of flight upon him, half rolled and half ran into a distant corner of the room, where, heaped upon the ground, he struck his foot out to defend himself.

"Get up!" said the Chemist. "You have not forgotten me?"

"You let me alone!" returned the boy. "This is the woman's house – not yours."

The Chemist's steady eye controlled him somewhat, or inspired him with enough submission to be raised upon his feet, and looked at.

"Who washed them, and put those bandages where they were bruised and cracked?" asked the Chemist, pointing to their altered state.

"The woman did."

"And is it she who has made you cleaner in the face, too?"

"Yes, the woman."

Redlaw asked these questions to attract his eyes towards himself, and with the same intent now held him by the chin, and threw his wild hair back, though he loathed to touch him. The boy watched his eyes keenly, as if he thought it needful to his own defence, not knowing what he might do next; and Redlaw could see well that no change came over him.

"Where are they?" he inquired.

"The woman's out."

"I know she is. Where is the old man with the white hair, and his son?"

"The woman's husband, d'ye mean?" inquired the boy.

"Ay. Where are those two?"

"Out. Something's the matter, somewhere. They were fetched out in a hurry, and told me to stop here."

"Come with me," said the Chemist, "and I'll give you money."

"Come where? and how much will you give?"

"I'll give you more shillings than you ever saw, and bring you back soon. Do you know your way to where you came from?"

"You let me go," returned the boy, suddenly twisting out of his grasp. "I'm not a going to take you there. Let me be, or I'll heave some fire at you!"

He was down before it, and ready, with his savage little hand, to pluck the burning coals out.

What the Chemist had felt, in observing the effect of his charmed influence stealing over those with whom he came in contact, was not nearly equal to the cold vague terror with which he saw this baby-monster put it at defiance. It chilled his blood to look on the immovable impenetrable thing, in the likeness of a child, with its sharp malignant face turned up to his, and its almost infant hand, ready at the bars.

"Listen, boy!" he said. "You shall take me where you please, so that you take me where the people are very miserable or very wicked. I want to do them good, and not to harm them. You shall have money, as I have told you, and I will bring you back. Get up! Come quickly!" He made a hasty step towards the door, afraid of her returning.

"Will you let me walk by myself, and never hold me, nor yet touch me?" said the boy, slowly withdrawing the hand with which he threatened, and beginning to get up.

"I will!"

"And let me go, before, behind, or anyways I like?"

"I will!"

"Give me some money first, then, and go."

The Chemist laid a few shillings, one by one, in his extended hand. To count them was beyond the boy's knowledge, but he said "one," every time, and avariciously looked at each as it was given, and at the donor. He had nowhere to put them, out of his hand, but in his mouth; and he put them there.

Redlaw then wrote with his pencil on a leaf of his pocket-book, that the boy was with him; and laying it on the table, signed to him to follow. Keeping his rags together, as usual, the boy complied, and went out with his bare head and naked feet into the winter night.

Preferring not to depart by the iron gate by which he had entered, where they were in danger of meeting her whom he so anxiously avoided, the Chemist led the way, through some of those passages among which the boy had lost himself, and by that portion of the building where he lived, to a small door of which he had the key. When they got into the street, he stopped to ask his guide – who instantly retreated from him – if he knew where they were.

The savage thing looked here and there, and at length, nodding his head, pointed in the direction he designed to take. Redlaw going on at once, he followed, something less suspiciously; shifting his money from his mouth into his hand, and back again into his mouth, and stealthily rubbing it bright upon his shreds of dress, as he went along.

Three times, in their progress, they were side by side. Three times they stopped, being side by side. Three times the Chemist glanced down at his face, and shuddered as it forced upon him one reflection.

The first occasion was when they were crossing an old churchyard, and Redlaw stopped among the graves, utterly at a loss how to connect them with any tender, softening, or consolatory thought.

The second was, when the breaking forth of the moon induced him to look up at the Heavens, where he saw her in her glory, surrounded by a host of stars he still knew by the names and histories which human science has appended to them; but where he saw nothing else he had been wont to see, felt nothing he had been wont to feel, in looking up there, on a bright night.

The third was when he stopped to listen to a plaintive strain of music, but could only hear a tune, made manifest to him by the dry mechanism of the instruments and his own ears, with no address to any mystery within him, without a whisper in it of the past, or of the future, powerless upon him as the sound of last year's running water, or the rushing of last year's wind.

At each of these three times, he saw with horror that, in spite of the vast intellectual distance between them, and their being unlike each other in all physical respects, the expression on the boy's face was the expression on his own.

They journeyed on for some time – now through such crowded places, that he often looked over his shoulder thinking he had lost his guide, but generally finding him within his shadow on his other side; now by ways so quiet, that he could have counted his short, quick, naked footsteps coming on behind – until they arrived at a ruinous collection of houses, and the boy touched him and stopped.

"In there!" he said, pointing out one house where there were shattered lights in the windows, and a dim lantern in the doorway, with "Lodgings for Travellers" painted on it.

Redlaw looked about him; from the houses to the waste piece of ground on which the houses stood, or rather did not altogether tumble down, unfenced, undrained, unlighted, and bordered by a sluggish ditch; from that, to the sloping line of arches, part of some neighbouring viaduct or bridge with which it was surrounded, and which lessened gradually towards them, until the last but one was a mere kennel for a dog, the last a plundered little heap of bricks; from that, to the child, close to him, cowering and trembling with the cold, and limping on one little foot, while he coiled the other round his leg to warm it, yet staring at all these things with that frightful likeness of expression so apparent in his face, that Redlaw started from him.

"In there!" said the boy, pointing out the house again. "I'll wait."

"Will they let me in?" asked Redlaw.

"Say you're a doctor," he answered with a nod. "There's plenty ill here."

Looking back on his way to the house-door, Redlaw saw him trail himself upon the dust and crawl within the shelter of the smallest arch, as if he were a rat. He had no pity for the thing, but he was afraid of it; and when it looked out of its den at him, he hurried to the house as a retreat.

"Sorrow, wrong, and trouble," said the Chemist, with a painful effort at some more distinct remembrance, "at least haunt this place darkly. He can do no harm, who brings forgetfulness of such things here!"

With these words, he pushed the yielding door, and went in.

There was a woman sitting on the stairs, either asleep or forlorn, whose head was bent down on her hands and knees. As it was not easy to pass without treading on her, and as she was perfectly regardless of his near approach, he stopped, and touched her on the shoulder. Looking up, she showed him quite a young face, but one whose bloom and promise were all swept away, as if the haggard winter should unnaturally kill the spring.

With little or no show of concern on his account, she moved nearer to the wall to leave him a wider passage.

"What are you?" said Redlaw, pausing, with his hand upon the broken stair-rail.

"What do you think I am?" she answered, showing him her face again.

He looked upon the ruined Temple of God, so lately made, so soon disfigured; and something, which was not compassion – for the springs in which a true compassion for such miseries has its rise, were dried up in his breast – but which was nearer to it, for the moment, than any feeling that had lately struggled into the darkening, but not yet wholly darkened, night of his mind – mingled a touch of softness with his next words.

"I am come here to give relief, if I can," he said. "Are you thinking of any wrong?"

She frowned at him, and then laughed; and then her laugh prolonged itself into a shivering sigh, as she dropped her head again, and hid her fingers in her hair.

"Are you thinking of a wrong?" he asked once more.

"I am thinking of my life," she said, with a mometary look at him.

He had a perception that she was one of many, and that he saw the type of thousands, when he saw her, drooping at his feet.

"What are your parents?" he demanded.

"I had a good home once. My father was a gardener, far away, in the country."

"Is he dead?"

"He's dead to me. All such things are dead to me. You a gentleman, and not know that!" She raised her eyes again, and laughed at him.

"Girl!" said Redlaw, sternly, "before this death, of all such things, was brought about, was there no wrong done to you? In spite of all that you can do, does no remembrance of wrong cleave to you? Are there not times upon times when it is misery to you?"

So little of what was womanly was left in her appearance, that now, when she burst into tears, he stood amazed. But he was more amazed, and much disquieted, to note that in her awakened recollection of this wrong, the first trace of her old humanity and frozen tenderness appeared to show itself.

He drew a little off, and in doing so, observed that her arms were black, her face cut, and her bosom bruised.

"What brutal hand has hurt you so?" he asked.

"My own. I did it myself!" she answered quickly.

"It is impossible."

"I'll swear I did! He didn't touch me. I did it to myself in a passion, and threw myself down here. He wasn't near me. He never laid a hand upon me!"

In the white determination of her face, confronting him with this untruth, he saw enough of the last perversion and distortion of good surviving in that miserable breast, to be stricken with remorse that he had ever come near her.

"Sorrow, wrong, and trouble!" he muttered, turning his fearful gaze away. "All that connects her with the state from which she has fallen, has those roots! In the name of God, let me go by!"

Afraid to look at her again, afraid to touch her, afraid to think of having sundered the last thread by which she held upon the mercy of Heaven, he gathered his cloak about him, and glided swiftly up the stairs.

Opposite to him, on the landing, was a door, which stood partly open, and which, as he ascended, a man with a candle in his hand, came forward from within to shut. But this man, on seeing him, drew back, with much emotion in his manner, and, as if by a sudden impulse, mentioned his name aloud.

In the surprise of such a recognition there, he stopped, endeavouring to recollect the wan and startled face. He had no time to consider it, for, to his yet greater amazement, old Philip came out of the room, and took him by the hand.

"Mr. Redlaw," said the old man, "this is like you, this is like you, sir! you have heard of it, and have come after us to render any help you can. Ah, too late, too late!"

Redlaw, with a bewildered look, submitted to be led into the room. A man lay there, on a truckle-bed, and William Swidger stood at the bedside.

"Too late!" murmured the old man, looking wistfully into the Chemist's face; and the tears stole down his cheeks.

"That's what I say, father," interposed his son in a low voice. "That's where it is, exactly. To keep as quiet as ever we can while he's a dozing, is the only thing to do. You're right, father!"

Redlaw paused at the bedside, and looked down on the figure that was stretched upon the mattress. It was that of a man, who should have been in the vigour of his life, but on whom it was not likely the sun would ever shine again. The vices of his forty or fifty years' career had so branded him, that, in comparison with their effects upon his face, the heavy hand of Time upon the old man's face who watched him had been merciful and beautifying.

"Who is this?" asked the Chemist, looking round.

"My son George, Mr. Redlaw," said the old man, wringing his hands. "My eldest son, George, who was more his mother's pride than all the rest!"

Redlaw's eyes wandered from the old man's grey head, as he laid it down upon the bed, to the person who had recognised him, and who had kept aloof, in the remotest corner of the room. He seemed to be about his own age; and although he knew no such hopeless decay and broken man as he appeared to be, there was something in the turn of his figure, as he stood with his back towards him, and now went out at the door, that made him pass his hand uneasily across his brow.

"William," he said in a gloomy whisper, "who is that man?"

"Why you see, sir," returned Mr. William, "that's what I say, myself. Why should a man ever go and gamble, and the like of that, and let himself down inch by inch till he can't let himself down any lower!"

"Has *he* done so?" asked Redlaw, glancing after him with the same uneasy action as before.

"Just exactly that, sir," returned William Swidger, "as I'm told. He knows a little about medicine, sir, it seems; and having been wayfaring towards London with my unhappy brother that you see here," Mr. William passed his coat-sleeve across his eyes, "and being lodging up stairs for the night – what I say, you see, is that strange companions come together here sometimes – he looked in to attend upon him, and came for us at his request. What a mournful spectacle, sir! But that's where it is. It's enough to kill my father!"

Redlaw looked up, at these words, and, recalling where he was and with whom, and the spell he carried with him – which his surprise had obscured – retired a little, hurriedly, debating with himself whether to shun the house that moment, or remain.

Yielding to a certain sullen doggedness, which it seemed to be a part of his condition to struggle with, he argued for remaining.

"Was it only yesterday," he said, "when I observed the memory of this old man to be a tissue of sorrow and trouble, and shall I be afraid, to-night, to shake it? Are such remembrances as I can drive away, so precious to this dying man that I need fear for *him*? No! I'll stay here."

But he stayed in fear and trembling none the less for these words; and, shrouded in his black cloak with his face turned from them, stood away from the bedside, listening to what they said, as if he felt himself a demon in the place.

"Father!" murmured the sick man, rallying a little from stupor.

"My boy! My son George!" said old Philip.

"You spoke, just now, of my being mother's favourite, long ago. It's a dreadful thing to think now, of long ago!"

"No, no, no;" returned the old man. "Think of it. Don't say it's dreadful. It's not dreadful to me, my son."

"It cuts you to the heart, father." For the old man's tears were falling on him.

"Yes, yes," said Philip, "so it does; but it does me good. It's a heavy sorrow to think of that time, but it does me good, George. Oh, think of it too, think of it too, and your heart will be softened more and more! Where's my son William? William, my boy, your mother loved him dearly to the last, and with her latest breath said, 'Tell him I forgave him, blessed him, and prayed for him.' Those were her words to me. I have never forgotten them, and I'm eighty-seven!"

"Father!" said the man upon the bed, "I am dying, I know. I am so far gone, that I can hardly speak, even of what my mind most runs on. Is there any hope for me beyond this bed?"

"There is hope," returned the old man, "for all who are softened and penitent. There is hope for all such. Oh!" he exclaimed, clasping his hands and looking up, "I was thankful, only yesterday, that I could remember this unhappy son when he was an innocent child. But what a comfort it is, now, to think that even God himself has that remembrance of him!"

Redlaw spread his hands upon his face, and shrank, like a murderer.

"Ah!" feebly moaned the man upon the bed. "The waste since then, the waste of life since then!"

"But he was a child once," said the old man. "He played with children. Before he lay down on his bed at night, and fell into his guiltless rest, he said his prayers at his poor mother's knee. I have seen him do it, many a time; and seen her lay his head upon her breast, and kiss him. Sorrowful as it was to her and me, to think of this, when he went so wrong, and when our hopes and plans for him were all broken, this gave him still a hold upon us, that nothing else could have given. Oh, Father, so much better than the fathers upon earth! Oh, Father, so much more afflicted by the errors of Thy children! take this wanderer back! Not as he is, but as he was then, let him cry to Thee, as he has so often seemed to cry to us!"

As the old man lifted up his trembling hands, the son, for whom he made the supplication, laid his sinking head against him for support and comfort, as if he were indeed the child of whom he spoke.

When did man ever tremble, as Redlaw trembled, in the silence that ensued! He knew it must come upon them, knew that it was coming fast.

"My time is very short, my breath is shorter," said the sick man, supporting himself on one arm, and with the other groping in the air, "and I remember there is something on my mind concerning the man who was here just now, Father and William – wait! – is there really anything in black, out there?"

"Yes, yes, it is real," said his aged father.

"Is it a man?"

"What I say myself, George," interposed his brother, bending kindly over him. "It's Mr. Redlaw."

"I thought I had dreamed of him. Ask him to come here."

The Chemist, whiter than the dying man, appeared before him. Obedient to the motion of his hand, he sat upon the bed.

"It has been so ripped up, to-night, sir," said the sick man, laying his hand upon his heart, with a look in which the mute, imploring agony of his condition was concentrated, "by the sight of my poor old father, and the thought of all the trouble I have been the cause of, and all the wrong and sorrow lying at my door, that—"

Was it the extremity to which he had come, or was it the dawning of another change, that made him stop?

"—that what I *can* do right, with my mind running on so much, so fast, I'll try to do. There was another man here. Did you see him?"

Redlaw could not reply by any word; for when he saw that fatal sign he knew so well now, of the wandering hand upon the forehead, his voice died at his lips. But he made some indication of assent.

"He is penniless, hungry, and destitute. He is completely beaten down, and has no resource at all. Look after him! Lose no time! I know he has it in his mind to kill himself."

It was working. It was on his face. His face was changing, hardening, deepening in all its shades, and losing all its sorrow.

"Don't you remember? Don't you know him?" he pursued.

He shut his face out for a moment, with the hand that again wandered over his forehead, and then it lowered on Redlaw, reckless, ruffianly, and callous.

"Why, d-n you!" he said, scowling round, "what have you been doing to me here! I have lived bold, and I mean to die bold. To the Devil with you!"

And so lay down upon his bed, and put his arms up, over his head and ears, as resolute from that time to keep out all access, and to die in his indifference.

If Redlaw had been struck by lightning, it could not have struck him from the bedside with a more tremendous shock. But the old man, who had left the bed while his son was speaking to him, now returning, avoided it quickly likewise, and with abhorrence.

"Where's my boy William?" said the old man hurriedly. "William, come away from here. We'll go home."

"Home, father!" returned William. "Are you going to leave your own son?"

"Where's my own son?" replied the old man.

"Where? why, there!"

"That's no son of mine," said Philip, trembling with resentment. "No such wretch as that, has any claim on me. My children are pleasant to look at, and they wait upon me, and get my meat and drink ready, and are useful to me. I've a right to it! I'm eighty-seven!"

"You're old enough to be no older," muttered William, looking at him grudgingly, with his hands in his pockets. "I don't know what good you are, myself. We could have a deal more pleasure without you."

"*My* son, Mr. Redlaw!" said the old man. "*My* son, too! The boy talking to me of *my* son! Why, what has he ever done to give me any pleasure, I should like to know?"

"I don't know what you have ever done to give *me* any pleasure," said William, sulkily.

"Let me think," said the old man. "For how many Christmas times running, have I sat in my warm place, and never had to come out in the cold night air; and have made good cheer, without being disturbed by any such uncomfortable, wretched sight as him there? Is it twenty, William?"

"Nigher forty, it seems," he muttered. "Why, when I look at my father, sir, and come to think of it," addressing Redlaw, with an impatience and irritation that were quite new, "I'm whipped if I can see anything in him but a calendar of ever so many years of eating and drinking, and making himself comfortable, over and over again."

"I—I'm eighty-seven," said the old man, rambling on, childishly and weakly, "and I don't know as I ever was much put out by anything. I'm not going to begin now, because of what he calls my son. He's not my son. I've had a power of pleasant times. I recollect once – no I don't – no, it's broken off. It was something about a game of cricket and a friend of mine, but it's somehow broken off. I wonder who he was – I suppose I liked him? And I wonder what became of him – I suppose he died? But I don't know. And I don't care, neither; I don't care a bit."

In his drowsy chuckling, and the shaking of his head, he put his hands into his waistcoat pockets. In one of them he found a bit of holly (left there, probably last night), which he now took out, and looked at.

"Berries, eh?" said the old man. "Ah! It's a pity they're not good to eat. I recollect, when I was a little chap about as high as that, and out a walking with – let me see – who was I out a walking with? – no, I don't remember how that was. I don't remember as I ever walked with any one particular, or cared for any one, or any one for me. Berries, eh? There's good cheer when there's berries. Well; I ought to have my share of it, and to be waited on, and kept warm and comfortable; for I'm eighty-seven, and a poor old man. I'm eigh-ty-seven. Eigh-ty-seven!"

The drivelling, pitiable manner in which, as he repeated this, he nibbled at the leaves, and spat the morsels out; the cold, uninterested eye with which his youngest son (so changed) regarded him; the determined apathy with which his eldest son lay hardened in his sin; impressed themselves no more on Redlaw's observation, – for he broke his way from the spot to which his feet seemed to have been fixed, and ran out of the house.

His guide came crawling forth from his place of refuge, and was ready for him before he reached the arches.

"Back to the woman's?" he inquired.

"Back, quickly!" answered Redlaw. "Stop nowhere on the way!"

For a short distance the boy went on before; but their return was more like a flight than a walk, and it was as much as his bare feet could do, to keep pace with the Chemist's rapid strides. Shrinking from all who passed, shrouded in his cloak, and keeping it drawn closely about him, as though there were mortal contagion in any fluttering touch of his garments, he made no pause until they reached the door by which they had come out. He unlocked it with his key, went in, accompanied by the boy, and hastened through the dark passages to his own chamber.

The boy watched him as he made the door fast, and withdrew behind the table, when he looked round.

"Come!" he said. "Don't you touch me! You've not brought me here to take my money away."

Redlaw threw some more upon the ground. He flung his body on it immediately, as if to hide it from him, lest the sight of it should tempt him to reclaim it; and not until he saw him seated by his lamp, with his face hidden in his hands, began furtively to pick it up. When he had done so, he crept near the fire, and, sitting down in a great chair before it, took from his breast some broken scraps of food, and fell to munching, and to staring at the blaze, and now and then to glancing at his shillings, which he kept clenched up in a bunch, in one hand.

"And this," said Redlaw, gazing on him with increased repugnance and fear, "is the only one companion I have left on earth!"

How long it was before he was aroused from his contemplation of this creature, whom he dreaded so – whether half-an-hour, or half the night – he knew not. But the stillness of the room was broken by the boy (whom he had seen listening) starting up, and running towards the door.

"Here's the woman coming!" he exclaimed.

The Chemist stopped him on his way, at the moment when she knocked.

"Let me go to her, will you?" said the boy.

"Not now," returned the Chemist. "Stay here. Nobody must pass in or out of the room now. Who's that?"

"It's I, sir," cried Milly. "Pray, sir, let me in!"

"No! not for the world!" he said.

"Mr. Redlaw, Mr. Redlaw, pray, sir, let me in."

"What is the matter?" he said, holding the boy.

"The miserable man you saw, is worse, and nothing I can say will wake him from his terrible infatuation. William's father has turned childish in a moment, William himself is changed. The shock has been too sudden for him; I cannot understand him; he is not like himself. Oh, Mr. Redlaw, pray advise me, help me!"

"No! No! No!" he answered.

"Mr. Redlaw! Dear sir! George has been muttering, in his doze, about the man you saw there, who, he fears, will kill himself."

"Better he should do it, than come near me!"

"He says, in his wandering, that you know him; that he was your friend once, long ago; that he is the ruined father of a student here – my mind misgives me, of the young gentleman who has been ill. What is to be done? How is he to be followed? How is he to be saved? Mr. Redlaw, pray, oh, pray, advise me! Help me!"

All this time he held the boy, who was half-mad to pass him, and let her in.

"Phantoms! Punishers of impious thoughts!" cried Redlaw, gazing round in anguish, "look upon me! From the darkness of my mind, let the glimmering of contrition that I know is there, shine up and show my misery! In the material world as I have long taught, nothing can be spared; no step or atom in the wondrous structure could be lost, without a blank being made in the great universe. I know, now, that it is the same with good and evil, happiness and sorrow, in the memories of men. Pity me! Relieve me!"

There was no response, but her "Help me, help me, let me in!" and the boy's struggling to get to her.

"Shadow of myself! Spirit of my darker hours!" cried Redlaw, in distraction, "come back, and haunt me day and night, but take this gift away! Or, if it must still rest with me, deprive me of the dreadful power of giving it to others. Undo what I have done. Leave me benighted, but restore the day to those whom I have cursed. As I have spared this woman from the first, and as I never will go forth again, but will die here, with no hand to tend me, save this creature's who is proof against me, – hear me!"

The only reply still was, the boy struggling to get to her, while he held him back; and the cry, increasing in its energy, "Help! let me in. He was your friend once, how shall he be followed, how shall he be saved? They are all changed, there is no one else to help me, pray, pray, let me in!"

## Chapter III
## The Gift Reversed

**NIGHT WAS STILL** heavy in the sky. On open plains, from hill-tops, and from the decks of solitary ships at sea, a distant low-lying line, that promised by-and-by to change to light, was visible in the dim horizon; but its promise was remote and doubtful, and the moon was striving with the night-clouds busily.

The shadows upon Redlaw's mind succeeded thick and fast to one another, and obscured its light as the night-clouds hovered between the moon and earth, and kept the latter veiled in darkness. Fitful and uncertain as the shadows which the night-clouds cast, were their concealments from him, and imperfect revelations to him; and, like the night-clouds still, if the clear light broke forth for a moment, it was only that they might sweep over it, and make the darkness deeper than before.

Without, there was a profound and solemn hush upon the ancient pile of building, and its buttresses and angles made dark shapes of mystery upon the ground, which now seemed to retire into the smooth white snow and now seemed to come out of it, as the moon's path was more or less beset. Within, the Chemist's room was indistinct and murky, by the light of the expiring lamp; a ghostly silence had succeeded to the knocking and the voice outside; nothing was audible but, now and then, a low sound among the whitened ashes of the fire, as of its yielding up its last breath. Before it on the ground the boy lay fast asleep. In his chair, the Chemist sat, as he had sat there since the calling at his door had ceased – like a man turned to stone.

At such a time, the Christmas music he had heard before, began to play. He listened to it at first, as he had listened in the church-yard; but presently – it playing still, and being borne towards him on the night air, in a low, sweet, melancholy strain – he rose, and stood stretching his hands about him, as if there were some friend approaching within his reach, on whom his desolate touch might rest, yet do no harm. As he did this, his face became less fixed and wondering; a gentle trembling came upon him; and at last his eyes filled with tears, and he put his hands before them, and bowed down his head.

His memory of sorrow, wrong, and trouble, had not come back to him; he knew that it was not restored; he had no passing belief or hope that it was. But some dumb stir within him made him capable, again, of being moved by what was hidden, afar off, in the music. If it were only that it told him sorrowfully the value of what he had lost, he thanked Heaven for it with a fervent gratitude.

As the last chord died upon his ear, he raised his head to listen to its lingering vibration. Beyond the boy, so that his sleeping figure lay at its feet, the Phantom stood, immovable and silent, with its eyes upon him.

Ghastly it was, as it had ever been, but not so cruel and relentless in its aspect – or he thought or hoped so, as he looked upon it trembling. It was not alone, but in its shadowy hand it held another hand.

And whose was that? Was the form that stood beside it indeed Milly's, or but her shade and picture? The quiet head was bent a little, as her manner was, and her eyes were looking down, as if in pity, on the sleeping child. A radiant light fell on her face, but did not touch the Phantom; for, though close beside her, it was dark and colourless as ever.

"Spectre!" said the Chemist, newly troubled as he looked, "I have not been stubborn or presumptuous in respect of her. Oh, do not bring her here. Spare me that!"

"This is but a shadow," said the Phantom; "when the morning shines seek out the reality whose image I present before you."

"Is it my inexorable doom to do so?" cried the Chemist.

"It is," replied the Phantom.

"To destroy her peace, her goodness; to make her what I am myself, and what I have made of others!"

"I have said seek her out," returned the Phantom. "I have said no more."

"Oh, tell me," exclaimed Redlaw, catching at the hope which he fancied might lie hidden in the words. "Can I undo what I have done?"

"No," returned the Phantom.

"I do not ask for restoration to myself," said Redlaw. "What I abandoned, I abandoned of my own free will, and have justly lost. But for those to whom I have transferred the fatal gift; who never sought it; who unknowingly received a curse of which they had no warning, and which they had no power to shun; can I do nothing?"

"Nothing," said the Phantom.

"If I cannot, can any one?"

The Phantom, standing like a statue, kept its gaze upon him for a while; then turned its head suddenly, and looked upon the shadow at its side.

"Ah! Can she?" cried Redlaw, still looking upon the shade.

The Phantom released the hand it had retained till now, and softly raised its own with a gesture of dismissal. Upon that, her shadow, still preserving the same attitude, began to move or melt away.

"Stay," cried Redlaw with an earnestness to which he could not give enough expression. "For a moment! As an act of mercy! I know that some change fell upon me, when those sounds were in the air just now. Tell me, have I lost the power of harming her? May I go near her without dread? Oh, let her give me any sign of hope!"

The Phantom looked upon the shade as he did – not at him – and gave no answer.

"At least, say this – has she, henceforth, the consciousness of any power to set right what I have done?"

"She has not," the Phantom answered.

"Has she the power bestowed on her without the consciousness?"

The phantom answered: "Seek her out."

And her shadow slowly vanished.

They were face to face again, and looking on each other, as intently and awfully as at the time of the bestowal of the gift, across the boy who still lay on the ground between them, at the Phantom's feet.

"Terrible instructor," said the Chemist, sinking on his knee before it, in an attitude of supplication, "by whom I was renounced, but by whom I am revisited (in which, and in whose milder aspect, I would fain believe I have a gleam of hope), I will obey without inquiry, praying that the cry I have sent up in the anguish of my soul has been, or will be, heard, in behalf of those whom I have injured beyond human reparation. But there is one thing—"

"You speak to me of what is lying here," the phantom interposed, and pointed with its finger to the boy.

"I do," returned the Chemist. "You know what I would ask. Why has this child alone been proof against my influence, and why, why, have I detected in its thoughts a terrible companionship with mine?"

"This," said the Phantom, pointing to the boy, "is the last, completest illustration of a human creature, utterly bereft of such remembrances as you have yielded up. No softening memory of sorrow, wrong, or trouble enters here, because this wretched mortal from his birth has been abandoned to a worse condition than the beasts, and has, within his knowledge, no one contrast, no humanising touch, to make a grain of such a memory spring up in his hardened breast. All within this desolate creature is barren wilderness. All within the man bereft of what you have resigned, is the same barren wilderness. Woe to such a man! Woe, tenfold, to the nation that shall count its monsters such as this, lying here, by hundreds and by thousands!"

Redlaw shrank, appalled, from what he heard.

"There is not," said the Phantom, "one of these – not one – but sows a harvest that mankind MUST reap. From every seed of evil in this boy, a field of ruin is grown that shall be gathered in, and garnered up, and sown again in many places in the world, until regions are overspread with wickedness enough to raise the waters of another Deluge. Open and unpunished murder in a city's streets would be less guilty in its daily toleration, than one such spectacle as this."

It seemed to look down upon the boy in his sleep. Redlaw, too, looked down upon him with a new emotion.

"There is not a father," said the Phantom, "by whose side in his daily or his nightly walk, these creatures pass; there is not a mother among all the ranks of loving mothers in this land; there is no one risen from the state of childhood, but shall be responsible in his or her degree for this enormity. There is not a country throughout the earth on which it would not bring a curse. There is no religion upon earth that it would not deny; there is no people upon earth it would not put to shame."

The Chemist clasped his hands, and looked, with trembling fear and pity, from the sleeping boy to the Phantom, standing above him with his finger pointing down.

"Behold, I say," pursued the Spectre, "the perfect type of what it was your choice to be. Your influence is powerless here, because from this child's bosom you can banish nothing. His thoughts have been in 'terrible companionship' with yours, because you have gone down to his unnatural level. He is the growth of man's indifference; you are the growth of man's presumption. The beneficent design of Heaven is, in each case, overthrown, and from the two poles of the immaterial world you come together."

The Chemist stooped upon the ground beside the boy, and, with the same kind of compassion for him that he now felt for himself, covered him as he slept, and no longer shrank from him with abhorrence or indifference.

Soon, now, the distant line on the horizon brightened, the darkness faded, the sun rose red and glorious, and the chimney stacks and gables of the ancient building gleamed in the clear air, which turned the smoke and vapour of the city into a cloud of gold. The very sun-dial in his shady corner, where the wind was used to spin with such unwindy constancy, shook off the finer particles of snow that had accumulated on his dull old face in the night, and looked out at the little white wreaths eddying round and round him. Doubtless some blind groping of the morning made its way down into the forgotten crypt so cold and earthy, where the Norman arches were half buried in the ground, and stirred the dull sap in the lazy vegetation hanging to the walls, and quickened the slow principle of life within the little world of wonderful and delicate creation which existed there, with some faint knowledge that the sun was up.

The Tetterbys were up, and doing. Mr. Tetterby took down the shutters of the shop, and, strip by strip, revealed the treasures of the window to the eyes, so proof against their seductions, of Jerusalem Buildings. Adolphus had been out so long already, that he was halfway on to "Morning Pepper." Five small Tetterbys, whose ten round eyes were much inflamed by soap and friction, were in the tortures of a cool wash in the back kitchen; Mrs. Tetterby presiding. Johnny, who was pushed and hustled through his toilet with great rapidity when Moloch chanced to be in an exacting frame of mind (which was always the case), staggered up and down with his charge before the shop door, under greater difficulties than usual; the weight of Moloch being much increased by a complication of defences against the cold, composed of knitted worsted-work, and forming a complete suit of chain-armour, with a head-piece and blue gaiters.

It was a peculiarity of this baby to be always cutting teeth. Whether they never came, or whether they came and went away again, is not in evidence; but it had certainly cut enough, on the showing of Mrs. Tetterby, to make a handsome dental provision for the sign of the Bull and Mouth. All sorts of objects were impressed for the rubbing of its gums, notwithstanding that it always carried, dangling at its waist (which was immediately under its chin), a bone ring, large enough to have represented the rosary of a young nun. Knife-handles, umbrella-tops, the heads of walking-sticks selected from the stock, the fingers of the family in general, but especially of Johnny, nutmeg-graters, crusts, the handles of doors, and the cool knobs on the tops of pokers, were among the commonest instruments indiscriminately applied for this baby's relief. The amount of electricity that must have been rubbed out of it in a week, is not to be calculated. Still Mrs. Tetterby always said "it was coming through, and then the child would be herself;" and still it never did come through, and the child continued to be somebody else.

The tempers of the little Tetterbys had sadly changed with a few hours. Mr. and Mrs. Tetterby themselves were not more altered than their offspring. Usually they were an unselfish, good-natured, yielding little race, sharing short commons when it happened (which was pretty often) contentedly and even generously, and taking a great deal of enjoyment out of a very little meat. But they were fighting now, not only for the soap and water, but even for the breakfast which was yet in perspective. The hand of every little Tetterby was against the other little Tetterbys; and even Johnny's hand – the patient, much-enduring, and devoted Johnny – rose against the baby! Yes, Mrs. Tetterby, going to the door by mere accident, saw him viciously pick out a weak place in the suit of armour where a slap would tell, and slap that blessed child.

Mrs. Tetterby had him into the parlour by the collar, in that same flash of time, and repaid him the assault with usury thereto.

"You brute, you murdering little boy," said Mrs. Tetterby. "Had you the heart to do it?"

"Why don't her teeth come through, then," retorted Johnny, in a loud rebellious voice, "instead of bothering me? How would you like it yourself?"

"Like it, sir!" said Mrs. Tetterby, relieving him of his dishonoured load.

"Yes, like it," said Johnny. "How would you? Not at all. If you was me, you'd go for a soldier. I will, too. There an't no babies in the Army."

Mr. Tetterby, who had arrived upon the scene of action, rubbed his chin thoughtfully, instead of correcting the rebel, and seemed rather struck by this view of a military life.

"I wish I was in the Army myself, if the child's in the right," said Mrs. Tetterby, looking at her husband, "for I have no peace of my life here. I'm a slave – a Virginia slave:" some indistinct association with their weak descent on the tobacco trade perhaps suggested this aggravated expression to Mrs. Tetterby. "I never have a holiday, or any pleasure at all, from year's end to year's end! Why, Lord bless and save the child," said Mrs. Tetterby, shaking the baby with an irritability hardly suited to so pious an aspiration, "what's the matter with her now?"

Not being able to discover, and not rendering the subject much clearer by shaking it, Mrs. Tetterby put the baby away in a cradle, and, folding her arms, sat rocking it angrily with her foot.

"How you stand there, 'Dolphus," said Mrs. Tetterby to her husband. "Why don't you do something?"

"Because I don't care about doing anything," Mr. Tetterby replied.

"I am sure I don't," said Mrs. Tetterby.

"I'll take my oath I don't," said Mr. Tetterby.

A diversion arose here among Johnny and his five younger brothers, who, in preparing the family breakfast table, had fallen to skirmishing for the temporary possession of the loaf, and were buffeting one another with great heartiness; the smallest boy of all, with precocious discretion, hovering outside the knot of combatants, and harassing their legs. Into the midst of this fray, Mr. and Mrs. Tetterby both precipitated themselves with great ardour, as if such ground were the only ground on which they could now agree; and having, with no visible remains of their late soft-heartedness, laid about them without any lenity, and done much execution, resumed their former relative positions.

"You had better read your paper than do nothing at all," said Mrs. Tetterby.

"What's there to read in a paper?" returned Mr. Tetterby, with excessive discontent.

"What?" said Mrs. Tetterby. "Police."

"It's nothing to me," said Tetterby. "What do I care what people do, or are done to?"

"Suicides," suggested Mrs. Tetterby.

"No business of mine," replied her husband.

"Births, deaths, and marriages, are those nothing to you?" said Mrs. Tetterby.

"If the births were all over for good, and all today; and the deaths were all to begin to come off tomorrow; I don't see why it should interest me, till I thought it was a coming to my turn," grumbled Tetterby. "As to marriages, I've done it myself. I know quite enough about *them*."

To judge from the dissatisfied expression of her face and manner, Mrs. Tetterby appeared to entertain the same opinions as her husband; but she opposed him, nevertheless, for the gratification of quarrelling with him.

"Oh, you're a consistent man," said Mrs. Tetterby, "an't you? You, with the screen of your own making there, made of nothing else but bits of newspapers, which you sit and read to the children by the half-hour together!"

"Say used to, if you please," returned her husband. "You won't find me doing so any more. I'm wiser now."

"Bah! wiser, indeed!" said Mrs. Tetterby. "Are you better?"

The question sounded some discordant note in Mr. Tetterby's breast. He ruminated dejectedly, and passed his hand across and across his forehead.

"Better!" murmured Mr. Tetterby. "I don't know as any of us are better, or happier either. Better, is it?"

He turned to the screen, and traced about it with his finger, until he found a certain paragraph of which he was in quest.

"This used to be one of the family favourites, I recollect," said Tetterby, in a forlorn and stupid way, "and used to draw tears from the children, and make 'em good, if there was any little bickering or discontent among 'em, next to the story of the robin redbreasts in the wood. 'Melancholy case of destitution. Yesterday a small man, with a baby in his arms, and surrounded by half-a-dozen ragged little ones, of various ages between ten and two, the whole of whom were evidently in a famishing condition, appeared before the worthy magistrate, and made the following recital' – Ha! I don't understand it, I'm sure," said Tetterby; "I don't see what it has got to do with us."

"How old and shabby he looks," said Mrs. Tetterby, watching him. "I never saw such a change in a man. Ah! dear me, dear me, dear me, it was a sacrifice!"

"What was a sacrifice?" her husband sourly inquired.

Mrs. Tetterby shook her head; and without replying in words, raised a complete sea-storm about the baby, by her violent agitation of the cradle.

"If you mean your marriage was a sacrifice, my good woman—" said her husband.

"I *do* mean it," said his wife.

"Why, then I mean to say," pursued Mr. Tetterby, as sulkily and surlily as she, "that there are two sides to that affair; and that I was the sacrifice; and that I wish the sacrifice hadn't been accepted."

"I wish it hadn't, Tetterby, with all my heart and soul I do assure you," said his wife. "You can't wish it more than I do, Tetterby."

"I don't know what I saw in her," muttered the newsman, "I'm sure; – certainly, if I saw anything, it's not there now. I was thinking so, last night, after supper, by the fire. She's fat, she's ageing, she won't bear comparison with most other women."

"He's common-looking, he has no air with him, he's small, he's beginning to stoop and he's getting bald," muttered Mrs. Tetterby.

"I must have been half out of my mind when I did it," muttered Mr. Tetterby.

"My senses must have forsook me. That's the only way in which I can explain it to myself," said Mrs. Tetterby with elaboration.

In this mood they sat down to breakfast. The little Tetterbys were not habituated to regard that meal in the light of a sedentary occupation, but discussed it as a dance or trot; rather resembling a savage ceremony, in the occasionally shrill whoops, and brandishings of bread and butter, with which it was accompanied, as well as in the intricate filings off into the street and back again, and the hoppings up and down the door-steps, which were incidental to the performance. In the present instance, the contentions between these Tetterby children for the milk-and-water jug, common to all, which stood upon the table, presented so lamentable an instance of angry passions risen very high indeed, that it was an outrage on the memory of Dr. Watts. It was not until Mr. Tetterby had driven the whole herd out at the front door, that a moment's peace was secured; and even that was broken by the discovery that Johnny had surreptitiously come back, and was at that instant choking in the jug like a ventriloquist, in his indecent and rapacious haste.

"These children will be the death of me at last!" said Mrs. Tetterby, after banishing the culprit. "And the sooner the better, I think."

"Poor people," said Mr. Tetterby, "ought not to have children at all. They give *us* no pleasure."

He was at that moment taking up the cup which Mrs. Tetterby had rudely pushed towards him, and Mrs. Tetterby was lifting her own cup to her lips, when they both stopped, as if they were transfixed.

"Here! Mother! Father!" cried Johnny, running into the room. "Here's Mrs. William coming down the street!"

And if ever, since the world began, a young boy took a baby from a cradle with the care of an old nurse, and hushed and soothed it tenderly, and tottered away with it cheerfully, Johnny was that boy, and Moloch was that baby, as they went out together!

Mr. Tetterby put down his cup; Mrs. Tetterby put down her cup. Mr. Tetterby rubbed his forehead; Mrs. Tetterby rubbed hers. Mr. Tetterby's face began to smooth and brighten; Mrs. Tetterby's began to smooth and brighten.

"Why, Lord forgive me," said Mr. Tetterby to himself, "what evil tempers have I been giving way to? What has been the matter here!"

"How could I ever treat him ill again, after all I said and felt last night!" sobbed Mrs. Tetterby, with her apron to her eyes.

"Am I a brute," said Mr. Tetterby, "or is there any good in me at all? Sophia! My little woman!"

"'Dolphus dear," returned his wife.

"I—I've been in a state of mind," said Mr. Tetterby, "that I can't abear to think of, Sophy."

"Oh! It's nothing to what I've been in, Dolf," cried his wife in a great burst of grief.

"My Sophia," said Mr. Tetterby, "don't take on. I never shall forgive myself. I must have nearly broke your heart, I know."

"No, Dolf, no. It was me! Me!" cried Mrs. Tetterby.

"My little woman," said her husband, "don't. You make me reproach myself dreadful, when you show such a noble spirit. Sophia, my dear, you don't know what I thought. I showed it bad enough, no doubt; but what I thought, my little woman!"

"Oh, dear Dolf, don't! Don't!" cried his wife.

"Sophia," said Mr. Tetterby, "I must reveal it. I couldn't rest in my conscience unless I mentioned it. My little woman—"

"Mrs. William's very nearly here!" screamed Johnny at the door.

"My little woman, I wondered how," gasped Mr. Tetterby, supporting himself by his chair, "I wondered how I had ever admired you – I forgot the precious children you have brought about me, and thought you didn't look as slim as I could wish. I – I never gave a recollection," said Mr. Tetterby, with severe self-accusation, "to the cares you've had as my wife, and along of me and mine, when you might have had hardly any with another man, who got on better and was luckier than me (anybody might have found such a man easily I am sure); and I quarrelled with you for having aged a little in the rough years you have lightened for me. Can you believe it, my little woman? I hardly can myself."

Mrs. Tetterby, in a whirlwind of laughing and crying, caught his face within her hands, and held it there.

"Oh, Dolf!" she cried. "I am so happy that you thought so; I am so grateful that you thought so! For I thought that you were common-looking, Dolf; and so you are, my dear, and may you be the commonest of all sights in my eyes, till you close them with your own good hands. I thought that you were small; and so you are, and I'll make much of you because you are, and more of you because I love my husband. I thought that you began to stoop; and so you do, and you shall lean on me, and I'll do all I can to keep you up. I thought there was no air about you; but there is, and it's the air of home, and that's the purest and the best there is, and God bless home once more, and all belonging to it, Dolf!"

"Hurrah! Here's Mrs. William!" cried Johnny.

So she was, and all the children with her; and so she came in, they kissed her, and kissed one another, and kissed the baby, and kissed their father and mother, and then ran back and flocked and danced about her, trooping on with her in triumph.

Mr. and Mrs. Tetterby were not a bit behind-hand in the warmth of their reception. They were as much attracted to her as the children were; they ran towards her, kissed her hands, pressed round her, could not receive her ardently or enthusiastically enough. She came among them like the spirit of all goodness, affection, gentle consideration, love, and domesticity.

"What! are *you* all so glad to see me, too, this bright Christmas morning?" said Milly, clapping her hands in a pleasant wonder. "Oh dear, how delightful this is!"

More shouting from the children, more kissing, more trooping round her, more happiness, more love, more joy, more honour, on all sides, than she could bear.

"Oh dear!" said Milly, "what delicious tears you make me shed. How can I ever have deserved this! What have I done to be so loved?"

"Who can help it!" cried Mr. Tetterby.

"Who can help it!" cried Mrs. Tetterby.

"Who can help it!" echoed the children, in a joyful chorus. And they danced and trooped about her again, and clung to her, and laid their rosy faces against her dress, and kissed and fondled it, and could not fondle it, or her, enough.

"I never was so moved," said Milly, drying her eyes, "as I have been this morning. I must tell you, as soon as I can speak. – Mr. Redlaw came to me at sunrise, and with a tenderness in his manner, more as if I had been his darling daughter than myself, implored me to go with him to where William's brother George is lying ill. We went together, and all the way along he was so kind, and so subdued, and seemed to put such trust and hope in me, that I could not help crying with pleasure. When we got to the house, we met a woman at the door (somebody had bruised and hurt her, I am afraid), who caught me by the hand, and blessed me as I passed."

"She was right!" said Mr. Tetterby. Mrs. Tetterby said she was right. All the children cried out that she was right.

"Ah, but there's more than that," said Milly. "When we got up stairs, into the room, the sick man who had lain for hours in a state from which no effort could rouse him, rose up in his bed, and, bursting into tears, stretched out his arms to me, and said that he had led a mis-spent life, but that he was truly repentant now, in his sorrow for the past, which was all as plain to him as a great prospect, from which a dense black cloud had cleared away, and that he entreated me to ask his poor old father for his pardon and his blessing, and to say a prayer beside his bed. And when I did so, Mr. Redlaw joined in it so fervently, and then so thanked and thanked me, and thanked Heaven, that my heart quite overflowed, and I could have done nothing but sob and cry, if the sick man had not begged me to sit down by him, – which made me quiet of course. As I sat there, he held my hand in his until he sank in a doze; and even then, when I withdrew my hand to leave him to come here (which Mr. Redlaw was very earnest indeed in wishing me to do), his hand felt for mine, so that some one else was obliged to take my place and make believe to give him my hand back. Oh dear, oh dear," said Milly, sobbing. "How thankful and how happy I should feel, and do feel, for all this!"

While she was speaking, Redlaw had come in, and, after pausing for a moment to observe the group of which she was the centre, had silently ascended the stairs. Upon those stairs he now appeared again; remaining there, while the young student passed him, and came running down.

"Kind nurse, gentlest, best of creatures," he said, falling on his knee to her, and catching at her hand, "forgive my cruel ingratitude!"

"Oh dear, oh dear!" cried Milly innocently, "here's another of them! Oh dear, here's somebody else who likes me. What shall I ever do!"

The guileless, simple way in which she said it, and in which she put her hands before her eyes and wept for very happiness, was as touching as it was delightful.

"I was not myself," he said. "I don't know what it was – it was some consequence of my disorder perhaps – I was mad. But I am so no longer. Almost as I speak, I am restored. I heard the children crying out your name, and the shade passed from me at the very sound of it. Oh, don't weep! Dear Milly, if you could read my heart, and only knew with what affection and what grateful homage it is glowing, you would not let me see you weep. It is such deep reproach."

"No, no," said Milly, "it's not that. It's not indeed. It's joy. It's wonder that you should think it necessary to ask me to forgive so little, and yet it's pleasure that you do."

"And will you come again? and will you finish the little curtain?"

"No," said Milly, drying her eyes, and shaking her head. "You won't care for my needlework now."

"Is it forgiving me, to say that?"

She beckoned him aside, and whispered in his ear.

"There is news from your home, Mr. Edmund."

"News? How?"

"Either your not writing when you were very ill, or the change in your handwriting when you began to be better, created some suspicion of the truth; however that is – but you're sure you'll not be the worse for any news, if it's not bad news?"

"Sure."

"Then there's some one come!" said Milly.

"My mother?" asked the student, glancing round involuntarily towards Redlaw, who had come down from the stairs.

"Hush! No," said Milly.

"It can be no one else."

"Indeed?" said Milly, "are you sure?"

"It is not—" Before he could say more, she put her hand upon his mouth.

"Yes it is!" said Milly. "The young lady (she is very like the miniature, Mr. Edmund, but she is prettier) was too unhappy to rest without satisfying her doubts, and came up, last night, with a little servant-maid. As you always dated your letters from the college, she came there; and before I saw Mr. Redlaw this morning, I saw her. *She* likes me too!" said Milly. "Oh dear, that's another!"

"This morning! Where is she now?"

"Why, she is now," said Milly, advancing her lips to his ear, "in my little parlour in the Lodge, and waiting to see you."

He pressed her hand, and was darting off, but she detained him.

"Mr. Redlaw is much altered, and has told me this morning that his memory is impaired. Be very considerate to him, Mr. Edmund; he needs that from us all."

The young man assured her, by a look, that her caution was not ill-bestowed; and as he passed the Chemist on his way out, bent respectfully and with an obvious interest before him.

Redlaw returned the salutation courteously and even humbly, and looked after him as he passed on. He dropped his head upon his hand too, as trying to reawaken something he had lost. But it was gone.

The abiding change that had come upon him since the influence of the music, and the Phantom's reappearance, was, that now he truly felt how much he had lost, and could compassionate his own condition, and contrast it, clearly, with the natural state of those who were around him. In this, an interest in those who were around him was revived, and a meek, submissive sense of his calamity was bred, resembling that which sometimes obtains in age, when its mental powers are weakened, without insensibility or sullenness being added to the list of its infirmities.

He was conscious that, as he redeemed, through Milly, more and more of the evil he had done, and as he was more and more with her, this change ripened itself within him. Therefore, and because of the attachment she inspired him with (but without other hope), he felt that he was quite dependent on her, and that she was his staff in his affliction.

So, when she asked him whether they should go home now, to where the old man and her husband were, and he readily replied "yes" – being anxious in that regard – he put his arm through hers, and walked beside her; not as if he were the wise and learned man to whom the wonders of Nature were an open book, and hers were the uninstructed mind, but as if their two positions were reversed, and he knew nothing, and she all.

He saw the children throng about her, and caress her, as he and she went away together thus, out of the house; he heard the ringing of their laughter, and their merry voices; he saw their bright faces, clustering around him like flowers; he witnessed the renewed contentment and affection of their parents; he breathed the simple air of their poor home, restored to its tranquillity; he thought of the unwholesome blight he had shed upon it, and might, but for her, have been diffusing then; and perhaps it is no wonder that he walked submissively beside her, and drew her gentle bosom nearer to his own.

When they arrived at the Lodge, the old man was sitting in his chair in the chimney-corner, with his eyes fixed on the ground, and his son was leaning against the opposite side of the fire-place, looking at him. As she came in at the door, both started, and turned round towards her, and a radiant change came upon their faces.

"Oh dear, dear, dear, they are all pleased to see me like the rest!" cried Milly, clapping her hands in an ecstasy, and stopping short. "Here are two more!"

Pleased to see her! Pleasure was no word for it. She ran into her husband's arms, thrown wide open to receive her, and he would have been glad to have her there, with her head lying on his shoulder, through the short winter's day. But the old man couldn't spare her. He had arms for her too, and he locked her in them.

"Why, where has my quiet Mouse been all this time?" said the old man. "She has been a long while away. I find that it's impossible for me to get on without Mouse. I – where's my son William? – I fancy I have been dreaming, William."

"That's what I say myself, father," returned his son. "I have been in an ugly sort of dream, I think. – How are you, father? Are you pretty well?"

"Strong and brave, my boy," returned the old man.

It was quite a sight to see Mr. William shaking hands with his father, and patting him on the back, and rubbing him gently down with his hand, as if he could not possibly do enough to show an interest in him.

"What a wonderful man you are, father! – How are you, father? Are you really pretty hearty, though?" said William, shaking hands with him again, and patting him again, and rubbing him gently down again.

"I never was fresher or stouter in my life, my boy."

"What a wonderful man you are, father! But that's exactly where it is," said Mr. William, with enthusiasm. "When I think of all that my father's gone through, and all the chances and changes, and sorrows and troubles, that have happened to him in the course of his long life, and under which his head has grown grey, and years upon years have gathered on it, I feel as if we couldn't do enough to honour the old gentleman, and make his old age easy. – How are you, father? Are you really pretty well, though?"

Mr. William might never have left off repeating this inquiry, and shaking hands with him again, and patting him again, and rubbing him down again, if the old man had not espied the Chemist, whom until now he had not seen.

"I ask your pardon, Mr. Redlaw," said Philip, "but didn't know you were here, sir, or should have made less free. It reminds me, Mr. Redlaw, seeing you here on a Christmas morning, of the time when you was a student yourself, and worked so hard that you were backwards and forwards in our Library even at Christmas time. Ha! ha! I'm old enough to remember that; and I remember it right well, I do, though I am eighty-seven. It was after you left here that my poor wife died. You remember my poor wife, Mr. Redlaw?"

The Chemist answered yes.

"Yes," said the old man. "She was a dear creetur. – I recollect you come here one Christmas morning with a young lady – I ask your pardon, Mr. Redlaw, but I think it was a sister you was very much attached to?"

The Chemist looked at him, and shook his head. "I had a sister," he said vacantly. He knew no more.

"One Christmas morning," pursued the old man, "that you come here with her – and it began to snow, and my wife invited the lady to walk in, and sit by the fire that is always a burning on Christmas Day in what used to be, before our ten poor gentlemen commuted, our great Dinner Hall. I was there; and I recollect, as I was stirring up the blaze for the young lady to warm her pretty feet by, she read the scroll out loud, that is underneath that pictur, 'Lord, keep my memory green!' She and my poor wife fell a talking about it; and it's a strange thing to think of, now, that they both said (both being so unlike to die) that it was a good prayer, and that it was one they would put up very earnestly, if they were called away young, with reference to those who were dearest to them. 'My brother,' says the young lady – 'My husband,' says my poor wife. – 'Lord, keep his memory of me, green, and do not let me be forgotten!'"

Tears more painful, and more bitter than he had ever shed in all his life, coursed down Redlaw's face. Philip, fully occupied in recalling his story, had not observed him until now, nor Milly's anxiety that he should not proceed.

"Philip!" said Redlaw, laying his hand upon his arm, "I am a stricken man, on whom the hand of Providence has fallen heavily, although deservedly. You speak to me, my friend, of what I cannot follow; my memory is gone."

"Merciful power!" cried the old man.

"I have lost my memory of sorrow, wrong, and trouble," said the Chemist, "and with that I have lost all man would remember!"

To see old Philip's pity for him, to see him wheel his own great chair for him to rest in, and look down upon him with a solemn sense of his bereavement, was to know, in some degree, how precious to old age such recollections are.

The boy came running in, and ran to Milly.

"Here's the man," he said, "in the other room. I don't want *him*."

"What man does he mean?" asked Mr. William.

"Hush!" said Milly.

Obedient to a sign from her, he and his old father softly withdrew. As they went out, unnoticed, Redlaw beckoned to the boy to come to him.

"I like the woman best," he answered, holding to her skirts.

"You are right," said Redlaw, with a faint smile. "But you needn't fear to come to me. I am gentler than I was. Of all the world, to you, poor child!"

The boy still held back at first, but yielding little by little to her urging, he consented to approach, and even to sit down at his feet. As Redlaw laid his hand upon the shoulder of the child, looking on him with compassion and a fellow-feeling, he put out his other hand to Milly. She stooped down on that side of him, so that she could look into his face, and after silence, said:

"Mr. Redlaw, may I speak to you?"

"Yes," he answered, fixing his eyes upon her. "Your voice and music are the same to me."

"May I ask you something?"

"What you will."

"Do you remember what I said, when I knocked at your door last night? About one who was your friend once, and who stood on the verge of destruction?"

"Yes. I remember," he said, with some hesitation.

"Do you understand it?"

He smoothed the boy's hair – looking at her fixedly the while, and shook his head.

"This person," said Milly, in her clear, soft voice, which her mild eyes, looking at him, made clearer and softer, "I found soon afterwards. I went back to the house, and, with Heaven's help, traced him. I was not too soon. A very little and I should have been too late."

He took his hand from the boy, and laying it on the back of that hand of hers, whose timid and yet earnest touch addressed him no less appealingly than her voice and eyes, looked more intently on her.

"He *is* the father of Mr. Edmund, the young gentleman we saw just now. His real name is Longford. – You recollect the name?"

"I recollect the name."

"And the man?"

"No, not the man. Did he ever wrong me?"

"Yes!"

"Ah! Then it's hopeless – hopeless."

He shook his head, and softly beat upon the hand he held, as though mutely asking her commiseration.

"I did not go to Mr. Edmund last night," said Milly, – "You will listen to me just the same as if you did remember all?"

"To every syllable you say."

"Both, because I did not know, then, that this really was his father, and because I was fearful of the effect of such intelligence upon him, after his illness, if it should be. Since I have known who this person is, I have not gone either; but that is for another reason. He has long been separated from his wife and son – has been a stranger to his home almost from this son's infancy, I learn from him – and has abandoned and deserted what he should have held most dear. In all that time he has been falling from the state of a gentleman, more and more, until—" she rose up, hastily, and going out for a moment, returned, accompanied by the wreck that Redlaw had beheld last night.

"Do you know me?" asked the Chemist.

"I should be glad," returned the other, "and that is an unwonted word for me to use, if I could answer no."

The Chemist looked at the man, standing in self-abasement and degradation before him, and would have looked longer, in an ineffectual struggle for enlightenment, but that Milly resumed her late position by his side, and attracted his attentive gaze to her own face.

"See how low he is sunk, how lost he is!" she whispered, stretching out her arm towards him, without looking from the Chemist's face. "If you could remember all that is connected with him, do you not think it would move your pity to reflect that one you ever loved (do not let us mind how long ago, or in what belief that he has forfeited), should come to this?"

"I hope it would," he answered. "I believe it would."

His eyes wandered to the figure standing near the door, but came back speedily to her, on whom he gazed intently, as if he strove to learn some lesson from every tone of her voice, and every beam of her eyes.

"I have no learning, and you have much," said Milly; "I am not used to think, and you are always thinking. May I tell you why it seems to me a good thing for us, to remember wrong that has been done us?"

"Yes."

"That we may forgive it."

"Pardon me, great Heaven!" said Redlaw, lifting up his eyes, "for having thrown away thine own high attribute!"

"And if," said Milly, "if your memory should one day be restored, as we will hope and pray it may be, would it not be a blessing to you to recall at once a wrong and its forgiveness?"

He looked at the figure by the door, and fastened his attentive eyes on her again; a ray of clearer light appeared to him to shine into his mind, from her bright face.

"He cannot go to his abandoned home. He does not seek to go there. He knows that he could only carry shame and trouble to those he has so cruelly neglected; and that the best reparation he can make them now, is to avoid them. A very little money carefully bestowed, would remove him to some distant place, where he might live and do no wrong, and make such atonement as is left within his power for the wrong he has done. To the unfortunate lady who is his wife, and to his son, this would be the best and kindest boon that their best friend could give them – one too that they need never know of; and to him, shattered in reputation, mind, and body, it might be salvation."

He took her head between her hands, and kissed it, and said: "It shall be done. I trust to you to do it for me, now and secretly; and to tell him that I would forgive him, if I were so happy as to know for what."

As she rose, and turned her beaming face towards the fallen man, implying that her mediation had been successful, he advanced a step, and without raising his eyes, addressed himself to Redlaw.

"You are so generous," he said, "—you ever were – that you will try to banish your rising sense of retribution in the spectacle that is before you. I do not try to banish it from myself, Redlaw. If you can, believe me."

The Chemist entreated Milly, by a gesture, to come nearer to him; and, as he listened looked in her face, as if to find in it the clue to what he heard.

"I am too decayed a wretch to make professions; I recollect my own career too well, to array any such before you. But from the day on which I made my first step downward, in dealing falsely by you, I have gone down with a certain, steady, doomed progression. That, I say."

Redlaw, keeping her close at his side, turned his face towards the speaker, and there was sorrow in it. Something like mournful recognition too.

"I might have been another man, my life might have been another life, if I had avoided that first fatal step. I don't know that it would have been. I claim nothing for the possibility. Your sister is at rest, and better than she could have been with me, if I had continued even what you thought me: even what I once supposed myself to be."

Redlaw made a hasty motion with his hand, as if he would have put that subject on one side.

"I speak," the other went on, "like a man taken from the grave. I should have made my own grave, last night, had it not been for this blessed hand."

"Oh dear, he likes me too!" sobbed Milly, under her breath. "That's another!"

"I could not have put myself in your way, last night, even for bread. But, today, my recollection of what has been is so strongly stirred, and is presented to me, I don't know how, so vividly, that I have dared to come at her suggestion, and to take your bounty, and to thank you for it, and to beg you, Redlaw, in your dying hour, to be as merciful to me in your thoughts, as you are in your deeds."

He turned towards the door, and stopped a moment on his way forth.

"I hope my son may interest you, for his mother's sake. I hope he may deserve to do so. Unless my life should be preserved a long time, and I should know that I have not misused your aid, I shall never look upon him more."

Going out, he raised his eyes to Redlaw for the first time. Redlaw, whose steadfast gaze was fixed upon him, dreamily held out his hand. He returned and touched it – little more – with both his own; and bending down his head, went slowly out.

In the few moments that elapsed, while Milly silently took him to the gate, the Chemist dropped into his chair, and covered his face with his hands. Seeing him thus, when she came back, accompanied by her husband and his father (who were both greatly concerned for him), she avoided disturbing him, or permitting him to be disturbed; and kneeled down near the chair to put some warm clothing on the boy.

"That's exactly where it is. That's what I always say, father!" exclaimed her admiring husband. "There's a motherly feeling in Mrs. William's breast that must and will have went!"

"Ay, ay," said the old man; "you're right. My son William's right!"

"It happens all for the best, Milly dear, no doubt," said Mr. William, tenderly, "that we have no children of our own; and yet I sometimes wish you had one to love and cherish. Our little dead child that you built such hopes upon, and that never breathed the breath of life – it has made you quiet-like, Milly."

"I am very happy in the recollection of it, William dear," she answered. "I think of it every day."

"I was afraid you thought of it a good deal."

"Don't say, afraid; it is a comfort to me; it speaks to me in so many ways. The innocent thing that never lived on earth, is like an angel to me, William."

"You are like an angel to father and me," said Mr. William, softly. "I know that."

"When I think of all those hopes I built upon it, and the many times I sat and pictured to myself the little smiling face upon my bosom that never lay there, and the sweet eyes turned up to mine that never opened to the light," said Milly, "I can feel a greater tenderness, I think, for all the disappointed hopes in which there is no harm. When I see a beautiful child in its fond mother's arms, I love it all the better, thinking that my child might have been like that, and might have made my heart as proud and happy."

Redlaw raised his head, and looked towards her.

"All through life, it seems by me," she continued, "to tell me something. For poor neglected children, my little child pleads as if it were alive, and had a voice I knew, with which to speak to me. When I hear of youth in suffering or shame, I think that my child might have come to that, perhaps, and that God took it from me in His mercy. Even in age and grey hair, such as father's, it is present: saying that it too might have lived to be old, long and long after you and I were gone, and to have needed the respect and love of younger people."

Her quiet voice was quieter than ever, as she took her husband's arm, and laid her head against it.

"Children love me so, that sometimes I half fancy – it's a silly fancy, William – they have some way I don't know of, of feeling for my little child, and me, and understanding why their love is precious to me. If I have been quiet since, I have been more happy, William, in a hundred ways. Not least happy, dear, in this – that even when my little child was born and dead but a few days, and I was weak and sorrowful, and could not help grieving a little, the thought arose, that if I tried to lead a good life, I should meet in Heaven a bright creature, who would call me, Mother!"

Redlaw fell upon his knees, with a loud cry.

"O Thou," he said, "who through the teaching of pure love, hast graciously restored me to the memory which was the memory of Christ upon the Cross, and of all the good who perished in His cause, receive my thanks, and bless her!"

Then, he folded her to his heart; and Milly, sobbing more than ever, cried, as she laughed, "He is come back to himself! He likes me very much indeed, too! Oh, dear, dear, dear me, here's another!"

Then, the student entered, leading by the hand a lovely girl, who was afraid to come. And Redlaw so changed towards him, seeing in him and his youthful choice, the softened shadow of that chastening passage in his own life, to which, as to a shady tree, the dove so long imprisoned in his solitary ark might fly for rest and company, fell upon his neck, entreating them to be his children.

Then, as Christmas is a time in which, of all times in the year, the memory of every remediable sorrow, wrong, and trouble in the world around us, should be active with us, not less than our own experiences, for all good, he laid his hand upon the boy, and, silently calling Him to witness who laid His hand on children in old time, rebuking, in the majesty of His prophetic knowledge, those who kept them from Him, vowed to protect him, teach him, and reclaim him.

Then, he gave his right hand cheerily to Philip, and said that they would that day hold a Christmas dinner in what used to be, before the ten poor gentlemen commuted, their great Dinner Hall; and that they would bid to it as many of that Swidger family, who, his son had told him, were so numerous that they might join hands and make a ring round England, as could be brought together on so short a notice.

And it was that day done. There were so many Swidgers there, grown up and children, that an attempt to state them in round numbers might engender doubts, in the distrustful, of the veracity of this history. Therefore the attempt shall not be made. But there they were, by dozens and scores – and there was good news and good hope there, ready for them, of George, who had been visited again by his father and brother, and by Milly, and again left in a quiet sleep. There, present at the dinner, too, were the Tetterbys, including young Adolphus, who arrived in his prismatic comforter, in good time for the beef. Johnny and the baby were too late, of course, and came in all on one side, the one exhausted, the other in a supposed state of double-tooth; but that was customary, and not alarming.

It was sad to see the child who had no name or lineage, watching the other children as they played, not knowing how to talk with them, or sport with them, and more strange to the ways of childhood than a rough dog. It was sad, though in a different way, to see what an instinctive knowledge the youngest children there had of his being different from all the rest, and how they made timid approaches to him with soft words and touches, and with little presents, that he might not be unhappy. But he kept by Milly, and began to love her – that was another, as she said! – and, as they all liked her dearly, they were glad of that, and when they saw him peeping at them from behind her chair, they were pleased that he was so close to it.

All this, the Chemist, sitting with the student and his bride that was to be, Philip, and the rest, saw.

Some people have said since, that he only thought what has been herein set down; others, that he read it in the fire, one winter night about the twilight time; others, that the Ghost was but the representation of his gloomy thoughts, and Milly the embodiment of his better wisdom. *I* say nothing.

Except this. That as they were assembled in the old Hall, by no other light than that of a great fire (having dined early), the shadows once more stole out of their hiding-places, and danced about the room, showing the children marvellous shapes and faces on the walls, and gradually changing what was real and familiar there, to what was wild and magical. But that there was one thing in the Hall, to which the eyes of Redlaw, and of Milly and her husband, and of the old man, and of the student, and his bride that was to be, were often turned, which the shadows did not obscure or change. Deepened in its gravity by the fire-light, and gazing from the darkness of the panelled wall like life, the sedate face in the portrait, with the beard and ruff, looked down at them from under its verdant wreath of holly, as they looked up at it; and, clear and plain below, as if a voice had uttered them, were the words.

Lord keep my Memory green.

**If you enjoyed this, you might also like...**
The Baron of Grogzwig, see page 24
To Be Read at Dusk, see page 132

# To Be Read at Dusk

**ONE, TWO, THREE,** four, five. There were five of them.

Five couriers, sitting on a bench outside the convent on the summit of the Great St. Bernard in Switzerland, looking at the remote heights, stained by the setting sun as if a mighty quantity of red wine had been broached upon the mountain top, and had not yet had time to sink into the snow.

This is not my simile. It was made for the occasion by the stoutest courier, who was a German. None of the others took any more notice of it than they took of me, sitting on another bench on the other side of the convent door, smoking my cigar, like them, and – also like them – looking at the reddened snow, and at the lonely shed hard by, where the bodies of belated travellers, dug out of it, slowly wither away, knowing no corruption in that cold region.

The wine upon the mountain top soaked in as we looked; the mountain became white; the sky, a very dark blue; the wind rose; and the air turned piercing cold. The five couriers buttoned their rough coats. There being no safer man to imitate in all such proceedings than a courier, I buttoned mine.

The mountain in the sunset had stopped the five couriers in a conversation. It is a sublime sight, likely to stop conversation. The mountain being now out of the sunset, they resumed. Not that I had heard any part of their previous discourse; for indeed, I had not then broken away from the American gentleman, in the travellers' parlour of the convent, who, sitting with his face to the fire, had undertaken to realise to me the whole progress of events which had led to the accumulation by the Honourable Ananias Dodger of one of the largest acquisitions of dollars ever made in our country.

"My God!" said the Swiss courier, speaking in French, which I do not hold (as some authors appear to do) to be such an all-sufficient excuse for a naughty word, that I have only to write it in that language to make it innocent; "if you talk of ghosts—"

"But I *don't* talk of ghosts," said the German.

"Of what then?" asked the Swiss.

"If I knew of what then," said the German, "I should probably know a great deal more."

It was a good answer, I thought, and it made me curious. So, I moved my position to that corner of my bench which was nearest to them, and leaning my back against the convent wall, heard perfectly, without appearing to attend.

"Thunder and lightning!" said the German, warming, "when a certain man is coming to see you, unexpectedly; and, without his own knowledge, sends some invisible messenger, to put the idea of him into your head all day, what do you call that? When you walk along a crowded street – at Frankfort, Milan, London, Paris – and think that a passing stranger is like your friend Heinrich, and then that another passing stranger is like your friend Heinrich, and so begin to have a strange foreknowledge that presently you'll meet your friend Heinrich – which you do, though you believed him at Trieste – what do you call *that?*"

"It's not uncommon, either," murmured the Swiss and the other three.

"Uncommon!" said the German. "It's as common as cherries in the Black Forest. It's as common as maccaroni at Naples. And Naples reminds me! When the old Marchesa Senzanima shrieks at a card-party on the Chiaja – as I heard and saw her, for it happened in a Bavarian family of mine, and I was overlooking the service that evening – I say, when the old Marchesa starts up at the card-table, white through her rouge, and cries, "My sister in Spain is dead! I felt her cold touch on my back!" – and when that sister *is* dead at the moment – what do you call that?"

"Or when the blood of San Gennaro liquefies at the request of the clergy – as all the world knows that it does regularly once a-year, in my native city," said the Neapolitan courier after a pause, with a comical look, "what do you call that?"

"*That!*" cried the German. "Well, I think I know a name for that."

"Miracle?" said the Neapolitan, with the same sly face.

The German merely smoked and laughed; and they all smoked and laughed.

"Bah!" said the German, presently. "I speak of things that really do happen. When I want to see the conjurer, I pay to see a professed one, and have my money's worth. Very strange things do happen without ghosts. Ghosts! Giovanni Baptista, tell your story of the English bride. There's no ghost in that, but something full as strange. Will any man tell me what?"

As there was a silence among them, I glanced around. He whom I took to be Baptista was lighting a fresh cigar. He presently went on to speak. He was a Genoese, as I judged.

"The story of the English bride?" said he. "Basta! one ought not to call so slight a thing a story. Well, it's all one. But it's true. Observe me well, gentlemen, it's true. That which glitters is not always gold; but what I am going to tell, is true."

He repeated this more than once.

Ten years ago, I took my credentials to an English gentleman at Long's Hotel, in Bond Street, London, who was about to travel – it might be for one year, it might be for two. He approved of them; likewise of me. He was pleased to make inquiry. The testimony that he received was favourable. He engaged me by the six months, and my entertainment was generous.

He was young, handsome, very happy. He was enamoured of a fair young English lady, with a sufficient fortune, and they were going to be married. It was the wedding-trip, in short, that we were going to take. For three months' rest in the hot weather (it was early summer then) he had hired an old place on the Riviera, at an easy distance from my city, Genoa, on the road to Nice. Did I know that place? Yes; I told him I knew it well. It was an old palace with great gardens. It was a little bare, and it was a little dark and gloomy, being close surrounded by trees; but it was spacious, ancient, grand, and on the seashore. He said it had been so described to him exactly, and he was well pleased that I knew it. For its being a little bare of furniture, all such places were. For its being a little gloomy, he had hired it principally for the gardens, and he and my mistress would pass the summer weather in their shade.

"So all goes well, Baptista?" said he.

"Indubitably, signore; very well."

We had a travelling chariot for our journey, newly built for us, and in all respects complete. All we had was complete; we wanted for nothing. The marriage took place. They were happy. I was happy, seeing all so bright, being so well situated, going to my own city, teaching my language in the rumble to the maid, la bella Carolina, whose heart was gay with laughter: who was young and rosy.

The time flew. But I observed – listen to this, I pray! (and here the courier dropped his voice) – I observed my mistress sometimes brooding in a manner very strange; in a frightened manner; in an unhappy manner; with a cloudy, uncertain alarm upon her. I think that I began to notice this when I was walking up hills by the carriage side, and master had gone on in front. At any rate, I remember that it impressed itself upon my mind one evening in the South of France, when she called to me to call master back; and when he came back, and walked for a long way, talking encouragingly and affectionately to her, with his hand upon the open window, and hers in it. Now and then, he laughed in a merry way, as if he were bantering her out of something. By-and-by, she laughed, and then all went well again.

It was curious. I asked la bella Carolina, the pretty little one, Was mistress unwell? – No. – Out of spirits? – No. – Fearful of bad roads, or brigands? – No. And what made it more mysterious was, the pretty little one would not look at me in giving answer, but *would* look at the view.

But, one day she told me the secret.

"If you must know," said Carolina, "I find, from what I have overheard, that mistress is haunted."

"How haunted?"

"By a dream."

"What dream?"

"By a dream of a face. For three nights before her marriage, she saw a face in a dream – always the same face, and only One."

"A terrible face?"

"No. The face of a dark, remarkable-looking man, in black, with black hair and a grey moustache – a handsome man except for a reserved and secret air. Not a face she ever saw, or at all like a face she ever saw. Doing nothing in the dream but looking at her fixedly, out of darkness."

"Does the dream come back?"

"Never. The recollection of it is all her trouble."

"And why does it trouble her?"

Carolina shook her head.

"That's master's question," said la bella. "She don't know. She wonders why, herself. But I heard her tell him, only last night, that if she was to find a picture of that face in our Italian house (which she is afraid she will) she did not know how she could ever bear it."

Upon my word I was fearful after this (said the Genoese courier) of our coming to the old palazzo, lest some such ill-starred picture should happen to be there. I knew there were many there; and, as we got nearer and nearer to the place, I wished the whole gallery in the crater of Vesuvius. To mend the matter, it was a stormy dismal evening when we, at last, approached that part of the Riviera. It thundered; and the thunder of my city and its environs, rolling among the high hills, is very loud. The lizards ran in and out of the chinks in the broken stone wall of the garden, as if they were frightened; the frogs bubbled and croaked their loudest; the sea-wind moaned, and the wet trees dripped; and the lightning – body of San Lorenzo, how it lightened!

We all know what an old palace in or near Genoa is – how time and the sea air have blotted it – how the drapery painted on the outer walls has peeled off in great flakes of plaster – how the lower windows are darkened with rusty bars of iron – how the courtyard is overgrown with grass – how the outer buildings are dilapidated – how the whole pile seems devoted to ruin. Our palazzo was one of the true kind. It had been shut up close for months. Months? – years! – it had an earthy smell, like a tomb. The scent of the orange trees on the broad back terrace, and of the lemons ripening on the wall, and of some shrubs that grew around a broken fountain, had got into the house somehow, and had never been able to get out again. There was, in every room, an aged smell, grown faint with confinement. It pined in all the cupboards and drawers. In the little rooms of communication between great rooms, it was stifling. If you turned a picture – to come back to the pictures – there it still was, clinging to the wall behind the frame, like a sort of bat.

The lattice-blinds were close shut, all over the house. There were two ugly, grey old women in the house, to take care of it; one of them with a spindle, who stood winding and mumbling in the doorway, and who would as soon have let in the devil as the air. Master, mistress, la bella Carolina, and I, went all through the palazzo. I went first, though I have named myself last, opening the windows and the lattice-blinds, and shaking down on myself splashes of rain, and scraps of mortar, and now and then a dozing mosquito, or a monstrous, fat, blotchy, Genoese spider.

When I had let the evening light into a room, master, mistress, and la bella Carolina, entered. Then, we looked round at all the pictures, and I went forward again into another room. Mistress secretly had great fear of meeting with the likeness of that face – we all had; but there was no such thing. The Madonna and Bambino, San Francisco, San Sebastiano, Venus, Santa Caterina, Angels, Brigands, Friars, Temples at Sunset, Battles, White Horses, Forests, Apostles, Doges, all my old acquaintances many times repeated? – yes. Dark, handsome man in black, reserved and secret, with black hair and grey moustache, looking fixedly at mistress out of darkness? – no.

At last we got through all the rooms and all the pictures, and came out into the gardens. They were pretty well kept, being rented by a gardener, and were large and shady. In one place there was a rustic theatre, open to the sky; the stage a green slope; the coulisses, three entrances upon a side, sweet-smelling leafy screens. Mistress moved her bright eyes, even there, as if she looked to see the face come in upon the scene; but all was well.

"Now, Clara," master said, in a low voice, "you see that it is nothing? You are happy."

Mistress was much encouraged. She soon accustomed herself to that grim palazzo, and would sing, and play the harp, and copy the old pictures, and stroll with master under the green trees and vines all day. She was beautiful. He was happy. He would laugh and say to me, mounting his horse for his morning ride before the heat:

"All goes well, Baptista!"

"Yes, signore, thank God, very well."

We kept no company. I took la bella to the Duomo and Annunciata, to the Café, to the Opera, to the village Festa, to the Public Garden, to the Day Theatre, to the Marionetti. The pretty little one was charmed with all she saw. She learnt Italian – heavens! miraculously! Was mistress quite forgetful of that dream? I asked Carolina sometimes. Nearly, said la bella – almost. It was wearing out.

One day master received a letter, and called me.

"Baptista!"

"Signore!"

"A gentleman who is presented to me will dine here today. He is called the Signor Dellombra. Let me dine like a prince."

It was an odd name. I did not know that name. But, there had been many noblemen and gentlemen pursued by Austria on political suspicions, lately, and some names had changed. Perhaps this was one. Altro! Dellombra was as good a name to me as another.

When the Signor Dellombra came to dinner (said the Genoese courier in the low voice, into which he had subsided once before), I showed him into the reception-room, the great sala of the old palazzo. Master received him with cordiality, and presented him to mistress. As she rose, her face changed, she gave a cry, and fell upon the marble floor.

Then, I turned my head to the Signor Dellombra, and saw that he was dressed in black, and had a reserved and secret air, and was a dark, remarkable-looking man, with black hair and a grey moustache.

Master raised mistress in his arms, and carried her to her own room, where I sent la bella Carolina straight. La bella told me afterwards that mistress was nearly terrified to death, and that she wandered in her mind about her dream, all night.

Master was vexed and anxious – almost angry, and yet full of solicitude. The Signor Dellombra was a courtly gentleman, and spoke with great respect and sympathy of mistress's being so ill. The African wind had been blowing for some days (they had told him at his hotel of the Maltese Cross), and he knew that it was often hurtful. He hoped the beautiful lady would recover soon. He begged permission to retire, and to renew his visit when he should have the happiness of hearing that she was better. Master would not allow of this, and they dined alone.

He withdrew early. Next day he called at the gate, on horseback, to inquire for mistress. He did so two or three times in that week.

What I observed myself, and what la bella Carolina told me, united to explain to me that master had now set his mind on curing mistress of her fanciful terror. He was all kindness, but he was sensible and firm. He reasoned with her, that to encourage such fancies was to invite melancholy, if not madness. That it rested with herself to be herself. That if she once resisted her strange weakness, so successfully as to receive the Signor Dellombra as an English lady would receive any other guest, it was for ever conquered. To make an end, the signore came again, and mistress received him without marked distress (though with constraint and apprehension still), and the evening passed serenely. Master was so delighted with this change, and so anxious to confirm it, that the Signor Dellombra became a constant guest. He was accomplished in pictures, books, and music; and his society, in any grim palazzo, would have been welcome.

I used to notice, many times, that mistress was not quite recovered. She would cast down her eyes and droop her head, before the Signor Dellombra, or would look at him with a terrified and fascinated glance, as if his presence had some evil influence or power upon her. Turning from her to him, I used to see him in the shaded gardens, or the large half-lighted sala, looking, as I might say, 'fixedly upon her out of darkness.' But, truly, I had not forgotten la bella Carolina's words describing the face in the dream.

After his second visit I heard master say:

"Now, see, my dear Clara, it's over! Dellombra has come and gone, and your apprehension is broken like glass."

"Will he – will he ever come again?" asked mistress.

"Again? Why, surely, over and over again! Are you cold?" (she shivered).

"No, dear – but – he terrifies me: are you sure that he need come again?"

"The surer for the question, Clara!" replied master, cheerfully.

But, he was very hopeful of her complete recovery now, and grew more and more so every day. She was beautiful. He was happy.

"All goes well, Baptista?" he would say to me again.

"Yes, signore, thank God; very well."

We were all (said the Genoese courier, constraining himself to speak a little louder), we were all at Rome for the Carnival. I had been out, all day, with a Sicilian, a friend of mine, and a courier, who was there with an English family. As I returned at night to our hotel, I met the little Carolina, who never stirred from home alone, running distractedly along the Corso.

"Carolina! What's the matter?"

"O Baptista! O, for the Lord's sake! where is my mistress?"

"Mistress, Carolina?"

"Gone since morning – told me, when master went out on his day's journey, not to call her, for she was tired with not resting in the night (having been in pain), and would lie in bed until the evening; then get up refreshed. She is gone! – she is gone! Master has come back, broken down the door, and she is gone! My beautiful, my good, my innocent mistress!"

The pretty little one so cried, and raved, and tore herself that I could not have held her, but for her swooning on my arm as if she had been shot. Master came up – in manner, face, or voice, no more the master that I knew, than I was he. He took me (I laid the little one upon her bed in the hotel, and left her with the chamber-women), in a carriage, furiously through the darkness, across the desolate Campagna. When it was day, and we stopped at a miserable post-house, all the horses had been hired twelve hours ago, and sent away in different directions. Mark me! by the Signor Dellombra, who had passed there in a carriage, with a frightened English lady crouching in one corner.

I never heard (said the Genoese courier, drawing a long breath) that she was ever traced beyond that spot. All I know is, that she vanished into infamous oblivion, with the dreaded face beside her that she had seen in her dream.

"What do you call *that?*" said the German courier, triumphantly. "Ghosts! There are no ghosts *there!* What do you call this, that I am going to tell you? Ghosts! There are no ghosts *here!*"

*I* took an engagement once (pursued the German courier) with an English gentleman, elderly and a bachelor, to travel through my country, my Fatherland. He was a merchant who traded with my country and knew the language, but who had never been there since he was a boy – as I judge, some sixty years before.

His name was James, and he had a twin-brother John, also a bachelor. Between these brothers there was a great affection. They were in business together, at Goodman's Fields, but they did not live together. Mr. James dwelt in Poland Street, turning out of Oxford Street, London; Mr. John resided by Epping Forest.

Mr. James and I were to start for Germany in about a week. The exact day depended on business. Mr. John came to Poland Street (where I was staying in the house), to pass that week with Mr. James. But, he said to his brother on the second day, "I don't feel very well, James. There's not much the matter with me; but I think I am a little gouty. I'll go home and put myself under the care of my old housekeeper, who understands my ways. If I get quite better, I'll come back and see you before you go. If I don't feel well enough to resume my visit where I leave it off, why *you* will come and see me before you go." Mr.

James, of course, said he would, and they shook hands – both hands, as they always did – and Mr. John ordered out his old-fashioned chariot and rumbled home.

It was on the second night after that – that is to say, the fourth in the week – when I was awoke out of my sound sleep by Mr. James coming into my bedroom in his flannel-gown, with a lighted candle. He sat upon the side of my bed, and looking at me, said:

"Wilhelm, I have reason to think I have got some strange illness upon me."

I then perceived that there was a very unusual expression in his face.

"Wilhelm," said he, "I am not afraid or ashamed to tell you what I might be afraid or ashamed to tell another man. You come from a sensible country, where mysterious things are inquired into and are not settled to have been weighed and measured – or to have been unweighable and unmeasurable – or in either case to have been completely disposed of, for all time – ever so many years ago. I have just now seen the phantom of my brother."

I confess (said the German courier) that it gave me a little tingling of the blood to hear it.

"I have just now seen," Mr. James repeated, looking full at me, that I might see how collected he was, "the phantom of my brother John. I was sitting up in bed, unable to sleep, when it came into my room, in a white dress, and regarding me earnestly, passed up to the end of the room, glanced at some papers on my writing-desk, turned, and, still looking earnestly at me as it passed the bed, went out at the door. Now, I am not in the least mad, and am not in the least disposed to invest that phantom with any external existence out of myself. I think it is a warning to me that I am ill; and I think I had better be bled."

I got out of bed directly (said the German courier) and began to get on my clothes, begging him not to be alarmed, and telling him that I would go myself to the doctor. I was just ready, when we heard a loud knocking and ringing at the street door. My room being an attic at the back, and Mr. James's being the second-floor room in the front, we went down to his room, and put up the window, to see what was the matter.

"Is that Mr. James?" said a man below, falling back to the opposite side of the way to look up.

"It is," said Mr. James, "and you are my brother's man, Robert."

"Yes, Sir. I am sorry to say, Sir, that Mr. John is ill. He is very bad, Sir. It is even feared that he may be lying at the point of death. He wants to see you, Sir. I have a chaise here. Pray come to him. Pray lose no time."

Mr. James and I looked at one another. "Wilhelm," said he, "this is strange. I wish you to come with me!" I helped him to dress, partly there and partly in the chaise; and no grass grew under the horses' iron shoes between Poland Street and the Forest.

Now, mind! (said the German courier) I went with Mr. James into his brother's room, and I saw and heard myself what follows.

His brother lay upon his bed, at the upper end of a long bed-chamber. His old housekeeper was there, and others were there: I think three others were there, if not four, and they had been with him since early in the afternoon. He was in white, like the figure – necessarily so, because he had his night-dress on. He looked like the figure – necessarily so, because he looked earnestly at his brother when he saw him come into the room.

But, when his brother reached the bed-side, he slowly raised himself in bed, and looking full upon him, said these words:

"James, you have seen me before, to-night – and you know it!"

And so died!

I waited, when the German courier ceased, to hear something said of this strange story. The silence was unbroken. I looked round, and the five couriers were gone: so noiselessly that the ghostly mountain might have absorbed them into its eternal snows. By this time, I was by no means in a mood to sit alone in that awful scene, with the chill air coming solemnly upon me – or, if I may tell the truth, to sit alone anywhere. So I went back into the convent-parlour, and, finding the American gentleman still disposed to relate the biography of the Honourable Ananias Dodger, heard it all out.

**If you enjoyed this, you might also like...**

The Ghosts of the Mail, see page 11

The Signal-Man, see page 258

# A Christmas Tree

**I HAVE BEEN** looking on, this evening, at a merry company of children assembled round that pretty German toy, a Christmas Tree. The tree was planted in the middle of a great round table, and towered high above their heads. It was brilliantly lighted by a multitude of little tapers; and everywhere sparkled and glittered with bright objects. There were rosy-cheeked dolls, hiding behind the green leaves; there were real watches (with movable hands, at least, and an endless capacity of being wound up) dangling from innumerable twigs; there were French-polished tables, chairs, bedsteads, wardrobes, eight-day clocks, and various other articles of domestic furniture (wonderfully made, in tin, at Wolverhampton), perched among the boughs, as if in preparation for some fairy housekeeping; there were jolly, broad-faced little men, much more agreeable in appearance than many real men – and no wonder, for their heads took off, and showed them to be full of sugar-plums; there were fiddles and drums; there were tambourines, books, work-boxes, paint-boxes, sweetmeat-boxes, peep-show boxes, all kinds of boxes; there were trinkets for the elder girls, far brighter than any grown-up gold and jewels; there were baskets and pincushions in all devices; there were guns, swords, and banners; there were witches standing in enchanted rings of pasteboard, to tell fortunes; there were teetotums, humming-tops, needle-cases, pen-wipers, smelling-bottles, conversation cards, bouquet-holders; real fruit, made artificially dazzling with gold leaf; imitation apples, pears, and walnuts, crammed with surprises; in short, as a pretty child, before me, delightedly whispered to another pretty child, her bosom friend, "There was everything, and more." This motley collection of odd objects, clustering on the tree like magic fruit, and flashing back the bright looks directed towards it from every side – some of the diamond-eyes admiring it were hardly on a level with the table, and a few were languishing in timid wonder on the bosoms of pretty mothers, aunts, and nurses – made a lively realisation of the fancies of childhood; and set me thinking how all the trees that grow and all the things that come into existence on the earth, have their wild adornments at that well-remembered time.

Being now at home again, and alone, the only person in the house awake, my thoughts are drawn back, by a fascination which I do not care to resist, to my own childhood. I begin to consider, what do we all remember best upon the branches of the Christmas Tree of our own young Christmas days, by which we climbed to real life.

Straight, in the middle of the room, cramped in the freedom of its growth by no encircling walls or soon-reached ceiling, a shadowy tree arises; and, looking up into the dreamy brightness of its top – for I observe, in this tree, the singular property that it appears to grow downward towards the earth – I look into my youngest Christmas recollections!

All toys at first, I find. Up yonder, among the green holly and red berries, is the Tumbler with his hands in his pockets, who wouldn't lie down, but whenever he was put upon the floor, persisted in rolling his fat body about, until he rolled himself still, and brought those lobster eyes of his to bear upon me – when I affected to laugh very much, but in my heart of hearts was extremely doubtful of him. Close beside him is that infernal snuff-box, out of which there sprang a demoniacal Counsellor in a black gown, with an obnoxious head of hair, and a red cloth mouth, wide open, who was not to be endured on any terms, but could not be put away either; for he used suddenly, in a highly magnified state, to fly out of Mammoth Snuff-boxes in dreams, when least expected. Nor is the frog with cobbler's wax on his tail, far off; for there was no knowing where he wouldn't jump; and when he flew over the candle, and came upon one's hand with that spotted back – red on a green ground – he was horrible. The cardboard lady in a blue-silk skirt, who was stood up against the candlestick to dance, and whom I see on the same branch, was milder, and was beautiful; but I can't say as much for the larger cardboard man, who used to be hung against the wall and pulled by a string; there was a sinister expression in that nose of his; and when he got his legs round his neck (which he very often did), he was ghastly, and not a creature to be alone with.

When did that dreadful Mask first look at me? Who put it on, and why was I so frightened that the sight of it is an era in my life? It is not a hideous visage in itself; it is even meant to be droll; why then were its stolid features so intolerable? Surely not because it hid the wearer's face. An apron would have done as much; and though I should have preferred even the apron away, it would not have been absolutely insupportable, like the mask? Was it the immovability of the mask? The doll's face was immovable, but I was not afraid of *her*. Perhaps that fixed and set change coming over a real face, infused into my quickened heart some remote suggestion and dread of the universal change that is to come on every face, and make it still? Nothing reconciled me to it. No drummers, from whom proceeded a melancholy chirping on the turning of a handle; no regiment of soldiers, with a mute band, taken out of a box, and fitted, one by one, upon a stiff and lazy little set of lazy-tongs; no old woman, made of wires and a brown-paper composition, cutting up a pie for two small children; could give me permanent comfort, for a long time. Nor was it any satisfaction to be shown the Mask, and see that it was made of paper, or to have it locked up and be assured that no one wore it. The mere recollection of that fixed face, the mere knowledge of its existence anywhere, was sufficient to awake me in the night all perspiration and horror, with "O I know it's coming! O the mask!"

I never wondered what the dear old donkey with the panniers – there he is! – was made of, then! His hide was real to the touch, I recollect. And the great black horse with round red spots all over him – the horse that I could even get upon – I never wondered what had brought him to that strange condition, or thought that such a horse was not commonly seen at Newmarket. The four horses of no colour, next to him, that went into the waggon of cheeses, and could be taken out and stabled under the piano, appear to have bits of fur- tippet for their tails, and other bits for their manes, and to stand on pegs instead of legs, but it was not so when they were brought home for a Christmas present. They were all right, then; neither was their harness unceremoniously nailed into their chests, as appears to be the case now. The tinkling works of the music-cart, I *did* find out, to be made of quill tooth-picks and wire; and I always thought that little tumbler in his shirt sleeves, perpetually swarming up one side of a wooden frame, and coming down, head foremost, on the other, rather a weak-minded person – though good-natured; but the Jacob's Ladder, next him, made of little squares of red wood, that went flapping and clattering over one another, each developing a different picture, and the whole enlivened by small bells, was a mighty marvel and a great delight.

Ah! The Doll's house! – of which I was not proprietor, but where I visited. I don't admire the Houses of Parliament half so much as that stone-fronted mansion with real glass windows, and door-steps, and a real balcony – greener than I ever see now, except at watering-places; and even they afford but a pooi- imitation. And though it *did* open all at once, the entire house-front (which was a blow, I admit, as cancelling the fiction of a staircase), it was but to shut it up again, and I could believe. Even open, there were three distinct rooms in it: a sitting-room and bedroom, elegantly furnished, and, best of all, a kitchen, with uncommonly soft fire-irons, a plentiful assortment of diminutive utensils – oh, the warming-pan! – and a tin man-cook in profile, who was always going to fry two fish. What Barmecide justice have I done to the noble feasts wherein the set of wooden platters figured, each with its own peculiar delicacy, as a ham or turkey, glued tight on to it, and garnished with something green, which I recollect as moss! Could all the Temperance Societies of these later days, united, give me such a tea-drinking as I have had through the means of yonder little set of blue crockery, which really would hold liquid (it ran out of the small wooden cask, I recollect, and tasted of matches), and which made tea, nectar. And if the two legs of the ineffectual little sugar- tongs did tumble over one another, and want purpose, like Punch's hands, what does it matter? And if I did once shriek out, as a poisoned child, and strike the fashionable company with consternation, by reason of having drunk a little teaspoon, inadvertently dissolved in too hot tea, I was never the worse for it, except by a powder!

Upon the next branches of the tree, lower down, hard by the green roller and miniature gardening-tools, how thick the books begin to hang. Thin books, in themselves, at first, but many of them, and with deliciously smooth covers of bright red or green. What fat black letters to begin with! "A was an archer, and shot at a frog." Of course he was. He was an apple-pie also, and there he is! He was a good many things in his time, was A, and so were most of his friends, except X, who had so little versatility, that I never knew him to get beyond Xerxes or Xantippe – like Y, who was always confined to a Yacht or a Yew Tree; and Z condemned for ever to be a Zebra or a Zany. But, now, the very tree itself changes, and becomes a bean-stalk – the marvellous bean-stalk up which Jack climbed to the Giant's house! And now, those dreadfully interesting, double- headed giants, with their clubs over their shoulders, begin to stride along the boughs in a perfect throng, dragging knights and ladies home for dinner by the hair of their heads. And Jack – how noble, with his sword of sharpness, and his shoes of swiftness! Again those old meditations come upon me as I gaze up at him; and I debate within myself whether there was more than one Jack (which I am loth to believe possible), or only one genuine original admirable Jack, who achieved all the recorded exploits.

Good for Christmas time is the ruddy color of the cloak, in which – the tree making a forest of itself for her to trip through, with her basket – Little Red Riding-Hood comes to me one Christmas Eve, to give me information of the cruelty and treachery of that dissembling Wolf who ate her grandmother, without making any impression on his appetite, and then ate her, after making that ferocious joke about his teeth. She was my first love. I felt that if I could have married Little Red Riding-Hood, I should have known perfect bliss. But, it was not to be; and there was nothing for it but to look out the Wolf in the Noah's Ark there, and put him late in the procession on the table, as a monster who was to be degraded. O the wonderful Noah's Ark! It was not found seaworthy when put in a washing-tub, and the animals were crammed in at the roof, and needed to have their legs well shaken down before they could be got in, even there – and then, ten to one but they began to tumble out at the door, which was but imperfectly fastened with a wire latch – but what was *that* against it! Consider the noble fly, a size or two smaller than the elephant: the lady-bird, the butterfly – all triumphs of art! Consider the goose, whose feet were so small, and whose balance was so indifferent, that he usually tumbled forward, and knocked down all the animal creation. Consider Noah and his family, like idiotic tobacco-stoppers; and how the leopard stuck to warm little fingers; and how the tails of the larger animals used gradually to resolve themselves into frayed bits of string!

Hush! Again a forest, and somebody up in a tree – not Robin Hood, not Valentine, not the Yellow Dwarf (I have passed him and all Mother Bunch's wonders, without mention), but an Eastern King with a glittering scimitar and turban. By Allah! two Eastern Kings, for I see another, looking over his shoulder! Down upon the grass, at the tree's foot, lies the full length of a coal-black Giant, stretched asleep, with his head in a lady's lap; and near them is a glass box, fastened with four locks of shining steel, in which he keeps the lady prisoner when he is awake. I see the four keys at his girdle now. The lady makes signs to the two kings in the tree, who softly descend. It is the setting-in of the bright Arabian Nights.

Oh, now all common things become uncommon and enchanted to me! All lamps are wonderful; all rings are talismans. Common flower-pots are full of treasure, with a little earth scattered on the top; trees are for Ali Baba to hide in; beef-steaks are to throw down into the Valley of Diamonds, that the precious stones may stick to them, and be carried by the eagles to their nests, whence the traders, with loud cries, will scare them. Tarts are made, according to the recipe of the Vizier's son of Bussorah, who turned pastrycook after he was set down in his drawers at the gate of Damascus; cobblers are all Mustaphas, and in the habit of sewing up people cut into four pieces, to whom they are taken blindfold. Any iron ring let into stone is the entrance to a cave, which only waits for the magician, and the little fire, and the necromancy, that will make the earth shake. All the dates imported come from the same tree as that unlucky date, with whose shell the merchant knocked out the eye of the genie's invisible son. All olives are of the stock of that fresh fruit, concerning which the Commander of the Faithful overheard the boy conduct the fictitious trial of the fraudulent olive merchant; all apples are akin to the apple purchased (with two others) from the Sultan's gardener, for three sequins, and which the tall black slave stole from the child. All dogs are associated with the dog, really a transformed man, who jumped upon the baker's counter, and put his paw on the piece of bad money. All rice recalls the rice which the awful lady, who was a ghoule, could only peck by grains, because of her nightly feasts in the burial-place. My very rocking- horse, – there he is, with his nostrils turned completely inside-out, indicative of Blood! – should have a peg in his neck, by virtue thereof to fly away with me, as the wooden horse did with the Prince of Persia, in the sight of all his father's Court.

Yes, on every object that I recognise among those upper branches of my Christmas Tree, I see this fairy light! When I wake in bed, at daybreak, on the cold dark winter mornings, the white snow dimly beheld, outside, through the frost on the window-pane, I hear Dinarzade. "Sister, sister, if you are yet awake, I pray you finish the history of the Young King of the Black Islands." Scheherazade replies, "If my lord the Sultan will suffer me to live another day, sister, I will not only finish that, but tell you a more wonderful story yet." Then, the gracious Sultan goes out, giving no orders for the execution, and we all three breathe again.

At this height of my tree I begin to see, cowering among the leaves – it may be born of turkey, or of pudding, or mince pie, or of these many fancies, jumbled with Robinson Crusoe on his desert island, Philip Quarll among the monkeys, Sandford and Merton with Mr. Barlow, Mother Bunch, and the Mask – or it may be the result of indigestion, assisted by imagination and over-doctoring – a prodigious nightmare. It is so exceedingly indistinct, that I don't know why it's frightful but I know it is. I can only make out that it is an immense array of shapeless things, which appear to be planted on a vast exaggeration of the lazy- tongs that used to bear the toy soldiers, and to be slowly coming close to my eyes, and receding to an immeasurable distance. When it comes closest, it is worst. In connection with it, I descry remembrances of winter nights incredibly long; of being sent early to bed, as a punishment for some small offence, and waking in two hours, with a sensation of having been asleep two nights; of the leaden hopelessness of morning ever dawning; and the oppression of a weight of remorse.

And now, I see a wonderful row of little lights rise smoothly out of the ground, before a vast green curtain. Now, a bell rings – a magic bell, which still sounds in my ears unlike all other bells – and music plays, amidst a buzz of voices, and a fragrant smell of orange-peel and oil. Anon, the magic bell commands the music to cease, and the great green curtain rolls itself up majestically, and The Play begins! The devoted dog of Montargis avenges the death of his master, foully murdered in the Forest of Bondy; and a humorous Peasant with a red nose and a very little hat, whom I take from this hour forth to my bosom as a friend (I think he was a Waiter or an Hostler at a village Inn, but many years have passed since he and I have met), remarks that the sassigassity of that dog is indeed surprising; and evermore this jocular conceit will live in my remembrance fresh and unfading, overtopping all possible jokes, unto the end of time. Or now, I learn with bitter tears how poor Jane Shore, dressed all in white, and with her brown hair hanging down, went starving through the streets; or how George Barnwell killed the worthiest uncle that ever man had, and was afterwards so sorry for it that he ought to have been let off. Comes swift to comfort me, the Pantomime – stupendous Phenomenon! – when Clowns are shot from loaded mortars into the great chandelier, bright constellation that it is; when Harlequins, covered all over with scales of pure gold, twist and sparkle, like amazing fish; when Pantaloon (whom I deem it no irreverence to compare in my own mind to my grandfather) puts red-hot pokers in his pocket, and cries "Here's somebody coming!" or taxes the Clown with petty larceny, by saying "Now, I sawed you do it!" when Everything is capable, with the greatest ease, of being changed into Anything; and "Nothing is, but thinking makes it so." Now, too, I perceive my first experience of the dreary sensation – often to return in after-life – of being unable, next day, to get back to the dull, settled world; of wanting to live for ever in the bright atmosphere I have quitted; of doting on the little Fairy, with the wand like a celestial Barber's Pole, and pining for a Fairy immortality along with her. Ah she comes back, in many shapes, as my eye wanders down the branches of my Christmas Tree, and goes as often, and has never yet stayed by me!

Out of this delight springs the toy-theatre, – there it is, with its familiar proscenium, and ladies in feathers, in the boxes! – and all its attendant occupation with paste and glue, and gum, and water colors, in the getting-up of The Miller and his Men, and Elizabeth, or the Exile of Siberia. In spite of a few besetting accidents and failures (particularly an unreasonable disposition in the respectable Kelmar, and some others, to become faint in the legs, and double up, at exciting points of the drama), a teeming world of fancies so suggestive and all-embracing, that, far below it on my Christmas Tree, I see dark, dirty, real Theatres in the day-time, adorned with these associations as with the freshest garlands of the rarest flowers, and charming me yet.

But hark! The Waits are playing, and they break my childish sleep! What images do I associate with the Christmas music as I see them set forth on the Christmas Tree? Known before all the others, keeping far apart from all the others, they gather round my little bed. An angel, speaking to a group of shepherds in a field; some travellers, with eyes uplifted, following a star; a baby in a manger; a child in a spacious temple, talking with grave men; a solemn figure, with a mild and beautiful face, raising a dead girl by the hand; again, near a city-gate, calling back the son of a widow, on his bier, to life; a crowd of people looking through the opened roof of a chamber where he sits, and letting down a sick person on a bed, with ropes; the same, in a tempest, walking on the water to a ship; again, on a sea-shore, teaching a great multitude; again, with a child upon his knee, and other children round; again, restoring sight to the blind, speech to the dumb, hearing to the deaf, health to the sick, strength to the lame, knowledge to the ignorant; again, dying upon a Cross, watched by armed soldiers, a thick darkness coming on, the earth beginning to shake, and only one voice heard. "Forgive them, for they know not what they do!"

Still, on the lower and maturer branches of the Tree, Christmas associations cluster thick. School-books shut up; Ovid and Virgil silenced; the Rule of Three, with its cool impertinent enquiries, long disposed of; Terence and Plautus acted no more, in an arena of huddled desks and forms, all chipped, and notched, and inked; cricket-bats, stumps, and balls, left higher up, with the smell of trodden grass and the softened noise of shouts in the evening air; the tree is still fresh, still gay. If I no more come home at Christmas time, there will be girls and boys (thank Heaven!) while the World lasts; and they do! Yonder they dance and play upon the branches of my Tree, God bless them, merrily, and my heart dances and plays too!

And I *do* come home at Christmas. We all do, or we all should. We all come home, or ought to come home, for a short holiday – the longer, the better – from the great boarding-school, where we are for ever working at our arithmetical slates, to take, and give a rest. As to going a visiting, where can we not go, if we will; where have we not been, when we would; starting our fancy from our Christmas Tree!

Away into the winter prospect. There are many such upon the tree! On, by low-lying misty grounds, through fens and fogs, up long hills, winding dark as caverns between thick plantations, almost shutting out the sparkling stars; so, out on broad heights, until we stop at last, with sudden silence, at an avenue. The gate-bell has a deep, half-awful sound in the frosty air; the gate swings open on its hinges; and, as we drive up to a great house, the glancing lights grow larger in the windows, and the opposing rows of trees seem to fall solemnly back on either side, to give us place. At intervals, all day, a frightened hare has shot across this whitened turf; or the distant clatter of a herd of deer trampling the hard frost, has, for the minute, crushed the silence too. Their watchful eyes beneath the fern may be shining now, if we could see them, like the icy dewdrops on the leaves; but they are still, and all is still. And so, the lights growing larger, and the trees falling back before us, and closing up again behind us, as if to forbid retreat, we come to the house.

There is probably a smell of roasted chestnuts and other good comfortable things all the time, for we are telling Winter Stories – Ghost Stories, or more shame for us – round the Christmas fire; and we have never stirred, except to draw a little nearer to it. But, no matter for that. We came to the house, and it is an old house, full of great chimneys where wood is burnt on ancient dogs upon the hearth, and grim Portraits (some of them with grim Legends, too) lower distrustfully from the oaken panels of the walls. We are a middle- aged nobleman, and we make a generous supper with our host and hostess and their guests – it being Christmas-time, and the old house full of company – and then we go to bed. Our room is a very old room. It is hung with tapestry. We don't like the portrait of a cavalier in green, over the fireplace. There are great black beams in the ceiling, and there is a great black bedstead, supported at the foot by two great black figures, who seem to have come off a couple of tombs in the old Baronial Church in the Park, for our particular accommodation. But, we are not a superstitious nobleman, and we don't mind. Well! we dismiss our servant, lock the door, and sit before the fire in our dressing-gown, musing about a great many things. At length we go to bed. Well! we can't sleep. We toss and tumble, and can't sleep. The embers on the hearth burn fitfully and make the room look ghostly. We can't help peeping out over the counterpane, at the two black figures and the cavalier – that wicked-looking cavalier – in green. In the flickering light, they seem to advance and retire: which, though we are not by any means a superstitious nobleman, is not agreeable. Well! we get nervous – more and more nervous. We say "This is very foolish, but we can't stand this; we'll pretend to be ill, and knock up somebody." Well! we are just going to do it, when the locked door opens, and there comes in a young woman, deadly pale, and with long fair hair, who glides to the fire, and sits down in the chair we have left there, wringing her hands. Then, we notice that her clothes are wet. Our tongue cleaves to the roof of our mouth, and we can't speak; but, we observe her accurately. Her clothes are wet; her long hair is dabbled with moist mud; she is dressed in the fashion of two hundred years ago; and she has at her girdle a bunch of rusty keys. Well! there she sits, and we can't even faint, we are in such a state about it. Presently she gets up, and tries all the locks in the room with the rusty keys, which won't fit one of them; then, she fixes her eyes on the Portrait of the Cavalier in green, and says, in a low, terrible voice, "The stags know it!" After that, she wrings her hands again, passes the bedside, and goes out at the door. We hurry on our dressing- gown, seize our pistols (we always travel with pistols), and are following, when we find the door locked. We turn the key, look out into the dark gallery; no one there. We wander away, and try to find our servant. Can't be done. We pace the gallery till daybreak; then return to our deserted room, fall asleep, and are awakened by our servant (nothing ever haunts *him*) and the shining sun. Well! we make a wretched breakfast, and all the company say we look queer. After breakfast, we go over the house with our host, and then we take him to the Portrait of the Cavalier in green, and then it all comes out. He was false to a young housekeeper once attached to that family, and famous for her beauty, who drowned herself in a pond, and whose body was discovered, after a long time, because the stags refused to drink of the water. Since which, it has been whispered that she traverses the house at midnight (but goes especially to that room where the Cavalier in green was wont to sleep), trying the old locks with her rusty keys. Well! we tell our host of what we have seen, and a shade comes over his features, and he begs it may be hushed up; and so it is. But, it's all true; and we said so, before we died (we are dead now) to many responsible people.

There is no end to the old houses, with resounding galleries, and dismal state-bed-chambers, and haunted wings shut up for many years, through which we may ramble, with an agreeable creeping up our back, and encounter any number of Ghosts, but, (it is worthy of remark perhaps) reducible to a very few general types and classes; for, Ghosts have little originality, and 'walk' in a beaten track. Thus, it comes to pass, that a certain room in a certain old hall, where a certain bad Lord, Baronet, Knight, or Gentleman, shot himself, has certain planks in the floor from which the blood *will not* be taken out. You may scrape and scrape, as the present owner has done, or plane and plane, as his father did, or scrub and scrub, as his grandfather did, or burn and burn with strong acids, as his great-grandfather did, but, there the blood will still be – no redder and no paler – no more and no less – always just the same. Thus, in such another house there is a haunted door, that never will keep open; or another door that never will keep shut; or a haunted sound of a spinning-wheel, or a hammer, or a footstep, or a cry, or a sigh, or a horse's tramp, or the rattling of a chain. Or else, there is a turret-clock, which, at the midnight hour, strikes thirteen when the head of the family is going to die; or a shadowy, immovable black carriage which at such a time is always seen by somebody, waiting near the great gates in the stable- yard. Or thus, it came to pass how Lady Mary went to pay a visit at a large wild house in the Scottish Highlands, and, being fatigued with her long journey, retired to bed early, and innocently said, next morning, at the breakfast-table, "How odd, to have so late a party last night, in this remote place, and not to tell me of it, before I went to bed!" Then, every one asked Lady Mary what she meant? Then, Lady Mary replied, "Why, all night long, the carriages were driving round and round the terrace, underneath my window!" Then, the owner of the house turned pale, and so did his Lady, and Charles Macdoodle of Macdoodle signed to Lady Mary to say no more, and every one was silent. After breakfast, Charles Macdoodle told Lady Mary that it was a tradition in the family that those rumbling carriages on the terrace betokened death. And so it proved, for, two months afterwards, the Lady of the mansion died. And Lady Mary, who was a Maid of Honour at Court, often told this story to the old Queen Charlotte; by this token that the old King always said, "Eh, eh? What, what? Ghosts, Ghosts? No such thing, no such thing!" And never left off saying so, until he went to bed.

Or, a friend of somebody's, whom most of us know, when he was a young man at college, had a particular friend, with whom he made the compact that, if it were possible for the Spirit to return to this earth after its separation from the body, he of the twain who first died, should reappear to the other. In course of time, this compact was forgotten by our friend; the two young men having progressed in life, and taken diverging paths that were wide asunder. But, one night, many years afterwards, our friend, being in the North of England, and staying for the night in an Inn, on the Yorkshire Moors, happened to look out of bed; and there, in the moonlight, leaning on a Bureau near the window, stedfastly regarding him, saw his old College friend! The appearance being solemnly addressed, replied, in a kind of whisper, but very audibly, "Do not come near me. I am dead. I am here to redeem my promise. I come from another world, but may not disclose its secrets!" Then, the whole form becoming paler, melted, as it were, into the moonlight, and faded away.

Or, there was the daughter of the first occupier of the picturesque Elizabethan house, so famous in our neighbourhood. You have heard about her? No! Why, *She* went out one summer evening, at twilight, when she was a beautiful girl, just seventeen years of age, to gather flowers in the garden; and presently came running, terrified, into the hall to her father, saying, "Oh, dear father, I have met myself!" He took her in his arms, and told her it was fancy, but she said "Oh no! I met myself in the broad walk, and I was pale and gathering withered flowers, and I turned my head, and held them up!" And, that night, she died; and a picture of her story was begun, though never finished, and they say it is somewhere in the house to this day, with its face to the wall.

Or, the uncle of my brother's wife was riding home on horseback, one mellow evening at sunset, when, in a green lane close to his own house, he saw a man, standing before him, in the very centre of the narrow way. "Why does that man in the cloak stand there!" he thought. "Does he want me to ride over him?" But the figure never moved. He felt a strange sensation at seeing it so still, but slackened his trot and rode forward. When he was so close to it, as almost to touch it with his stirrup, his horse shied, and the figure glided up the bank, in a curious, unearthly manner – backward, and without seeming to use its feet – and was gone. The uncle of my brother's wife, exclaiming, "Good Heaven! It's my cousin Harry, from Bombay!" put spurs to his horse, which was suddenly in a profuse sweat, and, wondering at such strange behaviour, dashed round to the front of his house. There, he saw the same figure, just passing in at the long french window of the drawing-room, opening on the ground. He threw his bridle to a servant, and hastened in after it. His sister was sitting there, alone. "Alice, where's my cousin Harry?"

"Your cousin Harry, John?"

"Yes. From Bombay. I met him in the lane just now, and saw him enter here, this instant." Not a creature had been seen by any one; and in that hour and minute, as it afterwards appeared, this cousin died in India.

Or, it was a certain sensible old maiden lady, who died at ninety-nine, and retained her faculties to the last, who really did see the Orphan Boy; a story which has often been incorrectly told, but, of which the real truth is this – because it is, in fact, a story belonging to our family – and she was a connexion of our family. When she was about forty years of age, and still an uncommonly fine woman (her lover died young, which was the reason why she never married, though she had many offers), she went to stay at a place in Kent, which her brother, an India-Merchant, had newly bought. There was a story that this place had once been held in trust, by the guardian of a young boy: who was himself the next heir, and who killed the young boy by harsh and cruel treatment. She knew nothing of that. It has been said that there was a Cage in her bed-room in which the guardian used to put the boy. There was no such thing. There was only a closet. She went to bed, made no alarm whatever in the night, and in the morning said composedly to her maid when she came in, "Who is the pretty forlorn-looking child who has been peeping out of that closet all night?"

The maid replied by giving a loud scream, and instantly decamping. She was surprised; but, she was a woman of remarkable strength of mind, and she dressed herself and went down stairs, and closeted herself with her brother. "Now, Walter," she said," I have been disturbed all night by a pretty, forlorn-looking boy, who has been constantly peeping out of that closet in my room, which I can't open. This is some trick."

"I am afraid not, Charlotte," said he, "for it is the legend of the house. It is the Orphan Boy. What did he do?"

"He opened the door softly," said she, "and peeped out. Sometimes, he came a step or two into the room. Then, I called to him, to encourage him, and he shrunk, and shuddered, and crept in again, and shut the door."

"The closet has no communication, Charlotte," said her brother, "with any other part of the house, and it's nailed up." This was undeniably true, and it took two carpenters a whole fore- noon to get it open, for examination. Then, she was satisfied that she had seen the Orphan Boy. But, the wild and terrible part of the story is, that he was also seen by three of her brother's sons, in succession, who all died young. On the occasion of each child being taken ill, he came home in a heat, twelve hours before, and said, Oh,

Mamma, he had been playing under a particular oak-tree, in a certain meadow, with a strange boy – a pretty, forlorn-looking boy, who was very timid, and made signs! From fatal experience, the parents came to know that this was the Orphan Boy, and that the course of that child whom he chose for his little playmate was surely run.

Legion is the name of the German castles, where we sit up alone to wait for the Spectre – where we are shown into a room, made comparatively cheerful for our reception – where we glance round at the shadows, thrown on the blank walls by the crackling fire – where we feel very lonely when the village innkeeper and his pretty daughter have retired, after laying down a fresh store of wood upon the hearth, and setting forth on the small table such supper-cheer as a cold roast capon, bread, grapes, and a flask of old Rhine wine – where the reverberating doors close on their retreat, one after another, like so many peals of sullen thunder – and where, about the small hours of the night, we come into the knowledge of divers supernatural mysteries. Legion is the name of the haunted German students, in whose society we draw yet nearer to the fire, while the schoolboy in the corner opens his eyes wide and round, and flies off the foot-stool he has chosen for his seat, when the door accidentally blows open. Vast is the crop of such fruit, shining on our Christmas Tree; in blossom, almost at the very top; ripening all down the boughs!

Among the later toys and fancies hanging there – as idle often and less pure – be the images once associated with the sweet old Waits, the softened music in the night, ever unalterable! Encircled by the social thoughts of Christmas time, still let the benignant figure of my childhood stand unchanged! In every cheerful image and suggestion that the season brings, may the bright star that rested above the poor roof, be the star of all the Christian world! A moment's pause, O vanishing tree, of which the lower boughs are dark to me as yet, and let me look once more! I know there are blank spaces on thy branches, where eyes that I have loved, have shone and smiled; from which they are departed. But, far above, I see the raiser of the dead girl, and the Widow's Son; and God is good! If Age be hiding for me in the unseen portion of thy downward growth, O may I, with a grey head, turn a child's heart to that figure yet, and a child's trustfulness and confidence!

Now, the tree is decorated with bright merriment, and song, and dance, and cheerfulness. And they are welcome. Innocent and welcome be they ever held, beneath the branches of the Christmas Tree, which cast no gloomy shadow! But, as it sinks into the ground, I hear a whisper going through the leaves. "This, in commemoration of the law of love and kindness, mercy and compassion. This, in remembrance of Me!"

**If you enjoyed this, you might also like...**
The Trial for Murder, see page 251
A Christmas Carol, see page 30

# Mr. Testator's Visitation

THIS WAS A MAN who, though not more than thirty, had seen the world in divers irreconcilable capacities – had been an officer in a South American regiment among other odd things – but had not achieved much in any way of life, and was in debt, and in hiding. He occupied chambers of the dreariest nature in Lyons Inn; his name, however, was not up on the door, or door-post, but in lieu of it stood the name of a friend who had died in the chambers, and had given him the furniture. The story arose out of the furniture, and was to this effect: Let the former holder of the chambers, whose name was still upon the door and door-post, be Mr. Testator.

Mr. Testator took a set of chambers in Lyons Inn when he had but very scanty furniture for his bedroom, and none for his sitting-room. He had lived some wintry months in this condition, and had found it very bare and cold. One night, past midnight, when he sat writing and still had writing to do that must be done before he went to bed, he found himself out of coals. He had coals down-stairs, but had never been to his cellar; however the cellar-key was on his mantelshelf, and if he went down and opened the cellar it fitted, he might fairly assume the coals in that cellar to be his. As to his laundress, she lived among the coal-waggons and Thames watermen – for there were Thames watermen at that time – in some unknown rat-hole by the river, down lanes and alleys on the other side of the Strand. As to any other person to meet him or obstruct him, Lyons Inn was dreaming, drunk, maudlin, moody, betting, brooding over bill-discounting or renewing – asleep or awake, minding its own affairs. Mr. Testator took his coal-scuttle in one hand, his candle and key in the other, and descended to the dismallest underground dens of Lyons Inn, where the late vehicles in the streets became thunderous, and all the water-pipes in the neighbourhood seemed to have Macbeth's Amen sticking in their throats, and to be trying to get it out. After groping here and there among low doors to no purpose, Mr. Testator at length came to a door with a rusty padlock which his key fitted. Getting the door open with much trouble, and looking in, he found, no coals, but a confused pile of furniture. Alarmed by this intrusion on another man's property, he locked the door again, found his own cellar, filled his scuttle, and returned up-stairs.

But the furniture he had seen, ran on castors across and across Mr. Testator's mind incessantly, when, in the chill hour of five in the morning, he got to bed. He particularly wanted a table to write at, and a table expressly made to be written at, had been the piece of furniture in the foreground of the heap. When his laundress emerged from her burrow in the morning to make his kettle boil, he artfully led up to the subject of cellars and furniture; but the two ideas had evidently no connexion in her mind. When she left him, and he sat at his breakfast, thinking about the furniture, he recalled the rusty state of the padlock, and inferred that the furniture must have been stored in the cellars for a long time – was perhaps forgotten – owner dead, perhaps? After thinking it over, a few days, in the course of which he could pump nothing out of Lyons Inn about the furniture, he became desperate, and resolved to borrow that table. He did so, that night. He had not had the table long, when he determined to borrow an easy-chair; he had not had that long, when he made up his mind to borrow a bookcase; then, a couch; then, a carpet and rug. By that time, he felt he was 'in furniture stepped in so far,' as that it could be no worse to borrow it all. Consequently, he borrowed it all, and locked up the cellar for good. He had always locked it, after every visit. He had carried up every separate article in the dead of the night, and, at the best, had felt as wicked as a Resurrection Man. Every article was blue and furry when brought into his rooms, and he had had, in a murderous and guilty sort of way, to polish it up while London slept.

Mr. Testator lived in his furnished chambers two or three years, or more, and gradually lulled himself into the opinion that the furniture was his own. This was his convenient state of mind when, late one night, a step came up the stairs, and a hand passed over his door feeling for his knocker, and then one deep and solemn rap was rapped that might have been a spring in Mr. Testator's easy-chair to shoot him out of it; so promptly was it attended with that effect.

With a candle in his hand, Mr. Testator went to the door, and found there, a very pale and very tall man; a man who stooped; a man with very high shoulders, a very narrow chest, and a very red nose; a shabby-genteel man. He was wrapped in a long thread-bare black coat, fastened up the front with more pins than buttons, and under his arm he squeezed an umbrella without a handle, as if he were playing bagpipes. He said, "I ask your pardon, but can you tell me—" and stopped; his eyes resting on some object within the chambers.

"Can I tell you what?" asked Mr. Testator, noting his stoppage with quick alarm.

"I ask your pardon," said the stranger, "but – this is not the inquiry I was going to make – do I see in there, any small article of property belonging to me?"

Mr. Testator was beginning to stammer that he was not aware – when the visitor slipped past him, into the chambers. There, in a goblin way which froze Mr. Testator to the marrow, he examined, first, the writing-table, and said, "Mine;" then, the easy-chair, and said, "Mine;" then, the bookcase, and said, "Mine;" then, turned up a corner of the carpet, and said, "Mine!" in a word, inspected every item of furniture from the cellar, in succession, and said, "Mine!" Towards the end of this investigation, Mr. Testator perceived that he was sodden with liquor, and that the liquor was gin. He was not unsteady with gin, either in his speech or carriage; but he was stiff with gin in both particulars.

Mr. Testator was in a dreadful state, for (according to his making out of the story) the possible consequences of what he had done in recklessness and hardihood, flashed upon him in their fulness for the first time. When they had stood gazing at one another for a little while, he tremulously began:

"Sir, I am conscious that the fullest explanation, compensation, and restitution, are your due. They shall be yours. Allow me to entreat that, without temper, without even natural irritation on your part, we may have a little—"

"Drop of something to drink," interposed the stranger. "I am agreeable."

Mr. Testator had intended to say, "a little quiet conversation," but with great relief of mind adopted the amendment. He produced a decanter of gin, and was bustling about for hot water and sugar, when he found that his visitor had already drunk half of the decanter's contents. With hot water and sugar the visitor drank the remainder before he had been an hour in the chambers by the chimes of the church of St. Mary in the Strand; and during the process he frequently whispered to himself, "Mine!"

The gin gone, and Mr. Testator wondering what was to follow it, the visitor rose and said, with increased stiffness, "At what hour of the morning, sir, will it be convenient?" Mr. Testator hazarded, "At ten?"

"Sir," said the visitor, "at ten, to the moment, I shall be here." He then contemplated Mr. Testator somewhat at leisure, and said, "God bless you! How is your wife?" Mr. Testator (who never had a wife) replied with much feeling, "Deeply anxious, poor soul, but otherwise well." The visitor thereupon turned and went away, and fell twice in going down-stairs. From that hour he was never heard of. Whether he was a ghost, or a spectral illusion of conscience, or a drunken man who had no business there, or the drunken rightful owner of the furniture, with a transitory gleam of memory; whether he got safe home, or had no time to get to; whether he died of liquor on the way, or lived in liquor ever afterwards; he never was heard of more. This was the story, received with the furniture and held to be as substantial, by its second possessor in an upper set of chambers in grim Lyons Inn.

**If you enjoyed this, you might also like...**

The Lawyer and the Ghost, see page 22
The Haunted House, see opposite

# The Haunted House

## The Mortals in the House
### Charles Dickens

UNDER NONE of the accredited ghostly circumstances, and environed by none of the conventional ghostly surroundings, did I first make acquaintance with the house which is the subject of this Christmas piece. I saw it in the daylight, with the sun upon it. There was no wind, no rain, no lightning, no thunder, no awful or unwonted circumstance, of any kind, to heighten its effect. More than that: I had come to it direct from a railway station: it was not more than a mile distant from the railway station; and, as I stood outside the house, looking back upon the way I had come, I could see the goods train running smoothly along the embankment in the valley. I will not say that everything was utterly commonplace, because I doubt if anything can be that, except to utterly commonplace people – and there my vanity steps in; but, I will take it on myself to say that anybody might see the house as I saw it, any fine autumn morning.

The manner of my lighting on it was this.

I was travelling towards London out of the North, intending to stop by the way, to look at the house. My health required a temporary residence in the country; and a friend of mine who knew that, and who had happened to drive past the house, had written to me to suggest it as a likely place. I had got into the train at midnight, and had fallen asleep, and had woke up and had sat looking out of window at the brilliant Northern Lights in the sky, and had fallen asleep again, and had woke up again to find the night gone, with the usual discontented conviction on me that I hadn't been to sleep at all; – upon which question, in the first imbecility of that condition, I am ashamed to believe that I would have done wager by battle with the man who sat opposite me. That opposite man had had, through the night – as that opposite man always has – several legs too many, and all of them too long. In addition to this unreasonable conduct (which was only to be expected of him), he had had a pencil and a pocket-book, and had been perpetually listening and taking notes. It had appeared to me that these aggravating notes related to the jolts and bumps of the carriage, and I should have resigned myself to his taking them, under a general supposition that he was in the civil-engineering way of life, if he had not sat staring straight over my head whenever he listened. He was a goggle-eyed gentleman of a perplexed aspect, and his demeanour became unbearable.

It was a cold, dead morning (the sun not being up yet), and when I had out-watched the paling light of the fires of the iron country, and the curtain of heavy smoke that hung at once between me and the stars and between me and the day, I turned to my fellow-traveller and said:

"I *beg* your pardon, sir, but do you observe anything particular in me?" For, really, he appeared to be taking down, either my travelling-cap or my hair, with a minuteness that was a liberty.

The goggle-eyed gentleman withdrew his eyes from behind me, as if the back of the carriage were a hundred miles off, and said, with a lofty look of compassion for my insignificance:

"In you, sir? – B."

"B, sir?" said I, growing warm.

"I have nothing to do with you, sir," returned the gentleman; "pray let me listen – O."

He enunciated this vowel after a pause, and noted it down.

At first I was alarmed, for an Express lunatic and no communication with the guard, is a serious position. The thought came to my relief that the gentleman might be what is popularly called a Rapper: one of a sect for (some of) whom I have the highest respect, but whom I don't believe in. I was going to ask him the question, when he took the bread out of my mouth.

"You will excuse me," said the gentleman contemptuously, "if I am too much in advance of common humanity to trouble myself at all about it. I have passed the night – as indeed I pass the whole of my time now – in spiritual intercourse."

"O!" said I, somewhat snappishly.

"The conferences of the night began," continued the gentleman, turning several leaves of his note-book, "with this message: 'Evil communications corrupt good manners.'"

"Sound," said I; "but, absolutely new?"

"New from spirits," returned the gentleman.

I could only repeat my rather snappish "O!" and ask if I might be favoured with the last communication.

"'A bird in the hand,'" said the gentleman, reading his last entry with great solemnity, "'is worth two in the Bosh.'"

"Truly I am of the same opinion," said I; "but shouldn't it be Bush?"

"It came to me, Bosh," returned the gentleman.

The gentleman then informed me that the spirit of Socrates had delivered this special revelation in the course of the night. "My friend, I hope you are pretty well. There are two in this railway carriage. How do you do? There are seventeen thousand four hundred and seventy-nine spirits here, but you cannot see them. Pythagoras is here. He is not at liberty to mention it, but hopes you like travelling." Galileo likewise had dropped in, with this scientific intelligence. "I am glad to see you, *amico. Come sta?* Water will freeze when it is cold enough. *Addio!*" In the course of the night, also, the following phenomena had occurred. Bishop Butler had insisted on spelling his name, "Bubler," for which offence against orthography and good manners he had been dismissed as out of temper. John Milton (suspected of wilful mystification) had repudiated the authorship of Paradise Lost, and had introduced, as joint authors of that poem, two Unknown gentlemen, respectively named Grungers and Scadgingtone. And Prince Arthur, nephew of King John of England, had described himself as tolerably comfortable in the seventh circle, where he was learning to paint on velvet, under the direction of Mrs. Trimmer and Mary Queen of Scots.

If this should meet the eye of the gentleman who favoured me with these disclosures, I trust he will excuse my confessing that the sight of the rising sun, and the contemplation of the magnificent Order of the vast Universe, made me impatient of them. In a word, I was so impatient of them, that I was mightily glad to get out at the next station, and to exchange these clouds and vapours for the free air of Heaven.

By that time it was a beautiful morning. As I walked away among such leaves as had already fallen from the golden, brown, and russet trees; and as I looked around me on the wonders of Creation, and thought of the steady, unchanging, and harmonious laws by which they are sustained; the gentleman's spiritual intercourse seemed to me as poor a piece of journey-work as ever this world saw. In which heathen state of mind, I came within view of the house, and stopped to examine it attentively.

It was a solitary house, standing in a sadly neglected garden: a pretty even square of some two acres. It was a house of about the time of George the Second; as stiff, as cold, as formal, and in as bad taste, as could possibly be desired by the most loyal admirer of the whole quartet of Georges. It was uninhabited, but had, within a year or two, been cheaply repaired to render it habitable; I say cheaply, because the work had been done in a surface manner, and was already decaying as to the paint and plaster, though the colours were fresh. A lop-sided board drooped over the garden wall, announcing that it was "to let on very reasonable terms, well furnished." It was much too closely and heavily shadowed by trees, and, in particular, there were six tall poplars before the front windows, which were excessively melancholy, and the site of which had been extremely ill chosen.

It was easy to see that it was an avoided house – a house that was shunned by the village, to which my eye was guided by a church spire some half a mile off – a house that nobody would take. And the natural inference was, that it had the reputation of being a haunted house.

No period within the four-and-twenty hours of day and night is so solemn to me, as the early morning. In the summer-time, I often rise very early, and repair to my room to do a day's work before breakfast, and I am always on those occasions deeply impressed by the stillness and solitude around me. Besides that there is something awful in the being surrounded by familiar faces asleep – in the knowledge that those who are dearest to us and to whom we are dearest, are profoundly unconscious of us, in an impassive state, anticipative of that mysterious condition to which we are all tending – the stopped life, the broken threads of yesterday, the deserted seat, the closed book, the unfinished but abandoned occupation, all are images of Death. The tranquillity of the hour is the tranquillity of Death. The colour and the chill have the same association. Even a certain air that familiar household objects take upon them when they first emerge from the shadows of the night into the morning, of being newer, and as they used to be long ago, has its counterpart in the subsidence of the worn face of maturity or age, in death, into the old youthful look. Moreover, I once saw the apparition of my father, at this hour. He was alive and well, and nothing ever came of it, but I saw him in the daylight, sitting with his back towards me, on a seat that stood beside my bed. His head was resting on his hand, and whether he was slumbering or grieving, I could not discern. Amazed to see him there, I sat up, moved my position, leaned out of bed, and watched him. As he did not move, I spoke to him more than once. As he did not move then, I became alarmed and laid my hand upon his shoulder, as I thought – and there was no such thing.

For all these reasons, and for others less easily and briefly statable, I find the early morning to be my most ghostly time. Any house would be more or less haunted, to me, in the early morning; and a haunted house could scarcely address me to greater advantage than then.

I walked on into the village, with the desertion of this house upon my mind, and I found the landlord of the little inn, sanding his door-step. I bespoke breakfast, and broached the subject of the house.

"Is it haunted?" I asked.

The landlord looked at me, shook his head, and answered, "I say nothing."

"Then it *is* haunted?"

"Well!" cried the landlord, in an outburst of frankness that had the appearance of desperation— "I wouldn't sleep in it."

"Why not?"

"If I wanted to have all the bells in a house ring, with nobody to ring 'em; and all the doors in a house bang, with nobody to bang 'em; and all sorts of feet treading about, with no feet there; why, then," said the landlord, "I'd sleep in that house."

"Is anything seen there?"

The landlord looked at me again, and then, with his former appearance of desperation, called down his stable-yard for "Ikey!"

The call produced a high-shouldered young fellow, with a round red face, a short crop of sandy hair, a very broad humorous mouth, a turned-up nose, and a great sleeved waistcoat of purple bars, with mother-of-pearl buttons, that seemed to be growing upon him, and to be in a fair way – if it were not pruned – of covering his head and overrunning his boots.

"This gentleman wants to know," said the landlord, "if anything's seen at the Poplars."

"'Ooded woman with a howl," said Ikey, in a state of great freshness.

"Do you mean a cry?"

"I mean a bird, sir."

"A hooded woman with an owl. Dear me! Did you ever see her?"

"I seen the howl."

"Never the woman?"

"Not so plain as the howl, but they always keeps together."

"Has anybody ever seen the woman as plainly as the owl?"

"Lord bless you, sir! Lots."

"Who?"

"Lord bless you, sir! Lots."

"The general-dealer opposite, for instance, who is opening his shop?"

"Perkins? Bless you, Perkins wouldn't go a-nigh the place. No!" observed the young man, with considerable feeling; "he an't overwise, an't Perkins, but he an't such a fool as *that*."

(Here, the landlord murmured his confidence in Perkins's knowing better.)

"Who is – or who was – the hooded woman with the owl? Do you know?"

"Well!" said Ikey, holding up his cap with one hand while he scratched his head with the other, "they say, in general, that she was murdered, and the howl he 'ooted the while."

This very concise summary of the facts was all I could learn, except that a young man, as hearty and likely a young man as ever I see, had been took with fits and held down in 'em, after seeing the hooded woman. Also, that a personage, dimly described as "a hold chap, a sort of one-eyed tramp, answering to the name of Joby, unless you challenged him as Greenwood, and then he said, 'Why not? and even if so, mind your own business,'" had encountered the hooded woman, a matter of five or six times. But, I was not materially assisted by these witnesses: inasmuch as the first was in California, and the last was, as Ikey said (and he was confirmed by the landlord), Anywheres.

Now, although I regard with a hushed and solemn fear, the mysteries, between which and this state of existence is interposed the barrier of the great trial and change that fall on all the things that live; and although I have not the audacity to pretend that I know anything of them; I can no more reconcile the mere banging of doors, ringing of bells, creaking of boards, and such-like insignificances, with the majestic beauty and pervading analogy of all the Divine rules that I am permitted to understand, than I had been able, a little while before, to yoke the spiritual intercourse of my fellow-traveller to the chariot of the rising sun. Moreover, I had lived in two haunted houses – both abroad. In one of these, an old Italian palace, which bore the reputation of being very badly haunted indeed, and which had recently been twice abandoned on that account, I lived eight months, most tranquilly and pleasantly: notwithstanding that the house had a score of mysterious bedrooms, which were never used, and possessed, in one large room in which I sat reading, times out of number at all hours, and next to which I slept, a haunted chamber of the first pretensions. I gently hinted these considerations to the landlord. And as to this particular house having a bad name, I reasoned with him, Why, how many things had bad names undeservedly, and how easy it was to give bad names, and did he not think that if he and I were persistently to whisper in the village that any weird-looking, old drunken tinker of the neighbourhood had sold himself to the Devil, he would come in time to be suspected of that commercial venture! All this wise talk was perfectly ineffective with the landlord, I am bound to confess, and was as dead a failure as ever I made in my life.

To cut this part of the story short, I was piqued about the haunted house, and was already half resolved to take it. So, after breakfast, I got the keys from Perkins's brother-in-law (a whip and harness maker, who keeps the Post Office, and is under submission to a most rigorous wife of the Doubly Seceding Little Emmanuel persuasion), and went up to the house, attended by my landlord and by Ikey.

Within, I found it, as I had expected, transcendently dismal. The slowly changing shadows waved on it from the heavy trees, were doleful in the last degree; the house was ill-placed, ill-built, ill-planned, and ill-fitted. It was damp, it was not free from dry rot, there was a flavour of rats in it, and it was the gloomy victim of that indescribable decay which settles on all the work of man's hands whenever it's not turned to man's account. The kitchens and offices were too large, and too remote from each other. Above stairs and below, waste tracts of passage intervened between patches of fertility represented by rooms; and there was a mouldy old well with a green growth upon it, hiding like a murderous trap, near the bottom of the back-stairs, under the double row of bells. One of these bells was labelled, on a black ground in faded white letters, Master B. This, they told me, was the bell that rang the most.

"Who was Master B.?" I asked. "Is it known what he did while the owl hooted?"

"Rang the bell," said Ikey.

I was rather struck by the prompt dexterity with which this young man pitched his fur cap at the bell, and rang it himself. It was a loud, unpleasant bell, and made a very disagreeable sound. The other bells were inscribed according to the names of the rooms to which their wires were conducted: as "Picture Room," "Double Room," "Clock Room," and the like. Following Master B.'s bell to its source I found that young gentleman to have had but indifferent third-class accommodation in a triangular cabin under the cock-loft, with a corner fireplace which Master B. must have been exceedingly small if he were ever able to warm himself at, and a corner chimney-piece like a pyramidal staircase to the ceiling for Tom Thumb. The papering of one side of the room had dropped down bodily, with fragments of plaster adhering to it, and almost blocked up the door. It appeared that Master B., in his spiritual condition, always made a point of pulling the paper down. Neither the landlord nor Ikey could suggest why he made such a fool of himself.

Except that the house had an immensely large rambling loft at top, I made no other discoveries. It was moderately well furnished, but sparely. Some of the furniture – say, a third – was as old as the house; the rest was of various periods within the last half-century. I was referred to a corn-chandler in the market-place of the county town to treat for the house. I went that day, and I took it for six months.

It was just the middle of October when I moved in with my maiden sister (I venture to call her eight-and-thirty, she is so very handsome, sensible, and engaging). We took with us, a deaf stable-man, my bloodhound Turk, two women servants, and a young person called an Odd Girl. I have reason to record of the attendant last enumerated, who was one of the Saint Lawrence's Union Female Orphans, that she was a fatal mistake and a disastrous engagement.

The year was dying early, the leaves were falling fast, it was a raw cold day when we took possession, and the gloom of the house was most depressing. The cook (an amiable woman, but of a weak turn of intellect) burst into tears on beholding the kitchen, and requested that her silver watch might be delivered over to her sister (2 Tuppintock's Gardens, Liggs's Walk, Clapham Rise), in the event of anything happening to her from the damp. Streaker, the housemaid, feigned cheerfulness, but was the greater martyr. The Odd Girl, who had never been in the country, alone was pleased, and made arrangements for sowing an acorn in the garden outside the scullery window, and rearing an oak.

We went, before dark, through all the natural – as opposed to supernatural – miseries incidental to our state. Dispiriting reports ascended (like the smoke) from the basement in volumes, and descended from the upper rooms. There was no rolling-pin, there was no salamander (which failed to surprise me, for I don't know what it is), there was nothing in the house, what there was, was broken, the last people must have lived like pigs, what could the meaning of the landlord be? Through these distresses, the Odd Girl was cheerful and exemplary. But within four hours after dark we had got into a supernatural groove, and the Odd Girl had seen "Eyes," and was in hysterics.

My sister and I had agreed to keep the haunting strictly to ourselves, and my impression was, and still is, that I had not left Ikey, when he helped to unload the cart, alone with the women, or any one of them, for one minute. Nevertheless, as I say, the Odd Girl had "seen Eyes" (no other explanation could ever be drawn from her), before nine, and by ten o'clock had had as much vinegar applied to her as would pickle a handsome salmon.

I leave a discerning public to judge of my feelings, when, under these untoward circumstances, at about half-past ten o'clock Master B.'s bell began to ring in a most infuriated manner, and Turk howled until the house resounded with his lamentations!

I hope I may never again be in a state of mind so unchristian as the mental frame in which I lived for some weeks, respecting the memory of Master B. Whether his bell was rung by rats, or mice, or bats, or wind, or what other accidental vibration, or sometimes by one cause, sometimes another, and sometimes by collusion, I don't know; but, certain it is, that it did ring two nights out of three, until I conceived the happy idea of twisting Master B.'s neck – in other words, breaking his bell short off – and silencing that young gentleman, as to my experience and belief, for ever.

But, by that time, the Odd Girl had developed such improving powers of catalepsy, that she had become a shining example of that very inconvenient disorder. She would stiffen, like a Guy Fawkes endowed with unreason, on the most irrelevant occasions. I would address the servants in a lucid manner, pointing out to them that I had painted Master B.'s room and balked the paper, and taken Master B.'s bell away and balked the ringing, and if they could suppose that that confounded boy had lived and died, to clothe himself with no better behaviour than would most unquestionably have brought him and the sharpest particles of a birch-broom into close acquaintance in the present imperfect state of existence, could they also suppose a mere poor human being, such as I was, capable by those contemptible means of counteracting and limiting the powers of the disembodied spirits of the dead, or of any spirits? – I say I would become emphatic and cogent, not to say rather complacent, in such an address, when it would all go for nothing by reason of the Odd Girl's suddenly stiffening from the toes upward, and glaring among us like a parochial petrifaction.

Streaker, the housemaid, too, had an attribute of a most discomfiting nature. I am unable to say whether she was of an unusually lymphatic temperament, or what else was the matter with her, but this young woman became a mere Distillery for the production of the largest and most transparent tears I ever met with. Combined with these characteristics, was a peculiar tenacity of hold in those specimens, so that they didn't fall, but hung upon her face and nose. In this condition, and mildly and deplorably shaking her head, her silence would throw me more heavily than the Admirable Crichton could have done in a verbal disputation for a purse of money. Cook, likewise, always covered me with confusion as with a garment, by neatly winding up the session with the protest that the Ouse was wearing her out, and by meekly repeating her last wishes regarding her silver watch.

As to our nightly life, the contagion of suspicion and fear was among us, and there is no such contagion under the sky. Hooded woman? According to the accounts, we were in a perfect Convent of hooded women. Noises? With that contagion downstairs, I myself have sat in the dismal parlour, listening, until I have heard so many and such strange noises, that they would have chilled my blood if I had not warmed it by dashing out to make discoveries. Try this in bed, in the dead of the night: try this at your own comfortable fire-side, in the life of the night. You can fill any house with noises, if you will, until you have a noise for every nerve in your nervous system.

I repeat; the contagion of suspicion and fear was among us, and there is no such contagion under the sky. The women (their noses in a chronic state of excoriation from smelling-salts) were always primed and loaded for a swoon, and ready to go off with hair-triggers. The two elder detached the Odd Girl on all expeditions that were considered doubly hazardous, and she always established the reputation of such adventures by coming back cataleptic. If Cook or Streaker went overhead after dark, we knew we should presently hear a bump on the ceiling; and this took place so constantly, that it was as if a fighting man were engaged to go about the house, administering a touch of his art which I believe is called The Auctioneer, to every domestic he met with.

It was in vain to do anything. It was in vain to be frightened, for the moment in one's own person, by a real owl, and then to show the owl. It was in vain to discover, by striking an accidental discord on the piano, that Turk always howled at particular notes and combinations. It was in vain to be a Rhadamanthus with the bells, and if an unfortunate bell rang without leave, to have it down inexorably and silence it. It was in vain to fire up chimneys, let torches down the well, charge furiously into suspected rooms and recesses. We changed servants, and it was no better. The new set ran away, and a third set came, and it was no better. At last, our comfortable housekeeping got to be so disorganised and wretched, that I one night dejectedly said to my sister: "Patty, I begin to despair of our getting people to go on with us here, and I think we must give this up."

My sister, who is a woman of immense spirit, replied, "No, John, don't give it up. Don't be beaten, John. There is another way."

"And what is that?" said I.

"John," returned my sister, "if we are not to be driven out of this house, and that for no reason whatever, that is apparent to you or me, we must help ourselves and take the house wholly and solely into our own hands."

"But, the servants," said I.

"Have no servants," said my sister, boldly.

Like most people in my grade of life, I had never thought of the possibility of going on without those faithful obstructions. The notion was so new to me when suggested, that I looked very doubtful. "We know they come here to be frightened and infect one another, and we know they are frightened and do infect one another," said my sister.

"With the exception of Bottles," I observed, in a meditative tone.

(The deaf stable-man. I kept him in my service, and still keep him, as a phenomenon of moroseness not to be matched in England.)

"To be sure, John," assented my sister; "except Bottles. And what does that go to prove? Bottles talks to nobody, and hears nobody unless he is absolutely roared at, and what alarm has Bottles ever given, or taken! None."

This was perfectly true; the individual in question having retired, every night at ten o'clock, to his bed over the coach-house, with no other company than a pitchfork and a pail of water. That the pail of water would have been over me, and the pitchfork through me, if I had put myself without announcement in Bottles's way after that minute, I had deposited in my own mind as a fact worth remembering. Neither had Bottles ever taken the least notice of any of our many uproars. An imperturbable and speechless man, he had sat at his supper, with Streaker present in a swoon, and the Odd Girl marble, and had only put another potato in his cheek, or profited by the general misery to help himself to beefsteak pie.

"And so," continued my sister, "I exempt Bottles. And considering, John, that the house is too large, and perhaps too lonely, to be kept well in hand by Bottles, you, and me, I propose that we cast about among our friends for a certain selected number of the most reliable and willing – form a Society here for three months – wait upon ourselves and one another – live cheerfully and socially – and see what happens."

I was so charmed with my sister, that I embraced her on the spot, and went into her plan with the greatest ardour.

We were then in the third week of November; but, we took our measures so vigorously, and were so well seconded by the friends in whom we confided, that there was still a week of the month unexpired, when our party all came down together merrily, and mustered in the haunted house.

I will mention, in this place, two small changes that I made while my sister and I were yet alone. It occurring to me as not improbable that Turk howled in the house at night, partly because he wanted to get out of it, I stationed him in his kennel outside, but unchained; and I seriously warned the village that any man who came in his way must not expect to leave him without a rip in his own throat. I then casually asked Ikey if he were a judge of a gun? On his saying, "Yes, sir, I knows a good gun when I sees her," I begged the favour of his stepping up to the house and looking at mine.

"*She's* a true one, sir," said Ikey, after inspecting a double-barrelled rifle that I bought in New York a few years ago. "No mistake about *her,* sir."

"Ikey," said I, "don't mention it; I have seen something in this house."

"No, sir?" he whispered, greedily opening his eyes. "'Ooded lady, sir?"

"Don't be frightened," said I. "It was a figure rather like you."

"Lord, sir?"

"Ikey!" said I, shaking hands with him warmly: I may say affectionately; "if there is any truth in these ghost-stories, the greatest service I can do you, is, to fire at that figure. And I promise you, by Heaven and earth, I will do it with this gun if I see it again!"

The young man thanked me, and took his leave with some little precipitation, after declining a glass of liquor. I imparted my secret to him, because I had never quite forgotten his throwing his cap at the bell; because I had, on another occasion, noticed something very like a fur cap, lying not far from the bell, one night when it had burst out ringing; and because I had remarked that we were at our ghostliest whenever he came up in the evening to comfort the servants. Let me do Ikey no injustice. He was afraid of the house, and believed in its being haunted; and yet he would play false on the haunting side, so surely as he got an opportunity. The Odd Girl's case was exactly similar. She went about the house in a state of real terror, and yet lied monstrously and wilfully, and invented many of the alarms she spread, and made many of the sounds we heard. I had had my eye on the two, and I know it. It is not necessary for me, here, to account for this preposterous state of mind; I content myself with remarking that it is familiarly known to every intelligent man who has had fair medical, legal, or other watchful experience; that it is as well established and as common a state of mind as any with which observers are acquainted; and that it is one of the first elements, above all others, rationally to be suspected in, and strictly looked for, and separated from, any question of this kind.

To return to our party. The first thing we did when we were all assembled, was, to draw lots for bedrooms. That done, and every bedroom, and, indeed, the whole house, having been minutely examined by the whole body, we allotted the various household duties, as if we had been on a gipsy party, or a yachting party, or a hunting party, or were shipwrecked. I then recounted the floating rumours concerning the hooded lady, the owl, and Master B.: with others, still more filmy, which had floated about during our occupation, relative to some ridiculous old ghost of the female gender who went up and down, carrying the ghost of a round table; and also to an impalpable Jackass, whom nobody was ever able to catch. Some of these ideas I really believe our people below had communicated to one another in some diseased way, without conveying them in words. We then gravely called one another to witness, that we were not there to be deceived, or to deceive – which we considered pretty much the same thing – and that, with a serious sense of responsibility, we would be strictly true to one another, and would strictly follow out the truth. The understanding was established, that any one who heard unusual noises in the night, and who wished to trace them, should knock at my door; lastly, that on Twelfth Night, the last night of holy Christmas, all our individual experiences since that then present hour of our coming together in the haunted house, should be brought to light for the good of all; and that we would hold our peace on the subject till then, unless on some remarkable provocation to break silence.

We were, in number and in character, as follows:

First – to get my sister and myself out of the way – there were we two. In the drawing of lots, my sister drew her own room, and I drew Master B.'s. Next, there was our first cousin John Herschel, so called after the great astronomer: than whom I suppose a better man at a telescope does not breathe. With him, was his wife: a charming creature to whom he had been married in the previous spring. I thought it (under the circumstances) rather imprudent to bring her, because there is no knowing what even a false alarm may do at such a time; but I suppose he knew his own business best, and I must say that if she had been *my* wife, I never could have left her endearing and bright face behind. They drew the Clock Room. Alfred Starling, an uncommonly agreeable young fellow of eight-and-twenty for whom I have the greatest liking, was in the Double Room; mine, usually, and designated by that name from having a dressing-room within it, with two large and cumbersome windows, which no wedges *I* was ever able to make, would keep from shaking, in any weather, wind or no wind. Alfred is a young fellow who pretends to be "fast" (another word for loose, as I understand the term), but who is much too good and sensible for that nonsense, and who would have distinguished himself before now, if his father had not unfortunately left him a small independence of two hundred a year, on the strength of which his only occupation in life has been to spend six. I am in hopes, however, that his Banker may break, or that he may enter into some speculation guaranteed to pay twenty per cent.; for, I am convinced that if he could only be ruined, his fortune is made. Belinda Bates, bosom friend of my sister, and a most intellectual, amiable, and delightful girl, got the Picture Room. She has a fine genius for poetry, combined with real business earnestness, and "goes in" – to use an expression of Alfred's – for Woman's mission, Woman's rights, Woman's wrongs, and everything that is woman's with a capital W, or is not and ought to be, or is and ought not to be. "Most praiseworthy, my dear, and Heaven prosper you!" I whispered to her on the first night of my taking leave of her at the Picture-Room door, "but don't overdo it. And in respect of the great necessity there is, my darling, for more employments being within the reach of Woman than our civilisation has as yet assigned to her, don't fly at the unfortunate men, even those men who are at first sight in your way, as if they were the natural oppressors of your sex; for, trust me, Belinda, they do sometimes spend their wages among wives and daughters, sisters, mothers, aunts, and grandmothers; and the play is, really, not *all* Wolf and Red Riding-Hood, but has other parts in it." However, I digress.

Belinda, as I have mentioned, occupied the Picture Room. We had but three other chambers: the Corner Room, the Cupboard Room, and the Garden Room. My old friend, Jack Governor, "slung his hammock," as he called it, in the Corner Room. I have always regarded Jack as the finest-looking sailor that ever sailed. He is gray now, but as handsome as he was a quarter of a century ago – nay, handsomer. A portly, cheery, well-built figure of a broad-shouldered man, with a frank smile, a brilliant dark eye, and a rich dark eyebrow. I remember those under darker hair, and they look all the better for their silver setting. He has been wherever his Union namesake flies, has Jack, and I have met old shipmates of his, away in the Mediterranean and on the other side of the Atlantic, who have beamed and brightened at the casual mention of his name, and have cried, "You know Jack Governor? Then you know a prince of men!" That he is! And so unmistakably a naval officer, that if you were to meet him coming out of an Esquimaux snow-hut in seal's skin, you would be vaguely persuaded he was in full naval uniform.

Jack once had that bright clear eye of his on my sister; but, it fell out that he married another lady and took her to South America, where she died. This was a dozen years ago or more. He brought down with him to our haunted house a little cask of salt beef; for, he is always convinced that all salt beef not of his own pickling, is mere carrion, and invariably, when he goes to London, packs a piece in his portmanteau. He had also volunteered to bring with him one "Nat Beaver," an old comrade of his, captain of a merchantman. Mr.

Beaver, with a thick-set wooden face and figure, and apparently as hard as a block all over, proved to be an intelligent man, with a world of watery experiences in him, and great practical knowledge. At times, there was a curious nervousness about him, apparently the lingering result of some old illness; but, it seldom lasted many minutes. He got the Cupboard Room, and lay there next to Mr. Undery, my friend and solicitor: who came down, in an amateur capacity, "to go through with it," as he said, and who plays whist better than the whole Law List, from the red cover at the beginning to the red cover at the end.

I never was happier in my life, and I believe it was the universal feeling among us. Jack Governor, always a man of wonderful resources, was Chief Cook, and made some of the best dishes I ever ate, including unapproachable curries. My sister was pastrycook and confectioner. Starling and I were Cook's Mate, turn and turn about, and on special occasions the chief cook "pressed" Mr. Beaver. We had a great deal of out-door sport and exercise, but nothing was neglected within, and there was no ill-humour or misunderstanding among us, and our evenings were so delightful that we had at least one good reason for being reluctant to go to bed.

We had a few night alarms in the beginning. On the first night, I was knocked up by Jack with a most wonderful ship's lantern in his hand, like the gills of some monster of the deep, who informed me that he "was going aloft to the main truck," to have the weathercock down. It was a stormy night and I remonstrated; but Jack called my attention to its making a sound like a cry of despair, and said somebody would be "hailing a ghost" presently, if it wasn't done. So, up to the top of the house, where I could hardly stand for the wind, we went, accompanied by Mr. Beaver; and there Jack, lantern and all, with Mr. Beaver after him, swarmed up to the top of a cupola, some two dozen feet above the chimneys, and stood upon nothing particular, coolly knocking the weathercock off, until they both got into such good spirits with the wind and the height, that I thought they would never come down. Another night, they turned out again, and had a chimney-cowl off. Another night, they cut a sobbing and gulping water-pipe away. Another night, they found out something else. On several occasions, they both, in the coolest manner, simultaneously dropped out of their respective bedroom windows, hand over hand by their counterpanes, to "overhaul" something mysterious in the garden.

The engagement among us was faithfully kept, and nobody revealed anything. All we knew was, if any one's room were haunted, no one looked the worse for it.

## The Ghost in the Clock Room
### Hesba Stretton

**MY COUSIN,** John Herschel, turned rather red, and turned rather white, and said he could not deny that his room had been haunted. The Spirit of a woman had pervaded it. On being asked by several voices whether the Spirit had taken any terrible or ugly shape, my cousin drew his wife's arm through his own, and said decidedly, "No." To the question, had his wife been aware of the Spirit? he answered, "Yes." Had it spoken? "Oh clear, yes!" As to the question, "What did it say?" he replied apologetically, that he could have wished his wife would have undertaken the answer, for she would have executed it much better than he. However, she had made him promise to be the mouthpiece of the Spirit, and was very anxious that he should withhold nothing; so, he would do his best, subject to her correction. "Suppose the Spirit," added my cousin, as he finally prepared himself for beginning, "to be my wife here, sitting among us:"

I was an orphan from my infancy, with six elder half-sisters. A long and persistent course of training imposed upon me the yoke of a second and diverse nature, and I grew up as much the child of my eldest sister, Barbara, as I was the daughter of my deceased parents.

Barbara, in all her private plans, as in all her domestic decrees, inexorably decided that her sisters must be married; and, so powerful had been her single but inflexible will, that each of them had been advantageously settled, excepting myself, upon whom she built her highest hopes.

Most people know a character such as I had grown – a mindless, flirting girl, whose acknowledged vocation was the hunting and catching of an eligible match; rather pretty, lively, and just sentimental enough to make me a very pleasant companion for an idle hour or two, as I exacted and enjoyed the slight attentions an unemployed man is pleased to offer. There was scarcely a young man in the neighbourhood with whom I had not coquetted. I had served my seven years' apprenticeship to my profession, and had passed my twenty-fifth birthday without having achieved my purpose, when Barbara's patience was wearied, and she spoke to me with a decision and explicitness we had always avoided; for, on some subjects, it is better to have a silent understanding than an expressed opinion.

"Stella," she said, solemnly, "you are now five-and-twenty, and every one of your sisters were in homes of their own before they were your age; yet none of them had your advantages or your talents. But I must tell you frankly your chances are on the wane, and, unless you exert yourself, our plans must fail. I have observed an error into which you have fallen, and which I have not mentioned before. Besides your very open and indiscriminate flirtations which young men regard only as an amusing pastime you have a way with you of rallying and laughing at any one who begins to look really serious. Now your opportunity rests upon the moment when they begin to be earnest in their manner. Then you should seem confused and silenced; you ought to lose your vivacity, and half avoid them; seeming almost frightened and quite bewildered by the change. A little melancholy goes a deal further than the utmost cheerfulness; for, if a man believes you can live without him, he will not, give you a second thought. I could name half a dozen most eligible settlements you have lost by laughing at the wrong minute. Mortify a man's self-love, Stella, and you can never heal the wound."

I paused for a minute or two before I answered; for the original suppressed nature that I had inherited from my unknown mother, was stirring unwonted feeling in my heart.

"Barbara," I answered, with timidity, "among all the people I have known, I never saw one whom I could reverence, and look up to; nor, I am half ashamed to use the word, whom I could love."

"I do not wonder you are ashamed," said Barbara, severely. "At your age, you cannot expect to fall in love like a girl of seventeen. But I tell you, definitely and distinctly, it is necessary that you should marry; and we had better work in concert now. So, if you will decide upon any one, I will give you every assistance in my power, and, if you will only concentrate your wishes and abilities, you cannot fail. Propinquity is all you require, if you once make up your mind."

"I do not like any one I know," I replied, moodily; "and I have no chance with those who have known me; so I decide upon besieging Martin Fraser."

Barbara received this announcement with a snort of derisive anger.

The neighbourhood in which we lived was a populous iron district, where, though there were few families of ancient birth or high standing, there were many of our own station, forming a pleasant, hospitable, social class. Our residences were commodious modern houses, built at convenient distances from each other. Some of these, including our own, were the property of an infirm old man, who dwelt in his family mansion, the last of the many gabled, half-timbered, Elizabethan houses which had stood upon the undiscovered iron and coal fields. The last relics of the rural aristocracy of the district, Mr. Fraser and his son led a strictly recluse life, avoiding all communication with their neighbours, whose gaiety and hospitality they could not reciprocate. No one intruded upon their privacy, excepting for the most necessary business transactions. The elder man was almost bedridden, and the younger was said to be entirely absorbed in scientific pursuits. No wonder that Barbara laughed; but her ridicule only excited and confirmed my determination; and the very difficulty of the enterprise gave it the interest that all my other efforts had lacked. I argued obstinately with Barbara till I won her consent.

"You must write to old Mr. Fraser," I said. "Do not mention the young one, and say your youngest sister is studying astronomy, and, as he possesses the only telescope in the country, you will be greatly indebted to him if he would let her see it."

"There is one thing in your favour," Barbara remarked, as she sat down to write; "the old gentleman was once engaged to your mother."

Oh! I am humbled to think how shrewdly we managed our business, and extorted a kind invitation from Mr. Fraser to the "daughter of his old friend, Maria Horley."

It was an evening in February when, accompanied only by an old servant – for Barbara was not included in the invitation – I first crossed the threshold of Martin Fraser's home.

An air of profound peace pervaded the dwelling. I entered it with a vague, uneasy consciousness of unfitness and treachery. My attendant remained in the entrance-hall, and, as I was conducted to the library, a feeling of shyness stole over me, which was prompting me to retreat; but, with the recollection that I was becomingly dressed, I regained my confidence, and advanced smilingly into the room. It was a low, oaken-panelled room, sombre, with massive antique furniture that threw deep and curious shadows around, in the flickering light of a fire, by which stood, instead of the recluse, Martin Fraser whom I expected to meet, a quaint, little child, dressed in the garb of a woman, and with a woman's self-possession and ease of manner.

"I am very glad to see you. You are welcome," she said, advancing to meet me, and extending her hand to lead me to a seat. She clasped my hand with a firm and peculiar grasp; a clasp of guidance and assistance, quite unlike the ordinary timidity or inertness of a child's manner, and, placing me in a chair before the fire, she seated herself nearly opposite me.

I made a few embarrassed remarks, to which she replied, and then I noticed her furtively and in silence. A huge black retriever lay motionless at her feet, which rested upon him, covered with the folds of the long robe-like dress she wore. There was an expression of placidity, slightly pensive, upon her tiny features, heightened by a peculiar habit of closing the eyes, which is rarely seen in children, and always gives them a statuesque appearance. It seemed as though she had withdrawn herself into a solitary self-communing, of which there could be no expression either by words or looks. I grew afraid of the silent, weird-like creature, sitting without apparent breath or motion in the dancing fire-light, and I was glad when the door opened, and the object of my pursuit entered. I looked at him inquisitively, for I had recovered from my sense of treachery, and it amused me to think how unconscious he was of our definite plans concerning him. Hitherto the young men I had met had a fear of being caught, greater than my desire to catch them, so our contest had been an open and equal one; but Martin Fraser knew nothing of the wiles of woman. I remembered that my brown hair fell in curls round my face, and that my dark blue eyes were considered expressive, when I looked up to meet his gaze; but when he accosted me with an air of grave preoccupation and of courteous indifference that would not permit him to notice my personal charms, I trembled to think that all I knew of astronomy was what I had learned at school in Mangnall's Questions.

The grave, austere man said at once:

"My father, Mr. Fraser, is altogether confined to his own rooms, but he desires the favour of a visit from you. Upon me devolves the honour of showing you what you require to view through the telescope, and, while I adjust it, will you oblige him by conversing with him for a few minutes? Lucy Fraser will accompany you."

The child rose, and, taking my hand again in her firm hold, led me to the old man's sitting-room.

"You are like your mother, child," he said, after looking at me long; "you have her face and eyes; not a whit like your sister Barbara. How did you come by your out-of-the-way name, Stella?"

"My father named me after a favourite racer," I answered, for the first time giving the simple derivation of my name.

"Just like him," laughed the old man; "I remember the horse well. I knew your father as well as I do my son Martin. You have seen my son, young lady? Yes, I thought so; and this is my granddaughter, Lucy Fraser, the last chip of the old block; for my son is not a marrying man, and we have adopted her as our heir, and she is always to keep her name, and be the founder of another line of Frasers."

The child stood with pensive, downcast eyes, as though already bowed down by her weight of cares and responsibilities; the old man chatted on, till the deep tones of an organ resounded through the house.

"My uncle is ready for us," she said to me.

We paused at the library door, for I laid my hand restrainingly on Lucy Fraser's shoulder, and stood listening to the wonderful music the organ poured forth. It was such as I had never heard before; roaring and swelling like the ceaseless surging of the sea; and, here and there, a single wailing note which seemed to pierce me with an inexpressible pain. When it had ended, I stood before Martin Fraser silent and subdued.

The telescope had been carried out to the end of the terrace, where the house could not intercept our view; and thither Lucy Fraser and I followed the astronomer. We stood upon the highest point of an imperceptibly rising table-land, the horizon of which was from twenty to forty miles distant. An infinite dome of sky was expanded above us, an ocean of firmament of which the dwellers among houses and mountains can have but little conception. The troops of glittering stars, the dark, shrouding night, the unaccustomed voices of my companions, deepened the awe that oppressed me, and, as I stood between them, I became as earnest and occupied as themselves. I forgot everything but the incomprehensible grandeur of the universe revealed to me, and the majestic sweep of the planets across the field of the telescope. What a freshness of awe and delight came over me! What floods of thought came, wave upon wave, across my mind! And how insignificant I felt before this wilderness of worlds!

I asked, with the humility of a child – for all affectation had been charmed away – if I might come again soon?

Martin Fraser met my uplifted eyes with a keen and penetrating look. I did not quail under it, for I was thinking only of the stars. As he looked, his mouth relaxed into a pleased and genial smile.

"We shall always be glad to see you," he replied.

Barbara was sitting up for me when I returned, and was about to address me with some worldly speculative remark, when I interrupted her quickly. "Not one word, Barbara, not one question, or I never go near The Holmes again."

I cannot dwell upon details. I went often to the house. Into the dull routine of Mr. Fraser's and Lucy's life, I came (I suppose) like a streak of sunshine, lighting up the cloud that had been creeping over them. To both, I brought wholesome excitement and merriment, and so I became dear and necessary to them. But over myself, there came a great and an almost incredible change. I had been frivolous, self-seeking, soulless; but the solemn study I had begun, with other studies that came in its train, awoke me from my inanity, to a life of mental activity. I absolutely forgot my purpose; for I had at once perceived that Martin Fraser was as distant and as self-poised as the Polar Star. So I became to him merely a diligent and insatiable pupil, and he was to me only a grave and exacting master, to be propitiated by my most profound reverence. Each time I crossed the threshold of his quiet home, all the worldliness and coquetry of my nature fell from my soul like an unfit garment, and I entered as into a temple, simple, real, and worshipping.

The happy summer passed away, the autumn crept on, and for eight months I had visited the Frasers constantly, and had never, by word, or look, or tone, intentionally deceived them.

Lucy Fraser and I had long looked forward to an eclipse of the moon, which was visible early in October. I left my home alone in the twilight of that evening, my thoughts dwelling upon the coming pleasure, when, just as I drew near The Holmes, there overtook me one of the young men with whom I had flirted in former times.

"Good evening, Stella," he exclaimed familiarly, "I have not seen you for a long time. Ah! you are pursuing other game I suppose; but are you not aiming rather too high this time? Well, you are in luck just now, for if Martin Fraser does not come forward, there is George Yorke, just come home from Australia with an immense fortune, and he is longing to remind you of some tender passages between you before he went out. He was showing us a lock of your hair after dinner at the Crown yesterday."

I listened to this speech with no outward demonstration; but the reality and mortification of my degradation was gnawing me; and, hastening onward to my sanctuary, I sought the presence of my little Lucy Fraser.

"I have done wrong today," she said. "I have been deceitful. I think I ought to tell you, that you may not think too well of me; but I want you to love me as much as ever. I have not told a story, but I have acted one."

Lucy Fraser leaned her tiny brow upon her tiny fingers, and her eyes closed in silent self-reading.

"My uncle says," she continued, looking up for a moment, and blushing like a woman, "that women are, perhaps, less truthful than men. Because they cannot do things by strength, they do them by cunning. They live falsely. They deceive their own selves. Sometimes women deceive for amusement. He has taught me some words which I shall understand better some day:

*To thine own self be true,*
*And it will follow as the night the day,*
*Thou canst not then be false to any man."*

I stood before the child abashed and speechless, listening with burning cheeks.

"Grandpapa showed me a verse in the Bible which is awful to me. Listen. 'I find more bitter than death, the woman whose heart is snares and nets, and her hands as bands: whoso pleaseth God shall escape from her, but the sinner shall be taken by her.'"

I hid my face in my hands though no eye was on me; for Lucy Fraser had veiled hers with their tremulous lids; and, as I stood confounded and self-accused, a hand was laid upon my arm, and Martin Fraser's voice said, "The eclipse, Stella!"

I started at this first utterance of my name, which he had never spoken before. I was completely unnerved, when I found that Lucy Fraser was not to accompany us on the terrace. As Martin Fraser stooped to see if the telescope were rightly adjusted for my use, I shrank from him.

"What is the meaning of this, Stella?" he exclaimed, as I burst into tears. "Shall I speak to you now, Stella?" he said, "while there is yet time, before you leave us. Does your heart cling to us as our hearts cling to you, till we dare not think of the void there will be in our home when you are gone? We did not live before we knew you. You are our health and our life. I have noted you as I never watched a woman before, and I find no fault in you, my pearl, my jewel, my star. Hitherto, woman and deceit have been inseparably conjoined in my mind; but your innocent heart is the home of truth. I know you have had no thought of this, and my vehemence alarms you; but tell me plainly if you can love me?"

He had taken me in his arms, and my head rested against his strongly throbbing heart. His sternness and austerity were gone, and he offered me the undiminished wealth of a love that had not been wasted in fickle likings. My success was perfect, and how gladly would I have remained there till my silence had grown eloquent! But Barbara rose to my memory, and Lucy Fraser's words still tingled in my ears. The black shadow eating away the heart of the moon seemed to pause in its measured motion. All heaven looked down upon us through the solemn stars. The rustling leaves were hushed, and the scented autumn breeze ceased for a minute; a cloud of truth-compelling witnesses echoed the cry of my awakened conscience. I withdrew myself, sad and shame-stricken.

"Martin Fraser," I said, "your words constrain me to be true. I am the falsest woman you ever met. I came here with the sole and definite intention of attracting you; and if you had ever gone out into our circle, you would have heard of me only as a flirt, a heartless coquette. I dare not bring falsehood to your fireside, and the bitterness of death to your heart. Do not speak to me now; have patience, and I will write to you!"

He would have detained me, but I sprang away, and, running swiftly down the avenue, I passed out of my Eden, with the sentence of perpetual banishment in my heart. The eclipse was at the full, and a horror of darkness and dismay engulfed me, as I stood shivering and sobbing under the restless poplars.

Barbara met me as I hastened to hide myself in my own room, and, with her cold glittering eyes fixed inquiringly on me, said, "Well, what is the matter with you?"

"Nothing," I answered, "only I am tired of astronomy, and I shall not go to The Holmes again. It is of no use."

"I always said so," she replied. "However, to bring matters to a crisis, I gave Mr. Fraser notice we should leave at Christmas. Then you are satisfied that it would be a waste of time to continue going there?"

"Quite," I said, and passed on to my room, to learn, through the weary hours of that night, what desolation and hopelessness meant.

The next day I wrote to Martin Fraser, in every word sacred truth, excepting that, self-deceived, and with a false pride even in my utter humiliation, I told him I had not loved, and did not love him.

The first object upon which my eyes rested every joyless morning, were the tall poplar trees, waving round his house, and beckoning maddeningly to me. The last thing I saw at night was the steady light in his library, shining like a star among the laurels. But, him I could never see; for my letter had been too explicit to suggest a hope; and I could not, for shame, attempt to meet him in his walks. All that remained, for me was to return to my former life, if I could by any means feed my hungering and fainting soul with the husks that had once satisfied me.

George Yorke renewed his addresses to me, offering me wealth beyond our expectations. It was a sore temptation; for before me lay a monotonous and fretted life with Barbara, and a solitary, uncared for old age. Why could not I live as thousands of other women, who were not unhappy wives? But I remembered a passage I had read in one of Martin's books: "It is not always our duty to marry; but it is always our duty to abide by right; not to purchase happiness by loss of honour; not to avoid unweddedness by untruthfulness;" and, setting my face steadily to meet the bleakness and bareness of my lot, I rejected the proposal.

Barbara was terribly exasperated; and very miserable we both were, until she accepted an invitation to spend the Christmas with one of her sisters, while I was left, with my old nurse, to superintend the moving of the furniture. I wished to linger in our old home till the last moment; and I was glad to be alone on Christmas-day in the deserted house, that, in solitude, I might make my mental record of all its associations and remembrances, before the place knew me no more. So, on Christmas-eve, I wandered through the empty rooms, not more empty than my heart, which was being dismantled of its old memories and newer but deeper tendernesses, until I paused mechanically before the window, whence I had often looked across to The Holmes.

The air had been dense and murky all day, with thickly falling snow; but the storm was over, and the moonless sky bright with stars: while the glistening snow reflected light enough to show me where stood, like a dark mass against the sky, the house of Martin Fraser. His room was dark, as it had been for many nights before; but old Mr. Fraser's window, which was nearer to our house, emitted a brilliant light across the white lawn. I was exhausted with over-work and over-excitement, and leaning there, pressing my heated cheeks against the frosty panes, I rehearsed to myself all the incidents of my intercourse with them; and there followed through my mind picture after picture, dream within dream, visions of the happiness that might have been mine.

As I stood thus, with tears stealing through the clasped hands that covered my eyes, my nurse came in to close the shutters. She started nervously when she saw me.

"I thought you were your mother," she exclaimed. "I have seen her stand just so, hundreds of times."

"Susan, how was it that my mother did not marry Mr. Fraser?"

"They were like other people – didn't understand one another, much as they were in love," she answered. "Mr. Fraser's first marriage had been for money, and was not a happy one, so he had grown something stern. They quarrelled, and your mother was provoked to marry Mr. Gretton, your father. Well! Mr. Fraser became an old man all at once, and scarcely ever left his own house; so that she never saw him again, near as he lived: though I have often seen her, when your father was off to balls or races or public meetings, standing here just as you stood now. Only the last time you were in her arms, she was leaning against this window when I brought you in to say good night, and she whispered sofily, looking up to Heaven, "I have tried to do my duty to my husband and to my little child!"

"Nurse," I said, "leave me; do not shut the window yet." It was no longer a selfish emotion that possessed me. I had been murmuring that there was no sorrow like my sorrow; but my mother's error had been graver, and her trials deeper than mine. The burden she had borne had weighed her down into an early grave; but it had not passed away from earth with her. It rested now, heavily augmented by her death, upon the heart of the aged man, who, doubtless, in the contemplative time, was reviewing the events of his past life, and this, chiefly, because it was the saddest of them all. I longed to see him once again to see him who had mourned my mother's death more bitterly and lastingly than any other being, and I determined to steal secretly across the fields, and up the avenue, and, if his window were uncurtained as its brightness suggested, to look upon him once more in remembrance of my mother.

I hesitated upon our door-step, as though my mother and myself were both concerned in some doubtful enterprise; but, with the hardihood of my nature, I drove away the scruple, and passed on into the frosty night.

Yes, the window was uncurtained. I could tell that at the avenue gate; and I should see him, whom my mother loved, lying alone and uncheered upon his couch, as he would lie now all his weary years through, till Lucy Fraser was old enough to be a daughter to him. And then I remembered a rumour that the old man's grandchild was dying, which Susan had told me sorrowfully an hour or two ago; and, growing bewildered, I ran on swiftly until I stood before the window.

It was no longer an invalid's room; the couch was gone and the sheltering screen, and Lucy's little chair within it. Neither were there any appliances of modern luxury or wealth; no softness, nor colouring, nor gorgeousness: it was simply the library and workroom of a busy student, who was forgetful and negligent of comfort. Yet, such as it was, my heart recognised it as home. There Martin sat, deep, as was his wont, in complicated calculations, and frequent reference to the books that were strewn about.

Could it be possible that yonder absorbed man had once spoken passionately to me of love, and now he sat in light, and warmth, and indifference, almost within reach of my hand, while I, like an outcast, stood in cold, and darkness, and despair? Was there, then, no echo of my footstep lingering about the threshold, and no shadowy memory of my face coming between him and his studies? I had forfeited the right to sit beside him, reading the observations his pencil noted down, and chasing away the gloom that was deepening on his nature; and I had not the hope, which would have been really a hope and a consolation to me, that some other woman, more true and more worthy, would by-and-by own my forfeited right.

I heard a bell tinkle, and Martin rose and left the room. I wondered if I should have time to creep in, and steal but one scrap of paper which had been thrown aside carelessly; but, as I tremblingly held the handle of the glass door, he returned, bearing in his arms the emaciated form of little Lucy Fraser. He had wrapped her carefully in a large cloak, and now, as he wheeled a chair to the fire and placed her in it, every rigid lineament of his countenance was softened into tenderness. I stretched out my arms towards him with an intense yearning to be gathered again to his noble heart, and have this chill and darkness dissipated; I turned away, with this last tender image of him graven on my memory, to retrace my steps to my desolate home.

There was a sudden twittering in the ivy overhead, and a little bird, pushed out of its nest into the cold night air, came fluttering down, and flew against the lighted panes. In an instant, his dog, which had been uneasy at my vicinity before, stood baying at the window, and I had only time to escape and hide myself among the shrubs, when he opened it, and stepped out upon the terrace. The dog tracked down the path by which I had come, barking joyfully as he careered along the open fields; and, as Martin looked round, I cowered more closely into the deepest shadows. I knew he must find me; for my footmarks were plain upon the newly-fallen snow, and an extravagant sensation of shame and gladness overpowered me. I saw him lose the footprints once or twice, but at last he was upon the right trace, and, lifting the boughs beneath which I had hidden, he found me among the laurels. I was crouching, and he stooped down curiously.

"It is Stella," I said, faintly.

"Stella?" he echoed.

He lifted me from the ground like a truant child, whom he had expected home every hour, carried me across the terrace into the library, and set me down in the light and warmth of his own hearth. One little kiss to the child, whose eyes beamed with a strange light upon us; and then, taking both my hands in his, he bent down and read my face. I met his gaze unshrinkingly, eye to eye. We sounded the depths of each other's heart in that long, unwavering look. Never more could there be doubt or mistrust; never again deception or misconstruction, between us.

Our star had arisen, and full orbed, rounded into perfection, shed a soft and brilliant light upon the years to come. Chime after chime, like the marriage peal of our souls, came the sound of distant bells across the snow, and roused us from our reverie.

"I thought I had lost you altogether," said Martin to me. "I believed you would come back to me, somehow, at some time; but this evening I heard, that you were gone, and I was telling Lucy Fraser so, not long since. She has been pining to see you."

Now, he suffered me to take the child upon my lap, and she nestled closely to me, with a weary sigh, resting her head upon my bosom. Just then, we heard the carol singers coming up the avenue, and Martin drew the curtains over the window, before which they stationed themselves to sing the legend of the miraculous star in the East.

When the singers ended and raised their cry of "We wish you a merry Christmas, and a happy New Year!" he went out into the porch to speak to them, and I hid my face in the child's curls, and thanked God who had so changed me.

"But what is this, Martin?" I cried in terror, as I raised my head, on his return.

The child's downcast eyes were closely sealed, and her little firm hand had grown lax and nerveless. Insensible and breathless, she lay in my arms like a withering flower.

"It is only fainting," said Martin; "she has been drooping ever since you left us, Stella; and my only hope of her recovery rests in your ministering care."

All that night, I sat with the little child resting on my bosom; revived from her deathlike swoon, and sleeping calmly in my arms because she was already beginning to share in the life and joy and brightness of my heart. There was perfect silence and tranquillity enclosing us in a blissful oasis, interrupted only once by the entrance of my nurse, who had been found by Martin in a state of the utmost perplexity and alarm.

The happy Christmas morning dawned. I asked my nurse to arrange my hair in the style in which my mother used to wear hers. And when, after a long conversation with Susan, Mr. Fraser received me as his daughter with great emotion and affection, and oftener called me Maria than Stella, I was satisfied to be identified with my mother. Then, in the evening, sitting amongst them, a passion of trembling and weeping seized me, which could only be soothed by their fondest assurances. After which I sang them some old songs, with nothing in them but their simple melody; and Mr. Fraser talked freely of former years and of the times to come; and Lucy's eyes almost laughed.

Then Martin took me home along the familiar path, which I had so often traversed alone and fearless; but the excess of gladness made me timid, and at every unusual sound I crept closer to him, with a sweet sense of being protected.

One sunny day in spring, with blithe Lucy and triumphant dictatress Barbara for my bridesmaids, I accepted, humbly and joyfully, the blessed lot of being Martin Fraser's wife. And even in the scenes of the empty-headed folly of my girlhood, I thenceforth tried to be better, and to do my duty in love, gratitude, and devotion. Only, at first, Martin pretended not to believe that on that night I stole out to have a last glimpse, not of him, but of his father: I knowing nothing of the change that had transformed Mr. Fraser's sitting-room into his own study.

## The Ghost in the Double Room
### George Augustus Sala

**WAS THE NEXT** Ghost on my list. I had noted the rooms down in the order in which they were drawn, and this was the order we were to follow. I invoked the Spectre of the Double Room, with the least possible delay, because we all observed John Herschel's wife to be much affected, and we all refrained, as if by common consent, from glancing at one another. Alfred Starling, with the tact and good feeling which are never wanting in him, briskly responded to my call, and declared the Double Room to be haunted by the Ghost of the Ague.

"What is the Ghost of the Ague like?" asked every one, when there had been a laugh.

"Like?" said Alfred. "Like the Ague."

"What is the Ague like?" asked somebody.

"Don't you know?" said Alfred. "I'll tell you."

We had both, Tilly – by which affectionate diminutive I mean my adored Matilda – and your humble servant, agreed that it was not only inexpedient, but in the highest degree contrary to the duty we owed to the community at large, to wait any longer. I had a hundred arguments to bring forward against the baleful effects of long engagements; and Tilly began to quote poetry of a morbid tendency. Our parents and guardians entertained different opinions. My uncle Bonsor wanted us to wait till the shares in the Caerlyon-upon-Usk Something or Other Company, in which undertaking I was vicariously interested, were at a premium – they have been at a hopeless discount for years. Tilly's papa and mamma called Tilly a girl and self a boy, when we were nothing whatsoever of the kind, and only the most ardent and faithful pair of young lovers that had existed since the time of Abelard and Heloïse, or Florio and Biancafiore. As, however, our parents and guardians were not made of adamant or Roman cement, we were not permitted to add another couple to the catalogue of historically unfortunate lovers. Uncle Bonsor and Mr. and Mrs. Captain Standfast (my Tilly's papa and mamma) at last relented. Much was effected towards this desirable consummation by my arguments against celibacy, contained in eight pages foolscap, and of which I made copies in triplicate for the benefit of our hard-hearted relatives. More was done by Tilly threatening to poison herself. Most, however, was accomplished by our both making up our minds to tell a piece thereof to our parents and guardians, and telling them that if they did not acquiesce in our views we would run away and get married at the very first opportunity. There was no just cause or impediment. We were young, healthy, and had plenty of money between us. Loads of money – as we thought then. As to personal appearance, Tilly was simply Lovely, and my whiskers had not been ill spoken of in the best society in Dover. So it was all arranged, and on the twenty-seventh of December, eighteen fifty dash, being the morrow of Boxing-day, Alfred Starling, gent., was to be united in the holy bonds of matrimony to Matilda, only daughter of Captain Rockleigh Standfast, R.N., of Snargatestone Villa, Dover.

I had been left an orphan at a very early age, and the guardian of my moderate property (including the shares in the Caerlyon-upon-Usk Something or Other concern), and guardian of my person, was my uncle Bonsor. He sent me to Merchant Taylors', and afterwards for a couple of years to college at Bonn, on the Rhine. He afterwards – to keep me out of mischief, I believe – paid a handsome premium for my entrance into the counting-house of Messrs. Baum, Brömm, and Boompjees, German merchants, of Finsbury Circus, under whose tutelage I did as little as I liked in the corresponding department, and was much envied by my brother salaried clerks. My uncle Bonsor resided chiefly at Dover, where he was making large sums of money by government contracts, whose objects apparently consisted in boring holes in the chalk and then filling them up again. My uncle was, perhaps, the most respectable man in Europe, and was well known in the city of London as "Responsible Bonsor." He was one of those men who are confidently said to be "good for any amount." He had a waistcoat – worn winter and summer – a waistcoat that wavered in hue between a sunny buff and a stony drab, which looked so ineffably respectable that I am certain if it had been presented at the pay-counter of any bank in Lombard-street the clerks would have cashed it at once for any amount of notes or gold demanded. My uncle Bonsor entrenched himself behind this astonishing garment as behind a fortification, and fired guns of respectability at you. That waistcoat had carried resolutions, assuaged the ire of indignant shareholders, given stability to wavering schemes, and brought in thumping subscriptions for burnt-out Caffres and destitute Fee-jees. It was a safe waistcoat, and Bonsor was a safe man. He was mixed up with a good many companies; but whenever a projector or promoter came to him with a plan, my responsible uncle would confer with his waistcoat, and within five minutes would either tell the projector or promoter to walk out of his counting-house, or put his name down for a thousand pounds. And the scheme was made that Responsible Bonsor put his name down for.

It was arranged that I was to go down to Dover on Christmas-eve, staying at my uncle's, and that we were to dine all together at Captain Standfast's on Christmas-day. Boxing-day was to be devoted to bonnets on the part of my beloved, and to the signing and sealing of certain releases, deeds, covenants, and other documents connected with law and money, on the part of self, my uncle, and my prospective papa in-!aw, and on the twenty-seventh we were to be MARRIED.

Of course my connexion with Messrs. Baum, Brömm, and Boompjees was brought to an amicable termination. I gave the clerks a grand treat at a hostelry in Newgate-street, and had the pleasure of receiving, at a somewhat late hour, and at least eighty-seven times, a unanimous choral assurance, not unaccompanied by hiccups, that I was a "jolly good fellow." I was unwillingly compelled to defer my departure for Dover till the 8.30 p.m. express mail on Christmas-eve, being engaged to a farewell dinner at four, at the mansion of our Mr. Max Boompjees, junior and dinner-giving partner in the firm, in Finsbury Circus. A capital dinner it was, and very merry. I left the gentlemen over their wine, and had just time to pop into a cab and catch the mail train at London Bridge.

You know how quickly time passes on a railway journey when one has dined comfortably before starting. I seemed to have been telegraphed down to Dover, so rapidly were the eighty odd miles skimmed over. But it now becomes my duty to impart to you the knowledge of my Terrible Misfortune. In my youth, a little boy at a preparatory school near Ashford, I had experienced a touch of the dreadful disease of the Kentish marshes. How long this malady had lain concealed in my frame, and by what accident of time or temperature it became again evolved, I had no means of judging, but by the time the train arrived at Dover I was in the throes of acute AGUE.

It was a horrible, persistent, regular shivering and shaking, a racking palsy, a violent tremor, accompanied, I am sure, by fever, for my temples throbbed, and I experienced an almost deafening, jarring, rattling noise in the head. My blood seemed all in revolt, and surging backwards and forwards in my veins, and my unhappy body swayed from side to side with the distempered current. On the platform I staggered to and fro; and the porter, of whose arm I caught hold to steady myself, seemed, lantern and all, by mere communicated violence, to be shaken and buffeted about as I was. I had always been an abstemious young man, and had not exceeded in the consumption of the hospitable junior partner's rare old hock; besides, for all the noise in my head, I could think and talk – albeit my teeth chattered, and my tongue wagged in my mouth with aguish convulsions. I had never known before that railway porters were a hard hearted race, but one tall man in velveteen grinned most impertinently as I was helped into a fly, and I am certain that his companion, a short, fat fellow, with a leer in his eye, thrust his tongue into his cheek as he heaped, at my desire, great-coats and rugs over me, and bade the flyman drive to the Marine Parade, where my uncle resided. I had told every one at the station about my attack of ague.

"*He's* got his load," I heard the tall porter exclaim, as we drove off. Of course he meant that the flyman had got all my luggage.

It was a dreadful five minutes' ride to my uncle's. The fit was so strong on me that my head and limbs kept bumping against opposite sides of the fly, and once came in contact with the window-glass. And the noise in my head never ceased. I stumbled out, somehow, when the vehicle stopped, and, clinging to the knocker of the avuncular door, struck such a quivering peal of blows – I had previously scattered the cabman's fare on the pavement in the attempt to place the money in his hand – that Jakes, my uncle's confidential man, who opened the door, stared with astonishment.

"I'm very ill, Jakes," I stammered, when I had staggered into the hall. "I'm down with that dreadful Ague again."

"Yes, sir," answered Jakes, with something like a grin on *his* countenance too. "Compts of the season, sir. Hadn't you better go to bed, sir?"

Now the house was all lighted up, for there was to be a snapdragon party, and I knew that my Tilly and all the Standfasts were up-stairs with my uncle and his waistcoat, and that they were to wait for my arrival before lighting the bowl. And, ill as I was, I burned to see my darling.

"No, Jakes," I said, "I'll try and bear up. You had better bring me a little cognac, and some very hot water, into the dining-room. It will do me good, and the fit may leave me." What would you believe was the reply of this pampered domestic?

"Better not, sir," he had the hardihood to observe. "Christmas time, sir. Plenty more like you. Better go to bed, sir. Think of your head in the morning, sir."

"Fellow—" I began to retort, still violently trembling, when I saw my uncle Bonsor appear at the head of the staircase. There was a group of ladies and gentlemen in the background, and as well as I could see for shaking, there were the dear golden curls of my Tilly. But her face looked *so* scared and terrified.

"Alfred," said my uncle, sternly, from behind his waistcoat, "you ought to be ashamed of yourself. Go to bed directly, sir!"

"Uncle!" I cried, with a desperate attempt to keep myself steady, "do you think I'm—" Here I made an effort to ascend the staircase, but my foot caught either in the carpet or over one of the confounded brass rods, and, upon my word, I tumbled heels over heels into the hall. And yet, even as I lay recumbent, I shook worse than ever. I heard my uncle's responsible voice ordering the servants to carry me to bed. And I was carried too; Jakes and a long-legged foot-page conveying my shaking body to my bedroom.

The night was brief and terrible as in an access of fever, and I lay shaking and chattering in the burning bed. In the morning, my uncle sent word to say that my ague was all nonsense, and that I was to come down to breakfast.

I went down, determined on remonstrance, but holding on by the banisters and quivering in every limb. O! for the tribulations of that wretched Christmas-day. I was received with sneers, and advised to take very strong tea with a little cognac; yet soon afterwards my uncle shook hands with me, and said that it was only once a year, and that he supposed boys would be boys. Everybody wished me a merry Christmas; but I could only return the compliments of the season in a spasmodic stutter. I took a walk on the pier immediately after breakfast, but I nearly tumbled into the sea, and bumped against so many posts, that I had to be led home by a mariner in a yellow sou'-wester hat, who insisted that I should give him five shillings to drink my health. Then came a more appalling ordeal. I was to call at Snargatestone Villa to accompany my Tilly and the family to church. To my great relief, though I was shaking in every joint of my fingers and toes, nobody took any notice of my alarming complaint. I began to hope that it might be intermittent, and would pass off, but it wouldn't, and rather increased in violence. My darling girl patted me on the head, and hoped that I was "a good boy, now;" but when I began, shiveringly, to explain my attack of ague, she only laughed. We went to church, and then my ague soon brought me into disgrace again. First I created terrible scandal by knocking up against the old pauper women in the free seats, and nearly upsetting the beadle. Then I knocked the church services and hymn-books off the ledge of the pew. Then I kicked a hassock from beneath the very knees of my future mamma-in-law. Then I trod – accidentally I declare – on the toes of Mary Seaton, my Tilly's pretty cousin; whereupon she gave a little scream, and my beloved looked daggers at me; and as a climax, in the agony of that extraordinary horizontal shaking fit of mine, I burst the pew door open, and tumbled once more against the beadle, who in stern tones, and in the name of the churchwardens, desired me either to behave myself or to leave the church. I saw that it was no good contending against my complaint, so I did leave; but as I lurched out of the edifice I seemed to see the clergyman shaking in the reading-desk, and the clerk wagging to and fro beneath him; while the hatchments and tablets shook on the walls; and the organ in the gallery kept bumping now against the charity boys, now against the charity girls.

It wasn't vertigo: the head swims round under that circumstance. It was clearly ague, and of the very worst description; the body shaking from right to left, and the blood surging in the ears with fever.

At dinner-time – my agonies had never ceased, but had not attracted notice – I began literally to put my foot into it again. First, handing Mrs. Van Plank of Sandwich down to the dining-room – my uncle Bonsor escorted Tilly – I entangled myself in the bugle ornaments which that wealthy but obese woman persisted in wearing; and we came down together with alarming results. I was undermost, shaking miserably, with Mrs. Van Plank's large person pressing on my shirt-studs. When we were assisted to rise she would not be appeased. She would not join us at dinner. She ordered her fly and returned to Sandwich, and as the carriage drove away, Captain Standfast, R.N., looking at me as savagely as though he would have liked to have me up at the gangway and give me six dozen on the instant, said, "There goes poor Tilly's diamond bracelet. The old screw won't give it her now. I saw the case on the cushion of the fly."

Was it my fault! could I help my lamentable ague?

At dinner I went from bad to worse. Item: I spilt two ladlefuls of mock turtle soup over a new damask tablecloth. Item: I upset a glass of Madeira over Mary Seaton's blue moire dress. Item: in a convulsive fit of shaking, I nearly stabbed Lieutenant Lamb, of the Fifty-fourth Regiment, stationed on the Heights, with a silver fork; and, finally, in a maniacal attempt to carve a turkey, I sent the entire body or that Christmas bird, with a garland of sausages clinging to it, full butt into the responsible waistcoat of my uncle Bonsor.

The peace was made somehow; I'm sure I don't know in what manner, but half an hour afterwards we were all very pleasant and talkative over our dessert. When I say all, I of course except my unhappy self. There had been no solution of continuity in my shaking. Somebody, I think, proposed my health. In returning thanks, I hit the proposer a tremendous blow under the left eye with my elbow. Endeavouring to regain my equilibrium, I sent a full glass of claret into the embroidered cambric bosom of that unhappy Lieutenant Lamb. In desperation I caught hold of the tablecloth with both hands. I saw how it would be; the perfidious polished mahogany slid away from my grasp. I turned my foot frantically round the leg of the table nearest me, and with a great crash over went dining-table, cut-glass decanters, and dessert. Lieutenant Lamb was badly hit across the bridge of the nose with a pair of silver nut-crackers, and my uncle Bonsor's head was crowned, in quite a classic manner, with filberts and hot-house grapes.

The bleak December sun rose next morning upon ruin and catastrophe. As well as I can collect my scattered reminiscences of that dismal time, my offences against decorum were once more condoned: not in consequence of my complaint (in which my relatives and friends persisted in disbelieving), but on the ground that it was "only once a year." Lawyers came backwards and forwards to Snargatestone Villa during the forenoon. There was a great production of tin boxes, red tape, blue seals, foolscap paper, and parchment; and my uncle Bonsor was more responsible than ever. They brought me a paper to sign at last, whispering much among themselves as they did so;

and I protest that I could see nothing but a large pool of white, jogging about in a field of green tablecloth, while on the paper an infinity of crabbed characters seemed racing up and down in a crazed and furious manner. I endeavoured to nerve myself to the task of signing, I bit my lips, I clenched my left hand, I tried to screw my wagging head on to my neck, I cramped my toes up in my boots, I held my breath; but was it my fault, when I clutched the pen and tried to write my name, that the abominable goosequill began to dance, and skate, and leap, and plunge, and dig its nibs into the paper; that when, in despair, I seized the inkstand, to hold it nearer to the pen, I shook its sable contents, in horrid, horned, tasseled blots, all over a grave legal document? I finished my achievement by inflicting a large splash on my uncle's sacred waistcoat, and hitting Captain Standfast under the third rib with the pen.

"That will do," my papa-in-law cried, collaring me. "Leave the house, scoundrel!"

But I broke from his grasp, and fled to the drawing-room, knowing that my Tilly would be there with her bridesmaids and her bonnets.

"Tilly – my adored Matilda!" I cried.

"No further explanation is needed, sir," broke in my beloved, in an inexorable tone. "I have seen and heard quite enough. Alfred Starling, I would sooner wed the meanest hind that gathers samphire on yon cliff than become the bride of a profligate and drunkard. Go, sir; repent if you can; be ashamed if you can. Henceforth we are strangers. Slave of self-indulgence, adieu for ever!" And she swept out of the room, and I could hear her sobbing her pretty heart out in the boudoir beyond.

I was discarded and expelled for ever from Snargatestone Villa; my uncle Bonsor repudiated me, and disinherited me from any share in his waistcoat; I hurled myself into the next train at the station, and shook all the way back to town. At about dusk on that dreadful Boxing-day, I found myself wandering and jolting about the purlieus of Soho.

From Soho-square the south-west side, I think – branches a shabby, dingy little court, called Bateman's-buildings. I was standing shivering at the corner of this ill-favoured place, when I stumbled against a gentleman, who looked about seven-eighths soldier and one-eighth civilian.

"He was a little, dapper, clean-limbed, young-looking old man, with a yellow face, and grey hair and whiskers. Soldiers, save in the cavalry, didn't wear moustaches then. He wore a blue uniform coat, rather white at the seams, and a silver medal with a faded ribbon on his breast. He had a bunch of parti-coloured streamers in his undress cap; he carried a bamboo-cane under his arm; on each sleeve he wore golden stripes, much tarnished; on his scarlet collar was embroidered a golden lion; and on his shoulders he had a pair of little, light, golden epaulettes, that very much resembled two sets of teeth from a dentist's glass-case, covered with bullion.

"And how are you, my hearty?" said the military gentleman, cheerily.

I answered that I was the most miserable wretch in the world; upon which the military gentleman, slapping me on the back and calling me his gallant comrade, asked me to have a pint of beer, warmed with a little spice, and a dash of Old Tom in it, for the sake of Christmas.

"You're a roving buck," observed my new friend. "*I'm* a roving buck. Yon never happened to have a twin-brother named Siph, did you?"

"No," I answered, moodily.

"He was as like you as two peas," continued the military gentleman, who had by this time taken my arm, and was leading me all shaking and clattering towards a mouldy little tavern, on whose door-jambs were displayed a couple of coloured cartoons, framed and glazed and much fly-blown, and displaying, the one, the presentment of an officer in sky-blue uniform much belaced with silver, and the other a bombadier with an enormous shako ramming the charge into a cannon: the whole surmounted by a placard setting forth that smart young men were required for the Honourable East India Company's infantry, cavalry, and artillery, and earnestly exhorting all smart young men, as aforesaid, to apply forthwith to Sergeant-Major Chutnee, who was always to be heard of at the bar of the "Highland Laddie," or at the office in Bateman's-buildings.

"The last time I saw him," went on the man with the yellow face and the grey whiskers, when he had tilted me into the "Highland Laddie," pinned me, shaking, against the bar-counter, and ordered a pint of sophisticated beer, "he had left our service, and was a field-marshal in the army of the King of Oude. Many's the time I've seen him with his cocked-hat and di'mond epulets riding on a white elephant, with five-and-twenty black-fellows running after him to brush the flies away and draw the soda-water corks. Such brandy he'd have with it, and all through meeting me promiscuous in this very public."

It is useless to prolong the narrative of my conversation with the military gentleman; suffice it to say, that within an hour I had taken the fatal shilling, and enlisted in the service of the Honourable East India Company. I was not a beggar. I possessed property, over which my uncle Bonsor had no control. I had not committed any crime; but I felt lost, ruined, and desperate, and I enlisted. For a wonder, when I was brought before a magistrate to be attested, and before a surgeon to be examined respecting my sanitary fitness for the service, my ague seemed entirely to have left me. I stood firm and upright in the witness-box, and under the measuring standard, and was only deterred by shame and anguish at the misconstruction put upon my conduct at Dover from negotiating for my discharge.

I had scarcely reached the East India recruiting depôt at Brentwood, however, before the attacks of ague returned with redoubled severity. At first, on my stating that I had an ear for music, they began to train me for a bandsman, but I could not keep a wind instrument in my hands, and struck those that were played by my comrades from their grasp. Then, I was put into the awkward squad among the recruits, and the sergeants caned me; but I could never get beyond the preliminary drill of the goose-step, and I kept my own time, and not the squad's, even then. The depôt surgeons wouldn't place the slightest credence in my ague, and the sergeant-major of my company reported that I was a skulking, "malingering" impostor. Among my comrades who despised, without pitying me, I got the nickname of "Young Shivery-Shakery." And the most wonderful thing is, that, although I could have procured remittances at any time, the thought of purchasing my discharge never entered my poor, shaking, jarring head.

How they came to send such a trembling, infirm creature as a soldier to India, I can't make out; but sent I was, by long sea, in a troop-ship, with seven or eight hundred more recruits. My military career in the East came to a very speedy and inglorious termination. We had scarcely arrived at Bombay when the battalion of the European regiment into which I was draughted was sent up-country to the banks of the Sutlej, where the Sikh war was then raging. It was the campaign of Aliwal and Sobraon, but it was very little that I saw of that glorious epoch in our military annals. In contemptuous reference to my nervous disorder, I was only permitted to form part of the baggage-guard, and one night, after perhaps ten days' march, throughout which I had shaken most awfully, an attack was made on our rear for mere purposes of plunder by a few rascally budmashes or thieves. Nothing was easier than to put these paltry scoundrels to the rout. I had been brave enough as a lad and as a young man. I declare that on the present occasion I didn't run away; but my unhappy disease got the mastery of me. I shook my musket out of my hands, my shako off my head, and my knapsack off my back, and my wretched legs shook and jolted me, as it seemed, over miles of arid country. There was some talk of shooting me afterwards, and some of flogging me; but corporal punishment did not exist in the Company's army. They sent me to a vile place of incarceration called a "congee house," where I was fed principally on rice-water, and at last I was conveyed to Bombay, tried by court-martial, sentenced, and publicly drummed out of my regiment as a coward. Yes, I, the son of a gentleman, and the possessor of a genteel private property, had the facings cut off my uniform, and, to the sound of the "Rogues' March," was dismissed from the service of the Honourable East India Company with ignominy and disgrace.

I can scarcely tell how I reached England again; whether a berth was given me, whether I paid for it, or whether I worked my passage home. I can only remember that the ship in which I was a passenger broke her back in Algoa Bay, close to the Cape, and became a total wreck. There was not the slightest danger; we were surrounded by large and small craft, and every soul on board was saved; but I shook so terribly and incessantly while the boats were leaving the vessel, that the whole ship's company hooted and groaned at me when I was shoved over the side, and I was not allowed to go in the long-boat, but was towed alone and aft in the dingy to shore.

I took passage in another ship, which did nothing but shake all the way from the Cape to Plymouth, and at last I reached England. I wrote innumerable letters to my friends and relatives, to Tilly and to my uncle Bonsor; but the only answer I received was a few formal lines from my uncle's lawyer, telling me that my illegible scrawls had come to the hands of the persons for whom they were designed; but that no further notice could be taken of my communications. I was put into the possession of my property to the last penny, but it seems to me that I must have shaken it away either at dice or bagatelle, or ninepins or billiards. And I remember that I never made a stroke at the latter game without hitting my adversary with the cue in the chest, knocking down the marker, sending the balls scudding through the windows, disarranging the scores, and cutting holes in the cloth, for which I had to pay innumerable guineas to the proprietor of the rooms.

I remember one day going into a jeweller's shop in Regent-street to purchase a watch-key. I had only a silver one now, my gold repeater had been shaken away in some unaccountable manner. It was winter-time, and I wore an overcoat with long loose sleeves. While the shopkeeper was adjusting a key to my watch, my ague fit came upon me with demoniacal ferocity, and, to my horror and dismay, in catching hold of the counter to save myself, I tilted a trayful of diamond rings over. Some fell on the floor; but some, horror and anguish! fell into the sleeves of my overcoat. I shook so that I seemed to have shaken diamond rings into my hands, my pockets, my very boots. By some uncontrollable impulse I attempted flight, but was seized at the very shop door, and carried, shaking, to the police-station.

I was taken before a magistrate, and committed, still shaking, in a van, to gaol. I shook for some time in a whitewashed cell, when I was brought up, shaking, to the Central Criminal Court, and placed, shaking, on my trial for an attempted robbery of fifteen hundred pounds' worth of property. The evidence was clear against me. My counsel tried to plead something about "kleptomania," but in vain. My uncle Bonsor, who had come expressly up from Dover, spoke strongly against my character. I was found guilty; yes, I, the most innocent and unfortunate young man breathing, and sentenced to seven years' transportation! I can recal the awful scene vividly to memory now. The jury in a body were shaking their heads at me. So was the judge, so was my uncle Bonsor, so were the spectators in the gallery; and I was holding on by the spikes on the ledge of the dock, shaking from right to left like ten thousand million aspen-leaves. My skull was splitting, my brain was bursting, when— I WOKE.

I was lying in a very uncomfortable position in a first-class carriage of the Dover mail-train; everything in the carriage was shaking; the oil was surging to and fro in the lamp; my companions were swaying to and fro, and the sticks and umbrellas were rattling in the network above. The train was "at speed," and my frightful dream was simply due to the violent and unusual oscillation of the train. Then, sitting up, and rubbing my eyes, immensely relieved, but holding on by the compartments near me (so violently did the carriages shake from side to side), I began to remember what I had dreamed or heard of others' dreams before; while at sea, or while somebody was knocking loudly at the door; and of the odd connexions between unusual sound and motion on the thoughts of our innermost souls. And again with odd distinctness I remember that at one period of my distempered vision, namely, when I was attested and examined as a recruit, I had remained perfectly still and steady. This temporary freedom from ague I was fain to ascribe to the customary two or three minutes' stoppage of the train at Tunbridge Wells. But, thank Heaven, all this was but a dream!

"Enough to shake one's head off!" exclaimed the testy old lady opposite, alluding to the oscillation of the train, as the guard appeared at the window with a shout of "Do—VOR!"

"Well, mum, it have bin a shaking most unusual all the way down," replied that functionary. "Thought we should have bin off the line, more than once. Screws will be looked to tomorrow morning. "Night, sir!" – this was to me: I knew the man well. "Merry Christmas and a happy new year! You'll be wanting a fly to Snargatestone Villa, won't you, sir? Now, por—TER!"

I did want that fly, and I had it. I paid the driver liberally, and did not scatter his money over the pavement. Mr. Jakes insisted upon my having something hot in the dining-room the moment I arrived. The weather was so "woundy cold," he said. I joined the merry party upstairs, and was received by my Tilly with open arms, and by my uncle Bonsor with an open waistcoat. I partook in cheerful moderation of the snapdragon festivities of Christmas-eve. We all dined together on Christmas-day, and I helped the soup and carved a turkey, beautifully; and on the morrow, Boxing-day, was complimented by my uncle's lawyer on my remarkably neat caligraphy, as displayed in the signatures to the necessary legal documents. On the twenty-seventh of December, eighteen, forty-six, I was married to my darling Tilly, and was going to live happy ever afterwards, when I WOKE AGAIN – really did wake in bed in this Haunted House – and found that I had been very much shaken on the railway coming down, and that there was no marriage, no Tilly, no Mary Seaton, no Van Plank, no anything but myself and the Ghost of the Ague, and the two inner windows of the Double Room rattling like the ghosts of two departed watchmen who wanted spiritual assistance to carry me to the dead and gone old Watch-house.

# The Ghost in the Picture Room
## Adelaide Anne Procter

**BELINDA**, with a modest self-possession quite her own, promptly answered for this Spectre in a low, clear voice:

> *The lights extinguished; by the hearth I leant,*
> *Half weary with a listless discontent.*
> *The flickering giant shadows, gathering near,*
> *Closed round me with a dim and silent fear;*
> *All dull, all dark; save when the leaping flame,*
> *Glancing, lit up The Picture's ancient frame.*
> *Above the hearth it hung. Perhaps the night,*
> *My foolish tremors, or the gleaming light,*
> *Lent Power to that Portrait dark and quaint—*
> *A Portrait such as Rembrandt loved to paint—*
> *The likeness of a Nun. I seemed to trace*
> *A world of sorrow in the patient face,*
> *In the thin hands folded across her breast—*
> *Its own and the room's shadow hid the rest.*
> *I gazed and dreamed, and the dull embers stirred,*
> *Till an old legend that I once had heard*
> *Came back to me; linked to the mystic gloom*
> *Of the dark Picture in the ghostly room.*
> *In the far South, where clustering vines are hung;*
> *Where first the old chivalric lays were sung;*
> *Where earliest smiled that gracious child of France,*
> *Angel and Knight and Fairy, called Romance,*
> *I stood one day. The warm blue June was spread*
> *Upon the earth; blue summer overhead,*
> *Without a cloud to fleck its radiant glare,*
> *Without a breath to stir its sultry air.*
> *All still, all silent, save the sobbing rush*
> *Of rippling waves, that lapsed in silver hush*
> *Upon the beach; where, glittering towards the strand*
> *The purple Mediterranean kissed the land.*
> *All still, all peaceful; when a convent chime*
> *Broke on the mid-day silence for a time,*
> *Then trembling into quiet, seemed to cease,*
> *In deeper silence and more utter peace.*
> *So as I turned to gaze, where gleaming white,*
> *Half hid by shadowy trees from passers' sight,*
> *The convent lay, one who had dwelt for long*
> *In that fair home of ancient tale and song,*
> *Who knew the story of each cave and hill,*
> *And every haunting fancy lingering still*
> *Within the land, spake thus to me, and told*

*The convent's treasured legend, quaint and old:*
*Long years ago, a dense and flowering wood,*
*Still more concealed where the white convent stood,*
*Borne on its perfumed wings the title came:*
*"Our Lady of the Hawthorns" is its name.*
*Then did that bell, which still rings out today*
*Bid all the country rise, or eat, or pray.*
*Before that convent shrine, the haughty knight*
*Passed the lone vigil of his perilous fight;*
*For humbler cottage strife, or village brawl,*
*The abbess listened, prayed, and settled all.*
*Young hearts that came, weighed down by love or wrong,*
*Left her kind presence comforted and strong.*
*Each passing pilgrim, and each beggar's right*
*Was food, and rest, and shelter for the night.*
*But, more than this, the nuns could well impart*
*The deepest mysteries of the healing art;*
*Their store of herbs and simples was renowned,*
*And held in wondering faith for miles around.*
*Thus strife, love, sorrow, good and evil fate,*
*Found help and blessing at the convent gate.*
*Of all the nuns, no heart was half so light,*
*No eyelids veiling glances half as bright,*
*No step that glided with such noiseless feet,*
*No face that looked so tender or so sweet,*
*No voice that rose in choir so pure, so clear,*
*No heart to all the others half so dear*
*(So surely touched by others' pain or woe,*
*Guessing the grief her young life could not know),*
*No soul in childlike faith so undefiled,*
*As Sister Angela's, the "Convent Child."*
*For thus they loved to call her. She had known*
*No home, no love, no kindred, save their own—*
*An orphan, to their tender nursing given,*
*Child, plaything, pupil, now the bride of Heaven.*
*And she it was who trimmed the lamp's red light*
*That swung before the altar, day and night.*
*Her hands it was, whose patient skill could trace*
*The finest broidery, weave the costliest lace;*
*But most of all, her first and dearest care,*
*The office she would never miss or share,*
*Was every day to weave fresh garlands sweet,*
*To place before the shrine at Mary's feet.*
*Nature is bounteous in that region fair,*
*For even winter has her blossoms there.*
*Thus Angela loved to count each feast the best,*
*By telling with what flowers the shrine was dressed,*

In pomp supreme the countless Roses passed,
  Battalion on battalion thronging fast,
Each with a different banner, flaming bright,
Damask, or striped, or crimson, pink, or white,
Until they bowed before the new-born queen,
  And the pure virgin lily rose serene.
Though Angela always thought the Mother blest,
  Must love the time of her own hawthorns best
Each evening through the year, with equal care,
She placed her flowers; then kneeling down in
  prayer,
As their faint perfume rose before the shrine,
  So rose her thoughts, as pure and as divine.
She knelt until the shades grew dim without,
  Till one by one the altar lights shone out,
Till one by one the nuns, like shadows dim,
Gathered around to chant their vesper hymn;
Her voice then led the music's winged flight,
  And "Ave, Maris Stella" filled the night.
But wherefore linger on those days of peace?
When storms draw near, then quiet hours must cease.
  War, cruel war, defaced the land, and came
So near the convent with its breath of flame,
That, seeking shelter, frightened peasants fled,
Sobbing out tales of coming fear and dread.
  Till after a fierce skirmish, down the road,
One night came straggling soldiers, with their load
Of wounded, dying comrades; and the band,
  Half pleading, yet as if they could command,
Summoned the trembling sisters, craved their care,
  Then rode away, and left the wounded there.
But soon compassion bade all fear depart,
  And bidding every sister do her part,
Some prepare simples, healing salves, or bands,
The abbess chose the more experienced hands,
To dress the wounds needing most skilful care;
Yet even the youngest novice took her share,
  And thus to Angela, whose ready will
  And pity could not cover lack of skill,
The charge of a young wounded knight must fall,
A case which seemed least dangerous of them all.
  Day after day she watched beside his bed,
  And first in utter quiet the hours fled:
His feverish moans alone the silence stirred,
Or her soft voice, uttering some pious word.
  At last the fever left him; day by day
  The hours, no longer silent, passed away.

🏵 183 🏵

*What could she speak of? First, to still his plaints,*
*She told him legends of the martyr'd saints;*
*Described the pangs, which, through God's plenteous*
*grace.*
*Had gained their souls so high and bright a place.*
*This pious artifice soon found success —*
*Of buds and blossoms strewed her way with flowers.*
*The knight unwearied listened; till at last,*
*He too described the glories of his past;*
*Tourney, and joust, and pageant bright and fair,*
*And all the lovely ladies who were there.*
*But half incredulous she heard. Could this—*
*This be the world? this place of love and bliss!*
*Where, then, was hid the strange and hideous charm.*
*That never failed to bring the gazer harm?*
*She crossed herself, yet asked, and listened still,*
*And still the knight described with all his skill,*
*The glorious world of joy, all joys above,*
*Transfigured in the golden mist of love.*
*Spread, spread your wings, ye angel guardians*
*bright,*
*And shield these dazzling phantoms from her sight!*
*But no; days passed, matins and vespers rang,*
*And still the quiet nuns toiled, prayed, and sang,*
*And never guessed the fatal, coiling net*
*That every day drew near, and nearer yet.*
*Around their darling; for she went and came*
*About her duties, outwardly the same.*
*The same? ah, no! even when she knelt to pray,*
*Some charmed dream kept all her heart away.*
*So days went on, until the convent gate*
*Opened one night. Who durst go forth so late?*
*Across the moonlit grass, with stealthy tread,*
*Two silent, shrouded figures passed and fled.*
*And all was silent, save the moaning seas,*
*That sobbed and pleaded, and a wailing breeze*
*That sighed among the perfumed hawthorn trees.*
*What need to tell that dream so bright and brief,*
*Of joy unchequered by a dread of grief?*
*What need to tell how all such dreams must fade,*
*Before the slow foreboding, dreaded shade,*
*That floated nearer, until pomp and pride,*
*Pleasure and wealth, were summoned to her side,*
*To bid, at least, the noisy hours forget,*
*And clamour down the whispers of regret.*
*Still Angela strove to dream, and strove in vain;*
*Awakened once, she could not sleep again.*

She saw, each day and hour, more worthless grown
The heart for which she cast away her own;
And her soul learnt, through bitterest inward strife,
The slight, frail love for which she wrecked her life,
The phantom for which all her hope was given,
The cold bleak earth for which she bartered heaven!
But all in vain; what chance remained? what heart
Would stoop to take so poor an outcast's part?
Years fled, and she grew reckless more and more,
Until the humblest peasant closed his door,
And where she passed, fair dames, in scorn and pride,
Shuddered, and drew their rustling robes aside.
At last a yearning seemed to fill her soul,
A longing that was stronger than control:
Once more, just once again, to see the place
That knew her young and innocent; to retrace
The long and weary southern path; to gaze
Upon the haven of her childish days;
Once more beneath the convent roof to lie;
Once more to look upon her home—and die!
Weary and worn—her comrades, chill remorse
And black despair, yet a strange silent force
Within her heart, that drew her more and more—
Onward she crawled, and begged from door to door.
Weighed down with weary days, her failing strength
Grew less each hour, till one day's dawn at length,
As its first rays flooded the world with light,
Showed the broad waters, glittering blue and bright,
And where, amid the leafy hawthorn wood,
Just as of old the low white convent stood.
Would any know her? Nay, no fear. Her face
Had lost all trace of youth, of joy, of grace,
Of the pure happy soul they used to know—
The novice Angela—so long ago.
She rang the convent bell. The well-known sound
Smote on her heart, and bowed her to the ground.
And she, who had not wept for long dry years,
Felt the strange rush of unaccustomed tears;
Terror and anguish seemed to check her breath,
And stop her heart O God! could this be death?
Crouching against the iron gate, she laid
Her weary head against the bars, and prayed:
But nearer footsteps drew, then seemed to wait;
And then she heard the opening of the grate,
And saw the withered face, on which awoke
Pity and sorrow, as the portress spoke,
And asked the stranger's bidding: "Take me in,"

*She faltered, "Sister Monica, from sin,*
*And sorrow, and despair, that will not cease;*
*Oh take me in, and let me die in peace!"*
*With soothing words the sister bade her wait,*
*Until she brought the key to unbar the gate.*
*The beggar tried to thank her as she lay,*
*And heard the echoing footsteps die away.*
*But what soft voice was that which sounded near,*
*And stirred strange trouble in her heart to hear?*
*She raised her head; she saw—she seemed to know*
*A face that came from long, long years ago:*
*Herself; yet not as when she fled away,*
*The young and blooming Novice, fair and gay,*
*But a grave woman, gentle and serene:*
*The outcast knew it—what she might have been.*
*But as she gazed and gazed, a radiance bright*
*Filled all the place with strange and sudden light;*
*The nun was there no longer, but instead,*
*A figure with a circle round its head,*
*A ring of glory; and a face, so meek,*
*So soft, so tender... Angela strove to speak,*
*And stretched her hands out, crying, "Mary mild,*
*Mother of mercy, help me!–help your child!"*
*And Mary answered, "From thy bitter past,*
*Welcome, my child! oh, welcome home at last!*
*I filled thy place. Thy flight is known to none,*
*For all thy daily duties I have done;*
*Gathered thy flowers, and prayed, and sang, and*
*slept;*
*Didst thou not know, poor child, thy place was kept?*
*Kind hearts are here; yet would the tenderest one*
*Have limits to its mercy: God has none.*
*And man's forgiveness may be true and sweet,*
*But yet he stoops to give it. More complete*
*Is love that lays forgiveness at thy feet,*
*And pleads with thee to raise it. Only Heaven*
*Means crowned, not vanquished, when it says*
*'Forgiven!'*
*Back hurried Sister Monica; but where*
*Was the poor beggar she left lying there?*
*Gone; and she searched in vain, and sought the*
*place*
*For that wan woman, with the piteous face:*
*But only Angela at the gateway stood,*
*Laden with hawthorn blossoms from the wood.*

*And never did a day pass by again,*

But the old portress, with a sigh of pain,
Would sorrow for her loitering: with a prayer
That the poor beggar, in her wild despair,
Might not have come to any ill; and when
She ended, "God forgive her!" humbly then
Did Angela bow her head, and say "Amen!"
How pitiful her heart was! all could trace
Something that dimmed the brightness of her face
After that day, which none had seen before;
Not trouble — but a shadow — nothing more.
Years passed away. Then, one dark day of dread,
Saw all the sisters kneeling round a bed,
Where Angela lay dying; every breath
Struggling beneath the heavy hand of death.
But suddenly a flush lit up her cheek,
She raised her wan right hand, and strove to speak.
In sorrowing love they listened; not a sound
Or sigh disturbed the utter silence round;
The very taper's flames were scarcely stirred,
In such hushed awe the sisters knelt and heard.
And thro' that silence Angela told her life:
Her sin, her flight; the sorrow and the strife,
And the return; and then, clear, low, and calm,
"Praise God for me, my sisters;" and the psalm
Rang up to heaven, far, and clear, and wide,
Again and yet again, then sank and died;
While her white face had such a smile of peace,
They saw she never heard the music cease;
And weeping sisters laid her in her tomb,
Crowned with a wreath of perfumed hawthorn bloom.

And thus the legend ended. It may be
Something is hidden in the mystery,
Besides the lesson of God's pardon, shown
Never enough believed, or asked, or known.
Have we not all, amid life's petty strife,
Some pure ideal of a noble life
That once seemed possible? Did we not hear
The flutter of its wings, and feel it near,
And just within our reach? It was. And yet
We lost it in this daily jar and fret,
And now live idle in a vague regret;
But still our place is kept, and it will wait,
Ready for us to fill it, soon or late.
No star is ever lost we once have seen,
We always may be what we might have been
Since good, tho' only thought, has life and breath,

*God's life–can always be redeemed from death;*
*And evil, in its nature, is decay,*
*And any hour can blot it all away;*
*The hopes that, lost, in some far distance seem,*
*May be the truer life, and this the dream.*

## The Ghost in the Cupboard Room
### Wilkie Collins

MR. BEAVER, on being "spoke" (as his friend and ally, Jack Governor, called it), turned out of an imaginary hammock with the greatest promptitude, and went straight on duty. "As it's Nat Beaver's watch," said he, "there shall be no skulking." Jack looked at me, with an expectant and admiring turn of his eye on Mr. Beaver, full of complimentary implication. I noticed, by the way, that Jack, in a naval absence of mind with which he is greatly troubled at times, had his arm round my sister's waist. Perhaps this complaint originates in an old nautical requirement of having something to hold on by.

These were the terms of Mr. Beaver's revelation to us:

What I have got to put forward, will not take very long; and I shall beg leave to begin by going back to last night – just about the time when we all parted from one another to go to bed.

The members of this good company did a very necessary and customary thing, last night – they each took a bedroom candlestick, and lit the candle before they went up-stairs. I wonder whether any one of them noticed that I left my candlestick untouched, and my candle unlighted; and went to bed, in a Haunted House, of all the places in the world, in the dark? I don't think any one of them did.

That is, perhaps, rather curious to begin with. It is likewise curious, and just as true, that the bare sight of those candlesticks in the hands of this good company set me in a tremble, and made last night, a night's bad dream instead of a night's good sleep. The fact of the matter is – and I give you leave, ladies and gentlemen, to laugh at it as much as you please that the ghost which haunted me last night, which has haunted *me* off and on for many years past, and which will go on haunting me till I am a ghost myself (and consequently spirit-proof in all respects), is, nothing more or less than – a bedroom candlestick.

Yes, a bedroom candlestick and candle, or a flat candlestick and candle – put it which way you like – that is what haunts me. I wish it was something pleasanter and more out of the common way; a beautiful lady, or a mine of gold and silver, or a cellar of wine and a coach and horses, and such-like. But, being what it is, I must take it for what it is, and make the best of it – and I shall thank you all kindly if you will help me out by doing the same.

I am not a scholar myself; but I make bold to believe that the haunting of any man, with anything under the sun, begins with the frightening of him. At any rate, the haunting of me with a bedroom candlestick and candle began with the frightening of me with a bedroom candlestick and candle – the frightening of me half out of my life, ladies and gentlemen; and, for the time being, the frightening of me altogether out of my wits. That is not a very pleasant thing to confess to you all, before stating the particulars; but perhaps you will be the readier to believe that I am not a downright coward, because you find me bold enough to make a clean breast of it already, to my own great disadvantage, so far.

These are the particulars, as well as I can put them.

I was apprenticed to the sea when I was about as tall as my own walking-stick; and I made good enough use of my time to be fit for a mate's berth at the age of twenty-five years.

It was in the year eighteen hundred and eighteen, or nineteen, I am not quite certain which, that I reached the before-mentioned age of twenty-five. You will please to excuse my memory not being very good for dates, names, numbers, places, and such-like. No fear, though, about the particulars I have undertaken to tell you of; I have got them all ship-shape in my recollection; I can see them, at this moment, as clear as noonday in my own mind. But there is a mist over what went before, and, for the matter of that, a mist likewise over much that came after – and it's not very likely to lift, at my time of life, is it?

Well, in eighteen hundred and eighteen, or nineteen, when there was peace in our part of the world – and not before it was wanted, you will say – there was fighting, of a certain scampering, scrambling kind, going on in that old fighting ground, which we seafaring men know by the name of the Spanish Main. The possessions that belonged to the Spaniards in South America had broken into open mutiny and declared for themselves years before. There was plenty of bloodshed between the new government and the old; but the new had got the best of it, for the most part, under one General Bolivar – a famous man in his time, though he seems to have dropped out of people's memories now. Englishmen and Irishmen with a turn for fighting, and nothing particular to do at home, joined the general as volunteers; and some of our merchants here found it a good venture to send supplies across the ocean to the popular side. There was risk enough, of course, in doing this; but where one speculation of the kind succeeded, it made up for two, at the least, that failed. And that's the true principle of trade, wherever I have met with it, all the world over.

Among the Englishmen who were concerned in this Spanish-American business, I, your humble servant, happened, in a small way, to be one. I was then mate of a brig belonging to a certain firm in the City, which drove a sort of general trade, mostly in queer out-of-the-way places, as far from home as possible; and which freighted the brig, in the year I am speaking of, with a cargo of gunpowder for General Bolivar and his volunteers. Nobody knew anything about our instructions, when we sailed, except the captain; and he didn't half seem to like them. I can't rightly say how many barrels of powder we had on board, or how much each barrel held – I only know we had no other cargo. The name of the brig was The Good Intent – a queer name enough, you will tell me, for a vessel laden with gunpowder, and sent to help a revolution. And as far as this particular voyage was concerned, so it was. I meant that for a joke, ladies and gentlemen, and I'm sorry to find you don't laugh at it.

The Good Intent was the craziest old tub of a vessel I ever went to sea in, and the worst found in all respects. She was two hundred and thirty, or two hundred and eighty tons burden, I forget which; and she had a crew of eight, all told – nothing like as many as we ought by rights to have had to work the brig. However, we were well and honestly paid our wages; and we had to set that against the chance of foundering at sea, and, on this occasion, likewise, the chance of being blown up into the bargain. In consideration of the nature of our cargo, we were harassed with new regulations which we didn't at all like, relative to smoking our pipes and lighting our lanterns; and, as usual in such cases, the captain who made the regulations preached what he didn't practise. Not a man of us was allowed to have a bit of lighted candle in his hand when he went below

– except the skipper; and he used his light, when he turned in, or when he looked over his charts on the cabin table, just as usual. This light was a common kitchen candle or "dip," of the sort that goes eight or ten to the pound; and it stood in an old battered flat candlestick, with all the japan worn and melted off, and all the tin showing through. It would have been more seamanlike and suitable in every respect if he had had a lamp or a lantern; but he stuck to his old candlestick; and that same old candlestick, ladies and gentlemen, has ever afterwards stuck to *me*. That's another joke, if you please; and I'm much obliged to Miss Belinda in the corner for being good enough to laugh at it.

Well (I said "well" before, but it's a word that helps a man on like), we sailed in the brig, and shaped our course, first, for the Virgin Islands, in the West Indies; and, after sighting them, we made for the Leeward Islands next; and then stood on due south, till the look-out at the mast-head hailed the deck, and said he saw land. That land was the coast of South America. We had had a wonderful voyage so far. We had lost none of our spars or sails, and not a man of us had been harassed to death at the pumps. It wasn't often The Good Intent made such a voyage as that, I can tell you.

I was sent aloft to make sure about the land, and I did make sure of it. When I reported the same to the skipper, he went below, and had a look at his letter of instructions and the chart. When he came on deck again, he altered our course a trifle to the eastward – I forget the point on the compass, but that don't matter. What I do remember is, that it was dark before we closed in with the land. We kept the lead going, and hove the brig to in from four to five fathoms water, or it might be six – I can't say for certain. I kept a sharp eye to the drift of the vessel, none of us knowing how the currents ran on that coast. We all wondered why the skipper didn't anchor; but he said, No, he must first show a light at the foretop-mast-head, and wait for an answering light on shore. We did wait, and nothing of the sort appeared. It was starlight and calm. What little wind there was came in puffs off the land. I suppose we waited, drifting a little to the westward, as I made it out, best part of an hour before anything happened – and then, instead of seeing the light on shore, we saw a boat coming towards us, rowed by two men only.

We hailed them, and they answered, "Friends!" and hailed us by our name. They came on board. One of them was an Irishman, and the other was a coffee-coloured native pilot, who jabbered a little English. The Irishman handed a note to our skipper, who showed it to me. It informed us that the part of the coast we were off then, was not over safe for discharging our cargo, seeing that spies of the enemy (that is to say, of the old government) had been taken and shot in the neighbourhood the day before. We might trust the brig to the native pilot; and he had his instructions to take us to another part of the coast. The note was signed by the proper parties; so we let the Irishman go back alone in the boat, and allowed the pilot to exercise his lawful authority over the brig. He kept us stretching off from the land till noon the next day – his instructions, seemingly, ordering him to keep us well out of sight of the shore. We only altered our course, in the afternoon, so as to close in with the land again a little before midnight.

This same pilot was about as ill-looking a vagabond as ever I saw; a skinny, cowardly, quarrelsome mongrel, who swore at the men, in the vilest broken English, till they were every one of them ready to pitch him overboard. The skipper kept them quiet, and I kept them quiet, for the pilot being given us by our instructions, we were bound to make the best of him. Near nightfall, however, with the best will in the world to avoid it, I was unlucky enough to quarrel with him. He wanted to go below with his pipe, and I stopped him, of course, because it was contrary to orders. Upon that, he tried to hustle by me, and I put him away with my hand. I never meant to push him down; but, somehow, I did. Ho picked himself up as quick as lightning, and pulled out his knife. I snatched it out of his hand, slapped his murderous face for him, and threw his weapon overboard. He gave me one ugly look, and walked aft. I didn't think much of the look then; but I remembered it a little too well afterwards.

We were close in with the land again, just as the wind failed us, between eleven and twelve that night; and dropped our anchor by the pilot's directions. It was pitch dark, and a dead, airless calm. The skipper was on deck with two of our best men for watch. The rest were below, except the pilot, who coiled himself up, more like a snake than a man, on the forecastle. It was not my watch till four in the morning. But I didn't like the look of the night, or the pilot, or the state of things generally, and I shook myself down on deck to get my nap there, and be ready for anything at a moment's notice. The last I remember was the skipper whispering to me that he didn't like the look of things either, and that he would go below and consult his instructions again. That is the last I remember, before the slow, heavy, regular roll of the old brig on the ground swell rocked me off to sleep.

I was woke, ladies and gentlemen, by a scuffle on the forecastle, and a gag in my mouth. There was a man on my breast and a man on my legs; and I was bound hand and foot in half a minute. The brig was in the hands of the Spaniards. They were swarming all over her. I heard six heavy splashes in the water, one after another – I saw the captain stabbed to the heart as he came running up the companion – and I heard a seventh splash in the water. Except myself, every soul of us on board had been murdered and thrown into the sea. Why I was left, I couldn't think, till I saw the pilot stoop over me with a lantern, and look, to make sure of who I was. There was a devilish grin on his face, and he nodded his head at me, as much as to say, *You* were the man who hustled me down and slapped my face, and I mean to play the game of cat and mouse with *you* in return for it!

I could neither move nor speak; but I could see the Spaniards take off the main hatch and rig the purchases for getting up the cargo. A quarter of an hour afterwards, I heard the sweeps of a schooner, or other small vessel, in the water. The strange craft was laid alongside of us; and the Spaniards set to work to discharge our cargo into her. They all worked hard except the pilot; and he came, from time to time, with his lantern, to have another look at me, and to grin and nod always in the same devilish way. I am old enough now not to be ashamed of confessing the truth; and I don't mind acknowledging that the pilot frightened me.

The fright, and the bonds, and the gag, and the not being able to stir hand or foot, had pretty nigh worn me out, by the time the Spaniards gave over work. This was just as the dawn broke. They had shifted good part of our cargo on board their vessel, but nothing like all of it; and they were sharp enough to be off with what they had got, before daylight. I need hardly say that I had made up my mind, by this time, to the worst I could think of. The pilot, it was clear enough, was one of the spies of the enemy, who had wormed himself into the confidence of our consignees without being suspected. He, or more likely his employers, had got knowledge enough of us to suspect what our cargo was; we had been anchored for the night in the safest berth for them to surprise us in; and we had paid the penalty of having a small crew, and consequently an insufficient watch. All this was clear enough – but what did the pilot mean to do with *me?*

On the word of a man, it makes my flesh creep, now, only to tell you what he did with me.

After all the rest of them were out of the brig, except the pilot and two Spanish seamen, these last took me up, bound and gagged as I was, lowered me into the hold of the vessel, and laid me along on the floor; lashing me to it with ropes' ends, so that I could just turn from one side to the other, but could not roll myself fairly over, so as to change my place. They then left me. Both of them were the worse for liquor; but the devil of a pilot was sober – mind that! – as sober as I am at the present moment.

I lay in the dark for a little while, with my heart thumping as if it was going to jump out of me. I lay about five minutes so, when the pilot came down into the hold, alone. He had the captain's cursed flat candlestick and a carpenter's awl in one hand, and a long thin twist of cotton yarn, well oiled, in the other. He put the candlestick, with a new "dip" lighted in it, down on the floor, about two feet from my face, and close against the side of the vessel. The light was feeble enough; but it was sufficient to show a dozen barrels of gunpowder or more, left all round me in the hold of the brig. I began to suspect what he was after, the moment I noticed the barrels. The horrors laid hold of me from head to foot; and the sweat poured off my face like water.

I saw him go, next, to one of the barrels of powder standing against the side of the vessel, in a line with the candle, and about three feet, or rather better, away from it. He bored a hole in the side of the barrel with his awl; and the horrid powder came trickling out, as black as hell, and dripped into the hollow of his hand, which he held to catch it. When he had got a good handful, he stopped up the hole by jamming one end of his oiled twist of cotton-yarn fast into it; and he then rubbed the powder into the whole length of the yarn, till he had blackened every hairsbreadth of it. The next thing he did – as true as I sit here, as true as the heaven above us all – the next thing he did was to carry the free end of his long, lean, black, frightful slow-match to the lighted candle along-side my face, and to tie it, in several folds, round the tallow dip, about a third of the distance down, measuring from the flame of the wick to the lip of the candlestick. He did that; he looked to see that my lashings were all safe; and then he put his face down close to mine; and whispered in my ear, "Blow up with the brig!"

He was on deck again the moment after; and he and the two others shoved the hatch on over me. At the farthest end from where I lay, they had not fitted it down quite true, and I saw a blink of daylight glimmering in when I looked in that direction. I heard the sweeps of the schooner fall into the water – splash! splash! fainter and fainter, as they swept the vessel out in the dead calm, to be ready for the wind in the offing. Fainter and fainter, splash! splash! for a quarter of an hour or more.

While those sounds were in my ears, my eyes were fixed on the candle. It had been freshly lit – if left to itself it would burn for between six and seven hours – the slow-match was twisted round it about a third of the way down – and therefore the flame would be about two hours reaching it. There I lay, gagged, bound, lashed to the floor; seeing my own life burning down with the candle by my side – there I lay, alone on the sea, doomed to be blown to atoms, and to see that doom drawing on, nearer and nearer with every fresh second of time, through nigh on two hours to come; powerless to help myself and speechless to call for help to others. The wonder to me is that I didn't cheat the flame, the slow-match, and the powder, and die of the horror of my situation before my first half-hour was out in the hold of the brig.

I can't exactly say how long I kept the command of my senses after I had ceased to hear the splash of the schooner's sweeps in the water. I can trace back everything I did and everything I thought, up to a certain point; but, once past that, I get all abroad, and lose myself in my memory now, much as I lost myself in my own feelings at the time.

The moment the hatch was covered over me, I began, as every other man would have begun in my place, with a frantic effort to free my hands. In the mad panic I was in, I cut my flesh with the lashings as if they had been knife-blades; but I never stirred them. There was less chance still of freeing my legs, or of tearing myself from the fastenings that held me to the floor. I gave in, when I was all but suffocated for want of breath. The gag, you will please to remember, was a terrible enemy to me; I could only breathe freely through my nose – and that is but a poor vent when a man is straining his strength as far as ever it will go.

I gave in, and lay quiet, and got my breath again; my eyes glaring and straining at the candle all the time. While I was staring at it, the notion struck me of trying to blow out the flame by pumping a long breath at it suddenly through my nostrils. It was too high above me, and too far away from me, to be reached in that fashion. I tried, and tried, and tried – and then I gave in again and lay quiet again; always with my eyes glaring at the candle and the candle glaring at me. The splash of the schooner's sweeps was very faint by this time. I could only just hear them in the morning stillness. Splash! splash! – fainter and fainter – splash! splash!

Without exactly feeling my mind going, I began to feel it getting queer, as early as this: The snuff of the candle was growing taller and taller, and the length of tallow between the flame and the slow-match, which was the length of my life, was getting shorter and shorter. I calculated that I had rather less than an hour and a half to live. An hour and a half! Was there a chance, in that time, of a boat pulling off to the brig from shore? Whether the land near which the vessel was anchored was in possession of our side, or in possession of the enemy's side, I made it out that they must, sooner or later, send to hail the brig, merely because she was a stranger in those parts. The question for *me w*as, how soon? The sun had not risen yet, as I could tell by looking through the chink in the hatch. There was no coast village near us, as we all knew, before the brig was seized, by seeing no lights on shore. There was no wind, as I could tell by listening, to bring any strange vessel near. If I had had six hours to live, there might have been a chance for me, reckoning from sunrise to noon. But with an hour and a half, which had dwindled to an hour and a quarter by this time – or, in other words, with the earliness of the morning, the uninhabited coast, and the dead calm all against me – there was not the ghost of a chance. As I felt that, I had another struggle – the last – with my bonds; and only cut myself the deeper for my pains.

I gave in once more, and lay quiet, and listened for the splash of the sweeps. Gone! Not a sound could I hear but the blowing of a fish, now and then, on the surface of the sea, and the creak of the brig's crazy old spars, as she rolled gently from side to side with the little swell there was on the quiet water.

An hour and a quarter. The wick grew terribly, as the quarter slipped away; and the charred top of it began to thicken and spread out mushroom-shape. It would fall off soon. Would it fall off red-hot, and would the swing of the brig cant it over the side of the candle and let it down on the slow-match? If it would, I had about ten minutes to live instead of an hour. This discovery set my mind for a minute on a new tack altogether. I began to ponder with myself what sort of a death blowing-up might be. Painful? Well, it would be, surely, too sudden for that. Perhaps just one crash, inside me, or outside me, or both, and nothing more? Perhaps not even a crash; that and death and the scattering of this living body of mine into millions of fiery sparks, might all happen in the same instant? I couldn't make it out; I couldn't settle how it would be. The minute of calmness in my mind left it, before I had half done thinking; and I got all abroad again.

When I came back to my thoughts, or when they came back to me (I can't say which), the wick was awfully tall, the flame was burning with a smoke above it, the charred top was broad and red, and heavily spreading out to its fall. My despair and horror at seeing it, took me in a new way, which was good and right, at any rate, for my poor soul. I tried to pray; in my own heart, you will understand, for the gag put all lip-praying out of my power. I tried, but the candle seemed to bum it up in me. I struggled hard to force my eyes from the slow, murdering flame, and to look up through the chink in the hatch at the blessed daylight. I tried once, tried twice; and gave it up. I tried next only to shut my eyes, and keep them shut – once – twice and the second time I did it. "God bless old mother, and sister Lizzie; God keep them both, and forgive *me*." That was all I had time to say, in my own heart, before my eyes opened again, in spite of me, and the flame of the candle flew into them, flew all over me, and burnt up the rest of my thoughts in an instant.

I couldn't hear the fish blowing now; I couldn't hear the creak of the spars; I couldn't think; I couldn't feel the sweat of my own death agony on my face – I could only look at the heavy, charred top of the wick. It swelled, tottered, bent over to one side, dropped – red hot at the moment of its fall – black and harmless, even before the swing of the brig had canted it over into the bottom of the candle-stick.

I caught myself laughing. Yes! laughing at the safe fall of the bit of wick. But for the gag I should have screamed with laughing. As it was, I shook with it inside me – shook till the blood was in my head, and I was all but suffocated for want of breath. I had just sense enough left to feel that my own horrid laughter, at that awful moment, was a sign of my brain going at last. I had just sense enough left to make another struggle before my mind broke loose like a frightened horse, and ran away with me.

One comforting look at the blink of daylight through the hatch was what I tried for once more. The fight to force my eyes from the candle and to get that one look at the daylight, was the hardest I had had yet; and I lost the fight. The flame had hold of my eyes as fast as the lashings had hold of my hands. I couldn't look away from it. I couldn't even shut my eyes, when I tried that next, for the second time. There was the wick,

growing tall once more. There was the space of unburnt candle between the light and the slow match shortened to an inch or less. How much life did that inch leave me? Three-quarters of an hour? Half an hour? Fifty minutes Twenty minutes? Steady! an inch of tallow candle would burn longer than twenty minutes. An inch of tallow! the notion of a man's body and soul being kept together by an inch of tallow! Wonderful! Why, the greatest king that sits on a throne can't keep a man's body and soul together; and here's an inch of tallow that can do what the king can't! There's something to tell mother, when I get home, which will surprise her more than all the rest of my voyages put together. I laughed inwardly, again, at the thought of that; and shook and swelled and suffocated myself, till the light of the candle leaped in through my eyes, and licked up the laughter, and burnt it out of me, and made me all empty, and cold, and quiet once more.

Mother and Lizzie. I don't know when they came back; but they did come back – not, as it seemed to me, into my mind this time; but right down bodily before me, in the hold of the brig.

Yes: sure enough, there was Lizzie, just as light-hearted as usual, laughing at me. Laughing! Well why not? Who is to blame Lizzie for thinking I'm lying on my back, drunk in the cellar, with the beer barrels all round me? Steady! she's crying now – spinning round and round in a fiery mist, wringing her hands, screeching out for help – fainter and fainter, like the splash of the schooner's sweeps. Gone! – burnt up in the fiery mist. Mist? fire? no: neither one nor the other. It's mother makes the light – mother knitting, with ten flaming points at the ends of her fingers and thumbs, and slow-matches hanging in bunches all round her face instead of her own grey hair. Mother in her old arm-chair, and the pilot's long skinny hands hanging over the back of the chair, dripping with gunpowder. No! no gunpowder, no chair, no mother – nothing but the pilot's face, shining red hot, like a sun, in the fiery mist; turning upside down in the fiery mist; running backwards and forwards along the slow-match, in the fiery mist; spinning millions of miles in a minute, in the fiery mist – spinning itself smaller and smaller into one tiny point, and that point darting on a sudden straight into my head – and then, all fire and all mist – no hearing, no seeing, no thinking, no feeling – the brig, the sea, my own. self, the whole world, all gone together!

After what I've just told you, I know nothing and remember nothing, till I woke up, as it seemed to me in a comfortable bed, with two rough and ready men like myself sitting on each side of my pillow, and a gentleman standing watching me at the foot of the bed. It was about seven in the morning. My sleep (or what seemed like my sleep to me) had lasted better than eight months – I was among my own countrymen in the island of Trinidad – the men at each side of my pillow were my keepers, turn and turn about – and the gentleman standing at the foot of the bed was the doctor. What I said and did in those eight months, I never have known and never shall. I woke out of it, as if it had been one long sleep – that's all I know.

It was another two months or more before the doctor thought it safe to answer the questions I asked him.

The brig had been anchored, just as I had supposed, off a part of the coast which was lonely enough to make the Spaniards pretty sure of no interruption, so long as they managed their murderous work quietly under cover of night. My life had not been saved from the shore, but from the sea. An American vessel, becalmed in the offing, had made out the brig as the sun rose; and the captain, having his time on his hands in consequence of the calm, and seeing a vessel anchored where no vessel had any reason to be, had manned one of his boats and sent his mate with it, to look a little closer into the matter, and bring back a report of what he saw. What he saw, when he and his men found the brig deserted and boarded her, was a gleam of candlelight through the chink in the hatchway. The flame was within about a thread's breadth of the slow-match, when he lowered himself into the hold; and if he had not had the sense and coolness to cut the match in two with his knife, before he touched the candle, he and his men might have been blown up along with the brig, as well as me. The match caught and turned into sputtering red fire, in the very act of putting the candle out; and if the communication with the powder barrel had not been cut off, the Lord only knows what might have happened.

What became of the Spanish schooner and the pilot I have never heard from that day to this. As for the brig, the Yankees took her, as they took me, to Trinidad, and claimed their salvage, and got it, I hope, for their own sakes. I was landed just in the same state as when they rescued me from the brig, that is to say, clean out of my senses. But, please to remember it was a long time ago; and, take my word for it, I was discharged cured, as I have told you. Bless your hearts, I'm all right now, as you may see. I'm a little shaken by telling the story, ladies and gentlemen – a little shaken, that's all.

## The Ghost in Master B.'s Room
### Charles Dickens

**WHEN I ESTABLISHED** myself in the triangular garret which had gained so distinguished a reputation, my thoughts naturally turned to Master B. My speculations about him were uneasy and manifold. Whether his Christian name was Benjamin, Bissextile (from his having been born in Leap Year), Bartholomew, or Bill. Whether the initial letter belonged to his family name, and that was Baxter, Black, Brown, Barker, Buggins, Baker, or Bird. Whether he was a foundling, and had been baptized B. Whether he was a lion-hearted boy, and B. was short for Briton, or for Bull. Whether he could possibly have been kith and kin to an illustrious lady who brightened my own childhood, and had come of the blood of the brilliant Mother Bunch?

With these profitless meditations I tormented myself much. I also carried the mysterious letter into the appearance and pursuits of the deceased; wondering whether he dressed in Blue, wore Boots (he couldn't have been Bald), was a boy of Brains, liked Books, was good at Bowling, had any skill as a Boxer, even in his Buoyant Boyhood Bathed from a Bathing-machine at Bognor, Bangor, Bournemouth, Brighton, or Broadstairs, like a Bounding Billiard Ball?

So, from the first, I was haunted by the letter B.

It was not long before I remarked that I never by any hazard had a dream of Master B., or of anything belonging to him. But, the instant I awoke from sleep, at whatever hour of the night, my thoughts took him up, and roamed away, trying to attach his initial letter to something that would fit it and keep it quiet.

For six nights, I had been worried thus in Master B.'s room, when I began to perceive that things were going wrong.

The first appearance that presented itself was early in the morning when it was but just daylight and no more. I was standing shaving at my glass, when I suddenly discovered, to my consternation and amazement, that I was shaving – not myself – I am fifty – but a boy. Apparently Master B.!

I trembled and looked over my shoulder; nothing there. I looked again in the glass, and distinctly saw the features and expression of a boy, who was shaving, not to get rid of a beard, but to get one. Extremely troubled in my mind, I took a few turns in the room, and went back to the looking-glass, resolved to steady my hand and complete the operation in which I had been disturbed. Opening my eyes, which I had shut while recovering my firmness, I now met in the glass, looking straight at me, the eyes of a young man of four or five and twenty. Terrified by this new ghost, I closed my eyes, and made a strong effort to recover myself. Opening them again, I saw, shaving his cheek in the glass, my father, who has long been dead. Nay, I even saw my grandfather too, whom I never did see in my life.

Although naturally much affected by these remarkable visitations, I determined to keep my secret, until the time agreed upon for the present general disclosure. Agitated by a multitude of curious thoughts, I retired to my room, that night, prepared to encounter some new experience of a spectral character. Nor was my preparation needless, for, waking from an uneasy sleep at exactly two o'clock in the morning, what were my feelings to find that I was sharing my bed with the skeleton of Master B.!

I sprang up, and the skeleton sprang up also. I then heard a plaintive voice saying, "Where am I? What is become of me?" and, looking hard in that direction, perceived the ghost of Master B.

The young spectre was dressed in an obsolete fashion: or rather, was not so much dressed as put into a case of inferior pepper-and-salt cloth, made horrible by means of shining buttons. I observed that these buttons went, in a double row, over each shoulder of the young ghost, and appeared to descend his back. He wore a frill round his neck. His right hand (which I distinctly noticed to be inky) was laid upon his stomach; connecting this action with some feeble pimples on his countenance, and his general air of nausea, I concluded this ghost to be the ghost of a boy who had habitually taken a great deal too much medicine.

"Where am I?" said the little spectre, in a pathetic voice. "And why was I born in the Calomel days, and why did I have all that Calomel given me?"

I replied, with sincere earnestness, that upon my soul I couldn't tell him.

"Where is my little sister," said the ghost, "and where my angelic little wife, and where is the boy I went to school with?"

I entreated the phantom to be comforted, and above all things to take heart respecting the loss of the boy he went to school with. I represented to him that probably that boy never did, within human experience, come out well, when discovered. I urged that I myself had, in later life, turned up several boys whom I went to school with, and none of them had at all answered. I expressed my humble belief that that boy never did answer. I represented that he was a mythic character, a delusion, and a snare. I recounted how, the last time I found him, I found him at a dinner party behind a wall of white cravat, with an inconclusive opinion on every possible subject, and a power of silent boredom absolutely Titanic. I related how, on the strength of our having been together at "Old Doylance's," he had asked himself to breakfast with me (a social offence of the largest magnitude); how, fanning my weak embers of belief in Doylance's boys, I had let him in; and how, he had proved to be a fearful wanderer about the earth, pursuing the race of Adam with inexplicable notions concerning the currency, and with a proposition that the Bank of England should, on pain of being abolished, instantly strike off and circulate, God knows how many thousand millions of ten-and-sixpenny notes.

The ghost heard me in silence, and with a fixed stare. "Barber!" it apostrophised me when I had finished.

"Barber?" I repeated – for I am not of that profession.

"Condemned," said the ghost, "to shave a constant change of customers – now, me – now, a young man – now, thyself as thou art – now, thy father – now, thy grandfather; condemned, too, to lie down with a skeleton every night, and to rise with it every morning—"

(I shuddered on hearing this dismal announcement.)

"Barber! Pursue me!"

I had felt, even before the words were uttered, that I was under a spell to pursue the phantom. I immediately did so, and was in Master B.'s room no longer.

Most people know what long and fatiguing night journeys had been forced upon the witches who used to confess, and who, no doubt, told the exact truth – particularly as they were always assisted with leading questions, and the Torture was always ready. I asseverate that, during my occupation of Master B.'s room, I was taken by the ghost that haunted it, on expeditions fully as long and wild as any of those. Assuredly, I was presented to no shabby old man with a goat's horns and tail (something between Pan and an old clothesman), holding conventional receptions, as stupid as those of real life and less decent; but, I came upon other things which appeared to me to have more meaning.

Confident that I speak the truth and shall be believed, I declare without hesitation that I followed the ghost, in the first instance on a broom-stick, and afterwards on a rocking-horse. The very smell of the animal's paint – especially when I brought it out, by making him warm – I am ready to swear to. I followed the ghost, afterwards, in a hackney coach; an institution with the peculiar smell of which, the present generation is unacquainted, but to which I am again ready to swear as a combination of stable, dog with the mange, and very old bellows. (In this, I appeal to previous generations to confirm or refute me.) I pursued the phantom, on a headless donkey: at least, upon a donkey who was so interested in the state of his stomach that his head was always down there, investigating it; on ponies, expressly born to kick up behind; on roundabouts and swings, from fairs; in the first cab – another forgotten institution where the fare regularly got into bed, and was tucked up with the driver.

Not to trouble you with a detailed account of all my travels in pursuit of the ghost of Master B., which were longer and more wonderful than those of Sinbad the Sailor, I will confine myself to one experience from which you may judge of many.

I was marvellously changed. I was myself, yet not myself. I was conscious of something within me, which has been the same all through my life, and which I have always recognised under all its phases and varieties as never altering, and yet I was not the I who had gone to bed in Master B.'s room. I had the smoothest of faces and the shortest of legs, and I had taken another creature like myself, also with the smoothest of faces and the shortest of legs, behind a door, and was confiding to him a proposition of the most astounding nature.

This proposition was, that we should have a Seraglio.

The other creature assented warmly. He had no notion of respectability, neither had I. It was the custom of the East, it was the way of the good Caliph Haroun Alraschid (let me have the corrupted name again for once, it is so scented with sweet memories!), the usage was highly laudable, and most worthy of imitation. "O, yes! Let us," said the other creature with a jump, "have a Seraglio."

It was not because we entertained the faintest doubts of the meritorious character of the Oriental establishment we proposed to import, that we perceived it must be kept a secret from Miss Griffin. It was because we knew Miss Griffin to be bereft of human sympathies, and incapable of appreciating the greatness of the great Haroun. Mystery impenetrably shrouded from Miss Griffin then, let us entrust it to Miss Bule.

We were ten in Miss Griffin's establishment by Hampstead Ponds; eight ladies and two gentlemen. Miss Bule, whom I judge to have attained the ripe age of eight or nine, took the lead in society. I opened the subject to her in the course of the day, and proposed that she should become the Favourite.

Miss Bule, after struggling with the diffidence so natural to, and charming in, her adorable sex, expressed herself as flattered by the idea, but wished to know how it was proposed to provide for Miss Pipson? Miss Bule – who was understood to have vowed towards that young lady, a friendship, halves, and no secrets, until death, on the Church Service and Lessons complete in two volumes with case and lock – Miss Bule said she could not, as the friend of Pipson, disguise from herself, or me, that Pipson was not one of the common.

Now, Miss Pipson, having curly hair and blue eyes (which was my idea of anything mortal and feminine that was called Fair), I promptly replied that I regarded Miss Pipson in the light of a Fair Circassian.

"And what then?" Miss Bule pensively asked.

I replied that she must be inveigled by a Merchant, brought to me veiled, and purchased as a slave.

[The other creature had already fallen into the second male place in the State, and was set apart for Grand Vizier. He afterwards resisted this disposal of events, but had his hair pulled until he yielded.]

"Shall I not be jealous?" Miss Bule inquired, casting down her eyes.

"Zobeide, no," I replied; "you will ever be the favourite Sultana; the first place in my heart, and on my throne, will be ever yours."

Miss Bule, upon that assurance, consented to propound the idea to her seven beautiful companions. It occurring to me, in the course of the same day, that we knew we could trust a grinning and good-natured soul called Tabby, who was the serving drudge of the house, and had no more figure than one of the beds, and upon whose face there was always more or less black-lead, I slipped into Miss Bule's hand after supper, a little note to that effect; dwelling on the black-lead as being in a manner deposited by the finger of Providence, pointing Tabby out for Mesrour, the celebrated chief of the Blacks of the Hareem.

There were difficulties in the formation of the desired institution, as there are in all combinations. The other creature showed himself of a low character, and, when defeated in aspiring to the throne, pretended to have conscientious scruples about prostrating himself before the Caliph; wouldn't call him Commander of the Faithful; spoke of him slightingly and inconsistently as a mere "chap;" said he, the other creature, "wouldn't play" – Play! – and was otherwise coarse and offensive. This meanness of disposition was, however, put down by the general indignation of an united Seraglio, and I became blessed in the smiles of eight of the fairest of the daughters of men.

The smiles could only be bestowed when Miss Griffin was looking another way, and only then in a very wary manner, for there was a legend among the followers of the Prophet that she saw with a little round ornament in the middle of the pattern on the back of her shawl. But every day after dinner, for an hour, we were all together, and then the Favourite and the rest of the Royal Hareem competed who should most beguile the leisure of the Serene Haroun reposing from the cares of State – which were generally, as in most affairs of State, of an arithmetical character, the Commander of the Faithful being a fearful boggler at a sum.

On these occasions, the devoted Mesrour, chief of the Blacks of the Hareem, was always in attendance (Miss Griffin usually ringing for that officer, at the same time, with great vehemence), but never acquitted himself in a manner worthy of his historical reputation. In the first place, his bringing a broom into the Divan of the Caliph, even when Haroun wore on his shoulders the red robe of anger (Miss Pipson's pelisse), though it might be got over for the moment, was never to be quite satisfactorily accounted for. In the second place, his breaking out into grinning exclamations of "Lork you pretties!" was neither Eastern nor respectful. In the third place, when specially instructed to say "Bismillah!" he always said "Hallelujah!" This officer, unlike his class, was too good-humoured altogether, kept his mouth open far too wide, expressed approbation to an incongruous extent, and even once – it was on the occasion of the purchase of the Fair Circassian for five hundred thousand purses of gold, and cheap, too – embraced the Slave, the Favourite, and the Caliph, all round. (Parenthetically let me say God bless Mesrour, and may there have been sons and daughters on that tender bosom, softening many a hard day since!)

Miss Griffin was a model of propriety, and I am at a loss to imagine what the feelings of the virtuous woman would have been, if she had known, when she paraded us down the Hampstead Road two and two, that she was walking with a stately step at the head of Polygamy and Mahomedanism. I believe that a mysterious and terrible joy with which the contemplation of Miss Griffin, in this unconscious state, inspired us, and a grim sense prevalent among us that there was a dreadful power in our knowledge of what Miss Griffin (who knew all things that could be learnt out of book) didn't know, were the main-spring of the preservation of our secret. It was wonderfully kept, but was once upon the verge of self-betrayal. The danger and escape occurred upon a Sunday. We were all ten ranged in a conspicuous part of the gallery at church, with Miss Griffin at our head – as we were every Sunday – advertising the establishment in an unsecular sort of way – when the description of Solomon in his domestic glory happened to be read. The moment that monarch was thus referred to, conscience whispered me, "Thou, too, Haroun!" The officiating minister had a cast in his eye, and it assisted conscience by giving him the appearance of reading personally at me. A crimson blush, attended by a fearful perspiration, suffused my features. The Grand Vizier became more dead than alive, and the whole Seraglio reddened as if the sunset of Bagdad shone direct upon their lovely faces. At this portentous time the awful Griffin rose, and balefully surveyed the children of Islam. My own impression was, that Church and State had entered into a conspiracy with Miss Griffin to expose us, and that we should all be put into white sheets, and exhibited in the centre aisle. But, so Westerly – if I may be allowed the expression as opposite to Eastern associations – was Miss Griffin's sense of rectitude, that she merely suspected Apples, and we were saved.

I have called the Seraglio, united. Upon the question, solely, whether the Commander of the Faithful durst exercise a right of kissing in that sanctuary of the palace, were its peerless inmates divided. Zobeide asserted a counter-right in the Favourite to scratch, and the fair Circassian put her face, for refuge, into a green baize bag, originally designed for books. On the other hand, a young antelope of transcendent beauty from the fruitful plains of Camden Town (whence she had been brought, by traders, in the half-yearly caravan that crossed the intermediate desert after the holidays), held more liberal opinions, but stipulated for limiting the benefit of them to that dog, and son of a dog, the Grand Vizier – who had no rights, and was not in question. At length, the difficulty was compromised by the installation of a very youthful slave as Deputy. She, raised upon a stool, officially received upon her cheeks the salutes intended by the gracious Haroun for other Sultanas, and was privately rewarded from the coffers of the Ladies of the Hareem.

And now it was, at the full height of enjoyment of my bliss, that I became heavily troubled. I began to think of my mother, and what she would say to my taking home at Midsummer eight of the most beautiful of the daughters of men, but all unexpected. I thought of the number of beds we made up at our house, of my father's income, and of the baker, and my despondency redoubled. The Seraglio and malicious Vizier, divining the cause of their Lord's unhappiness, did their utmost to augment it. They professed unbounded fidelity, and declared that they would live and die with him. Reduced to the utmost wretchedness by these protestations of attachment, I lay awake, for hours at a time, ruminating on my frightful lot. In my despair, I think I might have taken an early opportunity of falling on my knees before Miss Griffin, avowing my resemblance to Solomon, and praying to be dealt with according to the outraged laws of my country, if an unthought-of means of escape had not opened before me.

One day, we were out walking, two and two – on which occasion the Vizier had his usual instructions to take note of the boy at the turnpike, and if he profanely gazed (which he always did) at the beauties of the Hareem, to have him bowstrung in the course of the night – and it happened that our hearts were veiled in gloom. An unaccountable action on the part of the antelope had plunged the State into disgrace. That charmer, on the representation that the previous day was her birthday, and that vast treasures had been sent in a hamper for its celebration (both baseless assertions), had secretly but most pressingly invited thirty-five neighbouring princes and princesses to a ball and supper: with a special stipulation that they were "not to be fetched till twelve." This wandering of the antelope's fancy, led to the surprising arrival at Miss Griffin's door, in divers equipages and under various escorts, of a great company in full dress, who were deposited on the top step in a flush of high expectancy, and who were dismissed in tears. At the beginning of the double knocks attendant on these ceremonies, the antelope had retired to a back attic, and bolted herself in; and at every new arrival, Miss Griffin had gone so much more and more distracted, that at last she had been seen to tear her front. Ultimate capitulation on the part of the offender, had been followed by solitude in the linen-closet, bread and water and a lecture to all, of vindictive length, in which Miss Griffin had used expressions: Firstly, "I believe you all of you knew of it;" Secondly, "Every one of you is as wicked as another;" Thirdly, "A pack of little wretches."

Under these circumstances, we were walking drearily along; and I especially, with my Moosulmaun responsibilities heavy on me, was in a very low state of mind; when a strange man accosted Miss Griffin, and, after walking on at her side for a little while and talking with her, looked at me. Supposing him to be a minion of the law, and that my hour was come, I instantly ran away, with the general purpose of making for Egypt.

The whole Seraglio cried out, when they saw me making off as fast as my legs would carry me (I had an impression that the first turning on the left, and round by the public-house, would be the shortest way to the Pyramids), Miss Griffin screamed after me, the faithless Vizier ran after me, and the boy at the turnpike dodged me into a corner, like a sheep, and cut me off. Nobody scolded me when I was taken and brought back; Miss Griffin only said, with a stunning gentleness, This was very curious! Why had I run away when the gentleman looked at me?

If I had had any breath to answer with, I dare say I should have made no answer; having no breath, I certainly made none. Miss Griffin and the strange man took me between them, and walked me back to the palace in a sort of state; but not at all (as I couldn't help feeling, with astonishment) in culprit state.

When we got there, we went into a room by ourselves, and Miss Griffin called in to her assistance, Mesrour, chief of the dusky guards of the Hareem. Mesrour, on being whispered to, began to shed tears. "Bless you, my precious!" said that officer, turning to me; "your Pa's took bitter bad!"

I asked, with a fluttered heart, "Is he very ill?"

"Lord temper the wind to you, my lamb!" said the good Mesrour, kneeling down, that I might have a comforting shoulder for my head to rest on, "your Pa's dead!"

Haroun Alraschid took to flight at the words; the Seraglio vanished; from that moment, I never again saw one of the eight of the fairest of the daughters of men.

I was taken home, and there was Debt at home as well as Death, and we had a sale there. My own little bed was so superciliously looked upon by a Power unknown to me, hazily called "The Trade," that a brass coal-scuttle, a roasting-jack, and a birdcage, were obliged to be put into it to make a Lot of it, and then it went for a song. So I heard mentioned, and I wondered what song, and thought what a dismal song it must have been to sing!

Then, I was sent to a great, cold, bare, school of big boys; where everything to eat and wear was thick and clumpy, without being enough; where everybody, large and small, was cruel; where the boys knew all about the sale, before I got there, and asked me what I had fetched, and who had bought me, and hooted at me, "Going, going, gone!" I never whispered in that wretched place that I had been Haroun, or had had a Seraglio: for, I knew that if I mentioned my reverses, I should be so worried, that I should have to drown myself in the muddy pond near the playground, which looked like the beer.

Ah me, ah me! No other ghost has haunted the boy's room, my friends, since I have occupied it, than the ghost of my own childhood, the ghost of my own innocence, the ghost of my own airy belief. Many a time have I pursued the phantom: never with this man's stride of mine to come up with it, never with these man's hands of mine to touch it, never more to this man's heart of mine to hold it in its purity. And here you see me working out, as cheerfully and thankfully as I may, my doom of shaving in the glass a constant change of customers, and of lying down and rising up with the skeleton allotted to me for my mortal companion.

## The Ghost in the Garden Room
### Elizabeth Gaskell

**MY FRIEND** and solicitor rubbed his bald forehead – which is quite Shakespearian – with his hand, after a manner he has when I consult him professionally, and took a very large pinch of snuff. "My bedroom," said he, "has been haunted by the Ghost of a Judge."

"Of a Judge?" said all the company.

"Of a Judge. In his wig and robes as he sits upon the Bench, at Assize-time. As I have lingered in the great white chair at the side of my fire, when we have all retired for the night to our respective rooms, I have seen and heard him. I never shall forget the description he gave me, and I never have forgotten it since I first heard it."

"Then you have seen and heard him before, Mr. Undery?" said my sister.

"Often."

"Consequently, he is not peculiar to this house?"

"By no means. He returns to me in many intervals of quiet leisure, and his story haunts me."

We one and all called for the story, that it might haunt us likewise.

"It fell within the range of his judicial experience," said my friend and solicitor, "and this was the Judge's manner of summing it up."

Those words did not apply, of course, to the great pinch of snuff that followed them, but to the words that followed the great pinch of snuff. They were these:

Not many years after the beginning of this century, a worthy couple of the name of Huntroyd occupied a small farm in the North Riding of Yorkshire. They had married late in life, although they were very young when they first began to "keep company" with each other. Nathan Huntroyd had been farm servant to Hester Rose's father, and had made up to her at a time when her parents thought she might do better; and so, without much consultation of her feelings, they had dismissed Nathan in somewhat cavalier fashion. He had drifted far away from his former connexions, when an uncle of his died, leaving Nathan – by this time upwards of forty years of age – enough money to stock a small farm, and yet to have something over to put in the bank against bad times. One of the consequences of this bequest was that Nathan was looking out for a wife and housekeeper in a kind or discreet and leisurely way, when, one day, he heard that his old love, Hester, was – not married and flourishing, as he had always supposed her to be – but a poor maid-of-all-work, in the town of Ripon. For her father had had a succession of misfortunes, which had brought him in his old age to the workhouse; her mother was dead; her only brother struggling to bring up a large family; and Hester herself, a hard-working, homely-looking (at thirty-seven) servant. Nathan had a kind of growling satisfaction (which only lasted for a minute or two, however) in hearing of these turns of Fortune's wheel. He did not make many intelligible remarks to his informant, and to no one else did he say a word. But, a few days afterwards, he presented himself, dressed in his Sunday best, at Mrs. Thompson's back door in Ripon.

Hester stood there in answer to the good sound knock his good sound oak stick made; she with the light full upon her, he in shadow. For a moment there was silence. He was scanning the face and figure of his old love, for twenty years unseen. The comely beauty of youth had faded away entirely; she was, as I have said, homely-looking, plain-featured, but with a clean skin, and pleasant, frank eyes. Her figure was no longer round, but tidily draped in a blue and white bedgown, tied round her waist by her white apron-strings, and her short red linsey petticoat showed her tidy feet and ankles. Her former lover fell into no ecstasies. He simply said to himself, "She'll do;" and forthwith began upon his business.

"Hester, thou dost not mind me. I am Nathan, as thy father turned off at a minute's notice, for thinking of thee for a wife, twenty year come Michaelmas next. I have not thought much upon matrimony since. But Uncle Ben has died, leaving me a small matter in the bank; and I have taken Nab-end Farm, and put in a bit of stock, and shall want a missus to see after it. Wilt like to come? I'll not mislead thee. It's dairy, and it might have been arable. But arable takes more horses than it suited me to buy, and I'd the offer of a tidy lot of kine. That's all. If thou'lt have me, I'll come for thee as soon as the hay is gotten in."

Hester only said, "Come in, and sit thee down."

He came in, and sat down. For a time she took no more notice of him than of his stick, bustling about to get dinner ready for the family whom she served. He meanwhile watched her brisk, sharp movements, and repeated to himself,

"She'll do!" After about twenty minutes of silence thus employed, he got up, saying:

"Well, Hester, I'm going. When shall I come back again?"

"Please thysel', and thou'lt please me," said Hester, in a tone that she tried to make light and indifferent; but he saw that her colour came and went, and that she trembled while she moved about. In another moment Hester was soundly kissed; but when she looked round to scold the middle-aged farmer, he appeared so entirely composed that she hesitated. He said:

"I have pleased mysel', and thee too, I hope. Is it a month's wage, and a month's warning? Today is the eighth. July eighth is our wedding-day. I have no time to spend a-wooing before then, and wedding must na take long. Two days is enough to throw away at our time o' life."

It was like a dream; but Hester resolved not to think more about it till her work was done. And when all was cleaned up for the evening, she went and gave her mistress warning, telling her all the history of her life in a very few words. That day month she was married from Mrs. Thompson's house.

The issue of the marriage was one boy, Benjamin. A few years after his birth, Hester's brother died at Leeds, leaving ten or twelve children. Hester sorrowed bitterly over this loss; and Nathan showed her much quiet sympathy, although he could not but remember that Jack Rose had added insult to the bitterness of his youth. He helped his wife to make ready to go by the waggon to Leeds. He made light of the household difficulties which came thronging into her mind after all was fixed for her departure. He filled her purse, that she might have wherewithal to alleviate the immediate wants of her brother's family. And as she was leaving, he ran after the waggon. "Stop, stop!" he cried. "Hetty, if thou wilt – if it wunnot be too much for thee – bring back one of Jack's wenches for company, like. We've enough and to spare; and a lass will make the house winsome, as a man may say."

The waggon moved on, while Hester had such a silent swelling of gratitude in her heart, as was both thanks to her husband, and thanksgiving to God.

And that was the way that little Bessy Rose came to be an inmate of the Nab's-end farm.

Virtue met with its own reward in this instance, and in a clear and tangible shape, too, which need not delude people in general into thinking that such is the usual nature of virtue's rewards. Bessy grew up a bright, affectionate, active girl; a daily comfort to her uncle and aunt. She was so much a darling in the household that they even thought her worthy of their only son Benjamin, who was perfection in their eyes. It is not often the case that two plain, homely people have a child of uncommon beauty; but it is sometimes, and Benjamin Huntroyd was one of these exceptional cases. The hard-working, labour and care-marked farmer, and the mother, who could never have been more than tolerably comely in her best days, produced a son who might have been an earl's son for grace and beauty. Even the hunting squires of the neighbourhood reined up their horses to admire him, as he opened the gates for them. He had no shyness, he was so accustomed to admiration from strangers, and adoration from his parents from his earliest years. As for Bessy Rose, he ruled imperiously over her heart from the time she first set eyes on him. And as she grew older, she grew on in loving, persuading herself that what her uncle and aunt loved so dearly it was her duty to love dearest of all. At every unconscious symptom of the young girl's love for her cousin, his parents smiled and winked: all was going on as they wished, no need to go far afield for Benjamin's wife. The household could go on as it was now; Nathan and Hester sinking into the rest of years, and relinquishing care and authority to those dear ones, who, in process of time, might bring other dear ones to share their love.

But Benjamin took it all very coolly. He had been sent to a day-school in the neighbouring town – a grammar-school, in the high state of neglect in which the majority of such schools were thirty years ago. Neither his father nor his mother knew much of learning. All that they knew (and that directed their choice of a school) was, that they could not, by any possibility, part with their darling to a boarding-school; that some schooling he must have, and that Squire Pollard's son went to Highminster Grammar School. Squire Pollard's son, and many another son destined to make his parents' hearts ache, went to this school. If it had not been so utterly bad a place of education, the simple farmer and his wife might have found it out sooner. But not only did the pupils there learn vice, they also learnt deceit. Benjamin was naturally too clever to remain a dunce, or else, if he had chosen so to be, there was nothing in Highminster Grammar School to hinder his being a dunce of the first water. But to all appearance he grew clever and gentlemanlike. His father and mother were even proud of his airs and graces when he came home for the holidays; taking them for proofs of his refinement, although the practical effect of such refinement was to make him express his contempt for his parents' homely ways and simple ignorance. By the time he was eighteen – an articled clerk in an attorney's office at Highminster, for he had quite declined becoming a "mere clod-hopper," that is to say a hard-working, honest farmer like his father – Bessy Rose was the only person who was dissatisfied with him. The little girl of fourteen instinctively felt there was something wrong about him. Alas! two years more, and the girl of sixteen worshipped his very shadow, and would not see that aught could be wrong with one so soft-spoken, so handsome, so kind as Cousin Benjamin. For Benjamin had found out that the way to cajole his parents out of money for every indulgence he fancied, was to pretend to forward their innocent scheme, and make love to his pretty cousin Bessy Rose. He cared just

enough for her to make this work of necessity not disagreeable at the time he was performing it. But he found it tiresome to remember her little claims upon him when she was no longer present. The letters he had promised her during his weekly absences at Highminster, the trifling commissions she had asked him to do for her, were all considered in the light of troubles; and even when he was with her he resented the inquiries she made as to his mode of passing his time, or what female acquaintances he had in Highminster.

When his apprenticeship was ended, nothing would serve him but that he must go up to London for a year or two. Poor Farmer Huntroyd was beginning to repent of his ambition of making his son Benjamin a gentleman. But it was too late to repine now. Both father and mother felt this, and, however sorrowful they might be, they were silent, neither demurring nor assenting to Benjamin's proposition when first he made it. But Bessy, through her tears, noticed that both her uncle and aunt seemed unusually tired that night, and sat hand-in-hand on the fireside settle, idly gazing into the bright flames as if they saw in it pictures of what they had once hoped their lives would have been. Bessy rattled about among the supper things as she put them away after Benjamin's departure, making more noise than usual – as if noise and bustle was what she needed to keep her from bursting out crying – and, having at one keen glance taken in the position and looks of Nathan and Hester, she avoided looking in that direction again, for fear the sight of their wistful faces should make her own tears overflow.

"Sit thee down lass – sit thee down. Bring the creepie-stool to the fire side, and let's have a bit of talk over the lad's plans," said Nathan at last, rousing himself to speak. Bessy came and sat down in front of the fire, and threw her apron over her face, as she rested her head on both hands. Nathan felt as if it was a chance which of the two women burst out crying first. So he thought he would speak, in hopes of keeping off the infection of tears.

"Didst ever hear of this mad plan afore, Bessy?"

"No, never!" Her voice came muffled, and changed from under her apron. Hester felt as if the tone, both of question and answer, implied blame, and this she could not bear.

"We should ha' looked to it when we bound him, for of necessity it would ha' come to this. There's examins, and catechizes, and I dunno what all for him to be put through in London. It's not his fault."

"Which on us said it were?" asked Nathan, rather put out. "Thof, for that matter, a few weeks would carry him over the mire, and make him as good a lawyer as any judge among 'em. Oud Lawson the attorney told me that, in a talk I had wi' him a bit sin. Na, na! it's the lad's own hankering after London that makes him want for to stay there for a year, let alone two."

Nathan shook his head.

"And if it be his own hankering," said Bessy, putting down her apron, her face all aflame, and her eyes swollen up, "I dunnot see harm in it. Lads aren't like lasses, to be teed to their own fireside like th' crook yonder. It's fitting for a young man to go abroad, and see the world afore he settles down."

Hester's hand sought Bessy's, and the two women sat in sympathetic defiance of any blame that should be thrown on the beloved absent. Nathan only said:

"Nay, wench, dunna wax up so; whatten's done, 's done; and worse, it's my doing. I mun needs make my bairn a gentleman; and we mun pay for it."

"Dear uncle! he wunna spend much, I'll answer for it; and I'll scrimp and save i' th' house to make it good."

"Wench!" said Nathan, solemnly, "it were not paying in cash I were speaking on: it were paying in heart's care, and heaviness of soul. Lunnon is a place where the devil keeps court as well as King George; and my poor chap has more nor once welly fallen into his clutches here. I dunno what he'll do when he gets close within sniff of him."

"Don't let him go, father!" said Hester, for the first time taking this view. Hitherto she had only thought of her own grief at parting with him. "Father, if you think so, keep him here, safe under our own eye."

"Nay!" said Nathan, "he's past time o' life for that. Why, there's not one on us knows where he is at this present time, and he not gone out of our sight an hour. He's too big to be put back i' th' go-cart, mother, or kept within doors with the chair turned bottom upwards."

"I wish he were a wee bairn lying in my arms again. It were a sore day when I weaned him; and I think life's been getten sorer and sorer at every turn he's ta'en towards manhood."

"Coom, lass, that's noan the way to be talking. Be thankful to Marcy that thou'st getten a man for the son as stands five foot eleven in's stockings, and ne'er a sick piece about him. We wunnot grudge him his fling, will we, Bess, my wench. He'll be coming back in a year, or mebby a bit more; and be a' for settling in a quiet town like, wi' a wife that's noan so fur fra' me at this very minute. An' we oud folk, as we get into years, must gi' up farm, and tak a bit on a house near Lawyer Benjamin."

And so the good Nathan, his own heart heavy enough, tried to soothe his womenkind. But, of the three, his eyes were longest in closing; his apprehensions the deepest founded.

"I misdoubt me I hanna done well by th' lad. I misdoubt me sore," was the thought that kept him awake till day began to dawn. "Summet's wrong about him, or folk would na look at me wi' such piteous-like een when they speak on him. I can see th' meaning of it, thof I'm too proud to let on. And Lawson, too, he holds his tongue more nor he should do, when I ax him how my lad's getting on, and whatten sort of a lawyer he'll mak. God be marciful to Hester an' me, if th' lad's gone away! God be marciful! But mebby it's this lying waking a'

the night through, that maks me so fearfu'. Why, when I were his age, I daur be bound I should ha' spent money fast enoof, i' I could ha' come by it. But I had to arn it; that maks a great differ'. Well! It were hard to thwart th' child of our old age, and we waiten so long for to have 'un!"

Next morning Nathan rode Moggy the cart horse into Highminster to see Mr. Lawson. Anybody who saw him ride out of his own yard would have been struck with the change in him which, when he returned; a change, more than a day's unusual exercise should have made in a man of his years. He scarcely held the reins at all. One jerk of Moggy's head would have plucked them out of his hands. His head was bent forward, his eyes looking on some unseen thing, with long unwinking gaze. But as he drew near home on his return, he made an effort to recover himself.

"No need fretting them," he said; "lads will be lads. But I didna think he had it in him to be so thowtless; young as he is. Well, well! he'll mebby get more wisdom i' Lunnon. Anyways it's best to cut him off fra such evil lads as Will Hawker, and such-like. It's they as have led my boy astray. He were a good chap till he knowed them – a good chap till he knowed them."

But he put all his cares in the background when he came into the houseplace, where both Bessy and his wife met him at the door, and both would fain lend a hand to take off his great-coat.

"Theer, wenches, theer! ye might let a man alone for to get out on's clothes! Why, I might ha' struck thee, lass." And he went on talking, trying to keep them off for a time from the subject that all had at heart. But there was no putting them off for ever; and, by dint of repeated questioning on his wife's part, more was got out than he had ever meant to tell – enough to grieve both his hearers sorely; and yet the brave old man still kept the worst in his own breast.

The next day Benjamin came home for a week or two before making his great start to London. His father kept him at a distance, and was solemn and quiet in his manner to the young man. Bessy, who had shown anger enough at first, and had uttered many a sharp speech, began to relent, and then to feel hurt and displeased that her uncle should persevere so long in his cold, reserved manner, and Benjamin just going to leave them. Her aunt went, tremblingly busy, about the clothes-presses and drawers, as if afraid of letting herself think either of the past or the future; only once or twice, coming behind her son, she suddenly stooped over his sitting figure, and kissed his cheek, and stroked his hair. Bessy remembered afterwards – long years afterwards – how he had tossed his head away with nervous irritability on one of these occasions, and had muttered – her aunt did not hear it, but Bessy did—

"Can't you leave a man alone?"

Towards Bessy herself he was pretty gracious. No other words express his manner: it was not warm, nor tender, nor cousinly, but there was an assumption of underbred politeness towards her as a young, pretty woman; which politeness was neglected in his authoritative or grumbling manner towards his mother, or his sullen silence before his father. He once or twice ventured on a compliment to Bessy on her personal appearance. She stood still, and looked at him with astonishment.

"How's my eyes changed sin last thou sawst them," she asked, "that thou must be telling me about 'em i' that fashion? I'd rayther by a deal see thee helping the mother when she's dropped her knitting-needle and canna see i' th' dusk for to pick it up."

But Bessy thought of his pretty speech about her eyes long after he had forgotten making it, and would have been puzzled to tell the colour of them. Many a day, after he was gone, did she look earnestly in the little oblong looking-glass, which hung up against the wall of her little sleeping-chamber, but which she used to take down in order to examine the eyes he had praised, murmuring to herself, "Pretty soft grey eyes! Pretty soft grey eyes!" until she would hang up the glass again with a sudden laugh and a rosy blush.

In the days, when he had gone away to the vague distance and vaguer place – the city called London – Bessy tried to forget all that had gone against her feeling of the affection and duty that a son owed to his parents; and she had many things to forget of this kind that would keep surging up into her mind. For instance, she wished that he had not objected to the home-spun, home-made shirts which his mother and she had had such pleasure in getting ready for him. He might not know, it was true – and so her love urged – how carefully and evenly the thread had been spun: how, content with bleaching the yarn in the sunniest meadow, the linen, on its return from the weaver's, had been spread out afresh on the sweet summer grass, and watered carefully night after night when there was no dew to perform the kindly office. He did not know – for no one but Bessy herself did – how many false or large stitches, made large and false by her aunt's failing eyes (who yet liked to do the choicest part of the stitching all by herself), Bessy had unpicked at night in her own room, and with dainty fingers had restitched; sewing eagerly in the dead of night. All this he did not know; or he could never have complained of the coarse texture; the old-fashioned make of these shirts; and urged on his mother to give him part of her little store of egg and butter money in order to buy newer-fashioned linen in Highminster.

When once that little precious store of his mother's was discovered, it was well for Bessy's peace of mind that she did not know how loosely her aunt counted up the coins, mistaking guineas for shillings, or just the other way, so that the amount was seldom the same in the old black spoutless teapot. Yet this son, this hope, this love, had yet a strange power of fascination over the household. The evening before he left, he sat between his parents, a hand in theirs on either side, and Bessy on the old creepie-stool,

her head lying on her aunt's knee, and looking up at him from time to time, as if to learn his face off by heart; till his glances meeting hers, made her drop her eyes, and only sigh.

He stopped up late that night with his father, long after the women had gone to bed. But not to sleep; for I will answer for it the grey-haired mother never slept a wink till the late dawn of the autumn day, and Bessy heard her uncle come up-stairs with heavy, deliberate footsteps, and go to the old stocking which served him for bank; and count out golden guineas – once he stopped, but again he went on afresh, as if resolved to crown his gift with liberality. Another long pause – in which she could but indistinctly hear continued words, it might have been advice, it might be a prayer, for it was in her uncle's voice; and then father and son came up to bed. Bessy's room was but parted from her cousin's by a thin wooden partition, and the last sound she distinctly heard, before her eyes, tired out with crying, closed themselves in sleep, was the guineas clinking down upon each other at regular intervals, as if Benjamin were playing at pitch and toss with his father's present.

After he was gone, Bessy wished he had asked her to walk part of the way with him into Highminster. She was all ready, her things laid out on the bed, but she could not accompany him without invitation.

The little household tried to close over the gap as best they might. They seemed to set themselves to their daily work with unusual vigour; but somehow when evening came, there had been little done. Heavy hearts never make light work, and there was no telling how much care and anxiety each had had to bear in secret in the field, at the wheel, or in the dairy. Formerly he was looked for every Saturday; looked for, though he might not come, or if he came, there were things to be spoken about, that made his visit anything but a pleasure: still he might come, and all things might go right, and then what sunshine, what gladness to those humble people. But now he was away, and dreary winter was come on; old folks' sight fails, and the evenings were long, and sad, in spite of all Bessy could do or say. And he did not write so often as he might – so every one thought; though every one would have been ready to defend him from either of the others who had expressed such a thought aloud. "Surely!" said Bessy to herself, when the first primroses peeped out in a sheltered and sunny hedge bank, and she gathered them as she passed home from afternoon church—"surely there never will be such a dreary, miserable winter again as this has been." There had been a great change in Nathan and Bessy Huntroyd during this last year. The spring before, when Benjamin was yet the subject of more hopes than fears, his father and mother looked what I may call an elderly middle-aged couple: people who had a good deal of hearty work in them yet. Now – it was not his absence alone that caused the change – they looked frail and old, as if each day's natural trouble was a burden more than they could bear. For Nathan had heard sad reports about his only child, and had told them solemnly to his wife, as things too bad to be believed, and yet, "God help us if indeed he is such a lad as this!" Their eyes were become too dry and hollow for many tears; they sat together, hand in hand; and shivered, and sighed, and did not speak many words, or dare to look at each other : and then Hester had said,

"We mauna tell th' lass. Young folks' hearts break wi' a little, and she'd be apt to fancy it were true." Here the old woman's voice broke into a kind of piping cry, but she struggled, and her next words were all right. "We mauna tell her, he's bound to be fond on her, and mebby, if she thinks well on him, and loves him, it will bring him straight."

"God grant it!" said Nathan.

"God shall grant it," said Hester, passionately moaning out her words; and then repeating them, alas! with a vain repetition.

"It's a bad place for lying, is Highminster," said she, at length, as if impatient of the silence. "I never knowed such a place for getting up stories. But Bessy knows nought on, and nother you nor me belie'es un; that's one blessing."

But if they did not in their hearts believe them, how came they to look so sad, and worn, beyond what mere age could do?

Then came round another year, another winter, yet more miserable than the last. This year, with the primroses, came Benjamin; a bad, hard, flipppant young man, with yet enough of specious manners and handsome countenance to make his appearance striking at first to those to whom the aspect of a London fast young man of the lowest order is strange and new. Just at first, as he sauntered in with a swagger and an air of indifference, which was partly assumed, partly real, his old parents felt a simple kind of awe of him, as if he were not their son, but a real gentleman; but they had too much fine instinct in their homely natures not to know, after a very few minutes had passed, that this was not a true prince.

"Whatten ever does he mean," said Hester to her niece, as soon as they were alone, "by a' them maks and wearlocks? And he minces his words as if his tongue were clipped short, or split like a magpie's. Hech! London is as bad as a hot day i' August for spoiling good flesh; for he were a good-looking lad when he went up; and now, look at him, with his skin gone into lines and flourishes, just like first page on a copy-book!"

"I think he looks a deal better, aunt, for them new-fashioned whiskers!" said Bessy, blushing still at the remembrance of the kiss he had given her on first seeing her – a pledge, she thought, poor girl, that, in spite of his long silence in letter-writing, he still looked upon her as his troth-plight wife. There were things about him which none of them liked, although they never spoke about them, yet there was also something to gratify them all in the way in which he remained quiet at Nab-end, instead of seeking variety, as he had formerly done, by constantly stealing off to the neighbouring town. His father had paid all the debts that he knew of, soon after Benjamin had gone up to London; so there were no duns that his parents knew of to alarm him, and keep him at home. And he went out in the morning with the old man, his father, and lounged by his side, as Nathan went round his fields, with busy yet infirm gait, having heart, as he would have expressed it, in all that was going on, because at length his son seemed to take an interest in all the farming affairs, and stood patiently by his side, while he compared his own small galloways with the great short-horns looming over his neighbour's hedge.

"It's a slovenly way, thou seest, that of selling th' milk; folk don't care whether it's good or not, so that they get their pint-measure full o' stuff that's watered afore it leaves th' beast, instead o' honest cheating by the help o' th' pump. But look at Bessy's butter, what skill it shows! part her own manner of making, and part good choice o' cattle. It's a pleasure to see her basket, a' packed ready for to go to market; and it's noan o' a pleasure for to see the buckets fu' of their blue starch-water as yon beasts give. I'm thinking they crossed th' breed wi' a pump, not long sin'. Hech! but our Bessy's a cleaver canny wench! I sometimes think thou'lt be for gi'ng up th' law, and taking to th' oud trade, when thou wedst wi' her!" This was intended to be a skilful way of ascertaining whether there was any ground for the old farmer's wish and prayer that Benjamin might give up the law, and return to the primitive occupation of his father. Nathan dared to hope it now, since his son had never made much by his profession, owing, as he had said, to his want of a connexion: and the farm, and the stock, and the clean wife, too, were ready to his hand; and Nathan could safely rely on himself never in his most unguarded moments, to reproach his son with the hardly-earned hundreds that had been spent on his education. So the old man listened with painful interest to the answer which his son was evidently struggling to make; coughing a little and blowing his nose before he spoke.

"Well! you see, father, law is a precarious livelihood; a man, as I may express myself, has no chance in the profession unless he is known – known to the judges, and tiptop barristers, and that sort of thing. Now you see my mother and you have no acquaintance that you may call exactly in that line. But luckily I have met with a man, a friend as I may say, who is really a first-rate fellow, knowing everybody, from the Lord Chancellor downwards; and he has offered me a share in his business a partnership in short—" He hesitated a little.

"I'm sure that's uncommon kind of the gentleman," said Nathan. "I should like for to thank him mysen; for it's not many as would pick up a young chap out o' th' dirt as it were, and say, 'Here's hauf my good fortune for you, sir, and your very good health.' Most on 'em, when they're gettin' a bit o' luck, run off wi' it to keep it a' to themselves, and gobble it down in a corner. What may be his name, for I should like for to know it?"

"You don't quite apprehend me, father. A great deal of what you've said is true to the letter. People don't like to share their good luck, as you say."

"The more credit to them as does," broke in Nathan.

"Ay, but you see even such a fine fellow as my friend Cavendish does not like to give away half his good practice for nothing. He expects an equivalent."

"An equivalent," said Nathan: his voice had dropped down an octave. "And what may that be? There's always some meaning in grand words, I take it, though I'm not book-larned enough to find it out."

"Why, in this case the equivalent he demands for taking me into partnership, and afterwards relinquishing the whole business to me, is three hundred pounds down."

Benjamin looked sideways from under his eyes to see how his father took the proposition. His father struck his stick deep down in the ground, and leaning one hand upon it, faced round at him.

"Then thy fine friend may go and be hanged. Three hunder pound! I'll be darned an' danged too, if I know where to get 'em, e'en if I'd be making a fool o' thee an' mysen too."

He was out of breath by this time. His son took his father's first words in dogged silence; it was but the burst of surprise he had led himself to expect, and did not daunt him for long.

"I should think, sir—"

"'Sir' – whatten for dost thou 'sir' me? Is them's your manners? I'm plain Nathan Huntroyd; who never took on to be a gentleman: but I have paid my way up to this time, which I shannot do much longer, if I'm to have a son coming an' asking me for three hunder pounds, just as if I were a cow, and had nothing to do but let down my milk to the first person as strokes me."

"Well, father," said Benjamin, with an affectation of frankness, "then there's nothing for me but to do as I have often planned before; go and emigrate."

"And *what?*" said his father, looking sharply and steadily at him.

"Emigrate. Go to America, or India, or some colony where there would be an opening for a young man of spirit."

Benjamin had reserved this proposition for his trump card, expecting by means of it to carry all before him. But to his surprise his father plucked his stick out of the hole he had made when he so vehemently thrust it into the ground, and walked on four or five steps in advance; there he stood still again, and there was a dead silence for a few minutes.

"It 'ud, mebby, be th' best thing thou couldst do," the father began. Benjamin set his teeth hard to keep in curses. It was well for poor Nathan he did not look round then, and see the look his son gave him. "But it would come hard like upon us, upon Hester and me, for, whether thou'rt a good 'un or not, thou'rt our flesh and blood, our only bairn, and if thou'rt not all as a man could wish it's mebby been the fault on our pride i' thee. It 'ud kill the missus if he went off to Amerikay, and Bess, too, the lass as thinks so much on him." The speech originally addressed to his son, had wandered off into a monologue – as keenly listened to by Benjamin, however, as if it had all been spoken to him. After a pause of consideration his father turned round. "Yon man – I wunnot call him a friend o' yourn, to think of asking you for such a mint o' money – is not th' only one, I'll be bound, as could give ye a start i' th' law? Other folks 'ud, mebby, do it for less?"

"Not one of 'em; to give me equal advantages," said Benjamin, thinking he perceived signs of relenting.

"Well, then, thou mayst tell him that it's neither he nor thee as 'll see th' sight o' three hunder pound o' my money. I'll not deny as I've a bit laid up again a rainy day; it's not so much as thatten though, and a part on it is for Bessy, as has been like a daughter to us."

"But Bessy is to be your real daughter some day, when I've a home to take her to," said Benjamin; for he played very fast and loose, even in his own mind, with his engagement with Bessy. Present with her, when she was looking her brightest and best, he behaved to her as if they were engaged lovers: absent from her, he looked upon her rather as a good wedge, to be driven into his parent's favour on his behalf. Now, however, he was not exactly untrue in speaking as if he meant to make her his wife; for the thought was in his mind, though he made use of it to work upon his father.

"It will be a dree day for us, then," said the old man. "But God'll have us in his keeping, and 'll mebby be taking more care on us i' heaven by that time than Bess, good lass as she is, has had on us at Nab-end. Her heart is set on thee, too. But, lad, I hanna gotten the three hunder; I keeps my cash i' th' stocking, thou knowst, till it reaches fifty pound, and then I takes it to Ripon Bank. Now the last scratch they're gi'en me, made it just two hunder, and I hanna but on to fifteen pound yet i' the stockin', and I meant one hunder an' the red cow's calf to be for Bess, she's ta'en such pleasure like i' rearing it."

Benjamin gave a sharp glance at his father to see if he was telling the truth; and, that a suspicion of the old man, his father, had entered into the son's head, tells enough of his own character.

"I canna do it – I canna do it, for sure – although I shall like to think as I had helped on the wedding. There's the black heifer to be sold yet, and she'll fetch a matter of ten pound; but a deal on't will be needed for seed-corn, for the arable did but bad last year, and I thought I would try – I'll tell thee what, lad! I'll make it as though Bess lent thee her hunder, only thou must give her a writ of hand for it, and thou shalt have a' the money i' Ripon Bank, and see if the lawyer wunnot let thee have a share of what he offered thee for three hunder, for two. I dunnot mean for to wrong him, but thou must get a fair share for the money. At times I think thou'rt done by folk; now, I wadna have you cheat a bairn of a brass farthing: same time I wadna have thee so soft as to be cheated."

To explain this, it should be told that some of the bills which Benjamin had received money from his father to pay, had been altered so as to include other and less creditable expenses which the young man had incurred; and the simple old farmer, who had still much faith left in him for his boy, was acute enough to perceive that he had paid above the usual price for the articles he had purchased.

After some hesitation, Benjamin agreed to receive this two hundred, and promised to employ it to the best advantage in setting himself up in business. He had, nevertheless, a strange hankering after the additional fifteen pounds that was left to accumulate in the stocking. It was his, he thought, as heir to his father, and he soon lost some of his usual complaisance for Bessy that evening, as he dwelt on the idea that there was money being laid by for her, and grudged it to her even in imagination. He thought more of this fifteen pound that he was not to have, than of all the hardly-earned and humbly-saved two hundred that he was to come into possession of. Meanwhile Nathan was in unusual spirits that evening. He was so generous and affectionate at heart that he had an unconscious satisfaction in having helped two people on the road to happiness by the sacrifice of the greater part of his property. The very fact of having trusted his son so largely, seemed to make Benjamin more worthy of trust in his father's estimation. The sole idea he tried to banish was, that, if all came to pass as he hoped, both Benjamin and Bessy would be settled far away from Nab-end; but then he had a child-like reliance that "God would take care of him and his missus, somehow or anodder. It wur o' no use looking too far ahead."

Bessy had to hear many unintelligible jokes from her uncle that night; for he made no doubt that Benjamin had told her all that had passed, whereas the truth was, his son had said never a word to his cousin on the subject.

When the old couple were in bed, Nathan told his wife of the promise he had made to his son, and the plan in life which the advance of the two hundred was to promote. Poor Hester was a little startled at the sudden change in the destination of the sum, which she had long thought of with secret pride as "money i' th' bank." But she was willing enough to part with it, if necessary, for Benjamin. Only, how such a sum could be necessary, was the puzzle. But even this perplexity was jostled out of her mind by the overwhelming idea, not only of "our Ben" settling in London, but of Bessy going there too as his wife. This great trouble swallowed up all care about money, and Hester shivered and sighed all the night through with distress. In the morning, as Bessy was kneading the bread, her aunt, who had been sitting by the fire in an unusual manner for one of her active habits, said:

"I reckon we mun go to th' shop for our bread, an' that's a thing I never thought to come to so long as I lived."

Bessy looked up from her kneading, surprised.

"I'm sure I'm noan going to eat their nasty stuff. What for do ye want to get baker's bread, aunt? This dough will rise as high as a kite in a south wind."

"I'm not up to kneading as I could do once; it welly breaks my back; and when thou'rt off in London, I reckon we mun buy our bread, first time in my life."

"I'm not a-going to London," said Bessy, kneading away with fresh resolution, and growing very red, either with the idea or the exertion.

"But our Ben is going partner wi' a great London lawyer, and thou know'st he'll not tarry long but what he'll fetch thee."

"Now, aunt," said Bessy, stripping her arms of the dough, but still not looking up, "if that's all, don't fret yourself. Ben will have twenty minds in his head afore he settles, eyther in business or in wedlock. I sometimes wonder," she said, with increasing vehemence, "why I go on thinking on him; for I dunnot think he thinks on me when I'm out o' sight. I've a month's mind to try and forget him this time when he leaves us – that I have!"

"For shame, wench! and he to be planning and purposing all for thy sake. It wur only yesterday as he wur talking to thy uncle, and mapping' it out so clever; only thou seest, wench, it'll be dree work for us when both thee and him is gone."

The old woman began to cry the kind of tearless cry of the aged. Bessy hastened to comfort her; and the two talked, and grieved, and hoped, and planned for the days that now were to be, till they ended, the one in being consoled, the other in being secretly happy.

Nathan and his son came back from Highminster that evening, with their business transacted in the round-about way, which was most satisfactory to the old man. If he had thought it necessary to take half as much pains in ascertaining the truth of the plausible details by which his son bore out the story of the offered partnership, as he did in trying to get his money conveyed to London in the most secure manner, it would have been well for him. But he knew nothing of all this, and acted in the way which satisfied his anxiety best. He came home tired, but content; not in such high spirits as on the night before, but as easy in his mind as he could be on the eve of his son's departure. Bessy, pleasantly agitated by her aunt's tale of the morning of her cousin's true love for her – what ardently we wish we long believe – and the plan which was to end in their marriage – end to her, the woman, at least – Bessy looked almost pretty in her bright, blushing comeliness, and more than once, as she moved about from kitchen to dairy, Benjamin pulled her towards him, and gave her a kiss. To all such proceedings the old couple were wilfully blind; and, as night drew on, every one became sadder and quieter, thinking of the parting that was to be on the morrow. As the hours drew on, Bessy, too, became subdued; and, by-and-by, her simple cunning was exerted to get Benjamin to sit down next his mother, whose very heart was yearning after him, as Bessy saw. When once her child was placed by her side, and she had got possession of his hand, the old woman kept stroking it, and murmuring long unused words of endearment, such as she had spoken to him while he was yet a little child. But all this was wearisome to him. As long as he might play with, and plague, and caress Bessy, he had not been sleepy; but now he yawned loudly. Bessy could have boxed his ears for not curbing this gaping; at any rate, he needed not to have done it so openly – so almost ostentatiously. His mother was more pitiful.

"Thou'rt tired, my lad!" said she, putting her hand fondly on his shoulder; but it fell off, as he stood up suddenly, and said:

"Yes, deuced tired! I'm off to bed." And with a rough careless kiss all round, even to Bessy, as if he was "deuced tired" of playing the lover, he was gone; leaving the three to gather up their thoughts slowly, and follow him up-stairs.

He seemed almost impatient at them for rising betimes to see him off the next morning, and made no more of a good-by than some such speech as this: "Well, good folk, when next I see you, I hope you'll have merrier faces than you have today. Why, you might be going to a funeral; it's enough to scare a man from the place; you look quite ugly to what you did last night, Bess."

He was gone; and they turned into the house, and settled to the long day's work without many words about their loss. They had no time for unnecessary talking, indeed, for much had been left undone during his short visit that ought to have been done; and they had now to work double tides. Hard work was their comfort for many a long day.

For some time, Benjamin's letters, if not frequent, were full of exultant accounts of his well-doing. It is true that the details of his prosperity were somewhat vague; but the fact was broadly and unmistakably stated. Then came longer pauses; shorter letters, altered in tone. About a year after he had left them, Nathan received a letter, which bewildered and irritated him exceedingly. Something had gone wrong – what, Benjamin did not say – but the letter ended with a request that was almost a demand, for the remainder of his father's savings, whether in the stocking or the bank. Now the year had not been prosperous with Nathan; there had been an epidemic among cattle, and he had suffered along with his neighbours; and, moreover, the price of cows, when he had bought some to repair his wasted stock, was higher than he had ever remembered it before. The fifteen pounds in the stocking, which Benjamim left, had diminished to little more than three; and to have that required of him in so peremptory a manner! Before Nathan imparted the contents of this letter to any one (Bessy and her aunt had gone to market on a neighbour's cart that day), he got pen and ink and paper, and wrote back an ill-spelt, but very implicit and stern negative. Benjamin had had his portion; and if he could not make it do, so much the worse for him; his father had no more to give him. That was the substance of the letter.

The letter was written, directed, and sealed, and given to the country postman, returning to Highminster after his day's distribution and collection of letters, before Hester and Bessy returned from market. It had been a pleasant day of neighbourly meeting and sociable gossip: prices had been high, and they were in good spirits, only agreeably tired, and full of small pieces of news. It was some time before they found out how flatly all their talk fell on the ears of the stay-at-home listener. But, when they saw that his depression was caused by something beyond their powers of accounting for by any little every day cause, they urged him to tell them what was the matter. His anger had not gone off. It had rather increased by dwelling upon it, and he spoke it out in good resolute terms; and, long ere he had ended, the two women were as sad, if not as angry, as himself. Indeed, it was many days before either feeling wore away in the minds of those who entertained them. Bessy was the soonest comforted, because she found a vent for her sorrow in action; an action that was half as a kind of compensation for many a sharp word that she had spoken when her cousin had done anything to displease her on his last visit, and half because she believed that he never could have written such a letter to his father unless his want of money had been very pressing and real; though how he could ever have wanted money so soon, after such a heap of it had been given to him, was more than she could justly say. Bessy got out all her savings of little presents of sixpences and shillings, ever since she had been a child, of all the money she had gained for the eggs of two hens, called her own, she put all together, and it was above two pound – two pound five and seven-pence, to speak accurately – and, leaving out the penny as a nest egg for her future savings, she put up the rest in a little parcel, and sent it, with a note, to Benjamin's address in London:

*From a well-wisher.*
*Dr BENJAMIN, – Unkle has lost 2 cows and a vast of monney. He is a good deal Angored, but more Troubled. So no more at present. Hopeing this will*

*finding you well As it leaves us. Tho' lost to Site, To Memory Dear. Repayment not kneeded.*
     *Your effectonet cousin,*
     *ELIZABETH ROSE.*

When this packet was once fairly sent off, Bessy began to sing again over her work. She never expected the mere form of acknowledgment; indeed, she had such faith in the carrier (who took parcels to York, whence they were forwarded to London by coach), that she felt sure that he would go on purpose to London to deliver anything entrusted to him, if he had not full confidence in the person, persons, coach and horses, to whom he committed it. Therefore she was not anxious that she did not hear of its arrival. "Giving a thing to a man as one knows," said she to herself, "is a vast different to poking a thing through a hole into a box, th' inside of which one has never clapped eyes on; and yet letters get safe some ways or another." (This belief in the infallibility of the post was destined a shock before long.) But she had a secret yearning for Benjamin's thanks, and some of the old words of love that she had been without so long. Nay, she even thought – when, day after day, week after week, passed by without a line – that he might be winding up his affairs in that weary, wasteful London, and coming back to Nab-end to thank her in person.

One day – her aunt was up-stairs, inspecting the summer's make of cheeses, her uncle out in the fields – the postman brought a letter into the kitchen to Bessy. A country postman, even now, is not much pressed for time, and in those days there were but few letters to distribute, and they were only sent out from Highminster once a week into the district in which Nab-end was situated; and on those occasions the letter-carrier usually paid morning calls on the various people for whom he had letters. So, half standing by the dresser, half sitting on it, he began to rummage out his bag. "It's a queer-like thing I've got for Nathan this time. I am afraid it will bear ill news in it, for there's 'Dead Letter Office' stamped on the top of it."

"Lord save us!" said Bessy, and sat down on the nearest chair, as white as a sheet. In an instant, however, she was up, and, snatching the ominous letter out of the man's hands, she pushed him before her out of the house, and said, "Be off wi' thee, afore aunt comes down;" and ran past him as hard as she could till she reached the field where she expected to find her uncle.

"Uncle," said she, breathless, "what is it? Oh, uncle, speak! Is he dead?"

Nathan's hands trembled, and his eyes dazzled. "Take it," he said, "and tell me what it is."

"It's a letter – it's from you to Benjamin, it is and there's words printed with it, 'Not known at the address given;' so they've sent it back to the writer – that's you, uncle. Oh, it gave me such a start, with them nasty words printed outside!"

Nathan had taken the letter back into his own hands, and was turning it over, while he strove to understand what the quick-witted Bessy had picked up at a glance. But he arrived at a different conclusion.

"He's dead?" said he. "The lad is dead, and he never knowed how as I were sorry I wrote to 'un so sharp. My lad! my lad!" Nathan sat down on the ground where he stood, and covered his face with his old, withered hands. The letter returned to him was one which he had written with infinite pains and at various times, to tell his child, in kinder words and at greater length than he had done before, the reasons why he could not send him the money demanded. And now Benjamin was dead; nay, the old man immediately jumped to the conclusion that his child had been starved to death, without money, in a wild, wide, strange place. All he could say at first was:

"My heart, Bess – my heart is broken!" And he put his hand to his side, still keeping his shut eyes covered with the other, as though he never wished to see the light of day again. Bessy was down by his side in an instant, holding him in her arms, chafing and kissing him.

"It's noan so bad, uncle; he's not dead; the letter does not say that, dunnot think it. He's flitted from that lodging, and the lazy tyke dunna know where to find him; and so, they just send y' back th' letter, instead of trying fra' house to house, as Mark Benson would. I've always heerd tell on south country folk for laziness. He's noan dead, uncle; he's just flitted, and he'll let us know afore long where he's getten to. Mebby it's a cheaper place, for that lawyer has cheated him, ye recklet, and he'll be trying to live for as little as can, that's all, uncle. Dunnot take on so, for it doesna say he's dead." By this time, Bessy was crying with agitation, although she firmly believed in her own view of the case, and had felt the opening of the ill-favoured letter as a great relief. Presently she began to urge both with word and action upon her uncle, that he should sit no longer on the damp grass. She pulled him up, for he was very stiff, and, as he said, "all shaken to dithers." She made him walk about, repeating over and over again her solution of the case, always in the same words, beginning again and again, "He's noan dead; it's just been a flitting," and so on. Nathan shook his head, and tried to be convinced; but it was a steady belief in his own heart for all that. He looked so deathly ill on his return home with Bessy (for she would not let him go on with his day's work), that his wife made sure he had taken cold, and he, weary and indifferent to life, was glad to subside into bed and the rest from exertion which his real bodily illness gave him. Neither Bessy nor he spoke of the letter again, even to each other, for many days; and Bessy found means to stop Mark Benson's tongue, and satisfy his kindly curiosity by giving him the rosy side of her own view of the case.

Nathan got up again an older man in looks and constitution by ten years for that week of bed. His wife gave him many a scolding on his imprudence for sitting down in the wet field, if ever so tired. But now she, too, was beginning to be uneasy at Benjamin's long-continued silence. She could not write herself, but she urged her husband many a time to send a letter to ask for news of her lad. He said nothing in reply for some time; at length he told her he would write next Sunday afternoon. Sunday was his general time for writing, and this Sunday he meant to go to church for the first time since his illness. On Saturday he was very persistent against his wife's wishes (backed by Bessy as hard as she could), in resolving to go into Highminster to market. The change would do him good, he said. But he came home tired, and a little mysterious in his ways. When he went to the shippon the last thing at night, he asked Bessy to go with him, and hold the lantern, while he looked at an ailing cow; and, when they were fairly out of the earshot of the house, he pulled out a little shop-parcel, and said to her, "Thou'lt put that on ma Sunday hat, wilt 'ou lass? It'll be a bit on a comfort to me; for I know my lad's dead and gone, though I dunna speak on it for fear o' grieving th' old woman and ye."

"I'll put it on, uncle, if – But he's noan dead." (Bessy was sobbing.)

"I know – I know, lass. I dunnot wish other folk to hold my opinion; but I'd like to wear a bit o' crape, out o' respect to my boy. It 'ud have done me good for to have ordered a black coat, but she'd see if I had na' on my wedding-coat, Sundays, for a' she's losing her eyesight, poor old wench! But she'll ne'er take notice o' a bit o' crape. Thou'll put it on all canny and tidy."

So Nathan went to church with a strip of crape as narrow as Bessy durst venture to make it round his hat. Such is the contradictoriness of human nature, that, though he was most anxious his wife should not hear of his conviction that their son was dead, he was half hurt that none of the neighbours noticed his sign of mourning so far as to ask him for whom he wore it.

But after a while, when they never heard a word from or about Benjamin, the household wonder as to what had become of him grew so painful and strong, that Nathan no longer kept his idea to himself. Poor Hester, however, rejected it with her whole will, heart, and soul. She could not and would not believe – nothing should make her believe – that her only child Benjamin had died without some sign of love or farewell to her. No arguments could shake her in this. She believed that if all natural means of communication between her and him had been cut off at the last supreme moment – if death had come upon him in an instant, sudden and unexpected – her intense love would, she believed, have been supernaturally made conscious of the blank. Nathan at times tried to feel glad that she could still hope to see the lad again; but at other moments he wanted her sympathy in his grief, his self-reproach, his weary wonder as to how and what they had done wrong in the treatment of their son, that he had been such a care and sorrow to his parents. Bessy was convinced, first by her aunt, and then by her uncle – honestly convinced – on both sides of the argument; and so, for the time, able to sympathise with each. But she lost her youth in a very few months; she looked set and middle aged long before she ought to have done; and rarely smiled and never sang again.

All sorts of new arrangements were required by the blow which told so miserably upon the energies of all the household at Nab-end. Nathan could no longer go about and direct his two men, taking a good turn of work himself at busy times. Hester lost her interest in her dairy; for which indeed her increasing loss of sight unfitted her. Bessy would either do field work, or attend to the cows, the shippon, or churn, or make cheese; she did all well, no longer merrily, but with something of stern cleverness. But she was not sorry when her uncle one evening told her aunt and her that a neighbouring farmer, Job Kirkby, had made him an offer to take so much of his land off his hands as would leave him only pasture enough for two cows, and no arable to attend to; while Farmer Kirkby did not wish to interfere with anything in the house, only would be glad to use some of the outbuildings for his fattening cattle.

"We can do wi' Hawky and Daisy; it'll leave us eight or ten pound o' butter to take to market i' summer time, and keep us fra' thinking ing too much, which is what I'm dreading on as I get into years."

"Ay," said his wife. "Thou'll not have to go so far afield, if it's only the Aster-Toft as is on thy hands. And Bess will have to gi' up her pride i' cheese, and tak' to making cream-butter. I'd allays a fancy for trying at cream-butter, but th' whey had to be used; else, where I come fra, they'd never ha' looked near whey-butter."

When Hester was left alone with Bessy, she said, in allusion to this change of plan, "I'm thankful to the Lord as it is as it is: for I were allays feared Nathan would have to gie up the house and farm altogether, and then the lad would na' know where to find us when he came back fra Merikay. He's gone there for to make his fortune, I'll be bound. Keep up thy heart, lass, he'll be home some day; and have sown his wild oats. Eh! but thatten's a pretty story i' the Gospels about the Prodigal who'd to eat the pigs' vittle at one time, but ended i' clover in his father's house. And I'm sure our Nathan 'll be ready to forgive him, and love him, and make much of him, mebby a deal more nor me, who never gave in to's death. It 'll be liken to a resurrection to our Nathan."

Farmer Kirkby then, took by far the greater part of the land belonging to Nab-end Farm; and the work about the rest, and about the two remaining cows was easily done by three pairs of willing hands with a little occasional assistance. The Kirkby family were pleasant enough to have to deal with. There was a son, a stiff, grave bachelor, who was very particular and methodical about his work, and rarely spoke to any one. But Nathan took it into his head that John Kirkby was looking after Bessy, and was a good deal troubled in his mind in consequence; for it was the first time he had to face the effects of his belief in his son's death; and he discovered to his own surprise that he had not that implicit faith which would make it easy for him to look upon Bessy as the wife of another man than the one to whom she had been betrothed in her youth. As, however, John Kirkby seemed in no hurry to make his intentions (if indeed he had any) clear to Bessy, it was only at times that this jealousy on behalf of his lost son seized upon Nathan.

But people, old, and in deep hopeless sorrow, grow irritable at times, however they may repent and struggle against their irritability. There were days when Bessy had to bear a good deal from her uncle; but she loved him so dearly and respected him so much, that high as her temper was to all other people she never returned him a rough or impatient word. And she had a reward in the conviction of his deep, true affection for her, and in her aunt's entire and most sweet dependence upon her.

One day, however – it was near the end of November – Bessy had had a good deal to bear that seemed more than usually unreasonable on behalf of her uncle. The truth was, that one of Kirkby's cows was ill, and John Kirkby was a good deal about in the farm-yard; Bessy was interested about the animal, and had helped in preparing a mash over their own fire, that had to be given warm to the sick creature. If John had been out of the way, there would have been no one more anxious about the affair than Nathan; both because he was naturally kind-hearted and neighbourly, and also because he was rather proud of his reputation for knowledge in the diseases of cattle. But because John was about, and Bessy helping a little in what had to be done, Nathan would do nothing, and chose to assume that "nothing to think on ailed th' beast, but lads and lasses were allays fain to be feared on something." Now John was upwards of forty, and Bessy nearly eight-and-twenty, so the terms lads and lasses did not exactly apply to their case.

When Bessy brought the milk in from their own cows towards half-past five o'clock, Nathan bade her make the doors, and not be running out i' the dark and cold about other folk's business; and, though Bessy was a little surprised and a good deal annoyed at his tone, she sat down to her supper without making a remonstrance. It had long been Nathan's custom to look out the last thing at night to see "what mak' o' weather it wur;" and, when towards half-past eight he got his stick and went out – two or three steps from the door which opened into the houseplace where they were sitting – Hester put her hand on her niece's shoulder and said: "He's gotten a touch o' the rheumatics, as twinges him and makes him speak so sharp. I didna like to ask thee afore him, but how's yon poor beast?"

"Very ailing, belike. John Kirkby wur off for th' cow-doctor when I cam in. I'll reckon they'll have to stop up wi't a' night."

Since their sorrows, her uncle had taken to reading a chapter in the Bible aloud, the last thing at night. He could not read fluently, and often hesitated long over a word, which he miscalled at length; but the very fact of opening the book seemed to soothe those old bereaved parents; for it made them feel quiet and safe in the presence of God, and took them out of the cares and troubles of this world into that futurity which, however dim and vague, was to their faithful hearts as a sure and certain rest. This little quiet time – Nathan sitting with his horn spectacles on; the tallow candle between him and his Bible, and throwing a strong light on his reverent, earnest face; Hester sitting on the other side of the fire, her head bowed in attentive listening, now and then shaking it, and moaning a little, but when a promise came, or any good tidings of great joy, saying "Amen." with fervour; Bessy by her aunt, perhaps her mind a little wandering to some household cares, or it might be on thoughts of those who were absent – this little quiet pause, I say, was grateful and soothing to this household, as a lullaby to a tired child. But this night, Bessy – sitting opposite to the long low window, only shaded by a few geraniums that grew in the sill, and the door alongside that window, through which her uncle had passed not a quarter of an hour before – saw the wooden latch of the door gently and almost noiselessly lifted up, as if some one were trying it from the outside.

She was startled; and watched again, intently; but it was perfectly still now. She thought it must have been that it had not fallen into its proper place when her uncle had come in and locked the door. It was just enough to make her uncomfortable, no more; and she almost persuaded herself it must have been fancy. Before she went up-stairs, however, she went to the window to look out into the darkness; but all was still. Nothing to be seen; nothing to be heard. So the three went quietly up-stairs to bed.

The house was little better than a cottage. The front door opened on a houseplace, over which was the old couple's bedroom. To the left, as you entered this pleasant houseplace and at close right angles with the entrance, was a door that led into the small parlour, which was Hester and Bessy's pride, although not half as comfortable as the houseplace, and never on any occasion used as a sitting-room. There were shells and bunches of honesty in the fireplace; the best chest of drawers, and a company-set of gaudy-coloured china, and a bright common carpet on the floor; but all failed to give it the aspect of the homely comfort and delicate cleanliness of the houseplace. Over this parlour was the bedroom which Benjamin had slept in when a boy – when at home. It was kept still in a kind of readiness for him. The bed was still there, in which none had slept since he, eight or nine years ago; and every now and then the warming-pan was taken quietly and silently up by his old mother, and the bed thoroughly aired. But this she did in her husband's absence, and without saying a word to any one; nor did Bessy offer to help her, though her eyes often filled with tears, as she saw her aunt still going through the hopeless service. But the room had become a receptacle for all unused things; and there was always a corner of it appropriated to the winter's store of apples. To the left of the houseplace, as you stood facing the fire, on the side opposite to the window and outer door, were two other doors; the one on the right opened into a kind of back kitchen, and had a lean-to roof, and a door opening on to the farm-yard and back premises; the left-hand door gave on the stairs, underneath which was a closet, in which various household treasures were kept, and beyond that the dairy, over which Bessy slept; her little chamber window opening just above the sloping roof of the back kitchen. There were neither blinds nor shutters to any of the windows, either up-stairs or down; the house was built of stone, and there was heavy framework of the same material round the little casement windows, and the long, low window of the houseplace was divided by what, in grander dwellings would be called mullions.

By nine o'clock this night of which I am speaking, all had gone up-stairs to bed: it was even later than usual, for the burning of candles was regarded so much in the light of extravagance, that the household kept early hours even for country-folk. But somehow this evening, Bessy could not sleep, although in general she was in deep slumber five minutes after her head touched the pillow. Her thoughts ran on the chances for John Kirkby's cow, and a little fear lest the disorder might be epidemic, and spread to their own cattle. Across all these homely cares came a vivid, uncomfortable recollection of the way in which the door latch went up and down without any sufficient agency to account for it. She felt more sure now, than she had done downstairs, that it was a real movement and no effect of her imagination. She wished that it had not happened just when her uncle was reading, that she might at once have gone quick to the door, and convinced herself of the cause. As it was, her thoughts ran uneasily on the supernatural; and thence to Benjamin, her dear cousin and playfellow, her early lover. She had long given him up as lost for ever to her, if not actually dead; but this very giving him up for ever involved a free, full forgiveness of all his wrongs to her. She thought tenderly of him, as of one who might have been led astray in his later years, but who existed rather in her recollection as the innocent child, the spirited lad, the handsome, dashing young man. If John Kirkby's quiet attentions had ever betrayed his wishes to Bessy – if indeed he ever had any wishes on the subject – her first feeling would have been to compare his weather-beaten, middle-aged face and figure with the face and figure she remembered well, but never more expected to see in this life. So thinking, she became very restless, and weary of bed, and, after long tossing and turning, ending in a belief that she should never get to sleep at all that night, she went off soundly and suddenly.

As suddenly as she wide awake, sitting up in bed, listening to some noise that must have awakened her, but which was not repeated for some time. Surely it was in her uncle's room – her uncle was up; but for a minute or two there was no further sound. Then she heard him open his door, and go down stairs, with hurried, stumbling steps. She now thought that her aunt must be ill, and hastily sprang out of bed, and was putting on her petticoat with hurried, trembling hands, and had just opened her chamber door, when she heard the front door undone, and a scuffle, as of the feet of several people, and many rude, passionate words, spoken hoarsely below the breath. Quick as thought she understood it all – the house was lonely – her uncle had the reputation of being well-to-do – they had pretended to be belated, and had asked their way or something. What a blessing that John Kirkby's cow was sick, for there were several men watching with him. She went back, opened her window, squeezed herself out, slid down the lean-to roof, and ran, barefoot and breathless, to the shippon.

"John, John, for the love of God come quick; there's robbers in the house, and uncle and aunt 'll be murdered!" she whispered, in terrified accents, through the closed and barred shippon door. In a moment it was undone, and John and the cow-doctor stood there, ready to act, if they but understood her rightly. Again she repeated her words, with broken, half-unintelligible explanations of what she as yet did not rightly understand.

"Front door is open, say'st thou?" said John, arming himself with a pitchfork, while the cow-doctor took some other implement. "Then I reckon we'd best make for that way o' getting into th' house, and catch 'em all in a trap."

"Run! run!" was all Bessy could say, taking hold of John Kirkby's arm, and pulling him along with her. Swiftly did the three run to the house, round the corner, and in at the open front door. The men carried the horn lantern they had been using in the shippon, and, by the sudden oblong light that it threw upon objects, Bessy saw the principal one of her anxiety, her uncle, lying stunned and helpless on the kitchen floor. Her first thought was for him; for she had no idea that her aunt was in any immediate danger, although she heard the noise of feet, and fierce subdued voices up-stairs.

"Make th' door behind us, lass. We'll not let them escape!" said brave John Kirkby, dauntless in a good cause, though he knew not how many there might be above. The cow-doctor fastened and locked the door, saying, "There!" in a defiant tone, as he put the key in his pocket. It was to be a struggle for life or for death, or, at any rate, for effectual capture or desperate escape. Bessy kneeled down by her uncle, who did not speak nor give any sign of consciousness. Bessy raised his head by drawing a pillow off the settle and putting it under him; she longed to go for water into the back kitchen, but the sound of a violent struggle, and of heavy blows, and of low, hard curses spoken through closed teeth, and muttered passion, as though breath were too much needed for action to be wasted in speech, kept her still and quiet by her uncle's side in the kitchen, where the darkness might almost be felt, so thick and deep was it. Once – in a pause of her own heart's beating – a sudden terror came over her; she perceived, in that strange way in which the presence of a living creature forces itself on our consciousness in the darkest room, that some one was near her, keeping as still as she. It was not the poor old man's breathing that she heard, nor the radiation of his presence that she felt: some one else was in the kitchen; another robber, perhaps, left to guard the old man with murderous intent if his consciousness returned. Now, Bessy was fully aware that self-preservation would keep her terrible companion quiet, as there was no motive for his betraying himself stronger than the desire of escape; any effort for which he, the unseen witness, must know would be rendered abortive by the fact of the door being locked. Yet the knowledge that he was there, close to her, still, silent as the grave, with fearful, it might be deadly, unspoken thoughts in his heart, possibly even with keener and stronger sight than hers, as longer accustomed to the darkness, able to discern her figure and posture, and glaring at her like some wild beast, Bessy could not fail to shrink from the vision that her fancy presented. And still the struggle went on up-stairs; feet slipping, blows sounding, and the wrench of intentioned aims, the strong gasps for breath, as the wrestlers paused for an instant. In one of these pauses Bessy felt conscious of a creeping movement close to her, which ceased when the noise of the strife above died away, and was resumed when it again began. She was aware of it by some subtle vibration of the air rather than by touch or sound. She was sure that he who had been close to her one minute as she knelt, was, the next, passing stealthily towards the inner door which led to the staircase. She thought he was going to join and strengthen his accomplices, and, with a great cry, she sprang after him; but, just as she came to the doorway, through which some dim portion of light from the upper chambers came, she saw one man thrown down stairs with such violence that he fell almost at her very feet, while the dark, creeping figure glided suddenly away to the left, and as suddenly entered the closet beneath the stairs. Bessy had no time to wonder as to his purpose in so doing, whether he had at first designed to aid his accomplices in their desperate fight. He was an enemy, a robber, that was all she knew, and she sprang to the door of the closet, and in a trice had locked it on the outside. And then she stood frightened, panting in that dark corner, sick with terror lest the man who lay before her was either John Kirkby or the cow-doctor. If it were either of those friendly two, what would become of the other – of her uncle, her aunt, herself? But, in a very few minutes, this wonder was ended; her two defenders came slowly and heavily down the stairs, dragging with them a man, fierce, sullen, despairing – disabled with terrible blows, which had made his face one bloody, swollen mass. As for that, neither John nor the cow-doctor were much more presentable. One of them bore the lantern in his teeth, for all their strength was taken up by the weight of the fellow they were bearing.

"Take care," said Bessy, from her corner; "there's a chap just beneath your feet. I dunno if he's dead or alive, and uncle lies on the floor just beyond." They stood still on the stairs for a moment. Just then the robber they had thrown down stairs stirred and moaned.

"Bessy," said John, "run off to th' stable and fetch ropes and gearing for to bind 'em, and we'll rid the house on 'em, and thou can'st go see after th' oud folks, who need it sadly."

Bessy was back in a very few minutes. When she came in, there was more light in the houseplace, for some one had stirred up the raked fire.

"That felly makes as though his leg were broken," said John, nodding towards the man still lying on the ground. Bessy felt almost sorry for him as they handled him – not over gently – and bound him, only half-conscious, as hardly and tightly as they had done his fierce, surly companion. She even felt so sorry for his evident agony, as they turned him over and over, that she ran to get him a cup of water to moisten his lips,

"I'm loth to leave yo' with him alone," said John, "though I'm thinking his leg is broken for sartain, and he can't stir, even if he comes to hissel, to do yo' any harm. But we'll just take off this chap, and make sure of him, and then one on us 'll come back to yo', and we can, mebby, find a gate or so for yo' to get shut on him out o' th' house. This felly's made safe enough, I'll be bound," said he, looking at the burglar, who stood, bloody and black, with fell hatred on his sullen face. His eye caught Bessy's as hers fell on him with dread so evident that it made him smile, and the look and the smile prevented the words from being spoken which were on Bessy's lips. She dared not tell, before him, that an able-bodied accomplice still remained in the house, lest, somehow, the door which kept him a prisoner should be broken open, and the fight renewed. So she only said to John, as he was leaving the house: "Thou'lt not be long away, for I'm afeard of being left wi' this man."

"He'll noan do thee harm," said John.

"No! but I'm feared lest he should die. And there's uncle and aunt. Come back soon, John!"

"Ay, ay!" said he, half-pleased; I'll be back, never fear me."

So Bessy shut the door after them, but did not lock if for fear of mischances in the house, and went once more to her uncle, whose breathing, by this time, was easier than when she had first returned into the houseplace with John and the doctor. By the light of the fire, too, she could now see that he had received a blow on the head which was probably the occasion of his stupor. Round this wound, which was now bleeding pretty freely, Bessy put cloths dipped in cold water, and then, leaving him for a time, she lighted a candle, and was about to go up-stairs to her aunt, when, just as she was passing the bound and disabled robber, she heard her name softly, urgently called.

"Bessy, Bessy!" At first the voice sounded so close that she thought it must be the unconscious wretch at her feet. But once again that voice thrilled through her:

"Bessy, Bessy! for God's sake, let me out!"

She went to the stair-closet door, and tried to speak, but could not, her heart beat so terribly. Again, close to her ear: "Bessy, Bessy! they'll be back directly; let me out, I say! For God's sake, let me out!" And he began to kick violently against the panels.

"Hush, hush!" she said, sick with a terrible dread, yet with a will strongly resisting her conviction. "Who are you?" But she knew – knew quite well.

"Benjamin." An oath. "Let me out, I say, and I'll be off, and out of England by tomorrow night never to come back, and you'll have all my father's money."

"D'ye think I care for that," said Bessy, vehemently, feeling with trembling hands for the lock; "I wish there was noan such a thing as money i' the world, afore yo'd come to this. There, yo're free, and I charge yo' never to let me see your face again. I'd ne'er ha let yo' loose but for fear o' breaking their hearts, if yo' hanna killed them already." But, before she had ended her speech, he was gone – off into the black darkness, leaving the door open wide. With a new terror in her mind Bessy shut it afresh – shut it and bolted it this time. Then she sat down on the first chair, and relieved her soul by giving a great and exceeding bitter cry. But she knew it was no time for giving way, and, lifting herself up with as much effort as if each of her limbs was a heavy weight, she went into the back-kitchen, and took a drink of cold water. To her surprise she heard her uncle's voice, saying feebly: "Carry me up, and lay me by her."

But Bessy could not carry him; she could only help his faint exertions to walk upstairs; and, by the time he was there sitting panting on the first chair she could find, John Kirkby and Atkinson returned. John came up now to her aid. Her aunt lay across the bed in a fainting fit, and her uncle sat in so utterly broken-down a state that Bessy feared immediate death for both. But John cheered her up, and lifted the old man into his bed again, and, while Bessy tried to compose poor Hester's limbs into a position of rest, John went down to hunt about for the little store of gin which was always kept in a corner cupboard against emergencies.

"They've had a sore fright," said he, shaking his head, as he poured a little gin and hot water into their mouths with a teaspoon, while Bessy chafed their cold feet; "and it and the cold have been welly too much for 'em, poor old folk!"

He looked tenderly at them, and Bessy blessed him in her heart – blessed him unaware, for that look.

"I mun be off. I sent Atkinson up to th' farm for to bring down Bob, and Jack came wi' him back to th' shippon for to look after other man. He began blackguarding us all round, so Bob and Jack were gagging him wi' bridles when I left."

"Ne'er give heed to what he says," cried poor Bessy, a new panic besetting her. "Folks o' his sort are allays for dragging other folks into their mischief. I'm right glad he were well gagged."

"Well! but what I were saying were this. Atkinson and me will take t'other chap, who seems quiet enough, to th' shippon, and it 'll be one piece o' work for to mind them, and the cow; and I'll saddle old bay mare, and ride for constables and doctor fra Highminster. I'll bring

Dr. Preston up to see Nathan and Hester first, and then I reckon th' broken-legged chap down below must have his turn, for all as he's met wi' his misfortunes in a wrong line o' life."

"Ay!" said Bessy. "We mun ha' the doctor sure enough, for look at them how they lie! like two stone statues on a church monument, so sad and solemn."

"There's a look o' sense come back into their faces, though, sin' they supped that gin-and-water. I'd keep on a-bathing his head and giving them a sup on't fra time to time, if I was you, Bessy."

Bessy followed him down stairs, and lighted the men out of the house. She dared not light them carrying their burden even, until they passed round the corner of the house; so strong was her fearful conviction that Benjamin was lurking near, seeking again to enter. She rushed back into the kitchen, bolted and barred the door, and pushed the end of the dresser against it, shutting her eyes as she passed the uncurtained window, for fear of catching a glimpse of a white face pressed against the glass, and gazing at her. The poor old couple lay quiet and speechless, although Hester's position had slightly altered: she had turned a little on her side towards her husband, and had laid one shrivelled arm around his neck. But he was just as Bessy had left him, with the wet clothes around his head, his eyes not wanting in a certain intelligence, but solemn, and unconscious to all that was passing around as the eyes of death.

His wife spoke a little from time to time – said a word of thanks, perhaps, or so; but he, never. All the rest of that terrible night Bessy tended the poor old couple with constant care, her own heart so stunned and bruised in its feelings that she went about her pious duties almost like one in a dream. The November morning was long in coming; nor did she perceive any change either for the worse or the better before the doctor came, about eight o'clock. John Kirkby brought him; and was full of the capture of the two burglars.

As far as Bessy could make out, the participation of that unnatural Third was unknown; it was a relief, almost sickening in the revulsion it gave her from her terrible fear, which now she felt had haunted and held possession of her all night long, and had in fact paralysed her from thinking. Now she felt and thought with acute and feverish vividness, owing no doubt in part to the sleepless night she had passed. She felt almost sure that her uncle (possibly her aunt too) had recognised Benjamin; but there was a faint chance that they had not done so, and wild horses should never tear the secret from her, nor should any inadvertent word betray the fact that there had been a third person concerned. As to Nathan, he had never uttered a word. It was her aunt's silence that made Bessy fear lest Hester knew, somehow, that her son was concerned.

The doctor examined them both closely; looked hard at the wound on Nathan's head; asked questions which Hester answered shortly and unwillingly, and Nathan not at all: shutting his eyes as if even the sight of a stranger was pain to him. Bessy replied in their stead to all that she could answer respecting their state; and followed the doctor down stairs with a beating heart. When they came into the houseplace, they found John had opened the outer door to let in some fresh air, had brushed the hearth and made up the fire, and put the chairs and table in their right places. He reddened a little as Bessy's eye fell upon his swollen and battered face, but tried to smile it off in a dry kind of way.

"Yo' see I'm an ould bachelor, and I just thought as I'd redd up things a bit. How dun yo' find 'em, doctor?"

"Well, the poor old couple have had a terrible shock. I shall send them some soothing medicine to bring down the pulse, and a lotion for the old man's head. It is very well it bled so much; there might have been a good deal of inflammation." And so he went on, giving directions to Bessy for keeping them quietly in bed through the day. From these directions she gathered that they were not, as she had feared all night long, near to death. The doctor expected them to recover, though they would require care. She almost wished it had been otherwise, and that they, and she too, might have just lain down to their rest in the churchyard – so cruel did life seem to her; so dreadful the recollection of that subdued voice of the hidden robber, smiting her with recognition.

All this time John was getting things ready for breakfast, with something of the handiness of a woman. Bessy half resented his officiousness in pressing Dr. Preston to have a cup of tea, she did so want him to begone and leave her alone with her thoughts. She did not know that all was done for love of her; that the hard-featured, short-spoken John was thinking all the time how ill and miserable she looked, and trying with tender artifices to make it incumbent upon her sense of hospitality to share Dr. Preston's meal.

"I've seen as the cows is milked," said he, "yourn and all; and Atkinson's brought ours round fine. Whatten a marcy it were as she were sick just very night! Yon two chaps 'ud ha' made short work on't if yo' hadna fetched us in; and as it were we had a sore tussle. One on 'em 'll bear the marks on't to his dying day, wunnot he, doctor?"

"He'll barely have his leg well enough to stand his trial at York Assizes; they're coming off in a fortnight from now."

"Ay, and that reminds me, Bessy, yo'll have to go witness before Justice Royds. Constables bade me tell yo', and gie yo' this summons. Dunnot be feared; it will not be a long job, though I'm not saying as it 'll be a pleasant one. Yo'll have to answer questions as to how, and all about it; and Jane" (his sister) "will come and stop wi' th' oud folks; and I'll drive yo' in the shandry."

No one knew why Bessy's colour blenched, and her eye clouded. No one knew how she apprehended lest she should have to say that Benjamin had been of the gang, if, indeed, in some way the law had not followed on his heels quick enough to catch him.

But that trial was spared her; she was warned by John to answer questions, and say no more than was necessary, for fear of making her story less clear; and as she was known, by character, at least to Justice Royds and his clerk, they made the examination as little formidable as possible.

When all was over, and John was driving her back again, he expressed his rejoicing that there would be evidence enough to convict the men without summoning Nathan and Hester to identify them. Bessy was so tired that she hardly understood what an escape it was; how far greater than even her companion understood.

Jane Kirkby stayed with her for a week or more, and was an unspeakable comfort. Otherwise she sometimes thought she should have gone mad, with the face of her uncle always reminding her in its stony expression of agony, of that fearful night. Her aunt was softer in her sorrow, as became one of her faithful and pious nature; but it was easy to see how her heart bled inwardly. She recovered her strength sooner than her husband; but as she recovered, the doctor perceived the rapid approach of total blindness. Every day, nay, every hour of the day, that Bessy dared, without fear of exciting their suspicions of her knowledge, she told them, as she had anxiously told them at first, that only two men, and those perfect strangers, had been discovered as being concerned in the burglary. Her uncle would never have asked a question about it, even if she had withheld all information about the affair; but she noticed the quick, watching, waiting glance of his eye whenever she returned from any person or place where she might have been supposed to gain intelligence if Benjamin were suspected or caught; and she hastened to relieve the old man's anxiety, by always telling all that she had heard; thankful that as the days passed on the danger she sickened to think of grew less and less.

Day by day Bessy had ground for thinking that her aunt knew more than she had apprehended at first. There was something so very humble and touching in Hester's blind way of feeling about for her husband – stern, woe-begone Nathan – and mutely striving to console him in the deep agony of which Bessy learnt from this loving, piteous manner, that her aunt was conscious. Her aunt's face looked blankly up into his, tears slowly running down from her sightless eyes, while from time to time, when she thought herself unheard by any save him, she would repeat such texts as she had heard at church in happier days, and which she thought, in her true, simple piety, might tend to console him. Yet day by day her aunt grew more and more sad.

Three or four days before assize-time, two summonses to attend the trial at York were sent to the old people. Neither Bessy, nor John, nor Jane, could understand this; for their own notices had come long before, and they had been told that their evidence would be enough to convict.

But alas! the fact was that the lawyer employed to defend the prisoners had heard from them that there was a third person engaged, and had heard who that third person was; and it was this advocate's business to diminish if possible the guilt of his clients, by proving that they were but tools in the hands of one who had, from his superior knowledge of the premises and the daily customs of the inhabitants, been the originator and planner of the whole affair. To do this it was necessary to have the evidence of the parents, who, as the prisoners had said, must have recognised the voice of the young man, their son. For no one knew that Bessy, too, could have borne witness to his having been present, and, as it was supposed that Benjamin had escaped out of England, there was no exact betrayal of him on the part of his accomplices.

Wondering, bewildered, and weary, the old couple reached York, in company with John and Bessy, on the eve of the day of trial. Nathan was still so self-contained, that Bessy could never guess what had been passing in his mind. He was almost passive under his old wife's trembling caresses; he seemed hardly conscious of them, so rigid was his demeanour.

She, Bessy feared at times, was becoming childish; for she had evidently so great and anxious a love for her husband, that her memory seemed going in her endeavours to melt the stoniness of his aspect and manners; she appeared occasionally to have forgotten why he was so changed, in her piteous little attempts to bring him back to his former self.

"They'll for sure never torture them when they see what old folks they are!" cried Bessy, on the morning of the trial, a dim fear looming over her mind. "They'll never be so cruel, for sure!"

But "for sure" it was so. The barrister looked up at the judge, almost apologetically, as he saw how hoary-headed and woeful an old man was put into the witness-box when the defence came on, and Nathan Huntroyd was called on for his evidence.

"It is necessary, on behalf of my clients, my lord, that I should pursue a course which, for all other reasons, I deplore."

"Go on!" said the judge. "What is right and legal must be done." But, an old man himself, he covered his quivering mouth with his hand as Nathan, with grey, unmoved face, and solemn, hollow eyes, placing his two hands on each side of the witness-box, prepared to give his answers to questions, the nature of which he was beginning to foresee, but would not shrink from replying to truthfully; "the very stones" (as he said to himself, with a kind of dulled sense of the Eternal Justice), "rise up against such a sinner."

"Your name is Nathan Huntroyd, I believe?"

"It is."

"You live at Nab-end Farm?"

"I do."

"Do you remember the night of November the twelfth?"

"Yes."

"You were awakened that night by some noise, I believe. What was it?"

The old man's eyes fixed themselves upon his questioner with a look of a creature brought to bay. That look the barrister never forgets. It will haunt him till his dying day.

"It was a throwing up of stones against our window."

"Did you hear it at first?"

"No."

"What awakened you, then?"

"She did."

"And then you both heard the stones. Did you hear nothing else?"

A long pause. Then a low, clear "Yes."

"What?"

"Our Benjamin asking us for to let him in. She said as it were him, leastways."

"And you thought it was him, did you not?"

"I told her" (this time in a louder voice) "for to get to sleep, and not to be thinking that every drunken chap as passed by were our Benjamin, for that he were dead and gone."

"And she?"

"She said as though she'd heerd our Benjamin afore she were welly awake, axing for to be let in. But I bade her ne'er heed her dreams, but turn on her other side, and get to sleep again."

"And did she?"

A long pause, – judge, jury, bar, audience, all held their breath. At length Nathan said, "No!"

"What did you do then? (My lord I am compelled to ask these painful questions.)"

"I saw she wadna be quiet; she had allays thought he would come back to us, like the Prodigal i' th' Gospels." (His voice choked a little, but he tried to make it steady, succeeded, and went on.) "She said if I wadna get up she would; and just then I heerd a voice. I'm not quite mysel, gentlemen – I've been ill and i' bed, an' it makes me trembling-like. Some one said, 'Father, mother, I'm here, starving i' the cold – wunnot yo' get up and let me in?'"

"And that voice was?"

"It were like our Benjamin's. I see whatten yo're driving at, sir, and I'll tell yo' truth, though it kills me to speak it. I dunnot say it were our Benjamin as spoke, mind yo' – I only say it were like—"

"That's all I want, my good fellow. And on the strength of that entreaty, spoken in your son's voice, you went down and opened the door to these two prisoners at the bar, and to a third man?"

Nathan nodded assent, and even that counsel was too merciful to force him to put more into words.

"Call Hester Huntroyd."

An old woman, with a face of which the eyes were evidently blind, with a sweet, gentle, care-worn face, came into the witness-box, and meekly curtseyed to the presence of those whom she had been taught to respect – a presence she could not see.

There was something in her humble, blind aspect, as she stood waiting to have something done to her – what, her poor troubled mind hardly knew – that touched all who saw her, inexpressibly. Again the counsel apologised, but the judge could not reply in words; his face was quivering all over, and the jury looked uneasily at the prisoners' counsel. That gentleman saw that he might go too far, and send their sympathies off on the other side; but one or two questions he must ask. So, hastily recapitulating much that he had learned from Nathan, he said, "You believed it was your son's voice asking to be let in?"

"Ay! Our Benjamin came home, I'm sure; choose where he is gone."

She turned her head about, as if listening for the voice of her child, in the hushed silence of the court.

"Yes; he came home that night – and your husband went down to let him in?"

"Well! I believe he did. There was a great noise of folk down stair."

"And you heard your son Benjamin's voice among the others?"

"Is it to do him harm, sir?" asked she, her face growing more intelligent and intent on the business in hand.

"That is not my object in questioning you. I believe he has left England, so nothing you can say will do him any harm. You heard your son's voice, I say?"

"Yes, sir. For sure, I did."

"And some men came up-stairs into your room? What did they say?"

"They axed where Nathan kept his stocking."

"'And you – did you tell them?"

"No, sir, for I knew Nathan would not like me to."

"What did you do then?"

A shade of reluctance came over her face, as if she began to perceive causes and consequences.

"I just screamed on Bessy – that's my niece, sir."

"And you heard some one shout out from the bottom of the stairs?"

She looked piteously at him, but did not answer.

"Gentlemen of the jury, I wish to call your particular attention to this fact: she acknowledges she heard some one shout – some third person, you observe – shout out to the two above. What did he say? That is the last question I shall trouble you with. What did the third person, left behind down stairs, say?"

Her face worked – her mouth opened two or three times as if to speak – she stretched out her arms imploringly; but no word came, and she fell back into the arms of those nearest to her. Nathan forced himself forward into the witness-box:

"My Lord Judge, a woman bore ye, as I reckon; it's a cruel shame to serve a mother so. It wur my son, my only child, as called out for us t' open door, and who shouted out for to hold th' oud woman's throat if she did na stop her noise, when hoo'd fain ha' cried for her niece to help. And now yo've truth, and a' th' truth, and I'll leave yo' to th' Judgment o' God for th' way yo've getten at it."

Before night the mother was stricken with paralysis, and lay on her death-bed. But the broken-hearted go Home, to be comforted of God.

# The Ghost in the Corner Room
## Charles Dickens

**I HAD** observed Mr. Governor growing fidgety as his turn – his "spell," he called it – approached, and he now surprised us all, by rising with a serious countenance, and requesting permission to "come aft" and have speech with me, before he spun his yarn. His great popularity led to a gracious concession of this indulgence, and we went out together into the hall.

"Old shipmate," said Mr. Governor to me; "ever since I have been aboard of this old hulk, I have been haunted, day and night."

""By what, Jack?"

Mr. Governor, clapping his hand on my shoulder and keeping it there, said:

"By something in the likeness of a Woman."

"Ah! Your old affliction. You'll never get over *that,* Jack, if you live to be a hundred."

"No, don't talk so, because I am very serious. All night long, I have been haunted by one figure. All day, the same figure has so bewildered me in the kitchen, that I wonder I haven't poisoned the whole ship's company. Now, there's no fancy here. Would you like to see the figure?"

"I should like to see it very much."

"Then here it is!" said Jack. Thereupon, he presented my sister, who had stolen out quietly, after us.

"Oh, indeed?" said I. "Then, I suppose, Patty, my dear, I have no occasion to ask whether *you* have been haunted?"

"Constantly, Joe," she replied.

The effect of our going back again, all three together, and of my presenting my sister as the Ghost from the Corner Room, and Jack as the Ghost from my Sister's Room, was triumphant – the crowning hit of the night. Mr. Beaver was "so particularly delighted, that he by-and-by declared "a very little would make him dance a hornpipe." Mr. Governor immediately supplied the very little, by offering to make it a double hornpipe; and there ensued such toe-and-heeling, and buckle-covering, and double-shuffling, and heel-sliding, and execution of all sorts of slippery manoeuvres with vibratory legs, as none of us ever saw before, or will ever see again. When we had all laughed and applauded till we were faint, Starling, not to be outdone, favoured us with a more modern saltatory entertainment in the Lancashire clog manner – to the best of my belief, the longest dance ever performed: in which the sound of his feet became a Locomotive going through cuttings, tunnels, and open country, and became a vast number of other things we should never have suspected, unless he had kindly told us what they were.

It was resolved before we separated that night, that our three months' period in the Haunted House should be wound up with the marriage of my sister and Mr. Governor. Belinda was nominated bridesmaid, and Starling was engaged for bridegroom's man.

In a word, we lived our term out, most happily, and were never for a moment haunted by anything more disagreeable than our own imaginations and remembrances. My cousin's wife, in her great love for her husband and in her gratitude to him for the change her love had wrought in her, had told us, through his lips, her own story; and I am sure there was not one of us who did not like her the better for it, and respect her the more.

So, at last, before the shortest month in the year was quite out, we all walked forth one morning to the church with the spire, as if nothing uncommon were going to happen; and there Jack and my sister were married, as sensibly as could be. It occurs to me to mention that I observed Belinda and Alfred Starling to be rather sentimental and low, on the occasion, and that they are since engaged to be married in the same church. I regard it as an excellent thing for both, and a kind of union very wholesome for the times in which we live. He wants a little poetry, and she wants a little prose, and the marriage of the two things is the happiest marriage I know for all mankind.

Finally, I derived this Christmas Greeting from the Haunted House, which I affectionately address with all my heart to all my readers: Let us use the great virtue, Faith, but not abuse it; and let us put it to its best use, by having faith in the great Christmas book of the New Testament, and in one another.

**If you enjoyed this, you might also like...**
Four Stories, see page 232
The Haunted Man and the Ghost's Bargain, see page 77

# Four Stories

## The First Story

**SOME FEW YEARS AGO** a well-known English artist received a commission from Lady F. to paint a portrait of her husband. It was settled that he should execute the commission at F. Hall, in the country, because his engagements were too many to permit his entering upon a fresh work till the London season should be over. As he happened to be on terms of intimate acquaintance with his employers, the arrangement was satisfactory to all concerned, and on the 13th of September he set out in good heart to perform his engagement.

He look the train for the station nearest to F. Hall, and found himself, when first starting, alone in a carriage. His solitude did not, however, continue long. At the first station out of London, a young lady entered the carriage, and took the corner opposite to him. She was very delicate looking, with a remarkable blending of sweetness and sadness in her countenance, which did not fail to attract the notice of a man of observation and sensibility. For some time neither uttered a syllable. But at length the gentleman made the remarks usual under such circumstances, on the weather and the country, and, the ice being broken, they entered into conversation. They spoke of painting. The artist was much surprised by the intimate knowledge the young lady seemed to have of himself and his doings. He was quite certain that he had never seen her before. His surprise was by no means lessened when she suddenly inquired whether he could make, from recollection, the likeness of a person whom he had seen only once, or at most twice? He was hesitating what to reply, when she added, "Do you think, for example, that you could paint me from recollection?"

He replied that he was not quite sure, but that perhaps he could.

"Well," she said, "look at me again. You may have to take a likeness of me."

He complied with this odd request, and she asked, rather eagerly:

"Now, do you think you could?"

"I think so," he replied; "but I cannot say for certain."

At this moment the train stopped. The young lady rose from her seat, smiled in a friendly manner on the painter, and bade him good-by: adding, as she quitted the carriage, "We shall meet again soon." The train rattled off, and Mr. H. (the artist) was left to his own reflections.

The station was reached in due time, and Lady F.'s carriage was there, to meet the expected guest. It carried him to the place of his destination, one of "the stately homes of England," after a pleasant drive, and deposited him at the hall door, where his host and hostess were standing to receive him. A kind greeting passed, and he was shown to his room: for the dinner-hour was close at hand.

Having completed his toilet, and descended to the drawing-room, Mr. H. was much surprised, and much pleased, to see, seated on one of the ottomans, his young companion of the railway carriage. She greeted him with a smile and a bow of recognition. She sat by his side at dinner, spoke to him two or three times, mixed in the general conversation, and seemed perfectly at home. Mr. H. had no doubt of her being an intimate friend of his hostess. The evening passed away pleasantly. The conversation turned a good deal upon the fine arts in general, and on painting in particular, and Mr. H. was entreated to show some of the sketches he had brought down with him from London. He readily produced them, and the young lady was much interested in them.

At a late hour the party broke up, and retired to their several apartments.

Next morning, early, Mr. H. was tempted by the bright sunshine to leave his room, and stroll out into the park. The drawing-room opened

into the garden; passing through it, he inquired of a servant who was busy arranging the furniture, whether the young lady had come down yet?

"What young lady, sir?" asked the man, with an appearance of surprise.

"The young lady who dined here last night."

"No young lady dined here last night, sir," replied the man, looking fixedly at him.

The painter said no more: thinking within himself that the servant was either very stupid or had a very bad memory. So, leaving the room, he sauntered out into the park.

He was returning to the house, when his host met him, and the usual morning salutations passed between them.

"Your fair young friend has left you?" observed the artist.

"What young friend?" inquired the lord of the manor.

"The young lady who dined here last night," returned Mr. H.

"I cannot imagine to whom you refer," replied the gentleman, very greatly surprised.

"Did not a young lady dine and spend the evening here yesterday?" persisted Mr. H., who in his turn was beginning to wonder.

"No," replied his host; "most certainly not. There was no one at table but yourself, my lady, and I."

The subject was never reverted to after this occasion, yet our artist could not bring himself to believe that he was labouring under a delusion. If the whole were a dream, it was a dream in two parts. As surely as the young lady had been his companion in the railway carriage, so surely she had sat beside him at the dinner- table. Yet she did not come again; and everybody in the house, except himself, appeared to be ignorant of her existence.

He finished the portrait on which he was engaged, and returned to London.

For two whole years he followed up his profession: growing in reputation, and working hard. Yet he never all the while forgot a single lineament in the fair young face of his fellow-traveller. He had no clue by which to discover where she had come from, or who she was. He often thought of her, but spoke to no one about her. There was a mystery about the matter which imposed silence on him. It was wild, strange, utterly unaccountable.

Mr. H. was called by business to Canterbury. An old friend of his – whom I will call Mr. Wylde – resided there. Mr. H., being anxious to see him, and having only a few hours at his disposal, wrote as soon as he reached the hotel, begging Mr. Wylde to call upon him there. At the time appointed the door of his room opened, and Mr. Wylde was announced. He was a complete stranger to the artist; and the meeting between the two was a little awkward. It appeared, on explanation, that Mr. H.'s friend had left Canterbury some time; that the gentleman now face to face with the artist was another Mr. Wylde; that the note intended for the absentee had been given to him; and that he had obeyed the summons, supposing some business matter to be the cause of it.

The first coldness and surprise dispelled, the two gentlemen entered into a more friendly conversation; for Mr. H. had mentioned his name, and it was not a strange one to his visitor. When they had conversed a little while, Mr. Wylde asked Mr. H. whether he had ever painted, or could undertake to paint, a portrait from mere description? Mr. H. replied, never.

"I ask you this strange question," said Mr. Wylde, "because, about two years ago, I lost a dear daughter. She was my only child, and I loved her very dearly. Her loss was a heavy affliction to me, and my regrets are the deeper that I have no likeness of her. You are a man of unusual genius. If you could paint me a portrait of my child, I should be very grateful."

Mr. Wylde then described the features and appearance of his daughter, and the colour of her eyes and hair, and tried to give an idea of the expression of her face. Mr. H. listened attentively, and, feeling great sympathy with his grief, made a sketch. He had no thought of its being like, but hoped the bereaved father might possibly think it so. But the father shook his head on seeing the sketch, and said, "No, it was not at all like." Again the artist tried, and again he failed. The features were pretty well, but the expression was not hers; and the father turned away from it, thanking Mr. H. for his kind endeavours, but quite hopeless of any successful result. Suddenly a thought struck the painter; he took another sheet of paper, made a rapid and vigorous sketch, and handed it to his companion. Instantly, a bright look of recognition and pleasure lighted up the father's face, and he exclaimed, "That is she! Surely you must have seen my child, or you never could have made so perfect a likeness!"

"When did your daughter die?" inquired the painter, with agitation.

"About two years ago; on the 13th of September. She died in the afternoon, after a few days' illness."

Mr. H. pondered, but said nothing. The image of that fair young face was engraven on his memory as with a diamond's point, and her strangely prophetic words were now fulfilled.

A few weeks after, having completed a beautiful full-length portrait of the young lady, he sent it to her father, and the likeness was declared, by all who had ever seen her, to be perfect.

## Second Story

AMONG THE FRIENDS of my family was a young Swiss lady, who, with an only brother, had been left an orphan in her childhood. She was brought up, as well as her brother, by an aunt; and the children, thus thrown very much upon each other, became very strongly attached. At the age of twenty-two the youth got some appointment in India, and the terrible day drew near when they must part. I need not describe the agony of persons so circumstanced. But the mode in which these two sought to mitigate the anguish of separation was singular. They agreed that if either should die before the young man's return, the dead should appear to the living.

The youth departed. The young lady by-and- by married a Scotch gentleman, and quitted her home, to be the light and ornament of his. She was a devoted wife, but she never forgot her brother. She corresponded with him regularly, and her brightest days in all the year were those which brought letters from India.

One cold winter's day, two or three years after her marriage, she was seated at work near a large bright fire, in her own bedroom up-stairs. It was about mid-day, and the room was full of light. She was very busy, when some strange impulse caused her to raise her head and look round. The door was slightly open, and, near the large antique bed, stood a figure, which she, at a glance, recognised as that of her brother. With a cry of delight she started up, and ran forward to meet him, exclaiming, "Oh, Henry! How could you surprise me so! You never told me you were coming!" But he waved his hand sadly, in a way that forbade approach, and she remained rooted to the spot. He advanced a step towards her, and said, in a low soft voice, "Do you remember our agreement? I have come to fulfil it;" and approaching nearer he laid his hand on her wrist. It was icy cold, and the touch made her shiver. Her brother smiled, a faint sad smile, and, again waving his hand, turned and left the room.

When the lady recovered from a long swoon there was a mark on her wrist, which never left it to her dying day. The next mail from India brought a letter, informing her that her brother had died on the very day, and at the very hour, when he presented himself to her in her room.

## Third Story

**OVERHANGING THE WATERS** of the Frith of Forth there lived, a good many years ago, a family of old standing in the kingdom of Fife: frank, hospitable, and hereditary Jacobites. It consisted of the squire, or laird – a man well advanced in years – his wife, three sons, and four daughters. The sons were sent out into the world, but not into the service of the reigning family. The daughters were all young and unmarried, and the eldest and the youngest were much attached to each other. They slept in the same room, shared the same bed, and had no secrets one from the other. It chanced that among the visitors to the old house there came a young naval officer, whose gun-brig often put in to the neighbouring harbours. He was well received, and between him and the elder of the two sisters a tender attachment sprang up.

But the prospect of such an alliance did not quite please the lady's mother, and, without being absolutely told that it should never take place, the lovers were advised to separate. The plea urged, was, that they could not then afford to marry, and that they must wait for better times. Those were times when parental authority – at all events in Scotland – was like the decree of fate, and the lady felt that she had nothing left to do, but to say farewell to her lover. Not so he. He was a fine gallant fellow, and, taking the old lady at her word, he determined to do his utmost to push his worldly fortunes.

There was war at that time with some northern power – I think with Prussia – and the lover, who had interest at the Admiralty, applied to be sent to the Baltic. He obtained his wish. Nobody interfered to prevent the young people from taking a tender farewell of each other, and, he full of hope, and she desponding, they parted. It was settled that he should write by every opportunity; and twice a week – on the post days at the neighbouring village – the younger sister would mount her pony and ride in for letters. There was much hidden joy over every letter that arrived, and then intense anxiety until the next arrived. And often and often the sisters would sit at the window a whole winter's night listening to the roar of the sea among the rocks, and hoping and praying that each light, as it shone far away, might be the signal-lamp hung at the mast-head to apprise them that the gun-brig was coming. So weeks stole on in hope deferred, and there came a lull in the correspondence. Post-day after post-day brought no letters from the Baltic, and the agony of the sisters, especially of the betrothed, became almost unbearable.

CHARLES DICKENS SUPERNATURAL SHORT STORIES

They slept, as I have said, in the same room, and their window looked down well-nigh into the waters of the Frith. One night, the younger sister was awakened by the heavy moanings of the elder. They had taken to burning a candle in their room, and placing it in the window: thinking, poor girls, that it would serve as a beacon to the brig. She saw by its light that her sister was tossing about, and was greatly disturbed in her sleep. After some hesitation she determined to awaken the sleeper, who sprang up with a wild cry, and, pushing back her long hair with her hands, exclaimed, "What have you done, what have you done!" Her sister tried to soothe her, and asked tenderly if anything had alarmed her. "Alarmed!" she answered, still very wildly, "no! But I saw him! He entered at that door, and came near the foot of the bed. He looked very pale, and his hair was wet. He was just going to speak to me, when you drove him away. O what have you done, what have you done."

I do not believe that her lover's ghost really appeared, but the fact is certain that the next mail from the Baltic brought intelligence that the gun-brig had gone down in a gale of wind, with all on board.

## Fourth Story

**WHEN MY MOTHER** was a girl about eight or nine years old, and living in Switzerland, the Count R. of Holstein, coming to Switzerland for his health, took a house at Vevay, with the intention of remaining there for two or three years. He soon became acquainted with my mother's parents, and between him and them acquaintance ripened into friendship. They met constantly, and liked each other more and more. Knowing the count's intentions respecting his stay in Switzerland, my grandmother was much surprised by receiving from him one morning a short hurried note, informing her that urgent and unexpected business obliged him to return that very day to Germany. He added, that he was very sorry to go, but that he must go; and he ended by bidding her farewell, and hoping they might meet again some day. He quitted Vevay that evening, and nothing more was heard of him or his mysterious business.

A few years after this departure, my grandmother and one of her sons went to spend some time at Hamburg. Count R., hearing that they were there, went to see them, and brought them to his castle of Breitenburg, where they were to stay a few days. It was a wild but beautiful district, and the castle, a huge pile, was a relic of the feudal times, which, like most old places of the sort, was said to be haunted. Never having heard the story upon which this belief was founded, my grandmother entreated the count to tell it. After some little hesitation and demur, he consented:

"There is a room in this house," he began, "in which no one is ever able to sleep. Noises are heard in it continually, which have never been accounted for, and which sound like the ceaseless turning over and upsetting of furniture. I have had the room emptied, I have had the old floor taken up and a new one laid down, but nothing would stop the noises. At last, in despair, I had it walled up. The story attached to the room is this:

"Some hundreds of years ago, there lived in this castle a countess, whose charity to the poor and kindness to all people were unbounded. She was known far and wide as 'the good Countess R.,' and everybody loved her. The room in question was her room. One night, she was awakened from her sleep by a voice near her; and looking out of bed, she saw, by the faint light of her lamp, a little tiny man, about a foot in height, standing near her bedside. She was greatly surprised, but he spoke, and said, 'Good Countess of

R., I have come to ask you to be godmother to my child. Will you consent?' She said she would, and he told her that he would come and fetch her in a few days, to attend the christening; with those words he vanished out of the room.

"Next morning, recollecting the incidents of the night, the countess came to the conclusion that she had had an odd dream, and thought no more of the matter. But, about a fortnight afterwards, when she had well-nigh forgotten the dream, she was again roused at the same hour and by the same small individual, who said he had come to claim the fulfilment of her promise. She rose, dressed herself, and followed her tiny guide down the stairs of the castle. In the centre of the court-yard there was, and still is, a large square well, very deep, and stretching underneath the building nobody knew how far. Having reached the side of this well, the little man blindfolded the countess, and bidding her not fear, but follow him, descended some unknown stairs. This was for the countess a strange and novel position, and she felt uncomfortable; but she determined at all hazards to see the adventure to the end, and descended bravely. They reached the bottom, and when her guide removed the bandage from her eyes, she found herself in a room full of small people like himself. The christening was performed, the countess stood godmother, and at the conclusion of the ceremony, as the lady was about to say good-by, the mother of the baby took a handful of wood shavings which lay in a corner, and put them into her visitor's apron.

"'You have been very kind, good Countess of R.,' she said, 'in coming to be godmother to my child, and your kindness shall not go unrewarded. When you rise tomorrow, these shavings will have turned into metal, and out of them you must immediately get made, two fishes and thirty silberlingen (a German coin). When you get them back, take great care of them, for so long as they all remain in your family everything will prosper with you; but, if one of them ever gets lost, then you will have troubles without end.' The countess thanked her, and bade them all farewell. Having again covered her eyes, the little man led her out of the well, and landed her safe in her own court-yard, where he removed the bandage, and she never saw him more.

"Next morning the countess awoke with a confused notion of some extraordinary dream. While at her toilet, she recollected all the incidents quite plainly, and racked her brain for some cause which might account for it. She was so employed when, stretching out her hand for her apron, she was astounded to find it tied up, and, within the folds, a number of metal shavings. How came they there? Was it a reality? Had she not dreamed of the little man and the christening? She told the story to the members of her family at breakfast, who all agreed that whatever the token might mean, it should not be disregarded. It was therefore settled that the fishes and the silberlingen should be made, and carefully kept among the archives of the family. Time passed; everything prospered with the house of R. The King of Denmark loaded them with honours and benefits, and gave the count high office in his household. For many years all went well with them.

"Suddenly, to the consternation of the family, one of the fishes disappeared, and, though strenuous efforts were made to discover what had become of it, they all failed. From this time everything went wrong. The count then living, had two sons; while out hunting together, one killed the other; whether accidentally or not, is uncertain, but, as the youths were known to be perpetually disagreeing, the case seemed doubtful. This was the beginning of sorrows. The king, hearing what had occurred, thought it necessary to deprive the count of the office he held. Other misfortunes followed. The family fell into discredit. Their lands were sold, or forfeited to the crown; till little was left but the old castle of Breitenburg and the narrow domain which surrounded it. This deteriorating process went on through two or three generations, and, to add to all other misfortunes, there was always in the family one mad member.

"And now," continued the count, "comes the strange part of the mystery. I had never placed much faith in these mysterious little relics, and I regarded the story in connexion with them as a fable. I should have continued in this belief, but for a very extraordinary circumstance. You remember my sojourn in Switzerland a few years ago, and how abruptly it terminated? Well. Just before leaving Holstein, I had received a curious wild letter from some knight in Norway, saying that he was very ill, but that he could not die without first seeing and conversing with me. I thought the man mad, because I had never heard of him before, and he could have no possible business to transact with me. So, throwing the letter aside, I did not give it another thought.

"My correspondent, however, was not satisfied. He wrote again. My agent, who in my absence opened and answered my letters, told him that I was in Switzerland for my health, and that, if he had anything to say, he had better say it in writing, as I could not possibly travel so far as Norway.

"This, however, did not satisfy the knight. He wrote a third time, beseeching me to come to him, and declaring that what he had to tell me was of the utmost importance to us both. My agent was so struck by the earnest tone of the letter, that he forwarded it to me: at the same time advising me not to refuse the entreaty. This was the cause of my sudden departure from Vevay, and I shall never cease to rejoice that I did not persist in my refusal.

"I had a long and weary journey, and once or twice I felt sorely tempted to stop short, but some strange impulse kept me going. I had to traverse well-nigh the whole of Norway; often for days on horseback, riding over wild moorland, heathery bogs, mountains and crags and lonely places, and ever at my left the rocky coast, lashed and torn by the surging waters.

"At last, after some fatigue and hardship, I reached the village named in the letter, on the northern coast of Norway. The knight's castle – a large round tower – was built on a small island off the coast, and communicated with the land by a drawbridge. I arrived there, late at night, and must admit that I felt misgivings when I crossed the bridge by the lurid glare of torchlight, and heard the dark waters surging under me. The gate was opened by a man, who, as soon as I entered, closed it behind me. My horse was taken from me, and I was led up to the knight's room. It was a small circular apartment, nearly at the top of the tower, and scantily furnished. There, on a bed, lay the old knight, evidently at the point of death. He tried to rise as I entered, and gave me such a look of gratitude aud relief that it repaid me for my pains.

"'I cannot thank you sufficiently, Count of R.,' said he, 'for granting rny request. Had I been in a state to travel I should have gone to you; but that was impossible, and I could not die without first seeing you. My business is short, though important. Do you know this?' And he drew from under his pillow, my long- lost fish. Of course I knew it; and he went on. 'How long it has been in this house, I do not know, nor by what means it came here, nor, till quite lately, was I at all aware to whom it rightfully belonged. It did not come here in my time, nor in my father's time, and who brought it is a mystery. When I fell ill, and my recovery was pronounced to be impossible, I heard one night, a voice telling me that I should not die till I had restored the fish to the Count R. of Breitenburg. I did not know you; I had never heard of you; and at first I took no heed of the voice. But it came again, every night, until at length in despair I wrote to you. Then the voice stopped. Your answer came, and again I heard the warning, that I must not die till you arrived. At last I heard that you were coming, and I have no language in which to thank you for your kindness. I feel sure I could not have died without seeing you.'

"That night the old man died. I waited to bury him, and then returned home, bringing my recovered treasure with me. It was carefully restored to its place. That same year, my eldest brother, whom you know to have been the inmate of a lunatic asylum for years, died, and I became the owner of this place. Last year, to my great surprise, I received a kind letter from the King of Denmark, restoring to me the office which my fathers once held. This year, I have been named governor to his eldest son, and the king has returned a great part of the confiscated property; so that the sun of prosperity seems to shine once more upon the house of Breitenburg. Not long ago, I sent one of the silberlingen to Paris, and another to Vienna, in order that they might be analysed, and the metal of which they are composed made known to me; but no one is able to decide that point." Thus ended the Count of R.'s story, after which he led his eager listener to the place where these precious articles were kept, and showed them to her.

**If you enjoyed this, you might also like...**
To Be Read at Dusk, see page 132
The Baron of Grogzwig, see page 24

# The Portrait Painter's Story

**THERE WAS LATELY** published in these pages a paper entitled 'Four Stories'. The first of those stories related the strange experience of "a well-known English artist, Mr. H." On the publication of that account, Mr. H. himself addressed the conductor of this Journal (to his great surprise), and forwarded to him his own narrative of the occurrences in question.

As Mr. H. wrote, without any concealment, in his own name in full, and from his own studio in London, and as there was no possible doubt of his being a real existing person and a responsible gentleman, it became a duty to read his communication attentively. And great injustice having been unconsciously done to it, in the version published as the first of the "Four Stories," it follows here exactly as received. It is, of course, published with the sanction and authority of Mr. H., and Mr. H. has himself corrected the proofs.

Entering on no theory of our own towards the explanation of any part of this remarkable narrative, we have prevailed on Mr. H. to present it without any introductory remarks whatever. It only remains to add, that no one has for a moment stood between us and Mr. H. in this matter. The whole communication is at first hand. On seeing the article, Four Stories, Mr. H. frankly and good humouredly wrote, "I am the Mr. H., the living man, of whom mention is made; how my story has been picked up, I do not know, but it is not correctly told; I have it by me, written by myself, and here it is."

I am a painter. One morning in May, 1858, I was seated in my studio at my usual occupation. At an earlier hour than that at which visits are usually made, I received one from a friend whose acquaintance I had made some year or two previously in Richmond Barracks, Dublin. My acquaintance was a captain in the 3rd West York Militia, and from the hospitable manner in which I had been received while a guest with that regiment, as well as from the intimacy that existed between us personally, it was incumbent on me to offer my visitor suitable refreshments; consequently, two o'clock found us well occupied in conversation, cigars, and a decanter of sherry. About that hour a ring at the bell reminded me of an engagement I had made with a model, or a young person who, having a pretty face and neck, earned a livelihood by sitting for them to artists. Not being in the humour for work, I arranged with her to come on the following day, promising, of course, to remunerate her for her loss of time, and she went away. In about five minutes she returned, and, speaking to me privately, stated that she had looked forward to the money for the day's sitting, and would be inconvenienced by the want of it; would I let her have a part? There being no difficulty on this point, she again went. Close to the street in which I live there is another of a very similar name, and persons who are not familiar with my address often go to it by mistake. The model's way lay directly through it, and, on arriving there, she was accosted by a lady and gentleman, who asked if she could inform them where I lived? They had forgotten my right address, and were endeavouring to find me by inquiring of persons whom they met; in a few more minutes they were shown into my room.

My new visitors were strangers to me. They had seen a portrait I had painted, and wished for likenesses of themselves and their children. The price I named did not deter them, and they asked to look round the studio to select the style and size they should prefer. My friend of the 3rd West York, with infinite address and humour, took upon himself the office of showman, dilating on the merits of the respective works in a manner that the diffidence that is expected in a professional man when speaking of his own productions would not have allowed me to adopt. The inspection proving satisfactory, they asked whether I could paint the pictures at their house in the country, and there being no difficulty on this point, an engagement was made for the following autumn, subject to my writing to fix the time when I might be able to leave town for the purpose. This being adjusted, the gentleman gave me his card, and they left. Shortly afterwards my friend went also, and on looking for the first time at the card left by the strangers, I was somewhat disappointed to find that though it contained the name of Mr. and Mrs. Kirkbeck, there was no address. I tried to find it by looking at the Court Guide, but it contained no such name, so I put the card in my writing-desk, and forgot for a time the entire transaction.

Autumn came, and with it a series of engagements I had made in the north of England. Towards the end of September, 1858, I was one of a dinner-party at a country-house on the confines of Yorkshire and Lincolnshire. Being a stranger to the family, it was by a mere accident that I was at the house at all. I had arranged to pass a day and a night with a friend in the neighbourhood, who was intimate at the house, and had received an invitation, and the dinner occurring on the evening in question, I had been asked to accompany him. The party was a numerous one, and as the meal approached its termination, and was about to subside into the dessert, the conversation became general. I should here mention that my hearing is defective; at some times more so than at others, and on this particular evening I was extra deaf – so much so, that the conversation only reached me in the form of a continued din. At one instant, however, I heard a word distinctly pronounced, though it was uttered by a person at a considerable distance from me, and that word was Kirkbeck. In the business of the London season I had forgotten all about the visitors of the spring, who had left their card without the address. The word reaching me under such circumstances, arrested my attention, and immediately recalled the transaction to my remembrance. On the first opportunity that offered, I asked a person whom I was conversing with if a family of the name in question was resident in the neighbourhood. I was told, in reply, that a Mr. Kirkbeck lived at A—, at the farther end of the county. The next morning I wrote to this person, saying that I believed lie called at my studio in the spring, and had made an arrangement with me, which I was prevented fulfilling by there being no address on his card; furthermore, that I should shortly be in his neighbourhood on my return from the north, but should I be mistaken in addressing him, I begged he would not trouble himself to reply to my note. I gave as my address, The Post-office, York. On applying there three days afterwards, I received a note from Mr. Kirkbeck, stating that he was very glad he had heard from me, and that if I would call on my return, he would arrange about the pictures; he also told me to write a day before I proposed coming, that he might not otherwise engage himself. It was ultimately arranged that I should go to his house the succeeding Saturday, stay till Monday morning, transact afterwards what matters I had to attend to in London, and return in a fortnight to execute the commissions.

The day having arrived for my visit, directly after breakfast I took my place in the morning train from York to London. The train would stop at Doncaster, and after that at Retford junction, where I should have to get out in order to take the line through Lincoln to A— . The day was cold, wet, foggy, and in every way as disagreeable as I have ever known a day to be in an English October. The carriage in which I was seated had no other occupant, than myself, but at Doncaster a lady got in. My place was back to the engine and next to the door. As that is considered the ladies' seat, I offered it to her; she, however, very graciously declined it, and took the corner opposite, saying, in a very agreeable voice, that she liked to feel the breeze on her cheek. The next few minutes were occupied in locating herself. There was the cloak to be spread under her, the skirts of the dress to be arranged, the gloves to be tightened, and such other trifling arrangements of plumage as ladies are wont to make before settling themselves comfortably at church or elsewhere, the last and most important being the placing back over her hat the veil that concealed her features. I could then see that the lady was young, certainly not more than two or three-and-twenty; but being moderately tall, rather robust in make, and decided in expression, she might have been two or three years younger. I suppose that her complexion would be termed a medium one; her hair being of a bright brown, or auburn, while her eyes and rather decidedly marked eyebrows were nearly black. The colour of her cheek was of that pale trasparent hue that sets off to such advantage large expressive eyes, and an equable firm expression of mouth. On the whole, the ensemble was rather handsome than beautiful, her expression having that agreeable depth and harmony about it that rendered her face and features, though not strictly regular, infinitely more attractive than if they had been modelled upon the strictest rules of symmetry.

It is no small advantage on a wet day and a dull long journey to have an agreeable companion, one who can converse, and whose conversation has sufficient substance in it to make one forget the length and the dreariness of the journey. In this respect I had no deficiency to complain of, the lady being decidedly and agreeably conversational. When she had settled herself to her satisfaction, she asked to be allowed to look at my Bradshaw, and not being a proficient in that difficult work, she requested my aid in ascertaining at what time the train passed through Retford again on its way back from London to York. The conversation turned afterwards on general topics, and, somewhat to my surprise, she led it into such particular subjects as I might be supposed to be more especially familiar with; indeed, I could not avoid remarking that her entire manner, while it was anything but forward, was that of one who had either known me personally or by report. There was in her manner a kind of confidential reliance when she listened to me that is not usually accorded to a stranger, and sometimes she actually seemed to refer to different circumstances with which I had been connected in times past. After about three-quarters of an hour's conversation the train arrived at Retford, where I was to change carriages. On my alighting and wishing her good morning, she made a slight movement of the hand as if she meant me to shake it, and on my doing so she said, by way of adieu, "I dare say we shall meet again;" to which I replied, 'I hope that we shall all meet again," and so parted, she going on the line towards London, and I through Lincolnshire to A—. The remainder of the journey was cold, wet, and dreary. I missed the agreeable conversation, and tried to supply its place with a book I had brought with me from York, and the Times newspaper, which I had procured at Retford. But the most disagreeable journey comes to an end at last, and half-past five in the evening found me at the termination of mine. A carriage was waiting for me at the station, where Mr. Kirkbeck was also expected by the same train, but as he did not appear it was concluded he would come by the next – half an hour later; accordingly, the carriage drove away with myself only.

The family being from home at the moment, and the dinner hour being seven, I went at once to my room to unpack and to dress; having completed these operations, I descended to the drawing-room. It probably wanted some time to the dinner hour, as the lamps were not lighted, but in their place a large blazing fire threw a flood of light into every corner of the room, and more especially over a lady who, dressed in deep black, was standing by the chimney-piece warming a very handsome foot on the edge of the fender. Her face being turned away from the door by which I had entered, I did not at first see her features; on my advancing into the middle of the room, however, the foot was immediately withdrawn, and she turned round to accost me, when, to my profound astonishment, I perceived that it was none other than my companion in the railway carriage. She betrayed no surprise at seeing me; on the contrary, with one of those agreeable joyous expressions that make the plainest woman appear beautiful, she accosted me with, "I said we should meet again."

My bewilderment at the moment almost deprived me of utterance. I knew of no railway or other means by which she could have come. I had certainly left her in a London train, and had seen it start, and the only conceivable way in which she could have come was by going on to Peterborough and then returning by a branch to A—, a circuit of about ninety miles. As soon as my surprise enabled me to speak, I said that I wished I had come by the same conveyance as herself.

"That would have been rather difficult," she rejoined.

At this moment the servant came with the lamps, and informed me that his master had just arrived and would be down in a few minutes.

The lady took up a book containing some engravings, and having singled one out (a portrait of Lady—), asked me to look at it well and tell her whether I thought it like her.

I was engaged trying to get up an opinion, when Mr. and Mrs. Kirkbeck entered, and shaking me heartily by the hand, apologised for not being at home to receive me; the gentleman ending by requesting me to take Mrs. Kirkbeck in to dinner.

The lady of the house having taken my arm, we marched on. I certainly hesitated a moment to allow Mr. Kirkbeck to pass on first with the mysterious lady in black, but Mrs. Kirkbeck not seeming to understand it, we passed on at once. The dinner-party consisting of us four only, we fell into our respective places at the table without difficulty, the mistress and master of the house at the top and bottom, the lady in black and myself on each side. The dinner passed much as is usual on such occasions. I, having to play the guest, directed my conversation principally, if not exclusively, to my host and hostess, and I cannot call to mind that I or any one else once addressed the lady opposite. Seeing this, and remembering something that looked like a slight want of attention to her on coming into the dining-room, I at once concluded that she was the governess. I observed, however, that she made an excellent dinner; she seemed to appreciate both the beef and the tart as well as a glass of claret afterwards; probably she had had no luncheon, or the journey had given her an appetite.

The dinner ended, the ladies retired, and after the usual port, Mr. Kirkbeck and I joined them in the drawing-room. By this time, however, a much larger party had assembled. Brothers and sisters-in-law had come in from their residences in the neighbourhood, and several children, with Miss Hardwick, their governess, were also introduced to me. I saw at once that my supposition as to the lady in black being the governess was incorrect. After passing the time necessarily occupied in complimenting the children, and saying something to the different persons to whom I was introduced, I found myself again engaged in conversation with the lady of the railway carriage, and as the topic of the evening had referred principally to portrait-painting, she continued the subject.

"Do you think you could paint my portrait?" the lady inquired.

"Yes, I think I could, if I had the opportunity."

"Now, look at my face well; do you think you should recollect my features?"

"Yes, I am sure I should never forget your features."

"Of course I might have expected you to say that; but do you think you could do me from recollection?"

"Well, if it be necessary, I will try; but can't you give me any sittings?"

"No, quite impossible; it could not be. It is said that the print I showed to you before dinner is like me; do you think so?"

"Not much," I replied; "it has not your expression. If you can give me only one sitting, it would be better than none."

"No; I don't see how it could be."

The evening being by this time rather far advanced, and the chamber candles being brought in, on the plea of being rather tired, she shook me heartily by the hand, and wished me good night. My mysterious acquaintance caused me no small pondering during the night. I had never been introduced to her, I had not seen her speak to any one during the entire evening, not even to wish them good night – how she got across the country was an inexplicable mystery. Then, why did she wish me to paint her from memory, and why could she not give me even one sitting? Finding the difficulties of a solution to these questions rather increase upon me, I made up my mind to defer further consideration of them till breakfast-time, when I supposed the matter would receive some elucidation.

The breakfast now came, but with it no lady in black. The breakfast over, we went to church, came home to luncheon, and so on through the day, but still no lady, neither any reference to her. I then concluded that she must be some relative, who had gone away early in the morning to visit another member of the family living close by. I was much puzzled, however, by no reference whatever being made to her, and finding no opportunity of leading any part of my conversation with the family towards the subject, I went to bed the second night more puzzled than ever. On the servant coming in in the morning, I ventured to ask him the name of the lady who dined at the table on the Saturday evening, to which he answered:

"A lady, sir? No lady, only Mrs. Kirkbeck, sir."

"Yes, the lady that sat opposite me dressed in black?"

"Perhaps, Miss Hardwick, the governess, sir?"

"No, not Miss Hardwick; she came down afterwards."

"No lady as I see, sir."

"Oh dear me, yes, the lady dressed in black that was in the drawing-room when I arrived, before Mr. Kirkbeck came home?"

The man looked at me with surprise as if he doubted my sanity, and only answered, "I never see any lady, sir," and then left.

The mystery now appeared more impenetrable than ever – I thought it over in every possible aspect, but could come to no conclusion upon it. Breakfast was early that morning, in order to allow of my catching the morning train to London. The same cause also slightly hurried us, and allowed no time for conversation beyond that having direct reference to the business that brought me there; so, after arranging to return to paint the portraits on that day three weeks, I made my adieus, and took my departure for town.

It is only necessary for me to refer to my second visit to that house, in order to state that I was assured most positively, both by Mr. and Mrs. Kirkbeck, that no fourth person dined at the table on the Saturday evening in question. Their recollection was clear on the subject, as they had debated whether they should ask Miss Hardwick, the governess, to take the vacant seat, but had decided not to do so; neither could they recal to mind any such person as I described in the whole circle of their acquaintance.

Some weeks passed. It was close upon Christmas. The light of a short winter day was drawing to a close, and I was seated at my table, writing letters for the evening post. My back was towards the folding-doors leading into the room in which my visitors usually waited. I had been engaged some minutes in writing, when, without hearing or seeing anything, I became aware that a person had come through the folding-doors, and was then standing beside me. I turned, and beheld the lady of the railway carriage. I suppose that my manner indicated that I was somewhat startled, as the lady, after the usual salutation, said, "Pardon me for disturbing you. You did not hear me come in." Her manner, though it was more quiet and subdued than I had known it before, was hardly to be termed grave, still less sorrowful. There was a change, but it was that kind of change only which may often be observed from the frank impulsiveness of an intelligent young lady, to the composure and self-possession of that same young lady when she is either betrothed or has recently become a matron. She asked me whether I had made any attempt at a likeness of her. I was obliged to confess that I had not. She regretted it much, as she wished one for her father. She had brought an engraving (a portrait of Lady M. A.) with her that she thought would assist me. It was like the one she had asked my opinion upon at the house in Lincolnshire. It had always been considered very like her, and she would leave it with me. Then (putting her hand impressively on my arm) she added, "She really would be most thankful and grateful to me if I would do it" (and, if I recollect rightly, she added), "*as much depended on it.*" Seeing she was so much in earnest, I took up my sketch-book, and by the dim light that was still remaining began to make a rapid pencil sketch of her. On observing my doing so, however, instead of giving me what assistance she was able, she turned away under pretence of looking at the pictures around the room, occasionally passing from one to another so as to enable me to catch a momentary glimpse of her features. In this manner I made two hurried but rather expressive sketches of her, which being all that the declining light would allow me to do, I shut my book, and she prepared to leave. This time, instead of the usual "Good morning," she wished me an impressively pronounced "Good-by," firmly holding rather than shaking my hand while she said it. I accompanied her to the door, outside of which she seemed rather to fade into the darkness than to pass through it. But I refer this impression to my own fancy.

I immediately inquired of the servant why she had not announced the visitor to me. She stated that she was not aware there had been one, and that any one who had entered must have done so when she had left the street door open about half an hour previously, while she went across the road for a moment.

Soon after this occurred I had to fulfil an engagement at a house near Bosworth field, in Leicestershire. I left town on a Friday, having sent some pictures, that were too large to take with me, by the luggage train a week previously, in order that they might be at the house on my arrival, and occasion me no loss of time in waiting for them. On getting to the house, however, I found that they had not been heard of, and on inquiring at the station, it was stated that a case similar to the one I described had passed through and gone on to Leicester, where it probably still was. It being Friday, and past the hour for the post, there was no possibility of getting a letter to Leicester before Monday morning, as the luggage office would be closed there on the Sunday; consequently, I could in no case expect the arrival of the pictures before the succeeding Tuesday or Wednesday. The loss of three days would be a serious one; therefore, to avoid it, I suggested to my host that I should leave immediately to transact some business in South Staffordshire, as I should be obliged to attend to it before my return to town, and if I could see about it in the vacant interval thus thrown upon my hands, it would be saving me the same amount of time after my visit to his house was concluded. This arrangement meeting with his ready assent, I hastened to the Atherstone station on the Trent Valley Railway. By reference to Bradshaw, I found that my route lay through L—, where I was to change carriages, to S—, in Staffordshire. I was just in time for the train that would put me down at L— at eight in the evening, and a train was announced to start from L— for S— at ten minutes after eight, answering, as I concluded, to the train in which I was about to travel. I therefore saw no reason to doubt but that I should get to my journey's end the same night; but on my arriving at L— I found my plans entirely frustrated. The train arrived punctually, and I got out intending to wait on the platform for the arrival of the carriages for the other line. I found, however, that though the two lines crossed at L—, they did not communicate with each other, the L— station on the Trent Valley line being on one side of the town, and the L— station on the South Staffordshire line on the other. I also found that there was not time to get to the other station so as to catch the train the same evening; indeed, the train had just that moment passed on a lower level beneath my feet, and to get to the other side of the town, where it would stop for two minutes only, was out of the question. There was, therefore, nothing for it but to put up at the Swan Hotel for the night. I have an especial dislike to passing an evening at an hotel in a country town. Dinner at such places I never take, as I had rather go without than have such as I am likely to get. Books are never to be had, the country newspapers do not interest me. The Times I have spelt through on my journey. The society I am likely to meet have few ideas in common with myself. Under such circumstances, I usually resort to a meat tea to while away the time, and when that is over, occupy myself in writing letters.

This was the first time I had been in L—, and while waiting for the tea, it occurred to me how, on two occasions within the past six months, I had been on the point of coming to that very place, at one time to execute a small commission for an old acquaintance, resident there, and another, to get the materials for a picture I proposed painting of an incident in the early life of Dr. Johnson. I should have come on each of these occasions had not other arrangements diverted my purpose and caused me to postpone the journey indefinitely. The thought, however, would occur to me, "How strange! Here I am at L—, by no intention of my own, though I have twice tried to get here and been balked." When I had done tea, I thought; I might as well write to an acquaintance I had known some years previously, and who lived in the Cathedral-close, asking him to come and pass an hour or two with me. Accordingly, I rang for the waitress and asked: "Does Mr. Lute live in Lichfield?"

"Yes, sir."

"Cathedral-close?"

"Yes, sir,"

"Can I send a note to him?"

"Yes, sir."

I wrote the note, saying where I was, and asking if he would come for an hour or two and talk over old matters. The note was taken; in about twenty minutes a person of gentlemanly appearance, and what might be termed the advanced middle age, entered the room with my note in his hand, saying that I had sent him a letter, he presumed, by mistake, as he did not know my name. Seeing instantly that he was not the person I intended to write to, I apologised, and asked whether there was not another Mr. Lute living in L—?

"No, there was none other."

"Certainly," I rejoined, "my friend must have given me his right address, for I had written to him on other occasions here. He was a fair young man, he succeeded to an estate in consequence of his uncle having been killed while hunting with the Quorn hounds, and he married about two years since a lady of the name of Fairbairn."

The stranger very composedly replied, "You are speaking of Mr. Clyne; he did live in the Cathedral-close, but he has now gone away."

The stranger was right, and in my surprise I exclaimed:

"Oh dear, to be sure, that is the name; what could have made me address you instead? I really beg your pardon; my writing to you, and unconsciously guessing your name, is one of the most extraordinary and unaccountable things I ever did. Pray pardon me."

He continued very quietly, "There is no need of apology; it happens that you are the very person I most wished to see. You are a painter, and I want you to paint a portrait of my daughter; can you come to my house immediately for the purpose?"

I was rather surprised at finding myself known by him, and the turn matters had taken being so entirely unexpected, I did not at the moment feel inclined to undertake the business; I therefore explained how I was situate, stating that I had only the next day and Monday at my disposal. He, however, pressed me so earnestly, that I arranged to do what I could for him in those two days, and having put up my baggage, and arranged other matters, I accompanied him to his house. During the walk home he scarcely spoke a word, but his taciturnity seemed only a continuance of his quiet composure at the inn. On our arrival he introduced me to his daughter Maria, and then left the room. Maria Lute was a fair and a decidedly handsome girl of about fifteen; her manner was, however, in advance of her years, and evinced that self-possession, and, in the favourable sense of the term, that womanliness, that is only seen at such an early age in girls that have been left motherless, or from other causes thrown much on their own resources.

She had evidently not been informed of the purpose of my coming, and only knew that I was to stay there for the night; she therefore excused herself for a few moments, that she might give the requisite directions to the servants as to preparing my room. When she returned, she told me that I should not see her father again that evening, the state of his health having obliged him to retire for the night; but she hoped I should be able to see him some time on the morrow. In the mean time, she hoped I would make myself quite at home, and call for anything I wanted. She, herself, was sitting in the drawing-room, but perhaps I should like to smoke and take something; if so, there was a fire in the housekeeper's room, and she would come and sit with me, as she expected the medical attendant every minute, and he would probably stay to smoke, and take something. As the little lady seemed to recommend this course, I readily complied. I did not smoke, or take anything, but sat down by the fire, when she immediately joined me. She conversed well and readily, and with a command of language singular in a person so young. Without being disagreeably inquisitive, or putting any question to me, she seemed desirous of learning the business that had brought me to the house. I told her that her father wished me to paint either her portrait or that of a sister of hers, if she had one.

She remained silent and thoughtful for a moment, and then seemed to comprehend it at once. She told me that a sister of hers, an only one, to whom her father was devotedly attached, died near four months previously; that her father had never yet recovered from the shock of her death. He had often expressed the most earnest wish for a portrait of her; indeed, it was his one thought, and she hoped, if something of the kind could be done, it would improve his health. Here she hesitated, stammered, and burst into tears. After a while she continued: "It is no use hiding from you what you must very soon be aware of. Papa is insane – he has been so ever since dear Caroline was buried. He says he is always seeing dear Caroline, and he is subject to fearful delusions. The doctor says he cannot tell how much worse he may be, and that everything dangerous, like knives or razors, are to be kept out of his reach. It was necessary you should not see him again this evening, as he was unable to converse properly, and I fear the same may be the case tomorrow; but perhaps you can stay over Sunday, and I may be able to assist you in doing what he wishes." I asked whether they had any materials for making a likeness – a photograph, a sketch, or anything else for me to go from. "No, they had nothing." "Could she describe her clearly?" She thought she could; and there was a print that was very much like her, but she had mislaid it. I mentioned that with such disadvantages, and in such an absence of materials, I did not anticipate a satisfactory result. I had painted portraits under such circumstances, but their success much depended upon the powers of description of the persons who were to assist me by their recollection; in some instances I had attained a certain amount of success, but in most the result was quite a failure. The medical attendant came, but I did not see him. I learnt, however, that he ordered a strict watch to be kept on his patient till he came again the next morning. Seeing the state of things, and how much the little lady had to attend to, I retired early to bed. The next morning I heard that her father was decidedly better; he had inquired earnestly on waking whether I was really in the house, and at breakfast-time he sent down to say that he hoped nothing would prevent my making an attempt at the portrait immediately, and he expected to be able to see me in the course of the day.

Directly after breakfast I set to work, aided by such description as the sister could give me. I tried again and again, but without success, or, indeed, the least prospect of it. The features, I was told, were separately like, but the expression was not. I toiled on the greater part of the day with no better result. The different studies I made were taken up to the invalid, but the same answer was always returned – no resemblance. I had exerted myself to the utmost, and, in fact, was not a little fatigued by so doing – a circumstance that the little lady evidently noticed, as she expressed herself most grateful for the interest she could see I took in the matter, and referred the unsuccessful result entirely to her want of powers of description. She also said it was so provoking! she had a print

– a portrait of a lady – that was so like, but it had gone – she had missed it from her book for three weeks past. It was the more disappointing, as she was sure it would have been of such great assistance. I asked if she could tell me who the print was of, as if I knew, I could easily procure one in London. She answered, Lady M. A. Immediately the name was uttered the whole scene of the lady of the railway carriage presented itself to me. I had my sketch-book in my portmanteau up-stairs, and, by a fortunate chance, fixed in it was the print in question, with the two pencil sketches. I instantly brought them down, and showed them to Maria Lute. She looked at them for a moment, turned her eyes full upon me, and said slowly, and with something like fear in her manner, "Where did you get these?" Then quicker, and without waiting for my answer, "Let me take them instantly to papa." She was away ten minutes, or more; when she returned, her father came with her. He did not wait for salutations, but said, in a tone and manner I had not observed in him before, "I was right all the time; it was you that I saw with her, and these sketches are from her, and from no one else. I value them more than all my possessions, except this dear child." The daughter also assured me that the print I had brought to the house must be the one taken from the book about three weeks before, in proof of which she pointed out to me the gum marks at the back, which exactly corresponded with those left on the blank leaf. From the moment the father saw these sketches his mental health returned.

I was not allowed to touch either of the pencil drawings in the sketch-book, as it was feared I might injure them; but an oil picture from them was commenced immediately, the father sitting by me hour after hour, directing my touches, conversing rationally, and indeed cheerfully, while he did so. He avoided direct reference to his delusions, but from time to time led the conversation to the manner in which I had originally obtained the sketches. The doctor came in the evening, and, after extolling the particular treatment he had adopted, pronounced his patient decidedly, and he believed permanently, improved.

The next day being Sunday, we all went to church. The father, for the first time since his bereavement. During a walk which he took with me after luncheon, he again approached the subject of the sketches, and after some seeming hesitation as to whether he should confide in me or not, said, "Your writing to me by name, from the inn at L—, was one of those inexplicable circumstances that I suppose it is impossible to clear up. I knew you, however, directly I saw you; when those about me considered that my intellect was disordered, and that I spoke incoherently, it was only because I saw things that they did not. Since her death, I know, with a certainty that nothing will ever disturb, that at different times I have been in the actual and visible presence of my dear daughter that is gone – oftener, indeed, just after her death than latterly. Of the many times that this has occurred, I distinctly remember once seeing her in a railway carriage, speaking to a person seated opposite; who that person was I could not ascertain, as my position seemed to be immediately behind him. I next saw her at a dinner-table, with others, and amongst those others unquestionably I saw yourself. I afterwards learnt that at that time I was considered to be in one of my longest and most violent paroxysms, as I continued to see her speaking to you, in the midst of a large assembly, for some hours. Again I saw her, standing by your side, while you were engaged in either writing or drawing. I saw her once again afterwards, but the next time I saw yourself was in the inn parlour."

The picture was proceeded with the next day, and on the day after the face was completed, and I afterwards brought it with me to London to finish.

I have often seen Mr. L. since that period; his health is perfectly re-established, and his manner and conversation are as cheerful as can be expected within a few years of so great a bereavement.

The portrait now hangs in his bedroom, with the print and the two sketches by the side, and written beneath is: "C. L., 13th September, 1858, aged 22."

**If you enjoyed this, you might also like...**
A Christmas Tree, see page 140
The Haunted Man and the Ghost's Bargain, see page 77

# The Trial for Murder

**I HAVE ALWAYS** noticed a prevalent want of courage, even among persons of superior intelligence and culture, as to imparting their own psychological experiences when those have been of a strange sort. Almost all men are afraid that what they could relate in such wise would find no parallel or response in a listener's internal life, and might be suspected or laughed at. A truthful traveller, who should have seen some extraordinary creature in the likeness of a sea-serpent, would have no fear of mentioning it; but the same traveller, having had some singular presentiment, impulse, vagary of thought, vision (so-called), dream, or other remarkable mental impression, would hesitate considerably before he would own to it. To this reticence I attribute much of the obscurity in which such subjects are involved. We do not habitually communicate our experiences of these subjective things as we do our experiences of objective creation. The consequence is, that the general stock of experience in this regard appears exceptional, and really is so, in respect of being miserably imperfect.

In what I am going to relate, I have no intention of setting up, opposing, or supporting, any theory whatever. I know the history of the Bookseller of Berlin, I have studied the case of the wife of a late Astronomer Royal as related by Sir David Brewster, and I have followed the minutest details of a much more remarkable case of Spectral Illusion occurring within my private circle of friends. It may be necessary to state as to this last, that the sufferer (a lady) was in no degree, however distant, related to me. A mistaken assumption on that head might suggest an explanation of a part of my own case, – but only a part, – which would be wholly without foundation. It cannot be referred to my inheritance of any developed peculiarity, nor had I ever before any at all similar experience, nor have I ever had any at all similar experience since.

It does not signify how many years ago, or how few, a certain murder was committed in England, which attracted great attention. We hear more than enough of murderers as they rise in succession to their atrocious eminence, and I would bury the memory of this particular brute, if I could, as his body was buried, in Newgate Jail. I purposely abstain from giving any direct clue to the criminal's individuality.

When the murder was first discovered, no suspicion fell – or I ought rather to say, for I cannot be too precise in my facts, it was nowhere publicly hinted that any suspicion fell – on the man who was afterwards brought to trial. As no reference was at that time made to him in the newspapers, it is obviously impossible that any description of him can at that time have been given in the newspapers. It is essential that this fact be remembered.

Unfolding at breakfast my morning paper, containing the account of that first discovery, I found it to be deeply interesting, and I read it with close attention. I read it twice, if not three times. The discovery had been made in a bedroom, and, when I laid down the paper, I was aware of a flash – rush – flow – I do not know what to call it, – no word I can find is satisfactorily descriptive, – in which I seemed to see that bedroom passing through my room, like a picture impossibly painted on a running river. Though almost instantaneous in its passing, it was perfectly clear; so clear that I distinctly, and with a sense of relief, observed the absence of the dead body from the bed.

It was in no romantic place that I had this curious sensation, but in chambers in Piccadilly, very near to the corner of St. James's Street. It was entirely new to me. I was in my easy-chair at the moment, and the sensation was accompanied with a peculiar shiver which started the chair from its position. (But it is to be noted that the chair ran easily on castors.) I went to one of the windows (there are two in the room, and the room is on the second floor) to refresh my eyes with the moving objects down in Piccadilly. It was a bright autumn morning, and the street was sparkling and cheerful. The wind was high. As I looked out, it brought down from the Park a quantity of fallen leaves, which a gust took, and whirled into a spiral pillar. As the pillar fell and the leaves dispersed, I saw two men on the opposite side of the way, going from West to East. They were one behind the other. The foremost man often looked back over his shoulder. The second man followed him, at a distance of some thirty paces, with his right hand menacingly raised. First, the singularity and steadiness of this threatening gesture in so public a thoroughfare attracted my attention; and next, the more remarkable circumstance that nobody heeded it. Both men threaded their way among the other passengers with a smoothness hardly consistent even with the action of walking on a pavement; and no single creature, that I could see, gave them place, touched them, or looked after them. In passing before my windows, they both stared up at me. I saw their two faces very distinctly, and I knew that I could recognise them anywhere. Not that I had consciously noticed anything very remarkable in either face, except that the man who went first had an unusually lowering appearance, and that the face of the man who followed him was of the colour of impure wax.

I am a bachelor, and my valet and his wife constitute my whole establishment. My occupation is in a certain Branch Bank, and I wish that my duties as head of a Department were as light as they are popularly supposed to be. They kept me in town that autumn, when I stood in need of change. I was not ill, but I was not well. My reader is to make the most that can be reasonably made of my feeling jaded, having a depressing sense upon me of a monotonous life, and being "slightly dyspeptic." I am assured by my renowned doctor that my real state of health at that time justifies no stronger description, and I quote his own from his written answer to my request for it.

As the circumstances of the murder, gradually unravelling, took stronger and stronger possession of the public mind, I kept them away from mine by knowing as little about them as was possible in the midst of the universal excitement. But I knew that a verdict of Wilful Murder had been found against the suspected murderer, and that he had been committed to Newgate for trial. I also knew that his trial had been postponed over one Sessions of the Central Criminal Court, on the ground of general prejudice and want of time for the preparation of the defence. I may further have known, but I believe I did not, when, or about when, the Sessions to which his trial stood postponed would come on.

My sitting-room, bedroom, and dressing-room, are all on one floor. With the last there is no communication but through the bedroom. True, there is a door in it, once communicating with the staircase; but a part of the fitting of my bath has been – and had then been for some years – fixed across it. At the same period, and as a part of the same arrangement, – the door had been nailed up and canvased over.

I was standing in my bedroom late one night, giving some directions to my servant before he went to bed. My face was towards the only available door of communication with the dressing-room, and it was closed. My servant's back was towards that door. While I was speaking to him, I saw it open, and a man look in, who very earnestly and mysteriously beckoned to me. That man was the man who had gone second of the two along Piccadilly, and whose face was of the colour of impure wax.

The figure, having beckoned, drew back, and closed the door. With no longer pause than was made by my crossing the bedroom, I opened the dressing-room door, and looked in. I had a lighted candle already in my hand. I felt no inward expectation of seeing the figure in the dressing-room, and I did not see it there.

Conscious that my servant stood amazed, I turned round to him, and said: "Derrick, could you believe that in my cool senses I fancied I saw a—" As I there laid my hand upon his breast, with a sudden start he trembled violently, and said, "O Lord, yes, sir! A dead man beckoning!"

Now I do not believe that this John Derrick, my trusty and attached servant for more than twenty years, had any impression whatever of having seen any such figure, until I touched him. The change in him was so startling, when I touched him, that I fully believe he derived his impression in some occult manner from me at that instant.

I bade John Derrick bring some brandy, and I gave him a dram, and was glad to take one myself. Of what had preceded that night's phenomenon, I told him not a single word. Reflecting on it, I was absolutely certain that I had never seen that face before, except on the one occasion in Piccadilly. Comparing its expression when beckoning at the door with its expression when it had stared up at me as I stood at my window, I came to the conclusion that on the first occasion it had sought to fasten itself upon my memory, and that on the second occasion it had made sure of being immediately remembered.

I was not very comfortable that night, though I felt a certainty, difficult to explain, that the figure would not return. At daylight I fell into a heavy sleep, from which I was awakened by John Derrick's coming to my bedside with a paper in his hand.

This paper, it appeared, had been the subject of an altercation at the door between its bearer and my servant. It was a summons to me to serve upon a Jury at the forthcoming Sessions of the Central Criminal Court at the Old Bailey. I had never before been summoned on such a Jury, as John Derrick well knew. He believed – I am not certain at this hour whether with reason or otherwise – that that class of Jurors were customarily chosen on a lower qualification than mine, and he had at first refused to accept the summons. The man who served it had taken the matter very coolly. He had said that my attendance or non-attendance was nothing to him; there the summons was; and I should deal with it at my own peril, and not at his.

For a day or two I was undecided whether to respond to this call, or take no notice of it. I was not conscious of the slightest mysterious bias, influence, or attraction, one way or other. Of that I am as strictly sure as of every other statement that I make here. Ultimately I decided, as a break in the monotony of my life, that I would go.

The appointed morning was a raw morning in the month of November. There was a dense brown fog in Piccadilly, and it became positively black and in the last degree oppressive East of Temple Bar. I found the passages and staircases of the Court-House flaringly lighted with gas, and the Court itself similarly illuminated. I *think* that, until I was conducted by officers into the Old Court and saw its crowded state, I did not know that the Murderer was to be tried that day. I *think* that, until I was so helped into the Old Court with considerable difficulty, I did not know into which of the two Courts sitting my summons would take me. But this must not be received as a positive assertion, for I am not completely satisfied in my mind on either point.

I took my seat in the place appropriated to Jurors in waiting, and I looked about the Court as well as I could through the cloud of fog and breath that was heavy in it. I noticed the black vapour hanging like a murky curtain outside the great windows, and I noticed the stifled sound of wheels on the straw or tan that was littered in the street; also, the hum of the people gathered there, which a shrill whistle, or a louder song or hail than the rest, occasionally pierced. Soon afterwards the Judges, two in number, entered, and took their seats. The buzz in the Court was awfully hushed. The direction was given to put the Murderer to the bar. He appeared there. And in that same instant I recognised in him the first of the two men who had gone down Piccadilly.

If my name had been called then, I doubt if I could have answered to it audibly. But it was called about sixth or eighth in the panel, and I was by that time able to say, "Here!" Now, observe. As I stepped into the box, the prisoner, who had been looking on attentively, but with no sign of concern, became violently agitated, and beckoned to his attorney. The prisoner's wish to challenge me was so manifest, that it occasioned a pause, during which the attorney, with his hand upon the dock, whispered with his client, and shook his head. I afterwards had it from that gentleman, that the prisoner's first affrighted words to him were, "*At all hazards, challenge that man!*" But that, as he would give no reason for it, and admitted that he had not even known my name until he heard it called and I appeared, it was not done.

Both on the ground already explained, that I wish to avoid reviving the unwholesome memory of that Murderer, and also because a detailed account of his long trial is by no means indispensable to my narrative, I shall confine myself closely to such incidents in the ten days and nights during which we, the Jury, were kept together, as directly bear on my own curious personal experience. It is in that, and not in the Murderer, that I seek to interest my reader. It is to that, and not to a page of the Newgate Calendar, that I beg attention.

I was chosen Foreman of the Jury. On the second morning of the trial, after evidence had been taken for two hours (I heard the church clocks strike), happening to cast my eyes over my brother jurymen, I found an inexplicable difficulty in counting them. I counted them several times, yet always with the same difficulty. In short, I made them one too many.

I touched the brother juryman whose place was next me, and I whispered to him, "Oblige me by counting us." He looked surprised by the request, but turned his head and counted. "Why," says he, suddenly, "we are Thirt—; but no, it's not possible. No. We are twelve."

According to my counting that day, we were always right in detail, but in the gross we were always one too many. There was no appearance – no figure – to account for it; but I had now an inward foreshadowing of the figure that was surely coming.

The Jury were housed at the London Tavern. We all slept in one large room on separate tables, and we were constantly in the charge and under the eye of the officer sworn to hold us in safe-keeping. I see no reason for suppressing the real name of that officer. He was intelligent, highly polite, and obliging, and (I was glad to hear) much respected in the City. He had an agreeable presence, good eyes, enviable black whiskers, and a fine sonorous voice. His name was Mr. Harker.

When we turned into our twelve beds at night, Mr. Harker's bed was drawn across the door. On the night of the second day, not being disposed to lie down, and seeing Mr.

Harker sitting on his bed, I went and sat beside him, and offered him a pinch of snuff. As Mr. Harker's hand touched mine in taking it from my box, a peculiar shiver crossed him, and he said, "Who is this?"

Following Mr. Harker's eyes, and looking along the room, I saw again the figure I expected, – the second of the two men who had gone down Piccadilly. I rose, and advanced a few steps; then stopped, and looked round at Mr. Harker. He was quite unconcerned, laughed, and said in a pleasant way, "I thought for a moment we had a thirteenth juryman, without a bed. But I see it is the moonlight."

Making no revelation to Mr. Harker, but inviting him to take a walk with me to the end of the room, I watched what the figure did. It stood for a few moments by the bedside of each of my eleven brother jurymen, close to the pillow. It always went to the right-hand side of the bed, and always passed out crossing the foot of the next bed. It seemed, from the action of the head, merely to look down pensively at each recumbent figure. It took no notice of me, or of my bed, which was that nearest to Mr. Harker's. It seemed to go out where the moonlight came in, through a high window, as by an aërial flight of stairs.

Next morning at breakfast, it appeared that everybody present had dreamed of the murdered man last night, except myself and Mr. Harker.

I now felt as convinced that the second man who had gone down Piccadilly was the murdered man (so to speak), as if it had been borne into my comprehension by his immediate testimony. But even this took place, and in a manner for which I was not at all prepared.

On the fifth day of the trial, when the case for the prosecution was drawing to a close, a miniature of the murdered man, missing from his bedroom upon the discovery of the deed, and afterwards found in a hiding-place where the Murderer had been seen digging, was put in evidence. Having been identified by the witness under examination, it was handed up to the Bench, and thence handed down to be inspected by the Jury. As an officer in a black gown was making his way with it across to me, the figure of the second man who had gone down Piccadilly impetuously started from the crowd, caught the miniature from the officer, and gave it to me with his own hands, at the same time saying, in a low and hollow tone, – before I saw the miniature, which was in a locket, – "*I was younger then, and my face was not then drained of blood.*" It also came between me and the brother juryman to whom I would have given the miniature, and between him and the brother juryman to whom he would have given it, and so passed it on through the whole of our number, and back into my possession. Not one of them, however, detected this.

At table, and generally when we were shut up together in Mr. Harker's custody, we had from the first naturally discussed the day's proceedings a good deal. On that fifth day, the case for the prosecution being closed, and we having that side of the question in a completed shape before us, our discussion was more animated and serious. Among our number was a vestryman, – the densest idiot I have ever seen at large, – who met the plainest evidence with the most preposterous objections, and who was sided with by two flabby parochial parasites; all the three impanelled from a district so delivered over to Fever that they ought to have been upon their own trial for five hundred Murders. When these mischievous blockheads were at their loudest, which was towards midnight, while some of us were already preparing for bed, I again saw the murdered man. He stood grimly behind them, beckoning to me. On my going towards them, and striking into the conversation, he immediately retired. This was the beginning of a separate series of appearances, confined to that long room in which we were confined. Whenever a knot of my brother jurymen laid their heads together, I saw the head of the murdered man among theirs. Whenever their comparison of notes was going against him, he would solemnly and irresistibly beckon to me.

It will be borne in mind that down to the production of the miniature, on the fifth day of the trial, I had never seen the Appearance in Court. Three changes occurred now that we entered on the case for the defence. Two of them I will mention together, first. The figure was now in Court continually, and it never there addressed itself to me, but always to the person who was speaking at the time. For instance: the throat of the murdered man had been cut straight across. In the opening speech for the defence, it was suggested that the deceased might have cut his own throat. At that very moment, the figure, with its throat in the dreadful condition referred to (this it had concealed before), stood at the speaker's elbow, motioning across and across its windpipe, now with the right hand, now with the left, vigorously suggesting to the speaker himself the impossibility of such a wound having been self-inflicted by either hand. For another instance: a witness to character, a woman, deposed to the prisoner's being the most amiable of mankind. The figure at that instant stood on the floor before her, looking her full in the face, and pointing out the prisoner's evil countenance with an extended arm and an outstretched finger.

The third change now to be added impressed me strongly as the most marked and striking of all. I do not theorise upon it; I accurately state it, and there leave it. Although the Appearance was not itself perceived by those whom it addressed, its coming close to such persons was invariably attended by some trepidation or disturbance on their part. It seemed to me as if it were prevented, by laws to which I was not amenable, from fully revealing itself to others, and yet as if it could invisibly, dumbly, and darkly overshadow their minds. When the leading counsel for the defence suggested that hypothesis of suicide, and the figure stood at the learned gentleman's elbow, frightfully sawing at its severed throat, it is undeniable that the counsel faltered in his speech, lost for a few seconds the thread of his ingenious discourse, wiped his forehead with his handkerchief, and turned extremely pale. When the witness to character was confronted by the Appearance, her eyes most certainly did follow the direction of its pointed finger, and rest in great hesitation and trouble upon the prisoner's face. Two additional illustrations will suffice. On the eighth day of the trial, after the pause which was every day made early in the afternoon for a few minutes' rest and refreshment, I came back into Court with the rest of the Jury some little time before the return of the Judges. Standing up in the box and looking about me, I thought the figure was not there, until, chancing to raise my eyes to the gallery, I saw it bending forward, and leaning over a very decent woman, as if to assure itself whether the Judges had resumed their seats or not. Immediately afterwards that woman screamed, fainted, and was carried out. So with the venerable, sagacious, and patient Judge who conducted the trial. When the case was over, and he settled himself and his papers to sum up, the murdered man, entering by the Judges' door, advanced to his Lordship's desk, and looked eagerly over his shoulder at the pages of his notes which he was turning. A change came over his Lordship's face; his hand stopped; the peculiar shiver, that I knew so well, passed over him; he faltered, "Excuse me, gentlemen, for a few moments. I am somewhat oppressed by the vitiated air;" and did not recover until he had drunk a glass of water.

Through all the monotony of six of those interminable ten days, – the same Judges and others on the bench, the same Murderer in the dock, the same lawyers at the table, the same tones of question and answer rising to the roof of the court, the same scratching of the Judge's pen, the same ushers going in and out, the same lights kindled at the same hour when there had been any natural light of day, the same foggy curtain outside the great windows when it was foggy, the same rain pattering and dripping when it was rainy, the same footmarks of turnkeys and prisoner day after day on the same sawdust, the same keys locking and unlocking the same heavy doors, – through all the wearisome monotony which made me feel as if I had been Foreman of the Jury for a vast period of time, and Piccadilly had flourished coevally with Babylon, the murdered man never lost one trace of his distinctness in my eyes, nor was he at any moment less distinct than anybody else. I must not omit, as a matter of fact, that I never once saw the Appearance which I call by the name of the murdered man look at the Murderer. Again and again I wondered, "Why does he not?" But he never did.

Nor did he look at me, after the production of the miniature, until the last closing minutes of the trial arrived. We retired to consider, at seven minutes before ten at night. The idiotic vestryman and his two parochial parasites gave us so much trouble that we twice returned into Court to beg to have certain extracts from the Judge's notes re-read. Nine of us had not the smallest doubt about those passages, neither, I believe, had any one in the Court; the dunder-headed triumvirate, having no idea but obstruction, disputed them for that very reason. At length we prevailed, and finally the Jury returned into Court at ten minutes past twelve.

The murdered man at that time stood directly opposite the Jury-box, on the other side of the Court. As I took my place, his eyes rested on me with great attention; he seemed satisfied, and slowly shook a great gray veil, which he carried on his arm for the first time, over his head and whole form. As I gave in our verdict, "Guilty," the veil collapsed, all was gone, and his place was empty.

The Murderer, being asked by the Judge, according to usage, whether he had anything to say before sentence of Death should be passed upon him, indistinctly muttered something which was described in the leading newspapers of the following day as "a few rambling, incoherent, and half-audible words, in which he was understood to complain that he had not had a fair trial, because the Foreman of the Jury was prepossessed against him." The remarkable declaration that he really made was this: "*My Lord, I knew I was a doomed man, when the Foreman of my Jury came into the box. My Lord, I knew he would never let me off, because, before I was taken, he somehow got to my bedside in the night, woke me, and put a rope round my neck.*"

**If you enjoyed this, you might also like...**
Four Stories, see page 232
Mr. Testator's Visitation, see page 150

# The Signal-Man

**"HALLOA!** Below there!"

When he heard a voice thus calling to him, he was standing at the door of his box, with a flag in his hand, furled round its short pole. One would have thought, considering the nature of the ground, that he could not have doubted from what quarter the voice came; but instead of looking up to where I stood on the top of the steep cutting nearly over his head, he turned himself about, and looked down the Line. There was something remarkable in his manner of doing so, though I could not have said for my life what. But I know it was remarkable enough to attract my notice, even though his figure was foreshortened and shadowed, down in the deep trench, and mine was high above him, so steeped in the glow of an angry sunset, that I had shaded my eyes with my hand before I saw him at all.

"Halloa! Below!"

From looking down the Line, he turned himself about again, and, raising his eyes, saw my figure high above him.

"Is there any path by which I can come down and speak to you?"

He looked up at me without replying, and I looked down at him without pressing him too soon with a repetition of my idle question. Just then there came a vague vibration in the earth and air, quickly changing into a violent pulsation, and an oncoming rush that caused me to start back, as though it had force to draw me down. When such vapour as rose to my height from this rapid train had passed me, and was skimming away over the landscape, I looked down again, and saw him refurling the flag he had shown while the train went by.

I repeated my inquiry. After a pause, during which he seemed to regard me with fixed attention, he motioned with his rolled-up flag towards a point on my level, some two or three hundred yards distant. I called down to him, "All right!" and made for that point. There, by dint of looking closely about me, I found a rough zigzag descending path notched out, which I followed.

The cutting was extremely deep, and unusually precipitate. It was made through a clammy stone, that became oozier and wetter as I went down. For these reasons, I found the way long enough to give me time to recall a singular air of reluctance or compulsion with which he had pointed out the path.

When I came down low enough upon the zigzag descent to see him again, I saw that he was standing between the rails on the way by which the train had lately passed, in an attitude as if he were waiting for me to appear. He had his left hand at his chin, and that left elbow rested on his right hand, crossed over his breast. His attitude was one of such expectation and watchfulness that I stopped a moment, wondering at it.

I resumed my downward way, and stepping out upon the level of the railroad, and drawing nearer to him, saw that he was a dark, sallow man, with a dark beard and rather heavy eyebrows. His post was in as solitary and dismal a place as ever I saw. On either side, a dripping-wet wall of jagged stone, excluding all view but a strip of sky; the perspective one way only a crooked prolongation of this great dungeon; the shorter perspective in the other direction terminating in a gloomy red light, and the gloomier entrance to a black tunnel, in whose massive architecture there was a barbarous, depressing, and forbidding air. So little sunlight ever found its way to this spot, that it had an earthy, deadly smell; and so much cold wind rushed through it, that it struck chill to me, as if I had left the natural world.

Before he stirred, I was near enough to him to have touched him. Not even then removing his eyes from mine, he stepped back one step, and lifted his hand.

This was a lonesome post to occupy (I said), and it had riveted my attention when I looked down from up yonder. A visitor was a rarity, I should suppose; not an unwelcome rarity, I hoped? In me, he merely saw a man who had been shut up within narrow limits all his life, and who, being at last set free, had a newly-awakened interest in these great works. To such purpose I spoke to him; but I am far from sure of the terms I used; for, besides that I am not happy in opening any conversation, there was something in the man that daunted me.

He directed a most curious look towards the red light near the tunnel's mouth, and looked all about it, as if something were missing from it, and then looked at me.

That light was part of his charge? Was it not?

He answered in a low voice, – "Don't you know it is?"

The monstrous thought came into my mind, as I perused the fixed eyes and the saturnine face, that this was a spirit, not a man. I have speculated since, whether there may have been infection in his mind.

In my turn, I stepped back. But in making the action, I detected in his eyes some latent fear of me. This put the monstrous thought to flight.

"You look at me," I said, forcing a smile, "as if you had a dread of me."

"I was doubtful," he returned, "whether I had seen you before."

"Where?"

He pointed to the red light he had looked at.

"There?" I said.

Intently watchful of me, he replied (but without sound), "Yes."

"My good fellow, what should I do there? However, be that as it may, I never was there, you may swear."

"I think I may," he rejoined. "Yes; I am sure I may."

His manner cleared, like my own. He replied to my remarks with readiness, and in well-chosen words. Had he much to do there? Yes; that was to say, he had enough responsibility to bear; but exactness and watchfulness were what was required of him, and of actual work – manual labour – he had next to none. To change that signal, to trim those lights, and to turn this iron handle now and then, was all he had to do under that head. Regarding those many long and lonely hours of which I seemed to make so much, he could only say that the routine of his life had shaped itself into that form, and he had grown used to it. He had taught himself a language down here, – if only to know it by sight, and to have formed his own crude ideas of its pronunciation, could be called learning it. He had also worked at fractions and decimals, and tried a little algebra; but he was, and had been as a boy, a poor hand at figures. Was it necessary for him when on duty always to remain in that channel of damp air, and could he never rise into the sunshine from between those high stone walls? Why, that depended upon times and circumstances. Under some conditions there would be less upon the Line than under others, and the same held good as to certain hours of the day and night. In bright weather, he did choose occasions for getting a little above these lower shadows; but, being at all times liable to be called by his electric bell, and at such times listening for it with redoubled anxiety, the relief was less than I would suppose.

He took me into his box, where there was a fire, a desk for an official book in which he had to make certain entries, a telegraphic instrument with its dial, face, and needles, and the little bell of which he had spoken. On my trusting that he would excuse the remark that he had been well educated, and (I hoped I might say without offence) perhaps educated above that station, he observed that instances of slight incongruity in such wise would rarely be found wanting among large bodies of men; that he had heard it was so in workhouses, in the police force, even in that last desperate resource, the army; and that he knew it was so, more or less, in any great railway staff. He had been, when young (if I could believe it, sitting in that hut, – he scarcely could), a student of natural philosophy, and had attended lectures; but he had run wild, misused his opportunities, gone down, and never risen again. He had no complaint to offer about that. He had made his bed, and he lay upon it. It was far too late to make another.

All that I have here condensed he said in a quiet manner, with his grave, dark regards divided between me and the fire. He threw in the word, "Sir," from time to time, and especially when he referred to his youth, – as though to request me to understand that he claimed to be nothing but what I found him. He was several times interrupted by the little bell, and had to read off messages, and send replies. Once he had to stand without the door, and display a flag as a train passed, and make some verbal communication to the driver. In the discharge of his duties, I observed him to be remarkably exact and vigilant, breaking off his discourse at a syllable, and remaining silent until what he had to do was done.

In a word, I should have set this man down as one of the safest of men to be employed in that capacity, but for the circumstance that while he was speaking to me he twice broke off with a fallen colour, turned his face towards the little bell when it did NOT ring, opened the door of the hut (which was kept shut to exclude the unhealthy damp), and looked out towards the red light near the mouth of the tunnel. On both of those occasions, he came back to the fire with the inexplicable air upon him which I had remarked, without being able to define, when we were so far asunder.

Said I, when I rose to leave him, "You almost make me think that I have met with a contented man."

(I am afraid I must acknowledge that I said it to lead him on.)

"I believe I used to be so," he rejoined, in the low voice in which he had first spoken; "but I am troubled, sir, I am troubled."

He would have recalled the words if he could. He had said them, however, and I took them up quickly.

"With what? What is your trouble?"

"It is very difficult to impart, sir. It is very, very difficult to speak of. If ever you make me another visit, I will try to tell you."

"But I expressly intend to make you another visit. Say, when shall it be?"

"I go off early in the morning, and I shall be on again at ten tomorrow night, sir."

"I will come at eleven."

He thanked me, and went out at the door with me. "I'll show my white light, sir," he said, in his peculiar low voice, "till you have found the way up. When you have found it, don't call out! And when you are at the top, don't call out!"

His manner seemed to make the place strike colder to me, but I said no more than, "Very well."

"And when you come down tomorrow night, don't call out! Let me ask you a parting question. What made you cry, 'Halloa! Below there!' to-night?"

"Heaven knows," said I. "I cried something to that effect—"

"Not to that effect, sir. Those were the very words. I know them well."

"Admit those were the very words. I said them, no doubt, because I saw you below."

"For no other reason?"

"What other reason could I possibly have?"

"You had no feeling that they were conveyed to you in any supernatural way?"

"No."

He wished me good-night, and held up his light. I walked by the side of the down Line of rails (with a very disagreeable sensation of a train coming behind me) until I found the path. It was easier to mount than to descend, and I got back to my inn without any adventure.

Punctual to my appointment, I placed my foot on the first notch of the zigzag next night, as the distant clocks were striking eleven. He was waiting for me at the bottom, with his white light on. "I have not called out," I said, when we came close together; "may I speak now?"

"By all means, sir."

"Good-night, then, and here's my hand."

"Good-night, sir, and here's mine." With that we walked side by side to his box, entered it, closed the door, and sat down by the fire.

"I have made up my mind, sir," he began, bending forward as soon as we were seated, and speaking in a tone but a little above a whisper, "that you shall not have to ask me twice what troubles me. I took you for some one else yesterday evening. That troubles me."

"That mistake?"

"No. That some one else."

"Who is it?"

"I don't know."

"Like me?"

"I don't know. I never saw the face. The left arm is across the face, and the right arm is waved, – violently waved. This way."

I followed his action with my eyes, and it was the action of an arm gesticulating, with the utmost passion and vehemence, "For God's sake, clear the way!"

"One moonlight night," said the man, "I was sitting here, when I heard a voice cry, 'Halloa! Below there!' I started up, looked from that door, and saw this Some one else standing by the red light near the tunnel, waving as I just now showed you. The voice seemed hoarse with shouting, and it cried, 'Look out! Look out!' And then again, 'Halloa! Below there! Look out!' I caught up my lamp, turned it on red, and ran towards the figure, calling, 'What's wrong? What has happened? Where?' It stood just outside the blackness of the tunnel. I advanced so close upon it that I wondered at its keeping the sleeve across its eyes. I ran right up at it, and had my hand stretched out to pull the sleeve away, when it was gone."

"Into the tunnel?" said I.

"No. I ran on into the tunnel, five hundred yards. I stopped, and held my lamp above my head, and saw the figures of the measured distance, and saw the wet stains stealing down the walls and trickling through the arch. I ran out again faster than I had run in (for I had a mortal abhorrence of the place upon me), and I looked all round the red light with my own red light, and I went up the iron ladder to the gallery atop of it, and I came down again, and ran back here. I telegraphed both ways, 'An alarm has been given. Is anything wrong?' The answer came back, both ways, 'All well.'"

Resisting the slow touch of a frozen finger tracing out my spine, I showed him how that this figure must be a deception of his sense of sight; and how that figures, originating in disease of the delicate nerves that minister to the functions of the eye, were known to have often troubled patients, some of whom had become conscious of the nature of their affliction, and had even proved it by experiments upon themselves. "As to an imaginary cry," said I, "do but listen for a moment to the wind in this unnatural valley while we speak so low, and to the wild harp it makes of the telegraph wires."

That was all very well, he returned, after we had sat listening for a while, and he ought to know something of the wind and the wires, – he who so often passed long winter nights there, alone and watching. But he would beg to remark that he had not finished.

I asked his pardon, and he slowly added these words, touching my arm, –

"Within six hours after the Appearance, the memorable accident on this Line happened, and within ten hours the dead and wounded were brought along through the tunnel over the spot where the figure had stood."

A disagreeable shudder crept over me, but I did my best against it. It was not to be denied, I rejoined, that this was a remarkable coincidence, calculated deeply to impress his mind. But it was unquestionable that remarkable coincidences did continually occur, and they must be taken into account in dealing with such a subject. Though to be sure I must admit, I added (for I thought I saw that he was going to bring the objection to bear upon me), men of common sense did not allow much for coincidences in making the ordinary calculations of life.

He again begged to remark that he had not finished.

I again begged his pardon for being betrayed into interruptions.

"This," he said, again laying his hand upon my arm, and glancing over his shoulder with hollow eyes, "was just a year ago. Six or seven months passed, and I had recovered from the surprise and shock, when one morning, as the day was breaking, I, standing at the door, looked towards the red light, and saw the spectre again." He stopped, with a fixed look at me.

"Did it cry out?"

"No. It was silent."

"Did it wave its arm?"

"No. It leaned against the shaft of the light, with both hands before the face. Like this."

Once more I followed his action with my eyes. It was an action of mourning. I have seen such an attitude in stone figures on tombs.

"Did you go up to it?"

"I came in and sat down, partly to collect my thoughts, partly because it had turned me faint. When I went to the door again, daylight was above me, and the ghost was gone."

"But nothing followed? Nothing came of this?"

He touched me on the arm with his forefinger twice or thrice giving a ghastly nod each time:

"That very day, as a train came out of the tunnel, I noticed, at a carriage window on my side, what looked like a confusion of hands and heads, and something waved. I saw it just in time to signal the driver, Stop! He shut off, and put his brake on, but the train drifted past here a hundred and fifty yards or more. I ran after it, and, as I went along, heard terrible screams and cries. A beautiful young lady had died instantaneously in one of the compartments, and was brought in here, and laid down on this floor between us."

Involuntarily I pushed my chair back, as I looked from the boards at which he pointed to himself.

"True, sir. True. Precisely as it happened, so I tell it you."

I could think of nothing to say, to any purpose, and my mouth was very dry. The wind and the wires took up the story with a long lamenting wail.

He resumed. "Now, sir, mark this, and judge how my mind is troubled. The spectre came back a week ago. Ever since, it has been there, now and again, by fits and starts."

"At the light?"

"At the Danger-light."

"What does it seem to do?"

He repeated, if possible with increased passion and vehemence, that former gesticulation of, "For God's sake, clear the way!"

Then he went on. "I have no peace or rest for it. It calls to me, for many minutes together, in an agonised manner, 'Below there! Look out! Look out!' It stands waving to me. It rings my little bell—"

I caught at that. "Did it ring your bell yesterday evening when I was here, and you went to the door?"

"Twice."

"Why, see," said I, "how your imagination misleads you. My eyes were on the bell, and my ears were open to the bell, and if I am a living man, it did NOT ring at those times. No, nor at any other time, except when it was rung in the natural course of physical things by the station communicating with you."

He shook his head. "I have never made a mistake as to that yet, sir. I have never confused the spectre's ring with the man's. The ghost's ring is a strange vibration in the bell that it derives from nothing else, and I have not asserted that the bell stirs to the eye. I don't wonder that you failed to hear it. But *I* heard it."

"And did the spectre seem to be there, when you looked out?"

"It WAS there."

"Both times?"

He repeated firmly: "Both times."

"Will you come to the door with me, and look for it now?"

He bit his under lip as though he were somewhat unwilling, but arose. I opened the door, and stood on the step, while he stood in the doorway. There was the Danger-light. There was the dismal mouth of the tunnel. There were the high, wet stone walls of the cutting. There were the stars above them.

"Do you see it?" I asked him, taking particular note of his face. His eyes were prominent and strained, but not very much more so, perhaps, than my own had been when I had directed them earnestly towards the same spot.

"No," he answered. "It is not there."

"Agreed," said I.

We went in again, shut the door, and resumed our seats. I was thinking how best to improve this advantage, if it might be called one, when he took up the conversation in such a matter-of-course way, so assuming that there could be no serious question of fact between us, that I felt myself placed in the weakest of positions.

"By this time you will fully understand, sir," he said, "that what troubles me so dreadfully is the question, What does the spectre mean?"

I was not sure, I told him, that I did fully understand.

"What is its warning against?" he said, ruminating, with his eyes on the fire, and only by times turning them on me. "What is the danger? Where is the danger? There is danger overhanging somewhere on the Line. Some dreadful calamity will happen. It is not to be doubted this third time, after what has gone before. But surely this is a cruel haunting of me. What can I do?"

He pulled out his handkerchief, and wiped the drops from his heated forehead.

"If I telegraph Danger, on either side of me, or on both, I can give no reason for it," he went on, wiping the palms of his hands. "I should get into trouble, and do no good. They would think I was mad. This is the way it would work, – Message: 'Danger! Take care!' Answer: 'What Danger? Where?' Message: 'Don't know. But, for God's sake, take care!' They would displace me. What else could they do?"

His pain of mind was most pitiable to see. It was the mental torture of a conscientious man, oppressed beyond endurance by an unintelligible responsibility involving life.

"When it first stood under the Danger-light," he went on, putting his dark hair back from his head, and drawing his hands outward across and across his temples in an extremity of feverish distress, "why not tell me where that accident was to happen, – if it must happen? Why not tell me how it could be averted, – if it could have been averted? When on its second coming it hid its face, why not tell me, instead, 'She is going to die. Let them keep her at home'? If it came, on those two occasions, only to show me that its warnings were true, and so to prepare me for the third, why not warn me plainly now? And I, Lord help me! A mere poor signal-man on this solitary station! Why not go to somebody with credit to be believed, and power to act?"

When I saw him in this state, I saw that for the poor man's sake, as well as for the public safety, what I had to do for the time was to compose his mind. Therefore, setting aside all question of reality or unreality between us, I represented to him that whoever thoroughly discharged his duty must do well, and that at least it was his comfort that he understood his duty, though he did not understand these confounding Appearances. In this effort I succeeded far better than in the attempt to reason him out of his conviction. He became calm; the occupations incidental to his post as the night advanced began to make larger demands on his attention: and I left him at two in the morning. I had offered to stay through the night, but he would not hear of it.

That I more than once looked back at the red light as I ascended the pathway, that I did not like the red light, and that I should have slept but poorly if my bed had been under it, I see no reason to conceal. Nor did I like the two sequences of the accident and the dead girl. I see no reason to conceal that either.

But what ran most in my thoughts was the consideration how ought I to act, having become the recipient of this disclosure? I had proved the man to be intelligent, vigilant, painstaking, and exact; but how long might he remain so, in his state of mind? Though in a subordinate position, still he held a most important trust, and would I (for instance) like to stake my own life on the chances of his continuing to execute it with precision?

Unable to overcome a feeling that there would be something treacherous in my communicating what he had told me to his superiors in the Company, without first being plain with himself and proposing a middle course to him, I ultimately resolved to offer to accompany him (otherwise keeping his secret for the present) to the wisest medical practitioner we could hear of in those parts, and to take his opinion. A change in his time of duty would come round next night, he had apprised me, and he would be off an hour or two after sunrise, and on again soon after sunset. I had appointed to return accordingly.

Next evening was a lovely evening, and I walked out early to enjoy it. The sun was not yet quite down when I traversed the field-path near the top of the deep cutting. I would extend my walk for an hour, I said to myself, half an hour on and half an hour back, and it would then be time to go to my signal-man's box.

Before pursuing my stroll, I stepped to the brink, and mechanically looked down, from the point from which I had first seen him. I cannot describe the thrill that seized upon me, when, close at the mouth of the tunnel, I saw the appearance of a man, with his left sleeve across his eyes, passionately waving his right arm.

The nameless horror that oppressed me passed in a moment, for in a moment I saw that this appearance of a man was a man indeed, and that there was a little group of other men, standing at a short distance, to whom he seemed to be rehearsing the gesture he made. The Danger-light was not yet lighted. Against its shaft, a little low hut, entirely new to me, had been made of some wooden supports and tarpaulin. It looked no bigger than a bed.

With an irresistible sense that something was wrong, – with a flashing self-reproachful fear that fatal mischief had come of my leaving the man there, and causing no one to be sent to overlook or correct what he did, – I descended the notched path with all the speed I could make.

"What is the matter?" I asked the men.

"Signal-man killed this morning, sir."

"Not the man belonging to that box?"

"Yes, sir."

"Not the man I know?"

"You will recognise him, sir, if you knew him," said the man who spoke for the others, solemnly uncovering his own head, and raising an end of the tarpaulin, "for his face is quite composed."

"O, how did this happen, how did this happen?" I asked, turning from one to another as the hut closed in again.

"He was cut down by an engine, sir. No man in England knew his work better. But somehow he was not clear of the outer rail. It was just at broad day. He had struck the light, and had the lamp in his hand. As the engine came out of the tunnel, his back was towards her, and she cut him down. That man drove her, and was showing how it happened. Show the gentleman, Tom."

The man, who wore a rough dark dress, stepped back to his former place at the mouth of the tunnel.

"Coming round the curve in the tunnel, sir," he said, "I saw him at the end, like as if I saw him down a perspective-glass. There was no time to check speed, and I knew him to be very careful. As he didn't seem to take heed of the whistle, I shut it off when we were running down upon him, and called to him as loud as I could call."

"What did you say?"

"I said, 'Below there! Look out! Look out! For God's sake, clear the way!'"

I started.

"Ah! it was a dreadful time, sir. I never left off calling to him. I put this arm before my eyes not to see, and I waved this arm to the last; but it was no use."

Without prolonging the narrative to dwell on any one of its curious circumstances more than on any other, I may, in closing it, point out the coincidence that the warning of the Engine-Driver included, not only the words which the unfortunate Signal-man had repeated to me as haunting him, but also the words which I myself – not he – had attached, and that only in my own mind, to the gesticulation he had imitated.

**If you enjoyed this, you might also like...**
The Lawyer and the Ghost, see page 22
The Haunted Man and the Ghost's Bargain, see page 77

# The Ghost in the Bride's Chamber

**THE HOUSE** was a genuine old house of a very quaint description, teeming with old carvings, and beams, and panels, and having an excellent old staircase, with a gallery or upper staircase, cut off from it by a curious fence-work of old oak, or of the old Honduras Mahogany wood. It was, and is, and will be, for many a long year to come, a remarkably picturesque house; and a certain grave mystery lurking in the depth of the old mahogany panels, as if they were so many deep pools of dark water – such, indeed, as they had been much among when they were trees – gave it a very mysterious character after nightfall.

When Mr. Goodchild and Mr. Idle had first alighted at the door, and stepped into the sombre, handsome old hall, they had been received by half-a-dozen noiseless old men in black, all dressed exactly alike, who glided up the stairs with the obliging landlord and waiter – but without appearing to get into their way, or to mind whether they did or no – and who had filed off to the right and left on the old staircase, as the guests entered their sitting-room. It was then broad, bright day. But, Mr. Goodchild had said, when their door was shut, "Who on earth are those old men?" And afterwards, both on going out and coming in, he had noticed that there were no old men to be seen.

Neither, had the old men, or any one of the old men, reappeared since. The two friends had passed a night in the house, but had seen nothing more of the old men. Mr. Goodchild, in rambling about it, had looked along passages, and glanced in at doorways, but had encountered no old men; neither did it appear that any old men were, by any member of the establishment, missed or expected.

Another odd circumstance impressed itself on their attention. It was, that the door of their sitting-room was never left untouched for a quarter of an hour. It was opened with hesitation, opened with confidence, opened a little way, opened a good way, – always clapped-to again without a word of explanation. They were reading, they were writing, they were eating, they were drinking, they were talking, they were dozing; the door was always opened at an unexpected moment, and they looked towards it, and it was clapped-to again, and nobody was to be seen. When this had happened fifty times or so, Mr. Goodchild had said to his companion, jestingly: "I begin to think, Tom, there was something wrong with those six old men."

Night had come again, and they had been writing for two or three hours: writing, in short, a portion of the lazy notes from which these lazy sheets are taken. They had left off writing, and glasses were on the table between them. The house was closed and quiet. Around the head of Thomas Idle, as he lay upon his sofa, hovered light wreaths of fragrant smoke. The temples of Francis Goodchild, as he leaned back in his chair, with his two hands clasped behind his head, and his legs crossed, were similarly decorated.

They had been discussing several idle subjects of speculation, not omitting the strange old men, and were still so occupied, when Mr. Goodchild abruptly changed his attitude to wind up his watch. They were just becoming drowsy enough to be stopped in their talk by any such slight check. Thomas Idle, who was speaking at the moment, paused and said, "How goes it?"

"One," said Goodchild.

As if he had ordered One old man, and the order were promptly executed (truly, all orders were so, in that excellent hotel), the door opened, and One old man stood there.

He did not come in, but stood with the door in his hand.

"One of the six, Tom, at last!" said Mr. Goodchild, in a surprised whisper. – "Sir, your pleasure?"

"Sir, *your* pleasure?" said the One old man.

"I didn't ring."

"The bell did," said the One old man.

He said Bell, in a deep, strong way, that would have expressed the church Bell.

"I had the pleasure, I believe, of seeing you, yesterday?" said Goodchild.

"I cannot undertake to say for certain," was the grim reply of the One old man.

"I think you saw me? Did you not?"

"Saw *you*?" said the old man. "O yes, I saw you. But, I see many who never see me."

A chilled, slow, earthy, fixed old man. A cadaverous old man of measured speech. An old man who seemed as unable to wink, as if his eyelids had been nailed to his forehead. An old man whose eyes – two spots of fire – had no more motion than if they had been connected with the back of his skull by screws driven through it, and rivetted and bolted outside, among his grey hair.

The night had turned so cold, to Mr. Goodchild's sensations, that he shivered. He remarked lightly, and half apologetically, "I think somebody is walking over my grave."

"No," said the weird old man, "there is no one there."

Mr. Goodchild looked at Idle, but Idle lay with his head enwreathed in smoke.

"No one there?" said Goodchild.

"There is no one at your grave, I assure you," said the old man.

He had come in and shut the door, and he now sat down. He did not bend himself to sit, as other people do, but seemed to sink bolt upright, as if in water, until the chair stopped him.

"My friend, Mr. Idle," said Goodchild, extremely anxious to introduce a third person into the conversation.

"I am," said the old man, without looking at him, "at Mr. Idle's service."

"If you are an old inhabitant of this place," Francis Goodchild resumed.

"Yes."

"Perhaps you can decide a point my friend and I were in doubt upon, this morning. They hang condemned criminals at the Castle, I believe?"

"*I* believe so," said the old man.

"Are their faces turned towards that noble prospect?"

"Your face is turned," replied the old man, "to the Castle wall. When you are tied up, you see its stones expanding and contracting violently, and a similar expansion and contraction seem to take place in your own head and breast. Then, there is a rush of fire and an earthquake, and the Castle springs into the air, and you tumble down a precipice."

His cravat appeared to trouble him. He put his hand to his throat, and moved his neck from side to side. He was an old man of a swollen character of face, and his nose was immoveably hitched up on one side, as if by a little hook inserted in that nostril. Mr. Goodchild felt exceedingly uncomfortable, and began to think the night was hot, and not cold.

"A strong description, sir," he observed.

"A strong sensation," the old man rejoined.

Again, Mr. Goodchild looked to Mr. Thomas Idle; but Thomas lay on his back with his face attentively turned towards the One old man, and made no sign. At this time Mr. Goodchild believed that he saw threads of fire stretch from the old man's eyes to his own, and there attach themselves. (Mr. Goodchild writes the present account of his experience, and, with the utmost solemnity, protests that he had the strongest sensation upon him of being forced to look at the old man along those two fiery films, from that moment.)

"I must tell it to you," said the old man, with a ghastly and a stony stare.

"What?" asked Francis Goodchild.

"You know where it took place. Yonder!"

Whether he pointed to the room above, or to the room below, or to any room in that old house, or to a room in some other old house in that old town, Mr. Goodchild was not, nor is, nor ever can be, sure. He was confused by the circumstance that the right forefinger of the One old man seemed to dip itself in one of the threads of fire, light itself, and make a fiery start in the air, as it pointed somewhere. Having pointed somewhere, it went out.

"You know she was a Bride," said the old man.

"I know they still send up Bride-cake," Mr. Goodchild faltered. "This is a very oppressive air."

"She was a Bride," said the old man. "She was a fair, flaxen-haired, large-eyed girl, who had no character, no purpose. A weak, credulous, incapable, helpless nothing. Not like her mother. No, no. It was her father whose character she reflected.

"Her mother had taken care to secure everything to herself, for her own life, when the father of this girl (a child at that time) died—of sheer helplessness; no other disorder – and then He renewed the acquaintance that had once subsisted between the mother and Him. He had been put aside for the flaxen-haired, large-eyed man (or nonentity) with Money. He could overlook that for Money. He wanted compensation in Money.

"So, he returned to the side of that woman the mother, made love to her again, danced attendance on her, and submitted himself to her whims. She wreaked upon him every whim she had, or could invent. He bore it. And the more he bore, the more he wanted compensation in Money, and the more he was resolved to have it.

"But, lo! Before he got it, she cheated him. In one of her imperious states, she froze, and never thawed again. She put her hands to her head one night, uttered a cry, stiffened, lay in that attitude certain hours, and died. And he had got no compensation from her in Money, yet. Blight and Murrain on her! Not a penny.

"He had hated her throughout that second pursuit, and had longed for retaliation on her. He now counterfeited her signature to an instrument, leaving all she had to leave, to her daughter – ten years old then – to whom the property passed absolutely, and appointing himself the daughter's Guardian. When He slid it under the pillow of the bed on which she lay, He bent down in the deaf ear of Death, and whispered: 'Mistress Pride, I have determined a long time that, dead or alive, you must make me compensation in Money.'"

"So, now there were only two left. Which two were, He, and the fair flaxen-haired, large-eyed foolish daughter, who afterwards became the Bride.

"He put her to school. In a secret, dark, oppressive, ancient house, he put her to school with a watchful and unscrupulous woman. 'My worthy lady,' he said, 'here is a mind to be formed; will you help me to form it?' She accepted the trust. For which she, too, wanted compensation in Money, and had it.

"The girl was formed in the fear of him, and in the conviction, that there was no escape from him. She was taught, from the first, to regard him as her future husband – the man who must marry her – the destiny that overshadowed her – the appointed certainty that could never be evaded. The poor fool was soft white wax in their hands, and took the impression that they put upon her. It hardened with time. It became a part of herself. Inseparable from herself, and only to be torn away from her, by tearing life away from her.

"Eleven years she had lived in the dark house and its gloomy garden. He was jealous of the very light and air getting to her, and they kept her close. He stopped the wide chimneys, shaded the little windows, left the strong-stemmed ivy to wander where it would over the house-front, the moss to accumulate on the untrimmed fruit-trees in the red-walled garden, the weeds to over-run its green and yellow walks. He surrounded her with images of sorrow and desolation. He caused her to be filled with fears of the place and of the stories that were told of it, and then on pretext of correcting them, to be left in it in solitude, or made to shrink about it in the dark. When her mind was most depressed and fullest of terrors, then, he would come out of one of the hiding-places from which he overlooked her, and present himself as her sole resource.

"Thus, by being from her childhood the one embodiment her life presented to her of power to coerce and power to relieve, power to bind and power to loose, the ascendency over her weakness was secured. She was twenty-one years and twenty-one days old, when he brought her home to the gloomy house, his half-witted, frightened, and submissive Bride of three weeks.

"He had dismissed the governess by that time – what he had left to do, he could best do alone – and they came back, upon a rain night, to the scene of her long preparation. She turned to him upon the threshold, as the rain was dripping from the porch, and said:

"'O sir, it is the Death-watch ticking for me!'

"'Well!' he answered. 'And if it were?'

"'O sir!' she returned to him, 'look kindly on me, and be merciful to me! I beg your pardon. I will do anything you wish, if you will only forgive me!'

"That had become the poor fool's constant song: 'I beg your pardon,' and 'Forgive me!'

"She was not worth hating; he felt nothing but contempt for her. But, she had long been in the way, and he had long been weary, and the work was near its end, and had to be worked out.

"'You fool,' he said. 'Go up the stairs!'

"She obeyed very quickly, murmuring, 'I will do anything you wish!' When he came into the Bride's Chamber, having been a little retarded by the heavy fastenings of the great door (for they were alone in the house, and he had arranged that the people who attended on them should come and go in the day), he found her withdrawn to the furthest corner, and there standing pressed against the paneling as if she would have shrunk through it: her flaxen hair all wild about her face, and her large eyes staring at him in vague terror.

"'What are you afraid of? Come and sit down by me.'

"'I will do anything you wish. I beg your pardon, sir. Forgive me!' Her monotonous tune as usual.

"'Ellen, here is a writing that you must write out tomorrow, in your own hand. You may as well be seen by others, busily engaged upon it. When you have written it all fairly, and corrected all mistakes, call in any two people there may be about the house, and sign your name to it before them. Then, put it in your bosom to keep it safe, and when I sit here again tomorrow night, give it to me.'

"'I will do it all, with the greatest care. I will do anything you wish.'

"'Don't shake and tremble, then.'

"'I will try my utmost not to do it – if you will only forgive me!'

"Next day, she sat down at her desk, and did as she had been told. He often passed in and out of the room, to observe her, and always saw her slowly and laboriously writing: repeating to herself the words she copied, in appearance quite mechanically, and without caring or endeavouring to comprehend them, so that she did her task. He saw her follow the directions she had received, in all particulars; and at night, when they were alone again in the same Bride's Chamber, and he drew his chair to the hearth, she timidly approached him from her distant seat, took the paper from her bosom, and gave it into his hand.

"It secured all her possessions to him, in the event of her death. He put her before him, face to face, that he might look at her steadily; and he asked her, in so many plain words, neither fewer nor more, did she know that?

"There were spots of ink upon the bosom of her white dress, and they made her face look whiter and her eyes look larger as she nodded her head. There were spots of ink upon the hand with which she stood before him, nervously plaiting and folding her white skirts.

"He took her by the arm, and looked her, yet more closely and steadily, in the face. 'Now, die! I have done with you.'

"She shrunk, and uttered a low, suppressed cry.

"'I am not going to kill you. I will not endanger my life for yours. Die!'

"He sat before her in the gloomy Bride's Chamber, day after day, night after night, looking the word at her when he did not utter it. As often as her large unmeaning eyes were raised from the hands in which she rocked her head, to the stern figure, sitting with crossed arms and knitted forehead, in the chair, they read in it, 'Die!' When she dropped asleep in exhaustion, she was called back to shuddering consciousness, by the whisper, 'Die!' When she fell upon her old entreaty to be pardoned, she was answered 'Die!' When she had out-watched and out-suffered the long night, and the rising sun flamed into the sombre room, she heard it hailed with, 'Another day and not dead? – Die!'

"Shut up in the deserted mansion, aloof from all mankind, and engaged alone in such a struggle without any respite, it came to this – that either he must die, or she. He knew it very well, and concentrated his strength against her feebleness. Hours upon hours he held her by the arm when her arm was black where he held it, and bade her Die!

"It was done, upon a windy morning, before sunrise. He computed the time to be half-past four; but, his forgotten watch had run down, and he could not be sure. She had broken away from him in the night, with loud and sudden cries – the first of that kind to which she had given vent – and he had had to put his hands over her mouth. Since then, she had been quiet in the corner of the paneling where she had sunk down; and he had left her, and had gone back with his folded arms and his knitted forehead to his chair.

"Paler in the pale light, more colourless than ever in the leaden dawn, he saw her coming, trailing herself along the floor towards him – a white wreck of hair, and dress, and wild eyes, pushing itself on by an irresolute and bending hand.

"'O, forgive me! I will do anything. O, sir, pray tell me I may live!'

"'Die!'

"'Are you so resolved? Is there no hope for me?'

"'Die!'

"Her large eyes strained themselves with wonder and fear; wonder and fear changed to reproach; reproach to blank nothing. It was done. He was not at first so sure it was done, but that the morning sun was hanging jewels in her hair – he saw the diamond, emerald, and ruby, glittering among it in little points, as he stood looking down at her – when he lifted her and laid her on her bed.

"She was soon laid in the ground. And now they were all gone, and he had compensated himself well.

"He had a mind to travel. Not that he meant to waste his Money, for he was a pinching man and liked his Money dearly (liked nothing else, indeed), but, that he had grown tired of the desolate house and wished to turn his back upon it and have done with it. But, the house was worth Money, and Money must not be thrown away. He determined to sell it before he went. That it might look the less wretched and bring a better price, he hired some labourers to work in the overgrown garden; to cut out the dead wood, trim the ivy that drooped in heavy masses over the windows and gables, and clear the walks in which the weeds were growing mid-leg high.

"He worked, himself, along with them. He worked later than they did, and, one evening at dusk, was left working alone, with his bill-hook in his hand. One autumn evening, when the Bride was five weeks dead.

"'It grows too dark to work longer,' he said to himself, 'I must give over for the night.'

"He detested the house, and was loath to enter it. He looked at the dark porch waiting for him like a tomb, and felt that it was an accursed house. Near to the porch, and near to where he stood, was a tree whose branches waved before the old bay-window of the Bride's Chamber, where it had been done. The tree swung suddenly, and made him start. It swung again, although the night was still. Looking up into it, he saw a figure among the branches.

"It was the figure of a young man. The face looked down, as his looked up; the branches cracked and swayed; the figure rapidly descended, and slid upon its feet before him. A slender youth of about her age, with long light brown hair.

"'What thief are you?' he said, seizing the youth by the collar.

"The young man, in shaking himself free, swung him a blow with his arm across the face and throat. They closed, but the young man got from him and stepped back, crying, with great eagerness and horror, 'Don't touch me! I would as lieve be touched by the Devil!'

"He stood still, with his bill-hook in his hand, looking at the young man. For, the young man's look was the counterpart of her last look, and he had not expected ever to see that again.

"'I am no thief. Even if I were, I would not have a coin of your wealth, if it would buy me the Indies. You murderer!'

"'What!'

"'I climbed it,' said the young man, pointing up into the tree, 'for the first time, nigh four years ago. I climbed it, to look at her. I saw her. I spoke to her. I have climbed it, many a time, to watch and listen for her. I was a boy, hidden among its leaves, when from that bay-window she gave me this!'

"He showed a tress of flaxen hair, tied with a mourning ribbon.

"'Her life,' said the young man, 'was a life of mourning. She gave me this, as a token of it, and a sign that she was dead to every one but you. If I had been older, if I had seen her sooner, I might have saved her from you. But, she was fast in the web when I first climbed the tree, and what could I do then to break it!'

"In saying those words, he burst into a fit of sobbing and crying: weakly at first, then passionately.

"'Murderer! I climbed the tree on the night when you brought her back. I heard her, from the tree, speak of the Death-watch at the door. I was three times in the tree while you were shut up with her, slowly killing her. I saw her, from the tree, lie dead upon her bed. I have watched you, from the tree, for proofs and traces of your guilt. The manner of it, is a mystery to me yet, but I will pursue you until you have rendered up your life to the hangman. You shall never, until then, be rid of me. I loved her! I can know no relenting towards you. Murderer, I loved her!'

"The youth was bare-headed, his hat having fluttered away in his descent from the tree. He moved towards the gate. He had to pass – Him – to get to it. There was breadth for two old-fashioned carriages abreast; and the youth's abhorrence, openly expressed in every feature of his face and limb of his body, and very hard to bear, had verge enough to keep itself at a distance in. He (by which I mean the other) had not stirred hand or foot, since he had stood still to look at the boy. He faced round, now, to follow him with his eyes. As the back of the bare light-brown head was turned to him, he saw a red curve stretch from his hand to it. He knew, before he threw the bill-hook, where it had alighted – I say, had alighted, and not, would alight; for, to his clear perception the thing was done before he did it. It cleft the head, and it remained there, and the boy lay on his face.

"He buried the body in the night, at the foot of the tree. As soon as it was light in the morning, he worked at turning up all the ground near the tree, and hacking and hewing at the neighbouring bushes and undergrowth. When the labourers came, there was nothing suspicious, and nothing suspected.

"But, he had, in a moment, defeated all his precautions, and destroyed the triumph of the scheme he had so long concerted, and so successfully worked out. He had got rid of the Bride, and had acquired her fortune without endangering his life; but now, for a death by which he had gained nothing, he had evermore to live with a rope around his neck.

"Beyond this, he was chained to the house of gloom and horror, which he could not endure. Being afraid to sell it or to quit it, lest discovery should be made, he was forced to live in it. He hired two old people, man and wife, for his servants; and dwelt in it, and dreaded it. His great difficulty, for a long time, was the garden. Whether he should keep it trim, whether he should suffer it to fall into its former state of neglect, what would be the least likely way of attracting attention to it?

"He took the middle course of gardening, himself, in his evening leisure, and of then calling the old serving-man to help him; but, of never letting him work there alone. And he made himself an arbour over against the tree, where he could sit and see that it was safe.

"As the seasons changed, and the tree changed, his mind perceived dangers that were always changing. In the leafy time, he perceived that the upper boughs were growing into the form of the young man – that they made the shape of him exactly, sitting in a forked branch swinging in the wind. In the time of the falling leaves, he perceived that they came down from the tree, forming tell-tale letters on the path, or that they had a tendency to heap themselves into a churchyard mound above the grave. In the winter, when the tree was bare, he perceived that the boughs swung at him the ghost of the blow the young man had given, and that they threatened him openly. In the spring, when the sap was mounting in the trunk, he asked himself, were the dried-up particles of blood mounting with it: to make out more obviously this year than last, the leaf-screened figure of the young man, swinging in the wind?

"However, he turned his Money over and over, and still over. He was in the dark trade, the gold-dust trade, and most secret trades that yielded great returns. In ten years, he had turned his Money over, so many times, that the traders and shippers who had dealings with him, absolutely did not lie – for once – when they declared that he had increased his fortune, Twelve Hundred Per Cent.

"He possessed his riches one hundred years ago, when people could be lost easily. He had heard who the youth was, from hearing of the search that was made after him; but, it died away, and the youth was forgotten.

"The annual round of changes in the tree had been repeated ten times since the night of the burial at its foot, when there was a great thunder-storm over this place. It broke at midnight, and roared until morning. The first intelligence he heard from his old serving-man that morning, was, that the tree had been struck by Lightning.

"It had been riven down the stem, in a very surprising manner, and the stem lay in two blighted shafts: one resting against the house, and one against a portion of the old red garden-wall in which its fall had made a gap. The fissure went down the tree to a little above the earth, and there stopped. There was great curiosity to see the tree, and, with most of his former fears revived, he sat in his arbour – grown quite an old man – watching the people who came to see it.

"They quickly began to come, in such dangerous numbers, that he closed his garden-gate and refused to admit any more. But, there were certain men of science who travelled from a distance to examine the tree, and, in an evil hour, he let them in! – Blight and Murrain on them, let them in!

"They wanted to dig up the ruin by the roots, and closely examine it, and the earth about it. Never, while he lived! They offered money for it. They! Men of science, whom he could have bought by the gross, with a scratch of his pen! He showed them the garden-gate again, and locked and barred it.

"But they were bent on doing what they wanted to do, and they bribed the old serving-man – a thankless wretch who regularly complained when he received his wages, of being underpaid – and they stole into the garden by night with their lanterns, picks, and shovels, and fell to at the tree. He was lying in a turret-room on the other side of the house (the Bride's Chamber had been unoccupied ever since), but he soon dreamed of picks and shovels, and got up.

"He came to an upper window on that side, whence he could see their lanterns, and them, and the loose earth in a heap which he had himself disturbed and put back, when it was last turned to the air. It was found! They had that minute lighted on it. They were all bending over it. One of them said, 'The skull is fractured;' and another, 'See here the bones;' and another, 'See here the clothes;' and then the first struck in again, and said, 'A rusty bill-hook!'

"He became sensible, next day, that he was already put under a strict watch, and that he could go nowhere without being followed. Before a week was out, he was taken and laid in hold. The circumstances were gradually pieced together against him, with a desperate malignity, and an appalling ingenuity. But, see the justice of men, and how it was extended to him! He was further accused of having poisoned that girl in the Bride's Chamber. He, who had carefully and expressly avoided imperilling a hair of his head for her, and who had seen her die of her own incapacity!

"There was doubt for which of the two murders he should be first tried; but, the real one was chosen, and he was found Guilty, and cast for death. Bloodthirsty wretches! They would have made him Guilty of anything, so set they were upon having his life.

"His money could do nothing to save him, and he was hanged. *I* am He, and I was hanged at Lancaster Castle with my face to the wall, a hundred years ago!"

At this terrific announcement, Mr. Goodchild tried to rise and cry out. But, the two fiery lines extending from the old man's eyes to his own, kept him down, and he could not utter a sound. His sense of hearing, however, was acute, and he could hear the clock strike Two. No sooner had he heard the clock strike Two, than he saw before him Two old men!

Two.

The eyes of each, connected with his eyes by two films of fire: each, exactly like the other: each, addressing him at precisely one and the same instant: each, gnashing the same teeth in the same head, with the same twitched nostril above them, and the same suffused expression around it. Two old men. Differing in nothing, equally distinct to the sight, the copy no fainter than the original, the second as real as the first.

"At what time," said the Two old men, "did you arrive at the door below?"

"At Six."

"And there were Six old men upon the stairs!"

Mr. Goodchild having wiped the perspiration from his brow, or tried to do it, the Two old men proceeded in one voice, and in the singular number:

"I had been anatomised, but had not yet had my skeleton put together and re-hung on an iron hook, when it began to be whispered that the Bride's Chamber was haunted. It *was* haunted, and I was there.

"*We* were there. She and I were there. I, in the chair upon the hearth; she, a white wreck again, trailing itself towards me on the floor. But, I was the speaker no more, and the one word that she said to me from midnight until dawn was, 'Live!'

"The youth was there, likewise. In the tree outside the window. Coming and going in the moonlight, as the tree bent and gave. He has, ever since, been there, peeping in at me in my torment; revealing to me by snatches, in the pale lights and slatey shadows where he comes and goes, bare-headed – a bill-hook, standing edgewise in his hair.

"In the Bride's Chamber, every night from midnight until dawn – one month in the year excepted, as I am going to tell you – he hides in the tree, and she comes towards me on the floor; always approaching; never coming nearer; always visible as if by moon-light, whether the moon shines or no; always saying, from mid-night until dawn, her one word, 'Live!'

"But, in the month wherein I was forced out of this life – this present month of thirty days – the Bride's Chamber is empty and quiet. Not so my old dungeon. Not so the rooms where I was restless and afraid, ten years. Both are fitfully haunted then. At One in the morning. I am what you saw me when the clock struck that hour – One old man. At Two in the morning, I am Two old men. At Three, I am Three. By Twelve at noon, I am Twelve old men, One for every hundred per cent. of old gain. Every one of the Twelve, with Twelve times my old power of suffering and agony. From that hour until Twelve at night, I, Twelve old men in anguish and fearful foreboding, wait for the coming of the executioner. At Twelve at night, I, Twelve old men turned off, swing invisible outside Lancaster Castle, with Twelve faces to the wall!

"When the Bride's Chamber was first haunted, it was known to me that this punishment would never cease, until I could make its nature, and my story, known to two living men together. I waited for the coming of two living men together into the Bride's Chamber, years upon years. It was infused into my knowledge (of the means I am ignorant) that if two living men, with their eyes open, could be in the Bride's Chamber at One in the morning, they would see me sitting in my chair.

"At length, the whispers that the room was spiritually troubled, brought two men to try the adventure. I was scarcely struck upon the hearth at midnight (I come there as if the Lightning blasted me into being), when I heard them ascending the stairs. Next, I saw them enter. One of them was a bold, gay, active man, in the prime of life, some five and forty years of age; the other, a dozen years younger. They brought provisions with them in a basket, and bottles. A young woman accompanied them, with wood and coals for the lighting of the fire. When she had lighted it, the bold, gay, active man accompanied her along the gallery outside the room, to see her safely down the staircase, and came back laughing.

"He locked the door, examined the chamber, put out the contents of the basket on the table before the fire – little recking of me, in my appointed station on the hearth, close to him – and filled the glasses, and ate and drank. His companion did the same, and was as cheerful and confident as he: though he was the leader. When they had supped, they laid pistols on the table, turned to the fire, and began to smoke their pipes of foreign make.

"They had travelled together, and had been much together, and had an abundance of subjects in common. In the midst of their talking and laughing, the younger man made a reference to the leader's being always ready for any adventure; that one, or any other. He replied in these words:

"'Not quite so, Dick; if I am afraid of nothing else, I am afraid of myself.'

"His companion seeming to grow a little dull, asked him, in what sense? How?

"'Why, thus,' he returned. 'Here is a Ghost to be disproved. Well! I cannot answer for what my fancy might do if I were alone here, or what tricks my senses might play with me if they had me to themselves. But, in company with another man, and especially with Dick, I would consent to outface all the Ghosts that were ever of in the universe.'

"'I had not the vanity to suppose that I was of so much importance to-night,' said the other.

"'Of so much,' rejoined the leader, more seriously than he had spoken yet, 'that I would, for the reason I have given, on no account have undertaken to pass the night here alone.'

"It was within a few minutes of One. The head of the younger man had drooped when he made his last remark, and it drooped lower now.

"'Keep awake, Dick!' said the leader, gaily. 'The small hours are the worst.'

"He tried, but his head drooped again.

"'Dick!' urged the leader. 'Keep awake!'

"'I can't,' he indistinctly muttered. 'I don't know what strange influence is stealing over me. I can't.'

"His companion looked at him with a sudden horror, and I, in my different way, felt a new horror also; for, it was on the stroke of One, and I felt that the second watcher was yielding to me, and that the curse was upon me that I must send him to sleep.

"'Get up and walk, Dick!' cried the leader. 'Try!'

"It was in vain to go behind the slumber's chair and shake him. One o'clock sounded, and I was present to the elder man, and he stood transfixed before me.

"To him alone, I was obliged to relate my story, without hope of benefit. To him alone, I was an awful phantom making a quite useless confession. I foresee it will ever be the same. The two living men together will never come to release me. When I appear, the senses of one of the two will be locked in sleep; he will neither see nor hear me; my communication will ever be made to a solitary listener, and will ever be unserviceable. Woe! Woe! Woe!"

As the Two old men, with these words, wrung their hands, it shot into Mr. Goodchild's mind that he was in the terrible situation of being virtually alone with the spectre, and that Mr. Idle's immoveability was explained by his having been charmed asleep at One o'clock. In the terror of this sudden discovery which produced an indescribable dread, he struggled so hard to get free from the four fiery threads, that he snapped them, after he had pulled them out to a great width. Being then out of bonds, he caught up Mr. Idle from the sofa and rushed downstairs with him.

**If you enjoyed this, you might also like...**
The Trial for Murder, see page 251
To Be Read at Dusk, see page 132

# Murder & Revenge

# A Madman's Manuscript

**YES!** – a madman's! How that word would have struck to my heart, many years ago! How it would have roused the terror that used to come upon me sometimes, sending the blood hissing and tingling through my veins, till the cold dew of fear stood in large drops upon my skin, and my knees knocked together with fright! I like it now though. It's a fine name. Show me the monarch whose angry frown was ever feared like the glare of a madman's eye – whose cord and axe were ever half so sure as a madman's gripe. Ho! ho! It's a grand thing to be mad! to be peeped at like a wild lion through the iron bars – to gnash one's teeth and howl, through the long still night, to the merry ring of a heavy chain and to roll and twine among the straw, transported with such brave music. Hurrah for the madhouse! Oh, it's a rare place!

I remember days when I was afraid of being mad; when I used to start from my sleep, and fall upon my knees, and pray to be spared from the curse of my race; when I rushed from the sight of merriment or happiness, to hide myself in some lonely place, and spend the weary hours in watching the progress of the fever that was to consume my brain. I knew that madness was mixed up with my very blood, and the marrow of my bones! that one generation had passed away without the pestilence appearing among them, and that I was the first in whom it would revive. I knew it must be so: that so it always had been, and so it ever would be: and when I cowered in some obscure corner of a crowded room, and saw men whisper, and point, and turn their eyes towards me, I knew they were telling each other of the doomed madman; and I slunk away again to mope in solitude.

I did this for years; long, long years they were. The nights here are long sometimes – very long; but they are nothing to the restless nights, and dreadful dreams I had at that time. It makes me cold to remember them. Large dusky forms with sly and jeering faces crouched in the corners of the room, and bent over my bed at night, tempting me to madness. They told me in low whispers, that the floor of the old house in which my father died, was stained with his own blood, shed by his own hand in raging madness. I drove my fingers into my ears, but they screamed into my head till the room rang with it, that in one generation before him the madness slumbered, but that his grandfather had lived for years with his hands fettered to the ground, to prevent his tearing himself to pieces. I knew they told the truth – I knew it well. I had found it out years before, though they had tried to keep it from me. Ha! ha! I was too cunning for them, madman as they thought me.

At last it came upon me, and I wondered how I could ever have feared it. I could go into the world now, and laugh and shout with the best among them. I knew I was mad, but they did not even suspect it. How I used to hug myself with delight, when I thought of the fine trick I was playing them after their old pointing and leering, when I was not mad, but only dreading that I might one day become so! And how I used to laugh for joy, when I was alone, and thought how well I kept my secret, and how quickly my kind friends would have fallen from me, if they had known the truth. I could have screamed with ecstasy when I dined alone with some fine roaring fellow, to think how pale he would have turned, and how fast he would have run, if he had known that the dear friend who sat close to him, sharpening a bright, glittering knife, was a madman with all the power, and half the will, to plunge it in his heart. Oh, it was a merry life!

Riches became mine, wealth poured in upon me, and I rioted in pleasures enhanced a thousandfold to me by the consciousness of my well-kept secret. I inherited an estate. The law – the eagle-eyed law itself – had been deceived, and had handed over disputed thousands to a madman's hands. Where was the wit of the sharp-sighted men of sound mind? Where the dexterity of the lawyers, eager to discover a flaw? The madman's cunning had overreached them all.

I had money. How I was courted! I spent it profusely. How I was praised! How those three proud, overbearing brothers humbled themselves before me! The old, white-headed father, too – such deference – such respect – such devoted friendship – he worshipped me! The old man had a daughter, and the young men a sister; and all the five were poor. I was rich; and when I married the girl, I saw a smile of triumph play upon the faces of her needy relatives, as they thought of their well-planned scheme, and their fine prize. It was for me to smile. To smile! To laugh outright, and tear my hair, and roll upon the ground with shrieks of merriment. They little thought they had married her to a madman.

Stay. If they had known it, would they have saved her? A sister's happiness against her husband's gold. The lightest feather I blow into the air, against the gay chain that ornaments my body!

In one thing I was deceived with all my cunning. If I had not been mad – for though we madmen are sharp-witted enough, we get bewildered sometimes – I should have known that the girl would rather have been placed, stiff and cold in a dull leaden coffin, than borne an envied bride to my rich, glittering house. I should have known that her heart was with the dark-eyed boy whose name I once heard her breathe in her troubled sleep; and that she had been sacrificed to me, to relieve the poverty of the old, white-headed man and the haughty brothers.

I don't remember forms or faces now, but I know the girl was beautiful. I know she was; for in the bright moonlight nights, when I start up from my sleep, and all is quiet about me, I see, standing still and motionless in one corner of this cell, a slight and wasted figure with long black hair, which, streaming down her back, stirs with no earthly wind, and eyes that fix their gaze on me, and never wink or close. Hush! the blood chills at my heart as I write it down – that form is *her's*; the face is very pale, and the eyes are glassy bright; but I know them well. That figure never moves; it never frowns and mouths as others do, that fill this place sometimes; but it is much more dreadful to me, even than the spirits that tempted me many years ago – it comes fresh from the grave; and is so very death-like.

For nearly a year I saw that face grow paler; for nearly a year I saw the tears steal down the mournful cheeks, and never knew the cause. I found it out at last though. They could not keep it from me long. She had never liked me; I had never thought she did: she despised my wealth, and hated the splendour in which she lived; but I had not expected that. She loved another. This I had never thought of. Strange feelings came over me, and thoughts, forced upon me by some secret power, whirled round and round my brain. I did not hate her, though I hated the boy she still wept for. I pitied – yes, I pitied – the wretched life to which her cold and selfish relations had doomed her. I knew that she could not live long; but the thought that before her death she might give birth to some ill-fated being, destined to hand down madness to its offspring, determined me. I resolved to kill her.

For many weeks I thought of poison, and then of drowning, and then of fire. A fine sight, the grand house in flames, and the madman's wife smouldering away to cinders. Think of the jest of a large reward, too, and of some sane man swinging in the wind for a deed he never did, and all through a madman's cunning! I thought often of this, but I gave it up at last. Oh! the pleasure of stropping the razor day after day, feeling the sharp edge, and thinking of the gash one stroke of its thin, bright edge would make!

At last the old spirits who had been with me so often before whispered in my ear that the time was come, and thrust the open razor into my hand. I grasped it firmly, rose softly from the bed, and leaned over my sleeping wife. Her face was buried in her hands. I withdrew them softly, and they fell listlessly on her bosom. She had been weeping; for the traces of the tears were still wet upon her cheek. Her face was calm and placid; and even as I looked upon it, a tranquil smile lighted up her pale features. I laid my hand softly on her shoulder. She started – it was only a passing dream. I leaned forward again. She screamed, and woke.

One motion of my hand, and she would never again have uttered cry or sound. But I was startled, and drew back. Her eyes were fixed on mine. I knew not how it was, but they cowed and frightened me; and I quailed beneath them. She rose from the bed, still gazing fixedly and steadily on me. I trembled; the razor was in my hand, but I could not move. She made towards the door. As she neared it, she turned, and withdrew her eyes from my face. The spell was broken. I bounded forward, and clutched her by the arm. Uttering shriek upon shriek, she sank upon the ground.

Now I could have killed her without a struggle; but the house was alarmed. I heard the tread of footsteps on the stairs. I replaced the razor in its usual drawer, unfastened the door, and called loudly for assistance.

They came, and raised her, and placed her on the bed. She lay bereft of animation for hours; and when life, look, and speech returned, her senses had deserted her, and she raved wildly and furiously.

Doctors were called in – great men who rolled up to my door in easy carriages, with fine horses and gaudy servants. They were at her bedside for weeks. They had a great meeting and consulted together in low and solemn voices in another room. One, the cleverest and most celebrated among them, took me aside, and bidding me prepare for the worst, told me – me, the madman! – that my wife was mad. He stood close beside me at an open window, his eyes looking in my face, and his hand laid upon my arm. With one effort, I could have hurled him into the street beneath. It would have been rare sport to have done it; but my secret was at stake, and I let him go. A few days after, they told me I must place her under some restraint: I must provide a keeper for her. I! I went into the open fields where none could hear me, and laughed till the air resounded with my shouts!

She died next day. The white-headed old man followed her to the grave, and the proud brothers dropped a tear over the insensible corpse of her whose sufferings they had regarded in her lifetime with muscles of iron. All this was food for my secret mirth, and I laughed behind the white handkerchief which I held up to my face, as we rode home, till the tears came into my eyes.

But though I had carried my object and killed her, I was restless and disturbed, and I felt that before long my secret must be known. I could not hide the wild mirth and joy which boiled within me, and made me when I was alone, at home, jump up and beat my hands together, and dance round and round, and roar aloud. When I went out, and saw the busy crowds hurrying about the streets; or to the theatre, and heard the sound of music, and beheld the people dancing, I felt such glee, that I could have rushed among them, and torn them to pieces limb from limb, and howled in transport. But I ground my teeth, and struck my feet upon the floor, and drove my sharp nails into my hands. I kept it down; and no one knew I was a madman yet.

I remember – though it's one of the last things I can remember: for now I mix up realities with my dreams, and having so much to do, and being always hurried here, have no time to separate the two, from some strange confusion in which they get involved – I remember how I let it out at last. Ha! ha! I think I see their frightened looks now, and feel the ease with which I flung them from me, and dashed my clenched fist into their white faces, and then flew like the wind, and left them screaming and shouting far behind. The strength of a giant comes upon me when I think of it. There – see how this iron bar bends beneath my furious wrench. I could snap it like a twig, only there are long galleries here with many doors – I don't think I could find my way along them; and even if I could, I know there are iron gates below which they keep locked and barred. They know what a clever madman I have been, and they are proud to have me here, to show.

Let me see: yes, I had been out. It was late at night when I reached home, and found the proudest of the three proud brothers waiting to see me – urgent business he said: I recollect it well. I hated that man with all a madman's hate. Many and many a time had my fingers longed to tear him. They told me he was there. I ran swiftly upstairs. He had a word to say to me. I dismissed the servants. It was late, and we were alone together – for the first time.

I kept my eyes carefully from him at first, for I knew what he little thought – and I gloried in the knowledge – that the light of madness gleamed from them like fire. We sat in silence for a few minutes. He spoke at last. My recent dissipation, and strange remarks, made so soon after his sister's death, were an insult to her memory. Coupling together many circumstances which had at first escaped his observation, he thought I had not treated her well. He wished to know whether he was right in inferring that I meant to cast a reproach upon her memory, and a disrespect upon her family. It was due to the uniform he wore, to demand this explanation.

This man had a commission in the army – a commission, purchased with my money, and his sister's misery! This was the man who had been foremost in the plot to ensnare me, and grasp my wealth. This was the man who had been the main instrument in forcing his sister to wed me; well knowing that her heart was given to that puling boy. Due to his uniform! The livery of his degradation! I turned my eyes upon him – I could not help it – but I spoke not a word.

I saw the sudden change that came upon him beneath my gaze. He was a bold man, but the colour faded from his face, and he drew back his chair. I dragged mine nearer to him; and I laughed – I was very merry then – I saw him shudder. I felt the madness rising within me. He was afraid of me.

"You were very fond of your sister when she was alive," I said. "Very."

He looked uneasily round him, and I saw his hand grasp the back of his chair; but he said nothing.

"You villain," said I, "I found you out: I discovered your hellish plots against me; I know her heart was fixed on some one else before you compelled her to marry me. I know it – I know it."

He jumped suddenly from his chair, brandished it aloft, and bid me stand back – for I took care to be getting closer to him all the time I spoke.

I screamed rather than talked, for I felt tumultuous passions eddying through my veins, and the old spirits whispering and taunting me to tear his heart out.

"Damn you," said I, starting up, and rushing upon him; "I killed her. I am a madman. Down with you. Blood, blood! I will have it!"

I turned aside with one blow the chair he hurled at me in his terror, and closed with him; and with a heavy crash we rolled upon the floor together.

It was a fine struggle that; for he was a tall, strong man, fighting for his life; and I, a powerful madman, thirsting to destroy him. I knew no strength could equal mine, and I was right. Right again, though a madman! His struggles grew fainter. I knelt upon his chest, and clasped his brawny throat firmly with both hands. His face grew purple; his eyes were starting from his head, and with protruded tongue, he seemed to mock me. I squeezed the tighter.

The door was suddenly burst open with a loud noise, and a crowd of people rushed forward, crying aloud to each other to secure the madman.

My secret was out; and my only struggle now was for liberty and freedom. I gained my feet before a hand was on me, threw myself among my assailants, and cleared my way with my strong arm, as if I bore a hatchet in my hand, and hewed them down before me. I gained the door, dropped over the banisters, and in an instant was in the street.

Straight and swift I ran, and no one dared to stop me. I heard the noise of the feet behind, and redoubled my speed. It grew fainter and fainter in the distance, and at length died away altogether; but on I bounded, through marsh and rivulet, over fence and wall, with a wild shout which was taken up by the strange beings that flocked around me on every side, and swelled the sound, till it pierced the air. I was borne upon the arms of demons who swept along upon the wind, and bore down bank and hedge before them, and spun me round and round with a rustle and a speed that made my head swim, until at last they threw me from them with a violent shock, and I fell heavily upon the earth. When I woke I found myself here – here in this gray cell, where the sunlight seldom comes, and the moon steals in, in rays which only serve to show the dark shadows about me, and that silent figure in its old corner. When I lie awake, I can sometimes hear strange shrieks and cries from distant parts of this large place. What they are, I know not; but they neither come from that pale form, nor does it regard them. For from the first shades of dusk till the earliest light of morning, it still stands motionless in the same place, listening to the music of my iron chain, and watching my gambols on my straw bed.

**If you enjoyed this, you might also like...**
Captain Murderer and the Devil's Bargain, see page 309
The Mother's Eyes, see page 298

# The Convict's Return

**WHEN I FIRST** settled in this village, which is now just five-and-twenty years ago, the most notorious person among my parishioners was a man of the name of Edmunds, who leased a small farm near this spot. He was a morose, savage-hearted, bad man; idle and dissolute in his habits; cruel and ferocious in his disposition. Beyond the few lazy and reckless vagabonds with whom he sauntered away his time in the fields, or sotted in the ale-house, he had not a single friend or acquaintance; no one cared to speak to the man whom many feared, and every one detested – and Edmunds was shunned by all.

This man had a wife and one son, who, when I first came here, was about twelve years old. Of the acuteness of that woman's sufferings, of the gentle and enduring manner in which she bore them, of the agony of solicitude with which she reared that boy, no one can form an adequate conception. Heaven forgive me the supposition, if it be an uncharitable one, but I do firmly and in my soul believe, that the man systematically tried for many years to break her heart; but she bore it all for her child's sake, and, however strange it may seem to many, for his father's too; for brute as he was, and cruelly as he had treated her, she had loved him once; and the recollection of what he had been to her, awakened feelings of forbearance and meekness under suffering in her bosom, to which all God's creatures, but women, are strangers.

They were poor – they could not be otherwise when the man pursued such courses; but the woman's unceasing and unwearied exertions, early and late, morning, noon, and night, kept them above actual want. These exertions were but ill repaid. People who passed the spot in the evening – sometimes at a late hour of the night – reported that they had heard the moans and sobs of a woman in distress, and the sound of blows; and more than once, when it was past midnight, the boy knocked softly at the door of a neighbour's house, whither he had been sent, to escape the drunken fury of his unnatural father.

During the whole of this time, and when the poor creature often bore about her marks of ill-usage and violence which she could not wholly conceal, she was a constant attendant at our little church. Regularly every Sunday, morning and afternoon, she occupied the same seat with the boy at her side; and though they were both poorly dressed – much more so than many of their neighbours who were in a lower station – they were always neat and clean. Every one had a friendly nod and a kind word for "poor Mrs. Edmunds"; and sometimes, when she stopped to exchange a few words with a neighbour at the conclusion of the service in the little row of elm-trees which leads to the church porch, or lingered behind to gaze with a mother's pride and fondness upon her healthy boy, as he sported before her with some little companions, her careworn face would lighten up with an expression of heartfelt gratitude; and she would look, if not cheerful and happy, at least tranquil and contented.

Five or six years passed away; the boy had become a robust and well-grown youth. The time that had strengthened the child's slight frame and knit his weak limbs into the strength of manhood had bowed his mother's form, and enfeebled her steps; but the arm that should have supported her was no longer locked in hers; the face that should have cheered her, no more looked upon her own. She occupied her old seat, but there was a vacant one beside her. The Bible was kept as carefully as ever, the places were found and folded down as they used to be: but there was no one to read it with her; and the tears fell thick and fast upon the book, and blotted the words from her eyes. Neighbours were as kind as they were wont to be of old, but she shunned their greetings with averted head. There was no lingering among the old elm-trees now – no cheering anticipations of happiness yet in store. The desolate woman drew her bonnet closer over her face, and walked hurriedly away.

Shall I tell you that the young man, who, looking back to the earliest of his childhood's days to which memory and consciousness extended, and carrying his recollection down to that moment, could remember nothing which was not in some way connected with a long series of voluntary privations suffered by his mother for his sake, with ill-usage, and insult, and violence, and all endured for him – shall I tell you, that he, with a reckless disregard for her breaking heart, and a sullen, wilful forgetfulness of all she had done and borne for him, had linked himself with depraved and abandoned men, and was madly pursuing a headlong career, which must bring death to him, and shame to her? Alas for human nature! You have anticipated it long since.

The measure of the unhappy woman's misery and misfortune was about to be completed. Numerous offences had been committed in the neighbourhood; the perpetrators remained undiscovered, and their boldness increased. A robbery of a daring and aggravated nature occasioned a vigilance of pursuit, and a strictness of search, they had not calculated on. Young Edmunds was suspected, with three companions. He was apprehended – committed – tried – condemned – to die.

The wild and piercing shriek from a woman's voice, which resounded through the court when the solemn sentence was pronounced, rings in my ears at this moment. That cry struck a terror to the culprit's heart, which trial, condemnation – the approach of death itself, had failed to awaken. The lips which had been compressed in dogged sullenness throughout, quivered and parted involuntarily; the face turned ashy pale as the cold perspiration broke forth from every pore; the sturdy limbs of the felon trembled, and he staggered in the dock.

In the first transports of her mental anguish, the suffering mother threw herself on her knees at my feet, and fervently sought the Almighty Being who had hitherto supported her in all her troubles to release her from a world of woe and misery, and to spare the life of her only child. A burst of grief, and a violent struggle, such as I hope I may never have to witness again, succeeded. I knew that her heart was breaking from that hour; but I never once heard complaint or murmur escape her lips.

It was a piteous spectacle to see that woman in the prison-yard from day to day, eagerly and fervently attempting, by affection and entreaty, to soften the hard heart of her obdurate son. It was in vain. He remained moody, obstinate, and unmoved. Not even the unlooked-for commutation of his sentence to transportation for fourteen years, softened for an instant the sullen hardihood of his demeanour.

But the spirit of resignation and endurance that had so long upheld her, was unable to contend against bodily weakness and infirmity. She fell sick. She dragged her tottering limbs from the bed to visit her son once more, but her strength failed her, and she sank powerless on the ground.

And now the boasted coldness and indifference of the young man were tested indeed; and the retribution that fell heavily upon him nearly drove him mad. A day passed away and his mother was not there; another flew by, and she came not near him; a third evening arrived, and yet he had not seen her, and in four-and-twenty hours he was to be separated from her, perhaps for ever. Oh! how the long-forgotten thoughts of former days rushed upon his mind, as he almost ran up and down the narrow yard – as if intelligence would arrive the sooner for his hurrying – and how bitterly a sense of his helplessness and desolation rushed upon him, when he heard the truth! His mother, the only parent he had ever known, lay ill – it might be, dying – within one mile of the ground he stood on; were he free and unfettered, a few minutes would place him by her side. He rushed to the gate, and grasping the iron rails with the energy of desperation, shook it till it rang again, and threw himself against the thick wall as if to force a passage through the stone; but the strong building mocked his feeble efforts, and he beat his hands together and wept like a child.

I bore the mother's forgiveness and blessing to her son in prison; and I carried the solemn assurance of repentance, and his fervent supplication for pardon, to her sick-bed. I heard, with pity and compassion, the repentant man devise a thousand little plans for her comfort and support when he returned; but I knew that many months before he could reach his place of destination, his mother would be no longer of this world.

He was removed by night. A few weeks afterwards the poor woman's soul took its flight, I confidently hope, and solemnly believe, to a place of eternal happiness and rest. I performed the burial service over her remains. She lies in our little churchyard. There is no stone at her grave's head. Her sorrows were known to man; her virtues to God.

It had been arranged previously to the convict's departure, that he should write to his mother as soon as he could obtain permission, and that the letter should be addressed to me. The father had positively refused to see his son from the moment of his apprehension; and it was a matter of indifference to him whether he lived or died. Many years passed over without any intelligence of him; and when more than half his term of transportation had expired, and I had received no letter, I concluded him to be dead, as, indeed, I almost hoped he might be.

Edmunds, however, had been sent a considerable distance up the country on his arrival at the settlement; and to this circumstance, perhaps, may be attributed the fact, that though several letters were despatched, none of them ever reached my hands. He remained in the same place during the whole fourteen years. At the expiration of the term, steadily adhering to his old resolution and the pledge he gave his mother, he made his way back to England amidst innumerable difficulties, and returned, on foot, to his native place.

On a fine Sunday evening, in the month of August, John Edmunds set foot in the village he had left with shame and disgrace seventeen years before. His nearest way lay through the churchyard. The man's heart swelled as he crossed the stile. The tall old elms, through whose branches the declining sun cast here and there a rich ray of light upon the shady part, awakened the associations of his earliest days. He pictured himself as he was then, clinging to his mother's hand, and walking peacefully to church. He remembered how he used to look up into her pale face; and how her eyes would sometimes fill with tears as she gazed upon his features – tears which fell hot upon his forehead as she stooped to kiss him, and made him weep too, although he little knew then what bitter tears hers were. He thought how often he had run merrily down that path with some childish playfellow, looking back, ever and again, to catch his mother's smile, or hear her gentle voice; and then a veil seemed lifted from his memory, and words of kindness unrequited, and warnings despised, and promises broken, thronged upon his recollection till his heart failed him, and he could bear it no longer.

He entered the church. The evening service was concluded and the congregation had dispersed, but it was not yet closed. His steps echoed through the low building with a hollow sound, and he almost feared to be alone, it was so still and quiet. He looked round him. Nothing was changed. The place seemed smaller than it used to be; but there were the old monuments on which he had gazed with childish awe a thousand times; the little pulpit with its faded cushion; the Communion table before which he had so often repeated the Commandments he had reverenced as a child, and forgotten as a man. He approached the old seat; it looked cold and desolate. The cushion had been removed, and the Bible was not there. Perhaps his mother now occupied a poorer seat, or possibly she had grown infirm and could not reach the church alone. He dared not think of what he feared. A cold feeling crept over him, and he trembled violently as he turned away. 'An old man entered the porch just as he reached it. Edmunds started back, for he knew him well; many a time he had watched him digging graves in the churchyard. What would he say to the returned convict?

The old man raised his eyes to the stranger's face, bade him "good-evening," and walked slowly on. He had forgotten him.

He walked down the hill, and through the village. The weather was warm, and the people were sitting at their doors, or strolling in their little gardens as he passed, enjoying the serenity of the evening, and their rest from labour. Many a look was turned towards him, and many a doubtful glance he cast on either side to see whether any knew and shunned him. There were strange faces in almost every house; in some he recognised the burly form of some old schoolfellow – a boy when he last saw him – surrounded by a troop of merry children; in others he saw, seated in an easy-chair at a cottage door, a feeble and infirm old man, whom he only remembered as a hale and hearty labourer; but they had all forgotten him, and he passed on unknown.

The last soft light of the setting sun had fallen on the earth, casting a rich glow on the yellow corn sheaves, and lengthening the shadows of the orchard trees, as he stood before the old house – the home of his infancy – to which his heart had yearned with an intensity of affection not to be described, through long and weary years of captivity and sorrow. The paling was low, though he well remembered the time that it had seemed a high wall to him; and he looked over into the old garden. There were more seeds and gayer flowers than there used to be, but there were the old trees still – the very tree under which he had lain a thousand times when tired of playing in the sun, and felt the soft, mild sleep of happy boyhood steal gently upon him. There were voices within the house. He listened, but they fell strangely upon his ear; he knew them not. They were merry too; and he well knew that his poor old mother could not be cheerful, and he away. The door opened, and a group of little children bounded out, shouting and romping. The father, with a little boy in his arms, appeared at the door, and they crowded round him, clapping their tiny hands, and dragging him out, to join their joyous sports. The convict thought on the many times he had shrunk from his father's sight in that very place. He remembered how often he had buried his trembling head beneath the bedclothes, and heard the harsh word, and the hard stripe, and his mother's wailing; and though the man sobbed aloud with agony of mind as he left the spot, his fist was clenched, and his teeth were set, in a fierce and deadly passion.

And such was the return to which he had looked through the weary perspective of many years, and for which he had undergone so much suffering! No face of welcome, no look of forgiveness, no house to receive, no hand to help him – and this too in the old village. What was his loneliness in the wild, thick woods, where man was never seen, to this!

He felt that in the distant land of his bondage and infamy, he had thought of his native place as it was when he left it; and not as it would be when he returned. The sad reality struck coldly at his heart, and his spirit sank within him. He had not courage to make inquiries, or to present himself to the only person who was likely to receive him with kindness and compassion. He walked slowly on; and shunning the roadside like a guilty man, turned into a meadow he well remembered; and covering his face with his hands, threw himself upon the grass.

He had not observed that a man was lying on the bank beside him; his garments rustled as he turned round to steal a look at the new-comer; and Edmunds raised his head.

The man had moved into a sitting posture. His body was much bent, and his face was wrinkled and yellow. His dress denoted him an inmate of the workhouse: he had the appearance of being very old, but it looked more the effect of dissipation or disease, than the length of years. He was staring hard at the stranger, and though his eyes were lustreless and heavy at first, they appeared to glow with an unnatural and alarmed expression after they had been fixed upon him for a short time, until they seemed to be starting from their sockets. Edmunds gradually raised himself to his knees, and looked more and more earnestly on the old man's face. They gazed upon each other in silence.

The old man was ghastly pale. He shuddered and tottered to his feet. Edmunds sprang to his. He stepped back a pace or two. Edmunds advanced.

"Let me hear you speak," said the convict, in a thick, broken voice.

"Stand off!" cried the old man, with a dreadful oath. The convict drew closer to him.

"Stand off!" shrieked the old man. Furious with terror, he raised his stick, and struck Edmunds a heavy blow across the face.

"Father – devil!" murmured the convict between his set teeth. He rushed wildly forward, and clenched the old man by the throat – but he was his father; and his arm fell powerless by his side.

The old man uttered a loud yell which rang through the lonely fields like the howl of an evil spirit. His face turned black, the gore rushed from his mouth and nose, and dyed the grass a deep, dark red, as he staggered and fell. He had ruptured a blood-vessel, and he was a dead man before his son could raise him.

* * *

In that corner of the churchyard of which I have before spoken, there lies buried a man who was in my employment for three years after this event, and who was truly contrite, penitent, and humbled, if ever man was. No one save myself knew in that man's lifetime who he was, or whence he came – it was John Edmunds, the returned convict.

**If you enjoyed this, you might also like...**
The Trial for Murder, see page 251
Well-Authenticated Rappings, see page 303

# The Old Man's Tale About the Queer Client

**IT MATTERS** little where, or how, I picked up this brief history. If I were to relate it in the order in which it reached me, I should commence in the middle, and when I had arrived at the conclusion, go back for a beginning. It is enough for me to say that some of its circumstances passed before my own eyes; for the remainder I know them to have happened, and there are some persons yet living, who will remember them but too well.

In the Borough High Street, near St. George's Church, and on the same side of the way, stands, as most people know, the smallest of our debtors' prisons, the Marshalsea. Although in later times it has been a very different place from the sink of filth and dirt it once was, even its improved condition holds out but little temptation to the extravagant, or consolation to the improvident. The condemned felon has as good a yard for air and exercise in Newgate, as the insolvent debtor in the Marshalsea Prison. [Better. But this is past, in a better age, and the prison exists no longer.]

It may be my fancy, or it may be that I cannot separate the place from the old recollections associated with it, but this part of London I cannot bear. The street is broad, the shops are spacious, the noise of passing vehicles, the footsteps of a perpetual stream of people – all the busy sounds of traffic, resound in it from morn to midnight; but the streets around are mean and close; poverty and debauchery lie festering in the crowded alleys; want and misfortune are pent up in the narrow prison; an air of gloom and dreariness seems, in my eyes at least, to hang about the scene, and to impart to it a squalid and sickly hue.

Many eyes, that have long since been closed in the grave, have looked round upon that scene lightly enough, when entering the gate of the old Marshalsea Prison for the first time; for despair seldom comes with the first severe shock of misfortune. A man has confidence in untried friends, he remembers the many offers of service so freely made by his boon companions when he wanted them not; he has hope – the hope of happy inexperience – and however he may bend beneath the first shock, it springs up in his bosom, and flourishes there for a brief space, until it droops beneath the blight of disappointment and neglect. How soon have those same eyes, deeply sunken in the head, glared from faces wasted with famine, and sallow from confinement, in days when it was no figure of speech to say that debtors rotted in prison, with no hope of release, and no prospect of liberty! The atrocity in its full extent no longer exists, but there is enough of it left to give rise to occurrences that make the heart bleed.

Twenty years ago, that pavement was worn with the footsteps of a mother and child, who, day by day, so surely as the morning came, presented themselves at the prison gate; often after a night of restless misery and anxious thoughts, were they there, a full hour too soon, and then the young mother turning meekly away, would lead the child to the old bridge, and raising him in her arms to show him the glistening water, tinted with the light of the morning's sun, and stirring with all the bustling preparations for business and pleasure that the river presented at that early hour, endeavour to interest his thoughts in the objects before him. But she would quickly set him down, and hiding her face in her shawl, give vent to the tears that blinded her; for no expression of interest or amusement lighted up his thin and sickly face. His recollections were few enough, but they were all of one kind – all connected with the poverty and misery of his parents. Hour after hour had he sat on his mother's knee, and with childish sympathy watched the tears that stole down her face, and then crept quietly away into some dark corner, and sobbed himself to sleep. The hard realities of the world, with many of its worst privations – hunger and thirst, and cold and want – had all come home to him, from the first dawnings of reason; and though the form of childhood was there, its light heart, its merry laugh, and sparkling eyes were wanting.

The father and mother looked on upon this, and upon each other, with thoughts of agony they dared not breathe in words. The healthy, strong-made man, who could have borne almost any fatigue of active exertion, was wasting beneath the close confinement and unhealthy atmosphere of a crowded prison. The slight and delicate woman was sinking beneath the combined effects of bodily and mental illness. The child's young heart was breaking.

Winter came, and with it weeks of cold and heavy rain. The poor girl had removed to a wretched apartment close to the spot of her husband's imprisonment; and though the change had been rendered necessary by their increasing poverty, she was happier now, for she was nearer him. For two months, she and her little companion watched the opening of the gate as usual. One day she failed to come, for the first time. Another morning arrived, and she came alone. The child was dead.

They little know, who coldly talk of the poor man's bereavements, as a happy release from pain to the departed, and a merciful relief from expense to the survivor – they little know, I say, what the agony of those bereavements is. A silent look of affection and regard when all other eyes are turned coldly away – the consciousness that we possess the sympathy and affection of one being when all others have deserted us – is a hold, a stay, a comfort, in the deepest affliction, which no wealth could purchase, or power bestow. The child had sat at his parents' feet for hours together, with his little hands patiently folded in each other, and his thin wan face raised towards them. They had seen him pine away, from day to day; and though his brief existence had been a joyless one, and he was now removed to that peace and rest which, child as he was, he had never known in this world, they were his parents, and his loss sank deep into their souls.

It was plain to those who looked upon the mother's altered face, that death must soon close the scene of her adversity and trial. Her husband's fellow-prisoners shrank from obtruding on his grief and misery, and left to himself alone, the small room he had previously occupied in common with two companions. She shared it with him; and lingering on without pain, but without hope, her life ebbed slowly away.

She had fainted one evening in her husband's arms, and he had borne her to the open window, to revive her with the air, when the light of the moon falling full upon her face, showed him a change upon her features, which made him stagger beneath her weight, like a helpless infant.

"Set me down, George," she said faintly. He did so, and seating himself beside her, covered his face with his hands, and burst into tears.

"It is very hard to leave you, George," she said; "but it is God's will, and you must bear it for my sake. Oh! how I thank Him for having taken our boy! He is happy, and in heaven now. What would he have done here, without his mother!"

"You shall not die, Mary, you shall not die;" said the husband, starting up. He paced hurriedly to and fro, striking his head with his clenched fists; then reseating himself beside her, and supporting her in his arms, added more calmly, "Rouse yourself, my dear girl. Pray, pray do. You will revive yet."

"Never again, George; never again," said the dying woman. "Let them lay me by my poor boy now, but promise me, that if ever you leave this dreadful place, and should grow rich, you will have us removed to some quiet country churchyard, a long, long way off – very far from here – where we can rest in peace. Dear George, promise me you will."

"I do, I do," said the man, throwing himself passionately on his knees before her. "Speak to me, Mary, another word; one look – but one!"

He ceased to speak: for the arm that clasped his neck grew stiff and heavy. A deep sigh escaped from the wasted form before him; the lips moved, and a smile played upon the face; but the lips were pallid, and the smile faded into a rigid and ghastly stare. He was alone in the world.

That night, in the silence and desolation of his miserable room, the wretched man knelt down by the dead body of his wife, and called on God to witness a terrible oath, that from that hour, he devoted himself to revenge her death and that of his child; that thenceforth to the last moment of his life, his whole energies should be directed to this one object; that his revenge should be protracted and terrible; that his hatred should be undying and inextinguishable; and should hunt its object through the world.

The deepest despair, and passion scarcely human, had made such fierce ravages on his face and form, in that one night, that his companions in misfortune shrank affrighted from him as he passed by. His eyes were bloodshot and heavy, his face a deadly white, and his body bent as if with age. He had bitten his under lip nearly through in the violence of his mental suffering, and the blood which had flowed from the wound had trickled down his chin, and stained his shirt and neckerchief. No tear, or sound of complaint escaped him; but the unsettled look, and disordered haste with which he paced up and down the yard, denoted the fever which was burning within.

It was necessary that his wife's body should be removed from the prison, without delay. He received the communication with perfect calmness, and acquiesced in its propriety. Nearly all the inmates of the prison had assembled to witness its removal; they fell back on either side when the widower appeared; he walked hurriedly forward, and stationed himself, alone, in a little railed area close to the lodge gate, from whence the crowd, with an instinctive feeling of delicacy, had retired. The rude coffin was borne slowly forward on men's shoulders. A dead silence pervaded the throng, broken only by the audible lamentations of the women, and the shuffling steps of the bearers on the stone pavement. They reached the spot where the bereaved husband stood: and stopped. He laid his hand upon the coffin, and mechanically adjusting the pall with which it was covered, motioned them onward. The turnkeys in the prison lobby took off their hats as it passed through, and in another moment the heavy gate closed behind it. He looked vacantly upon the crowd, and fell heavily to the ground.

Although for many weeks after this, he was watched, night and day, in the wildest ravings of fever, neither the consciousness of his loss, nor the recollection of the vow he had made, ever left him for a moment. Scenes changed before his eyes, place succeeded place, and event followed event, in all the hurry of delirium; but they were all connected in some way with the great object of his mind. He was sailing over a boundless expanse of sea, with a blood-red sky above, and the angry waters, lashed into fury beneath, boiling and eddying up, on every side. There was another vessel before them, toiling and labouring in the howling storm; her canvas fluttering in ribbons from the mast, and her deck thronged with figures who were lashed to the sides, over which huge waves every instant burst, sweeping away some devoted creatures into the foaming sea. Onward they bore, amidst the roaring mass of water, with a speed and force which nothing could resist; and striking the stem of the foremost vessel, crushed her beneath their keel. From the huge whirlpool which the sinking wreck occasioned, arose a shriek so loud and shrill – the death-cry of a hundred drowning creatures, blended into one fierce yell – that it rung far above the war-cry of the elements, and echoed, and re-echoed till it seemed to pierce air, sky, and ocean. But what was that – that old gray head that rose above the water's surface, and with looks of agony, and screams for aid, buffeted with the waves! One look, and he had sprung from the vessel's side, and with vigorous strokes was swimming towards it. He reached it; he was close upon it. They were *his* features. The old man saw him coming, and vainly strove to elude his grasp. But he clasped him tight, and dragged him beneath the water. Down, down with him, fifty fathoms down; his struggles grew fainter and fainter, until they wholly ceased. He was dead; he had killed him, and had kept his oath.

He was traversing the scorching sands of a mighty desert, barefoot and alone. The sand choked and blinded him; its fine thin grains entered the very pores of his skin, and irritated him almost to madness. Gigantic masses of the same material, carried forward by the wind, and shone through by the burning sun, stalked in the distance like pillars of living fire. The bones of men, who had perished in the dreary waste, lay scattered at his feet; a fearful light fell on everything around; so far as the eye could reach, nothing but objects of dread and horror presented themselves. Vainly striving to utter a cry of terror, with his tongue cleaving to his mouth, he rushed madly forward. Armed with supernatural strength, he waded through the sand, until, exhausted with fatigue and thirst, he fell senseless on the earth. What fragrant coolness revived him; what gushing sound was that? Water! It was indeed a well; and the clear fresh stream was running at his feet. He drank deeply of it, and throwing his aching limbs upon the bank, sank into a delicious trance. The sound of approaching footsteps roused him. An old gray-headed man tottered forward to slake his burning thirst. It was *he* again! He wound his arms round the old man's body, and held him back. He struggled, and shrieked for water – for but one drop of water to save his life! But he held the old man firmly, and watched his agonies with greedy eyes; and when his lifeless head fell forward on his bosom, he rolled the corpse from him with his feet.

When the fever left him, and consciousness returned, he awoke to find himself rich and free, to hear that the parent who would have let him die in jail – *would*! who *had* let those who were far dearer to him than his own existence die of want, and sickness of heart that medicine cannot cure – had been found dead in his bed of down. He had had all the heart to leave his son a beggar, but proud even of his health and strength, had put off the act till it was too late, and now might gnash his teeth in the other world, at the thought of the wealth his remissness had left him. He awoke to this, and he awoke to more. To recollect the purpose for which he lived, and to remember that his enemy was his wife's own father – the man who had cast him into prison, and who, when his daughter and her child sued at his feet for mercy, had spurned them from his door. Oh, how he cursed the weakness that prevented him from being up, and active, in his scheme of vengeance!

He caused himself to be carried from the scene of his loss and misery, and conveyed to a quiet residence on the sea-coast; not in the hope of recovering his peace of mind or happiness, for both were fled for ever; but to restore his prostrate energies, and meditate on his darling object. And here, some evil spirit cast in his way the opportunity for his first, most horrible revenge.

It was summer-time; and wrapped in his gloomy thoughts, he would issue from his solitary lodgings early in the evening, and wandering along a narrow path beneath the cliffs, to a wild and lonely spot that had struck his fancy in his ramblings, seat himself on some fallen fragment of the rock, and burying his face in his hands, remain there for hours – sometimes until night had completely closed in, and the long shadows of the frowning cliffs above his head cast a thick, black darkness on every object near him.

He was seated here, one calm evening, in his old position, now and then raising his head to watch the flight of a sea-gull, or carry his eye along the glorious crimson path, which, commencing in the middle of the ocean, seemed to lead to its very verge where the sun was setting, when the profound stillness of the spot was broken by a loud cry for help; he listened, doubtful of his having heard aright, when the cry was repeated with even greater vehemence than before, and, starting to his feet, he hastened in the direction whence it proceeded.

The tale told itself at once: some scattered garments lay on the beach; a human head was just visible above the waves at a little distance from the shore; and an old man, wringing his hands in agony, was running to and fro, shrieking for assistance. The invalid, whose strength was now sufficiently restored, threw off his coat, and rushed towards the sea, with the intention of plunging in, and dragging the drowning man ashore.

"Hasten here, Sir, in God's name; help, help, sir, for the love of Heaven. He is my son, Sir, my only son!" said the old man frantically, as he advanced to meet him. "My only son, Sir, and he is dying before his father's eyes!"

At the first word the old man uttered, the stranger checked himself in his career, and, folding his arms, stood perfectly motionless.

"Great God!" exclaimed the old man, recoiling, "Heyling!"

The stranger smiled, and was silent.

"Heyling!" said the old man wildly; "my boy, Heyling, my dear boy, look, look!" Gasping for breath, the miserable father pointed to the spot where the young man was struggling for life.

"Hark!" said the old man. "He cries once more. He is alive yet. Heyling, save him, save him!"

The stranger smiled again, and remained immovable as a statue.

"I have wronged you," shrieked the old man, falling on his knees, and clasping his hands together. "Be revenged; take my all, my life; cast me into the water at your feet, and, if human nature can repress a struggle, I will die, without stirring hand or foot. Do it, Heyling, do it, but save my boy; he is so young, Heyling, so young to die!"

"Listen," said the stranger, grasping the old man fiercely by the wrist; "I will have life for life, and here is *one*. *My* child died, before his father's eyes, a far more agonising and painful death than that young slanderer of his sister's worth is meeting while I speak. You laughed – laughed in your daughter's face, where death had already set his hand – at our sufferings, then. What think you of them now! See there, see there!"

As the stranger spoke, he pointed to the sea. A faint cry died away upon its surface; the last powerful struggle of the dying man agitated the rippling waves for a few seconds;

and the spot where he had gone down into his early grave, was undistinguishable from the surrounding water.

Three years had elapsed, when a gentleman alighted from a private carriage at the door of a London attorney, then well known as a man of no great nicety in his professional dealings, and requested a private interview on business of importance. Although evidently not past the prime of life, his face was pale, haggard, and dejected; and it did not require the acute perception of the man of business, to discern at a glance, that disease or suffering had done more to work a change in his appearance, than the mere hand of time could have accomplished in twice the period of his whole life.

"I wish you to undertake some legal business for me," said the stranger.

The attorney bowed obsequiously, and glanced at a large packet which the gentleman carried in his hand. His visitor observed the look, and proceeded.

"It is no common business," said he; "nor have these papers reached my hands without long trouble and great expense."

The attorney cast a still more anxious look at the packet; and his visitor, untying the string that bound it, disclosed a quantity of promissory notes, with copies of deeds, and other documents.

"Upon these papers," said the client, "the man whose name they bear, has raised, as you will see, large sums of money, for years past. There was a tacit understanding between him and the men into whose hands they originally went – and from whom I have by degrees purchased the whole, for treble and quadruple their nominal value – that these loans should be from time to time renewed, until a given period had elapsed. Such an understanding is nowhere expressed. He has sustained many losses of late; and these obligations accumulating upon him at once, would crush him to the earth."

"The whole amount is many thousands of pounds," said the attorney, looking over the papers.

"It is," said the client.

"What are we to do?" inquired the man of business.

"Do!" replied the client, with sudden vehemence. "Put every engine of the law in force, every trick that ingenuity can devise and rascality execute; fair means and foul; the open oppression of the law, aided by all the craft of its most ingenious practitioners. I would have him die a harassing and lingering death. Ruin him, seize and sell his lands and goods, drive him from house and home, and drag him forth a beggar in his old age, to die in a common jail."

"But the costs, my dear Sir, the costs of all this," reasoned the attorney, when he had recovered from his momentary surprise. "If the defendant be a man of straw, who is to pay the costs, Sir?"

"Name any sum," said the stranger, his hand trembling so violently with excitement, that he could scarcely hold the pen he seized as he spoke— "any sum, and it is yours. Don't be afraid to name it, man. I shall not think it dear, if you gain my object."

The attorney named a large sum, at hazard, as the advance he should require to secure himself against the possibility of loss; but more with the view of ascertaining how far his client was really disposed to go, than with any idea that he would comply with the demand. The stranger wrote a cheque upon his banker, for the whole amount, and left him.

The draft was duly honoured, and the attorney, finding that his strange client might be safely relied upon, commenced his work in earnest. For more than two years afterwards,

Mr. Heyling would sit whole days together, in the office, poring over the papers as they accumulated, and reading again and again, his eyes gleaming with joy, the letters of remonstrance, the prayers for a little delay, the representations of the certain ruin in which the opposite party must be involved, which poured in, as suit after suit, and process after process, was commenced. To all applications for a brief indulgence, there was but one reply – the money must be paid. Land, house, furniture, each in its turn, was taken under some one of the numerous executions which were issued; and the old man himself would have been immured in prison had he not escaped the vigilance of the officers, and fled.

The implacable animosity of Heyling, so far from being satiated by the success of his persecution, increased a hundredfold with the ruin he inflicted. On being informed of the old man's flight, his fury was unbounded. He gnashed his teeth with rage, tore the hair from his head, and assailed with horrid imprecations the men who had been intrusted with the writ. He was only restored to comparative calmness by repeated assurances of the certainty of discovering the fugitive. Agents were sent in quest of him, in all directions; every stratagem that could be invented was resorted to, for the purpose of discovering his place of retreat; but it was all in vain. Half a year had passed over, and he was still undiscovered.

At length late one night, Heyling, of whom nothing had been seen for many weeks before, appeared at his attorney's private residence, and sent up word that a gentleman wished to see him instantly. Before the attorney, who had recognised his voice from above stairs, could order the servant to admit him, he had rushed up the staircase, and entered the drawing-room pale and breathless. Having closed the door, to prevent being overheard, he sank into a chair, and said, in a low voice—

"Hush! I have found him at last."

"No!" said the attorney. "Well done, my dear sir, well done."

"He lies concealed in a wretched lodging in Camden Town," said Heyling. "Perhaps it is as well we *did* lose sight of him, for he has been living alone there, in the most abject misery, all the time, and he is poor – very poor."

"Very good," said the attorney. "You will have the caption made tomorrow, of course?"

"Yes," replied Heyling. "Stay! No! The next day. You are surprised at my wishing to postpone it," he added, with a ghastly smile; "but I had forgotten. The next day is an anniversary in his life: let it be done then."

"Very good," said the attorney. "Will you write down instructions for the officer?"

"No; let him meet me here, at eight in the evening, and I will accompany him myself."

They met on the appointed night, and, hiring a hackney-coach, directed the driver to stop at that corner of the old Pancras Road, at which stands the parish workhouse. By the time they alighted there, it was quite dark; and, proceeding by the dead wall in front of the Veterinary Hospital, they entered a small by-street, which is, or was at that time, called Little College Street, and which, whatever it may be now, was in those days a desolate place enough, surrounded by little else than fields and ditches.

Having drawn the travelling-cap he had on half over his face, and muffled himself in his cloak, Heyling stopped before the meanest-looking house in the street, and knocked gently at the door. It was at once opened by a woman, who dropped a curtsey of recognition, and Heyling, whispering the officer to remain below, crept gently upstairs, and, opening the door of the front room, entered at once.

The object of his search and his unrelenting animosity, now a decrepit old man, was seated at a bare deal table, on which stood a miserable candle. He started on the entrance of the stranger, and rose feebly to his feet.

"What now, what now?" said the old man. "What fresh misery is this? What do you want here?"

"A word with *you*," replied Heyling. As he spoke, he seated himself at the other end of the table, and, throwing off his cloak and cap, disclosed his features.

The old man seemed instantly deprived of speech. He fell backward in his chair, and, clasping his hands together, gazed on the apparition with a mingled look of abhorrence and fear.

"This day six years," said Heyling, "I claimed the life you owed me for my child's. Beside the lifeless form of your daughter, old man, I swore to live a life of revenge. I have never swerved from my purpose for a moment's space; but if I had, one thought of her uncomplaining, suffering look, as she drooped away, or of the starving face of our innocent child, would have nerved me to my task. My first act of requital you well remember: this is my last."

The old man shivered, and his hands dropped powerless by his side.

"I leave England tomorrow," said Heyling, after a moment's pause. "To-night I consign you to the living death to which you devoted her – a hopeless prison—"

He raised his eyes to the old man's countenance, and paused. He lifted the light to his face, set it gently down, and left the apartment.

"You had better see to the old man," he said to the woman, as he opened the door, and motioned the officer to follow him into the street. "I think he is ill." The woman closed the door, ran hastily upstairs, and found him lifeless.

Beneath a plain gravestone, in one of the most peaceful and secluded churchyards in Kent, where wild flowers mingle with the grass, and the soft landscape around forms the fairest spot in the garden of England, lie the bones of the young mother and her gentle child. But the ashes of the father do not mingle with theirs; nor, from that night forward, did the attorney ever gain the remotest clue to the subsequent history of his queer client.

**If you enjoyed this, you might also like...**
A Madman's Manuscript, see page 279
The Ghost in the Bride's Chamber, see page 267

# The Mother's Eyes

**I HELD** a lieutenant's commission in his Majesty's army, and served abroad in the campaigns of 1677 and 1678. The treaty of Nimeguen being concluded, I returned home, and retiring from the service, withdrew to a small estate lying a few miles east of London, which I had recently acquired in right of my wife.

This is the last night I have to live, and I will set down the naked truth without disguise. I was never a brave man, and had always been from my childhood of a secret, sullen, distrustful nature. I speak of myself as if I had passed from the world; for while I write this, my grave is digging, and my name is written in the black-book of death.

Soon after my return to England, my only brother was seized with mortal illness. This circumstance gave me slight or no pain; for since we had been men, we had associated but very little together. He was open-hearted and generous, handsomer than I, more accomplished, and generally beloved. Those who sought my acquaintance abroad or at home, because they were friends of his, seldom attached themselves to me long, and would usually say, in our first conversation, that they were surprised to find two brothers so unlike in their manners and appearance. It was my habit to lead them on to this avowal; for I knew what comparisons they must draw between us; and having a rankling envy in my heart, I sought to justify it to myself.

We had married two sisters. This additional tie between us, as it may appear to some, only estranged us the more. His wife knew me well. I never struggled with any secret jealousy or gall when she was present but that woman knew it as well as I did. I never raised my eyes at such times but I found hers fixed upon me; I never bent them on the ground or looked another way but I felt that she overlooked me always. It was an inexpressible relief to me when we quarrelled, and a greater relief still when I heard abroad that she was dead. It seems to me now as if some strange and terrible foreshadowing of what has happened since must have hung over us then. I was afraid of her; she haunted me; her fixed and steady look comes back upon me now, like the memory of a dark dream, and makes my blood run cold.

She died shortly after giving birth to a child – a boy. When my brother knew that all hope of his won recovery was past, he called my wife to his bedside, and confided this orphan, a child of four years old, to her protection. He bequeathed to him all the property he had, and willed that, in the case of his child's death, it should pass to my wife, as the only acknowledgement he could make her for her care and love. He exchanged a few brotherly words with me, deploring our long separation; and being exhausted, fell into slumber, from which he never awoke.

We had no children; and as there had been a strong affection between the sisters, and my wife had almost supplied the place of a mother to this boy, she loved him as if he had been her own. The child was ardently attached to her; but he was his mother's image in face and spirit, and always mistrusted me.

I can scarcely fix the date when the feeling first came upon me; but I soon began to be uneasy when this child was by. I never roused myself from some moody train of thought but I marked him looking at me; not with mere childish wonder, but with something of the purpose and meaning that I had so often noted in his mother. It was no effort of my fancy, founded on close resemblance of feature and expression. I never could look the boy down. He feared me, but seemed by some instinct to despise me while he did so; and even when he drew back beneath my gaze – as he would when we were alone, to get nearer to the door – he would keep his bright eyes on me still.

Perhaps I hide the truth from myself, but I do think that, when this began, I meditated to do him any wrong. I may have thought how serviceable his inheritance would be to us, and may have wished him dead; but I believe I had no thought of compassing his death. Neither did the idea come upon me at once, but by very slow degrees, presenting itself at first in dim shapes at a very great distance, as men may think of an earthquake or the last day; then drawing nearer and nearer, and losing something of its horror and improbability; then coming to be part and parcel – nay nearly the whole sum and substance – of my daily thoughts, and resolving itself into a question of means and safety; not of doing or abstaining from the deed.

While this was going on within me, I never could bear that the child should see me looking at him, and yet I was under a fascination which made it a kind of business with me to contemplate his slight and fragile figure and think how easily it might be done. Sometimes I would steal upstairs and watch him as he slept; but usually I hovered in the garden near the window of the room in which he learnt his little tasks; and there, as he sat upon a low seat beside my wife, I would peer at him for hours together from behind a tree; starting like the guilty wretch I was, at every rustling of a leaf, and still gliding back to look and start again.

Hard by our cottage, but quite out of sight, and (if there were any wind astir) of hearing too, was a deep sheet of water. I spent days in shaping with my pocket-knife a rough model of a boat, which I finished at last and dropped in the child's way. Then I withdrew to a secret place, which he must pass if he stole away alone to swim this bauble, and lurked there for his coming. He came neither that day not the next, though I waited from noon till nightfall. I was sure that I had him in my net, for I had heard him prattling of the toy, and knew that in his infant pleasure he kept it by his side in bed. I felt no weariness or fatigue, but waited patiently, and on the third day he passed me, running joyously along, with his silken hair streaming in the wind, and he singing – god have mercy upon me! – singing a merry ballad – who could hardly lisp the words.

I stole down after him, creeping under certain shrubs which grow in that place, and none but devils know with what terror I, a strong, full-grown man, tracked the footsteps of that baby as he approached the water's brink. I was close upon him, had sunk upon my knee and raised my hand to thrust him in, when he saw my shadow in the stream and turned him round.

His mother's ghost was looking from his eyes. The sun burst forth from behind a cloud; it shone in the bright sky, the glistening earth, the clear water, the sparkling drops of rain upon the leaves. There were eyes in everything. The whole great universe of light was there to see the murder done. I know not what he said; he came out of bold and manly blood, and, child as he was, he did not crouch or fawn upon me. I heard him cry that he would try to love me – not that he did – and then I saw him running back towards the house. The next I saw was my own sword naked in my hand, and he at my feet stark dead – dabbled here and there with blood, but otherwise no different from what I had seen him in his sleep – in the same attitude too, with his cheek resting upon his little hand.

I took him in my arms and laid him – very gently now that he was dead – in a thicket. My wife was from home that day, and would not return until the next. Our bedroom window, the only sleeping-room on that side of the house, was but a few feet from the ground, and I resolved to descend from it at night and bury him in the garden. I had no thought that I had failed in my design, no thought that the water would be dragged and nothing found, that the money must now lie waste, since I must encourage the idea that the child was lost or stolen. All my thoughts were bound up and knotted together in the one absorbing necessity of hiding what I had done.

How I felt when they came to tell me that the child was missing, when I ordered scouts in all directions, when I gasped and trembled at every one's approach, no tongue can tell or mind of man can conceive. I buried him that night. When I parted the boughs and looked into the dark thicket, there was a glow-worm shining like the visible spirit of God upon the murdered child. I glanced down into his grave when I had placed him there, and still it gleamed upon his breast; an eye of fire looking up to Heaven in supplication to the stars that watched me at my work.

I had to meet my wife, and break the news, and give her hope that the child would soon be found. All this I did – with some appearance, I suppose, of being sincere, for I was the object of no suspicion. This done, I sat at the bedroom window all day long, and watched the spot where the dreadful secret lay.

It was in a piece of ground which had been dug up to be newly turfed, and which I had chosen on that account, as the traces of my spade were less likely to attract attention. The men who laid down the grass must have thought me mad. I called to them continually to expedite their work, ran out and worked beside them, trod down the earth with my feet, and hurried them with frantic eagerness. They had finished their task before night, and then I thought myself comparatively safe.

I slept – not as men do who awake refreshed and cheerful, but I did sleep, passing from vague and shadowy dreams of being hunted down, to visions of the plot of grass, through which now had a hand, and now a foot, and now the head itself was starting out. At this point I always woke and stole to the window, to make sure that it was really not so. That done, I crept to bed again; and thus I spent the night in fits and starts, getting up and lying down a full twenty times, and dreaming the same dream over and over again – which was far worse than lying awake, for every dream had a whole night's suffering of its own. Once I thought the child was alive, that I had never tried to kill him. To wake from that dream was the most dreadful agony of all.

The next day I sat at the window again, never once taking my eyes from the place, which, although it was covered by the grass, was as plain to me – its shape, its size, its depth, its jagged sides, and all – as if it had been open to the light of day. When a servant walked across it, I felt as if he must sink in; when he had passed, I looked to see that his feet had not worn the edges. If a bird lighted there, I was in terror lest by some tremendous interposition it should be instrumental in the discovery; if a breath of air sighed across it, to me is whispered murder. There was not a sight or a sound – how ordinary, mean, or unimportant soever – but was fraught with fear.

On the fourth there came to a gate one who had served with me abroad, accompanied by a brother officer of whom I had never seen. I felt that I could not bear to be out of sight of the place. It was a summer evening, and I bade my people take a table and a flask of wine into the garden. Then I sat down WITH MY CHAIR UPON THE GRAVE and being assured that nobody could disturb it now without my knowledge, tried to drink and talk.

They hoped that my wife was well – that she was not obliged to keep her chamber – that they had not frightened her away. What could I do but tell them with a faltering tongue about the child? The officer whom I did not know was a down-looking man, and kept his eyes upon the ground while I was speaking. Even that terrified me. I could not divest myself of the idea that he saw something there which caused him to suspect the truth. I asked him hurriedly if he supposed that – and stopped. "That the child has been murdered?" said he, looking mildly at me: "O no! What could a man gain by murdering a poor child?" I could have told him what a man gained by such a deed, no one better: but I held my peace and shivered as with an ague.

Mistaking my emotion, they were endeavouring to cheer me with the hope that the boy would certainly be found – great cheer that was for me! – when we heard a low deep howl, and presently there sprung over the wall two great dogs, who, bounding into the garden, repeated the baying sound we had heard before.

"Bloodhounds!" cried my visitors.

What need to tell me that! I had never seen one of that kind in all my life, but I knew what they were and for what purpose they had come. I grasped the elbows of my chair, and neither spoke a word nor moved.

"They are of the genuine breed," said the man whom I had known abroad, "and being out for exercise have no doubt escaped from their keeper."

Both he and his friend turned to look at the dogs, who with their noses to the ground moved restlessly about, running to and fro, and up and down, and across, and round in circles, careering about like wild things, and all this time taking no notice of us, but ever and again repeating the yell we had heard already, then dropping their noses to the ground again and tracking earnestly here and there. They now began to snuff the earth more eagerly than they had done yet, and although they were still very restless, no longer beat about in such wide circuits, but kept near to one spot, and constantly diminished the distance between themselves and me.

At last they came up close to the chair upon which I sat, and raising their frightful howl once more, tried to tear away the wooden rails that kept them from the ground beneath. I saw how I looked, in the faces of the two who were with me.

"They scent some prey," said they, both together.

"They scent no prey!" cried I.

"in heaven's name, move!" said the one I knew, very earnestly, "or you will be torn to pieces."

"Let them tear me limb from limb, I'll never leave this place!" cried I. "Are dogs to hurry men to shameful deaths? Hew them down, cut them in pieces."

"There is some foul mystery here!" said the officer whom I did not know, drawing his sword. "In King Charles's name, assist me to secure this man."

They both set upon me and forced me away, though I fought and bit and caught at them like a madman. After a struggle, they got me quietly between them; and then, my God! I saw the angry dogs tearing at the earth and throwing it up into the air like water.

What more have I to tell? That I fell upon my knees, and with chattering teeth confessed the truth, and prayed to be forgiven. That I have since denied, and now confess to it again. That I have been tried for the crime, found guilty, and sentenced. That I have not the courage to anticipate my doom, or to bear up manfully against it. That I have no compassion, no consolation, no hope, no friend. That my wife has happily lost for the time those faculties which would enable her to know my misery or hers. That I am alone in this stone dungeon with my evil spirit, and that I die tomorrow.

**If you enjoyed this, you might also like...**
The Ghost in the Bride's Chamber, see page 267
The Convict's Return, see page 284

# Well-Authenticated Rappings

**THE WRITER,** who is about to record three spiritual experiences of his own in the present truthful article, deems it essential to state that, down to the time of his being favored therewith, he had not been a believer in rappings, or tippings. His vulgar notions of the spiritual world, represented its inhabitants as probably advanced, even beyond the intellectual supremacy of Peckham or New York; and it seemed to him, considering the large amount of ignorance, presumption, and folly with which this earth is blessed, so very unnecessary to call in immaterial Beings to gratify mankind with bad spelling and worse nonsense, that the presumption was strongly against those respected films taking the trouble to come here, for no better purpose than to make supererogatory idiots of themselves.

This was the writer's gross and fleshy state of mind at so late a period as the twenty-sixth of December last. On that memorable morning, at about two hours after daylight, – that is to say, at twenty minutes before ten by the writer's watch, which stood on a table at his bedside, and which can be seen at the publishing-office, and identified as a demi-chronometer made by BAUTTE of Geneva, and numbered 67,709 – on that memorable morning, at about two hours after daylight, the writer, starting up in bed with his hand to his forehead, distinctly felt seventeen heavy throbs or beats in that region. They were accompanied by a feeling of pain in the locality, and by a general sensation not unlike that which is usually attendant on biliousness. Yielding to a sudden impulse, the writer asked:

"What is this?"

The answer immediately returned (in throbs or beats upon the forehead) was, "Yesterday."

The writer then demanded, being as yet but imperfectly awake:

"What was yesterday?"

Answer: "Christmas Day."

The writer, being now quite come to himself, inquired, "Who is the Medium in this case?"

Answer: "Clarkins."

Question: "Mrs. Clarkins, or Mr. Clarkins?"

Answer: "Both."

Question: "By Mr., do you mean Old Clarkins, or Young Clarkins?"

Answer: "Both."

Now, the writer had dined with his friend Clarkins (who can be appealed to, at the State-Paper Office) on the previous day, and spirits had actually been discussed at that dinner, under various aspects. It was in the writer's remembrance, also, that both Clarkins Senior and Clarkins Junior had been very active in such discussion, and had rather pressed it on the company. Mrs. Clarkins too had joined in it with animation, and had observed, in a joyous if not an exuberant tone, that it was "only once a year."

Convinced by these tokens that the rapping was of spiritual origin, the writer proceeded as follows:

"Who are you?"

The rapping on the forehead was resumed, but in a most incoherent manner. It was for some time impossible to make sense of it. After a pause, the writer (holding his head) repeated the inquiry in a solemn voice, accompanied with a groan:

"Who ARE you?"

Incoherent rappings were still the response.

The writer then asked, solemnly as before, and with another groan:

"What is your name?"

The reply was conveyed in a sound exactly resembling a loud hiccough. It afterwards appeared that this spiritual voice was distinctly heard by Alexander Pumpion, the writer's footboy (seventh son of Widow Pumpion, mangler), in an adjoining chamber.

Question: "Your name cannot be Hiccough? Hiccough is not a proper name?"

No answer being returned, the writer said: "I solemnly charge you, by our joint knowledge of Clarkins the Medium – of Clarkins Senior, Clarkins Junior, and Clarkins Mrs. – to reveal your name!"

The reply rapped out with extreme unwillingness, was, "Sloe-Juice, Logwood, Blackberry."

This appeared to the writer sufficiently like a parody on Cobweb, Moth, and Mustard-Seed, in the Midsummer Night's Dream, to justify the retort:

"*That* is not your name?"

The rapping spirit admitted, "No."

"Then what do they generally call you?"

A pause.

"I ask you, what do they generally call you?"

The spirit, evidently under coercion, responded, in a most solemn manner, "Port!"

This awful communication caused the writer to lie prostrate, on the verge of insensibility, for a quarter of an hour: during which the rappings were continued with violence, and a host of spiritual appearances passed before his eyes, of a black hue, and greatly resembling tadpoles endowed with the power of occasionally spinning themselves out into musical notes as they swam down into space. After contemplating a vast Legion of these appearances, the writer demanded of the rapping spirit:

"How am I to present you to myself? What, upon the whole, is most like you?"

The terrific reply was, "Blacking."

As soon as the writer could command his emotion, which was now very great, he inquired:

"Had I better take something?"

Answer: "Yes."

Question: "Can I write for something?"

Answer: "Yes."

A pencil and a slip of paper which were on the table at the bedside immediately bounded into the writer's hand, and he found himself forced to write (in a curiously unsteady character and all down-hill, whereas his own writing is remarkably plain and straight) the following spiritual note.

"Mr. O. D. S. Pooney presents his compliments to Messrs. Bell and Company, Pharmaceutical chemists, Oxford Street, opposite to Portland Street, and begs them to have the goodness to send him by Bearer a five- grain genuine blue pill and a genuine black draught of corresponding power."

But, before entrusting this document to Alexander Pumpion (who unfortunately lost it on his return, if he did not even lay himself open to the suspicion of having wilfully inserted it into one of the holes of a perambulating chesnut-roaster, to see how it would flare), the writer resolved to test the rapping spirit with one conclusive question. He therefore asked, in a slow and impressive voice:

"Will these remedies make my stomach ache?"

It is impossible to describe the prophetic confidence of the reply. "YES." The assurance was fully borne out by the result, as the writer will long remember; and after this experience it were needless to observe that he could no longer doubt.

The next communication of a deeply interesting character with which the writer was favored, occurred on one of the leading lines of railway. The circumstances under which the revelation was made to him – on the second day of January in the present year – were these: He had recovered from the effects of the previous remarkable visitation, and had again been partaking of the compliments of the season. The preceding day had been passed in hilarity. He was on his way to a celebrated town, a well-known commercial emporium where he had business to transact, and had lunched in a somewhat greater hurry than is usual on railways, in consequence of the train being behind time. His lunch had been very reluctantly administered to him by a young lady behind a counter. She had been much occupied at the time with the arrangement of her hair and dress, and her expressive countenance had denoted disdain. It will be seen that this young lady proved to be a powerful Medium.

The writer had returned to the first-class carriage in which he chanced to be travelling alone, the train had resumed its motion, he had fallen into a doze, and the unimpeachable watch already mentioned recorded forty-five minutes to have elapsed since his interview with the Medium, when he was aroused by a very singular musical instrument. This instrument, he found to his admiration not unmixed with alarm, was performing in his inside. Its tones were of a low and rippling character, difficult to describe; but, if such a comparison may be admitted, resembling a melodious heart-burn. Be this as it may, they suggested that humble sensation to the writer.

Concurrently with his becoming aware of the phenomenon in question, the writer perceived that his attention was being solicited by a hurried succession of angry raps in the stomach, and a pressure on the chest. A sceptic no more, he immediately communed with the spirit. The dialogue was as follows:

Question: "Do I know your name?"

Answer: "*I* should think so!"

Question: "Does it begin with a P?"

Answer (second time): "*I* should think so!"

Question: "Have you two names, and does each begin with a P?"

Answer (third time): "*I* should think so!"

Question: "I charge you to lay aside this levity, and inform me what you are called."

The spirit, after reflecting for a few seconds, spelt out P. O. R. K. The musical instrument then performed a short and fragmentary strain. The spirit then recommenced, and spelt out the word "P. I. E."

Now, this precise article of pastry, this particular viand or comestible, actually had formed – let the scoffer know – the staple of the writer's lunch, and actually had been handed to him by the young lady whom he now knew to be a powerful Medium! Highly gratified by the conviction thus forced upon his mind that the knowledge with which he conversed was not of this world, the writer pursued the dialogue.

Question: "They call you Pork Pie?"

Answer: "Yes."

Question (which the writer timidly put,

after struggling with some natural reluctance), "Are you, in fact, Pork Pie?"

Answer: "Yes."

It were vain to attempt a description of the mental comfort and relief which the writer derived from this important answer. He proceeded:

Question: "Let us understand each other. A part of you is Pork, and a part of you is Pie?"

Answer: "Exactly so."

Question: "What is your Pie-part made of?"

Answer: "Lard." Then came a sorrowful strain from the musical instrument. Then the word "Dripping."

Question: "How am I to present you to my mind? What are you most like?"

Answer (very quickly): "Lead."

A sense of despondency overcame the writer at this point. When he had in some measure conquered it, he resumed:

Question: "Your other nature is a Porky nature. What has that nature been chiefly sustained upon?"

Answer (in a sprightly manner): "Pork, to be sure!"

Question: "Not so. Pork is not fed upon Pork?"

Answer: "Isn't it, though!"

A strange internal feeling, resembling a flight of pigeons, seized upon the writer. He then became illuminated in a surprising manner, and said:

"Do I understand you to hint that the human race, incautiously attacking the indigestible fortresses called by your name, and not having time to storm them, owing to the great solidity of their almost impregnable walls, are in the habit of leaving much of their contents in the hands of the Mediums, who with such pig nourish the pigs of future pies?"

Answer: "That's it!"

Question: "Then to paraphrase the words of our immortal bard—"

Answer (interrupting):

"The same pork in its time, makes many pies, Its least being seven pasties."

The writer's emotion was profound. But, again desirous still further to try the Spirit, and to ascertain whether, in the poetic phraseology of the advanced seers of the United States, it hailed from one of the inner and more elevated circles, he tested its knowledge with the following

Question: "In the wild harmony of the musical instrument within me, of which I am again conscious, what other substances are there airs of, besides those you have mentioned?"

Answer: "Cape. Gamboge. Camomile. Treacle. Spirits of wine. Distilled Potatoes."

Question: "Nothing else?"

Answer: "Nothing worth mentioning."

Let the scorner tremble and do homage; let the feeble sceptic blush! The writer at his lunch had demanded of the powerful Medium, a glass of Sherry, and likewise a small glass of Brandy. Who can doubt that the articles of commerce indicated by the Spirit were supplied to him from that source under those two names?

One other instance may suffice to prove that experiences of the foregoing nature are no longer to be questioned, and that it ought to be made capital to attempt to explain them away. It is an exquisite case of Tipping.

The writer's Destiny had appointed him to entertain a hopeless affection for Miss L. B., of Bungay, in the county of Suffolk. Miss L. B. had not, at the period of the occurrence of the Tipping, openly rejected the writer's offer of his hand and heart; but it has since seemed probable that she had been withheld from doing so, by filial fear of her father, Mr. B., who was favourable to the writer's pretensions. Now, mark the Tipping. A young man, obnoxious to all well-constituted minds (since married to Miss L. B.), was visiting at the house. Young B., was also home from school. The writer was present. The family party were assembled about a round table. It was the spiritual time of twilight in the month of July. Objects could not be discerned with any degree of distinctness. Suddenly, Mr. B. whose senses had been lulled to repose, infused terror into all our breasts, by uttering a passionate roar or ejaculation. His words (his education was neglected in his youth) were exactly these: "Damme, here's somebody a shoving of a letter into my hand, under my own mahogany!" Consternation seized the assembled group. Mrs. B. augmented the prevalent dismay by declaring that somebody had been softly treading on her toes, at intervals, for half-an-hour. Greater consternation seized the assembled group. Mr. B. called for lights. Now, mark the Tipping. Young B. cried (I quote his expressions accurately), "It's the spirits, father! They've been at it with me this last fortnight." Mr. B. demanded with irascibility, "What do you mean, sir? What have they been at?" Young B. replied, "Wanting to make a regular Post-office of me, father. They're always handing impalpable letters to me, father. A letter must have come creeping round to you by mistake. I must be a Medium, father. O here's a go!" cried young B. "If I an't a jolly Medium!" The boy now became violently convulsed, spluttering exceedingly, and jerking out his legs and arms in a manner calculated to cause me (and which did cause me) serious inconvenience; for, I was supporting his respected mother within range of his boots, and he conducted himself like a telegraph before the invention of the electric one. All this time Mr. B. was looking about under the table for the letter, while the obnoxious young man, since married to Miss L. B., protected that young lady in an obnoxious manner. "O here's a go!" Young B. continued to cry without intermission, "If I an't a jolly Medium, father! Here's a go! There'll be a Tipping presently, father. Look out for the table!" Now mark the Tipping. The table tipped so violently as to strike Mr. B. a good half-dozen times on his bald head while he was looking under it; which caused Mr. B. to come out with great agility, and rub it with much tenderness (I refer to his head), and to imprecate it with much violence (I refer to the table). I observed that the tipping of the table was uniformly in the direction of the magnetic current; that is to say, from south to north, or from young B. to Mr. B. I should have made some further observations on this deeply interesting point, but that the table suddenly revolved, and tipped over on myself, bearing me to the ground with a force increased by the momentum imparted to it by young B., who came over with it in a state of mental exaltation, and could not be displaced for some time. In the interval, I was aware of being crushed by his weight and the table's, and also of his constantly calling out to his sister and the obnoxious young man, that he foresaw there would be another Tipping presently.

None such, however, took place. He recovered after taking a short walk with them in the dark, and no worse effects of the very beautiful experience with which we had been favoured, were perceptible in him during the rest of the evening, than a slight tendency to hysterical laughter, and a noticeable attraction (I might almost term it fascination) of his left hand, in the direction of his heart or waistcoat-pocket.

Was this, or was it not a case of Tipping? Will the sceptic and the scoffer reply?

**If you enjoyed this, you might also like...**
A Madman's Manuscript, see page 279
The Mother's Eyes, see page 298

# Captain Murderer and the Devil's Bargain

**THERE ARE NOT** many places that I find it more agreeable to revisit when I am in an idle mood, than some places to which I have never been. For, my acquaintance with those spots is of such long standing, and has ripened into an intimacy of so affectionate a nature, that I take a particular interest in assuring myself that they are unchanged.

I never was in Robinson Crusoe's Island, yet I frequently return there. The colony he established on it soon faded away, and it is uninhabited by any descendants of the grave and courteous Spaniards, or of Will Atkins and the other mutineers, and has relapsed into its original condition. Not a twig of its wicker houses remains, its goats have long run wild again, its screaming parrots would darken the sun with a cloud of many flaming colours if a gun were fired there, no face is ever reflected in the waters of the little creek which Friday swam across when pursued by his two brother cannibals with sharpened stomachs. After comparing notes with other travellers who have similarly revisited the Island and conscientiously inspected it, I have satisfied myself that it contains no vestige of Mr. Atkins's domesticity or theology, though his track on the memorable evening of his landing to set his captain ashore, when he was decoyed about and round about until it was dark, and his boat was stove, and his strength and spirits failed him, is yet plainly to be traced. So is the hill-top on which Robinson was struck dumb with joy when the reinstated captain pointed to the ship, riding within half a mile of the shore, that was to bear him away, in the nine-and-twentieth year of his seclusion in that lonely place. So is the sandy beach on which the memorable footstep was impressed, and where the savages hauled up their canoes when they came ashore for those dreadful public dinners, which led to a dancing worse than speech-making. So is the cave where the flaring eyes of the old goat made such a goblin appearance in the dark. So is the site of the hut where Robinson lived with the dog and the parrot and the cat, and where he endured those first agonies of solitude, which – strange to say – never involved any ghostly fancies; a circumstance so very remarkable, that perhaps he left out something in writing his record? Round hundreds of such objects, hidden in the dense tropical foliage, the tropical sea breaks evermore; and over them the tropical sky, saving in the short rainy season, shines bright and cloudless.

Neither, was I ever belated among wolves, on the borders of France and Spain; nor, did I ever, when night was closing in and the ground was covered with snow, draw up my little company among some felled trees which served as a breastwork, and there fire a train of gunpowder so dexterously that suddenly we had three or four score blazing wolves illuminating the darkness around us. Nevertheless, I occasionally go back to that dismal region and perform the feat again; when indeed to smell the singeing and the frying of the wolves afire, and to see them setting one another alight as they rush and tumble, and to behold them rolling in the snow vainly attempting to put themselves out, and to hear their howlings taken up by all the echoes as well as by all the unseen wolves within the woods, makes me tremble.

I was never in the robbers' cave, where Gil Blas lived, but I often go back there and find the trap-door just as heavy to raise as it used to be, while that wicked old disabled Black lies everlastingly cursing in bed. I was never in Don Quixote's study where he read his books of chivalry until he rose and hacked at imaginary giants, and then refreshed himself with great draughts of water, yet you couldn't move a book in it without my knowledge, or with my consent. I was never (thank Heaven) in company with the little old woman who hobbled out of the chest and told the merchant Abudah to go in search of the Talisman of Oromanes, yet I make it my business to know that she is well preserved and as intolerable as ever. I was never at the school where the boy Horatio Nelson got out of bed to steal the pears: not because he wanted any, but because every other boy was afraid: yet I have several times been back to this Academy, to see him let down out of the window with a sheet. So with Damascus, and Bagdad, and Brobdingnag (which has the curious fate of being usually misspelt when written), and Lilliput, and Laputa, and the Nile, and Abyssinia, and the Ganges, and the North Pole, and many hundreds of places – I was never at them, yet it is an affair of my life to keep them intact, and I am always going back to them.

But when I was in Dullborough one day, revisiting the associations of my childhood as recorded in previous pages of these notes, my experience in this wise was made quite inconsiderable and of no account, by the quantity of places and people – utterly impossible places and people, but none the less alarmingly real – that I found I had been introduced to by my nurse before I was six years old, and used to be forced to go back to at night without at all wanting to go. If we all knew our own minds (in a more enlarged sense than the popular acceptation of that phrase), I suspect we should find our nurses responsible for most of the dark corners we are forced to go back to, against our wills.

The first diabolical character that intruded himself on my peaceful youth (as I called to mind that day at Dullborough), was a certain Captain Murderer. This wretch must have been an offshoot of the Blue Beard family, but I had no suspicion of the consanguinity in those times. His warning name would seem to have awakened no general prejudice against him, for he was admitted into the best society and possessed immense wealth. Captain Murderer's mission was matrimony, and the gratification of a cannibal appetite with tender brides. On his marriage morning, he always caused both sides of the way to church to be planted with curious flowers; and when his bride said, "Dear Captain Murderer, I never saw flowers like these before: what are they called?" he answered, "They are called Garnish for house-lamb," and laughed at his ferocious practical joke in a horrid manner, disquieting the minds of the noble bridal company, with a very sharp show of teeth, then displayed for the first time. He made love in a coach and six, and married in a coach and twelve, and all his horses were milk-white horses with one red spot on the back which he caused to be hidden by the harness. For, the spot *would* come there, though every horse was milk white when Captain Murderer bought him. And the spot was young bride's blood. (To this terrific point I am indebted for my first personal experience of a shudder and cold beads on the forehead.) When Captain Murderer had made an end of feasting and revelry, and had dismissed the noble guests, and was alone with his wife on the day month after their marriage, it was his whimsical custom to produce a golden rolling-pin and a silver pie- board. Now, there was this special feature in the Captain's courtships, that he always asked if the young lady could make pie-crust;

and if she couldn't by nature or education, she was taught. Well. When the bride saw Captain Murderer produce the golden rolling-pin and silver pie-board, she remembered this, and turned up her laced-silk sleeves to make a pie. The Captain brought out a silver pie-dish of immense capacity, and the Captain brought out flour and butter and eggs and all things needful, except the inside of the pie; of materials for the staple of the pie itself, the Captain brought out none. Then said the lovely bride, "Dear Captain Murderer, what pie is this to be?" He replied, "A meat pie." Then said the lovely bride, "Dear Captain Murderer, I see no meat." The Captain humorously retorted, "Look in the glass." She looked in the glass, but still she saw no meat, and then the Captain roared with laughter, and, suddenly frowning and drawing his sword, bade her roll out the crust. So she rolled out the crust, dropping large tears upon it all the time because he was so cross, and when she had lined the dish with crust and had cut the crust all ready to fit the top, the Captain called out, "*I* see the meat in the glass!" And the bride looked up at the glass, just in time to see the Captain cutting her head off; and he chopped her in pieces, and peppered her, and salted her, and put her in the pie, and sent it to the baker's, and ate it all, and picked the bones.

Captain Murderer went on in this way, prospering exceedingly, until he came to choose a bride from two twin sisters, and at first didn't know which to choose. For, though one was fair and the other dark, they were both equally beautiful. But the fair twin loved him, and the dark twin hated him, so he chose the fair one. The dark twin would have prevented the marriage if she could, but she couldn't; however, on the night before it, much suspecting Captain Murderer, she stole out and climbed his garden wall, and looked in at his window through a chink in the shutter, and saw him having his teeth filed sharp. Next day she listened all day, and heard him make his joke about the house-lamb. And that day month, he had the paste rolled out, and cut the fair twin's head off, and chopped her in pieces, and peppered her, and salted her, and put her in the pie, and sent it to the baker's, and ate it all, and picked the bones.

Now, the dark twin had had her suspicions much increased by the filing of the Captain's teeth, and again by the house-lamb joke. Putting all things together when he gave out that her sister was dead, she divined the truth, and determined to be revenged. So she went up to Captain Murderer's house, and knocked at the knocker and pulled at the bell, and when the Captain came to the door, said: "Dear Captain Murderer, marry me next, for I always loved you and was jealous of my sister." The Captain took it as a compliment, and made a polite answer, and the marriage was quickly arranged. On the night before it, the bride again climbed to his window, and again saw him having his teeth filed sharp. At this sight, she laughed such a terrible laugh, at the chink in the shutter, that the Captain's blood curdled, and he said: "I hope nothing has disagreed with me!" At that, she laughed again, a still more terrible laugh, and the shutter was opened and search made, but she was nimbly gone and there was no one. Next day they went to church in the coach and twelve, and were married. And that day month, she rolled the pie-crust out, and Captain Murderer cut her head off, and chopped her in pieces, and peppered her, and salted her, and put her in the pie, and sent it to the baker's, and ate it all, and picked the bones.

But before she began to roll out the paste she had taken a deadly poison of a most awful character, distilled from toads' eyes and spiders' knees; and Captain Murderer had hardly picked her last bone, when he began to swell, and to turn blue, and to be all over spots, and to scream. And he went on swelling and turning bluer and being more all over spots and screaming, until he reached from floor to ceiling and from wall to

CHARLES DICKENS SUPERNATURAL SHORT STORIES

wall; and then, at one o'clock in the morning, he blew up with a loud explosion. At the sound of it, all the milk-white horses in the stables broke their halters and went mad, and then they galloped over everybody in Captain Murderer's house (beginning with the family blacksmith who had filed his teeth) until the whole were dead, and then they galloped away.

Hundreds of times did I hear this legend of Captain Murderer, in my early youth, and added hundreds of times was there a mental compulsion upon me in bed, to peep in at his window as the dark twin peeped, and to revisit his horrible house, and look at him in his blue and spotty and screaming stage, as he reached from floor to ceiling and from wall to wall. The young woman who brought me acquainted with Captain Murderer, had a fiendish enjoyment of my terrors, and used to begin, I remember – as a sort of introductory overture – by clawing the air with both hands, and uttering a long low hollow groan. So acutely did I suffer from this ceremony in combination with this infernal Captain, that I sometimes used to plead I thought I was hardly strong enough and old enough to hear the story again just yet. But she never spared me one word of it, and indeed commended the awful chalice to my lips as the only preservative known to science against "The Black Cat" – a weird and glaring-eyed supernatural Tom, who was reputed to prowl about the world by night, sucking the breath of infancy, and who was endowed with a special thirst (as I was given to understand) for mine.

This female bard – may she have been repaid my debt of obligation to her in the matter of nightmares and perspirations! – reappears in my memory as the daughter of a shipwright. Her name was Mercy, though she had none on me. There was something of a ship-building flavour in the following story. As it always recurs to me in a vague association with calomel pills, I believe it to have been reserved for dull nights when I was low with medicine.

There was once a shipwright, and he wrought in a Government Yard, and his name was Chips. And his father's name before him was Chips, and *his* father's name before *him* was Chips, and they were all Chipses. And Chips the father had sold himself to the Devil for an iron pot and a bushel of tenpenny nails and half a ton of copper and a rat that could speak; and Chips the grandfather had sold himself to the Devil for an iron pot and a bushel of tenpenny nails and half a ton of copper and a rat that could speak; and Chips the great-grandfather had disposed of himself in the same direction on the same terms; and the bargain had run in the family for a long long time. So one day when young Chips was at work in the Dock Slip all alone, down in the dark hold of an old Seventy- four that was hauled up for repairs, the Devil presented himself, and remarked: "A Lemon has pips, And a Yard has ships, And *I*'ll have Chips!"

(I don't know why, but this fact of the Devil's expressing himself in rhyme was peculiarly trying to me.) Chips looked up when he heard the words, and there he saw the Devil with saucer eyes that squinted on a terrible great scale, and that struck out sparks of blue fire continually. And whenever he winked his eyes, showers of blue sparks came out, and his eyelashes made a clattering like flints and steels striking lights. And hanging over one of his arms by the handle was an iron pot, and under that arm was a bushel of tenpenny nails, and under his other arm was half a ton of copper, and sitting on one of his shoulders was a rat that could speak. So the Devil said again: "A Lemon has pips, And a Yard has ships, And *I*'ll have Chips!"

(The invariable effect of this alarming tautology on the part of the Evil Spirit was to deprive me of my senses for some moments.) So Chips answered never a word, but went on with his work. "What are you doing, Chips?" said the rat that could speak. "I am putting in new planks where you and your gang have eaten old away," said Chips. "But we'll eat them too," said the rat that could speak; "and we'll let in the water, and we'll drown the crew, and we'll eat them too." Chips, being only a shipwright, and not a Man-of-war's man, said, "You are welcome to it." But he couldn't keep his eyes off the half a ton of copper or the bushel of tenpenny nails; for nails and copper are a shipwright's sweethearts, and shipwrights will run away with them whenever they can. So the Devil said, "I see what you are looking at, Chips. You had better strike the bargain. You know the terms. Your father before you was well acquainted with them, and so were your grandfather and great-grandfather before him." Says Chips, "I like the copper, and I like thé nails, and I don't mind the pot, but I don't like the rat." Says the Devil, fiercely, "You can't have the metal without him – and *he's* a curiosity. I'm going." Chips, afraid of losing the half a ton of copper and the bushel of nails, then said, "Give us hold!" So he got the copper and the nails and the pot and the rat that could speak, and the Devil vanished.

Chips sold the copper, and he sold the nails, and he would have sold the pot; but whenever he offered it for sale, the rat was in it, and the dealers dropped it, and would have nothing to say to the bargain. So Chips resolved to kill the rat, and, being at work in the Yard one day with a great kettle of hot pitch on one side of him and the iron pot with the rat in it on the other, he turned the scalding pitch into the pot, and filled it full. Then he kept his eye upon it till it cooled and hardened, and then he let it stand for twenty days, and then he heated the pitch again and turned it back into the kettle, and then he sank the pot in water for twenty days more, and then he got the smelters to put it in the furnace for twenty days more, and then they gave it him out, red hot, and looking like red-hot glass instead of iron – yet there was the rat in it, just the same as ever! And the moment it caught his eye, it said with a jeer:

"A Lemon has pips, And a Yard has ships, And *I'll* have Chips!"

(For this Refrain I had waited since its last appearance, with inexpressible horror, which now culminated.) Chips now felt certain in his own mind that the rat would stick to him; the rat, answering his thought, said, "I will – like pitch!"

Now, as the rat leaped out of the pot when it had spoken, and made off, Chips began to hope that it wouldn't keep its word. But a terrible thing happened next day. For, when dinner-time came and the Dock-bell rang to strike work, he put his rule into the long pocket at the side of his trousers, and there he found a rat – not that rat, but another rat. And in his hat, he found another; and in his pocket-handkerchief, another; and in the sleeves of his coat, when he pulled it on to go to dinner, two more. And from that time he found himself so frightfully intimate with all the rats in the Yard, that they climbed up his legs when he was at work, and sat on his tools while he used them. And they could all speak to one another, and he understood what they said. And they got into his lodging, and into his bed, and into his teapot, and into his beer, and into his boots. And he was going to be married to a corn-chandler's daughter; and when he gave her a workbox he had himself made for her, a rat jumped out of it; and when he put his arm round her waist, a rat clung about her; so the marriage was broken off, though the banns were already twice put up – which the parish clerk well remembers, for, as he handed the book to the clergyman for the second time of asking, a large fat rat ran over the leaf. (By this time a special cascade of rats was rolling down my back, and the whole of my small listening person was overrun with them. At intervals ever since, I have been morbidly afraid of my own pocket, lest my exploring hand should find a specimen or two of those vermin in it.)

You may believe that all this was very terrible to Chips; but even all this was not the worst. He knew besides, what the rats were doing, wherever they were. So sometimes he would cry aloud, when he was at his club at night, "Oh! Keep the rats out of the convicts' burying-ground! Don't let them do that!" Or, "There's one of them at the cheese down stairs!" Or, "There's two of them smelling at the baby in the garret!" Or, other things of that sort. At last, he was voted mad, and lost his work in the Yard, and could get no other work. But King George wanted men, so before very long he got pressed for a sailor. And so he was taken off in a boat one evening to his ship, lying at Spithead, ready to sail. And so the first thing he made out in her as he got near her, was the figure-head of the old Seventy-four, where he had seen the Devil. She was called the Argonaut, and they rowed right under the bowsprit where the figure-head of the Argonaut, with a sheepskin in his hand and a blue gown on, was looking out to sea; and sitting staring on his forehead was the rat who could speak, and his exact words were these: "Chips ahoy! Old boy! We've pretty well eat them too, and will drown the crew, and will eat them too!" (Here I always became exceedingly faint, and would have asked for water, but that I was speechless.)

The ship was bound for the Indies; and if you don't know where that is, you ought to it, and angels will never love you. (Here I felt myself an outcast from a future state.) The ship set sail that very night, and she sailed, and sailed, and sailed. Chips's feelings were dreadful. Nothing ever equalled his terrors. No wonder. At last, one day he asked leave to speak to the Admiral. The Admiral giv' leave. Chips went down on his knees in the Great State Cabin.

"Your Honour, unless your Honour, without a moment's loss of time makes sail for the nearest shore, this is a doomed ship, and her name is the Coffin!"

"Young man, your words are a madman's words."

"Your Honour no; they are nibbling us away."

"They?"

"Your Honour, them dreadful rats. Dust and hollowness where solid oak ought to be! Rats nibbling a grave for every man on board! Oh! Does your Honour love your Lady and your pretty children?"

"Yes, my man, to be sure."

"Then, for God's sake, make for the nearest shore, for at this present moment the rats are all stopping in their work, and are all looking straight towards you with bare teeth, and are all saying to one another that you shall never, never, never, never, see your Lady and your children more."

"My poor fellow, you are a case for the doctor. Sentry, take care of this man!"

So he was bled and he was blistered, and he was this and that, for six whole days and nights. So then he again asked leave to speak to the Admiral. The Admiral giv' leave. He went down on his knees in the Great State Cabin. "Now, Admiral, you must die! You took no warning; you must die! The rats are never wrong in their calculations, and they make out that they'll be through, at twelve to-night. So, you must die! – With me and all the rest!" And so at twelve o'clock there was a great leak reported in the ship, and a torrent of water rushed in and nothing could stop it, and they all went down, every living soul. And what the rats – being water-rats – left of Chips, at last floated to shore, and sitting on him was an immense overgrown rat, laughing, that dived when the corpse touched the beach and never came up. And there was a deal of seaweed on the remains. And if you get thirteen bits of seaweed, and dry them and burn them in the fire, they will go – off – like in these thirteen words as plain as plain can be: "A Lemon has pips, And a Yard has ships, And *I*'ve got Chips!"

The same female bard – descended, possibly, from those terrible old Scalds who seem to have existed for the express purpose of addling the brains of mankind when they begin to investigate languages – made a standing pretence which greatly assisted in forcing me back to a number of hideous places that I would by all means have avoided. This pretence was, that all her ghost stories had occurred to her own relations. Politeness towards a meritorious family, therefore forbade my doubting them, and they acquired an air of authentication that impaired my digestive powers for life. There was a narrative concerning an unearthly animal foreboding death, which appeared in the open street to a parlour-maid who "went to fetch the beer" for supper: first (as I now recall it) assuming the likeness of a black dog, and gradually rising on its hind-legs and swelling into the semblance of some quadruped greatly surpassing a hippopotamus: which apparition – not because I deemed it in the least improbable, but because I felt it to be really too large to bear – I feebly endeavoured to explain away. But on Mercy's retorting with wounded dignity that the parlour- maid was her own sister-in-law, I perceived there was no hope, and resigned myself to this zoological phenomenon as one of my many pursuers. There was another narrative describing the apparition of a young woman who came out of a glass-case and haunted another young woman until the other young woman questioned it and elicited that its bones (Lord! To think of its being so particular about its bones!) were buried under the glass-case, whereas she required them to be interred, with every Undertaking solemnity up to twenty-four pound ten, in another particular place. This narrative I considered I had a personal interest in disproving, because we had glass-cases at home, and how, otherwise, was I to be guaranteed from the intrusion of young women requiring *me* to bury them up to twenty- four pound ten, when I had only twopence a week? But my remorseless nurse cut the ground from under my tender feet, by informing me that She was the other young woman; and I couldn't say "I don't believe you;" it was not possible.

Such are a few of the uncommercial journeys that I was forced to make, against my will, when I was very young and unreasoning. And really, as to the latter part of them, it is not so very long ago – now I come to think of it – that I was asked to undertake them once again, with a steady countenance.

**If you enjoyed this, you might also like...**
A Madman's Manuscript, see page 279
The Trial for Murder, see page 251

# Fantasy & Adventure

# The True Legend of Prince Bladud

**LESS THAN** two hundred years ago, on one of the public baths in this city, there appeared an inscription in honour of its mighty founder, the renowned Prince Bladud. That inscription is now erased.

For many hundred years before that time, there had been handed down, from age to age, an old legend, that the illustrious prince being afflicted with leprosy, on his return from reaping a rich harvest of knowledge in Athens, shunned the court of his royal father, and consorted moodily with husbandman and pigs. Among the herd (so said the legend) was a pig of grave and solemn countenance, with whom the prince had a fellow-feeling – for he too was wise – a pig of thoughtful and reserved demeanour; an animal superior to his fellows, whose grunt was terrible, and whose bite was sharp. The young prince sighed deeply as he looked upon the countenance of the majestic swine; he thought of his royal father, and his eyes were bedewed with tears.

This sagacious pig was fond of bathing in rich, moist mud. Not in summer, as common pigs do now, to cool themselves, and did even in those distant ages (which is a proof that the light of civilisation had already begun to dawn, though feebly), but in the cold, sharp days of winter. His coat was ever so sleek, and his complexion so clear, that the prince resolved to essay the purifying qualities of the same water that his friend resorted to. He made the trial. Beneath that black mud, bubbled the hot springs of Bath. He washed, and was cured. Hastening to his father's court, he paid his best respects, and returning quickly hither, founded this city and its famous baths.

He sought the pig with all the ardour of their early friendship – but, alas! the waters had been his death. He had imprudently taken a bath at too high a temperature, and the natural philosopher was no more! He was succeeded by Pliny, who also fell a victim to his thirst for knowledge.

This was the legend. Listen to the true one.

A great many centuries since, there flourished, in great state, the famous and renowned Lud Hudibras, king of Britain. He was a mighty monarch. The earth shook when he walked – he was so very stout. His people basked in the light of his countenance – it was so red and glowing. He was, indeed, every inch a king. And there were a good many inches of him, too, for although he was not very tall, he was a remarkable size round, and the inches that he wanted in height, he made up in circumference. If any degenerate monarch of modern times could be in any way compared with him, I should say the venerable King Cole would be that illustrious potentate.

This good king had a queen, who eighteen years before, had had a son, who was called Bladud. He was sent to a preparatory seminary in his father's dominions until he was ten years old, and was then despatched, in charge of a trusty messenger, to a finishing school at Athens; and as there was no extra charge for remaining during the holidays, and no notice required previous to the removal of a pupil, there he remained for eight long years, at the expiration of which time, the king his father sent the lord chamberlain over, to settle the bill, and to bring him home; which, the lord chamberlain doing, was received with shouts, and pensioned immediately.

When King Lud saw the prince his son, and found he had grown up such a fine young man, he perceived what a grand thing it would be to have him married without delay, so that his children might be the means of perpetuating the glorious race of Lud, down to the very latest ages of the world. With this view, he sent a special embassy, composed of great noblemen who had nothing particular to do, and wanted lucrative employment, to a neighbouring king, and demanded his fair daughter in marriage for his son; stating at the same time that he was anxious to be on the most affectionate terms with his brother and friend, but that if they couldn't agree in arranging this marriage, he should be under the unpleasant necessity of invading his kingdom and putting his eyes out. To this, the other king (who was the weaker of the two) replied that he was very much obliged to his friend and brother for all his goodness and magnanimity, and that his daughter was quite ready to be married, whenever Prince Bladud liked to come and fetch her.

This answer no sooner reached Britain, than the whole nation was transported with joy. Nothing was heard, on all sides, but the sounds of feasting and revelry – except the chinking of money as it was paid in by the people to the collector of the royal treasures, to defray the expenses of the happy ceremony. It was upon this occasion that King Lud, seated on the top of his throne in full council, rose, in the exuberance of his feelings, and commanded the lord chief justice to order in the richest wines and the court minstrels – an act of graciousness which has been, through the ignorance of traditionary historians, attributed to King Cole, in those celebrated lines in which his Majesty is represented as

> *Calling for his pipe, and calling for his pot,*
> *And calling for his fiddlers three.*

Which is an obvious injustice to the memory of King Lud, and a dishonest exaltation of the virtues of King Cole.

But, in the midst of all this festivity and rejoicing, there was one individual present, who tasted not when the sparkling wines were poured forth, and who danced not, when the minstrels played. This was no other than Prince Bladud himself, in honour of whose happiness a whole people were, at that very moment, straining alike their throats and purse-strings. The truth was, that the prince, forgetting the undoubted right of the minister for foreign affairs to fall in love on his behalf, had, contrary to every precedent of policy and diplomacy, already fallen in love on his own account, and privately contracted himself unto the fair daughter of a noble Athenian.

Here we have a striking example of one of the manifold advantages of civilisation and refinement. If the prince had lived in later days, he might at once have married the object of his father's choice, and then set himself seriously to work, to relieve himself of the burden which rested heavily upon him. He might have endeavoured to break her heart by a systematic course of insult and neglect; or, if the spirit of her sex, and a proud consciousness of her many wrongs had upheld her under this ill-treatment, he might have sought to take her life, and so get rid of her effectually. But neither mode of relief suggested itself to Prince Bladud; so he solicited a private audience, and told his father.

It is an old prerogative of kings to govern everything but their passions. King Lud flew into a frightful rage, tossed his crown up to the ceiling, and caught it again – for in those days kings kept their crowns on their heads, and not in the Tower – stamped the ground, rapped his forehead, wondered why his own flesh and blood rebelled against him, and, finally, calling in his guards, ordered the prince away to instant Confinement in a lofty turret; a course of treatment which the kings of old very generally pursued towards their sons, when their matrimonial inclinations did not happen to point to the same quarter as their own.

When Prince Bladud had been shut up in the lofty turret for the greater part of a year, with no better prospect before his bodily eyes than a stone wall, or before his mental vision than prolonged imprisonment, he naturally began to ruminate on a plan of escape, which, after months of preparation, he managed to accomplish; considerately leaving his dinner-knife in the heart of his jailer, lest the poor fellow (who had a family) should be considered privy to his flight, and punished accordingly by the infuriated king.

The monarch was frantic at the loss of his son. He knew not on whom to vent his grief and wrath, until fortunately bethinking himself of the lord chamberlain who had brought him home, he struck off his pension and his head together.

Meanwhile, the young prince, effectually disguised, wandered on foot through his father's dominions, cheered and supported in all his hardships by sweet thoughts of the Athenian maid, who was the innocent cause of his weary trials. One day he stopped to rest in a country village; and seeing that there were gay dances going forward on the green, and gay faces passing to and fro, ventured to inquire of a reveller who stood near him, the reason for this rejoicing.

"Know you not, O stranger," was the reply, "of the recent proclamation of our gracious king?"

"Proclamation! No. What proclamation?" rejoined the prince – for he had travelled along the by and little-frequented ways, and knew nothing of what had passed upon the public roads, such as they were.

"Why," replied the peasant, "the foreign lady that our prince wished to wed, is married to a foreign noble of her own country, and the king proclaims the fact, and a great public festival besides; for now, of course, Prince Bladud will come back and marry the lady his father chose, who they say is as beautiful as the noonday sun. Your health, sir. God save the king!"

The prince remained to hear no more. He fled from the spot, and plunged into the thickest recesses of a neighbouring wood. On, on, he wandered, night and day; beneath the blazing sun, and the cold pale moon; through the dry heat of noon, and the damp cold of night; in the gray light of morn, and the red glare of eve. So heedless was he of time or object, that being bound for Athens, he wandered as far out of his way as Bath.

There was no city where Bath stands, then. There was no vestige of human habitation, or sign of man's resort, to bear the name; but there was the same noble country, the same broad expanse of hill and dale, the same beautiful channel stealing on, far away, the same lofty mountains which, like the troubles of life, viewed at a distance, and partially obscured by the bright mist of its morning, lose their ruggedness and asperity, and seem all ease and softness. Moved by the gentle beauty of the scene, the prince sank upon the green turf, and bathed his swollen feet in his tears.

"Oh!" said the unhappy Bladud, clasping his hands, and mournfully raising his eyes towards the sky, "would that my wanderings might end here! Would that these grateful tears with which I now mourn hope misplaced, and love despised, might flow in peace for ever!"

The wish was heard. It was in the time of the heathen deities, who used occasionally to take people at their words, with a promptness, in some cases, extremely awkward. The ground opened beneath the prince's feet; he sank into the chasm; and instantaneously it closed upon his head for ever, save where his hot tears welled up through the earth, and where they have continued to gush forth ever since.

It is observable that, to this day, large numbers of elderly ladies and gentlemen who have been disappointed in procuring partners, and almost as many young ones who are anxious to obtain them, repair annually to Bath to drink the waters, from which they derive much strength and comfort. This is most complimentary to the virtue of Prince Bladud's tears, and strongly corroborative of the veracity of this legend.

**If you enjoyed this, you might also like...**
A Child's Dream of a Star, see page 386
The Magic Fishbone, see page 466

# The Queer Chair

**ONE WINTER'S EVENING,** about five o'clock, just as it began to grow dusk, a man in a gig might have been seen urging his tired horse along the road which leads across Marlborough Downs, in the direction of Bristol. I say he might have been seen, and I have no doubt he would have been, if anybody but a blind man had happened to pass that way; but the weather was so bad, and the night so cold and wet, that nothing was out but the water, and so the traveller jogged along in the middle of the road, lonesome and dreary enough. If any bagman of that day could have caught sight of the little neck-or-nothing sort of gig, with a clay-coloured body and red wheels, and the vixenish, ill tempered, fast-going bay mare, that looked like a cross between a butcher's horse and a twopenny post-office pony, he would have known at once, that this traveller could have been no other than Tom Smart, of the great house of Bilson and Slum, Cateaton Street, City. However, as there was no bagman to look on, nobody knew anything at all about the matter; and so Tom Smart and his clay-coloured gig with the red wheels, and the vixenish mare with the fast pace, went on together, keeping the secret among them, and nobody was a bit the wiser.

There are many pleasanter places even in this dreary world, than Marlborough Downs when it blows hard; and if you throw in beside, a gloomy winter's evening, a miry and sloppy road, and a pelting fall of heavy rain, and try the effect, by way of experiment, in your own proper person, you will experience the full force of this observation.

The wind blew – not up the road or down it, though that's bad enough, but sheer across it, sending the rain slanting down like the lines they used to rule in the copy-books at school, to make the boys slope well. For a moment it would die away, and the traveller would begin to delude himself into the belief that, exhausted with its previous fury, it had quietly laid itself down to rest, when, whoo! he could hear it growling and whistling in the distance, and on it would come rushing over the hill-tops, and sweeping along the plain, gathering sound and strength as it drew nearer, until it dashed with a heavy gust against horse and man, driving the sharp rain into their ears, and its cold damp breath into their very bones; and past them it would scour, far, far away, with a stunning roar, as if in ridicule of their weakness, and triumphant in the consciousness of its own strength and power.

The bay mare splashed away, through the mud and water, with drooping ears; now and then tossing her head as if to express her disgust at this very ungentlemanly behaviour of the elements, but keeping a good pace notwithstanding, until a gust of wind, more furious than any that had yet assailed them, caused her to stop suddenly and plant her four feet firmly against the ground, to prevent her being blown over. It's a special mercy that she did this, for if she had been blown over, the vixenish mare was so light, and the gig was so light, and Tom Smart such a light weight into the bargain, that they must infallibly have all gone rolling over and over together, until they reached the confines of earth, or until the wind fell; and in either case the probability is, that neither the vixenish mare, nor the clay-coloured gig with the red wheels, nor Tom Smart, would ever have been fit for service again.

"Well, damn my straps and whiskers," says Tom Smart (Tom sometimes had an unpleasant knack of swearing) – "damn my straps and whiskers," says Tom, "if this ain't pleasant, blow me!"

You'll very likely ask me why, as Tom Smart had been pretty well blown already, he expressed this wish to be submitted to the same process again. I can't say – all I know is, that Tom Smart said so – or at least he always told my uncle he said so, and it's just the same thing.

"Blow me," says Tom Smart; and the mare neighed as if she were precisely of the same opinion.

"Cheer up, old girl," said Tom, patting the bay mare on the neck with the end of his whip. "It won't do pushing on, such a night as this; the first house we come to we'll put up at, so the faster you go the sooner it's over. Soho, old girl – gently – gently."

Whether the vixenish mare was sufficiently well acquainted with the tones of Tom's voice to comprehend his meaning, or whether she found it colder standing still than moving on, of course I can't say. But I can say that Tom had no sooner finished speaking, than she pricked up her ears, and started forward at a speed which made the clay-coloured gig rattle until you would have supposed every one of the red spokes were going to fly out on the turf of Marlborough Downs; and even Tom, whip as he was, couldn't stop or check her pace, until she drew up of her own accord, before a roadside inn on the right-hand side of the way, about half a quarter of a mile from the end of the Downs.

Tom cast a hasty glance at the upper part of the house as he threw the reins to the hostler, and stuck the whip in the box. It was a strange old place, built of a kind of shingle, inlaid, as it were, with cross-beams, with gabled-topped windows projecting completely over the pathway, and a low door with a dark porch, and a couple of steep steps leading down into the house, instead of the modern fashion of half a dozen shallow ones leading up to it. It was a comfortable-looking place though, for there was a strong, cheerful light in the bar window, which shed a bright ray across the road, and even lighted up the hedge on the other side; and there was a red flickering light in the opposite window, one moment but faintly discernible, and the next gleaming strongly through the drawn curtains, which intimated that a rousing fire was blazing within. Marking these little evidences with the eye of an experienced traveller, Tom dismounted with as much agility as his half-frozen limbs would permit, and entered the house.

In less than five minutes' time, Tom was ensconced in the room opposite the bar – the very room where he had imagined the fire blazing – before a substantial, matter-of-fact, roaring fire, composed of something short of a bushel of coals, and wood enough to make half a dozen decent gooseberry bushes, piled half-way up the chimney, and roaring and crackling with a sound that of itself would have warmed the heart of any reasonable man. This was comfortable, but this was not all; for a smartly-dressed girl, with a bright eye and a neat ankle, was laying a very clean white cloth on the table; and as Tom sat with his slippered feet on the fender, and his back to the open door, he saw a charming prospect of the bar reflected in the glass over the chimney-piece, with delightful rows of green bottles and gold labels, together with jars of pickles and preserves, and cheeses and boiled hams, and rounds of beef, arranged on shelves in the most tempting and delicious array. Well, this was comfortable too; but even this was not all – for in the bar, seated at tea at the nicest possible little table, drawn close up before the brightest possible little fire, was a buxom widow of somewhere about eight-and-forty or thereabouts, with a face as comfortable as the bar, who was evidently the landlady of the house, and the supreme ruler over all these agreeable possessions. There was only one drawback to the beauty of the whole picture, and that was a tall man – a very tall man – in a brown coat and bright basket buttons, and black whiskers and wavy black hair, who was seated at tea with the widow, and who it required no great penetration to discover was in a fair way of persuading her to be a widow no longer, but to confer upon him the privilege of sitting down in that bar, for and during the whole remainder of the term of his natural life.

Tom Smart was by no means of an irritable or envious disposition, but somehow or other the tall man with the brown coat and the bright basket buttons did rouse what little gall he had in his composition, and did make him feel extremely indignant, the more especially as he could now and then observe, from his seat before the glass, certain little affectionate familiarities passing between the tall man and the widow, which sufficiently denoted that the tall man was as high in favour as he was in size. Tom was fond of hot punch – I may venture to say he was very fond of hot punch – and after he had seen the vixenish mare well fed and well littered down, and had eaten every bit of the nice little hot dinner which the widow tossed up for him with her own hands, he just ordered a tumbler of it by way of experiment. Now, if there was one thing in the whole range of domestic art, which the widow could manufacture better than another, it was this identical article; and the first tumbler was adapted to Tom Smart's taste with such peculiar nicety, that he ordered a second with the least possible delay. Hot punch is a pleasant thing, gentlemen – an extremely pleasant thing under any circumstances – but in that snug old parlour, before the roaring fire, with the wind blowing outside till every timber in the old house creaked again, Tom Smart found it perfectly delightful. He ordered another tumbler, and then another – I am not quite certain whether he didn't order another after that – but the more he drank of the hot punch, the more he thought of the tall man.

"Confound his impudence!" said Tom to himself, "what business has he in that snug bar? Such an ugly villain too!" said Tom. "If the widow had any taste, she might surely pick up some better fellow than that." Here Tom's eye wandered from the glass on the chimney-piece to the glass on the table; and as he felt himself becoming gradually sentimental, he emptied the fourth tumbler of punch and ordered a fifth.

Tom Smart, gentlemen, had always been very much attached to the public line. It had been long his ambition to stand in a bar of his own, in a green coat, knee-cords, and tops. He had a great notion of taking the chair at convivial dinners, and he had often thought how well he could preside in a room of his own in the talking way, and what a capital example he could set to his customers in the drinking department. All these things passed rapidly through Tom's mind as he sat drinking the hot punch by the roaring fire, and he felt very justly and properly indignant that the tall man should be in a fair way of keeping such an excellent house, while he, Tom Smart, was as far off from it as ever. So, after deliberating over the two last tumblers, whether he hadn't a perfect right to pick a quarrel with the tall man for having contrived to get into the good graces of the buxom widow, Tom Smart at last arrived at the satisfactory conclusion that he was a very ill-used and persecuted individual, and had better go to bed.

Up a wide and ancient staircase the smart girl preceded Tom, shading the chamber candle with her hand, to protect it from the currents of air which in such a rambling old place might have found plenty of room to disport themselves in, without blowing the candle out, but which did blow it out nevertheless – thus affording Tom's enemies an opportunity of asserting that it was he, and not the wind, who extinguished the candle, and that while he pretended to be blowing it alight again, he was in fact kissing the girl.

Be this as it may, another light was obtained, and Tom was conducted through a maze of rooms, and a labyrinth of passages, to the apartment which had been prepared for his reception, where the girl bade him good-night and left him alone.

It was a good large room with big closets, and a bed which might have served for a whole boarding-school, to say nothing of a couple of oaken presses that would have held the baggage of a small army; but what struck Tom's fancy most was a strange, grim-looking, high backed chair, carved in the most fantastic manner, with a flowered damask cushion, and the round knobs at the bottom of the legs carefully tied up in red cloth, as if it had got the gout in its toes. Of any other queer chair, Tom would only have thought it was a queer chair, and there would have been an end of the matter; but there was something about this particular chair, and yet he couldn't tell what it was, so odd and so unlike any other piece of furniture he had ever seen, that it seemed to fascinate him. He sat down before the fire, and stared at the old chair for half an hour. – Damn the chair, it was such a strange old thing, he couldn't take his eyes off it.

"Well," said Tom, slowly undressing himself, and staring at the old chair all the while, which stood with a mysterious aspect by the bedside, "I never saw such a rum concern as that in my days. Very odd," said Tom, who had got rather sage with the hot punch – "very odd." Tom shook his head with an air of profound wisdom, and looked at the chair again. He couldn't make anything of it though, so he got into bed, covered himself up warm, and fell asleep.

In about half an hour, Tom woke up with a start, from a confused dream of tall men and tumblers of punch; and the first object that presented itself to his waking imagination was the queer chair.

"I won't look at it any more," said Tom to himself, and he squeezed his eyelids together, and tried to persuade himself he was going to sleep again. No use; nothing but queer chairs danced before his eyes, kicking up their legs, jumping over each other's backs, and playing all kinds of antics.

"I may as well see one real chair, as two or three complete sets of false ones," said Tom, bringing out his head from under the bedclothes. There it was, plainly discernible by the light of the fire, looking as provoking as ever.

Tom gazed at the chair; and, suddenly as he looked at it, a most extraordinary change seemed to come over it. The carving of the back gradually assumed the lineaments and expression of an old, shrivelled human face; the damask cushion became an antique, flapped waistcoat; the round knobs grew into a couple of feet, encased in red cloth slippers; and the whole chair looked like a very ugly old man, of the previous century, with his arms akimbo. Tom sat up in bed, and rubbed his eyes to dispel the illusion. No. The chair was an ugly old gentleman; and what was more, he was winking at Tom Smart.

Tom was naturally a headlong, careless sort of dog, and he had had five tumblers of hot punch into the bargain; so, although he was a little startled at first, he began to grow rather indignant when he saw the old gentleman winking and leering at him with such an impudent air. At length he resolved that he wouldn't stand it; and as the old face still kept winking away as fast as ever, Tom said, in a very angry tone –

"What the devil are you winking at me for?"

"Because I like it, Tom Smart," said the chair; or the old gentleman, whichever you like to call him. He stopped winking though, when Tom spoke, and began grinning like a superannuated monkey.

"How do you know my name, old nut-cracker face?" inquired Tom Smart, rather staggered; though he pretended to carry it off so well.

"Come, come, Tom," said the old gentleman, "that's not the way to address solid Spanish mahogany. Damme, you couldn't treat me with less respect if I was veneered." When the old gentleman said this, he looked so fierce that Tom began to grow frightened.

"I didn't mean to treat you with any disrespect, Sir," said Tom, in a much humbler tone than he had spoken in at first.

"Well, well," said the old fellow, "perhaps not – perhaps not. Tom—"

"Sir—"

"I know everything about you, Tom; everything. You're very poor, Tom."

"I certainly am," said Tom Smart. "But how came you to know that?"

"Never mind that," said the old gentleman; "you're much too fond of punch, Tom."

Tom Smart was just on the point of protesting that he hadn't tasted a drop since his last birthday, but when his eye encountered that of the old gentleman he looked so knowing that Tom blushed, and was silent.

"Tom," said the old gentleman, "the widow's a fine woman – remarkably fine woman – eh, Tom?" Here the old fellow screwed up his eyes, cocked up one of his wasted little legs, and looked altogether so unpleasantly amorous, that Tom was quite disgusted with the levity of his behaviour – at his time of life, too!

"I am her guardian, Tom," said the old gentleman.

"Are you?" inquired Tom Smart.

"I knew her mother, Tom," said the old fellow: "and her grandmother. She was very fond of me – made me this waistcoat, Tom."

"Did she?" said Tom Smart.

"And these shoes," said the old fellow, lifting up one of the red cloth mufflers; "but don't mention it, Tom. I shouldn't like to have it known that she was so much attached to me. It might occasion some unpleasantness in the family." When the old rascal said this, he looked so extremely impertinent, that, as Tom Smart afterwards declared, he could have sat upon him without remorse.

"I have been a great favourite among the women in my time, Tom," said the profligate old debauchee; "hundreds of fine women have sat in my lap for hours together. What do you think of that, you dog, eh!" The old gentleman was proceeding to recount some other exploits of his youth, when he was seized with such a violent fit of creaking that he was unable to proceed.

"Just serves you right, old boy," thought Tom Smart; but he didn't say anything.

"Ah!" said the old fellow, "I am a good deal troubled with this now. I am getting old, Tom, and have lost nearly all my nails. I have had an operation performed, too – a small piece let into my back – and I found it a severe trial, Tom."

"I dare say you did, Sir," said Tom Smart.

"However," said the old gentleman, "that's not the point. Tom! I want you to marry the widow."

"Me, Sir!" said Tom.

"You," said the old gentleman.

"Bless your reverend locks," said Tom (he had a few scattered horse-hairs left) – "bless your reverend locks, she wouldn't have me." And Tom sighed involuntarily, as he thought of the bar.

"Wouldn't she?" said the old gentleman firmly.

CHARLES DICKENS SUPERNATURAL SHORT STORIES

"No, no," said Tom; "there's somebody else in the wind. A tall man – a confoundedly tall man – with black whiskers."

"Tom," said the old gentleman; "she will never have him."

"Won't she?" said Tom. "If you stood in the bar, old gentleman, you'd tell another story."

"Pooh, pooh," said the old gentleman. "I know all about that."

"About what?" said Tom.

"The kissing behind the door, and all that sort of thing, Tom," said the old gentleman. And here he gave another impudent look, which made Tom very wroth, because as you all know, gentlemen, to hear an old fellow, who ought to know better, talking about these things, is very unpleasant – nothing more so.

"I know all about that, Tom," said the old gentleman. "I have seen it done very often in my time, Tom, between more people than I should like to mention to you; but it never came to anything after all."

"You must have seen some queer things," said Tom, with an inquisitive look.

"You may say that, Tom," replied the old fellow, with a very complicated wink. "I am the last of my family, Tom," said the old gentleman, with a melancholy sigh.

"Was it a large one?" inquired Tom Smart.

"There were twelve of us, Tom," said the old gentleman; "fine, straight-backed, handsome fellows as you'd wish to see. None of your modern abortions – all with arms, and with a degree of polish, though I say it that should not, which it would have done your heart good to behold."

"And what's become of the others, Sir?" asked Tom Smart.

The old gentleman applied his elbow to his eye as he replied, "Gone, Tom, gone. We had hard service, Tom, and they hadn't all my constitution. They got rheumatic about the legs and arms, and went into kitchens and other hospitals; and one of 'em, with long service and hard usage, positively lost his senses – he got so crazy that he was obliged to be burnt. Shocking thing that, Tom."

"Dreadful!" said Tom Smart.

The old fellow paused for a few minutes, apparently struggling with his feelings of emotion, and then said –

"However, Tom, I am wandering from the point. This tall man, Tom, is a rascally adventurer. The moment he married the widow, he would sell off all the furniture, and run away. What would be the consequence? She would be deserted and reduced to ruin, and I should catch my death of cold in some broker's shop."

"Yes, but—"

"Don't interrupt me," said the old gentleman. "Of you, Tom, I entertain a very different opinion; for I well know that if you once settled yourself in a public-house, you would never leave it, as long as there was anything to drink within its walls."

"I am very much obliged to you for your good opinion, Sir," said Tom Smart.

"Therefore," resumed the old gentleman, in a dictatorial tone, "you shall have her, and he shall not."

"What is to prevent it?" said Tom Smart eagerly.

"This disclosure," replied the old gentleman; "he is already married."

"How can I prove it?" said Tom, starting half out of bed.

The old gentleman untucked his arm from his side, and having pointed to one of the oaken presses, immediately replaced it, in its old position.

"He little thinks," said the old gentleman, "that in the right-hand pocket of a pair of trousers in that press, he has left a letter, entreating him to return to his disconsolate wife, with six – mark me, Tom – six babes, and all of them small ones."

As the old gentleman solemnly uttered these words, his features grew less and less distinct, and his figure more shadowy. A film came over Tom Smart's eyes. The old man seemed gradually blending into the chair, the damask waistcoat to resolve into a cushion, the red slippers to shrink into little red cloth bags. The light faded gently away, and Tom Smart fell back on his pillow, and dropped asleep.

Morning aroused Tom from the lethargic slumber, into which he had fallen on the disappearance of the old man. He sat up in bed, and for some minutes vainly endeavoured to recall the events of the preceding night. Suddenly they rushed upon him. He looked at the chair; it was a fantastic and grim-looking piece of furniture, certainly, but it must have been a remarkably ingenious and lively imagination, that could have discovered any resemblance between it and an old man.

"How are you, old boy?" said Tom. He was bolder in the daylight – most men are.

The chair remained motionless, and spoke not a word.

"Miserable morning," said Tom. No. The chair would not be drawn into conversation.

"Which press did you point to? – you can tell me that," said Tom. Devil a word, gentlemen, the chair would say.

"It's not much trouble to open it, anyhow," said Tom, getting out of bed very deliberately. He walked up to one of the presses. The key was in the lock; he turned it, and opened the door. There was a pair of trousers there. He put his hand into the pocket, and drew forth the identical letter the old gentleman had described!

"Queer sort of thing, this," said Tom Smart, looking first at the chair and then at the press, and then at the letter, and then at the chair again. "Very queer," said Tom. But, as there was nothing in either, to lessen the queerness, he thought he might as well dress himself, and settle the tall man's business at once – just to put him out of his misery.

Tom surveyed the rooms he passed through, on his way downstairs, with the scrutinising eye of a landlord; thinking it not impossible, that before long, they and their contents would be his property. The tall man was standing in the snug little bar, with his hands behind him, quite at home. He grinned vacantly at Tom. A casual observer might have supposed he did it, only to show his white teeth; but Tom Smart thought that a consciousness of triumph was passing through the place where the tall man's mind would have been, if he had had any. Tom laughed in his face; and summoned the landlady.

"Good-morning ma'am," said Tom Smart, closing the door of the little parlour as the widow entered.

"Good-morning, Sir," said the widow. "What will you take for breakfast, sir?"

Tom was thinking how he should open the case, so he made no answer.

"There's a very nice ham," said the widow, "and a beautiful cold larded fowl. Shall I send 'em in, Sir?"

These words roused Tom from his reflections. His admiration of the widow increased as she spoke. Thoughtful creature! Comfortable provider!

"Who is that gentleman in the bar, ma'am?" inquired Tom.

"His name is Jinkins, Sir," said the widow, slightly blushing.

"He's a tall man," said Tom.

"He is a very fine man, Sir," replied the widow, "and a very nice gentleman."

"Ah!" said Tom.

"Is there anything more you want, Sir?" inquired the widow, rather puzzled by Tom's manner.

"Why, yes," said Tom. "My dear ma'am, will you have the kindness to sit down for one moment?"

The widow looked much amazed, but she sat down, and Tom sat down too, close beside her. I don't know how it happened, gentlemen – indeed my uncle used to tell me that Tom Smart said he didn't know how it happened either – but somehow or other the palm of Tom's hand fell upon the back of the widow's hand, and remained there while he spoke.

"My dear ma'am," said Tom Smart – he had always a great notion of committing the amiable – "my dear ma'am, you deserve a very excellent husband – you do indeed."

"Lor, Sir!" said the widow – as well she might; Tom's mode of commencing the conversation being rather unusual, not to say startling; the fact of his never having set eyes upon her before the previous night being taken into consideration. "Lor, Sir!"

"I scorn to flatter, my dear ma'am," said Tom Smart. "You deserve a very admirable husband, and whoever he is, he'll be a very lucky man." As Tom said this, his eye involuntarily wandered from the widow's face to the comfort around him.

The widow looked more puzzled than ever, and made an effort to rise. Tom gently pressed her hand, as if to detain her, and she kept her seat. Widows, gentlemen, are not usually timorous, as my uncle used to say.

"I am sure I am very much obliged to you, Sir, for your good opinion," said the buxom landlady, half laughing; "and if ever I marry again—"

"If," said Tom Smart, looking very shrewdly out of the right-hand corner of his left eye. "If—"

"Well," said the widow, laughing outright this time, "when I do, I hope I shall have as good a husband as you describe."

"Jinkins, to wit," said Tom.

"Lor, sir!" exclaimed the widow.

"Oh, don't tell me," said Tom, "I know him."

"I am sure nobody who knows him, knows anything bad of him," said the widow, bridling up at the mysterious air with which Tom had spoken.

"Hem!" said Tom Smart.

The widow began to think it was high time to cry, so she took out her handkerchief, and inquired whether Tom wished to insult her, whether he thought it like a gentleman to take away the character of another gentleman behind his back, why, if he had got anything to say, he didn't say it to the man, like a man, instead of terrifying a poor weak woman in that way; and so forth.

"I'll say it to him fast enough," said Tom, "only I want you to hear it first."

"What is it?" inquired the widow, looking intently in Tom's countenance.

"I'll astonish you," said Tom, putting his hand in his pocket.

"If it is, that he wants money," said the widow, "I know that already, and you needn't trouble yourself." "Pooh, nonsense, that's nothing," said Tom Smart, "I want money. 'Tain't that."

"Oh, dear, what can it be?" exclaimed the poor widow.

"Don't be frightened," said Tom Smart. He slowly drew forth the letter, and unfolded it. "You won't scream?" said Tom doubtfully.

"No, no," replied the widow; "let me see it."

"You won't go fainting away, or any of that nonsense?" said Tom.

"No, no," returned the widow hastily.

"And don't run out, and blow him up," said Tom; "because I'll do all that for you. You had better not exert yourself."

"Well, well," said the widow, "let me see it."

"I will," replied Tom Smart; and, with these words, he placed the letter in the widow's hand.

Gentlemen, I have heard my uncle say, that Tom Smart said the widow's lamentations when she heard the disclosure would have pierced a heart of stone. Tom was certainly very tender-hearted, but they pierced his, to the very core. The widow rocked herself to and fro, and wrung her hands.

"Oh, the deception and villainy of the man!" said the widow.

"Frightful, my dear ma'am; but compose yourself," said Tom Smart.

"Oh, I can't compose myself," shrieked the widow. "I shall never find anyone else I can love so much!"

"Oh, yes you will, my dear soul," said Tom Smart, letting fall a shower of the largest-sized tears, in pity for the widow's misfortunes. Tom Smart, in the energy of his compassion, had put his arm round the widow's waist; and the widow, in a passion of grief, had clasped Tom's hand. She looked up in Tom's face, and smiled through her tears. Tom looked down in hers, and smiled through his.

I never could find out, gentlemen, whether Tom did or did not kiss the widow at that particular moment. He used to tell my uncle he didn't, but I have my doubts about it. Between ourselves, gentlemen, I rather think he did.

At all events, Tom kicked the very tall man out at the front door half an hour later, and married the widow a month after. And he used to drive about the country, with the clay-coloured gig with the red wheels, and the vixenish mare with the fast pace, till he gave up business many years afterwards, and went to France with his wife; and then the old house was pulled down.

**If you enjoyed this, you might also like...**
The Story of the Goblins Who Stole a Sexton, see page 330
The Chimes, see page 337

# The Story of the Goblins Who Stole a Sexton

**IN AN OLD ABBEY TOWN,** down in this part of the country, a long, long while ago – so long, that the story must be a true one, because our great grandfathers implicitly believed it – there officiated as sexton and grave-digger in the church-yard, one Gabriel Grub. It by no means follows that because a man is a sexton, and constantly surrounded by emblems of mortality, therefore he should be a morose and melancholy man; your undertakers are the merriest fellows in the world, and I once had the honour of being on intimate terms with a mute, who in private life, and off duty, was as comical and jocose a little fellow as ever chirped out a devil-may-care song, without a hitch in his memory, or drained off a good stiff glass of grog without stopping for breath. But notwithstanding these precedents to the contrary, Gabriel Grub was an ill-conditioned, cross-grained, surly fellow – a morose and lonely man, who consorted with nobody but himself, and an old wicker bottle which fitted into his large deep waistcoat pocket; and who eyed each merry face as it passed him by, with such a deep scowl of malice and ill-humour, as it was difficult to meet without feeling something the worse for.

A little before twilight one Christmas Eve, Gabriel shouldered his spade, lighted his lantern, and betook himself towards the old church-yard, for he had got a grave to finish by next morning, and feeling very low he thought it might raise his spirits perhaps, if he went on with his work at once. As he wended his way up the ancient street, he saw the cheerful light of the blazing fires gleam through the old casements, and heard the loud laugh and the cheerful shouts of those who were assembled around them; he marked the bustling preparations for next day's good cheer, and smelt the numerous savoury odours consequent thereupon, as they steamed up from the kitchen windows in clouds. All this was gall and wormwood to the heart of Gabriel Grub; and as groups of children bounded out of the houses, tripped across the road, and were met, before they could knock at the opposite door, by half a dozen curly-headed little rascals who crowded round them as they flocked up stairs to spend the evening in their Christmas games, Gabriel smiled grimly, and clutched the handle of his spade with a firmer grasp, as he thought of measles, scarlet-fever, thrush, hooping-cough, and a good many other sources of consolation beside.

In this happy frame of mind, Gabriel strode along, returning a short, sullen growl to the good-humoured greetings of such of his neighbours as now and then passed him, until he turned into the dark lane which led to the church-yard. Now Gabriel had been looking forward to reaching the dark lane, because it was, generally speaking, a nice gloomy mournful place, into which the towns-people did not much care to go, except in broad daylight, and when the sun was shining; consequently he was not a little indignant to hear a young urchin roaring out some jolly song about a merry Christmas, in this very sanctuary, which had been called Coffin Lane ever since the days of the old abbey, and the time of the shaven-headed monks. As Gabriel walked on, and the voice drew nearer, he found it proceeded from a small boy, who was hurrying along, to join one of the little parties in the old street, and who, partly to keep himself company, and partly to prepare himself for the occasion, was shouting out the song at the highest pitch of his lungs. So Gabriel waited till the boy came up, and then dodged him into a corner, and rapped him over the head with his lantern five or six times, just to teach him to modulate his voice. And as the boy hurried away with his hand to his head, singing quite a different sort of tune, Gabriel Grub chuckled very heartily to himself, and entered the church-yard, locking the gate behind him.

He took off his coat, set down his lantern, and getting into the unfinished grave, worked at it for an hour or so, with right good-will. But the earth was hardened with the frost, and it was no very easy matter to break it up, and shovel it out; and although there was a moon, it was a very young one, and shed little light upon the grave, which was in the shadow of the church. At any other time, these obstacles would have made Gabriel Grub very moody and miserable, but he was so well pleased with having stopped the small boy's singing, that he took little heed of the scanty progress he had made, and looked down into the grave when he had finished work for the night, with grim satisfaction, murmuring as he gathered up his things –

> *Brave lodgings for one, brave lodgings for one,*
> *A few feet of cold earth, when life is done;*
> *A stone at the head, a stone at the feet,*
> *A rich, juicy meal for the worms to eat;*
> *Rank grass over head, and damp clay around,*
> *Brave lodgings for one, these, in holy ground!*

"Ho! ho!" laughed Gabriel Grub, as he sat himself down on a flat tombstone which was a favourite resting place of his and drew forth his wicker bottle. "A coffin at Christmas – a Christmas Box. Ho! ho! ho!"

"Ho! ho! ho!" repeated a voice which sounded close behind him.

Gabriel paused in some alarm, in the act of raising the wicker bottle to his lips, and looked round. The bottom of the oldest grave about him, was not more still and quiet, than the church-yard in the pale moonlight. The cold hoar frost glistened on the tombstones, and sparkled like rows of gems among the stone carvings of the old church. The snow lay hard and crisp upon the ground, and spread over the thickly-strewn mounds of earth, so white and smooth a cover, that it seemed as if corpses lay there, hidden only by their winding sheets. Not the faintest rustle broke the profound tranquillity of the solemn scene. Sound itself appeared to be frozen up, all was so cold and still.

"It was the echoes," said Gabriel Grub, raising the bottle to his lips again.

"It was *not*," said a deep voice.

Gabriel started up, and stood rooted to the spot with astonishment and terror; for his eyes rested on a form which made his blood run cold.

Seated on an upright tombstone, close to him, was a strange unearthly figure, whom Gabriel felt at once, was no being of this world. His long fantastic legs which might have reached the ground, were cocked up, and crossed after a quaint, fantastic fashion; his sinewy arms were bare, and his hands rested on his knees. On his short round body he wore a close covering, ornamented with small slashes; and a short cloak dangled at his back; the collar was cut into curious peaks, which served the goblin in lieu of ruff or neckerchief; and his shoes curled up at the toes into long points. On his head he wore a broad-brimmed sugar loaf hat, garnished with a single feather. The hat was covered with the white frost, and the goblin looked as if he had sat on the same tombstone very comfortably, for two or three hundred years. He was sitting perfectly still; his tongue was put out, as if in derision; and he was grinning at Gabriel Grub with such a grin as only a goblin could call up.

"It was *not* the echoes," said the goblin.

Gabriel Grub was paralysed, and could make no reply.

"What do you do here on Christmas eve?" said the goblin, sternly.

"I came to dig a grave Sir," stammered Gabriel Grub.

"What man wanders among graves and church-yards on such a night as this?" said the goblin.

"Gabriel Grub! Gabriel Grub!" screamed a wild chorus of voices that seemed to fill the church-yard. Gabriel looked fearfully round – nothing was to be seen.

"What have you got in that bottle?" said the goblin.

"Hollands, Sir," replied the sexton, trembling more than ever; for he had bought it of the smugglers, and he thought that perhaps his questioner might be in the excise department of the goblins.

"Who drinks Hollands alone, and in a church-yard, on such a night as this?" said the goblin.

"Gabriel Grub! Gabriel Grub!" exclaimed the wild voices again.

The goblin leered maliciously at the terrified sexton, and then raising his voice, exclaimed –

"And who, then, is our fair and lawful prize?"

To this inquiry the invisible chorus replied, in a strain that sounded like the voices of many choristers singing to the mighty swell of the old church organ – a strain that seemed borne to the sexton's ears upon a gentle wind, and to die away as its soft breath passed onward – but the burden of the reply was still the same, "Gabriel Grub! Gabriel Grub!"

The goblin grinned a broader grin than before, as he said, "Well, Gabriel, what do you say to this?"

The sexton gasped for breath.

"What do you think of this, Gabriel?" said the goblin, kicking up his feet in the air on either side the tombstone, and looking at the turned-up points with as much complacency as if he had been contemplating the most fashionable pair of Wellingtons in all Bond Street.

"It's – it's – very curious, Sir," replied the sexton, half dead with fright, "very curious, and very pretty, but I think I'll go back and finish my work, Sir, if you please."

"Work!" said the goblin, "what work?"

"The grave, Sir, making the grave," stammered the sexton.

"Oh, the grave, eh?" said the goblin, "who makes graves at a time when all other men are merry, and takes a pleasure in it?"

Again the mysterious voices replied, "Gabriel Grub! Gabriel Grub!"

"I'm afraid my friends want you, Gabriel," said the goblin, thrusting his tongue further into his cheek than ever – and a most astonishing tongue it was – "I'm afraid my friends want you, Gabriel," said the goblin.

"Under favour, Sir," replied the horror-struck sexton, "I don't think they can, Sir; they don't know me, Sir, I don't think the gentlemen have ever seen me, Sir."

"Oh yes they have," replied the goblin; "we know the man with the sulky face and the grim scowl, that came down the street to-night, throwing his evil looks at the children, and grasping his burying spade the tighter. We know the man that struck the boy in the envious malice of his heart, because the boy could be merry, and he could not. We know him, we know him."

Here the goblin gave a loud shrill laugh, that the echoes returned twenty-fold, and throwing his legs up in the air, stood upon his head, or rather upon the very point of his sugar-loaf hat, on the narrow edge of the tombstone, from whence he threw a summerset with extraordinary agility, right to the sexton's feet, at which he planted himself in the attitude in which tailors generally sit upon the shop-board.

"I – I – am afraid I must leave you, Sir," said the sexton, making an effort to move.

"Leave us!" said the goblin, "Gabriel Grub going to leave us. Ho! ho! ho!"

As the goblin laughed, the sexton observed for one instant a brilliant illumination within the windows of the church, as if the whole building were lighted up; it disappeared, the organ pealed forth a lively air, and whole troops of goblins, the very counterpart of the first one, poured into the church-yard, and began playing at leap-frog with the tombstones, never stopping for an instant to take breath, but overing the highest among them, one after the other, with the most marvellous dexterity. The first goblin was a most astonishing leaper, and none of the others could come near him; even in the extremity of his terror the sexton could not help observing, that while his friends were content to leap over the common-sized gravestones, the first one took the family vaults, iron railings and all, with as much ease as if they had been so many street posts.

At last the game reached to a most exciting pitch; the organ played quicker and quicker, and the goblins leaped faster and faster, coiling themselves up, rolling head over heels upon the ground, and bounding over the tombstones like foot-balls. The sexton's brain whirled round with the rapidity of the motion he beheld, and his legs reeled beneath him, as the spirits flew before his eyes, when the goblin king suddenly darting towards him, laid his hand upon his collar, and sank with him through the earth.

When Gabriel Grub had had time to fetch his breath, which the rapidity of his descent had for the moment taken away, he found himself in what appeared to be a large cavern, surrounded on all sides by crowds of goblins, ugly and grim; in the centre of the room, on an elevated seat, was stationed his friend of the church-yard; and close beside him stood Gabriel Grub himself, without the power of motion.

"Cold to-night," said the king of the goblins, "very cold. A glass of something warm, here."

At this command, half a dozen officious goblins, with a perpetual smile upon their faces, whom Gabriel Grub imagined to be courtiers, on that account, hastily disappeared, and presently returned with a goblet of liquid fire, which they presented to the king.

"Ah!" said the goblin, whose cheeks and throat were quite transparent, as he tossed down the flame, "This warms one, indeed: bring a bumper of the same, for Mr. Grub."

It was in vain for the unfortunate sexton to protest that he was not in the habit of taking anything warm at night; for one of the goblins held him while another poured the blazing liquid down his throat, and the whole assembly screeched with laughter as he coughed and choked, and wiped away the tears which gushed plentifully from his eyes, after swallowing the burning draught.

"And now," said the king, fantastically poking the taper corner of his sugar-loaf hat into the sexton's eye, and thereby occasioning him the most exquisite pain – "And now, show the man of misery and gloom a few of the pictures from our own great storehouse."

As the goblin said this, a thick cloud which obscured the further end of the cavern, rolled gradually away, and disclosed, apparently at a great distance, a small and scantily furnished, but neat and clean apartment. A crowd of little children were gathered round a bright fire, clinging to their mother's gown, and gambolling round her chair. The mother occasionally rose, and drew aside the window-curtain as if to look for some expected object; a frugal meal was ready spread upon the table, and an elbow chair was placed near the fire. A knock was heard at the door: the mother opened it, and the children crowded round her, and clapped their hands for joy, as their father entered. He was wet and weary, and shook the snow from his garments, as the children crowded round him, and seizing his cloak, hat, stick, and gloves, with busy zeal, ran with them from the room. Then as he sat down to his meal before the fire, the children climbed about his knee, and the mother sat by his side, and all seemed happiness and comfort.

But a change came upon the view, almost imperceptibly. The scene was altered to a small bed-room, where the fairest and youngest child lay dying; the roses had fled from his cheek, and the light from his eye; and even as the sexton looked upon him with an interest he had never felt or known before, he died. His young brothers and sisters crowded round his little bed, and seized his tiny hand, so cold and heavy; but they shrunk back from its touch, and looked with awe on his infant face; for calm and tranquil as it was, and sleeping in rest and peace as the beautiful child seemed to be, they saw that he was dead, and they knew that he was an angel looking down upon, and blessing them, from a bright and happy Heaven.

Again the light cloud passed across the picture, and again the subject changed. The father and mother were old and helpless now, and the number of those about them was diminished more than half; but content and cheerfulness sat on every face, and beamed in every eye, as they crowded round the fireside, and told and listened to old stories of earlier and bygone days. Slowly and peacefully the father sank into the grave, and, soon after, the sharer of all his cares and troubles followed him to a place of rest and peace. The few, who yet survived them, knelt by their tomb, and watered the green turf which covered it with their tears; then rose and turned away, sadly and mournfully, but not with bitter cries, or despairing lamentations, for they knew that they should one day meet again; and once more they mixed with the busy world, and their content and cheerfulness were restored. The cloud settled upon the picture, and concealed it from the sexton's view.

"What do you think of *that*?" said the goblin, turning his large face towards Gabriel Grub.

Gabriel murmured out something about its being very pretty, and looked somewhat ashamed, as the goblin bent his fiery eyes upon him.

"*You* a miserable man!" said the goblin, in a tone of excessive contempt. "You!" He appeared disposed to add more, but indignation choked his utterance, so he lifted up one of his very pliable legs, and flourishing it above his head a little, to insure his aid, administered a good sound kick to Gabriel Grub; immediately after which, all the goblins in waiting crowded round the wretched sexton, and kicked him without mercy, according to the established and invariable custom of courtiers upon earth, who kick whom royalty kicks, and hug whom royalty hugs.

"Show him some more," said the king of the goblins.

At these words the cloud was again dispelled, and a rich and beautiful landscape was disclosed to view – there is just such another to this day, within half a mile of the old abbey town. The sun shone from out the clear blue sky, the water sparkled beneath his rays, and the trees looked greener, and the flowers more gay, beneath his cheering influence. The water rippled on, with a pleasant sound, the trees rustled in the light wind that murmured among their leaves, the birds sang upon the boughs, and the lark carolled on high, her welcome to the morning. Yes, it was morning, the bright, balmy morning of summer; the minutest leaf, the smallest blade of grass, was instinct with life. The ant crept forth to her daily toil, the butterfly fluttered and basked in the warm rays of the sun; myriads of insects spread their transparent wings, and revelled in their brief but happy existence. Man walked forth, elated with the scene; and all was brightness and splendour.

"*You* a miserable man!" said the king of the goblins, in a more contemptuous tone than before. And again the king of the goblins gave his leg a flourish; again it descended on the shoulders of the sexton; and again the attendant goblins imitated the example of their chief.

Many a time the cloud went and came, and many a lesson it taught to Gabriel Grub, who although his shoulders smarted with pain from the frequent applications of the goblin's feet thereunto, looked on with an interest which nothing could diminish. He saw that men who worked hard, and earned their scanty bread with lives of labour, were cheerful and happy; and that to the most ignorant, the sweet face of nature was a never-failing source of cheerfulness and joy. He saw those who had been delicately nurtured, and tenderly brought up, cheerful under privations, and superior to suffering, that would have crushed many of a rougher grain, because they bore within their own bosoms the materials of happiness, contentment, and peace. He saw that women, the tenderest and most fragile of all God's creatures, were the oftenest superior to sorrow, adversity, and distress; and he saw that it was because they bore in their own hearts an inexhaustible wellspring of affection and devotedness. Above all, he saw that men like himself, who snarled at the mirth and cheerfulness of others, were the foulest weeds on the fair surface of the earth; and setting all the good of the world against the evil, he came to the conclusion that it was a very decent and respectable sort of world after all. No sooner had he formed it, than the cloud which had closed over the last picture, seemed to settle on his senses, and lull him to repose. One by one, the goblins faded from his sight, and as the last one disappeared, he sunk to sleep.

\* \* \*

The day had broken when Gabriel Grub awoke, and found himself lying at full length on the flat gravestone in the church-yard, with the wicker bottle lying empty by his side, and his coat, spade, and lantern, all well whitened by the last night's frost, scattered on the ground. The stone on which he had first seen the goblin seated, stood bolt upright before him, and the grave at which he had worked, the night before, was not far off. At first he began to doubt the reality of his adventures, but the acute pain in his shoulders when he attempted to rise, assured him that the kicking of the goblins was certainly not ideal. He was staggered again, by observing no traces of footsteps in the snow on which the goblins had played at leap-frog with the gravestones, but he speedily accounted for this circumstance when he remembered that being spirits, they would leave no visible impression behind them. So Gabriel Grub got on his feet as well as he could, for the pain in his back; and brushing the frost off his coat, put it on, and turned his face towards the town.

But he was an altered man, and he could not bear the thought of returning to a place where his repentance would be scoffed at, and his reformation disbelieved. He hesitated for a few moments; and then turned away to wander where he might, and seek his bread elsewhere.

The lantern, the spade, and the wicker bottle, were found that day in the church-yard. There were a great many speculations about the sexton's fate at first, but it was speedily determined that he had been carried away by the goblins; and there were not wanting some very credible witnesses who had distinctly seen him whisked through the air on the back of a chestnut horse blind of one eye, with the hind quarters of a lion, and the tail of a bear. At length all this was devoutly believed; and the new sexton used to exhibit to the curious for a trifling emolument, a good-sized piece of the church weathercock which had been accidentally kicked off by the aforesaid horse in his aërial flight, and picked up by himself in the church-yard, a year or two afterwards.

Unfortunately these stories were somewhat disturbed by the unlooked-for reappearance of Gabriel Grub himself, some ten years afterwards, a ragged, contented, rheumatic old man. He told his story to the clergyman, and also to the mayor; and in course of time it began to be received as a matter of history, in which form it has continued down to this very day. The believers in the weathercock tale, having misplaced their confidence once, were not easily prevailed upon to part with it again, so they looked as wise as they could, shrugged their shoulders, touched their foreheads, and murmured something about Gabriel Grub's having drunk all the Hollands, and then fallen asleep on the flat tombstone; and they affected to explain what he supposed he had witnessed in the goblin's cavern, by saying that he had seen the world, and grown wiser. But this opinion, which was by no means a popular one at any time, gradually died off; and be the matter how it may, as Gabriel Grub was afflicted with rheumatism to the end of his days, this story has at least one moral, if it teach no better one – and that is, that if a man turns sulky and drinks by himself at Christmas time, he may make up his mind to be not a bit the better for it, let the spirits be ever so good, or let them be even as many degrees beyond proof, as those which Gabriel Grub saw, in the goblin's cavern.

**If you enjoyed this, you might also like...**
The True Legend of Prince Bladud, see page 317
A Message from the Sea, see page 388

# The Chimes
## A Goblin Story

## Chapter I
## First Quarter

**THERE ARE NOT** many people – and as it is desirable that a story-teller and a story-reader should establish a mutual understanding as soon as possible, I beg it to be noticed that I confine this observation neither to young people nor to little people, but extend it to all conditions of people: little and big, young and old: yet growing up, or already growing down again – there are not, I say, many people who would care to sleep in a church. I don't mean at sermon-time in warm weather (when the thing has actually been done, once or twice), but in the night, and alone. A great multitude of persons will be violently astonished, I know, by this position, in the broad bold Day. But it applies to Night. It must be argued by night, and I will undertake to maintain it successfully on any gusty winter's night appointed for the purpose, with any one opponent chosen from the rest, who will meet me singly in an old churchyard, before an old church-door; and will previously empower me to lock him in, if needful to his satisfaction, until morning.

For the night-wind has a dismal trick of wandering round and round a building of that sort, and moaning as it goes; and of trying, with its unseen hand, the windows and the doors; and seeking out some crevices by which to enter. And when it has got in; as one not finding what it seeks, whatever that may be, it wails and howls to issue forth again: and not content with stalking through the aisles, and gliding round and round the pillars, and tempting the deep organ, soars up to the roof, and strives to rend the rafters: then flings itself despairingly upon the stones below, and passes, muttering, into the vaults. Anon, it comes up stealthily, and creeps along the walls, seeming to read, in whispers, the Inscriptions sacred to the Dead. At some of these, it breaks out shrilly, as with laughter; and at others, moans and cries as if it were lamenting. It has a ghostly sound too, lingering within the altar; where it seems to chaunt, in its wild way, of Wrong and Murder done, and false Gods worshipped, in defiance of the Tables of the Law, which look so fair and smooth, but are so flawed and broken. Ugh! Heaven preserve us, sitting snugly round the fire! It has an awful voice, that wind at Midnight, singing in a church!

But, high up in the steeple! There the foul blast roars and whistles! High up in the steeple, where it is free to come and go through many an airy arch and loophole, and to twist and twine itself about the giddy stair, and twirl the groaning weathercock; and make the very tower shake and shiver! High up in the steeple, where the belfry is, and iron rails are ragged with rust, and sheets of lead and copper, shrivelled by the changing weather, crackle and heave beneath the unaccustomed tread; and birds stuff shabby nests into corners of old oaken joists and beams; and dust grows old and grey; and speckled spiders, indolent and fat with long security, swing idly to and fro in the vibration of the bells, and never loose their hold upon their thread-spun castles in the air, or climb up sailor-like in quick alarm, or drop upon the ground and ply a score of nimble legs to save one life! High up in the steeple of an old church, far above the light and murmur of the town and far below the flying clouds that shadow it, is the wild and dreary place at night: and high up in the steeple of an old church, dwelt the Chimes I tell of.

They were old Chimes, trust me. Centuries ago, these Bells had been baptized by bishops: so many centuries ago, that the register of their baptism was lost long, long before the memory of man, and no one knew their names. They had had their Godfathers and Godmothers, these Bells (for my own part, by the way, I would rather incur the responsibility of being Godfather to a Bell than a Boy), and had their silver mugs no doubt, besides. But Time had mowed down their sponsors, and Henry the Eighth had melted down their mugs; and they now hung, nameless and mugless, in the church-tower.

Not speechless, though. Far from it. They had clear, loud, lusty, sounding voices, had these Bells; and far and wide they might be heard upon the wind. Much too sturdy Chimes were they, to be dependent on the pleasure of the wind, moreover; for, fighting gallantly against it when it took an adverse whim, they would pour their cheerful notes into a listening ear right royally; and bent on being heard on stormy nights, by some poor mother watching a sick child, or some lone wife whose husband was at sea, they had been sometimes known to beat a blustering Nor' Wester; aye, 'all to fits,' as Toby Veck said; – for though they chose to call him Trotty Veck, his name was Toby, and nobody could make it anything else either (except Tobias) without a special act of parliament; he having been as lawfully christened in his day as the Bells had been in theirs, though with not quite so much of solemnity or public rejoicing.

For my part, I confess myself of Toby Veck's belief, for I am sure he had opportunities enough of forming a correct one. And whatever Toby Veck said, I say. And I take my stand by Toby Veck, although he *did* stand all day long (and weary work it was) just outside the church-door. In fact he was a ticket-porter, Toby Veck, and waited there for jobs.

And a breezy, goose-skinned, blue-nosed, red-eyed, stony-toed, tooth-chattering place it was, to wait in, in the winter-time, as Toby Veck well knew. The wind came tearing round the corner – especially the east wind – as if it had sallied forth, express, from the confines of the earth, to have a blow at Toby. And oftentimes it seemed to come upon him sooner than it had expected, for bouncing round the corner, and passing Toby, it would suddenly wheel round again, as if it cried 'Why, here he is!' Incontinently his little white apron would be caught up over his head like a naughty boy's garments, and his feeble little cane would be seen to wrestle and struggle unavailingly in his hand, and his legs would undergo tremendous agitation, and Toby himself all aslant, and facing now in this direction, now in that, would be so banged and buffeted, and touzled, and worried, and hustled, and lifted off his feet, as to render it a state of things but one degree removed from a positive miracle, that he wasn't carried up bodily into the air as a colony of frogs or snails or other very portable creatures sometimes are, and rained down again, to the great astonishment of the natives, on some strange corner of the world where ticket-porters are unknown.

But, windy weather, in spite of its using him so roughly, was, after all, a sort of holiday for Toby. That's the fact. He didn't seem to wait so long for a sixpence in the wind, as at other times; the having to fight with that boisterous element took off his attention, and quite freshened him up, when he was getting hungry and low-spirited. A hard frost too, or a fall of snow, was an Event; and it seemed to do him good, somehow or other – it would have been hard to say in what respect though, Toby! So wind and frost and snow, and perhaps a good stiff storm of hail, were Toby Veck's red-letter days.

Wet weather was the worst; the cold, damp, clammy wet, that wrapped him up like a moist great-coat – the only kind of great-coat Toby owned, or could have added to his comfort by dispensing with. Wet days, when the rain came slowly, thickly, obstinately down; when the street's throat, like his own, was choked with mist; when smoking umbrellas passed and re-passed, spinning round and round like so many teetotums, as they knocked against each other on the crowded footway, throwing off a little whirlpool of uncomfortable sprinklings; when gutters brawled and waterspouts were full and noisy; when the wet from the projecting stones and ledges of the church fell drip, drip, drip, on Toby, making the wisp of straw on which he stood mere mud in no time; those were the days that tried him. Then, indeed, you might see Toby looking anxiously out from his shelter in an angle of the church wall – such a meagre shelter that in summer time it never cast a shadow thicker than a good-sized walking stick upon the sunny pavement – with a disconsolate and lengthened face. But coming out, a minute afterwards, to warm himself by exercise, and trotting up and down some dozen times, he would brighten even then, and go back more brightly to his niche.

They called him Trotty from his pace, which meant speed if it didn't make it. He could have walked faster perhaps; most likely; but rob him of his trot, and Toby would have taken to his bed and died. It bespattered him with mud in dirty weather; it cost him a world of trouble; he could have walked with infinitely greater ease; but that was one reason for his clinging to it so tenaciously. A weak, small, spare old man, he was a very Hercules, this Toby, in his good intentions. He loved to earn his money. He delighted to believe – Toby was very poor, and couldn't well afford to part with a delight – that he was worth his salt. With a shilling or an eighteenpenny message or small parcel in hand, his courage always high, rose higher. As he trotted on, he would call out to fast Postmen ahead of him, to get out of the way; devoutly believing that in the natural course of things he must inevitably overtake and run them down; and he had perfect faith – not often tested – in his being able to carry anything that man could lift.

Thus, even when he came out of his nook to warm himself on a wet day, Toby trotted. Making, with his leaky shoes, a crooked line of slushy footprints in the mire; and blowing on his chilly hands and rubbing them against each other, poorly defended from the searching cold by threadbare mufflers of grey worsted, with a private apartment only for the thumb, and a common room or tap for the rest of the fingers; Toby, with his knees bent and his cane beneath his arm, still trotted. Falling out into the road to look up at the belfry when the Chimes resounded, Toby trotted still.

He made this last excursion several times a day, for they were company to him; and when he heard their voices, he had an interest in glancing at their lodging-place, and thinking how they were moved, and what hammers beat upon them. Perhaps he was the more curious about these Bells, because there were points of resemblance between themselves and him. They hung there, in all weathers, with the wind and rain driving in upon them; facing only the outsides of all those houses; never getting any nearer to the blazing fires that gleamed and shone upon the windows, or came puffing out of the chimney tops; and incapable of participation in any of the good things that were constantly being handed through the street doors and the area railings, to prodigious cooks. Faces came and went at many windows: sometimes pretty faces, youthful faces, pleasant faces: sometimes the reverse: but Toby knew no more (though he often speculated on these trifles, standing idle in the streets) whence they came, or where they went, or whether, when the lips moved, one kind word was said of him in all the year, than did the Chimes themselves.

Toby was not a casuist – that he knew of, at least – and I don't mean to say that when he began to take to the Bells, and to knit up his first rough acquaintance with them into something of a closer and more delicate woof, he passed through these considerations one by one, or held any formal review or great field-day in his thoughts. But what I mean to say, and do say is, that as the functions of Toby's body, his digestive organs for example, did of their own cunning, and by a great many operations of which he was altogether ignorant, and the knowledge of which would have astonished him very much, arrive at a certain end; so his mental faculties, without his privity or concurrence, set all these wheels and springs in motion, with a thousand others, when they worked to bring about his liking for the Bells.

And though I had said his love, I would not have recalled the word, though it would scarcely have expressed his complicated feeling. For, being but a simple man, he invested them with a strange and solemn character. They were so mysterious, often heard and never seen; so high up, so far off, so full of such a deep strong melody, that he regarded them with a species of awe; and sometimes when he looked up at the dark arched windows in the tower, he half expected to be beckoned to by something which was not a Bell, and yet was what he had heard so often sounding in the Chimes. For all this, Toby scouted with indignation a certain flying rumour that the Chimes were haunted, as implying the possibility of their being connected with any Evil thing. In short, they were very often in his ears, and very often in his thoughts, but always in his good opinion; and he very often got such a crick in his neck by staring with his mouth wide open, at the steeple where they hung, that he was fain to take an extra trot or two, afterwards, to cure it.

The very thing he was in the act of doing one cold day, when the last drowsy sound of Twelve o'clock, just struck, was humming like a melodious monster of a Bee, and not by any means a busy bee, all through the steeple!

"Dinner-time, eh!" said Toby, trotting up and down before the church. "Ah!"

Toby's nose was very red, and his eyelids were very red, and he winked very much, and his shoulders were very near his ears, and his legs were very stiff, and altogether he was evidently a long way upon the frosty side of cool.

"Dinner-time, eh!" repeated Toby, using his right-hand muffler like an infantine boxing-glove, and punishing his chest for being cold. "Ah-h-h-h!"

He took a silent trot, after that, for a minute or two.

"There's nothing," said Toby, breaking forth afresh – but here he stopped short in his trot, and with a face of great interest and some alarm, felt his nose carefully all the way up. It was but a little way (not being much of a nose) and he had soon finished.

"I thought it was gone," said Toby, trotting off again. "It's all right, however. I am sure I couldn't blame it if it was to go. It has a precious hard service of it in the bitter weather, and precious little to look forward to; for I don't take snuff myself. It's a good deal tried, poor creetur, at the best of times; for when it *does* get hold of a pleasant whiff or so (which an't too often) it's generally from somebody else's dinner, a-coming home from the baker's."

The reflection reminded him of that other reflection, which he had left unfinished.

"There's nothing," said Toby, "more regular in its coming round than dinner-time, and nothing less regular in its coming round than dinner. That's the great difference between 'em. It's took me a long time to find it out. I wonder whether it would be worth any gentleman's while, now, to buy that obserwation for the Papers; or the Parliament!"

Toby was only joking, for he gravely shook his head in self-depreciation.

"Why! Lord!" said Toby. "The Papers is full of obserwations as it is; and so's the Parliament. Here's last week's paper, now;" taking a very dirty one from his pocket, and holding it from him at arm's length; "full of obserwations! Full of obserwations! I like to know the news as well as any man," said Toby, slowly; folding it a little smaller, and putting it in his pocket again: "but it almost goes against the grain with me to read a paper now. It frightens me almost. I don't know what we poor people are coming to. Lord send we may be coming to something better in the New Year nigh upon us!"

"Why, father, father!" said a pleasant voice, hard by.

But Toby, not hearing it, continued to trot backwards and forwards: musing as he went, and talking to himself.

"It seems as if we can't go right, or do right, or be righted," said Toby. "I hadn't much schooling, myself, when I was young; and I can't make out whether we have any business on the face of the earth, or not. Sometimes I think we must have – a little; and sometimes I think we must be intruding. I get so puzzled sometimes that I am not even able to make up my mind whether there is any good at all in us, or whether we are born bad. We seem to be dreadful things; we seem to give a deal of trouble; we are always being complained of and guarded against. One way or other, we fill the papers. Talk of a New Year!" said Toby, mournfully. "I can bear up as well as another man at most times; better than a good many, for I am as strong as a lion, and all men an't; but supposing it should really be that we have no right to a New Year – supposing we really *are* intruding—"

"Why, father, father!" said the pleasant voice again.

Toby heard it this time; started; stopped; and shortening his sight, which had been directed a long way off as seeking the enlightenment in the very heart of the approaching year, found himself face to face with his own child, and looking close into her eyes.

Bright eyes they were. Eyes that would bear a world of looking in, before their depth was fathomed. Dark eyes, that reflected back the eyes which searched them; not flashingly, or at the owner's will, but with a clear, calm, honest, patient radiance, claiming kindred with that light which Heaven called into being. Eyes that were beautiful and true, and beaming with Hope. With Hope so young and fresh; with Hope so buoyant, vigorous, and bright, despite the twenty years of work and poverty on which they had looked; that they became a voice to Trotty Veck, and said: "I think we have some business here – a little!"

Trotty kissed the lips belonging to the eyes, and squeezed the blooming face between his hands.

"Why, Pet," said Trotty. "What's to do? I didn't expect you today, Meg."

"Neither did I expect to come, father," cried the girl, nodding her head and smiling as she spoke. "But here I am! And not alone; not alone!"

"Why you don't mean to say," observed Trotty, looking curiously at a covered basket which she carried in her hand, "that you—"

"Smell it, father dear," said Meg. "Only smell it!"

Trotty was going to lift up the cover at once, in a great hurry, when she gaily interposed her hand.

"No, no, no," said Meg, with the glee of a child. "Lengthen it out a little. Let me just lift up the corner; just the lit-tle ti-ny cor-ner, you know," said Meg, suiting the action to the word with the utmost gentleness, and speaking very softly, as if she were afraid of being overheard by something inside the basket; "there. Now. What's that?"

Toby took the shortest possible sniff at the edge of the basket, and cried out in a rapture:

"Why, it's hot!"

"It's burning hot!" cried Meg. "Ha, ha, ha! It's scalding hot!"

"Ha, ha, ha!" roared Toby, with a sort of kick. "It's scalding hot!"

"But what is it, father?" said Meg. "Come. You haven't guessed what it is. And you must guess what it is. I can't think of taking it out, till you guess what it is. Don't be in such a hurry! Wait a minute! A little bit more of the cover. Now guess!"

Meg was in a perfect fright lest he should guess right too soon; shrinking away, as she held the basket towards him; curling up her pretty shoulders; stopping her ear with her hand, as if by so doing she could keep the right word out of Toby's lips; and laughing softly the whole time.

Meanwhile Toby, putting a hand on each knee, bent down his nose to the basket, and took a long inspiration at the lid; the grin upon his withered face expanding in the process, as if he were inhaling laughing gas.

"Ah! It's very nice," said Toby. "It an't – I suppose it an't Polonies?"

"No, no, no!" cried Meg, delighted. "Nothing like Polonies!"

"No," said Toby, after another sniff. "It's – it's mellower than Polonies. It's very nice. It improves every moment. It's too decided for Trotters. An't it?"

Meg was in an ecstasy. He could not have gone wider of the mark than Trotters – except Polonies.

"Liver?" said Toby, communing with himself. "No. There's a mildness about it that don't answer to liver. Pettitoes? No. It an't faint enough for pettitoes. It wants the stringiness of Cocks' heads. And I know it an't sausages. I'll tell you what it is. It's chitterlings!"

"No, it an't!" cried Meg, in a burst of delight. "No, it an't!"

"Why, what am I a-thinking of!" said Toby, suddenly recovering a position as near the perpendicular as it was possible for him to assume. "I shall forget my own name next. It's tripe!"

Tripe it was; and Meg, in high joy, protested he should say, in half a minute more, it was the best tripe ever stewed.

"And so," said Meg, busying herself exultingly with the basket, "I'll lay the cloth at once, father; for I have brought the tripe in a basin, and tied the basin up in a pocket-handkerchief; and if I like to be proud for once, and spread that for a cloth, and call it a cloth, there's no law to prevent me; is there, father?"

"Not that I know of, my dear," said Toby. "But they're always a-bringing up some new law or other."

"And according to what I was reading you in the paper the other day, father; what the Judge said, you know; we poor people are supposed to know them all. Ha ha! What a mistake! My goodness me, how clever they think us!"

"Yes, my dear," cried Trotty; "and they'd be very fond of any one of us that *did* know 'em all. He'd grow fat upon the work he'd get, that man, and be popular with the gentlefolks in his neighbourhood. Very much so!"

"He'd eat his dinner with an appetite, whoever he was, if it smelt like this," said Meg, cheerfully. "Make haste, for there's a hot potato besides, and half a pint of fresh-drawn beer in a bottle. Where will you dine, father? On the Post, or on the Steps? Dear, dear, how grand we are. Two places to choose from!"

"The steps today, my Pet," said Trotty. "Steps in dry weather. Post in wet. There's a greater conveniency in the steps at all times, because of the sitting down; but they're rheumatic in the damp."

"Then here," said Meg, clapping her hands, after a moment's bustle; "here it is, all ready! And beautiful it looks! Come, father. Come!"

Since his discovery of the contents of the basket, Trotty had been standing looking at her – and had been speaking too – in an abstracted manner, which showed that though she was the object of his thoughts and eyes, to the exclusion even of tripe, he neither saw nor thought about her as she was at that moment, but had before him some imaginary rough sketch or drama of her future life. Roused, now, by her cheerful summons, he shook off a melancholy shake of the head which was just coming upon him, and trotted to her side. As he was stooping to sit down, the Chimes rang.

"Amen!" said Trotty, pulling off his hat and looking up towards them.

"Amen to the Bells, father?" cried Meg.

"They broke in like a grace, my dear," said Trotty, taking his seat. "They'd say a good one, I am sure, if they could. Many's the kind thing they say to me."

"The Bells do, father!" laughed Meg, as she set the basin, and a knife and fork, before him. "Well!"

"Seem to, my Pet," said Trotty, falling to with great vigour. "And where's the difference? If I hear 'em, what does it matter whether they speak it or not? Why bless you, my dear," said Toby, pointing at the tower with his fork, and becoming more animated under the influence of dinner, "how often have I heard them bells say, "Toby Veck, Toby Veck, keep a good heart, Toby! Toby Veck, Toby Veck, keep a good heart, Toby!" A million times? More!"

"Well, I never!" cried Meg.

She had, though – over and over again. For it was Toby's constant topic.

"When things is very bad," said Trotty; "very bad indeed, I mean; almost at the worst; then it's 'Toby Veck, Toby Veck, job coming soon, Toby! Toby Veck, Toby Veck, job coming soon, Toby!' That way."

"And it comes – at last, father," said Meg, with a touch of sadness in her pleasant voice.

"Always," answered the unconscious Toby. "Never fails."

While this discourse was holding, Trotty made no pause in his attack upon the savoury meat before him, but cut and ate, and cut and drank, and cut and chewed, and dodged about, from tripe to hot potato, and from hot potato back again to tripe, with an unctuous and unflagging relish. But happening now to look all round the street – in case anybody should be beckoning from any door or window, for a porter – his eyes, in coming back again, encountered Meg: sitting opposite to him, with her arms folded and only busy in watching his progress with a smile of happiness.

"Why, Lord forgive me!" said Trotty, dropping his knife and fork. "My dove! Meg! why didn't you tell me what a beast I was?"

"Father?"

"Sitting here," said Trotty, in penitent explanation, "cramming, and stuffing, and gorging myself; and you before me there, never so much as breaking your precious fast, nor wanting to, when—"

"But I have broken it, father," interposed his daughter, laughing, "all to bits. I have had my dinner."

"Nonsense," said Trotty. "Two dinners in one day! It an't possible! You might as well tell me that two New Year's Days will come together, or that I have had a gold head all my life, and never changed it."

"I have had my dinner, father, for all that," said Meg, coming nearer to him. "And if you'll go on with yours, I'll tell you how and where; and how your dinner came to be brought; and – and something else besides."

Toby still appeared incredulous; but she looked into his face with her clear eyes, and laying her hand upon his shoulder, motioned him to go on while the meat was hot. So Trotty took up his knife and fork again, and went to work. But much more slowly than before, and shaking his head, as if he were not at all pleased with himself.

"I had my dinner, father," said Meg, after a little hesitation, "with – with Richard. His dinner-time was early; and as he brought his dinner with him when he came to see me, we – we had it together, father."

Trotty took a little beer, and smacked his lips. Then he said, "Oh!" – because she waited.

"And Richard says, father—" Meg resumed. Then stopped.

"What does Richard say, Meg?" asked Toby.

"Richard says, father—" Another stoppage.

"Richard's a long time saying it," said Toby.

"He says then, father," Meg continued, lifting up her eyes at last, and speaking in a tremble, but quite plainly; "another year is nearly gone, and where is the use of waiting on from year to year, when it is so unlikely we shall ever be better off than we are now? He says we are poor now, father, and we shall be poor then, but we are young now, and years will make us old before we know it. He says that if we wait: people in our condition: until we see our way quite clearly, the way will be a narrow one indeed – the common way – the Grave, father."

A bolder man than Trotty Veck must needs have drawn upon his boldness largely, to deny it. Trotty held his peace.

"And how hard, father, to grow old, and die, and think we might have cheered and helped each other! How hard in all our lives to love each other; and to grieve, apart, to see each other working, changing, growing old and grey. Even if I got the better of it, and forgot him (which I never could), oh father dear, how hard to have a heart so full as mine is now, and live to have it slowly drained out every drop, without the recollection of one happy moment of a woman's life, to stay behind and comfort me, and make me better!"

Trotty sat quite still. Meg dried her eyes, and said more gaily: that is to say, with here a laugh, and there a sob, and here a laugh and sob together:

"So Richard says, father; as his work was yesterday made certain for some time to come, and as I love him, and have loved him full three years – ah! longer than that, if he knew it! – will I marry him on New Year's Day; the best and happiest day, he says, in the whole year, and one that is almost sure to bring good fortune with it. It's a short notice, father – isn't it? – but I haven't my fortune to be settled, or my wedding dresses to be made, like the great ladies, father, have I? And he said so much, and said it in his way; so strong and earnest, and all the time so kind and gentle; that I said I'd come and talk to you, father. And as they paid the money for that work of mine this morning (unexpectedly, I am sure!) and as you have fared very poorly for a whole week, and as I couldn't help wishing there should be something to make this day a sort of holiday to you as well as a dear and happy day to me, father, I made a little treat and brought it to surprise you."

"And see how he leaves it cooling on the step!" said another voice.

It was the voice of this same Richard, who had come upon them unobserved, and stood before the father and daughter; looking down upon them with a face as glowing as the iron on which his stout sledge-hammer daily rung. A handsome, well-made, powerful youngster he was; with eyes that sparkled like the red-hot droppings from a furnace fire; black hair that curled about his swarthy temples rarely; and a smile – a smile that bore out Meg's eulogium on his style of conversation.

"See how he leaves it cooling on the step!" said Richard. "Meg don't know what he likes. Not she!"

Trotty, all action and enthusiasm, immediately reached up his hand to Richard, and was going to address him in great hurry, when the house-door opened without any warning, and a footman very nearly put his foot into the tripe.

"Out of the vays here, will you! You must always go and be a-settin on our steps, must you! You can't go and give a turn to none of the neighbours never, can't you! *Will* you clear the road, or won't you?"

Strictly speaking, the last question was irrelevant, as they had already done it.

"What's the matter, what's the matter!" said the gentleman for whom the door was opened; coming out of the house at that kind of light-heavy pace – that peculiar compromise between a walk and a jog-trot – with which a gentleman upon the smooth down-hill of life, wearing creaking boots, a watch-chain, and clean linen, *may* come out of his house: not only without any abatement of his dignity, but with an expression of having important and wealthy engagements elsewhere. "What's the matter! What's the matter!"

"You're always a-being begged, and prayed, upon your bended knees you are," said the footman with great emphasis to Trotty Veck, "to let our door-steps be. Why don't you let 'em be? Can't you let 'em be?"

"There! That'll do, that'll do!" said the gentleman. "Halloa there! Porter!" beckoning with his head to Trotty Veck. "Come here. What's that? Your dinner?"

"Yes, sir," said Trotty, leaving it behind him in a corner.

"Don't leave it there," exclaimed the gentleman. "Bring it here, bring it here. So! This is your dinner, is it?"

"Yes, sir," repeated Trotty, looking with a fixed eye and a watery mouth, at the piece of tripe he had reserved for a last delicious tit-bit; which the gentleman was now turning over and over on the end of the fork.

Two other gentlemen had come out with him. One was a low-spirited gentleman of middle age, of a meagre habit, and a disconsolate face; who kept his hands continually in the pockets of his scanty pepper-and-salt trousers, very large and dog's-eared from that custom; and was not particularly well brushed or washed. The other, a full-sized, sleek, well-conditioned gentleman, in a blue coat with bright buttons, and a white cravat. This gentleman had a very red face, as if an undue proportion of the blood in his body were squeezed up into his head; which perhaps accounted for his having also the appearance of being rather cold about the heart.

He who had Toby's meat upon the fork, called to the first one by the name of Filer; and they both drew near together. Mr. Filer being exceedingly short-sighted, was obliged to go so close to the remnant of Toby's dinner before he could make out what it was, that Toby's heart leaped up into his mouth. But Mr. Filer didn't eat it.

"This is a description of animal food, Alderman," said Filer, making little punches in it with a pencil-case, "commonly known to the labouring population of this country, by the name of tripe."

The Alderman laughed, and winked; for he was a merry fellow, Alderman Cute. Oh, and a sly fellow too! A knowing fellow. Up to everything. Not to be imposed upon. Deep in the people's hearts! He knew them, Cute did. I believe you!

"But who eats tripe?" said Mr. Filer, looking round. "Tripe is without an exception the least economical, and the most wasteful article of consumption that the markets of this country can by possibility produce. The loss upon a pound of tripe has been found to be, in the boiling, seven-eights of a fifth more than the loss upon a pound of any other animal substance whatever. Tripe is more expensive, properly understood, than the hothouse pine-apple. Taking into account the number of animals slaughtered yearly within the bills of mortality alone; and forming a low estimate of the quantity of tripe which the carcases of those animals, reasonably well butchered, would yield; I find that the waste on that amount of tripe, if boiled, would victual a garrison of five hundred men for five months of thirty-one days each, and a February over. The Waste, the Waste!"

Trotty stood aghast, and his legs shook under him. He seemed to have starved a garrison of five hundred men with his own hand.

"Who eats tripe?" said Mr. Filer, warmly. "Who eats tripe?"

Trotty made a miserable bow.

"You do, do you?" said Mr. Filer. "Then I'll tell you something. You snatch your tripe, my friend, out of the mouths of widows and orphans."

"I hope not, sir," said Trotty, faintly. "I'd sooner die of want!"

"Divide the amount of tripe before-mentioned, Alderman," said Mr. Filer, "by the estimated number of existing widows and orphans, and the result will be one pennyweight of tripe to each. Not a grain is left for that man. Consequently, he's a robber."

Trotty was so shocked, that it gave him no concern to see the Alderman finish the tripe himself. It was a relief to get rid of it, anyhow.

"And what do you say?" asked the Alderman, jocosely, of the red-faced gentleman in the blue coat. "You have heard friend Filer. What do *you say*?"

"What's it possible to say?" returned the gentleman. "What *is* to be said? Who can take any interest in a fellow like this," meaning Trotty; "in such degenerate times as these? Look at him. What an object! The good old times, the grand old times, the great old times! *Those* were the times for a bold peasantry, and all that sort of thing. Those were the times for every sort of thing, in fact. There's nothing now-a-days. Ah!" sighed the red-faced gentleman. "The good old times, the good old times!"

The gentleman didn't specify what particular times he alluded to; nor did he say whether he objected to the present times, from a disinterested consciousness that they had done nothing very remarkable in producing himself.

"The good old times, the good old times," repeated the gentleman. "What times they were! They were the only times. It's of no use talking about any other times, or discussing what the people are in *these* times. You don't call these, times, do you? I don't. Look into Strutt's Costumes, and see what a Porter used to be, in any of the good old English reigns."

"He hadn't, in his very best circumstances, a shirt to his back, or a stocking to his foot; and there was scarcely a vegetable in all England for him to put into his mouth," said Mr. Filer. "I can prove it, by tables."

But still the red-faced gentleman extolled the good old times, the grand old times, the great old times. No matter what anybody else said, he still went turning round and round in one set form of words concerning them; as a poor squirrel turns and turns in its revolving cage; touching the mechanism, and trick of which, it has probably quite as distinct perceptions, as ever this red-faced gentleman had of his deceased Millennium.

It is possible that poor Trotty's faith in these very vague Old Times was not entirely destroyed, for he felt vague enough at that moment. One thing, however, was plain to him, in the midst of his distress; to wit, that however these gentlemen might differ in details, his misgivings of that morning, and of many other mornings, were well founded. "No, no. We can't go right or do right," thought Trotty in despair. "There is no good in us. We are born bad!"

But Trotty had a father's heart within him; which had somehow got into his breast in spite of this decree; and he could not bear that Meg, in the blush of her brief joy, should have her fortune read by these wise gentlemen. "God help her," thought poor Trotty. "She will know it soon enough."

He anxiously signed, therefore, to the young smith, to take her away. But he was so busy, talking to her softly at a little distance, that he only became conscious of this desire, simultaneously with Alderman Cute. Now, the Alderman had not yet had his say, but *he* was a philosopher, too – practical, though! Oh, very practical – and, as he had no idea of losing any portion of his audience, he cried "Stop!"

"Now, you know," said the Alderman, addressing his two friends, with a self-complacent smile upon his face which was habitual to him, "I am a plain man, and a practical man; and I go to work in a plain practical way. That's my way. There is not the least mystery or difficulty in dealing with this sort of people if you only understand 'em, and can talk to 'em in their own manner. Now, you Porter! Don't you ever tell me, or anybody else, my friend, that you haven't always enough to eat, and of the best; because I know better. I have tasted your tripe, you know, and you can't 'chaff' me. You understand what 'chaff' means, eh? That's the right word, isn't it? Ha, ha, ha! Lord bless you," said the Alderman, turning to his friends again, "it's the easiest thing on earth to deal with this sort of people, if you understand 'em."

Famous man for the common people, Alderman Cute! Never out of temper with them! Easy, affable, joking, knowing gentleman!

"You see, my friend," pursued the Alderman, "there's a great deal of nonsense talked about Want – 'hard up,' you know; that's the phrase, isn't it? ha! ha! ha! – and I intend to Put it Down. There's a certain amount of cant in vogue about Starvation, and I mean to Put it Down. That's all! Lord bless you," said the Alderman, turning to his friends again, "you may Put Down anything among this sort of people, if you only know the way to set about it."

Trotty took Meg's hand and drew it through his arm. He didn't seem to know what he was doing though.

"Your daughter, eh?" said the Alderman, chucking her familiarly under the chin.

Always affable with the working classes, Alderman Cute! Knew what pleased them! Not a bit of pride!

"Where's her mother?" asked that worthy gentleman.

"Dead," said Toby. "Her mother got up linen; and was called to Heaven when She was born."

"Not to get up linen *there*, I suppose," remarked the Alderman pleasantly.

Toby might or might not have been able to separate his wife in Heaven from her old pursuits. But query: If Mrs. Alderman Cute had gone to Heaven, would Mr. Alderman Cute have pictured her as holding any state or station there?

"And you're making love to her, are you?" said Cute to the young smith.

"Yes," returned Richard quickly, for he was nettled by the question. "And we are going to be married on New Year's Day."

"What do you mean!" cried Filer sharply. "Married!"

"Why, yes, we're thinking of it, Master," said Richard. "We're rather in a hurry, you see, in case it should be Put Down first."

"Ah!" cried Filer, with a groan. "Put *that* down indeed, Alderman, and you'll do something. Married! Married!! The ignorance of the first principles of political economy on the part of these people; their improvidence; their wickedness; is, by Heavens! enough to— Now look at that couple, will you!"

Well? They were worth looking at. And marriage seemed as reasonable and fair a deed as they need have in contemplation.

"A man may live to be as old as Methuselah," said Mr. Filer, "and may labour all his life for the benefit of such people as those; and may heap up facts on figures, facts on figures, facts on figures, mountains high and dry; and he can no more hope to persuade 'em that they have no right or business to be married, than he can hope to persuade 'em that they have no earthly right or business to be born. And *that* we know they haven't. We reduced it to a mathematical certainty long ago!"

Alderman Cute was mightily diverted, and laid his right forefinger on the side of his nose, as much as to say to both his friends, "Observe me, will you! Keep your eye on the practical man!" – and called Meg to him.

"Come here, my girl!" said Alderman Cute.

The young blood of her lover had been mounting, wrathfully, within the last few minutes; and he was indisposed to let her come. But, setting a constraint upon himself, he came forward with a stride as Meg approached, and stood beside her. Trotty kept her hand within his arm still, but looked from face to face as wildly as a sleeper in a dream.

"Now, I'm going to give you a word or two of good advice, my girl," said the Alderman, in his nice easy way. "It's my place to give advice, you know, because I'm a Justice. You know I'm a Justice, don't you?"

Meg timidly said, "Yes." But everybody knew Alderman Cute was a Justice! Oh dear, so active a Justice always! Who such a mote of brightness in the public eye, as Cute!

"You are going to be married, you say," pursued the Alderman. "Very unbecoming and indelicate in one of your sex! But never mind that. After you are married, you'll quarrel with your husband and come to be a distressed wife. You may think not; but you will, because I tell you so. Now, I give you fair warning, that I have made up my mind to Put distressed wives Down. So, don't be brought before me. You'll have children – boys. Those boys will grow up bad, of course, and run wild in the streets, without shoes and stockings. Mind, my young friend! I'll convict 'em summarily, every one, for I am determined to Put boys without shoes and stockings, Down. Perhaps your husband will die young (most likely) and leave you with a baby. Then you'll be turned out of doors, and wander up and down the streets. Now, don't wander near me, my dear, for I am resolved, to Put all wandering mothers Down. All young mothers, of all sorts and kinds, it's my determination to Put Down. Don't think to plead illness as an excuse with me; or babies as an excuse with me; for all sick persons and young children (I hope you know the church-service, but I'm afraid not) I am determined to Put Down. And if you attempt, desperately, and ungratefully, and impiously, and fraudulently attempt, to drown yourself, or hang yourself, I'll have no pity for you, for I have made up my mind to Put all suicide Down! If there is one thing," said the Alderman, with his self-satisfied smile, "on which I can be said to have made up my mind more than on another, it is to Put suicide Down. So don't try it on. That's the phrase, isn't it? Ha, ha! now we understand each other."

Toby knew not whether to be agonised or glad, to see that Meg had turned a deadly white, and dropped her lover's hand.

"And as for you, you dull dog," said the Alderman, turning with even increased cheerfulness and urbanity to the young smith, "what are you thinking of being married for? What do you want to be married for, you silly fellow? If I was a fine, young, strapping chap like you, I should be ashamed of being milksop enough to pin myself to a woman's apron-strings! Why, she'll be an old woman before you're a middle-aged man! And a pretty figure you'll cut then, with a draggle-tailed wife and a crowd of squalling children crying after you wherever you go!"

O, he knew how to banter the common people, Alderman Cute!

"There! Go along with you," said the Alderman, "and repent. Don't make such a fool of yourself as to get married on New Year's Day. You'll think very differently of it, long before next New Year's Day: a trim young fellow like you, with all the girls looking after you. There! Go along with you!"

They went along. Not arm in arm, or hand in hand, or interchanging bright glances; but, she in tears; he, gloomy and down-looking. Were these the hearts that had so lately made old Toby's leap up from its faintness? No, no. The Alderman (a blessing on his head!) had Put *them* Down.

"As you happen to be here," said the Alderman to Toby, "you shall carry a letter for me. Can you be quick? You're an old man."

Toby, who had been looking after Meg, quite stupidly, made shift to murmur out that he was very quick, and very strong.

"How old are you?" inquired the Alderman.

"I'm over sixty, sir," said Toby.

"O! This man's a great deal past the average age, you know," cried Mr. Filer breaking in as if his patience would bear some trying, but this really was carrying matters a little too far.

"I feel I'm intruding, sir," said Toby. "I – I misdoubted it this morning. Oh dear me!"

The Alderman cut him short by giving him the letter from his pocket. Toby would have got a shilling too; but Mr. Filer clearly showing that in that case he would rob a certain given number of persons of ninepence-halfpenny a-piece, he only got sixpence; and thought himself very well off to get that.

Then the Alderman gave an arm to each of his friends, and walked off in high feather; but, he immediately came hurrying back alone, as if he had forgotten something.

"Porter!" said the Alderman.

"Sir!" said Toby.

"Take care of that daughter of yours. She's much too handsome."

"Even her good looks are stolen from somebody or other, I suppose," thought Toby, looking at the sixpence in his hand, and thinking of the tripe. "She's been and robbed five hundred ladies of a bloom a-piece, I shouldn't wonder. It's very dreadful!"

CHARLES DICKENS SUPERNATURAL SHORT STORIES

"She's much too handsome, my man," repeated the Alderman. "The chances are, that she'll come to no good, I clearly see. Observe what I say. Take care of her!" With which, he hurried off again.

"Wrong every way. Wrong every way!" said Trotty, clasping his hands. "Born bad. No business here!"

The Chimes came clashing in upon him as he said the words. Full, loud, and sounding – but with no encouragement. No, not a drop.

"The tune's changed," cried the old man, as he listened. "There's not a word of all that fancy in it. Why should there be? I have no business with the New Year nor with the old one neither. Let me die!"

Still the Bells, pealing forth their changes, made the very air spin. Put 'em down, Put 'em down! Good old Times, Good old Times! Facts and Figures, Facts and Figures! Put 'em down, Put 'em down! If they said anything they said this, until the brain of Toby reeled.

He pressed his bewildered head between his hands, as if to keep it from splitting asunder. A well-timed action, as it happened; for finding the letter in one of them, and being by that means reminded of his charge, he fell, mechanically, into his usual trot, and trotted off.

## Chapter II
### Second Quarter

**THE LETTER** Toby had received from Alderman Cute, was addressed to a great man in the great district of the town. The greatest district of the town. It must have been the greatest district of the town, because it was commonly called 'the world' by its inhabitants. The letter positively seemed heavier in Toby's hand, than another letter. Not because the Alderman had sealed it with a very large coat of arms and no end of wax, but because of the weighty name on the superscription, and the ponderous amount of gold and silver with which it was associated.

"How different from us!" thought Toby, in all simplicity and earnestness, as he looked at the direction. "Divide the lively turtles in the bills of mortality, by the number of gentlefolks able to buy 'em; and whose share does he take but his own! As to snatching tripe from anybody's mouth – he'd scorn it!"

With the involuntary homage due to such an exalted character, Toby interposed a corner of his apron between the letter and his fingers.

"His children," said Trotty, and a mist rose before his eyes; "his daughters – Gentlemen may win their hearts and marry them; they may be happy wives and mothers; they may be handsome like my darling M-e—"

He couldn't finish the name. The final letter swelled in his throat, to the size of the whole alphabet.

"Never mind," thought Trotty. "I know what I mean. That's more than enough for me." And with this consolatory rumination, trotted on.

It was a hard frost, that day. The air was bracing, crisp, and clear. The wintry sun, though powerless for warmth, looked brightly down upon the ice it was too weak to melt, and set a radiant glory there. At other times, Trotty might have learned a poor man's lesson from the wintry sun; but, he was past that, now.

The Year was Old, that day. The patient Year had lived through the reproaches and misuses of its slanderers, and faithfully performed its work. Spring, summer, autumn, winter. It had laboured through the destined round, and now laid down its weary head to die. Shut out from hope, high impulse, active happiness, itself, but active messenger of many joys to others, it made appeal in its decline to have its toiling days and patient hours remembered, and to die in peace. Trotty might have read a poor man's allegory in the fading year; but he was past that, now.

And only he? Or has the like appeal been ever made, by seventy years at once upon an English labourer's head, and made in vain!

The streets were full of motion, and the shops were decked out gaily. The New Year, like an Infant Heir to the whole world, was waited for, with welcomes, presents, and rejoicings. There were books and toys for the New Year, glittering trinkets for the New Year, dresses for the New Year, schemes of fortune for the New Year; new inventions to beguile it. Its life was parcelled out in almanacks and pocket-books; the coming of its moons, and stars, and tides, was known beforehand to the moment; all the workings of its seasons in their days and nights, were calculated with as much precision as Mr. Filer could work sums in men and women.

The New Year, the New Year. Everywhere the New Year! The Old Year was already looked upon as dead; and its effects were selling cheap, like some drowned mariner's aboardship. Its patterns were Last Year's, and going at a sacrifice, before its breath was gone. Its treasures were mere dirt, beside the riches of its unborn successor!

Trotty had no portion, to his thinking, in the New Year or the Old.

"Put 'em down, Put 'em down! Facts and Figures, Facts and Figures! Good old Times, Good old Times! Put 'em down, Put 'em down!" – his trot went to that measure, and would fit itself to nothing else.

But, even that one, melancholy as it was, brought him, in due time, to the end of his journey. To the mansion of Sir Joseph Bowley, Member of Parliament.

The door was opened by a Porter. Such a Porter! Not of Toby's order. Quite another thing. His place was the ticket though; not Toby's.

This Porter underwent some hard panting before he could speak; having breathed himself by coming incautiously out of his chair, without first taking time to think about it and compose his mind. When he had found his voice – which it took him a long time to do, for it was a long way off, and hidden under a load of meat – he said in a fat whisper,

"Who's it from?"

Toby told him.

"You're to take it in, yourself," said the Porter, pointing to a room at the end of a long passage, opening from the hall. "Everything goes straight in, on this day of the year. You're not a bit too soon; for the carriage is at the door now, and they have only come to town for a couple of hours, a' purpose."

Toby wiped his feet (which were quite dry already) with great care, and took the way pointed out to him; observing as he went that it was an awfully grand house, but hushed and covered up, as if the family were in the country. Knocking at the room-door, he was told to enter from within; and doing so found himself in a spacious library, where, at a table strewn with files and papers, were a stately lady in a bonnet; and a not very stately gentleman in black who wrote from her dictation; while another, and an older, and a much statelier gentleman, whose hat and cane were on the table, walked up and down, with one hand in his breast, and looked complacently from time to time at his own picture – a full length; a very full length – hanging over the fireplace.

"What is this?" said the last-named gentleman. "Mr. Fish, will you have the goodness to attend?"

Mr. Fish begged pardon, and taking the letter from Toby, handed it, with great respect.

"From Alderman Cute, Sir Joseph."

"Is this all? Have you nothing else, Porter?" inquired Sir Joseph.

Toby replied in the negative.

"You have no bill or demand upon me – my name is Bowley, Sir Joseph Bowley – of any kind from anybody, have you?" said Sir Joseph. "If you have, present it. There is a cheque-book by the side of Mr. Fish. I allow nothing to be carried into the New Year. Every description of account is settled in this house at the close of the old one. So that if death was to – to—"

"To cut," suggested Mr. Fish.

"To sever, sir," returned Sir Joseph, with great asperity, "the cord of existence – my affairs would be found, I hope, in a state of preparation."

"My dear Sir Joseph!" said the lady, who was greatly younger than the gentleman. "How shocking!"

"My lady Bowley," returned Sir Joseph, floundering now and then, as in the great depth of his observations, "at this season of the year we should think of – of – ourselves. We should look into our – our accounts. We should feel that every return of so eventful a period in human transactions, involves a matter of deep moment between a man and his – and his banker."

Sir Joseph delivered these words as if he felt the full morality of what he was saying; and desired that even Trotty should have an opportunity of being improved by such discourse. Possibly he had this end before him in still forbearing to break the seal of the letter, and in telling Trotty to wait where he was, a minute.

"You were desiring Mr. Fish to say, my lady—" observed Sir Joseph.

"Mr. Fish has said that, I believe," returned his lady, glancing at the letter. "But, upon my word, Sir Joseph, I don't think I can let it go after all. It is so very dear."

"What is dear?" inquired Sir Joseph.

"That Charity, my love. They only allow two votes for a subscription of five pounds. Really monstrous!"

"My lady Bowley," returned Sir Joseph, "you surprise me. Is the luxury of feeling in proportion to the number of votes; or is it, to a rightly constituted mind, in proportion to the number of applicants, and the wholesome state of mind to which their canvassing reduces them? Is there no excitement of the purest kind in having two votes to dispose of among fifty people?"

"Not to me, I acknowledge," replied the lady. "It bores one. Besides, one can't oblige one's acquaintance. But you are the Poor Man's Friend, you know, Sir Joseph. You think otherwise."

"I *am* the Poor Man's Friend," observed Sir Joseph, glancing at the poor man present. "As such I may be taunted. As such I have been taunted. But I ask no other title."

"Bless him for a noble gentleman!" thought Trotty.

"I don't agree with Cute here, for instance," said Sir Joseph, holding out the letter. "I don't agree with the Filer party. I don't agree with any party. My friend the Poor Man, has no business with anything of that sort, and nothing of that sort has any business with him. My friend the Poor Man, in my district, is my business. No man or body of men has any right to interfere between my friend and me. That is the ground I take. I assume a – a paternal character towards my friend. I say, 'My good fellow, I will treat you paternally.'"

Toby listened with great gravity, and began to feel more comfortable.

"Your only business, my good fellow," pursued Sir Joseph, looking abstractedly at Toby; "your only business in life is with me. You needn't trouble yourself to think about anything. I will think for you; I know what is good for you; I am your perpetual parent. Such is the dispensation of an all-wise Providence! Now, the design of your creation is – not that you should swill, and guzzle, and associate your enjoyments, brutally, with food;" Toby thought remorsefully of the tripe; "but that you should feel the Dignity of Labour. Go forth erect into the cheerful morning air, and – and stop there. Live hard and temperately, be respectful, exercise your self-denial, bring up your family on next to nothing, pay your rent as regularly as the clock strikes, be punctual in your dealings (I set you a good example; you will find Mr. Fish, my confidential secretary, with a cash-box before him at all times); and you may trust to me to be your Friend and Father."

"Nice children, indeed, Sir Joseph!" said the lady, with a shudder. "Rheumatisms, and fevers, and crooked legs, and asthmas, and all kinds of horrors!"

"My lady," returned Sir Joseph, with solemnity, "not the less am I the Poor Man's Friend and Father. Not the less shall he receive encouragement at my hands. Every quarter-day he will be put in communication with Mr. Fish. Every New Year's Day, myself and friends will drink his health. Once every year, myself and friends will address him with the deepest feeling. Once in his life, he may even perhaps receive; in public, in the presence of the gentry; a Trifle from a Friend. And when, upheld no more by these stimulants, and the Dignity of Labour, he sinks into his comfortable grave, then, my lady" – here Sir Joseph blew his nose – "I will be a Friend and a Father – on the same terms – to his children."

Toby was greatly moved.

"O! You have a thankful family, Sir Joseph!" cried his wife.

"My lady," said Sir Joseph, quite majestically, "Ingratitude is known to be the sin of that class. I expect no other return."

"Ah! Born bad!" thought Toby. "Nothing melts us."

"What man can do, I do," pursued Sir Joseph. "I do my duty as the Poor Man's Friend and Father; and I endeavour to educate his mind, by inculcating on all occasions the one great moral lesson which that class requires. That is, entire Dependence on myself. They have no business whatever with – with themselves. If wicked and designing persons tell them otherwise, and they become impatient and discontented, and are guilty of insubordinate conduct and black-hearted ingratitude; which is undoubtedly the case; I am their Friend and Father still. It is so Ordained. It is in the nature of things."

With that great sentiment, he opened the Alderman's letter; and read it.

"Very polite and attentive, I am sure!" exclaimed Sir Joseph. "My lady, the Alderman is so obliging as to remind me that he has had "the distinguished honour" – he is very good – of meeting me at the house of our mutual friend Deedles, the banker; and he does me the favour to inquire whether it will be agreeable to me to have Will Fern put down."

"Most agreeable!" replied my Lady Bowley. "The worst man among them! He has been committing a robbery, I hope?"

"Why no," said Sir Joseph, referring to the letter. "Not quite. Very near. Not quite. He came up to London, it seems, to look for employment (trying to better himself – that's his story), and being found at night asleep in a shed, was taken into custody, and carried next morning before the Alderman. The Alderman observes (very properly) that he is determined to put this sort of thing down; and that if it will be agreeable to me to have Will Fern put down, he will be happy to begin with him."

CHARLES DICKENS SUPERNATURAL SHORT STORIES

"Let him be made an example of, by all means," returned the lady. "Last winter, when I introduced pinking and eyelet-holing among the men and boys in the village, as a nice evening employment, and had the lines,

> *O let us love our occupations,*
> *Bless the squire and his relations,*
> *Live upon our daily rations,*
> *And always know our proper stations,*

set to music on the new system, for them to sing the while; this very Fern – I see him now – touched that hat of his, and said, 'I humbly ask your pardon, my lady, but *an't* I something different from a great girl?' I expected it, of course; who can expect anything but insolence and ingratitude from that class of people! That is not to the purpose, however. Sir Joseph! Make an example of him!"

"Hem!" coughed Sir Joseph. "Mr. Fish, if you'll have the goodness to attend—"

Mr. Fish immediately seized his pen, and wrote from Sir Joseph's dictation.

"Private. My dear Sir. I am very much indebted to you for your courtesy in the matter of the man William Fern, of whom, I regret to add, I can say nothing favourable. I have uniformly considered myself in the light of his Friend and Father, but have been repaid (a common case, I grieve to say) with ingratitude, and constant opposition to my plans. He is a turbulent and rebellious spirit. His character will not bear investigation. Nothing will persuade him to be happy when he might. Under these circumstances, it appears to me, I own, that when he comes before you again (as you informed me he promised to do tomorrow, pending your inquiries, and I think he may be so far relied upon), his committal for some short term as a Vagabond, would be a service to society, and would be a salutary example in a country where – for the sake of those who are, through good and evil report, the Friends and Fathers of the Poor, as well as with a view to that, generally speaking, misguided class themselves – examples are greatly needed. And I am," and so forth.

"It appears," remarked Sir Joseph when he had signed this letter, and Mr. Fish was sealing it, "as if this were Ordained: really. At the close of the year, I wind up my account and strike my balance, even with William Fern!"

Trotty, who had long ago relapsed, and was very low-spirited, stepped forward with a rueful face to take the letter.

"With my compliments and thanks," said Sir Joseph. "Stop!"

"Stop!" echoed Mr. Fish.

"You have heard, perhaps," said Sir Joseph, oracularly, "certain remarks into which I have been led respecting the solemn period of time at which we have arrived, and the duty imposed upon us of settling our affairs, and being prepared. You have observed that I don't shelter myself behind my superior standing in society, but that Mr. Fish – that gentleman – has a cheque-book at his elbow, and is in fact here, to enable me to turn over a perfectly new leaf, and enter on the epoch before us with a clean account. Now, my friend, can you lay your hand upon your heart, and say, that you also have made preparations for a New Year?"

"I am afraid, sir," stammered Trotty, looking meekly at him, "that I am a – a – little behind-hand with the world."

"Behind-hand with the world!" repeated Sir Joseph Bowley, in a tone of terrible distinctness.

"I am afraid, sir," faltered Trotty, "that there's a matter of ten or twelve shillings owing to Mrs. Chickenstalker."

"To Mrs. Chickenstalker!" repeated Sir Joseph, in the same tone as before.

"A shop, sir," exclaimed Toby, "in the general line. Also a – a little money on account of rent. A very little, sir. It oughtn't to be owing, I know, but we have been hard put to it, indeed!"

Sir Joseph looked at his lady, and at Mr. Fish, and at Trotty, one after another, twice all round. He then made a despondent gesture with both hands at once, as if he gave the thing up altogether.

"How a man, even among this improvident and impracticable race; an old man; a man grown grey; can look a New Year in the face, with his affairs in this condition; how he can lie down on his bed at night, and get up again in the morning, and— There!" he said, turning his back on Trotty. "Take the letter. Take the letter!"

"I heartily wish it was otherwise, sir," said Trotty, anxious to excuse himself. "We have been tried very hard."

Sir Joseph still repeating "Take the letter, take the letter!" and Mr. Fish not only saying the same thing, but giving additional force to the request by motioning the bearer to the door, he had nothing for it but to make his bow and leave the house. And in the street, poor Trotty pulled his worn old hat down on his head, to hide the grief he felt at getting no hold on the New Year, anywhere.

He didn't even lift his hat to look up at the Bell tower when he came to the old church on his return. He halted there a moment, from habit: and knew that it was growing dark, and that the steeple rose above him, indistinct and faint, in the murky air. He knew, too, that the Chimes would ring immediately; and that they sounded to his fancy, at such a time, like voices in the clouds. But he only made the more haste to deliver the Alderman's letter, and get out of the way before they began; for he dreaded to hear them tagging "Friends and Fathers, Friends and Fathers," to the burden they had rung out last.

Toby discharged himself of his commission, therefore, with all possible speed, and set off trotting homeward. But what with his pace, which was at best an awkward one in the street; and what with his hat, which didn't improve it; he trotted against somebody in less than no time, and was sent staggering out into the road.

"I beg your pardon, I'm sure!" said Trotty, pulling up his hat in great confusion, and between the hat and the torn lining, fixing his head into a kind of bee-hive. "I hope I haven't hurt you."

As to hurting anybody, Toby was not such an absolute Samson, but that he was much more likely to be hurt himself: and indeed, he had flown out into the road, like a shuttlecock. He had such an opinion of his own strength, however, that he was in real concern for the other party: and said again,

"I hope I haven't hurt you?"

The man against whom he had run; a sun-browned, sinewy, country-looking man, with grizzled hair, and a rough chin; stared at him for a moment, as if he suspected him to be in jest. But, satisfied of his good faith, he answered:

"No, friend. You have not hurt me."

"Nor the child, I hope?" said Trotty.

"Nor the child," returned the man. "I thank you kindly."

As he said so, he glanced at a little girl he carried in his arms, asleep: and shading her face with the long end of the poor handkerchief he wore about his throat, went slowly on.

The tone in which he said "I thank you kindly," penetrated Trotty's heart. He was so jaded and foot-sore, and so soiled with travel, and looked about him so forlorn and strange, that it was a comfort to him to be able to thank any one: no matter for how little. Toby stood gazing after him as he plodded wearily away, with the child's arm clinging round his neck.

At the figure in the worn shoes – now the very shade and ghost of shoes – rough leather leggings, common frock, and broad slouched hat, Trotty stood gazing, blind to the whole street. And at the child's arm, clinging round its neck.

Before he merged into the darkness the traveller stopped; and looking round, and seeing Trotty standing there yet, seemed undecided whether to return or go on. After doing first the one and then the other, he came back, and Trotty went half-way to meet him.

"You can tell me, perhaps," said the man with a faint smile, "and if you can I am sure you will, and I'd rather ask you than another – where Alderman Cute lives."

"Close at hand," replied Toby. "I'll show you his house with pleasure."

"I was to have gone to him elsewhere tomorrow," said the man, accompanying Toby, "but I'm uneasy under suspicion, and want to clear myself, and to be free to go and seek my bread – I don't know where. So, maybe he'll forgive my going to his house to-night."

"It's impossible," cried Toby with a start, "that your name's Fern!"

"Eh!" cried the other, turning on him in astonishment.

"Fern! Will Fern!" said Trotty.

"That's my name," replied the other.

"Why then," said Trotty, seizing him by the arm, and looking cautiously round, "for Heaven's sake don't go to him! Don't go to him! He'll put you down as sure as ever you were born. Here! come up this alley, and I'll tell you what I mean. Don't go to *him*."

His new acquaintance looked as if he thought him mad; but he bore him company nevertheless. When they were shrouded from observation, Trotty told him what he knew, and what character he had received, and all about it.

The subject of his history listened to it with a calmness that surprised him. He did not contradict or interrupt it, once. He nodded his head now and then – more in corroboration of an old and worn-out story, it appeared, than in refutation of it; and once or twice threw back his hat, and passed his freckled hand over a brow, where every furrow he had ploughed seemed to have set its image in little. But he did no more.

"It's true enough in the main," he said, "master, I could sift grain from husk here and there, but let it be as 'tis. What odds? I have gone against his plans; to my misfortun'. I can't help it; I should do the like tomorrow. As to character, them gentlefolks will search and search, and pry and pry, and have it as free from spot or speck in us, afore they'll help us to a dry good word! – Well! I hope they don't lose good opinion as easy as we do, or their lives is strict indeed, and hardly worth the keeping. For myself, master, I never took with that hand" – holding it before him – "what wasn't my own; and never held it back from work, however hard, or poorly paid. Whoever can deny it, let him chop it off! But when work won't maintain me like a human creetur; when my living is so bad, that I am Hungry, out of doors and in; when I see a whole working life begin that way, go on that way, and end that way, without a chance or change; then I say to the gentlefolks 'Keep away from me! Let my cottage be. My doors is dark enough without your darkening of 'em more. Don't look for me to come up into the Park to help the show when there's a Birthday, or a fine Speechmaking, or what not. Act your Plays and Games without me, and be welcome to 'em, and enjoy 'em. We've nowt to do with one another. I'm best let alone!'"

Seeing that the child in his arms had opened her eyes, and was looking about her in wonder, he checked himself to say a word or two of foolish prattle in her ear, and stand her on the ground beside him. Then slowly winding one of her long tresses round and round his rough forefinger like a ring, while she hung about his dusty leg, he said to Trotty:

"I'm not a cross-grained man by natu', I believe; and easy satisfied, I'm sure. I bear no ill-will against none of 'em. I only want to live like one of the Almighty's creeturs. I can't – I don't – and so there's a pit dug between me, and them that can and do. There's others like me. You might tell 'em off by hundreds and by thousands, sooner than by ones."

Trotty knew he spoke the Truth in this, and shook his head to signify as much.

"I've got a bad name this way," said Fern; "and I'm not likely, I'm afeared, to get a better. 'Tan't lawful to be out of sorts, and I am out of sorts, though God knows I'd sooner bear a cheerful spirit if I could. Well! I don't know as this Alderman could hurt *me* much by sending me to jail; but without a friend to speak a word for me, he might do it; and you see!" pointing downward with his finger, at the child.

"She has a beautiful face," said Trotty.

"Why yes!" replied the other in a low voice, as he gently turned it up with both his hands towards his own, and looked upon it steadfastly. "I've thought so, many times. I've thought so, when my hearth was very cold, and cupboard very bare. I thought so t'other night, when we were taken like two thieves. But they – they shouldn't try the little face too often, should they, Lilian? That's hardly fair upon a man!"

He sunk his voice so low, and gazed upon her with an air so stern and strange, that Toby, to divert the current of his thoughts, inquired if his wife were living.

"I never had one," he returned, shaking his head. "She's my brother's child: a orphan. Nine year old, though you'd hardly think it; but she's tired and worn out now. They'd have taken care on her, the Union – eight-and-twenty mile away from where we live – between four walls (as they took care of my old father when he couldn't work no more, though he didn't trouble 'em long); but I took her instead, and she's lived with me ever since. Her mother had a friend once, in London here. We are trying to find her, and to find work too; but it's a large place. Never mind. More room for us to walk about in, Lilly!"

Meeting the child's eyes with a smile which melted Toby more than tears, he shook him by the hand.

"I don't so much as know your name," he said, "but I've opened my heart free to you, for I'm thankful to you; with good reason. I'll take your advice, and keep clear of this—"

"Justice," suggested Toby.

"Ah!" he said. "If that's the name they give him. This Justice. And tomorrow will try whether there's better fortun' to be met with, somewheres near London. Good night. A Happy New Year!"

"Stay!" cried Trotty, catching at his hand, as he relaxed his grip. "Stay! The New Year never can be happy to me, if we part like this. The New Year never can be happy to me, if I see the child and you go wandering away, you don't know where, without a shelter for your heads. Come home with me! I'm a poor man, living in a poor place; but I can give you lodging for one night and never miss it. Come home with me! Here! I'll take her!" cried Trotty, lifting up the child. "A pretty one! I'd carry twenty times her weight, and never know I'd got it. Tell me if I go too quick for you. I'm very fast. I always was!" Trotty said this, taking about six of his trotting paces to one stride of his fatigued companion; and with his thin legs quivering again, beneath the load he bore.

"Why, she's as light," said Trotty, trotting in his speech as well as in his gait; for he couldn't bear to be thanked, and dreaded a moment's pause; "as light as a feather. Lighter than a Peacock's feather – a great deal lighter. Here we are and here we go! Round this first turning to the right, Uncle Will, and past the pump, and sharp off up the passage to the left, right opposite the public-house. Here we are and here we go! Cross over, Uncle Will, and mind the kidney pieman at the corner! Here we are and here we go! Down the Mews here, Uncle Will, and stop at the black door, with "T. Veck, Ticket Porter," wrote upon a board; and here we are and here we go, and here we are indeed, my precious. Meg, surprising you!"

With which words Trotty, in a breathless state, set the child down before his daughter in the middle of the floor. The little visitor looked once at Meg; and doubting nothing in that face, but trusting everything she saw there; ran into her arms.

"Here we are and here we go!" cried Trotty, running round the room, and choking audibly. "Here, Uncle Will, here's a fire you know! Why don't you come to the fire? Oh here we are and here we go! Meg, my precious darling, where's the kettle? Here it is and here it goes, and it'll bile in no time!"

Trotty really had picked up the kettle somewhere or other in the course of his wild career and now put it on the fire: while Meg, seating the child in a warm corner, knelt down on the ground before her, and pulled off her shoes, and dried her wet feet on a cloth. Ay, and she laughed at Trotty too – so pleasantly, so cheerfully, that Trotty could have blessed her where she kneeled; for he had seen that, when they entered, she was sitting by the fire in tears.

"Why, father!" said Meg. "You're crazy to-night, I think. I don't know what the Bells would say to that. Poor little feet. How cold they are!"

"Oh, they're warmer now!" exclaimed the child. "They're quite warm now!"

"No, no, no," said Meg. "We haven't rubbed 'em half enough. We're so busy. So busy! And when they're done, we'll brush out the damp hair; and when that's done, we'll bring some colour to the poor pale face with fresh water; and when that's done, we'll be so gay, and brisk, and happy!"

The child, in a burst of sobbing, clasped her round the neck; caressed her fair cheek with its hand; and said, "Oh Meg! oh dear Meg!"

Toby's blessing could have done no more. Who could do more!

"Why, father!" cried Meg, after a pause.

"Here I am and here I go, my dear!" said Trotty.

"Good Gracious me!" cried Meg. "He's crazy! He's put the dear child's bonnet on the kettle, and hung the lid behind the door!"

"I didn't go for to do it, my love," said Trotty, hastily repairing this mistake. "Meg, my dear?"

Meg looked towards him and saw that he had elaborately stationed himself behind the chair of their male visitor, where with many mysterious gestures he was holding up the sixpence he had earned.

"I see, my dear," said Trotty, "as I was coming in, half an ounce of tea lying somewhere on the stairs; and I'm pretty sure there was a bit of bacon too. As I don't remember where it was exactly, I'll go myself and try to find 'em."

With this inscrutable artifice, Toby withdrew to purchase the viands he had spoken of, for ready money, at Mrs. Chickenstalker's; and presently came back, pretending he had not been able to find them, at first, in the dark.

"But here they are at last," said Trotty, setting out the tea-things, "all correct! I was pretty sure it was tea, and a rasher. So it is. Meg, my pet, if you'll just make the tea, while your unworthy father toasts the bacon, we shall be ready, immediate. It's a curious circumstance," said Trotty, proceeding in his cookery, with the assistance of the toasting-fork, "curious, but well known to my friends, that I never care, myself, for rashers, nor for tea. I like to see other people enjoy 'em," said Trotty, speaking very loud, to impress the fact upon his guest, "but to me, as food, they're disagreeable."

Yet Trotty sniffed the savour of the hissing bacon – ah! – as if he liked it; and when he poured the boiling water in the tea-pot, looked lovingly down into the depths of that snug cauldron, and suffered the fragrant steam to curl about his nose, and wreathe his head and face in a thick cloud. However, for all this, he neither ate nor drank, except at the very beginning, a mere morsel for form's sake, which he appeared to eat with infinite relish, but declared was perfectly uninteresting to him.

No. Trotty's occupation was, to see Will Fern and Lilian eat and drink; and so was Meg's. And never did spectators at a city dinner or court banquet find such high delight in seeing others feast: although it were a monarch or a pope: as those two did, in looking on that night. Meg smiled at Trotty, Trotty laughed at Meg. Meg shook her head, and made belief to clap her hands, applauding Trotty; Trotty conveyed, in dumb-show, unintelligible narratives of how and when and where he had found their visitors, to Meg; and they were happy. Very happy.

"Although," thought Trotty, sorrowfully, as he watched Meg's face; "that match is broken off, I see!"

"Now, I'll tell you what," said Trotty after tea. "The little one, she sleeps with Meg, I know."

"With good Meg!" cried the child, caressing her. "With Meg."

"That's right," said Trotty. "And I shouldn't wonder if she kiss Meg's father, won't she? *I'm* Meg's father."

Mightily delighted Trotty was, when the child went timidly towards him, and having kissed him, fell back upon Meg again.

"She's as sensible as Solomon," said Trotty. "Here we come and here we – no, we don't – I don't mean that – I – what was I saying, Meg, my precious?"

Meg looked towards their guest, who leaned upon her chair, and with his face turned from her, fondled the child's head, half hidden in her lap.

"To be sure," said Toby. "To be sure! I don't know what I'm rambling on about, to-night. My wits are wool-gathering, I think. Will Fern, you come along with me. You're tired to death, and broken down for want of rest. You come along with me." The man still played with the child's curls, still leaned upon Meg's chair, still turned away his face. He didn't speak, but in his rough coarse fingers, clenching and expanding in the fair hair of the child, there was an eloquence that said enough.

"Yes, yes," said Trotty, answering unconsciously what he saw expressed in his daughter's face. "Take her with you, Meg. Get her to bed. There! Now, Will, I'll show you where you lie. It's not much of a place: only a loft; but, having a loft, I always say, is one of the great conveniences of living in a mews; and till this coach-house and stable gets a better let, we live here cheap. There's plenty of sweet hay up there, belonging to a neighbour; and it's as clean as hands, and Meg, can make it. Cheer up! Don't give way. A new heart for a New Year, always!"

The hand released from the child's hair, had fallen, trembling, into Trotty's hand. So Trotty, talking without intermission, led him out as tenderly and easily as if he had been a child himself. Returning before Meg, he listened for an instant at the door of her little chamber; an adjoining room. The child was murmuring a simple Prayer before lying down to sleep; and when she had remembered Meg's name, "Dearly, Dearly" – so her words ran – Trotty heard her stop and ask for his.

It was some short time before the foolish little old fellow could compose himself to mend the fire, and draw his chair to the warm hearth. But, when he had done so, and had trimmed the light, he took his newspaper from his pocket, and began to read. Carelessly at first, and skimming up and down the columns; but with an earnest and a sad attention, very soon.

For this same dreaded paper re-directed Trotty's thoughts into the channel they had taken all that day, and which the day's events had so marked out and shaped. His interest in the two wanderers had set him on another course of thinking, and a happier one, for the time; but being alone again, and reading of the crimes and violences of the people, he relapsed into his former train.

In this mood, he came to an account (and it was not the first he had ever read) of a woman who had laid her desperate hands not only on her own life but on that of her young child. A crime so terrible, and so revolting to his soul, dilated with the love of Meg, that he let the journal drop, and fell back in his chair, appalled!

"Unnatural and cruel!" Toby cried. "Unnatural and cruel! None but people who were bad at heart, born bad, who had no business on the earth, could do such deeds. It's too true, all I've heard today; too just, too full of proof. We're Bad!"

The Chimes took up the words so suddenly – burst out so loud, and clear, and sonorous – that the Bells seemed to strike him in his chair.

And what was that, they said?

"Toby Veck, Toby Veck, waiting for you Toby! Toby Veck, Toby Veck, waiting for you Toby! Come and see us, come and see us, Drag him to us, drag him to us, Haunt and hunt him, haunt and hunt him, Break his slumbers, break his slumbers! Toby Veck Toby Veck, door open wide Toby, Toby Veck Toby Veck, door open wide Toby—" then fiercely back to their impetuous strain again, and ringing in the very bricks and plaster on the walls.

Toby listened. Fancy, fancy! His remorse for having run away from them that afternoon! No, no. Nothing of the kind. Again, again, and yet a dozen times again. "Haunt and hunt him, haunt and hunt him, Drag him to us, drag him to us!" Deafening the whole town!

"Meg," said Trotty softly: tapping at her door. "Do you hear anything?"

"I hear the Bells, father. Surely they're very loud to-night."

"Is she asleep?" said Toby, making an excuse for peeping in.

"So peacefully and happily! I can't leave her yet though, father. Look how she holds my hand!"

"Meg," whispered Trotty. "Listen to the Bells!"

She listened, with her face towards him all the time. But it underwent no change. She didn't understand them.

Trotty withdrew, resumed his seat by the fire, and once more listened by himself. He remained here a little time.

It was impossible to bear it; their energy was dreadful.

"If the tower-door is really open," said Toby, hastily laying aside his apron, but never thinking of his hat, "what's to hinder me from going up into the steeple and satisfying myself? If it's shut, I don't want any other satisfaction. That's enough."

He was pretty certain as he slipped out quietly into the street that he should find it shut and locked, for he knew the door well, and had so rarely seen it open, that he couldn't reckon above three times in all. It was a low arched portal, outside the church, in a dark nook behind a column; and had such great iron hinges, and such a monstrous lock, that there was more hinge and lock than door.

But what was his astonishment when, coming bare-headed to the church; and putting his hand into this dark nook, with a certain misgiving that it might be unexpectedly seized, and a shivering propensity to draw it back again; he found that the door, which opened outwards, actually stood ajar!

He thought, on the first surprise, of going back; or of getting a light, or a companion, but his courage aided him immediately, and he determined to ascend alone.

"What have I to fear?" said Trotty. "It's a church! Besides, the ringers may be there, and have forgotten to shut the door." So he went in, feeling his way as he went, like a blind man; for it was very dark. And very quiet, for the Chimes were silent.

The dust from the street had blown into the recess; and lying there, heaped up, made it so soft and velvet-like to the foot, that there was something startling, even in that. The narrow stair was so close to the door, too, that he stumbled at the very first; and shutting the door upon himself, by striking it with his foot, and causing it to rebound back heavily, he couldn't open it again.

This was another reason, however, for going on. Trotty groped his way, and went on. Up, up, up, and round, and round; and up, up, up; higher, higher, higher up!

It was a disagreeable staircase for that groping work; so low and narrow, that his groping hand was always touching something; and it often felt so like a man or ghostly figure standing up erect and making room for him to pass without discovery, that he would rub the smooth wall upward searching for its face, and downward searching for its feet, while a chill tingling crept all over him. Twice or thrice, a door or niche broke the monotonous surface; and then it seemed a gap as wide as the whole church; and he felt on the brink of an abyss, and going to tumble headlong down, until he found the wall again.

Still up, up, up; and round and round; and up, up, up; higher, higher, higher up!

At length, the dull and stifling atmosphere began to freshen: presently to feel quite windy: presently it blew so strong, that he could hardly keep his legs. But, he got to an arched window in the tower, breast high, and holding tight, looked down upon the house-tops, on the smoking chimneys, on the blur and blotch of lights (towards the place where Meg was wondering where he was and calling to him perhaps), all kneaded up together in a leaven of mist and darkness.

This was the belfry, where the ringers came. He had caught hold of one of the frayed ropes which hung down through apertures in the oaken roof. At first he started, thinking it was hair; then trembled at the very thought of waking the deep Bell. The Bells themselves were higher. Higher, Trotty, in his fascination, or in working out the spell upon him, groped his way. By ladders now, and toilsomely, for it was steep, and not too certain holding for the feet.

Up, up, up; and climb and clamber; up, up, up; higher, higher, higher up!

Until, ascending through the floor, and pausing with his head just raised above its beams, he came among the Bells. It was barely possible to make out their great shapes in the gloom; but there they were. Shadowy, and dark, and dumb.

A heavy sense of dread and loneliness fell instantly upon him, as he climbed into this airy nest of stone and metal. His head went round and round. He listened, and then raised a wild "Holloa!" Holloa! was mournfully protracted by the echoes.

Giddy, confused, and out of breath, and frightened, Toby looked about him vacantly, and sunk down in a swoon.

## Chapter III
## Third Quarter

**BLACK ARE THE BROODING** clouds and troubled the deep waters, when the Sea of Thought, first heaving from a calm, gives up its Dead. Monsters uncouth and wild, arise in premature, imperfect resurrection; the several parts and shapes of different things are joined and mixed by chance; and when, and how, and by what wonderful degrees, each separates from each, and every sense and object of the mind resumes its usual form and lives again, no man – though every man is every day the casket of this type of the Great Mystery – can tell.

So, when and how the darkness of the night-black steeple changed to shining light; when and how the solitary tower was peopled with a myriad figures; when and how the whispered "Haunt and hunt him," breathing monotonously through his sleep or swoon, became a voice exclaiming in the waking ears of Trotty, "Break his slumbers;" when and how he ceased to have a sluggish and confused idea that such things were, companioning a host of others that were not; there are no dates or means to tell. But, awake and standing on his feet upon the boards where he had lately lain, he saw this Goblin Sight.

He saw the tower, whither his charmed footsteps had brought him, swarming with dwarf phantoms, spirits, elfin creatures of the Bells. He saw them leaping, flying, dropping, pouring from the Bells without a pause. He saw them, round him on the ground; above him, in the air; clambering from him, by the ropes below; looking down upon him, from the massive iron-girded beams; peeping in upon him, through the chinks and loopholes in the walls; spreading away and away from him in enlarging circles, as the water ripples give way to a huge stone that suddenly comes plashing in among them. He saw them, of all aspects and all shapes. He saw them ugly, handsome, crippled, exquisitely formed. He saw them young, he saw them old, he saw them kind, he saw them cruel, he saw them merry, he saw them grim; he saw them dance, and heard them sing; he saw them tear their hair, and heard them howl. He saw the air thick with them. He saw them come and go, incessantly. He saw them riding downward, soaring upward, sailing off afar, perching near at hand, all restless and all violently active. Stone, and brick, and slate, and tile, became transparent to him as to them. He saw them *in* the houses, busy at the sleepers' beds. He saw them soothing people in their dreams; he saw them beating them with knotted whips; he saw them yelling in their ears; he saw them playing softest music on their pillows; he saw them cheering some with the songs of birds and the perfume of flowers; he saw them flashing awful faces on the troubled rest of others, from enchanted mirrors which they carried in their hands.

He saw these creatures, not only among sleeping men but waking also, active in pursuits irreconcilable with one another, and possessing or assuming natures the most opposite. He saw one buckling on innumerable wings to increase his speed; another loading himself with chains and weights, to retard his. He saw some putting the hands of clocks forward, some putting the hands of clocks backward, some endeavouring to stop the clock entirely. He saw them representing, here a marriage ceremony, there a funeral; in this chamber an election, in that a ball he saw, everywhere, restless and untiring motion.

Bewildered by the host of shifting and extraordinary figures, as well as by the uproar of the Bells, which all this while were ringing, Trotty clung to a wooden pillar for support, and turned his white face here and there, in mute and stunned astonishment.

As he gazed, the Chimes stopped. Instantaneous change! The whole swarm fainted! their forms collapsed, their speed deserted them; they sought to fly, but in the act of falling died and melted into air. No fresh supply succeeded them. One straggler leaped down pretty briskly from the surface of the Great Bell, and alighted on his feet, but he was dead and gone before he could turn round. Some few of the late company who had gambolled in the tower, remained there, spinning over and over a little longer; but these became at every turn more faint, and few, and feeble, and soon went the way of the rest. The last of all was one small hunchback, who had got into an echoing corner, where he twirled and twirled, and floated by himself a long time; showing such perseverance, that at last he dwindled to a leg and even to a foot, before he finally retired; but he vanished in the end, and then the tower was silent.

Then and not before, did Trotty see in every Bell a bearded figure of the bulk and stature of the Bell – incomprehensibly, a figure and the Bell itself. Gigantic, grave, and darkly watchful of him, as he stood rooted to the ground.

Mysterious and awful figures! Resting on nothing; poised in the night air of the tower, with their draped and hooded heads merged in the dim roof; motionless and shadowy. Shadowy and dark, although he saw them by some light belonging to themselves – none else was there – each with its muffled hand upon its goblin mouth.

He could not plunge down wildly through the opening in the floor; for all power of motion had deserted him. Otherwise he would have done so – aye, would have thrown himself, headforemost, from the steeple-top, rather than have seen them watching him with eyes that would have waked and watched although the pupils had been taken out.

Again, again, the dread and terror of the lonely place, and of the wild and fearful night that reigned there, touched him like a spectral hand. His distance from all help; the long, dark, winding, ghost-beleaguered way that lay between him and the earth on which men lived; his being high, high, high, up there, where it had made him dizzy to see the birds fly in the day; cut off from all good people, who at such an hour were safe at home and sleeping in their beds; all this struck coldly through him, not as a reflection but a bodily sensation. Meantime his eyes and thoughts and fears, were fixed upon the watchful figures; which, rendered unlike any figures of this world by the deep gloom and shade enwrapping and enfolding them, as well as by their looks and forms and supernatural hovering above the floor, were nevertheless as plainly to be seen as were the stalwart oaken frames, cross-pieces, bars and beams, set up there to support the Bells. These hemmed them, in a very forest of hewn timber; from the entanglements, intricacies, and depths of which, as from among the boughs of a dead wood blighted for their phantom use, they kept their darksome and unwinking watch.

A blast of air – how cold and shrill! – came moaning through the tower. As it died away, the Great Bell, or the Goblin of the Great Bell, spoke.

"What visitor is this!" it said. The voice was low and deep, and Trotty fancied that it sounded in the other figures as well.

"I thought my name was called by the Chimes!" said Trotty, raising his hands in an attitude of supplication. "I hardly know why I am here, or how I came. I have listened to the Chimes these many years. They have cheered me often."

"And you have thanked them?" said the Bell.

"A thousand times!" cried Trotty.

"How?"

"I am a poor man," faltered Trotty, "and could only thank them in words."

"And always so?" inquired the Goblin of the Bell. "Have you never done us wrong in words?"

"No!" cried Trotty eagerly.

"Never done us foul, and false, and wicked wrong, in words?" pursued the Goblin of the Bell.

Trotty was about to answer, "Never!" But he stopped, and was confused.

"The voice of Time," said the Phantom, "cries to man, Advance! Time is for his advancement and improvement; for his greater worth, his greater happiness, his better life; his progress onward to that goal within its knowledge and its view, and set there, in the period when Time and He began. Ages of darkness, wickedness, and violence, have come and gone – millions uncountable, have suffered, lived, and died – to point the way before him. Who seeks to turn him back, or stay him on his course, arrests a mighty engine which will strike the meddler dead; and be the fiercer and the wilder, ever, for its momentary check!"

"I never did so to my knowledge, sir," said Trotty. "It was quite by accident if I did. I wouldn't go to do it, I'm sure."

"Who puts into the mouth of Time, or of its servants," said the Goblin of the Bell, "a cry of lamentation for days which have had their trial and their failure, and have left deep traces of it which the blind may see – a cry that only serves the present time, by showing men how much it needs their help when any ears can listen to regrets for such a past – who does this, does a wrong. And you have done that wrong, to us, the Chimes."

Trotty's first excess of fear was gone. But he had felt tenderly and gratefully towards the Bells, as you have seen; and when he heard himself arraigned as one who had offended them so weightily, his heart was touched with penitence and grief.

"If you knew," said Trotty, clasping his hands earnestly – "or perhaps you do know – if you know how often you have kept me company; how often you have cheered me up when I've been low; how you were quite the plaything of my little daughter Meg (almost the only one she ever had) when first her mother died, and she and me were left alone; you won't bear malice for a hasty word!"

"Who hears in us, the Chimes, one note bespeaking disregard, or stern regard, of any hope, or joy, or pain, or sorrow, of the many-sorrowed throng; who hears us make response to any creed that gauges human passions and affections, as it gauges the amount of miserable food on which humanity may pine and wither; does us wrong. That wrong you have done us!" said the Bell.

"I have!" said Trotty. "Oh forgive me!"

"Who hears us echo the dull vermin of the earth: the Putters Down of crushed and broken natures, formed to be raised up higher than such maggots of the time can crawl or can conceive," pursued the Goblin of the Bell; "who does so, does us wrong. And you have done us wrong!"

"Not meaning it," said Trotty. "In my ignorance. Not meaning it!"

"Lastly, and most of all," pursued the Bell. "Who turns his back upon the fallen and disfigured of his kind; abandons them as vile; and does not trace and track with pitying eyes the unfenced precipice by which they fell from good – grasping in their fall some tufts and shreds of that lost soil, and clinging to them still when bruised and dying in the gulf below; does wrong to Heaven and man, to time and to eternity. And you have done that wrong!"

"Spare me!" cried Trotty, falling on his knees; "for Mercy's sake!"

"Listen!" said the Shadow.

"Listen!" cried the other Shadows.

"Listen!" said a clear and childlike voice, which Trotty thought he recognised as having heard before.

The organ sounded faintly in the church below. Swelling by degrees, the melody ascended to the roof, and filled the choir and nave. Expanding more and more, it rose up, up; up, up; higher, higher, higher up; awakening agitated hearts within the burly piles of oak: the hollow bells, the iron-bound doors, the stairs of solid stone; until the tower walls were insufficient to contain it, and it soared into the sky.

No wonder that an old man's breast could not contain a sound so vast and mighty. It broke from that weak prison in a rush of tears; and Trotty put his hands before his face.

"Listen!" said the Shadow.

"Listen!" said the other Shadows.

"Listen!" said the child's voice.

A solemn strain of blended voices, rose into the tower.

It was a very low and mournful strain – a Dirge – and as he listened, Trotty heard his child among the singers.

"She is dead!" exclaimed the old man. "Meg is dead! Her Spirit calls to me. I hear it!"

"The Spirit of your child bewails the dead, and mingles with the dead – dead hopes, dead fancies, dead imaginings of youth," returned the Bell, "but she is living. Learn from her life, a living truth. Learn from the creature dearest to your heart, how bad the bad are born. See every bud and leaf plucked one by one from off the fairest stem, and know how bare and wretched it may be. Follow her! To desperation!"

Each of the shadowy figures stretched its right arm forth, and pointed downward.

"The Spirit of the Chimes is your companion," said the figure.

"Go! It stands behind you!"

Trotty turned, and saw – the child! The child Will Fern had carried in the street; the child whom Meg had watched, but now, asleep!

"I carried her myself, to-night," said Trotty. "In these arms!"

"Show him what he calls himself," said the dark figures, one and all.

The tower opened at his feet. He looked down, and beheld his own form, lying at the bottom, on the outside: crushed and motionless.

"No more a living man!" cried Trotty. "Dead!"

"Dead!" said the figures all together.

"Gracious Heaven! And the New Year—"

"Past," said the figures.

"What!" he cried, shuddering. "I missed my way, and coming on the outside of this tower in the dark, fell down – a year ago?"

"Nine years ago!" replied the figures.

As they gave the answer, they recalled their outstretched hands; and where their figures had been, there the Bells were.

And they rung; their time being come again. And once again, vast multitudes of phantoms sprung into existence; once again, were incoherently engaged, as they had been before; once again, faded on the stopping of the Chimes; and dwindled into nothing.

"What are these?" he asked his guide. "If I am not mad, what are these?"

"Spirits of the Bells. Their sound upon the air," returned the child. "They take such shapes and occupations as the hopes and thoughts of mortals, and the recollections they have stored up, give them."

"And you," said Trotty wildly. "What are you?"

"Hush, hush!" returned the child. "Look here!"

In a poor, mean room; working at the same kind of embroidery which he had often, often seen before her; Meg, his own dear daughter, was presented to his view. He made no effort to imprint his kisses on her face; he did not strive to clasp her to his loving heart; he knew that such endearments were, for him, no more. But, he held his trembling breath, and brushed away the blinding tears, that he might look upon her; that he might only see her.

Ah! Changed. Changed. The light of the clear eye, how dimmed. The bloom, how faded from the cheek. Beautiful she was, as she had ever been, but Hope, Hope, Hope, oh where was the fresh Hope that had spoken to him like a voice!

She looked up from her work, at a companion. Following her eyes, the old man started back.

In the woman grown, he recognised her at a glance. In the long silken hair, he saw the self-same curls; around the lips, the child's expression lingering still. See! In the eyes, now turned inquiringly on Meg, there shone the very look that scanned those features when he brought her home!

Then what was this, beside him!

Looking with awe into its face, he saw a something reigning there: a lofty something, undefined and indistinct, which made it hardly more than a remembrance of that child – as yonder figure might be – yet it was the same: the same: and wore the dress.

Hark. They were speaking!

"Meg," said Lilian, hesitating. "How often you raise your head from your work to look at me!"

"Are my looks so altered, that they frighten you?" asked Meg.

"Nay, dear! But you smile at that, yourself! Why not smile, when you look at me, Meg?"

"I do so. Do I not?" she answered: smiling on her.

"Now you do," said Lilian, "but not usually. When you think I'm busy, and don't see you, you look so anxious and so doubtful, that I hardly like to raise my eyes. There is little cause for smiling in this hard and toilsome life, but you were once so cheerful."

"Am I not now!" cried Meg, speaking in a tone of strange alarm, and rising to embrace her. "Do I make our weary life more weary to you, Lilian!"

"You have been the only thing that made it life," said Lilian, fervently kissing her; "sometimes the only thing that made me care to live so, Meg. Such work, such work! So many hours, so many days, so many long, long nights of hopeless, cheerless, never-ending work – not to heap up riches, not to live grandly or gaily, not to live upon enough, however coarse; but to earn bare bread; to scrape together just enough to toil upon, and want upon, and keep alive in us the consciousness of our hard fate! Oh Meg, Meg!" she raised her voice and twined her arms about her as she spoke, like one in pain. "How can the cruel world go round, and bear to look upon such lives!"

"Lilly!" said Meg, soothing her, and putting back her hair from her wet face. "Why, Lilly! You! So pretty and so young!"

"Oh Meg!" she interrupted, holding her at arm's-length, and looking in her face imploringly. "The worst of all, the worst of all! Strike me old, Meg! Wither me, and shrivel me, and free me from the dreadful thoughts that tempt me in my youth!"

Trotty turned to look upon his guide. But the Spirit of the child had taken flight. Was gone.

Neither did he himself remain in the same place; for, Sir Joseph Bowley, Friend and Father of the Poor, held a great festivity at Bowley Hall, in honour of the natal day of Lady Bowley. And as Lady Bowley had been born on New Year's Day (which the local newspapers considered an especial pointing of the finger of Providence to number One, as Lady Bowley's destined figure in Creation), it was on a New Year's Day that this festivity took place.

Bowley Hall was full of visitors. The red-faced gentleman was there, Mr. Filer was there, the great Alderman Cute was there – Alderman Cute had a sympathetic feeling with great people, and had considerably improved his acquaintance with Sir Joseph Bowley on the strength of his attentive letter: indeed had become quite a friend of the family since then – and many guests were there. Trotty's ghost was there, wandering about, poor phantom, drearily; and looking for its guide.

There was to be a great dinner in the Great Hall. At which Sir Joseph Bowley, in his celebrated character of Friend and Father of the Poor, was to make his great speech. Certain plum-puddings were to be eaten by his Friends and Children in another Hall first; and, at a given signal, Friends and Children flocking in among their Friends and Fathers, were to form a family assemblage, with not one manly eye therein unmoistened by emotion.

But, there was more than this to happen. Even more than this. Sir Joseph Bowley, Baronet and Member of Parliament, was to play a match at skittles – real skittles – with his tenants!

"Which quite reminds me," said Alderman Cute, "of the days of old King Hal, stout King Hal, bluff King Hal. Ah! Fine character!"

"Very," said Mr. Filer, dryly. "For marrying women and murdering 'em. Considerably more than the average number of wives by the bye."

"You'll marry the beautiful ladies, and not murder 'em, eh?" said Alderman Cute to the heir of Bowley, aged twelve. "Sweet boy! We shall have this little gentleman in Parliament now," said the Alderman, holding him by the shoulders, and looking as reflective as he could, "before we know where we are. We shall hear of his successes at the poll; his speeches in the House; his overtures from Governments; his brilliant achievements of all kinds; ah! we shall make our little orations about him in the Common Council, I'll be bound; before we have time to look about us!"

"Oh, the difference of shoes and stockings!" Trotty thought. But his heart yearned towards the child, for the love of those same shoeless and stockingless boys, predestined (by the Alderman) to turn out bad, who might have been the children of poor Meg.

"Richard," moaned Trotty, roaming among the company, to and fro; "where is he? I can't find Richard! Where is Richard?" Not likely to be there, if still alive! But Trotty's grief and solitude confused him; and he still went wandering among the gallant company, looking for his guide, and saying, "Where is Richard? Show me Richard!"

He was wandering thus, when he encountered Mr. Fish, the confidential Secretary: in great agitation.

"Bless my heart and soul!" cried Mr. Fish. "Where's Alderman Cute? Has anybody seen the Alderman?"

Seen the Alderman? Oh dear! Who could ever help seeing the Alderman? He was so considerate, so affable, he bore so much in mind the natural desires of folks to see him, that if he had a fault, it was the being constantly On View. And wherever the great people were, there, to be sure, attracted by the kindred sympathy between great souls, was Cute.

Several voices cried that he was in the circle round Sir Joseph. Mr. Fish made way there; found him; and took him secretly into a window near at hand. Trotty joined them. Not of his own accord. He felt that his steps were led in that direction.

"My dear Alderman Cute," said Mr. Fish. "A little more this way. The most dreadful circumstance has occurred. I have this moment received the intelligence. I think it will be best not to acquaint Sir Joseph with it till the day is over. You understand Sir Joseph, and will give me your opinion. The most frightful and deplorable event!"

"Fish!" returned the Alderman. "Fish! My good fellow, what is the matter? Nothing revolutionary, I hope! No – no attempted interference with the magistrates?"

"Deedles, the banker," gasped the Secretary. "Deedles Brothers – who was to have been here today – high in office in the Goldsmiths' Company—"

"Not stopped!" exclaimed the Alderman, "It can't be!"

"Shot himself."

"Good God!"

"Put a double-barrelled pistol to his mouth, in his own counting house," said Mr. Fish, "and blew his brains out. No motive. Princely circumstances!"

"Circumstances!" exclaimed the Alderman. "A man of noble fortune. One of the most respectable of men. Suicide, Mr. Fish! By his own hand!"

"This very morning," returned Mr. Fish.

"Oh the brain, the brain!" exclaimed the pious Alderman, lifting up his hands. "Oh the nerves, the nerves; the mysteries of this machine called Man! Oh the little that unhinges it: poor creatures that we are! Perhaps a dinner, Mr. Fish. Perhaps the conduct of his son, who, I have heard, ran very wild, and was in the habit of drawing bills upon him without the least authority! A most respectable man. One of the most respectable men I ever knew! A lamentable instance, Mr. Fish. A public calamity! I shall make a point of wearing the deepest mourning. A most respectable man! But there is One above. We must submit, Mr. Fish. We must submit!"

What, Alderman! No word of Putting Down? Remember, Justice, your high moral boast and pride. Come, Alderman! Balance those scales. Throw me into this, the empty one, no dinner, and Nature's founts in some poor woman, dried by starving misery and rendered obdurate to claims for which her offspring *has* authority in holy mother Eve. Weigh me the two, you Daniel, going to judgment, when your day shall come! Weigh them, in the eyes of suffering thousands, audience (not unmindful) of the grim farce you play. Or supposing that you strayed from your five wits – it's not so far to go, but that it might be – and laid hands upon that throat of yours, warning your fellows (if you have a fellow) how they croak their comfortable wickedness to raving heads and stricken hearts. What then?

The words rose up in Trotty's breast, as if they had been spoken by some other voice within him. Alderman Cute pledged himself to Mr. Fish that he would assist him in breaking the melancholy catastrophe to Sir Joseph when the day was over. Then, before they parted, wringing Mr. Fish's hand in bitterness of soul, he said, "The most respectable of men!" And added that he hardly knew (not even he), why such afflictions were allowed on earth.

"It's almost enough to make one think, if one didn't know better," said Alderman Cute, "that at times some motion of a capsizing nature was going on in things, which affected the general economy of the social fabric. Deedles Brothers!"

The skittle-playing came off with immense success. Sir Joseph knocked the pins about quite skilfully; Master Bowley took an innings at a shorter distance also; and everybody said that now, when a Baronet and the Son of a Baronet played at skittles, the country was coming round again, as fast as it could come.

At its proper time, the Banquet was served up. Trotty involuntarily repaired to the Hall with the rest, for he felt himself conducted thither by some stronger impulse than his own free will. The sight was gay in the extreme; the ladies were very handsome; the visitors delighted, cheerful, and good-tempered. When the lower doors were opened, and the people flocked in, in their rustic dresses, the beauty of the spectacle was at its height; but Trotty only murmured more and more, "Where is Richard! He should help and comfort her! I can't see Richard!"

There had been some speeches made; and Lady Bowley's health had been proposed; and Sir Joseph Bowley had returned thanks, and had made his great speech, showing by various pieces of evidence that he was the born Friend and Father, and so forth; and had given as a Toast, his Friends and Children, and the Dignity of Labour; when a slight disturbance at the bottom of the Hall attracted Toby's notice. After some confusion, noise, and opposition, one man broke through the rest, and stood forward by himself.

Not Richard. No. But one whom he had thought of, and had looked for, many times. In a scantier supply of light, he might have doubted the identity of that worn man, so old, and grey, and bent; but with a blaze of lamps upon his gnarled and knotted head, he knew Will Fern as soon as he stepped forth.

"What is this!" exclaimed Sir Joseph, rising. "Who gave this man admittance? This is a criminal from prison! Mr. Fish, sir, *will* you have the goodness—"

"A minute!" said Will Fern. "A minute! My Lady, you was born on this day along with a New Year. Get me a minute's leave to speak."

She made some intercession for him. Sir Joseph took his seat again, with native dignity.

The ragged visitor – for he was miserably dressed – looked round upon the company, and made his homage to them with a humble bow.

"Gentlefolks!" he said. "You've drunk the Labourer. Look at me!"

"Just come from jail," said Mr. Fish.

"Just come from jail," said Will. "And neither for the first time, nor the second, nor the third, nor yet the fourth."

Mr. Filer was heard to remark testily, that four times was over the average; and he ought to be ashamed of himself.

"Gentlefolks!" repeated Will Fern. "Look at me! You see I'm at the worst. Beyond all hurt or harm; beyond your help; for the time when your kind words or kind actions could have done me good," – he struck his hand upon his breast, and shook his head, "is gone, with the scent of last year's beans or clover on the air. Let me say a word for these," pointing to the labouring people in the Hall; "and when you're met together, hear the real Truth spoke out for once."

"There's not a man here," said the host, "who would have him for a spokesman."

"Like enough, Sir Joseph. I believe it. Not the less true, perhaps, is what I say. Perhaps that's a proof on it. Gentlefolks, I've lived many a year in this place. You may see the cottage from the sunk fence over yonder. I've seen the ladies draw it in their books, a hundred times. It looks well in a picter, I've heerd say; but there an't weather in picters, and maybe 'tis fitter for that, than for a place to live in. Well! I lived there. How hard – how bitter hard, I lived there, I won't say. Any day in the year, and every day, you can judge for your own selves."

He spoke as he had spoken on the night when Trotty found him in the street. His voice was deeper and more husky, and had a trembling in it now and then; but he never raised it passionately, and seldom lifted it above the firm stern level of the homely facts he stated.

"'Tis harder than you think for, gentlefolks, to grow up decent, commonly decent, in such a place. That I growed up a man and not a brute, says something for me – as I was then. As I am now, there's nothing can be said for me or done for me. I'm past it."

"I am glad this man has entered," observed Sir Joseph, looking round serenely. "Don't disturb him. It appears to be Ordained. He is an example: a living example. I hope and trust, and confidently expect, that it will not be lost upon my Friends here."

"I dragged on," said Fern, after a moment's silence, "somehow. Neither me nor any other man knows how; but so heavy, that I couldn't put a cheerful face upon it, or make believe that I was anything but what I was. Now, gentlemen – you gentlemen that sits at Sessions – when you see a man with discontent writ on his face, you says to one another, 'He's suspicious. I has my doubts,' says you, 'about Will Fern. Watch that fellow!' I don't say, gentlemen, it ain't quite nat'ral, but I say 'tis so; and from that hour, whatever Will Fern does, or lets alone – all one – it goes against him."

Alderman Cute stuck his thumbs in his waistcoat-pockets, and leaning back in his chair, and smiling, winked at a neighbouring chandelier. As much as to say, "Of course! I told you so. The common cry! Lord bless you, we are up to all this sort of thing – myself and human nature."

"Now, gentlemen," said Will Fern, holding out his hands, and flushing for an instant in his haggard face, "see how your laws are made to trap and hunt us when we're brought to this. I tries to live elsewhere. And I'm a vagabond. To jail with him! I comes back here. I goes a-nutting in your woods, and breaks – who don't? – a limber branch or two. To jail with him! One of your keepers sees me in the broad day, near my own patch of garden, with a gun. To jail with him! I has a nat'ral angry word with that man, when I'm free again. To jail with him! I cuts a stick. To jail with him! I eats a rotten apple or a turnip. To jail with him! It's twenty mile away; and coming back I begs a trifle on the road. To jail with him! At last, the constable, the keeper – anybody – finds me anywhere, a-doing anything. To jail with him, for he's a vagrant, and a jail-bird known; and jail's the only home he's got."

The Alderman nodded sagaciously, as who should say, "A very good home too!"

"Do I say this to serve my cause!" cried Fern. "Who can give me back my liberty, who can give me back my good name, who can give me back my innocent niece? Not all the Lords and Ladies in wide England. But, gentlemen, gentlemen, dealing with other men like me, begin at the right end. Give us, in mercy, better homes when we're a-lying in our cradles; give us better food when we're a-working for our lives; give us kinder laws to bring us back when we're a-going wrong; and don't set jail, jail, jail, afore us, everywhere we turn. There an't a condescension you can show the Labourer then, that he won't take, as ready and as grateful as a man can be; for, he has a patient, peaceful, willing heart. But you must put his rightful spirit in him first; for, whether he's a wreck and ruin such as me, or is like one of them that stand here now, his spirit is divided from you at this time. Bring it back, gentlefolks, bring it back! Bring it back, afore the day comes when even his Bible changes in his altered mind, and the words seem to him to read, as they have sometimes read in my own eyes – in jail: 'Whither thou goest, I can Not go; where thou lodgest, I do Not lodge; thy people are Not my people; Nor thy God my God!'"

A sudden stir and agitation took place in Hall. Trotty thought at first, that several had risen to eject the man; and hence this change in its appearance. But, another moment showed him that the room and all the company had vanished from his sight, and that his daughter was again before him, seated at her work. But in a poorer, meaner garret than before; and with no Lilian by her side.

The frame at which she had worked, was put away upon a shelf and covered up. The chair in which she had sat, was turned against the wall. A history was written in these little things, and in Meg's grief-worn face. Oh! who could fail to read it!

Meg strained her eyes upon her work until it was too dark to see the threads; and when the night closed in, she lighted her feeble candle and worked on. Still her old father was invisible about her; looking down upon her; loving her – how dearly loving her! – and talking to her in a tender voice about the old times, and the Bells. Though he knew, poor Trotty, though he knew she could not hear him.

A great part of the evening had worn away, when a knock came at her door. She opened it. A man was on the threshold. A slouching, moody, drunken sloven, wasted by intemperance and vice, and with his matted hair and unshorn beard in wild disorder; but, with some traces on him, too, of having been a man of good proportion and good features in his youth.

He stopped until he had her leave to enter; and she, retiring a pace or two from the open door, silently and sorrowfully looked upon him. Trotty had his wish. He saw Richard.

"May I come in, Margaret?"

"Yes! Come in. Come in!"

It was well that Trotty knew him before he spoke; for with any doubt remaining on his mind, the harsh discordant voice would have persuaded him that it was not Richard but some other man.

There were but two chairs in the room. She gave him hers, and stood at some short distance from him, waiting to hear what he had to say.

He sat, however, staring vacantly at the floor; with a lustreless and stupid smile. A spectacle of such deep degradation, of such abject hopelessness, of such a miserable downfall, that she put her hands before her face and turned away, lest he should see how much it moved her.

Roused by the rustling of her dress, or some such trifling sound, he lifted his head, and began to speak as if there had been no pause since he entered.

"Still at work, Margaret? You work late."

"I generally do."

"And early?"

"And early."

"So she said. She said you never tired; or never owned that you tired. Not all the time you lived together. Not even when you fainted, between work and fasting. But I told you that, the last time I came."

"You did," she answered. "And I implored you to tell me nothing more; and you made me a solemn promise, Richard, that you never would."

"A solemn promise," he repeated, with a drivelling laugh and vacant stare. "A solemn promise. To be sure. A solemn promise!" Awakening, as it were, after a time; in the same manner as before; he said with sudden animation:

"How can I help it, Margaret? What am I to do? She has been to me again!"

"Again!" cried Meg, clasping her hands. "O, does she think of me so often! Has she been again!"

"Twenty times again," said Richard. "Margaret, she haunts me. She comes behind me in the street, and thrusts it in my hand. I hear her foot upon the ashes when I'm at my work (ha, ha! that an't often), and before I can turn my head, her voice is in my ear, saying, 'Richard, don't look round. For Heaven's love, give her this!' She brings it where I live: she sends it in letters; she taps at the window and lays it on the sill. What *can* I do? Look at it!"

He held out in his hand a little purse, and chinked the money it enclosed.

"Hide it," said Meg. "Hide it! When she comes again, tell her, Richard, that I love her in my soul. That I never lie down to sleep, but I bless her, and pray for her. That, in my solitary work, I never cease to have her in my thoughts. That she is with me, night and day. That if I died tomorrow, I would remember her with my last breath. But, that I cannot look upon it!"

He slowly recalled his hand, and crushing the purse together, said with a kind of drowsy thoughtfulness:

"I told her so. I told her so, as plain as words could speak. I've taken this gift back and left it at her door, a dozen times since then. But when she came at last, and stood before me, face to face, what could I do?"

"You saw her!" exclaimed Meg. "You saw her! O, Lilian, my sweet girl! O, Lilian, Lilian!"

"I saw her," he went on to say, not answering, but engaged in the same slow pursuit of his own thoughts. "There she stood: trembling! "How does she look, Richard? Does she ever speak of me? Is she thinner? My old place at the table: what's in my old place? And the frame she taught me our old work on – has she burnt it, Richard!" There she was. I heard her say it."

Meg checked her sobs, and with the tears streaming from her eyes, bent over him to listen. Not to lose a breath.

With his arms resting on his knees; and stooping forward in his chair, as if what he said were written on the ground in some half legible character, which it was his occupation to decipher and connect; he went on.

"'Richard, I have fallen very low; and you may guess how much I have suffered in having this sent back, when I can bear to bring it in my hand to you. But you loved her once, even in my memory, dearly. Others stepped in between you; fears, and jealousies, and doubts, and vanities, estranged you from her; but you did love her, even in my memory!' I suppose I did," he said, interrupting himself for a moment. "I did! That's neither here nor there – 'O Richard, if you ever did; if you have any memory for what is gone and lost, take it to her once more. Once more! Tell her how

I laid my head upon your shoulder, where her own head might have lain, and was so humble to you, Richard. Tell her that you looked into my face, and saw the beauty which she used to praise, all gone: all gone: and in its place, a poor, wan, hollow cheek, that she would weep to see. Tell her everything, and take it back, and she will not refuse again. She will not have the heart!'"

So he sat musing, and repeating the last words, until he woke again, and rose.

"You won't take it, Margaret?"

She shook her head, and motioned an entreaty to him to leave her.

"Good night, Margaret."

"Good night!"

He turned to look upon her; struck by her sorrow, and perhaps by the pity for himself which trembled in her voice. It was a quick and rapid action; and for the moment some flash of his old bearing kindled in his form. In the next he went as he had come. Nor did this glimmer of a quenched fire seem to light him to a quicker sense of his debasement.

In any mood, in any grief, in any torture of the mind or body, Meg's work must be done. She sat down to her task, and plied it. Night, midnight. Still she worked.

She had a meagre fire, the night being very cold; and rose at intervals to mend it. The Chimes rang half-past twelve while she was thus engaged; and when they ceased she heard a gentle knocking at the door. Before she could so much as wonder who was there, at that unusual hour, it opened.

O Youth and Beauty, happy as ye should be, look at this. O Youth and Beauty, blest and blessing all within your reach, and working out the ends of your Beneficent Creator, look at this!

She saw the entering figure; screamed its name; cried "Lilian!"

It was swift, and fell upon its knees before her: clinging to her dress.

"Up, dear! Up! Lilian! My own dearest!"

"Never more, Meg; never more! Here! Here! Close to you, holding to you, feeling your dear breath upon my face!"

"Sweet Lilian! Darling Lilian! Child of my heart – no mother's love can be more tender – lay your head upon my breast!"

"Never more, Meg. Never more! When I first looked into your face, you knelt before me. On my knees before you, let me die. Let it be here!"

"You have come back. My Treasure! We will live together, work together, hope together, die together!"

"Ah! Kiss my lips, Meg; fold your arms about me; press me to your bosom; look kindly on me; but don't raise me. Let it be here. Let me see the last of your dear face upon my knees!"

O Youth and Beauty, happy as ye should be, look at this! O Youth and Beauty, working out the ends of your Beneficent Creator, look at this!

"Forgive me, Meg! So dear, so dear! Forgive me! I know you do, I see you do, but say so, Meg!"

She said so, with her lips on Lilian's cheek. And with her arms twined round – she knew it now – a broken heart.

"His blessing on you, dearest love. Kiss me once more! He suffered her to sit beside His feet, and dry them with her hair. O Meg, what Mercy and Compassion!"

As she died, the Spirit of the child returning, innocent and radiant, touched the old man with its hand, and beckoned him away.

# Chapter IV
## Fourth Quarter

**SOME NEW REMEMBRANCE** of the ghostly figures in the Bells; some faint impression of the ringing of the Chimes; some giddy consciousness of having seen the swarm of phantoms reproduced and reproduced until the recollection of them lost itself in the confusion of their numbers; some hurried knowledge, how conveyed to him he knew not, that more years had passed; and Trotty, with the Spirit of the child attending him, stood looking on at mortal company.

Fat company, rosy-cheeked company, comfortable company. They were but two, but they were red enough for ten. They sat before a bright fire, with a small low table between them; and unless the fragrance of hot tea and muffins lingered longer in that room than in most others, the table had seen service very lately. But all the cups and saucers being clean, and in their proper places in the corner-cupboard; and the brass toasting-fork hanging in its usual nook and spreading its four idle fingers out as if it wanted to be measured for a glove; there remained no other visible tokens of the meal just finished, than such as purred and washed their whiskers in the person of the basking cat, and glistened in the gracious, not to say the greasy, faces of her patrons.

This cosy couple (married, evidently) had made a fair division of the fire between them, and sat looking at the glowing sparks that dropped into the grate; now nodding off into a doze; now waking up again when some hot fragment, larger than the rest, came rattling down, as if the fire were coming with it.

It was in no danger of sudden extinction, however; for it gleamed not only in the little room, and on the panes of window-glass in the door, and on the curtain half drawn across them, but in the little shop beyond. A little shop, quite crammed and choked with the abundance of its stock; a perfectly voracious little shop, with a maw as accommodating and full as any shark's. Cheese, butter, firewood, soap, pickles, matches, bacon, table-beer, peg-tops, sweetmeats, boys' kites, bird-seed, cold ham, birch brooms, hearth-stones, salt, vinegar, blacking, red-herrings, stationery, lard, mushroom-ketchup, staylaces, loaves of bread, shuttlecocks, eggs, and slate pencil; everything was fish that came to the net of this greedy little shop, and all articles were in its net. How many other kinds of petty merchandise were there, it would be difficult to say; but balls of packthread, ropes of onions, pounds of candles, cabbage-nets, and brushes, hung in bunches from the ceiling, like extraordinary fruit; while various odd canisters emitting aromatic smells, established the veracity of the inscription over the outer door, which informed the public that the keeper of this little shop was a licensed dealer in tea, coffee, tobacco, pepper, and snuff.

Glancing at such of these articles as were visible in the shining of the blaze, and the less cheerful radiance of two smoky lamps which burnt but dimly in the shop itself, as though its plethora sat heavy on their lungs; and glancing, then, at one of the two faces by the parlour-fire; Trotty had small difficulty in recognising in the stout old lady, Mrs. Chickenstalker: always inclined to corpulency, even in the days when he had known her as established in the general line, and having a small balance against him in her books.

The features of her companion were less easy to him. The great broad chin, with creases in it large enough to hide a finger in; the astonished eyes, that seemed to expostulate with themselves for sinking deeper and deeper into the yielding fat of the soft face; the nose afflicted with that disordered action of its functions which is generally termed The Snuffles; the short thick throat and labouring chest, with other beauties of the like description; though calculated to impress the memory, Trotty could at first allot to nobody he had ever known: and yet he had some recollection of them too. At length, in Mrs. Chickenstalker's partner in the general line, and in the crooked and eccentric line of life, he recognised the former porter of Sir Joseph Bowley; an apoplectic innocent, who had connected himself in Trotty's mind with Mrs. Chickenstalker years ago, by giving him admission to the mansion where he had confessed his obligations to that lady, and drawn on his unlucky head such grave reproach.

Trotty had little interest in a change like this, after the changes he had seen; but association is very strong sometimes; and he looked involuntarily behind the parlour-door, where the accounts of credit customers were usually kept in chalk. There was no record of his name. Some names were there, but they were strange to him, and infinitely fewer than of old; from which he argued that the porter was an advocate of ready-money transactions, and on coming into the business had looked pretty sharp after the Chickenstalker defaulters.

So desolate was Trotty, and so mournful for the youth and promise of his blighted child, that it was a sorrow to him, even to have no place in Mrs. Chickenstalker's ledger.

"What sort of a night is it, Anne?" inquired the former porter of Sir Joseph Bowley, stretching out his legs before the fire, and rubbing as much of them as his short arms could reach; with an air that added, "Here I am if it's bad, and I don't want to go out if it's good."

"Blowing and sleeting hard," returned his wife; "and threatening snow. Dark. And very cold."

"I'm glad to think we had muffins," said the former porter, in the tone of one who had set his conscience at rest. "It's a sort of night that's meant for muffins. Likewise crumpets. Also Sally Lunns."

The former porter mentioned each successive kind of eatable, as if he were musingly summing up his good actions. After which he rubbed his fat legs as before, and jerking them at the knees to get the fire upon the yet unroasted parts, laughed as if somebody had tickled him.

"You're in spirits, Tugby, my dear," observed his wife.

The firm was Tugby, late Chickenstalker.

"No," said Tugby. "No. Not particular. I'm a little elewated. The muffins came so pat!"

With that he chuckled until he was black in the face; and had so much ado to become any other colour, that his fat legs took the strangest excursions into the air. Nor were they reduced to anything like decorum until Mrs. Tugby had thumped him violently on the back, and shaken him as if he were a great bottle.

"Good gracious, goodness, lord-a-mercy bless and save the man!" cried Mrs. Tugby, in great terror. "What's he doing?"

Mr. Tugby wiped his eyes, and faintly repeated that he found himself a little elewated.

"Then don't be so again, that's a dear good soul," said Mrs. Tugby, "if you don't want to frighten me to death, with your struggling and fighting!"

Mr. Tugby said he wouldn't; but, his whole existence was a fight, in which, if any judgment might be founded on the constantly-increasing shortness of his breath, and the deepening purple of his face, he was always getting the worst of it.

"So it's blowing, and sleeting, and threatening snow; and it's dark, and very cold, is it, my dear?" said Mr. Tugby, looking at the fire, and reverting to the cream and marrow of his temporary elevation.

"Hard weather indeed," returned his wife, shaking her head.

"Aye, aye! Years," said Mr. Tugby, "are like Christians in that respect. Some of 'em die hard; some of 'em die easy. This one hasn't many days to run, and is making a fight for it. I like him all the better. There's a customer, my love!"

Attentive to the rattling door, Mrs. Tugby had already risen.

"Now then!" said that lady, passing out into the little shop. "What's wanted? Oh! I beg your pardon, sir, I'm sure. I didn't think it was you."

She made this apology to a gentleman in black, who, with his wristbands tucked up, and his hat cocked loungingly on one side, and his hands in his pockets, sat down astride on the table-beer barrel, and nodded in return.

"This is a bad business up-stairs, Mrs. Tugby," said the gentleman. "The man can't live."

"Not the back-attic can't!" cried Tugby, coming out into the shop to join the conference.

"The back-attic, Mr. Tugby," said the gentleman, "is coming down-stairs fast, and will be below the basement very soon."

Looking by turns at Tugby and his wife, he sounded the barrel with his knuckles for the depth of beer, and having found it, played a tune upon the empty part.

"The back-attic, Mr. Tugby," said the gentleman: Tugby having stood in silent consternation for some time: "is Going."

"Then," said Tugby, turning to his wife, "he must Go, you know, before he's Gone."

"I don't think you can move him," said the gentleman, shaking his head. "I wouldn't take the responsibility of saying it could be done, myself. You had better leave him where he is. He can't live long."

"It's the only subject," said Tugby, bringing the butter-scale down upon the counter with a crash, by weighing his fist on it, "that we've ever had a word upon; she and me; and look what it comes to! He's going to die here, after all. Going to die upon the premises. Going to die in our house!"

"And where should he have died, Tugby?" cried his wife.

"In the workhouse," he returned. "What are workhouses made for?"

"Not for that," said Mrs. Tugby, with great energy. "Not for that! Neither did I marry you for that. Don't think it, Tugby. I won't have it. I won't allow it. I'd be separated first, and never see your face again. When my widow's name stood over that door, as it did for many years: this house being known as Mrs. Chickenstalker's far and wide, and never known but to its honest credit and its good report: when my widow's name stood over that door, Tugby, I knew him as a handsome, steady, manly, independent youth; I knew her as the sweetest-looking, sweetest-tempered girl, eyes ever saw; I knew her father (poor old creetur, he fell down from the steeple walking in his sleep, and killed himself), for the simplest, hardest-working, childest-hearted man, that ever drew the breath of life; and when I turn them out of house and home, may angels turn me out of Heaven. As they would! And serve me right!"

Her old face, which had been a plump and dimpled one before the changes which had come to pass, seemed to shine out of her as she said these words; and when she dried her eyes, and shook her head and her handkerchief at Tugby, with an expression of firmness which it was quite clear was not to be easily resisted, Trotty said, "Bless her! Bless her!"

Then he listened, with a panting heart, for what should follow. Knowing nothing yet, but that they spoke of Meg.

If Tugby had been a little elevated in the parlour, he more than balanced that account by being not a little depressed in the shop, where he now stood staring at his wife, without attempting a reply; secretly conveying, however – either in a fit of abstraction or as a precautionary measure – all the money from the till into his own pockets, as he looked at her.

The gentleman upon the table-beer cask, who appeared to be some authorised medical attendant upon the poor, was far too well accustomed, evidently, to little differences of opinion between man and wife, to interpose any remark in this instance. He sat softly whistling, and turning little drops of beer out of the tap upon the ground, until there was a perfect calm: when he raised his head, and said to Mrs. Tugby, late Chickenstalker:

"There's something interesting about the woman, even now. How did she come to marry him?"

"Why that," said Mrs. Tugby, taking a seat near him, "is not the least cruel part of her story, sir. You see they kept company, she and Richard, many years ago. When they were a young and beautiful couple, everything was settled, and they were to have been married on a New Year's Day. But, somehow, Richard got it into his head, through what the gentlemen told him, that he might do better, and that he'd soon repent it, and that she wasn't good enough for him, and that a young man of spirit had no business to be married. And the gentlemen frightened her, and made her melancholy, and timid of his deserting her, and of her children coming to the gallows, and of its being wicked to be man and wife, and a good deal more of it. And in short, they lingered and lingered, and their trust in one another was broken, and so at last was the match. But the fault was his. She would have married him, sir, joyfully. I've seen her heart swell many times afterwards, when he passed her in a proud and careless way; and never did a woman grieve more truly for a man, than she for Richard when he first went wrong."

"Oh! he went wrong, did he?" said the gentleman, pulling out the vent-peg of the table-beer, and trying to peep down into the barrel through the hole.

"Well, sir, I don't know that he rightly understood himself, you see. I think his mind was troubled by their having broke with one another; and that but for being ashamed before the gentlemen, and perhaps for being uncertain too, how she might take it, he'd have gone through any suffering or trial to have had Meg's promise and Meg's hand again. That's my belief. He never said so; more's the pity! He took to drinking, idling, bad companions: all the fine resources that were to be so much better for him than the Home he might have had. He lost his looks, his character, his health, his strength, his friends, his work: everything!"

"He didn't lose everything, Mrs. Tugby," returned the gentleman, "because he gained a wife; and I want to know how he gained her."

"I'm coming to it, sir, in a moment. This went on for years and years; he sinking lower and lower; she enduring, poor thing, miseries enough to wear her life away. At last, he was so cast down, and cast out, that no one would employ or notice him; and doors were shut upon him, go where he would. Applying from place to place, and door to door; and coming for the hundredth time to one gentleman who had often and often tried him (he was a good workman to the very end); that gentleman, who knew his history, said, "I believe you are incorrigible; there is only one person in the world who has a chance of reclaiming you; ask me to trust you no more, until she tries to do it." Something like that, in his anger and vexation."

"Ah!" said the gentleman. "Well?"

"Well, sir, he went to her, and kneeled to her; said it was so; said it ever had been so; and made a prayer to her to save him."

"And she? – Don't distress yourself, Mrs. Tugby."

"She came to me that night to ask me about living here. "What he was once to me,"
she said, "is buried in a grave, side by side with what I was to him. But I have thought
of this; and I will make the trial. In the hope of saving him; for the love of the light-
hearted girl (you remember her) who was to have been married on a New Year's Day;
and for the love of her Richard." And she said he had come to her from Lilian, and
Lilian had trusted to him, and she never could forget that. So they were married; and
when they came home here, and I saw them, I hoped that such prophecies as parted
them when they were young, may not often fulfil themselves as they did in this case,
or I wouldn't be the makers of them for a Mine of Gold."

The gentleman got off the cask, and stretched himself, observing:

"I suppose he used her ill, as soon as they were married?"

"I don't think he ever did that," said Mrs. Tugby, shaking her head, and wiping her
eyes. "He went on better for a short time; but, his habits were too old and strong to be
got rid of; he soon fell back a little; and was falling fast back, when his illness came so
strong upon him. I think he has always felt for her. I am sure he has. I have seen him,
in his crying fits and tremblings, try to kiss her hand; and I have heard him call her
"Meg," and say it was her nineteenth birthday. There he has been lying, now, these
weeks and months. Between him and her baby, she has not been able to do her old
work; and by not being able to be regular, she has lost it, even if she could have done
it. How they have lived, I hardly know!"

"I know," muttered Mr. Tugby; looking at the till, and round the shop, and at his
wife; and rolling his head with immense intelligence. "Like Fighting Cocks!"

He was interrupted by a cry – a sound of lamentation – from the upper story of the
house. The gentleman moved hurriedly to the door.

"My friend," he said, looking back, "you needn't discuss whether he shall be
removed or not. He has spared you that trouble, I believe."

Saying so, he ran up-stairs, followed by Mrs. Tugby; while Mr. Tugby panted and
grumbled after them at leisure: being rendered more than commonly short-winded
by the weight of the till, in which there had been an inconvenient quantity of copper.
Trotty, with the child beside him, floated up the staircase like mere air.

"Follow her! Follow her! Follow her!" He heard the ghostly voices in the Bells
repeat their words as he ascended. "Learn it, from the creature dearest to your heart!"

It was over. It was over. And this was she, her father's pride and joy! This haggard,
wretched woman, weeping by the bed, if it deserved that name, and pressing to her
breast, and hanging down her head upon, an infant. Who can tell how spare, how
sickly, and how poor an infant! Who can tell how dear!

"Thank God!" cried Trotty, holding up his folded hands. "O, God be thanked! She
loves her child!"

The gentleman, not otherwise hard-hearted or indifferent to such scenes, than
that he saw them every day, and knew that they were figures of no moment in the
Filer sums – mere scratches in the working of these calculations – laid his hand
upon the heart that beat no more, and listened for the breath, and said, "His pain
is over. It's better as it is!" Mrs. Tugby tried to comfort her with kindness. Mr. Tugby
tried philosophy.

"Come, come!" he said, with his hands in his pockets, "you mustn't give way, you
know. That won't do. You must fight up. What would have become of me if *I* had given

way when I was porter, and we had as many as six runaway carriage-doubles at our door in one night! But, I fell back upon my strength of mind, and didn't open it!"

Again Trotty heard the voices saying, "Follow her!" He turned towards his guide, and saw it rising from him, passing through the air. "Follow her!" it said. And vanished.

He hovered round her; sat down at her feet; looked up into her face for one trace of her old self; listened for one note of her old pleasant voice. He flitted round the child: so wan, so prematurely old, so dreadful in its gravity, so plaintive in its feeble, mournful, miserable wail. He almost worshipped it. He clung to it as her only safeguard; as the last unbroken link that bound her to endurance. He set his father's hope and trust on the frail baby; watched her every look upon it as she held it in her arms; and cried a thousand times, "She loves it! God be thanked, she loves it!"

He saw the woman tend her in the night; return to her when her grudging husband was asleep, and all was still; encourage her, shed tears with her, set nourishment before her. He saw the day come, and the night again; the day, the night; the time go by; the house of death relieved of death; the room left to herself and to the child; he heard it moan and cry; he saw it harass her, and tire her out, and when she slumbered in exhaustion, drag her back to consciousness, and hold her with its little hands upon the rack; but she was constant to it, gentle with it, patient with it. Patient! Was its loving mother in her inmost heart and soul, and had its Being knitted up with hers as when she carried it unborn.

All this time, she was in want: languishing away, in dire and pining want. With the baby in her arms, she wandered here and there, in quest of occupation; and with its thin face lying in her lap, and looking up in hers, did any work for any wretched sum; a day and night of labour for as many farthings as there were figures on the dial. If she had quarrelled with it; if she had neglected it; if she had looked upon it with a moment's hate; if, in the frenzy of an instant, she had struck it! No. His comfort was, She loved it always.

She told no one of her extremity, and wandered abroad in the day lest she should be questioned by her only friend: for any help she received from her hands, occasioned fresh disputes between the good woman and her husband; and it was new bitterness to be the daily cause of strife and discord, where she owed so much.

She loved it still. She loved it more and more. But a change fell on the aspect of her love. One night.

She was singing faintly to it in its sleep, and walking to and fro to hush it, when her door was softly opened, and a man looked in.

"For the last time," he said.

"William Fern!"

"For the last time."

He listened like a man pursued: and spoke in whispers.

"Margaret, my race is nearly run. I couldn't finish it, without a parting word with you. Without one grateful word."

"What have you done?" she asked: regarding him with terror.

He looked at her, but gave no answer.

After a short silence, he made a gesture with his hand, as if he set her question by; as if he brushed it aside; and said:

"It's long ago, Margaret, now: but that night is as fresh in my memory as ever 'twas. We little thought, then," he added, looking round, "that we should ever meet like this. Your child, Margaret? Let me have it in my arms. Let me hold your child."

He put his hat upon the floor, and took it. And he trembled as he took it, from head to foot.

"Is it a girl?"

"Yes."

He put his hand before its little face.

"See how weak I'm grown, Margaret, when I want the courage to look at it! Let her be, a moment. I won't hurt her. It's long ago, but – What's her name?"

"Margaret," she answered, quickly.

"I'm glad of that," he said. "I'm glad of that!" He seemed to breathe more freely; and after pausing for an instant, took away his hand, and looked upon the infant's face. But covered it again, immediately.

"Margaret!" he said; and gave her back the child. "It's Lilian's."

"Lilian's!"

"I held the same face in my arms when Lilian's mother died and left her."

"When Lilian's mother died and left her!" she repeated, wildly.

"How shrill you speak! Why do you fix your eyes upon me so? Margaret!"

She sunk down in a chair, and pressed the infant to her breast, and wept over it. Sometimes, she released it from her embrace, to look anxiously in its face: then strained it to her bosom again. At those times, when she gazed upon it, then it was that something fierce and terrible began to mingle with her love. Then it was that her old father quailed.

"Follow her!" was sounded through the house. "Learn it, from the creature dearest to your heart!"

"Margaret," said Fern, bending over her, and kissing her upon the brow: "I thank you for the last time. Good night. Good bye! Put your hand in mine, and tell me you'll forget me from this hour, and try to think the end of me was here."

"What have you done?" she asked again.

"There'll be a Fire to-night," he said, removing from her. "There'll be Fires this winter-time, to light the dark nights, East, West, North, and South. When you see the distant sky red, they'll be blazing. When you see the distant sky red, think of me no more; or, if you do, remember what a Hell was lighted up inside of me, and think you see its flames reflected in the clouds. Good night. Good bye!" She called to him; but he was gone. She sat down stupefied, until her infant roused her to a sense of hunger, cold, and darkness. She paced the room with it the livelong night, hushing it and soothing it. She said at intervals, "Like Lilian, when her mother died and left her!" Why was her step so quick, her eye so wild, her love so fierce and terrible, whenever she repeated those words?

"But, it is Love," said Trotty. "It is Love. She'll never cease to love it. My poor Meg!"

She dressed the child next morning with unusual care – ah, vain expenditure of care upon such squalid robes! – and once more tried to find some means of life. It was the last day of the Old Year. She tried till night, and never broke her fast. She tried in vain.

She mingled with an abject crowd, who tarried in the snow, until it pleased some officer appointed to dispense the public charity (the lawful charity; not that once preached upon a Mount), to call them in, and question them, and say to this one, "Go to such a place," to that one, "Come next week;" to make a football of another wretch, and pass him here and there, from hand to hand, from house to house, until he wearied and lay down to die; or started up and robbed, and so became a higher sort of criminal, whose claims allowed of no delay. Here, too, she failed.

She loved her child, and wished to have it lying on her breast. And that was quite enough.

It was night: a bleak, dark, cutting night: when, pressing the child close to her for warmth, she arrived outside the house she called her home. She was so faint and giddy, that she saw no one standing in the doorway until she was close upon it, and about to enter. Then, she recognised the master of the house, who had so disposed himself – with his person it was not difficult – as to fill up the whole entry.

"O!" he said softly. "You have come back?"

She looked at the child, and shook her head.

"Don't you think you have lived here long enough without paying any rent? Don't you think that, without any money, you've been a pretty constant customer at this shop, now?" said Mr. Tugby.

She repeated the same mute appeal.

"Suppose you try and deal somewhere else," he said. "And suppose you provide yourself with another lodging. Come! Don't you think you could manage it?"

She said in a low voice, that it was very late. Tomorrow.

"Now I see what you want," said Tugby; "and what you mean. You know there are two parties in this house about you, and you delight in setting 'em by the ears. I don't want any quarrels; I'm speaking softly to avoid a quarrel; but if you don't go away, I'll speak out loud, and you shall cause words high enough to please you. But you shan't come in. That I am determined."

She put her hair back with her hand, and looked in a sudden manner at the sky, and the dark lowering distance.

"This is the last night of an Old Year, and I won't carry ill-blood and quarrellings and disturbances into a New One, to please you nor anybody else," said Tugby, who was quite a retail Friend and Father. "I wonder you an't ashamed of yourself, to carry such practices into a New Year. If you haven't any business in the world, but to be always giving way, and always making disturbances between man and wife, you'd be better out of it. Go along with you."

"Follow her! To desperation!"

Again the old man heard the voices. Looking up, he saw the figures hovering in the air, and pointing where she went, down the dark street.

"She loves it!" he exclaimed, in agonised entreaty for her. "Chimes! she loves it still!"

"Follow her!" The shadow swept upon the track she had taken, like a cloud.

He joined in the pursuit; he kept close to her; he looked into her face. He saw the same fierce and terrible expression mingling with her love, and kindling in her eyes. He heard her say, "Like Lilian! To be changed like Lilian!" and her speed redoubled.

O, for something to awaken her! For any sight, or sound, or scent, to call up tender recollections in a brain on fire! For any gentle image of the Past, to rise before her!

"I was her father! I was her father!" cried the old man, stretching out his hands to the dark shadows flying on above. "Have mercy on her, and on me! Where does she go? Turn her back! I was her father!"

But they only pointed to her, as she hurried on; and said, "To desperation! Learn it from the creature dearest to your heart!" A hundred voices echoed it. The air was made of breath expended in those words. He seemed to take them in, at every gasp he drew. They were everywhere, and not to be escaped. And still she hurried on; the same light in her eyes, the same words in her mouth, "Like Lilian! To be changed like Lilian!" All at once she stopped.

"Now, turn her back!" exclaimed the old man, tearing his white hair. "My child! Meg! Turn her back! Great Father, turn her back!"

In her own scanty shawl, she wrapped the baby warm. With her fevered hands, she smoothed its limbs, composed its face, arranged its mean attire. In her wasted arms she folded it, as though she never would resign it more. And with her dry lips, kissed it in a final pang, and last long agony of Love.

Putting its tiny hand up to her neck, and holding it there, within her dress, next to her distracted heart, she set its sleeping face against her: closely, steadily, against her: and sped onward to the River.

To the rolling River, swift and dim, where Winter Night sat brooding like the last dark thoughts of many who had sought a refuge there before her. Where scattered lights upon the banks gleamed sullen, red, and dull, as torches that were burning there, to show the way to Death. Where no abode of living people cast its shadow, on the deep, impenetrable, melancholy shade.

To the River! To that portal of Eternity, her desperate footsteps tended with the swiftness of its rapid waters running to the sea. He tried to touch her as she passed him, going down to its dark level: but, the wild distempered form, the fierce and terrible love, the desperation that had left all human check or hold behind, swept by him like the wind.

He followed her. She paused a moment on the brink, before the dreadful plunge. He fell down on his knees, and in a shriek addressed the figures in the Bells now hovering above them.

"I have learnt it!" cried the old man. "From the creature dearest to my heart! O, save her, save her!"

He could wind his fingers in her dress; could hold it! As the words escaped his lips, he felt his sense of touch return, and knew that he detained her.

The figures looked down steadfastly upon him.

"I have learnt it!" cried the old man. "O, have mercy on me in this hour, if, in my love for her, so young and good, I slandered Nature in the breasts of mothers rendered desperate! Pity my presumption, wickedness, and ignorance, and save her." He felt his hold relaxing. They were silent still.

"Have mercy on her!" he exclaimed, "as one in whom this dreadful crime has sprung from Love perverted; from the strongest, deepest Love we fallen creatures know! Think what her misery must have been, when such seed bears such fruit! Heaven meant her to be good. There is no loving mother on the earth who might not come to this, if such a life had gone before. O, have mercy on my child, who, even at this pass, means mercy to her own, and dies herself, and perils her immortal soul, to save it!"

She was in his arms. He held her now. His strength was like a giant's.

"I see the Spirit of the Chimes among you!" cried the old man, singling out the child, and speaking in some inspiration, which their looks conveyed to him. "I know that our inheritance is held in store for us by Time. I know there is a sea of Time to rise one day, before which all who wrong us or oppress us will be swept away like leaves. I see it, on the flow! I know that we must trust and hope, and neither doubt ourselves, nor doubt the good in one another. I have learnt it from the creature dearest to my heart. I clasp her in my arms again. O Spirits, merciful and good, I take your lesson to my breast along with her! O Spirits, merciful and good, I am grateful!"

He might have said more; but, the Bells, the old familiar Bells, his own dear, constant, steady friends, the Chimes, began to ring the joy-peals for a New Year: so lustily, so merrily, so happily, so gaily, that he leapt upon his feet, and broke the spell that bound him.

"And whatever you do, father," said Meg, "don't eat tripe again, without asking some doctor whether it's likely to agree with you; for how you *have* been going on, Good gracious!"

She was working with her needle, at the little table by the fire; dressing her simple gown with ribbons for her wedding. So quietly happy, so blooming and youthful, so full of beautiful promise, that he uttered a great cry as if it were an Angel in his house; then flew to clasp her in his arms.

But, he caught his feet in the newspaper, which had fallen on the hearth; and somebody came rushing in between them.

"No!" cried the voice of this same somebody; a generous and jolly voice it was! "Not even you. Not even you. The first kiss of Meg in the New Year is mine. Mine! I have been waiting outside the house, this hour, to hear the Bells and claim it. Meg, my precious prize, a happy year! A life of happy years, my darling wife!"

And Richard smothered her with kisses.

You never in all your life saw anything like Trotty after this. I don't care where you have lived or what you have seen; you never in all your life saw anything at all approaching him! He sat down in his chair and beat his knees and cried; he sat down in his chair and beat his knees and laughed; he sat down in his chair and beat his knees and laughed and cried together; he got out of his chair and hugged Meg; he got out of his chair and hugged Richard; he got out of his chair and hugged them both at once; he kept running up to Meg, and squeezing her fresh face between his hands and kissing it, going from her backwards not to lose sight of it, and running up again like a figure in a magic lantern; and whatever he did, he was constantly sitting himself down in his chair, and never stopping in it for one single moment; being – that's the truth – beside himself with joy.

"And tomorrow's your wedding-day, my pet!" cried Trotty. "Your real, happy wedding-day!"

"Today!" cried Richard, shaking hands with him. "Today. The Chimes are ringing in the New Year. Hear them!"

They were ringing! Bless their sturdy hearts, they were ringing! Great Bells as they were; melodious, deep-mouthed, noble Bells; cast in no common metal; made by no common founder; when had they ever chimed like that, before!

"But, today, my pet," said Trotty. "You and Richard had some words today."

"Because he's such a bad fellow, father," said Meg. "An't you, Richard? Such a headstrong, violent man! He'd have made no more of speaking his mind to that great Alderman, and putting *him* down I don't know where, than he would of—"

"—Kissing Meg," suggested Richard. Doing it too!

"No. Not a bit more," said Meg. "But I wouldn't let him, father. Where would have been the use!"

"Richard my boy!" cried Trotty. "You was turned up Trumps originally; and Trumps you must be, till you die! But, you were crying by the fire to-night, my pet, when I came home! Why did you cry by the fire?"

"I was thinking of the years we've passed together, father. Only that. And thinking that you might miss me, and be lonely."

Trotty was backing off to that extraordinary chair again, when the child, who had been awakened by the noise, came running in half-dressed.

"Why, here she is!" cried Trotty, catching her up. "Here's little Lilian! Ha ha ha! Here we are and here we go! O here we are and here we go! And here we are and here we go!

and Uncle Will too!" Stopping in his trot to greet him heartily. "O, Uncle Will, the vision that I've had to-night, through lodging you! O, Uncle Will, the obligations that you've laid me under, by your coming, my good friend!"

Before Will Fern could make the least reply, a band of music burst into the room, attended by a lot of neighbours, screaming "A Happy New Year, Meg!" "A Happy Wedding!" "Many of 'em!" and other fragmentary good wishes of that sort. The Drum (who was a private friend of Trotty's) then stepped forward, and said:

"Trotty Veck, my boy! It's got about, that your daughter is going to be married tomorrow. There an't a soul that knows you that don't wish you well, or that knows her and don't wish her well. Or that knows you both, and don't wish you both all the happiness the New Year can bring. And here we are, to play it in and dance it in, accordingly."

Which was received with a general shout. The Drum was rather drunk, by-the-bye; but, never mind.

"What a happiness it is, I'm sure," said Trotty, "to be so esteemed! How kind and neighbourly you are! It's all along of my dear daughter. She deserves it!"

They were ready for a dance in half a second (Meg and Richard at the top); and the Drum was on the very brink of feathering away with all his power; when a combination of prodigious sounds was heard outside, and a good-humoured comely woman of some fifty years of age, or thereabouts, came running in, attended by a man bearing a stone pitcher of terrific size, and closely followed by the marrow-bones and cleavers, and the bells; not *the* Bells, but a portable collection on a frame.

Trotty said, "It's Mrs. Chickenstalker!" And sat down and beat his knees again.

"Married, and not tell me, Meg!" cried the good woman. "Never! I couldn't rest on the last night of the Old Year without coming to wish you joy. I couldn't have done it, Meg. Not if I had been bed-ridden. So here I am; and as it's New Year's Eve, and the Eve of your wedding too, my dear, I had a little flip made, and brought it with me."

Mrs. Chickenstalker's notion of a little flip did honour to her character. The pitcher steamed and smoked and reeked like a volcano; and the man who had carried it, was faint.

"Mrs. Tugby!" said Trotty, who had been going round and round her, in an ecstasy. – "I *should* say, Chickenstalker – Bless your heart and soul! A Happy New Year, and many of 'em! Mrs. Tugby," said Trotty when he had saluted her; – "I *should* say, Chickenstalker – This is William Fern and Lilian."

The worthy dame, to his surprise, turned very pale and very red.

"Not Lilian Fern whose mother died in Dorsetshire!" said she.

Her uncle answered "Yes," and meeting hastily, they exchanged some hurried words together; of which the upshot was, that Mrs. Chickenstalker shook him by both hands; saluted Trotty on his cheek again of her own free will; and took the child to her capacious breast.

"Will Fern!" said Trotty, pulling on his right-hand muffler. "Not the friend you was hoping to find?"

"Ay!" returned Will, putting a hand on each of Trotty's shoulders. "And like to prove a'most as good a friend, if that can be, as one I found."

"O!" said Trotty. "Please to play up there. Will you have the goodness!"

To the music of the band, and, the bells, the marrow-bones and cleavers, all at once; and while the Chimes were yet in lusty operation out of doors; Trotty, making Meg and Richard, second couple, led off Mrs. Chickenstalker down the dance, and danced it in a step unknown before or since; founded on his own peculiar trot.

Had Trotty dreamed? Or, are his joys and sorrows, and the actors in them, but a dream; himself a dream; the teller of this tale a dreamer, waking but now? If it be so, O listener, dear to him in all his visions, try to bear in mind the stern realities from which these shadows come; and in your sphere – none is too wide, and none too limited for such an end – endeavour to correct, improve, and soften them. So may the New Year be a happy one to you, happy to many more whose happiness depends on you! So may each year be happier than the last, and not the meanest of our brethren or sisterhood debarred their rightful share, in what our Great Creator formed them to enjoy.

**If you enjoyed this, you might also like...**
The Story of the Goblins Who Stole a Sexton, see page 330
The Queer Chair, see page 321

# A Child's Dream of a Star

HERE WAS ONCE a child, and he strolled about a good deal, and thought of a number of things. He had a sister, who was a child too, and his constant companion. These two used to wonder all day long. They wondered at the beauty of the flowers; they wondered at the height and blueness of the sky; they wondered at the depth of the bright water; they wondered at the goodness and the power of God, who made the lovely world.

They used to say to one another, sometimes, Supposing all the children upon earth were to die, would the flowers and the water and the sky be sorry? They believed they would be sorry. For, said they, the buds are the children of the flowers, and the little playful streams that gambol down the hillsides are the children of the water; and the smallest bright specks playing at hide-and-seek in the sky all night must surely be the children of the stars; and they would all be grieved to see their playmates, the children of men, no more.

There was one clear shining star that used to come out in the sky before the rest, near the church-spire, above the graves. It was larger and more beautiful, they thought, than all the others, and every night they watched for it, standing hand in hand at a window. Whoever saw it first cried out, "I see the star!" And often they cried out both together, knowing so well when it would rise and where. So they grew to be such friends with it, that, before lying down in their beds, they always looked out once again, to bid it good night; and when they were turning round to sleep, they used to say, "God bless the star!"

But while she was still very young, O, very, very young, the sister drooped, and came to be so weak that she could no longer stand in the window at night; and then the child looked sadly out by himself, and when he saw the star, turned round and said to the patient pale face on the bed, "I see the star!" And then a smile would come upon the face, and a little weak voice used to say, "God bless my brother and the star!"

And so the time came, all too soon! when the child looked out alone, and when there was no face on the bed; and when there was a little grave among the graves, not there before; and when the star made long rays down towards him, as he saw it through his tears.

Now, these rays were so bright, and they seemed to make such a shining way from earth to heaven, that when the child went to his solitary bed, he dreamed about the star; and dreamed that, lying where he was, he saw a train of people taken up that sparkling road by angels. And the star, opening, showed him a great world of light, where many more such angels waited to receive them.

All these angels, who were waiting, turned their beaming eyes upon the people who were carried up into the star; and some came out from the long rows in which they stood, and fell upon the people's necks, and kissed them tenderly, and went away with them down avenues of light, and were so happy in their company, that, lying in his bed, he wept for joy.

But there were many angels who did not go with them, and among them one he knew. The patient face that once had lain upon the bed was glorified and radiant, but his heart found out his sister among all the host.

His sister's angel lingered near the entrance of the star, and said to the leader among those who had brought the people thither, "Is my brother come?"

And he said, "No."

She was turning hopefully away, when the child stretched out his arms, and cried, "O sister, I am here! Take me!" And then she turned her beaming eyes upon him, and it was night; and the star was shining into the room, making long rays down towards him as he saw it through his tears.

From that hour forth, the child looked out upon the star as on the home he was to go to, when his time should come; and he thought that he did not belong to the earth alone, but to the star too, because of his sister's angel gone before.

There was a baby born to be a brother to the child; and while he was so little that he never yet had spoken word, he stretched his tiny form out on his bed, and died.

Again the child dreamed of the opened star, and of the company of angels, and the train of people, and the rows of angels with their beaming eyes all turned upon those people's faces.

Said his sister's angel to the leader, "Is my brother come?"

And he said, "Not that one, but another."

As the child beheld his brother's angel in her arms, he cried, "O sister, I am here! Take me!" And she turned and smiled upon him, and the star was shining.

He grew to be a young man, and was busy at his books when an old servant came to him and said, "Thy mother is no more. I bring her blessing on her darling son!"

Again at night he saw the star, and all that former company. Said his sister's angel to the leader, "Is my brother come?"

And he said, "Thy mother!"

A mighty cry of joy went forth through all the star, because the mother was reunited to her two children. And he stretched out his arms and cried, "O mother, sister, and brother, I am here! Take me!"

And they answered him, "Not yet." And the star was shining.

He grew to be a man, whose hair was turning gray; and he was sitting in his chair by the fireside, heavy with grief, and with his face bedewed with tears, when the star opened once again.

Said his sister's angel to the leader, "Is my brother come?"

And he said, "Nay, but his maiden daughter."

And the man who had been the child saw his daughter, newly lost to him, a celestial creature among those three, and he said, "My daughter's head is on my sister's bosom, and her arm is round my mother's neck, and at her feet there is the baby of old time, and I can bear the parting from her, God be praised!"

And the star was shining.

Thus the child came to be an old man, and his once smooth face was wrinkled, and his steps were slow and feeble, and his back was bent. And one night as he lay upon his bed, his children standing round, he cried, as he had cried so long ago, "I see the star!"

They whispered one another, "He is dying."

And he said, "I am. My age is falling from me like a garment, and I move towards the star as a child. And O my Father, now I thank thee that it has so often opened to receive those dear ones who await me!"

And the star was shining; and it shines upon his grave.

**If you enjoyed this, you might also like...**

The Queer Chair, see page 321
The Magic Fishbone, see page 466

# A Message from the Sea

### *Charles Dickens and Wilkie Collins*

## Chapter I
## The Village

**"AND A MIGHTY** sing'lar and pretty place it is, as ever I saw in all the days of my life!" said Captain Jorgan, looking up at it.

Captain Jorgan had to look high to look at it, for the village was built sheer up the face of a steep and lofty cliff. There was no road in it, there was no wheeled vehicle in it, there was not a level yard in it. From the sea-beach to the cliff-top, two irregular rows of white houses, placed opposite to one another, and twisting here and there and there and here, rose, like the sides of a long succession of stages of crooked ladders, and you climbed up the village or climbed down the village by the staves between: some six feet wide or so, and made of sharp irregular stones. The old pack-saddle, long laid aside in most parts of England as one of the appendages of its infancy, nourished here intact. Strings of pack-horses and pack-donkeys toiled slowly up the staves of the ladders, bearing fish, and coal, and such other cargo as was unshipping at the pier from the dancing fleet of village boats, and from two or three little coasting traders. As the beasts of burden ascended laden, or descended light, they got so lost at intervals in the floating clouds of village smoke, that they seemed to dive down some of the village chimneys and come to the surface again far off, high above others. No two houses in the village were alike, in chimney, size, shape, door, window, gable, roof-tree, anything. The sides of the ladders were musical with water, running clear and bright. The staves were musical with the clattering feet of the pack-horses and pack-donkeys, and the voices of the fishermen urging them up, mingled with the voices of the fishermen's wives and their many children. The pier was musical with the wash of the sea, the creaking of capstans and windlasses, and the airy fluttering of little vanes and sails. The rough sea-bleached boulders of which the pier was made, and the whiter boulders of the shore, were brown with drying nets. The red-brown cliffs, richly wooded to their extremest verge, had their softened and beautiful forms reflected in the bluest water, under the clear North Devonshire sky of a November day without a cloud. The village itself was so steeped in autumnal foliage, from the houses giving on the pier, to the topmost round of the topmost ladder, that one might have fancied it was out a birds'-nesting, and was (as indeed it was) a wonderful climber. And mentioning birds, the place was not without some music from them too; for, the rook was very busy on the higher levels, and the gull with his flapping wings was fishing in the bay, and the lusty little robin was hopping among the great stone blocks and iron rings of the breakwater, fearless in the faith of his ancestors and the Children in the Wood.

Thus it came to pass that Captain Jorgan, sitting balancing himself on the pier-wall, struck his leg with his open hand, as some men do when they are pleased – and as he always did when he was pleased – and said: "A mighty sing'lar and pretty place it is, as ever I saw in all the days of my life!"

Captain Jorgan had not been through the village, but had come down to the pier by a winding side-road, to have a preliminary look at it from the level of his own natural element. He had seen many things and places, and had stowed them all away in a shrewd intellect and a vigorous memory. He was an American born, was Captain Jorgan – a New Englander – but he was a citizen of the world, and a combination of most of the best qualities of most of its best countries.

For Captain Jorgan to sit anywhere in his long-skirted blue coat and blue trousers, without holding converse with everybody within speaking distance, was a sheer impossibility. So, the captain fell to talking with the fishermen, and to asking them knowing questions about the fishery, and the tides, and the currents, and the race of water off that point yonder, and what you kept in your eye and got into a line with what else when you ran into the little harbour; and other nautical profundities. Among the men who exchanged ideas with the captain, was a young fellow who exactly hit his fancy – a young fisherman of two or three-and-twenty, in the rough sea-dress of his craft, with a brown face, dark curling hair, and bright modest eyes under his Sou'-Wester hat, and with a frank but simple and retiring manner which the captain found uncommonly taking. "I'd bet a thousand dollars," said the captain to himself, "that your father was an honest man!"

"Might you be married now?" asked the captain when he had had some talk with this new acquaintance.

"Not yet."

"Going to be?" said the captain.

"I hope so."

The captain's keen glance followed the slightest possible turn of the dark eye, and the slightest possible tilt of the Sou'-Wester hat. The captain then slapped both his legs, and said to himself: "Never knew such a good thing in all my life! There's his sweetheart looking over the wall!"

There was a very pretty girl looking over the wall, from a little platform of cottage, vine, and fuchsia; and she certainly did not look as if the presence of this young fisherman in the landscape, made it any the less sunny and hopeful for her.

Captain Jorgan, having doubled himself up to laugh with that hearty good nature which is quite exultant in the innocent happiness of other people, had undoubled himself and was going to start a new subject, when there appeared coming down the lower ladders of stones a man whom he hailed as "Tom Pettifer Ho!" Tom Pettifer Ho responded with alacrity, and in speedy course descended on the pier.

"Afraid of a sunstroke in England in November, Tom, that you wear your tropical hat, strongly paid outside and paper-lined inside, here?" said the captain, eyeing it.

"It's as well to be on the safe side, sir," replied Tom.

"Safe side!" repeated the captain, laughing. "You'd guard against a sunstroke with that old hat, in an Ice Pack. Wa'al! What have you made out at the Post-office?"

"It *is* the Post-office, sir."

"What's the Post-office?" said the captain.

"The name, sir. The name keeps the Post-office."

"A coincidence!" said the captain. "A lucky hit! Show me where it is. Good-by, shipmates, for the present! I shall come and have another look at you, afore I leave, this afternoon."

This was addressed to all there, but especially the young fisherman; so, all there acknowledged it, but especially the young fisherman. "He's a sailor!" said one to another, as they looked after the captain moving away. That he was; and so outspeaking was the sailor in him, that although his dress had nothing nautical about it with the single exception of its colour, but was a suit of a shore-going shape and form, too long, in the sleeves, and too short in the legs, and too unaccommodating everywhere, terminating earthward in a pair of Wellington boots, and surmounted by a tall stiff hat which no mortal could have worn at sea in any wind under Heaven; nevertheless, a glimpse of his sagacious weather-beaten face or his strong brown hand would have established the captain's calling. Whereas, Mr. Pettifer – a man of a certain plump neatness with a curly whisker, and elaborately nautical in a jacket and shoes and all things correspondent – looked no more like a seaman, beside Captain Jorgan, than he looked like a sea-serpent.

The two climbed high up the village – which had the most arbitrary turns and twists in it, so that the cobbler's house came dead across the ladder, and to have held a reasonable course you must have gone through his house, and through, him too, as he sat at his work between two little windows, with one eye microscopically on the geological formation of that part of Devonshire, and the other telescopically on the open sea – the two climbed high up the village, and stopped before a quaint little house, on which was painted "MRS. RAYBROCK, DRAPER;" and also, "POST-OFFICE." Before it, ran a rill of murmuring water, and access to it was gained by a little plank-bridge.

"Here's the name," said Captain Jorgan, "sure enough. You can come in if you like, Tom."

The captain opened the door, and passed into an odd little shop about six feet high, with a great variety of beams and bumps in the ceiling, and, besides the principal window giving on the ladder of stones, a purblind little window of a single pane of glass: peeping out of an abutting corner at the sun-lighted ocean, and winking at its brightness.

"How do you do, ma'am?" said the captain. "I am very glad to see you. I have come a long way to see you."

"*Have* you, sir? Then I am sure I am very glad to see *you*, though I don't know you from. Adam."

Thus, a comely elderly woman, short of stature, plump of form, sparkling and dark of eye, who, perfectly clean and neat herself, stood in the midst of her perfectly clean and neat arrangements, and surveyed Captain Jorgan with smiling curiosity. "Ah! but you are a sailor, sir," she added, almost immediately, and with a slight movement of her hands, that was not very unlike wringing them; "then you are heartily welcome."

"Thankee, ma'am," said the captain. "I don't know what it is, I am sure, that brings out the salt in me, but everybody seems to see it on the crown of my hat and the collar of my coat. Yes, ma'am, I am in that way of life."

"And the other gentleman, too," said Mrs. Raybrock.

"Well now, ma'am," said the captain, glancing shrewdly at the other gentleman, "you are that nigh right, that he goes to sea – if that makes him a sailor. This is my steward, ma'am, Tom Pettifer; he's been a'most all trades you could name, in the course of his life – would have bought all your chairs and tables, once, if you had wished to sell 'em – but now he's my steward. My name's Jorgan, and I'm a shipowner, and I sail my own and my partners' ships, and have done so this five-and-twenty year. According to custom I am called Captain Jordan, but I am no more a captain, bless your heart! than you are."

"Perhaps you'll come into my parlour, sir, and take a chair?" said Mrs. Raybrock.

"Ex-actly what I was going to propose myself, ma'am. After you."

Thus replying, and enjoining Tom to give an eye to the shop, Captain Jorgan followed Mrs. Raybrock into the little low back-room – decorated with divers plants in pots, tea-trays, old china teapots, and punch-bowls which was at once the private sitting-room of the Raybrock family, and the inner cabinet of the post-office of the village of Steepways.

"Now, ma'am," said the captain, "it don't signify a cent to you where I was born, except—" But, here the shadow of some one entering, fell upon the captain's figure, and he broke off to double himself up, slap both his legs, and ejaculate, "Never knew such a thing in all my life! Here he is again! How are you?"

These words referred to the young fellow who had so taken Captain Jorgan's fancy down at the pier. To make it all quite complete he came in accompanied by the sweetheart whom the captain had detected looking over the wall. A prettier sweetheart the sun could not have shone upon, that shining day. As she stood before the captain, with her rosy lips just parted in surprise, her brown eyes a little wider open than was usual from the same cause, and her breathing a little quickened by the ascent (and possibly by some mysterious hurry and flurry at the parlour door, in which the captain had observed her face to be for a moment totally eclipsed by the Sou'-Wester hat), she looked so charming, that the captain felt himself under a moral obligation to slap both his legs again. She was very simply dressed, with no other ornament than an autumnal flower in her bosom. She wore neither hat nor bonnet, but merely a scarf or kerchief, folded squarely back over the head, to keep the sun off – according to a fashion that may be sometimes seen in the more genial parts of England as well as of Italy, and which is probably the first fashion of head-dress that came into the world when grasses and leaves went out.

"In my country," said the captain, rising to give her his chair, and dexterously sliding it close to another chair on which the young fisherman must necessarily establish himself "in my country we should call Devonshire beauty, first-rate!"

Whenever a frank manner is offensive, it is because it is strained or feigned; for, there may be quite as much intolerable affectation in plainness, as in mincing nicety. All that the captain said and did, was honestly according to his nature, and his nature was open nature and good nature; therefore, when he paid this little compliment, and expressed with a sparkle or two of his knowing eye, "I see how it is, and nothing could be better," he had established a delicate confidence on that subject with the family.

"I was saying to your worthy mother," said the captain to the young man, after again introducing himself by name and occupation: "I was saying to your mother (and you're very like her) that it didn't signify where I was born except that I was raised on question-asking ground, where the babies as soon as ever they come into the world, inquire of their mothers 'Neow, how old may *you* be, and wa'at air you a goin' to name me?' – which is a fact." Here he slapped his leg. "Such being the case, I may be excused for asking you if your name's Alfred?"

"Yes, sir, my name is Alfred," returned the young man.

"I am not a conjuror," pursued the captain, "and don't think me so, or I shall right soon undeceive you. Likewise don't think, if you please, though I *do* come from that country of the babies, that I am asking questions for question-asking's sake, for I am not. Somebody belonging to you, went to sea?"

"My elder brother Hugh," returned the young man. He said it in an altered and lower voice, and glanced at his mother: who raised her hands hurriedly, and put them together across her black gown, and looked eagerly at the visitor.

"No! For God's sake, don't think that!" said the captain, in a solemn way; "I bring no good tidings of him."

There was a silence, and the mother turned her face to the fire and put her hand between it and her eyes. The young fisherman slightly motioned towards the window, and the captain, looking in that direction, saw a young widow sitting at a neighbouring window across a little garden, engaged in needlework, with a young child sleeping on her bosom. The silence continued until the captain asked of Alfred: "How long is it since it happened?"

"He shipped for his last voyage, better than three years ago."

"Ship struck upon some reef or rock, as I take it," said the captain, "and all hands lost?"

"Yes."

"Wa'al!" said the captain, after a shorter silence. "Here I sit who may come to the same end, like enough. He holds the seas in the hollow of His hand. We must all strike somewhere and go down. Our comfort, then, for ourselves and one another, is, to have done our duty. I'll wager your brother did his!"

"He did!" answered the young fisherman.

"If ever man strove faithfully on all occasions to do his duty, my brother did. My brother was not a quick man (anything but that), but he was a faithful, true, and just man. We were the sons of only a small tradesman in this county, sir; yet our father was as watchful of his good name as if he had been a king."

"A precious sight more so, I hope – bearing in mind the general run of that class of crittur," said the captain. "But I interrupt."

"My brother considered that our father left the good name to us, to keep clear and true."

"Your brother considered right," said the captain; "and you couldn't take care of a better legacy. But again I interrupt."

"No; for I have nothing more to say. We know that Hugh lived well for the good name, and we feel certain that he died well for the good name. And now it has come into my keeping. And that's all."

"Well spoken!" cried the captain. "Well spoken, young man! Concerning the manner of your brother's death;" by this time, the captain had released the hand he had shaken, and sat with his own broad brown hands spread out on his knees, and spoke aside; "concerning the manner of your brother's death, it may be that I have some information to give you; though it may not be, for I am far from sure. Can we have a little talk alone?"

The young man rose; but, not before the captain's quick eye had noticed that, on the pretty sweetheart's turning to the window to greet the young widow with a nod and a wave of the hand, the young widow had held up to her the needlework on which she was engaged, with a patient and pleasant smile. So the captain said, being on his legs: "What might she be making now?"

"What is Margaret making, Kitty?" asked the young fisherman – with one of his arms apparently mislaid somewhere.

As Kitty only blushed in reply, the captain doubled himself up, as far as he could, standing, and said, with a slap of his leg:

"In my country we should call it wedding-clothes, fact! We should, I do assure you."

But, it seemed to strike the captain in another light too; for, his laugh was not a long one, and he added in quite a gentle tone:

"And it's very pretty, my dear, to see her – poor young thing, with her fatherless child upon her bosom giving up her thoughts to your home and your happiness. It's very pretty, my dear, and it's very good. May your marriage be more prosperous than hers, and be a comfort to her, too. May the blessed sun see you all happy together, in possession of the good name, long after I have done ploughing the great salt field that is never sown!"

Kitty answered very earnestly. "O! Thank you, sir, with all my heart!" And, in her loving little way, kissed her hand to him, and possibly by implication to the young fisherman too, as the latter held the parlour door open for the captain to pass out.

## Chapter II
## The Money

**"THE STAIRS** are very narrow, sir," said Alfred Raybrock to Captain Jorgan.

"Like my cabin-stairs," returned the captain, "on many a voyage."

"And they are rather inconvenient for the head."

"If my head can't take care of itself by this time, after all the knocking about the world it has had," replied the captain, as unconcernedly as if he had no connexion with it, "it's not worth looking after."

Thus, they came into the young fisherman's bedroom, which was as perfectly neat and clean as the shop and parlour below: though it was but a little place, with a sliding window, and a phrenological ceiling expressive of all the peculiarities of the house-roof. Here the captain sat down on the foot of the bed, and, glancing at a dreadful libel on Kitty which ornamented the wall – the production of some wandering limner, whom the captain secretly admired, as having studied portraiture from the figure-heads of ships – motioned to the young man to take the rush-chair on the other side of the small round table. That done, the captain put his hand into the deep breast-pocket of his long-skirted blue coat, and took out of it a strong square case-bottle – not a large bottle, but such as may be seen in any ordinary ship's medicine chest. Setting this bottle on the table without removing his hand from it, Captain Jorgan then spake as follows.

"In my last voyage homeward-bound," said the captain, "and that's the voyage off of which I now come straight, I encountered such weather off the Horn, as is not very often met with, even there. I have rounded that stormy Cape pretty often, and I believe I first beat about there in the identical storms that blew the devil's horns and tail off, and led to the horns being worked up into toothpicks for the plantation overseers in my country, who may be seen (if you travel down South, or away West, fur enough) picking their teeth with 'em, while the whips, made of the tail, flog hard. In this last voyage, homeward-bound for Liverpool from South America, I say to you my young friend, it blew. Whole measures! No half measures, nor making believe to blow; it blew! Now, I warn't blown clean out of the water into the sky – though I expected to be even that but I was blown clean out of my course; and when at last it fell calm, it fell dead calm, and a strong current set one way, day and night, night and day, and I drifted – drifted – drifted – out of all the ordinary tracks and courses of ships, and drifted yet, and yet drifted. It behoves a man who takes charge of fellow-critturs' lives, never to rest from making himself master of his calling. I never did rest, and consequently I knew pretty well (specially looking over the side in the dead calm at that strong current), what dangers to expect, and what precautions to take against 'em. In short, we were driving head on, to an island. There was no Island in the chart, and, therefore, you may say it was ill manners in the Island to be there; I don't dispute its bad breeding, but there it was. Thanks be to Heaven, I was as ready for the Island as the Island was ready for me. I made it out myself from the masthead, and I got enough way upon her in good time, to keep her off. I ordered a boat to be lowered and manned, and went in that boat myself to explore the Island. There was a reef outside it, and, floating in a corner of the smooth water within the reef, was a heap of seaweed, and entangled in that seaweed was this bottle."

Here, the captain took his hand from the bottle for a moment, that the young fisherman might direct a wondering glance at it; and then replaced his hand and went on: "if ever you come – or even if ever you don't come – to a desert place, use you your eyes and your spy-glass well; for the smallest thing you see, may prove of use to you, and may have some information or some warning in it. That's the principle on which I came to see this bottle. I picked up the bottle and ran the boat alongside the Island and made fast and went ashore, armed, with a part of my boat's crew. We found that every scrap of vegetation on the Island (I give it you as in my opinion, but scant and scrubby at the best of times) had been consumed by fire. As we were making our way, cautiously and toilsomely, over the pulverised embers, one of my people sank into the earth, breast high. He turned pale, and 'Haul me out smart, shipmates,' says he, 'for my feet are among bones.' We soon got him on his legs again, and then we dug up the spot, and we found that the man was right, and that his feet had been among bones. More than that, they were human bones; though whether the remains of one man, or of two or three men, what with calcination and ashes, and what with a poor practical knowledge of anatomy, I can't undertake to say. We examined the whole Island and made out nothing else, save and except that, from its opposite side, I sighted a considerable tract of land, which land I was able to identify, and according to the bearings of which (not to trouble you with my log) I took a fresh departure. When I got aboard again, I opened the bottle, which was oilskin-covered as you see, and glass-stoppered as you see. Inside of it," pursued the captain, suiting his action to his words, "I found this little crumpled folded paper, just as you see. Outside of it was written, as you see, these words: *'Whoever finds this, is solemnly entreated by the dead, to convey it unread to Alfred Raybrock, Steepways, North Devon, England.'* A sacred charge," said the captain, concluding his narrative, "and, Alfred Raybrock, there it is!"

"This is my poor brother's writing!"

"I supposed so," said Captain Jorgan. "I'll take a look out of this little window while you read it."

"Pray no, sir! I should be hurt. We should all be hurt. My brother couldn't know it would fall into such hands as yours."

The captain sat down again on the foot of the bed, and the young man opened the folded paper with a trembling hand, and spread it on the table. The ragged paper, evidently creased and torn both before and after being written on, was much blotted and stained, and the ink had faded and run, and many words were wanting.

The young fisherman had become more and more agitated, as the writing had become clearer to him. He now left it lying before the captain, over whose shoulder he had been reading it, and, dropping into his former seat, leaned forward on the table and laid his face in his hands.

"What, man," urged the captain, "don't give in! Be up and doing, *like* a man!"

"It is selfish, I know – but doing what, doing what?" cried the young fisherman, in complete despair, and stamping his sea-boot on the ground.

"Doing what?" returned the captain.

"Something! I'd go down to the little breakwater below, yonder, and take a wrench at one of the salt-rusted iron-rings there, and either wrench it up by the roots or wrench my teeth out of my head, sooner than I'd do nothing. Nothing!" ejaculated the captain. "Any fool or faint-heart can do *that*, and nothing can come of nothing – Which was pretended to be found out, I believe, by one of them Latin critturs," said the captain, with the deepest disdain; "as if Adam hadn't found it out, afore ever he so much as named the beasts!"

Yet the captain saw, in spite of his bold words, that there was some greater reason than he yet understood for the young man's distress. And he eyed him with a sympathising curiosity.

"Come, come!" continued the captain. "Speak out. What is it, boy?"

"You have seen how beautiful she is, sir," said the young man, looking up for the moment, with a flushed face and rumpled hair.

"Did any man ever say she warn't beautiful?" retorted the captain. "If so, go and lick him."

The young man laughed fretfully in spite of himself, and said, "It's not that, it's not that."

"Wa'al, then, what is it?" said the captain, in a more soothing tone.

The young fisherman mournfully composed himself to tell the captain what it was, and began: "We were to have been married next Monday week—"

"Were to have been!" interrupted Captain Jorgan. "And are to be? Hey?"

Young Raybrock shook his head, and traced out with his forefinger the words *"poor father's five hundred pounds,"* in the written paper.

"Go along." said the captain. "Five hundred pounds? Yes?"

"That sum of money," pursued the young fisherman, entering with the greatest earnestness on his demonstration, while the captain eyed him with equal earnestness, "was all my late father possessed. When he died, he owed no man more than he left means to pay, but he had been able to lay by only five hundred pounds."

"Five hundred pounds," repeated the captain. "Yes?"

"In his lifetime, years before, he had expressly laid the money aside, to leave to my mother – like to settle upon her, if I make myself understood."

"Yes?"

"He had risked it once – my father put down in writing at that time, respecting the money – and was resolved never to risk it again."

"Not a spec'lator," said the captain. "My country wouldn't have suited him. Yes?"

"My mother has never touched the money till now. And now it was to have been laid out, this very next week, in buying me a handsome share in our neighbouring fishery here, to settle me in life with Kitty."

The captain's face fell, and he passed and repassed his sun-browned right hand over his thin hair, in a discomfited manner.

"Kitty's father has no more than enough to live on, even in the sparing way in which we live about here. He is a kind of bailiff or steward of manor rights here, and they are not much, and it is but a poor little office. He was better off once, and Kitty must never marry to mere drudgery and hard living."

The captain still sat stroking his thin hair, and looking at the young fisherman.

"I am as certain that my father had no knowledge that any one was wronged as to this money, or that any restitution ought to be made, as I am certain that the sun now shines. But, after this solemn warning from my brother's grave in the sea, that the money is Stolen Money," said Young Raybrock, forcing himself to the utterance of the words, "can I doubt it? Can I touch it?"

"About not doubting, I ain't so sure," observed the captain; "but about not touching – no – I don't think you can."

"See, then," said Young Raybrock, "why I am so grieved. Think of Kitty. Think what I have got to tell her!"

His heart quite failed him again when he had come round to that, and he once more beat his sea-boot softly on the floor. But, not for long; he soon began again, in a quietly resolute tone.

"However! Enough of that! You spoke some brave words to me just now, Captain Jorgan, and they shall not be spoken in vain. I have got to do Something. What I have got to do, before all other things, is to trace out the meaning of this paper, for the sake of the Good Name that has no one else to put it right or keep it right. And still, for the sake of the Good Name, and my father's memory, not a word of this writing must be breathed to my mother, or to Kitty, or to any human creature. You agree in this?"

"I don't know what they'll think of us, below," said the captain, "but for certain I can't oppose it. Now, as to tracing. How will you do?"

They both, as by consent, bent over the paper again, and again carefully puzzled out the whole of the writing.

"I make out that this would stand, if all the writing was here, 'Inquire among the old men living there, for' – some one. Most like, you'll go to this village named here?" said the captain, musing, with his finger on the name.

"Yes! And Mr. Tregarthen is a Cornishman, and – to be sure! – comes from Lanrean."

"Does he?" said the captain, quietly. "As I ain't acquainted with him, who may he be?"

"Mr. Tregarthen is Kitty's father."

"Ay, ay!" cried the captain. "Now, you speak! Tregarthen knows this village of Lanrean, then?"

"Beyond all doubt he does. I have often heard him mention it, as being his native place. He knows it well."

"Stop half a moment," said the captain. "We want a name here. You could ask Tregarthen (or if you couldn't, I could) what names of old men he remembers in his time in those diggings? Hey?"

"I can go straight to his cottage, and ask him now."

"Take me with you," said the captain, rising in a solid way that had a most comfortable reliability in it, "and just a word more, first. I knocked about harder than you, and have got along further than you. I have had, all my sea-going life long, to keep my wits polished bright with acid and friction, like the brass cases of the ship's instruments. I'll keep you company on this expedition. Now, you don't live by talking, any more than I do. Clench that hand of yours in this hand of mine, and that's a speech on both sides."

Captain Jorgan took command of the expedition with that hearty shake. He at once refolded the paper exactly as before, replaced it in the bottle, put the stopper in, put the oilskin over the stopper, confided the whole to Young Raybrock's keeping, and led the way down stairs.

But it was harder navigation below stairs than above. The instant they set foot in the parlour, the quick womanly eye detected that there was something wrong. Kitty exclaimed, frightened, as she ran to her lover's side, "Alfred! What's the matter?" Mrs. Raybrock cried out to the captain, "Gracious! what have you done to my son to change him like this, all in a minute!" And the young widow – who was there with her work upon her arm was at first so agitated, that she frightened the little girl she held in her hand, who hid her face in her mother's skirts and screamed. The captain, conscious of being held responsible for this domestic change, contemplated it with quite a guilty expression of countenance, and looked to the young fisherman to come to his rescue.

"Kitty darling," said Young Raybrock, "Kitty, dearest love, I must go away to Lanrean, and I don't know where else or how much farther, this very day. Worse than that – our marriage, Kitty, must be put off, and I don't know for how long."

Kitty stared at him, in doubt and wonder and in anger, and pushed him from her with her hand

"Put off?" cried Mrs. Raybrock. "The marriage put off? And you going to Lanrean! Why, in the name of the dear Lord?"

"Mother dear, I can't say why, I must not say why. It would be dishonourable and undutiful to say why."

"Dishonourable and undutiful?" returned the dame. "And is there nothing dishonourable or undutiful in the boy's breaking the heart of his own plighted love, and his mother's heart too, for the sake of the dark secrets and counsels of a wicked stranger? Why did you ever come here?" she apostrophised the innocent captain. "Who wanted you? Where did you come from? Why couldn't you rest in your own bad place, wherever it is, instead of disturbing the peace of quiet unoffending folk like us?"

"And what," sobbed the poor little Kitty, "have I ever done to you, you hard and cruel captain, that you should come and serve me so?"

And then they both began to weep most pitifully, while the captain could only look from the one to the other, and lay hold of himself by the coat-collar.

"Margaret," said the poor young fisherman, on his knees at Kitty's feet, while Kitty kept both her hands before her tearful face, to shut out the traitor from her view – but kept her fingers wide asunder and looked at him all the time: "Margaret, you have suffered so much, so uncomplainingly, and are always so careful and considerate! Do take my part, for poor Hugh's sake!"

The quiet Margaret was not appealed to in vain. "I will, Alfred," she returned, "and I do. I wish this gentleman had never come near us;" whereupon the captain laid hold of himself the tighter; "but I take your part, for all that. I am sure you have some strong reason and some sufficient reason for what you do, strange as it is, and even for not saying why you do it, strange as that is. And, Kitty darling, you are bound to think so, more than any one, for true love believes everything, and bears everything, and trusts everything. And mother dear, you are bound to think so too, for you know you have been blest with good sons, whose word was always as good as their oath, and who were brought up in as true a sense of honour as any gentlemen in this land. And I am sure you have no more call, mother, to doubt your living son than to doubt your dead son; and for the sake of the dear dead, I stand up for the dear living."

"Wa'al now," the captain struck in, with enthusiasm, "this I say. That whether your opinions flatter me or not, you are a young woman of sense and spirit and feeling; and I'd sooner have you by my side, in the hour of danger, than a good half of the men I've ever fallen in with – or fallen out with, ayther."

Margaret did not return the captain's compliment, or appear fully to reciprocate his good opinion, but she applied herself to the consolation of Kitty and of Kitty's mother-in-law that was to have been next Monday week, and soon restored the parlour to a quiet condition.

'Kitty, my darling,' said the young fisher-man, "I must go to your father to entreat him still to trust me in spite of this wretched change and mystery, and to ask him for some directions concerning Lanrean. Will you come home? Will you come with me, Kitty?"

Kitty answered not a word, but rose sobbing, with the end of her simple head-dress at her eyes. Captain Jorgan followed the lovers out, quite sheepishly: pausing in the shop to give an instruction to Mr. Pettifer.

"Here, Tom!" said the captain, in a low voice. "Here's something in your line. Here's an old lady poorly and low in her spirits. Cheer her up a bit, Tom. Cheer 'em all up."

Mr. Pettifer, with a brisk nod of intelligence, immediately assumed his steward face, and went with his quiet helpful steward step into the parlour: where the captain had the great satisfaction of seeing him, through the glass door, take the child in his arms (who offered no objection), and bend over Mrs. Raybrock, administering soft words of consolation.

"Though what he finds to say, unless he's telling her that it'll soon be over, or that most people is so at first, or that it'll do her good afterwards, I can not imaginate!" was the captain's reflection as he followed the lovers.

He had not far to follow them, since it was but a short descent down the stony ways to the cottage of Kitty's father. But, short as the distance was, it was long enough to enable the captain to observe that he was fast becoming the village Ogre; for, there was not a woman standing working at her door, or a fisherman coming up or going down, who saw Young Raybrock unhappy and little Kitty in tears, but she or he instantly darted a suspicious and indignant glance at the captain, as the foreigner who must somehow be responsible for this unusual spectacle. Consequently, when they came into Tregarthen's little garden – which formed the platform from which the captain had seen Kitty peeping over the wall – the captain brought to, and stood off and on at the gate, while Kitty hurried to hide her tears in her own room, and Alfred spoke with her father who was working in the garden. He was a rather infirm man, but could scarcely be called old yet, with an agreeable face and a promising air of making the best of things. The conversation began on his side with great cheerfulness and good humour, but soon became distrustful and soon angry. That was the captain's cue for striking both into the conversation and the garden.

"Morning, sir!" said Captain Jorgan. "How do you do?"

"The gentleman I am going away with," said the young fisherman to Tregarthen.

"Oh!" returned Kitty's father, surveying the unfortunate captain with a look of extreme disfavour. "I confess that I can't say I am glad to see you."

"No," said the captain, "and, to admit the truth, that seems to be the general, opinion in these parts. But don't be hasty; you may think better of me, by-and-by."

"I hope so," observed Tregarthen.

"Wa'al, I hope so," observed the captain, quite at his ease; "more than that, I believe so – though you don't. Now, Mr. Tregarthen, you don't want to exchange words of mistrust with me; and if you did, you couldn't, because I wouldn't. You and I are old enough to know better than to judge against experience from surfaces and appearances; and if you haven't lived to find out the evil and injustice of such judgments, you are a lucky man."

The other seemed to shrink under this remark, and replied, "Sir, I *have* lived to feel it deeply."

"Wa'al," said the captain, mollified, "then I've made a good cast, without knowing it. Now, Tregarthen, there stands the lover of your only child, and here stand I who know his secret. I warrant it a righteous secret, and none of his making, though bound to be of his keeping. I want to help him out with it, and tewwards that end we ask you to favour us with the names of two or three old residents in the village of Lanrean. As I am taking out my pocket-book and pencil to put the names down, I may as well observe to you that this, wrote atop of the first page here, is my name and address: 'Silas Jonas Jorgan, Salem, Massachusetts, United States.' If ever you take it in your head to run over, any morning, I shall be glad to welcome you. Now, what may be the spelling of these said names?"

"There was an elderly man," said Tregarthen, "named David Polreath. He may be dead."

"Wa'al," said the captain, cheerfully, "if Polreath's dead and buried, and can be made of any service to us, Polreath won't object to our digging of him up. Polreath's down, anyhow."

"There was another, named Penrewen. I don't know his Christian name."

"Never mind his Chris'en name," said the captain. "Penrewen for short."

"There was another, named John Tredgear."

"And a pleasant-sounding name, too," said the captain;" John Tredgear's booked."

"I can recal no other, except old Parvis."

"One of old Parvis's fam'ly, I reckon," said the captain, "kept a dry-goods store in New York city, and realised a handsome competency by burning his house to ashes. Same name, anyhow. David Polreath, Unchris'en Penrewen, John Tredgear, and old Arson Parvis."

"I cannot recall any others, at the moment."

"Thankee," said the captain. "And so, Tregarthen, hoping for your good opinion yet, and likewise for the fair Devonshire Flower's, your daughter's, I give you my hand, sir, and wish you good day."

Young Raybrock accompanied him disconsolately; for, there was no Kitty at the window when he looked up, no Kitty in the garden when he shut the gate, no Kitty gazing after them along the stony ways when they began to climb back.

"Now I tell you what," said the captain. "Not being at present calc'lated to promote harmony in your family, I won't come in. You go and get your dinner at home, and I'll get mine at the little hotel. Let our hour of meeting be two o'clock, and you'll find me smoking a cigar in the sun afore the hotel door. Tell Tom Pettifer, my steward, to consider himself on duty, and to look after your people till we come back; you'll find he'll have made himself useful to 'em already, and will be quite acceptable."

All was done as Captain Jorgan directed. Punctually at two o'clock, the young fisherman, appeared with his knapsack at his back; and punctually at two o'clock, the captain jerked away the last feathery end of his cigar.

"Let me carry your baggage, Captain Jorgan; I can easily take it with mine."

"Thank'ee," said the captain, "I'll carry it myself. It's on'y a comb."

They climbed out of the village, and paused among the trees and fern on the summit of the hill above, to take breath and to look down at the beautiful sea. Suddenly, the captain gave his leg a resounding slap, and cried, "Never knew such a right thing in all my life!" – and ran away.

The cause of this abrupt retirement on the part of the captain, was little Kitty among the trees. The captain went out of sight and waited, and kept out of sight and waited, until it occurred to him to beguile the time with another cigar. He lighted it, and smoked it out, and still he was out of sight and waiting. He stole within sight at last, and saw the lovers, with their arms entwined and their bent heads touching, moving slowly among the trees. It was the golden time of the afternoon then, and the captain said to himself, "Golden sun, golden sea, golden sails, golden leaves, golden love, golden youth – a golden state of things altogether!"

Nevertheless, the captain found it necessary to hail his young companion before going out of sight again. In a few moments more, he came up, and they began their journey.

"That still young woman with the fatherless child," said Captain Jorgan as they fell into step, "didn't throw her words away; but good honest words are never thrown away. And now that I am conveying you off from that tender little thing that loves and relies and hopes, I feel just as if I was the snarling crittur in the picters, with the tight legs, the long nose, and the feather in his cap, the tips of whose mustachios get up nearer to his eyes, the wickeder he gets."

The young fisherman knew nothing of Mephistopheles; but, he smiled when the captain stopped to double himself up and slap his leg, and they went along in right good fellowship.

## Chapter III
### The Club Night

**A CORNISH MOOR**, when the east wind drives over it, is as cold and rugged a scene as a traveller is likely to find in a year's travel. A Cornish Moor in the dark, is as black a solitude as the traveller is likely to wish himself well out of, in the course of a life's wanderings. A Cornish Moor in a night fog, is a wilderness where the traveller needs to know his way well, or the chances are very strong that his life and his wanderings will soon perplex him no more.

Captain Jorgan and the young fisherman had faced the east and the south-east winds, from the first rising of the sun after their departure from the village of Steepways. Thrice, had the sun risen, and still all day long had the sharp wind blown at them like some malevolent spirit bent on forcing them back. But, Captain Jorgan was too familiar with all the winds that blow, and too much accustomed to circumvent their slightest weaknesses and get the better of them in the long run, to be beaten by any member of the airy family. Taking the year round, it was his opinion that it mattered little what wind blew, or how hard it blew; so, he was as indifferent to the wind on this occasion as a man could be who frequently observed "that it freshened him up," and who regarded it in the light of an old acquaintance. One might have supposed from his way, that there was even a kind of fraternal understanding between Captain Jorgan and the wind, as between two professed fighters often opposed to one another. The young fisherman, for his part, was accustomed within his narrower limits to hold hard weather cheap, and had his anxious object before him; so, the wind went by him too, little heeded, and went upon its way to kiss Kitty.

Their varied course had lain by the side of the sea where the brown rocks cleft it into fountains of spray, and inland where once barren moors were reclaimed and cultivated, and by lonely villages of poor-enough cabins with mud walls, and by a town or two with an old church and a market-place. But, always travelling through a sparely inhabited country and over a broad expanse, they had come at last upon the true Cornish Moor within reach of Lanrean. None but gaunt spectres of miners passed them here, with metallic masks of faces, ghastly with dust of copper and tin; anon, solitary works on remote hill-tops, and bare machinery of torturing wheels and cogs and chains, writhing up hill-sides, were the few scattered hints of human presence in the landscape; during long intervals, the bitter wind, howling and tearing at them like a fierce wild monster, had them all to itself.

"A sing'lar thing it is," said the captain, looking round at the brown desert of rank grass and poor moss, "how like this airth is, to the men that live upon it! Here's a spot of country rich with hidden metals, and it puts on the worst rags of clothes possible, and crouches and shivers and makes believe to be so poor that it can't so much as afford a feed for a beast. Just like a human miser, ain't it?"

"But they find the miser out," returned the young fisherman, pointing to where the earth by the watercourses and along the valleys was turned up, for miles, in trying for metal.

"Ay, they find him out," said the captain; "but he makes a struggle of it even then, and holds back all he can. He's a 'cute 'un."

The gloom of evening was already gathering on the dreary scene, and they were, at the shortest and best, a dozen miles from their destination. But, the captain, in his long-skirted blue coat, and his boots and his hat and his square shirt-collar, and without any extra defence against the weather, walked coolly along with his hands in his pockets: as if he lived underground somewhere hard by, and had just come up to show his friend the road.

"I'd have liked to have had a look at this place, too," said the captain, "when there was a monstrous sweep of water rolling over it, dragging the powerful great stones along and piling 'em atop of one another, and depositing the foundations for all manner of superstitions. Bless you! the old priests, smart mechanical critturs as they were, never piled up many of these stones. Water's the lever that moved 'em. When you see 'em thick and blunt tewwards one point of the compass, and fined away thin tewwards the opposite point, you may be as good as moral sure that the name of the ancient Druid that fixed 'em was Water."

The captain referred to some great blocks of stone presenting this characteristic, which were wonderfully balanced and heaped on one another, on a desolate hill. Looking back at these, as they stood out against the lurid glare of the west, just then expiring, they were not unlike enormous antediluvian birds, that had perched there on crags and peaks, and had been petrified there.

"But it's an interesting country," said the captain, "—fact! It's old in the annals of that said old Arch Druid, Water, and it's old in the annals of the said old parson-critturs too. It's a mighty interesting thing to set your boot (as I did this day) on a rough honey-combed old stone, with just nothing you can name but weather visible upon it: which the scholars that go about with hammers, chipping pieces off the universal airth, find to be an inscription, entreating prayers for the soul of some for-ages-bust-up crittur of a governor that over-taxed a people never heard of." Here the captain stopped to slap his leg. "It's a mighty interesting thing to come upon a score or two of stones set up on end in a desert, some short, some tall, some leaning here, some leaning there, and to know that they were pop'larly supposed – and may be still – to be a group of Cornish men that got changed into that geological formation for playing a game upon a Sunday. They wouldn't have it in my country, I reckon, even if they could get it – but it's very interesting."

In this, the captain, though it amused him, was quite sincere. Quite as sincere as when he added, after looking well about him: "That fog-bank coming up as the sun goes down, will spread, and we shall have to feel our way into Lanrean full as much as see it."

All the way along, the young fisherman had spoken at times to the captain, of his interrupted hopes, and of the family good name, and of the restitution that must be made, and of the cherished plans of his heart so near attainment, which must be set aside for it. In his simple faith and honour, he seemed incapable of entertaining the idea that it was within the bounds of possibility to evade the doing of what their inquiries should establish to be right. This was very agreeable to Captain Jorgan, and won his genuine admiration. Wherefore, he now turned the discourse back into that channel, and encouraged his companion to talk of Kitty, and to calculate how many years it would take, without a share in the fishery, to establish a home for her, and to relieve his honest heart by dwelling on its anxieties.

Meanwhile, it fell very dark, and the fog became dense, though the wind howled at them and bit them as savagely as ever. The captain had carefully taken the bearings of Lanrean from the map, and carried his pocket compass with him; the young fisherman, too, possessed that kind of cultivated instinct for shaping a course, which is often found among men of such pursuits. But, although they held a true course in the main, and corrected it when they lost the road by the aid of the compass and a light obtained with great difficulty in the roomy depths of the captain's hat, they could not help losing the road often. On such occasions they would become involved in the difficult ground of the spongy moor, and, after making a laborious loop, would emerge upon the road at some point they had passed before they left it, and thus would have a good deal of work to do twice over. But the young fisherman was not easily lost, and the captain (and his comb) would probably have turned up, with perfect coolness and self-possession, at any appointed spot on the surface of this globe. Consequently, they were no more than retarded in their progress to Lanrean, and arrived in that small place at nine o'clock. By that time, the captain's hat had fallen back over his ears and rested on the nape of his neck; but he still had his hands in his pockets, and showed no other sign of dilapidation.

They had almost run against a low stone house with red-curtained windows, before they knew they had hit upon the little hotel, the King Arthur's Arms. They could just descry through the mist, on the opposite side of the narrow road, other low stone buildings which were its outhouses and stables; and somewhere overhead, its invisible sign was being wrathfully swung by the wind.

"Now, wait a bit," said the captain. "They might be full here, or they might offer us cold quarters. Consequently, the policy is to take an observation, and, when we've found the warmest room, walk right slap into it."

The warmest room was evidently that from which fire and candle streamed reddest and brightest, and from which the sound of voices engaged in some discussion came out into the night. Captain Jorgan having established the bearings of this room, merely said to his young friend, "Follow me!" and was in it, before King Arthur's Arms had any notion that they enfolded a stranger.

"Order, order, order!" cried several voices, as the captain with his hat under his arm, stood within the door he had opened.

"Gentlemen," said the captain, advancing, "I am much beholden to you for the opportunity you give me of addressing you; but will not detain you with any lengthened observations. I have the honour to be a cousin of yours on the Uncle Sam side; this young friend of mine is a nearer relation of yours on the Devonshire side; we are both pretty nigh used up, and much in want of supper. I thank you for your welcome, and I am proud to take you by the hand, sir, and I hope I see you well."

These last words were addressed to a jolly looking chairman with a wooden hammer near him: which, but for the captain's friendly grasp, he would have taken up, and hammered the table with.

"How do you *do*, sir?" said the captain, shaking this chairman's hand with the greatest heartiness, while his new friend ineffectually eyed his hammer of office; "when you come to my country, I shall be proud to return your welcome, sir, and that of this good company."

The captain now took his seat near the fire, and invited his companion to do the like – whom he congratulated aloud, on their having "fallen on their feet."

The company, who might be about a dozen in number, were at a loss what to make of, or do with, the captain. But, one little old man in long flapping shirt collars: who, with only his face and them visible through a cloud of tobacco smoke, looked like a superannuated Cherubim: said sharply, "This is a Club."

"This is a Club," the captain repeated to his young friend. "Wa'al now, that's curious! Didn't I say, coming along, if we could only light upon a Club?"

The captain's doubling himself up and slapping his leg, finished the chairman. He had been softening towards the captain from the first, and he melted. "Gentlemen King Arthurs," said he, rising, "though it is not the custom to admit strangers, still, as we have broken the rule once to-night, I will exert my authority and break it again. And while the supper of these travellers is cooking;" here his eye fell on the landlord, who discreetly took the hint and withdrew to see about it; "I will recal you to the subject of the seafaring man."

"D'ye hear!" said the captain, aside to the young fisherman; "that's in our way. Who's the seafaring man, I wonder?"

"I see several old men here," returned the young fisherman, eagerly, for his thoughts were always on his object. "Perhaps one or more of the old men whose names you wrote down in your book, may be here."

"Perhaps," said the captain; "I've got my eye on 'em. But don't force it. Try if it won't come nat'ral."

Thus the two, behind their hands, while they sat warming them at the fire. Simultaneously, the Club beginning to be at its ease again, and resuming the discussion of the seafaring man, the captain winked to his fellow-traveller to let him attend to it.

As it was a kind of conversation not altogether unprecedented in such assemblages, where most of those who spoke at all, spoke all at once, and where half of those could put no beginning to what they had to say, and the other half could put no end, the tendency of the debate was discursive, and not very intelligible. All the captain had made out, down to the time when the separate little table laid for two was covered with a smoking broiled fowl and rashers of bacon, reduced itself to these heads. That, a seafaring man had arrived at The King Arthur's Arms, benighted, an hour or so earlier in the evening. That, the Gentlemen King Arthurs had admitted him, though all unknown, into the sanctuary of their Club. That, they had invited him to make his footing good by telling a story. That, he had, after some pressing, begun a story of adventure and shipwreck: at an interesting point of which he suddenly broke off, and positively refused to finish. That, he had thereupon taken up a candlestick, and gone to bed, and was now the sole occupant of a double-bedded room up-stairs. The question raised on these premises, appeared to be, whether the seafaring man was not in a state of contumacy and contempt, and ought not to be formally voted and declared in that condition. This deliberation involved the difficulty (suggested by the more jocose and irreverent of the Gentlemen King Arthurs) that it might make no sort of difference to the seafaring man whether he was so voted and declared, or not.

Captain Jorgan and the young fisherman ate their supper and drank their beer, and their knives and forks had ceased to rattle and their glasses had ceased to clink, and still the discussion showed no symptoms of coming to any conclusion. But, when they had left their little supper-table and had returned to their seats by the fire, the Chairman hammered himself into attention, and thus outspake.

"Gentlemen King Arthurs; when the night is so bad without, harmony should prevail within. When the moor is so windy, cold, and bleak, this room should be cheerful, convivial, and entertaining. Gentlemen, at present it is neither the one, nor yet the other, nor yet the other. Gentlemen King Arthurs, I recal you to yourselves. Gentlemen King Arthurs, what are you? You are inhabitants – old inhabitants – of the noble village of Lanrean. You are in council assembled. You are a monthly Club through all the winter months, and they are many. It is your perroud perrivilege, on a new member's entrance or on a member's birthday, to call upon that member to make good his footing by relating to you some transaction or adventure in his life, or in the life of a relation, or in the life of a friend, and then to depute me as your representative to spin a teetotum to pass it round. Gentlemen King Arthurs, your perroud perrivileges shall not suffer in my keeping. N—no! Therefore, as the member whose birthday the present occasion has the honour to be, has gratified you; and as the seafaring man overhead has *not* gratified you; I start you fresh, by spinning the teetotum attached to my office, and calling on the gentleman it falls to, to speak up when his name is declared."

The captain and his young friend looked hard at the teetotum as it whirled rapidly, and harder still when it gradually became intoxicated and began to stagger about the table in an ill-conducted and disorderly manner. Finally, it came into collision with a candlestick and leaped against the pipe of the old gentleman with the flapping shirt collars. Thereupon, the chairman struck the table once with his hammer and said: "Mr. Parvis!"

"D'ye hear that?" whispered the captain, greatly excited, to the young fisherman. "I'd have laid you a thousand dollars a good half-hour ago, that that old cherubim in the clouds was Arson Parvis!"

The respectable personage in question, after turning up one eye to assist his memory – at which time, he bore a very striking resemblance indeed to the conventional representations of his race as executed in oil by various ancient masters – commenced a narrative, of which the interest centred in a waistcoat. It appeared that the waistcoat was a yellow waistcoat with a green stripe, white sleeves, and a plain brass button. It also appeared that the waistcoat was made to order, by Nicholas Pendold of Penzance, who was thrown off the top of a four-horse coach coming down the hill on the Plymouth road, and, pitching on his head where he was not sensitive, lived two-and-thirty years afterwards, and considered himself the better for the accident – roused up, as it might be. It further appeared that the waistcoat belonged to Mr. Parvis's father, and had once attended him, in company with a pair of gaiters, to the annual feast of miners at St. Just: where the extraordinary circumstance which ever afterwards rendered it a waistcoat famous in story had occurred. But, the celebrity of the waistcoat was not thoroughly accounted for by Mr. Parvis, and had to be to some extent taken on trust by the company, in consequence of that gentleman's entirely forgetting all about the extraordinary circumstance that had handed it down to fame. Indeed, he was even unable, on a gentle cross-examination instituted for the assistance of his memory, to inform the Gentlemen King Arthurs whether it was a circumstance of a natural or supernatural character. Having thus responded to the teetotum, Mr. Parvis, after looking out from his clouds as if he would like to see the man who would beat that, subsided into himself.

The fraternity were plunged into a blank condition by Mr. Parvis's success, and the chairman was about to try another spin, when young Raybrock – whom Captain Jorgan had with difficulty restrained – rose, and said might he ask Mr. Parvis a question.

The Gentlemen King Arthurs holding, with loud cries of "Order!" that he might not, he asked the question as soon as he could possibly make himself heard.

Did the forgotten circumstance relate in any way to money? To a sum of money, such as five hundred pounds? To money supposed by its possessor to be honestly come by, but in reality ill-gotten and stolen?

A general surprise seized upon the club when this remarkable inquiry was preferred; which would have become resentment but for the captain's interposition.

"Strange as it sounds," said he, "and suspicious as it sounds, I pledge myself, gentlemen, that my young friend here has a manly stand-up Cornish reason for his words. Also, I pledge myself that they are inoffensive words. He and I are searching for information on a subject which those words generally describe. Such information we may get from the honestest and best of men may get, or not get, here or anywhere about here. I hope the Honourable Mr. Arson – I ask his pardon – Parvis will not object to quiet my young friend's mind by saying Yes or No.

After some time, the obtuse Mr. Parvis was with great trouble and difficulty induced to roar out "No!" For which concession the captain rose and thanked him.

"Now, listen to the next," whispered the captain to the young fisherman. "There may be more in him than in the other crittur. Don't interrupt him. Hear him out."

The chairman with all due formality spun the teetotum, and it reeled into the brandy-and-water of a strong brown man of sixty or so: John Tredgear: the manager of a neighbouring mine. He immediately began as follows, with a plain business-like air that gradually warmed as he proceeded.

IT happened that at one period of my life the path of my destiny (not a tin path then) lay along the highways and byways of France, and that I had occasion to make frequent stoppages at common French roadside cabarets – that kind of tavern which has a very bad name in French books and French plays. I had engaged myself in an undertaking which rendered such journeys necessary. A very old friend of mine had recently established himself at Paris in a wholesale commercial enterprise, into the nature of which it is not necessary for our present purpose to enter. He had proposed to me a certain share in the undertaking, and one of the duties of my post was to involve occasional journeys among the smaller towns and villages of France, with the view of establishing agencies and opening connexions. My friend had applied to me to undertake this function, rather than to a native, feeling that he could trust me better than a stranger. He knew also that, in consequence of my having been half my life at school in France, my knowledge of the language would be sufficient for every purpose that could be required.

I accepted my friend's proposal, and entered with such energy as I could command upon my new mode of life. Sometimes, my journeyings from place to place were accomplished by means of the railroad, or other public conveyance; but there were other occasions, and these last I liked the best, when it was necessary I should go to out-of-the-way places, and by such crossroads as rendered it more convenient for me to travel with a carriage and horse of my own. My carriage was a kind of phaeton without a coach-box, with a leather hood that would put up and down; and there was plenty of room at the back, for such specimens or samples of goods as it was necessary that I should carry with me. For my horse it was absolutely indispensable that it should be an animal of some value, as no horse but a very good one would be capable of performing the long courses day after day which my mode of travelling rendered necessary. He cost me two thousand francs, and was anything but dear at the price.

Many were the journeys we performed together over the broad acres of beautiful France. Many were the hotels, many the auberges, many the bad dinners, many the damp beds, and many the fleas which I encountered en route. Many were the dull old fortified towns over whose drawbridges I rolled; many the still more dull old towns without fortifications and without drawbridges, at which my avocations made it necessary for me to halt.

I don't know how it was that on the morning when I was to start from the town of Doulaise, with the intention of sleeping at Francy-le-Grand, I was an hour later in commencing my journey than I ought to have been. I have said I don't know how it was, but this is scarcely true. I do know how it was. It was because on that morning, to use a popular expression, everything went wrong. So, it was an hour later than it ought to have been, gentlemen, when I drew up the sheepskin lining of my carriage apron over my legs, and establishing my little dog comfortably on the seat beside me, set off on my journey. In all my expeditions I was accompanied by a favourite terrier of mine, which I had brought with me from England. I never travelled without her, and found her a companion.

It was a miserable day in the month of October. A perfectly grey sky, with white gleams about the horizon, gave unmistakable evidence that the small drizzle which was falling would continue for four-and-twenty hours at least. It was cold and cheerless weather, and on the deserted road I was pursuing, there was scarcely a human being (unless it was an occasional cantonnier, or road-mender) to break the solitude. A deserted way indeed, with poplars on each side of it, which had turned yellow in the autumn, and had shed their leaves in abundance all across the road, so that my mare's footsteps had quite a muffled sound as she trampled them under her hoofs. Widely-extending flats spread out on either side till the view was lost in an inconceivably melancholy scene, and the road itself was so perfectly straight, that you could see something like ten miles of it diminishing to a point in front of you, while a similar view was visible through the little window at the back of the carriage.

In the hurry of the morning's departure I had omitted to inquire, as I generally did in travelling an unknown road, at what village it would be best for me to stop, about noon, to bait, and what was the name of the most respectable house of public entertainment in my way; so that when I arrived between twelve and one o'clock at a certain place where four roads met; and when at one of the corners formed by their union I saw a great bare-looking inn, with the sign of the Tête Noire swinging in front; I had nothing for it but to put up there, without knowing anything of the character of the house.

The look of the place did not please me. It was a great bare uninhabited-looking house, which seemed much larger than was necessary, and presented a black and dirty appearance, which, considering the distance from any town, it was difficult to account for. All the doors and all the windows were shut; there was no sign of any living creature about the place; and niched into the wall above the principal entrance was a grim and ghastly-looking life-size figure of a Saint. For a moment I hesitated whether I should turn into the open gates of the stable-yard, or go further in search of some more attractive halting-place. But my mare was tired, I was more than half way on my road, and this would be the best division of the journey. Besides, Gentlemen; why not put up here? If I was only going to stop at such places of entertainment as completely satisfied me, externally as well as internally, I had better give up travelling altogether.

There were no more signs of life in the interior of the yard, than were presented by the external aspect of the house, as it fronted the road. Everything seemed shut up. All the stables and outhouses were characterised by closed doors, without so much as a straw clinging to their thresholds to indicate that these buildings were sometimes put to a practical use. I saw no manure strewed about the place, and no living creature: no pigs, no ducks, no fowls. It was perfectly still and quiet, and, as it was one of those days when a fine small rain descends quite straight, without a breath of air to drive it one way or other, the silence was complete and distressing. I gave a loud shout, and began undoing the harness while my summons was taking effect.

The first person whom the sound of my voice appeared to have reached, was a small but precocious boy: who opened a door in the back of the house, and, descending the flight of steps which led to it, approached to aid me in my task. I was just undoing the final buckle on my side of the harness, when, happening to turn round, I discovered, standing close behind me, a personage who had approached so quietly that it would have been a confusing thing to find him so near even if there had been nothing in his appearance which was calculated to startle one. He was the most ill-looking man,

Gentlemen, that it was ever my fortune to behold. Nearer fifty than any other age I could give him, his dry spare nature had kept him as light and active as a restless boy. An absence of flesh, however, was not the only want I felt to exist in the personal appearance of the landlord of the Tête Noire. There was a much more serious defect in him than this. A want of any hint of mercy, or conscience, or any accessible approach to the better side (if there was a better side) of the man's nature. When first I looked at his eyes, as he stood behind me in the open court, and as they rapidly glanced over the comely points of my horse, and thence to the packages inside my carriage and the portmanteau strapped on in front of it – at that time, the colour of his eyes appeared to me to be of an almost orange tinge; but when, a minute afterwards, we stood, together in the dark stable, I noted that a kind of blue phosphorescence gleamed upon their surface, veiling their real hue, and imparting to them a tigerish lustre. The moment when I remarked this, by-the-by, was when the organs I have been describing were fixed upon the very large gold ring which I had not ceased to wear when I adopted my adventurous life, and which you may see upon my finger now. There were two other things about this man that struck me. These were, a bald red projecting lump of flesh at the back of his head, and a deep scar, which a scrap of frouzy whisker on his cheek wholly declined to conceal.

"A nasty day for a journey of pleasure," said the landlord, looking at me with a satirical smile.

"Perhaps it is *not* a journey of pleasure," I answered, dryly.

"We have few such travellers on the road now," said the evil-faced man. "The railroads make the country a desert, and the roads are as wild as they were three hundred years ago."

"They are well enough," I answered, carelessly, "for those who are obliged to travel by them. Nobody else, I should think, would be likely to make use of them."

"Will you come into the house?" said the landlord, abruptly, looking me full in the face.

I never felt a stronger repugnance than I entertained towards the idea of entering this man's doors. Yet what other course was open to me. My mare was already half through the first instalment of her oats, so there was no more excuse for remaining in the stable. To take a walk in the drenching rain was out of the question, and to remain sitting in my calèche would have been a worse indication of suspicion and mistrust. Besides, I had had nothing since the morning's coffee, and I wanted something to eat and drink. There was nothing to be done, then, but to accept my ill-looking friend's offer. He led the way up the flight of steps which gave access to the interior of the building.

The room in which I found myself on passing through the door at the top of these steps, was one of those rooms which an excess of light not only fails to enliven, but seems even to invest with an additional degree of gloom. There is *sometimes* this character about light, and I have seen before now, a workhouse ward, and a barren schoolroom, which have owed a good share of their melancholy to an immoderate amount of cold grey daylight. This room, then, into which I was shown, was one of those which, on a wet day, seemed several degrees lighter than the open air. Of course it could not be really lighter than the thing that lit it, but it seemed so. It also appeared larger than the whole out-door world; and this, certainly, could not be either, but seemed so. Vast as it was, there appeared through two glass-doors in one of the walls another apartment of similar dimensions. It was not a square room, nor an oblong room, but was smaller at one end than at the other: a phenomenon which, as you have very likely observed, Gentlemen, has always an unpleasant effect. The billiard-table, which stood in the middle of the apartment, though really of the usual size, looked quite a trifling piece of furniture; and as to the other tables, which were planted sparingly here and there for purposes of refreshment, they were quite lost in the immensity of space about them. A cupboard, a rack of billiard cues, a marking-board, and a print of the murder of the Archbishop of Paris in a black frame, alone broke the uniformity of wall. The ceiling, as far as one could judge of anything at that altitude, appeared to be traversed by an enormous beam with rings fastened into it adapted for suicidal purposes, and splashed with the whitewash with which the ceiling itself and the walls had just been decorated. Even my little terrier, whom I had been obliged to take up in my arms on account of the disposition she had manifested to fly at the shins of our detested landlord, looked round the room with a gaze of horror as I set her down, and trembled and shivered as if she would come out of her skin.

"And so you don't like him, Nelly, and your little beads of eyes, that look up at me from under that hairy penthouse, with nothing but love in them, are all a-blaze with fury when they are turned upon his sinister face? And how did he get that scar, Nelly? Did he get it when he slaughtered his last traveller? And what do you think of his eyes, Nelly? And what do you think of the back of his head, my dog? What do you think he's about now, eh? What mischief do you think he's hatching? Don't you wish you were sitting by my side in the calèche, and that we were out on the free road again?"

To all these questions and remarks, my little companion responded very intelligibly by faint thumpings of the ground with her tail, and by certain flutterings of her ears, which, from long habits of intercourse, I understood very well to mean that whatever my opinion might be, she coincided in it.

I had ordered an omelette and some wine when I first entered the house, and, as I now sat waiting for it, I observed that my landlord would every now and then leave what he was about in the other room – where I concluded that he was engaged preparing my meal – and would come and peer at me furtively through the glass-doors which connected the room I was in, with that in which he was. Once, too, I heard him go out, and I felt sure that he had retired to the stables, to examine more minutely the value of my horse and carriage.

I took it into my head that my landlord was a desperate rogue; that his business was not sufficient to support him; that he had remarked that I was in possession of a very valuable horse, a carriage which would fetch something, and a quantity of luggage in which there were probably articles of price. I had other things of worth about my person, including a sum of money, without which I could not be travelling about, as he saw me, from place to place.

While my mind was amusing itself with these cheerful reflections, a little girl, of about twelve years old, entered the room through the glass-doors, and, after honouring me with a long stare, went to the cupboard at the other end of the apartment, and, opening it with a bunch of keys which she brought with her in her hand, took out a small white paper packet, about four inches square, and retired with it by the way by which she had entered; still staring at me so diligently that, from want of proper attention to where she was going, she got (I am happy to state) a severe bump against the door as she passed through it. She was a horrid little girl this, with eyes that in shirking the necessity of looking straight at anybody or anything, had got at last to look only at her nose – finding it, probably, as bad a nose as could be met with, and therefore a congenial companion. She had, moreover, frizzy and fluey hair, was excessively dirty, and had a slow crab-like way of going along without looking at what she was about, which was very noisome and detestable.

It was not long before this young lady reappeared, bearing in her hand a plate containing the omelette, which she placed upon the table without going through the previous form of laying a cloth. She next cut an immense piece of bread from a loaf shaped like a ring, and, having clapped this also down upon the dirtiest part of the table, and having further favoured me with a wiped knife and fork, disappeared once more. She disappeared to fetch the wine. When this had been brought, and some water, the preparations for my feast were considered complete, and I was left to enjoy it alone.

I must not omit to mention that the horrid waiting-maid appeared to excite as strong an antipathy in the breast of my little dog as that which my landlord himself had stirred up; and, I am happy to say, that as the child left the room I was obliged to interfere, to prevent Nelly from harassing her retreating calves.

Gentlemen, an experienced traveller soon learns that he must eat to support nature: closing his eyes, nose, and ears to all suggestions. I set to work, then, at the omelette with energy, and at the tough sour bread with good will, and had swallowed half a tumbler of wine and water, when a thought suddenly occurred to me which caused me to set the glass down upon the table. I had no sooner done this, than I raised it again to my lips, took a fresh sip, rolled the liquid about in my mouth two or three times, and spat it out upon the floor. But I uttered, as I did so, in an audible tone, the monosyllable "Pooh!"

"Pooh! Nelly," I said, looking down at my dog, who was watching me intensely with her head on one side – "pooh! Nelly," I repeated, "what frantic and inconceivable nonsense!"

And what was it that I thus stigmatised? What was it that had given me pause in the middle of my draught? What thought was it that caused me to set down my glass with half its contents remaining in it? It was a suspicion, driven straight and swift as an arrow into the innermost recesses of my soul, that the wine I had just been drinking, and which, contrary to my custom, I had mingled with water, was drugged!

There are some thoughts which, like noxious insects, come buzzing back into one's mind as often as we repulse them. We confute them in argument, prove them illogical, leave them not a leg to stand upon, and yet there they are the next moment as brisk as bees, and stronger on their pins than ever. It was just such a thought as this with which I had now to deal. It was well to say "Pooh!" it was well to remind myself that this was the nineteenth century, that I was not acting a part in a French melodrama, that such things as I was thinking of were only known in romances; it was well to argue that to set a respectable man down as a murderer, because he had peculiar coloured eyes and a scar upon his cheek, were ridiculous things to do. There seemed to be two separate parties within me: one possessed of great powers of argument and a cool judgment: the other, an irrational or opposition party, whose chief force consisted in a system of dogged assertion, which all the arguments of the rational party were insufficient to put down.

It was not long before an additional force was imparted to the tactics of the irrational party, by certain symptoms which began to develop themselves in my internal organisation, and which seemed favourable to the view of the case I was so anxious to refute. In spite of all my efforts to the contrary, I could not help feeling that some very remarkable sensations were slowly and gradually stealing over me. First of all, I began to find that I was a little at fault in my system of calculating distances: so that when I took up any object and attempted to replace it on the table, I either brought it into contact with that article of furniture with a crash, in consequence of conceiving it to be lower than it was; or else, imagining that the table was several inches nearer to the ceiling than was the case, I abandoned whatever I held in my hand sooner than I should, and found that I was confiding it to space again, my head felt light upon my shoulders, there was a slight tingling in my hands, and a sense that they, as well as my feet (which were very cold), were swelling to gigantic size, and were also surrounded with numerous rapidly revolving wheels of a light structure, like Catherine-wheels previous to ignition. It also appeared to me that when I spoke to my dog, my voice had a curious sound, and my words were very imperfectly articulated.

It would happen, too, that when I looked towards the glass-doors, my landlord was there, peering at me through the muslin curtains: or the horrid little girl would enter, with no obvious intention, and having loitered for a little time about the room, would leave it again. At length the landlord himself came in, and coolly walking up to the table at which I was seated, glanced at the hardly tasted wine before me.

"It would appear that the wine of the country is not to your taste," he said.

"It is good enough," I answered, as carelessly as I could; the words sounding to me as if they were uttered inside the cupola of St. Paul's, and were conveyed by iron tubes to the place I occupied.

I was in a strange state – perfectly conscious, but imperfectly able to control my thoughts, my words, my actions. I believe my landlord stood staring down at me as I sat staring up at him, and watching the Catherine-wheels as they revolved round his eyes and nose and chin – Gentlemen, they seemed absolutely to *fizz* when they got to the scar on his cheek.

At this time a noisy party entered the main room of the auberge, which I have described as being visible through the glass-doors, and the landlord had to leave me for a time, to go and attend to them. I think I must have fallen into a slight and strongly-resisted doze, and that when I started out of it, it was in consequence of the violent barking of my terrier. The landlord was in the room; he was just unlocking the cupboard from which the little girl had taken the paper parcel. He took out just such another paper parcel, and returned again through the doors. As he did so, I remember stupidly wondering what had become of the little girl. Presently his evil face appeared again at the door.

"I am going to prepare the coffee," said the landlord; "perhaps monsieur will like it better than the wine."

As the man disappeared, I started suddenly and violently upon my feet. I could deceive myself no longer. My thoughts were like lightning. "The wine having been taken in so small a quantity and so profusely mixed with water, has done its work (as this man can see) but imperfectly. The coffee will finish that work. He is now preparing it. The cupboard, the little parcel – there can be no doubt. I will leave this place while I yet can. Now or never; if those men whose voices I hear in the other room leave the house it will be too late. With so many witnesses, no attempt can be made to prevent my departure. I *will* not sleep – I *will* act – I *will* force my muscles to their work, and get away from this place."

Gentlemen; in compensation for a set of nerves of distressing sensitiveness, I have received from nature a remarkable power of controlling my nerves for a time. I staggered to the door, closing it after me more violently than I had intended, and descended – the fresh air making me feel very giddy – into the yard.

As I went down the steps, I saw the truculent little girl of whom I have already spoken entering the yard, followed by a blackmith, carrying a hammer and some other implements of his trade. Catching sight of me, the little girl spoke quickly to the blacksmith, and in an instant they both changed their course, which was directed towards the stable, and entered an outhouse on the other side of the yard. The thought entered my head that this man had been sent for to drive a nail into my horse's foot, so that in the event of the drugged wine failing I might still be unable to proceed. This horrible idea added new force to my exertions. I seized the shafts of my carriage and commenced dragging it out of the yard and round to the front of the house: feeling that if it was once in the highway, there would be less possibility of offering any impediment to my starting. I am conscious of having fallen twice to the ground, in my struggles to get the carriage out of the yard. Next, I hastened to the stable. My mare was still harnessed, with the exception of the headstall. I managed to get the bit into her mouth, and dragged her to the place where I had left the carriage. After I know not how many efforts to place the docile beast in the shafts – for I was as incapable of calculating distances as a drunken man – I recollect, but how I know not, securing the assistance of the boy I had seen. I was making a final effort to fasten the trace to its little pin, when a voice behind me said: "Are you going away without drinking your coffee?'

I turned round and saw my landlord standing close beside me. He was watching my bungling efforts to secure the harness, but he made no movement to assist me.

"I do not want any coffee," I answered.

"No coffee, and no wine! It would appear that the gentleman is not a great drinker. You have not given your horse much of a rest," he added, presently.

"I am in haste. What have I to pay?"

"You will take something else," said the landlord; "a glass of brandy before starting in the wet?"

"No, nothing more. What have I to pay?"

"You will at least come in for an instant, and warm your feet at the stove."

"No. Tell me at once how much I am to pay."

Baffled in all his efforts to get me again into the house, my detested landlord had nothing for it but to answer my demand.

"Four litres of oats," he muttered, "a half-truss of hay, breakfast, wine, coffee" he emphasised the last two words with a malignant grin— "seven francs fifty centimes."

My mare was by this time somehow or other buckled into the shafts, and now I had to get out my purse to pay this demand. My hands were cold, my head was giddy, my sight was dim, and, as I brought out my purse (which was a porte-monnaie, opening with a hinge), I managed while paying the bill to turn the purse over and to drop some gold pieces.

"Gold!" cried the boy who had been helping me to harness the horse: speaking as if by an irresistible impulse.

The landlord made a sudden dart at it, but instantly checked himself.

"People want plenty of gold," he said, "when they make a journey of pleasure."

I felt myself getting worse. I could not pick up the gold pieces as they lay on the ground. I fell on my knees, and my head bowed forward. I could not hit the place where a coin lay; I could see it but I could not guide my fingers to it. Still I did not yield. I got some of the money up, and the stable-boy, who was very officious in assisting me, gave me one or two pieces – to this day, I don't know how many he kept. I cast a hasty glance around, and, seeing no more gold on the ground, raised myself by a desperate effort and scrambled to my place in the carriage. I shook the reins instinctively, and the mare began to move.

The well-trained beast was beginning to trot away as cleverly as usual, when a thought suddenly flashed into my brain, as will sometimes happen when we are just going to sleep – a thought which woke me up like a pistol-shot, and caused me to spring forward and gather up the reins so violently as almost to bring the mare back upon her haunches.

"My dog, my dear little Nelly!" I had left her behind!

To abandon my little favourite was a thing that never entered my head. "No, I must return. I must go back to the horrible place I have just escaped from. He has seen my gold, too, now," I said to myself, as I turned my horse's head with many clumsy efforts; "the men who were drinking in the auberge are gone; and, what is worse than all, I feel more under the influence of the drugs I have swallowed."

As I approached the auberge once more, I remember noticing that its walls looked blacker than ever, that the rain was falling more heavily, that the landlord and the stable-boy were on the steps of the inn, evidently on the look-out for me. One thing more I noticed; on the road a small speck, as of some vehicle nearing the place.

"I have come back for my dog," said I.

"I know nothing of your dog."

"It is false! I left her shut up in the inner room."

"Go there and find her, then," retorted the man, throwing off all disguise.

"I will," was my answer.

I knew it was a trap to get me into the house; I knew I was lost if I entered it; but I did not care. I descended from the carriage, I clambered up the steps with the aid of the banisters, I heard the barking of my little Nelly as I passed through the outer room and approached the glass-doors, steadying myself as I went by the articles of furniture in the room. I burst the doors open, and my favourite bounded into my arms.

And now I felt that it was too late. As I approached the door that opened to the road, I saw my carriage being led round to the back of the house, and the form of the landlord appeared in the doorway blocking up the passage. I made an effort to push past him, but it was useless. My little Nelly fell out of my arm on the steps outside: the landlord slammed the door heavily; and I fell, without sense or knowledge, at his feet.

* * *

It was dark, Gentlemen, – dark and very cold. The little patch of sky I was looking up at, had in it a marvellous number of stars, which would have looked bright but for a blazing planet which seemed to eclipse, in the absence ol the moon, all the other luminaries round about it. To lie thus, was in spite of the cold, quite a luxurious sensation. As I turned my head to ease it a little (for it seemed to have been in this position some time), I felt stiff and weak. At this moment, too, I feel a stirring close beside me, and first a cold nose touching my hand, and then a hot tongue licking it. As to my other sensations, I was aware of a gentle rumbling sound, and I could feel that I was being carried slowly along, and that every now and then there was a slight jolt: one of which, perhaps, more marked than the rest, might be the cause of my being awake at all.

Presently, other matters began to dawn upon my mind through the medium of my senses. I could see the regular movement of a horse's ears walking in front of me; surely I saw, too, part of the figure of a man – a pair of sturdy shoulders, the hood of a coat, and a head with a wide-awake hat upon it. I could hear the occasional sounds of encouragement which seemed to emanate from this figure, and which were addressed to the horse. I could hear the tinkling of bells upon the animal's neck. Surely, too, I heard a rumbling sound behind us, and the tread of a horse's feet just as if there were another vehicle following close upon us. Was there anything more? Yes, in the distance I was able to detect the twinkling of. a light or two, as if a town were not far off.

Now, Gentlemen, as I lay and observed all these things, there was such a languor shed over my spirits, such a sense of utter but not unpleasant weakness, that I hardly cared to ask myself what it all meant, or to inquire where I was, or how I came there. A conviction that all was well with me, lay like an anodyne upon my heart, and it was only slowly and gradually that any curiosity as to how I came to be so, developed itself in my brain. I dare say we had been jogging along for a quarter of an hour during which I had been perfectly conscious, before I struggled up into a sitting posture, and recognised the hooded back of the man at the horse's head.

"Dufay?"

The man with the hooded coat who was walking by the side of the horse, suddenly cried out "Wo!" in a sturdy voice; then ran to the back of the carriage and cried out "Wo!" again; and then we came to a stand-still. In another moment he had mounted on the step of the carriage and had taken me cordially by the hand.

"What," he said, "awake at last? Thank Heaven! I had almost begun to despair of you."

"My dear friend, what does all this mean? Where am I? Where did you come from? This is not my calèche, that is not my horse."

"Both are safe behind," said Dufay, heartily; "and having told you so much, I will not utter another word till you are safe and warm at the Lion d'Or. See! There are the lights of the town. Now, not another word." And pulling the horsecloth under which I was lying, more closely over me, my friend dismounted from the step; started the vehicle with the customary cry of "Allons donc!" and a crack of the whip; and we were soon once more in motion.

Castaing Dufay was a man into whose company circumstances had thrown me very often, and with whom I had become intimate from choice. Of the numerous class to which he belonged, those men whose sturdy vehicles and sturdier horses are to be seen standing in the yards and stables of all the inns in provincial France – the class of the commis-voyageurs, or French commercial travellers – Castaing Dufay was more than a favourable specimen. I was very fond of him. In the course of our intimacy, I had been fortunate enough to have the opportunity of being useful to him in matters of some importance. I think, Gentlemen, we like those we have served, quite as well as they like us.

The town lights were, indeed, close by, and it was not long before we turned into the yard of the Lion d'Or and found ourselves in the midst of warmth and brightness, and surrounded by faces which, after the dangers I had passed through, looked perfectly angelic.

I had no idea, till I attempted to move, how weak and dazed I was. I was too far gone for dinner. A bed and a fire were the only things I coveted, and I was soon in possession of both.

I was no sooner snugly ensconced with my head on the pillow, watching the crackling logs as they sparkled – my little Nelly lying outside the counterpane – than my friend seated himself beside me and volunteered to relieve my curiosity as to the circumstances of my escape from the Tête Noire. It was now my turn to refuse to listen; as it had been his before, to refuse to speak.

"Not one word," I said, "till you have had a good dinner, after which you will come up and sit beside me, and tell me all I am longing to know. And stay – you will do one thing more for me, I know; when you come up you will bring a plateful of bones for Nelly; she will not leave me to-night, I swear, to save herself from starving."

"She deserves some dinner," said Dufay, as he left the room, "for I think it is through her instrumentality that you are alive at this moment."

The bliss in which I lay after Dufay had left the room, is known only to those who have passed through some great danger, or who, at least, are newly relieved from some condition of severe and protracted suffering. It was a state of perfect repose and happiness.

When my friend came back, he brought: not only a plate of fowl-bones for Nelly, but a basin of soup for me. When I had finished lapping it up, and while Nelly was still crunching the bones, Dufay spoke as follows:

"I said just now that it was to your little dog you owe the preservation of your life, and I must now tell you how it was. You remember that you left Doulaise this morning—"

"It seems a week ago," I interrupted.

"This morning," continued Dufay. "Well! You were hardly out of the inn-yard before I drove into it, having made a small stage before breakfast. I heard where you were gone, and, as I was going that way too, I determined to give my horse a rest of a couple of hours, while I breakfasted and transacted some business in the town, and then to set off after you. 'Have you any idea,' I said, as I left the inn at Doulaise, 'whether monsieur meant to stop en route, and if so, where?' The garçon did not know. 'Let me see,' I said, 'the Tête Noire at Mauconseil would be a likely place, wouldn't it?' 'No,' said the boy; 'the house does not enjoy a good character, and no one from here ever stops there.' 'Well,' said I, thinking no more of what he said, 'I shall be sure to find him. I will inquire after him as I go along.'

"The afternoon was getting on, when I came within sight of the inn of the Tête Noire. As you know, I am a little near-sighted, but I saw, as I drew near the auberge, that a conveyance of some kind was being taken round to the yard at the back of the house. This circumstance, however, I should have paid no attention to, had not my attention been suddenly caught by the violent barking of a dog, which seemed to be trying to gain admittance at the closed door of the inn. At a second glance I knew the dog to be yours. Pulling up my horse, I got down and ascended the steps of the auberge. One sniff at my shins was enough to convince Nelly that a friend was at hand, and her excitement as I approached the door was frantic.

CHARLES DICKENS SUPERNATURAL SHORT STORIES

"On my entering the house I did not at first see you, but on looking in the direction towards which your dog had hastened as soon as the door was opened, I saw a dark wooden staircase, which led out of one corner of the apartment I was standing in. I saw also, that you, my friend, were being dragged up the stairs in the arms of a very ill-looking man, assisted by (if possible) a still more ill-looking little girl, who had charge of your legs. At sight of me, the man deposited you upon the stairs, and advanced to meet me.

"'What are you doing with that gentleman?' I asked.

"'He is unwell,' replied the ill-looking man, 'and I am helping him up-stairs to bed.'

"'That gentleman is a friend of mine. What is the meaning of his being in this state?'

"'How should I know?' was the answer; 'I am not the guardian of the gentleman's health.'

"'Well, then, I *am*' said I, approaching the place where you were lying; 'and I prescribe, to begin with, that he shall leave this place at once.'

"I must own," continued Dufay, "that you were looking horribly ill, and, as I bent over, and felt your hardly fluttering pulse, I felt for a moment doubtful whether it was safe to move you. However, I determined to risk it.

"'Will you help me' I said, 'to move this gentleman to his carriage?'

"'No,' replied the ruffian, 'he is not fit to travel. Besides, what right have you over him?'

"'The right of being his friend.'

"'How do I know that?'

"'Because I tell you so. See, his dog knows me.'

"'And suppose I decline to accept that as evidence, and refuse to let this gentleman leave my house in his present state of health?'

"'You dare not do it.'

"'Why?'

"'Because,' I answered, slowly, 'I should go to the Gendarmerie in the village, and mention under what suspicious circumstances I found my friend here, and because your house has not the best of characters.'

"The man was silent for a moment, as if a little baffled. He seemed, however, determined to try once more.

"'And suppose I close my doors, and decline to let either of you go; what is to prevent me?'

"'In the first place,' I answered, '*I* will effectually prevent your detaining me single-handed. If you have assistance near, I am expected to-night at Francy, and if I do not arrive there, I shall soon be sought out. It was known that I left Doulaise this morning, and most people are aware that there is an auberge on the road which does not bear the best of reputations, and that its name is LaTête Noire. *Now*, will you help me?'

"'No,' replied the savage. 'I will have nothing to do with the affair.'

"It was not an easy task to drag you without assistance from the place where you were lying, out into the open air, down the steps, and to put you into my conveyance which was standing outside; but I managed to do it. The next thing I had to accomplish, was the feat of driving two carriages and two horses single-handed. I could see only one way of managing this. I led my own horse round to the gate of the stable-yard, where I could keep my eye upon him, while I went in search of your horse and carriage, which I had to get right without assistance. It was done at last. I fastened your horse's head by a halter, to the back of my carriage, and then leading my own beast by the bridle, I managed to start the procession. And so (though only at a foot pace) we turned our backs upon the Tête Noire. And now you know everything."

"I feel, Castaing, as if I should never be able to think of this adventure, or to speak of it again. It wears, somehow or other, such a ghastly aspect, that I sicken at the mere memory of it."

"Not a bit of it," said Dufay, cheerily; "you will live to tell it as a stirring tale some winter night, take my word for it."

Gentlemen, the prediction is verified. May the teetotum fall next time with more judgment!

"Wa'al, now!" said Captain Jorgan, rising, with his hand upon the sleeve of his fellow-traveller to keep him down; "I congratulate you, sir, upon that adventer; unpleasant at the time, but pleasant to look back upon; as many adventers in many lives are. Mr. Tredgear, you had a feeling for your money on that occasion, and it went hard on being Stolen Money. It was not a sum of five hundred pound, perhaps?"

"I wish it had been half as much," was the reply.

"Thank you, sir. Might I ask the question of you that has been already put? About this place of Lanrean, did you ever hear of any circumstances whatever, that might seem to have a bearing – any how – on that question?"

"Never."

"Thank you again for a straightfor'ard answer," said the captain, apologetically. "You see, we have been referred to Lanrean to make inquiries, and happening in among the inhabitants present, we use the opportunity. In my country, we always *do* use opportunities."

"And you turn them to good account, I believe, and prosper?"

"It's a fact, sir," said the captain, "that we get along. Yes, we get along, sir. – But I stop the teetotum."

It was twirled again, and fell to David Polreath; an iron-grey man; "as old as the hills," the captain whispered to young Raybrock, "and as hard as nails. – And I admire," added the captain, glancing about, "whether Unchrisen Penrewen is here, and which is he!"

David Polreath stroked down the long iron-grey hair that fell massively upon the shoulders of his large-buttoned coat, and spake thus:

THE question was, Did he throw himself over the cliff of set purpose, or did he lose his way in the dusk and fall over accidentally, or was he pushed over by some person or persons unknown?

His body was found nearly fifty yards below the fall, caught in the low branches of the trees that overhang the water at the foot of the track down the cliff. It was shockingly bruised and disfigured, so much so as to be hardly recognisable; but for his clothing, and the name on his linen, I doubt whether anybody could have identified him except myself. There was, however, no suspicion of foul play; the signs of rough usage might all have been caused by the body having been driven about amongst the stones that encumber the bed of the river a long way below the fall.

When I speak of the fall, I speak of the Ashenfall, by Ashendell village, within an hour's drive of this house. This, Gentlemen, is for the information of strangers.

He had been seen by many persons about the village during the day; I myself had seen him go up the hill past the parsonage towards the church: which I rather wondered at, considering who was buried there, and how, and why. I will even confess that I watched him; and he went – as I expected he would, since he had the heart to go near the place at all – round to the back of the church where Honor Livingston's grave is; and there he stayed, sitting by himself on the low wall for an hour or more. Sometimes, he turned to look across the valley – many a time and oft I had seen him there before, with Honor beside him, watching, while he sketched the beautiful landscape – and sometimes he had his back to it, and his head down, as if he were watching her grave. Not that there is anything pleasant or comforting to read there, as on the graves of good Christian people who have died in their beds; for, being a suicide, when they buried her on the north side of the church it was at dusk, and without any service, and, of course, no stone was allowed to be put up over it. Our clergyman has talked of having the mound levelled and turfed over, and I wish he would; it always hurts me when I go up to Sunday service, to see that ragged grave lying in the shadow of the wall, for I remember the pretty little lass ever since she could run alone; and though she was passionate, her heart was as good as gold. She had been religiously brought up, and I am quite sure in my own mind, let the coroner's inquest have said what it would, that she was out of herself, and Bedlam-mad when she did it.

The verdict on him was "accidental death," and he had a regular funeral – priest, bell, clerk, and sexton, complete; and there he lies, only a stone's throw from Honor, with a ton or two of granite over him, and an inscription, setting forth what a great man he was in his day, and what mighty engineering works he did at home and abroad, and how he sleeps now in the hope of a joyful resurrection with the just made perfect. These present strangers can read it for themselves; many strangers go up to look at it. His grave is as famous as the Ashenfall itself, and I have known folks come away with tears in their eyes after reading the flourishing inscription: believing it all like gospel, and saying how sad that so distinguished a man should have been cut off in the prime of his days. But I don't believe it. He was never any more than plain James Lawrence to me – a young fellow who, as a lad, had paddled bare-legged over the stones of the river as a guide across for visitors; who had been taken a fancy to by one of them, and decently educated; who had made the most of his luck, and done a clever thing or two in engineering; who had come back amongst us in all his glory, to dazzle most people's eyes, and break little Honor Livingston's heart. The one good thing I know of him was, that he pensioned his poor old mother; but he did not often come near her, and never after Honor Livingston was dead – no, not even in her last illness. It was a marvel to everybody what brought him over here, when we saw him the day before he was found dead; but it was his fate, and he couldn't keep away. That is my view of it. About his death, and the manner of it, all Lanrean had its speculation, and said its say; but I held my peace. I had my opinion, however, and I keep it. I have never seen reason to change it; but, on the contrary, I can show you evidence to establish it. I do not believe he either threw himself over the cliff, or fell over, or was pushed over; no, I believe he was drawn over – drawn over by something below. When you have heard the notes he made in a little book that was found amongst his things after he was dead, you will know what I mean. His cousin gave that book to me, knowing I am curious after odd stories of the neighbourhood; and what I am going to read, is written in his hand. I know his hand well, and certify to it.

*PASSAGES FROM JAMES LAWRENCE'S JOURNAL. London, August 11, 1829.*

Honor Livingston has kept her word with me. I saw her last night as plainly as I now see this pen I am writing with, and the ink-bottle I have just dipped it into. I saw her standing betwixt the two lights, looking at me, exactly as she looked the last time I saw her alive. I was neither asleep, nor dreaming-awake. I had only drunk a couple of glasses of wine at dinner, and was as much my own man as ever I was in my life. It is all nonsense to talk about fancy and optical delusions, in this case; I saw her with my eyes as distinctly as I ever saw her alive in the body. The hall clock had just struck eight, and it was growing dusk: exactly the time of evening, as I well remember, when she came creeping round by the cottage wall, and saw me through the open window, gathering up my books and making ready to go away from Ashendell. She was the last thought to have come into my mind at that moment, for I was just on the point of lighting my cigar and going out for a stroll, before turning in at the Daltons to chat with Anne. All at once, there she was, Honor herself! I could have sworn it, had I not seen them put her underground just a twelvemonth ago. I could not take my eyes off her; and there she stood, as nearly as I can tell, a minute – but it may have been an hour – and then the place she had filled was empty. I was so much bewildered, and out of myself as it were, that for a while I could neither think of anything, nor hear anything, but the mad heavy throbbing of my own pulses. I cannot say that I was scared exactly; for the time I was completely rapt away; the first actual sensation I had was of my own heart thumping in my breast like a sledge-hammer.

But I can call her up now and analyse her – a wan, vague, misty outline, with Honor's own eyes full upon me. I can almost fancy I hear her asking again, "Is it true you're going, James? You're not really going, James?"

Now, I am not the man to be frightened by a shadow, though that shadow be Honor Livingston, whom they say I as good as murdered. I always had a turn for investigating riddles, spiritual, physiological, and otherwise; and I shall follow this mystery up, and note whether she comes back to me year by year, as she promised. I have never kept a diary of personal matters before, not being one who cares to see spectres of himself, at remote periods of his life, talking to him again of his adventures and misadventures out of yellow old pages that had better never have been written; but this is a marked event worth commemorating, and a well-authenticated ghost-story to me who never believed in ghosts before.

It was a rather spiteful threat of Honor – "I'll haunt you till you come to the Ashenfall, where I'm going now!" I might have stopped her, but it never entered my mind what she meant, until it was done. I did not expect she would make a tragedy of a little love story; she did not look like that sort of thing. She was no ghost, bless her! in the flesh, but as round, rosy, dimpled a little creature as one would wish to see; and what could possess her to throw herself over the fall, Heaven only knows. Bah! Yes, / know; I need tell no lies here, I need not do any false swearing to myself – the poor little creature loved me, and I wanted her to love me, and I petted and plagued her into loving me, because I was idle, and I had the opportunity; and then I had nothing better to tell her than that I was only in jest— I could not marry her, for I was engaged to another woman. She would not believe it. That sounded, to her, more like jest than the other. And she did not believe it until she saw me making ready to go; and then, all in a moment, I suppose, madness seized her, and she neither knew where she went, nor what she did.

I fancy I can see her now, coming tripping down the fields leading her little brother by the hand, and I fancy I can see the saucy laugh she gave me over her shoulder as I asked her if she had any ripe cherries to sell. She looked the very mischief with those pretty eyes, and I was taken rather aback when she said, "I know you, Jemmy Lawrence." That was the beginning of it. Little Honor and her mother lived next door to mine, and she had not forgotten me though I had been full seven years away. I did not know her, the gipsy, but I must needs go in and see her that evening; and so we went on until I asked her if she remembered when we went to dame-school together and when she promised to be my little wife? *If* she remembered! Of course she did, every word of it, and more; and she was so pretty, and the lanes in the summer were so pleasant, that sometimes my fancy did play Anne Dalton false, and I believed I should like Honor better; and I said more than I meant, and she took it all in the grand serious manner.

I was not much to blame. I would not have injured her for the world; she was as good a little soul as ever lived. Love and jealousy, as passions, seem to find their strongholds under thatch. If Phillis, the milkmaid, is disappointed, she drowns herself in the mill-pool; if Lady Clara gets a cross of the heart, she indites a lachrymose sonnet, and marries a gouty peer. If Colin's sweetheart smiles on Lubin, Colin loads his gun and shoots them both; if Sir Harry's fair flouts him, he whistles her down the wind, and goes a-wooing elsewhere. Had little Honor been a fine lady, she would be living still. Oh, the pretty demure lips, and the shy glances and rosy blushes! When I saw Anne Dalton today I could not help comparing her frigid gentility with poor Honor. Anne loves herself better than she will ever love any man alive. But then I know she is the kind of wife to help a man up in the world, and that is the kind of wife for me.

Honor Livingston lying on her little bed, and her blind mother feeling her cold dead face! I wish I had never seen it. I would have given the world to keep away, but something compelled me to go in and look at her; and I did feel then, as it I had killed her. Last night she was a shadowy essence of this drowned Ophelia and of her living self. She was like, yet unlike; but I knew it was Honor; and I suppose, if she has her will, wherever her restless spirit may be condemned to bide between whiles—on the tenth of August she will always come back to me, and haunt me until I go to her.

**Hastings, August 11, 1830.**

Again! I had forgotten the day – forgotten everything about that wretched business of poor Honor Livingston, when last night I saw her.

Anne and I were sitting together out in the verandah, talking of all sorts of common-place things – our neighbours' affairs, money, this, that, and the other – the sea was looking beautiful, and I was on the point of proposing a row by moonlight, when Anne said, "How lovely the evenings are, James, in this place. Look at the sky over the down, how clear it is!" Turning my head, I saw Honor standing on the grass only a few paces off, her shadowy shape quite distinct against the reds and purples of the clouds.

Anne clutched my hand with a sudden cry, for she was looking at my face all the time, and asked me, passionately, what I saw. With that, Honor was gone, and, passing my hand over my

eyes, I put my wife off with an excuse about a spasm at my heart. And, indeed, it was no lie to say so, for this visitation gave me a terrible shock.

Anne insisted on my seeing the doctor. "It must be something dreadful, if not dangerous, that could make you look in that way; you had an awful face, James, for a moment."

I begged her not to talk about it, assured her that it was a thing of very rare recurrence with me, and that there was no cure for it. But this did not pacify her, and this morning no peace could be had until Dr. Hutchinson was sent for and she had given the old gentleman her own account of me. He said he would talk to me by-and-by. And when he got me by myself, I cannot tell how it was, but he absolutely contrived to worm the facts out of me, and I was fool enough to let him do it. He looked at me very oddly, with a sort of suspicious scrutiny in his eye; but I understood him, and said, laughing, "No, doctor, no, there is nothing wrong here," tapping my forehead as I spoke.

"I should say not, except this fancy for seeing ghosts," replied he, dryly. But I perceived, all the time he was with me, that I was the object of a furtive and carefully dissembled observation, which was excessively trying. I could with difficulty keep my temper under it, and I believe he saw the struggle.

I fancy he wanted to have some talk with Anne by herself; but I prevented that, by never losing sight of him until he was safely off the premises. If he proposed a private interview while I was out alone, I prevented that, too, by immediately ordering Anne to pack up our traps, and coming back to town that very day. I have not been well since. I feel out of spirits, bored, worried, sick of everything. If the feeling does not leave me, in spite of all Anne may say, I shall take that offer to go to South America, and start by the next packet. I should like to see Dr. Hutchinson's face when he calls at our lodgings to visit his patient, and finds the bird flown.

**London, August 20, 1830.**

This wretched state of things does not cease. One day I feel in full, firm, clear possession of my soul; and the next, perhaps, I am hurried to and fro with the most tormenting fancies. I see shadows of Honor wherever I turn, and she is no longer motionless as before, but beckons me with her hand, until I tremble in every limb. My heart is sick almost to death. For three days now, I have had no rest. I cannot sleep at nights for hideous dreams; and Anne watches me stealthily, I see, and never remains alone with me longer than she can help. I can perceive that she is afraid of me, and that she suspects something, without exactly knowing what. Today she must needs suggest my seeing a doctor here, and when I replied that I was going to South America, she told me I was not fit for it, in such a contemptuous tone of provocation that I lifted my hand and struck her. Then she quailed, and while shrinking under my eyes, she said, "James, your conduct is that of a madman!" Since then, I know she sits with me in silent terror, longing to escape and find some one to listen to her grievances. But I shall keep strict ward that she does nothing of the kind. I will not have my foes of my own household, and no spying relatives shall come between us to put asunder those whom God has joined together.

**Acapulco, March 17, 1831.**

It is six months since I wrote the above. In the interval I have been miserably ill, grievously tormented both in mind and body; but now that I have got safely away from them all, with the Atlantic between myself and my wicked wife, whose conduct towards me I will never forgive, I can collect my powers of mind, and bend them again to my work. Burton came out in the same ship with me to engage in the same enterprise. After a few days' rest we intend setting out on our journey to the mining districts, where we are to act. My head feels perfectly light and clear, all my impressions are distinct and vivid again, and I can get through a hard day's close study without inconvenience. There was nothing but my miserable liver to blame, and when that was set right, all my imaginary phantoms disappeared. Umpleby said it had been coming on gradually for months, and that there was nothing at all extraordinary in my delusions; my diseased state was one always so attended more or less. And Anne, in her cowardly malignity, would have consigned me for life to a lunatic asylum! It was Umpleby who saved me, and I have put his name down in my will for a handsome remembrance. As for Anne, she has chosen to return to her family, and they may keep her; she will never see my face again, of my free will, as long as I live.

The picturesqueness of this place is not noteworthy in any high degree. The harbour is enclosed by a chain of mountains, and has two entrances formed by the island of Roquetta; the castle of St. Diego commands the town and the bay, standing on a spur of the hills. Burton has been to and fro on his rambles ever since we landed; but I find the heat too great for much exertion, and when we begin our journey into the interior I shall have need of all my forces; therefore, better husband them now.

**Mexico, April 24, 1831.**

We are better off here than we anticipated. Burton has found an old fellow-pupil engaged as engineering tutor in the School of Mines, and there are civilised amusements which we neither of us had any hope of finding. The city is full of ancient relics, and Burton is on foot exploring, day by day. I prefer the living interests of this strange place, and sometimes early in the morning I betake myself to the market-place, and watch the Indians dress their stalls. No matter what they sell, they decorate their shops with fresh herbs and flowers until they are sheltered under a bower of verdure. They display their fruit in open basket-work, laying the pears and raisins below, and covering them above with odorous flowers. An artist might make a pretty picture here, when the Indians arrive at sunrise in their boats loaded with the produce of their floating gardens. Next week, Burton, his friend, and I, are to set out for the mines of Moran and Real del Monte. I should have preferred to delay our journey a while longer for reasons of my own, but Burton presses, and feels wo have already delayed longer than enough.

**Moran, July 4, 1831.**

I am sick of this place, but our business here is now on the verge of completion, and in a few days we start on our expedition to the mines of Guanamato. The director, Burton, and myself, are all of opinion that immense advantages are to be gained by improving the working of the mines, which is, at present, in a very defective condition. There is great mortality amongst the Indians, who are the beasts of burden of the mines; they carry on their backs, loads of metal of from two hundred and fifty to three hundred and fifty pounds at a time, ascending and descending thousands of steps, in files which contain old men of seventy, and mere children. I have not been very well here, having had some return of old symptoms, but under proper treatment they dispersed; however, I shall be thankful to be on the move again.

**Pascuaro, August 11, 1831.**

Can any man evade his thoughts, impalpable curses sitting on his heart, mocking like fiends? I cannot evade mine. All yesterday I was haunted by a terrible anxiety and dread. At every turn, at every moment, I expected to see Honor Livingston appear before me, but I did not see her. The day and the night passed, and I was freed from that great horror – how great I had not realised until its hour had gone and left no trace. This morning I am myself again; my spirits revive; I have escaped my enemy, and have proved that it was, indeed, but a subtle emanation of my own diseased body and mind. But these thoughts, these troublesome persistent thoughts, how combat them? Burton, very observant of me at all times, was yesterday watchful as an inquisitor; he said he hoped I was not going to have the frightful fever which is prevailing here, but I know he meant something else. I have not a doubt now, that Anne and all that confederacy warned him before we set sail, to beware of me, for I had been mad; that is the cursed lie they set abroad. Mad! All the world's mad, or on the way to it!

But if Honor had come back to me yesterday, we might have gone and have looked down together into hell, through the ovens of Jorulla. The missionaries cursed this frightful place, generations since; and it is accursed, if ever land was. Nothing more awful than this desolate burning waste, which the seas could not quench. When I remember it, and all I underwent yesterday, the confusion and horror return upon me again, and my brain swerves like the brain of a drunken man. I will write no more – sufficient to record that the appointed time came and went, and Honor Livingston did not keep her word with me.

**New Orleans, February, 1832.**

I left Burton still in Mexico, and came here alone. His care and considerateness were more than I could put up with, and after two or three ineffectual remonstrances, we came to a violent rupture, and I determined to throw up my engagement, rather than carry it out in conjunction with such a man. There was no avoiding the quarrel. Was I to be tutored day by day, and the wine-bottle removed out of my reach? He dared to tell me that when I was cool, clear – myself, in short – there was no man my master in our profession; but that when I had drunk freely I was unmanageable as a lunatic! A lie, of course; but unscrupulous persecutors are difficult to circumvent. Anne's malice pursues me even here. When I was out yesterday, my footsteps were dogged pertinaciously wherever I went, and perhaps an account of my doings will precede me home; but if they do, I defy them all to do their worst.

**Ashendell, August 9, 1839.**

This old book turned up today, amongst some traps that have lain by in London all the years that I have spent, first in Spain and afterwards in Russia. What fool's-talk it is; but I suppose it was true at the time. I know I was in a wretched condition while I was in Mexico and in the States, but I have been sane enough and sound enough ever since the illness I had at Baltimore. To prove how little hold on me my ancient horrors nave retained, I find myself at Ashendell in the very season of the year when Honor Livingston destroyed herself – tomorrow is the anniversary of her death. So I take my enemy by the throat, and crush him! These fantastical maladies will not stand against a determined will. At Moscow, at Cherson, at Archangel, the tenth of August has come and gone, unmarked. Honor failed of her threat everywhere except at Lisbon. I saw her there twice, just before we sailed. I saw her, when we were off that coast where we so nearly escaped wreck, rising and falling upon the waves. I saw her in London, that day I appointed to see Anne. But I know what it means: it means that I must put myself in Umpleby's hands for a few weeks, and that the shadows will forthwith vanish. Shadows they are, out of my own brain, and they take the shape of Honor because I have let her become a fixed idea in my mind. Yet it is very strange that the last time, she appeared to me, I heard her speak. I fancied she said that it was Almost time; and then louder, "I'll haunt you, James, until you come to the Ashenfall, where I am going now!" And with that she vanished. Fancy plays strange tricks with us, and makes cowards of us almost as cleverly as conscience.

**August 10.**

I have had a very unpleasant impression on me all day. I wish I had resisted Linchley's persuasions more steadily. I ought never to have come down here again. The excitement of its miserable recollections is too much for me. The man at the inn called me by my name this morning, and said he recollected me – looking up towards the church as he spoke. Damn him! All day I seem to have been acting against my will. What should possess me to go there, this afternoon? Round about among the graves, until I came to the grassy hillock on the north side of the church, where they buried Honor that night, without a prayer. I sat down on the low wall, and looked across to the hills beyond the river, listening to the monotonous sing-song of the fall. I would give all I possess today, to be able to tread back or to untread a score of the years of my life. It seems such a blank; of all I planned and schemed, how little have I accomplished! Watching by Honor's grave, I fell to thinking of her. What had either of us done that we should be so wretched? Is it part and parcel of the great injustice of life, that some must suffer so signally while others escape? The coarse grass is never cut at the north side of the church, nettles and brambles grow about the grave. Honor was mad, poor soul; they might have given her a prayer for rest, if they were forbidden to believe she died in hope. I prayed for her today – more need, perhaps, to pray for myself – and then there came a crazed whirl in my brain, and I set off to find Linchley. As I came down near the water, the fall sounded very tumultuous; it was sultry hot, and I should have liked to turn down by the river, but I said, "No, it is the tenth of August! If I am to meet Honor Livingston today, I'll not meet her by Ashenfall!" So I came home to our lodgings, to find that Linchley had gone over to Warfe, and had left a message that he should not return until tomorrow. I have the night before me alone; it is not like an English night at all; it is like the nights I remember at Cadiz, which always heralded a tremendous storm. And I think we shall have a storm here, too, before the morning.

\* \* \*

Those were the last words James Lawrence ever wrote, Gentlemen. Further than this, no man can speak of his death; it is plain to me that one of his mad fits was coming on before he left Lisbon; that it grew and increased until he came here; and that here it reached its climax and urged him to his death. I believe in the ghosts James Lawrence saw, as I believe in the haunting power of any great misdeed that has driven a fellow-creature into deadly sin.

When David Polreath had finished, the chairman gave the teetotum such a swift and sudden twirl, to be beforehand with any interruption, that it twirled among all the glasses and into all corners of the table, and finally, flew off the table and lodged in Captain Jorgan's waistcoat.

"A kind of a judgment!" said the captain, taking it out. "What's to be done now? *I* know no story, except Down Easters, and *they* didn't happen to myself, or any one of my acquaintance, and you couldn't enjoy 'em without going out of your minds first. And perhaps the company ain't prepared to do that?"

The chairman interposed by rising and declaring it to be his perroud perrivilege to stop preliminary observations.

"Wa'al," said the captain, "I defer to the President which an't at all what they do in my country, where they lay into him, head, limbs, and body." Here he slapped his leg. "But I beg to ask a preliminary question. Colonel Polreath has read from a diary. Might I read from a pipe-light?"

The chairman requested explanation.

"The history of the pipe-light," said the captain, "is just this: that it's verses, and was made on the voyage home by a passenger I brought over. And he was a quiet crittur of a middle-aged man with a pleasant countenance. And he wrote it on the head of a cask. And he was a most etarnal time about it tew. And he blotted it as if he had wrote it in a continual squall of ink. And then he took an indigestion, and I physicked him for want of a better doctor. And then to show his liking for me he copied it out fair, and gave it to me for a pipe-light. And it ain't been lighted yet, and that's a fact."

"Let it be read," said the chairman.

"With thanks to Colonel Polreath for setting the example," pursued the captain, "and with apologies to the Honourable A. Parvis and the whole of the present company for this passenger's having expressed his mind in verses – which he may have done along of bein' sea-sick, and he was very – the pipe-light, unrolled, comes to this:

> WE sit by the fire so wide and red,
> With the dance of the young within,
> Who have yet small learning of cold and dread,
> And of sorrow no more than of sin;
> Nor dream of a night on a sleepless bed
> Of waves, with their terrible wrecks o'erspread.
> We sit round the hearth as red as gold,
> And the legends beloved we tell,
> How battles were won by the nobles bold,
> Where hamlets of villains fell:
> And we praise our God, while we cut the bread,
> And share the wine round, for our heroes dead.
> And we talk of the Kings, those strong proud men,
> Who ravaged, confessed, and died;

*And of churls who rabbled them oft and again,*
*Perchance with a kindred pride—*
*Though the Kings built churches to pierce the sky,*
*And the rabbling churls in the cross-road lie.*
*Yet 'twixt the despot and slave half-free,*
*Old Truth may have message clear;*
*Since the hard black yew, and the lithe young tree,*
*Belong to an age – and a year,*
*And though distant in might and in leaf they be,*
*In right of the woods, they are near.*

And old Truth's message, perchance, may be:

*"Believe in thy kind, whate'er the degree,*
*Be it King on his throne, or serf on his knee,*
*While Our Lord showers light, in his bounty free,*
*On the rock and the vale – on the sand and the sea."*
*They are singing within, with their voices dear,*
*To tunes which are dear as well;*
*And we sit and dream while the words we hear,*
*Having tale of our own to tell—*
*Of a far midnight on the terrible sea,*
*Which comes back on the tune of their blithe old glee.*
*As old as the hills, and as old as the sky,—*
*As the King on his throne, – as the serf on his knee,*
*A song wherein rich can with poor agree,*
*With its chorus to make them laugh or cry—*
*Which the young are singing, with no thought nigh,*
*Of a night on a terrible sea:*
*"I care for nobody; no, not I,*
*Since nobody cares for me."*
*The storm had its will. There was wreck – there was*
*flight O'er an ocean of Alps, through the pitch-black*
*night, When a good ship sank, and a few got free,*
*To cope in their boat with the terrible sea.*
*And when the day broke, there was blood on the sea,*
*From the wild hot eye of the sun outshed,*
*For the heaven was a-flame as with fire from Hell,*
*And a scorching calm on the waters fell,*
*As if Ruin had won, and with fiendish glee,*
*Sailed forth in his galley to number the dead.*
*And they rowed their boat o'er the terrible sea,*
*As mute as a crew made of ghosts might be:*
*For the best in his heart had not manhood to say,*
*That the land was five hundred miles away.*
*A day – and a week – There was bread for one man;*
*The water was dry. And on this, the few*

Who were rowing their boat o'er the terrible sea,
To murmur, to curse, and to crave began.
And how 'twas agreed on, no one knew,
But the feeble and famished and scorched by the sun,
With his pitiless eye, drew lots to agree,
What their hideous morrow of meat must be.
O then were the faces frightful to read,
Of ravening hope, and of cowardly pride
That lies to the last, its sharp terror to hide;
And a stillness as though 'twere some game of the Dead,
While they waited the number their lot to decide—
There were nine in that boat on the terrible sea,
And he who drew NINE, was the victim to be.
You may think what a ghastly shiver there ran,
From mate to his mate, as the doom began.
SIX – had a wife with a wild rose cheek;
TWO – a brave boy, not a year yet old;
EIGHT – his last sister, lame and weak,
Who quivered with palsy more than with cold.
You may think what a breath the respited drew,
And how wildly still, sat the rest of the crew;
How the voice as it called spoke hoarser and slower;
The number it next dared to speak was – FOUR.
'Twas the rude black man, who had handled an oar
The best on that terrible sea of the few.
And ugly and grim in the sunshine glare
Were his thick parched lip, and his dull small eyes,
And the tangled fleece of his rusty hair—
'Ere the next of the breathless the death-lot drew,
His shout like a sword pierced the silence through.
"Let the play end, with your Number Four.
What need to draw? Live along, you few
Who have hopes to save and have wives to cry
O'er the cradles of children free!
What matter if folk without home should die.
And be eaten by land or sea?
I care for nobody; no, not I,
Since nobody cares for me!"
And with that, a knife – and a heart struck through—
And the warm red blood, and the cold black clay,
And the famine withdrawn from among the few,
By their horrible meal for another day!
So the eight, thus fed, came at last to land,
And the tale of their shipmate told,
As of water found in the burning sand,
Which braves not the thirsty, cold.
But the love of the listener, safe and free,

*Goes forth to that slave on that terrible sea.*
*For, fancies from hearth and from home will stray,*
*Though within are the dance and the song;*
*And a grave tale told, if the tune be gay,*
*Says little to scare the young.*
*While they sing, with their voices clear as can be,*
*Having called, once more, for the blithe old glee—*
*"I care for nobody, no, not I,*
*Since nobody cares for me."*
*But the careless tune, it saith to the old,*
*Who sit by the hearth as red as gold,*
*When they think of their tale of the terrible sea:*
*"Believe in thy kind, whate'er the degree, Be it King on his throne, or serf on*
*his knee, While Our Lord showert good from his bounty free, Over storm, over*
*calm, over land, over sea."*

Mr. Parvis had so greatly disquieted the minds of the Gentlemen King Arthurs for some minutes, by snoring with strong symptoms of apoplexy – which, in a mild form, was his normal state of health – that it was now deemed expedient to wake him and entreat him to allow himself to be escorted home. Mr. Parvis's reply to this friendly suggestion could not be placed on record without the aid of several dashes, and is therefore omitted. It was conceived in a spirit of the profoundest irritation, and executed with vehemence, contempt, scorn, and disgust. There was nothing for it, but to let the excellent gentleman alone, and he fell without loss of time into a defiant slumber.

The teetotum being twirled again, so buzzed and bowed in the direction of the young fisherman, that Captain Jorgan advised him to be bright and prepare for the worst. But, it started off at a tangent, late in its career, and fell before a well-looking bearded man (one who made working drawings for machinery, the captain was informed by his next neighbour), who promptly took it up like a challenger's glove.

"Oswald Penrewen!" said the chairman.

"Here's Unchris'en at last!" the captain whispered Alfred Raybrock. "Unchris'en goes ahead, right smart; don't he?"

He did, without one introductory word.

MINE is my brother's Ghost Story. It happened to my brother about thirty years ago, while he was wandering, sketch-book in hand, among the High Alps, picking up subjects for an illustrated work on Switzerland. Having entered the Oberland by the Brunig Pass, and filled his portfolio with what he used to call "bits" from the neighbourhood of Meyringen, he went over the Great Scheideck to Grindlewald, where he arrived one dusky September evening, about three-quarters of an hour after sunset. There had been a fair that day, and the place was crowded. In the best inn there was not an inch of space to spare – there were only two inns at Grindlewald, thirty years ago – so my brother went to one at the end of the covered bridge next the church, and there, with some difficulty, obtained the promise of a pile of rugs and a mattress, in a room which was already occupied by three other travellers.

The Adler was a primitive hostelry, half farm, half inn, with great rambling galleries outside, and a huge general room, like a barn. At the upper end of this room stood long stoves, like metal counters, laden with steaming-pans, and glowing underneath like furnaces. At the lower end, smoking, supping, and chatting, were congregated some thirty or forty guests, chiefly mountaineers, char drivers, and guides. Among these my brother took his seat, and was served, like the rest, with a bowl of soup, a platter of beef, a flagon of country wine, and a loaf made of Indian corn. Presently, a huge St. Bernard dog came and laid his nose upon my brother's arm. In the mean time he fell into conversation with two Italian youths, bronzed and dark-eyed, near whom he happened to be seated. They were Florentines. Their names, they told him, were Stefano and Battisto. They had been travelling for some months on commission, selling cameos, mosaics, sulphur casts, and the like pretty Italian trifles, and were now on their way to Interlaken and Geneva. Weary of the cold North, they longed, like children, for the moment which should take them back to their own blue hills and grey-green olives; to their workshop on the Ponte Vecchio, and their home down by the Arno.

It was quite a relief to my brother, on going up to bed, to find that these youths were to be two of his fellow-lodgers. The third was already there, and sound asleep, with his face to the wall. They scarcely looked at this third. They were all tired, and all anxious to rise at daybreak, having agreed to walk together over the Wengern Alp as far as Lauterbrunnen. So, my brother and the two youths exchanged a brief good night, and, before many minutes, were all as far away in the land of dreams as their unknown companion.

My brother slept profoundly – so profoundly that, being roused in the morning by a clamour of merry voices, he sat up dreamily in his rugs, and wondered where he was.

"Good day, signor," cried Battisto. "Here is a fellow-traveller going the same way as ourselves."

"Christien Baumann, native of Kandersteg, musical-box maker by trade, stands five feet eleven in his shoes, and is at monsieur's service to command," said the sleeper of the night before.

He was as fine a young fellow as one would wish to see. Light, and strong, and well proportioned, with curling brown hair, and bright, honest eyes that seemed to dance at every word he uttered.

"Good morning," said my brother. "You were asleep last night when we came up."

"Asleep! I should think so, after being all day in the fair, and walking from Meyringen the evening before. What a capital fair it was!"

"Capital, indeed," said Battisto. "We sold cameos and mosaics yesterday, for nearly fifty francs."

"Oh, you sell cameos and mosaics, you two! Show me your cameos, and I will show you my musical boxes. I have such pretty ones, with coloured views of Geneva and Chillon on the lids, playing two, four, six, and even eight tunes. Bah! I will give you a concert!"

And with this he unstrapped his pack, displayed his little boxes on the table, and wound them up, one after the other, to the delight of the Italians.

"I helped to make them myself, every one," said he, proudly. "Is it not pretty music? I sometimes set one of them when I go to bed at night, and fall asleep listening to it. I am sure, then, to have pleasant dreams! But let us see your cameos. Perhaps I may buy one for Marie, if they are not too dear. Marie is my sweetheart, and we are to be married next week."

"Next week!" exclaimed Stefano. "That is very soon. Battisto has a sweetheart also, up at Impruneta; but they will have to wait a long time before they can buy the ring."

Battisto blushed like a girl.

"Hush, brother!" said he. "Show the cameos to Christien, and give your tongue a holiday!"

But Christien was not so to be put off.

"What is her name?" said he. "Tush! Battisto, you must tell me her name! Is she pretty? Is she dark, or fair? Do you often see her when you are at home? Is she very fond of you? Is she as fond of you as Marie is of me?"

"Nay, how should I know that?" asked the soberer Battisto. "She loves me, and I love her – that is all."

"And her name?"

"Margherita."

"A charming name! And she is herself as pretty as her name, I'll engage. Did you say she was fair?"

"I said nothing about it one way or the other," said Battisto, unlocking a green box clamped with iron, and taking out tray after tray of his pretty wares. "There! Those pictures all inlaid in little bits are Roman mosaics – these flowers on a black ground are Florentine. The ground is of hard dark stone, and the flowers are made of thin slices of jasper, onyx, cornelian, and so forth. Those forget-me-nots, for instance, are bits of turquoise, and that poppy is cut from a piece of coral."

"I like the Roman ones best," said Christien. "What place is that with all the arches?"

"This is the Coliseum, and the one next to it is St. Peter's. But we Florentines care little for the Roman work. It is not half so fine or so valuable as ours. The Romans make their mosaics of composition."

"Composition or no, I like the little landscapes best," said Christien. "There is a lovely one, with a pointed building, and a tree, and mountains at the back. How I should like that one for Marie!"

"You may have it for eight francs," replied Battisto; "we sold two of them yesterday for ten each, it represents the tomb of Caius Cestius, near Rome."

"A tomb!" echoed Christien, considerably dismayed. "Diable! That would be a dismal present to one's bride."

"She would never guess that it was a tomb, if you did not tell her," suggested Stefano. Christien shook his head.

"That would be next door to deceiving her," said he.

"Nay," interposed my brother, "the owner of that tomb has been dead these eighteen or nineteen hundred years. One almost forgets that he was ever buried in it."

"Eighteen or nineteen hundred years? Then he was a heathen?"

"Undoubtedly, if by that you mean that he lived before Christ."

Christien's face lighted up immediately.

"Oh, that settles the question," said he, pulling out his little canvas purse, and paying his money down at once. "A heathen's tomb is as good as no tomb at all. I'll have it made into a brooch for her, at Interlaken. Tell me, Battisto, what shall you take home to Italy for your Margherita?"

Battisto, laughed, and chinked his eight francs. "That depends on trade," said he; "if we make good profits between this and Christmas, I may take her a Swiss muslin from Berne; but we have already been away seven months, and we have hardly made a hundred francs over and above our expenses."

And with this, the talk turned upon general matters, the Florentines locked away their treasures, Christien restrapped his pack, and my brother and all went down together, and breakfasted in the open air outside the inn.

It was a magnificent morning; cloudless and sunny, with a cool breeze that rustled in the vine upon the porch, and flecked the table with shifting shadows of green leaves. All around and about them stood the great mountains, with their blue-white glaciers bristling down to the verge of the pastures, and the pine-woods creeping darkly up their sides. To the left, the Wetterhorn; to the right, the Eigher; straight before them, dazzling and imperishable, like an obelisk of frosted silver, the Schreckhorn, or Peak of Terror. Breakfast over, they bade farewell to their hostess, and, mountain-staff in hand, took the path to the Wengern Alp. Half in light, half in shadow, lay the quiet valley, dotted over with farms, and traversed by a torrent that rushed, milk-white, from its prison in the glacier. The three lads walked briskly in advance, their voices chiming together every now and then in chorus of laughter. Somehow my brother felt sad. He lingered behind, and, plucking a little red flower from the bank, watched it hurry away with the torrent, like a life on the stream of time. Why was his heart so heavy, and why were their hearts so light?

As the day went on, my brother's melancholy, and the mirth of the young men, seemed to increase. Full of youth and hope, they talked of the joyous future, and built up pleasant castles in the air. Battisto, grown more communicative, admitted that to marry Margherita, and become a master mosaicist, would fulfil the dearest dream of his life. Stefano, not being in love, preferred to travel. Christien, who seemed to be the most prosperous, declared that it was his darling ambition to rent a farm in his native Kander Valley, and lead the patriarchal life of his fathers. As for the musical-box trade, he said, one should live in Geneva to make it answer; and, for his part, he loved the pine-forests and the snow-peaks, better than all the towns in Europe. Marie, too, had been born among the mountains, and it would break her heart, if she thought she were to live in Geneva all her life, and never see the Kander Thal again. Chatting thus, the morning wore on to noon, and the party rested awhile in the shade of a clump of gigantic firs festooned with trailing banners of grey-green moss.

Here they ate their lunch, to the silvery music of one of Christien's little boxes, and by-and-by heard the sullen echo of an avalanche far away on the shoulder of the Jungfrau.

Then they went on again in the burning afternoon, to heights where the Alp-rose fails from the sterile steep, and the brown lichen grows more and more scantily among the stones. Here, only the bleached and barren skeletons of a forest of pines varied the desolate monotony; and high on the summit of the pass, stood a little solitary inn, between them and the sky.

At this inn they rested again, and drank to the health of Christien and his bride, in a jug of country wine. He was in uncontrollable spirits and shook hands with them all, over and over again.

"By nightfall tomorrow," said he, "I shall hold her once more in my arms! It is now nearly two years since I came home to see her, at the end of my apprenticeship. Now I am foreman, with a salary of thirty francs a week, and well able to marry."

"Thirty francs a week!" echoed Battisto. "Corpo di Bacco! that is a little fortune."
Christien's face beamed.

"Yes," said he, "we shall be very happy; and, by-and-by – who knows? – we may end our days in the Kander Thal, and bring up our children to succeed us. Ah! If Marie knew that I should be there tomorrow night, how delighted she would be!"

"How so, Christien?" said my brother. "Does she not expect you?"

"Not a bit of it. She has no idea that I can be there till the day after tomorrow – nor could I, if I took the road all round by Unterseen and Frütigen. I mean to sleep to-night at Lauterbrunnen, and tomorrow morning shall strike across the Tschlingel glacier to Kandersteg. If I rise a little before daybreak, I shall be at home by sunset."

At this moment the path took a sudden turn, and began to descend in sight of an immense perspective of very distant valleys. Christien flung his cap into the air, and uttered a great shout.

"Look!" said he, stretching out his arms as if to embrace all the dear familiar scene: "O! Look! There are the hills and woods of Interlaken, and here, below the precipices on which we stand, lies Lauterbrunnen! God be praised, who has made our native land so beautiful!"

The Italians smiled at each other, thinking their own Arno valley far more fair; but my brother's heart warmed to the boy, and echoed his thanksgiving in that spirit which accepts all beauty as a birthright and an inheritance. And now their course lay across an immense plateau, all rich with corn-fields and meadows, and studded with substantial homesteads built of old brown wood, with huge sheltering eaves, and strings of Indian corn hanging like golden ingots along the carven balconies. Blue whortleberries grew beside the footway, and now and then they came upon a wild gentian, or a star-shaped immortelle. Then the path became a mere zigzag on the face of the precipice, and in less than half an hour they reached the lowest level of the valley. The glowing afternoon had not yet faded from the uppermost pines, when they were all dining together in the parlour of a little inn looking to the Jungfrau. In the evening my brother wrote letters, while the three lads strolled about the village. At nine o'clock they bade each other good night, and went to their several rooms.

Weary as he was, my brother found it impossible to sleep. The same unaccountable melancholy still possessed him, and when at last he dropped into an uneasy slumber, it was but to start over and over again from frightful dreams, faint with a nameless terror. Towards morning, he fell into a profound sleep, and never woke until the day was fast advancing towards noon. He then found, to his regret, that Christien had long since gone. He had risen before daybreak, breakfasted by candlelight, and started off in the grey dawn – "as merry," said the host, "as a fiddler at a fair."

Stefano and Battisto were still waiting to see my brother, being charged by Christien with a friendly farewell message to him, and an invitation to the wedding. They, too, were asked, and meant to go; so, my brother agreed to meet them at Interlaken on the following Tuesday, whence they might walk to Kandersteg by easy stages, reaching their destination on the Thursday morning, in time to go to church with the bridal party. My brother then bought some of the little Florentine cameos, wished the two boys every good fortune, and watched them down the road till he could see them no longer.

Left now to himself, he wandered out with his sketch-book, and spent the day in the upper valley; at sunset, he dined alone in his chamber, by the light of a single lamp. This meal despatched, he drew nearer to the fire, took out a pocket edition of Goethe's Essays on Art, and promised himself some hours of pleasant reading. (Ah, how well I know that very book, in its faded cover, and how often I have heard him describe that lonely evening!) The night had by this time set in cold and wet. The damp logs spluttered on the hearth, and a wailing wind swept down the valley, bearing the rain in sudden gusts against the panes. My brother soon found that to read was impossible. His attention wandered incessantly. He read the same sentence over and over again, unconscious of its meaning, and fell into long trains of thought leading far into the dim past.

Thus the hours went by, and at eleven o'clock he heard the doors closing below, and the household retiring to rest. He determined to yield no longer to this dreaming apathy. He threw on fresh logs, trimmed the lamp, and took several turns about the room. Then he opened the casement, and suffered the rain to beat against his face, and the wind to ruffle his hair, as it ruffled the acacia leaves in the garden below. Some minutes passed thus, and when, at length, he closed the window and came back into the room, his face and hair and all the front of his shirt were thoroughly saturated. To unstrap his knapsack and take out a dry shirt was, of course, his first impulse – to drop the garment, listen eagerly, and start to his feet, breathless and bewildered, was the next.

For, borne fitfully upon the outer breeze, now sweeping past the window, now dying in the distance, he heard a well-remembered strain of melody, subtle and silvery as the "sweet airs" of Prospero's isle, and proceeding unmistakably, from the musical-box which had, the day before, accompanied the lunch under the fir-trees of the Wengern Alp!

Had Christien come back, and was it thus that he announced his return? If so, where was he? Under the window? Outside in the corridor? Sheltering in the porch, and waiting for admittance? My brother threw open the casement again, and called him by his name.

"Christien! Is that you?"

All without was intensely silent. He could hear the last gust of wind and rain moaning farther and farther away upon its wild course down the valley, and the pine trees shivering, like living things.

"Christien!" he said again, and his own voice seemed to echo strangely on his ear. "Speak! Is it you?"

Still no one answered. He leaned out into the dark night; but could see nothing – not even the outline of the porch below. He began to think that his imagination had deceived him, when suddenly the strain burst forth again; – this time, apparently in his own chamber.

As he turned, expecting to find Christien at his elbow, the sounds broke off abruptly, and a sensation of intensest cold seized him in every limb – not the mere chill of nervous terror, not the mere physical result of exposure to wind and rain, but a deadly freezing of every vein, a paralysis of every nerve, an appalling consciousness that in a few moments more the lungs must cease to play, and the heart to beat! Powerless to speak or stir, he closed his eyes, and believed that he was dying.

This strange faintness lasted but a few seconds. Gradually the vital warmth returned, and, with it, strength to close the window, and stagger to a chair. As he did so, he found the breast of his shirt all stiff and frozen, and the rain clinging in solid icicles upon his hair.

He looked at his watch. It had stopped at twenty minutes before twelve. He took his thermometer from the chimney-piece, and found the mercury at sixty-eight. Heavenly powers! How were these things possible in a temperature of sixty-eight degrees, and with a large fire blazing on the hearth?

He poured out half a tumbler of cognac, and drank it at a draught. Going to bed was out of the question. He felt that he dared not sleep —that he scarcely dared to think. All he could do, was, to change his linen, pile on more logs, wrap himself in his blankets, and sit all night in an easy-chair before the fire.

My brother had not long sat thus, however, before the warmth, and probably the nervous reaction, drew him off to sleep. In the morning he found himself lying on the bed, without being able to remember in the least how or when he reached it.

It was again a glorious day. The rain and wind were gone, and the Silverhorn at the end of the valley lifted its head into an unclouded sky. Looking out upon the sunshine, he almost doubted the events of the night, and, but for the evidence of his watch, which still pointed to twenty minutes before twelve, would have been disposed to treat the whole matter as a dream. As it was, he attributed more than half his terrors to the prompting of an over-active and over-wearied brain. For all this, he still felt depressed and uneasy, and so very unwilling to pass another night at Lauterbrunnen, that he made up his mind to proceed that morning to Interlaken. While he was yet loitering over his breakfast, and considering whether he should walk the miles of road, or hire a vehicle, a char came rapidly up to the inn door, and a young man jumped out.

"Why, Battisto!" exclaimed my brother, in astonishment, as he came into the room; "what brings you here today? Where is Stefano?"

"I have left him at Interlaken, signor," replied the Italian.

Something there was in his voice, something in his face, both strange and startling.

"What is the matter?" asked my brother, breathlessly. "He is not ill? No accident has happened?"

Battisto shook his head, glanced furtively up and down the passage, and closed the door.

"Stefano is well, signor; but – but a circumstance has occurred – a circumstance so strange! Signor, do you believe in spirits?"

"In spirits, Battisto?"

"Ay, signor; for if ever the spirit of any man, dead or living, appealed to human ears, the spirit of Christien came to me last night, at twenty minutes before twelve o'clock."

"At twenty minutes before twelve o'clock!" repeated my brother.

"I was in bed, signor, and Stefano was sleeping in the same room. I had gone up quite warm, and had fallen asleep, full of pleasant thoughts. By-and-by, although I had plenty of bed-clothes, and a rug over me as well, I woke, frozen with cold and scarcely able to breathe. I tried to call to Stefano; but I had no power to utter the slightest sound. I thought my last moment was come. All at once, I heard a sound under the window – a sound which I knew to be Christien's musical box; and it played as it played when we lunched under the fir-trees, except that it was more wild and strange and melancholy and most solemn to hear – awful to hear! Then, signor, it grew fainter and fainter – and then it seemed to float past upon the wind, and die away. When it ceased, my frozen blood grew warm again, and I cried out to Stefano. When I told him what had happened, he declared I had been only dreaming. I made him strike a light, that I might look at my watch. It pointed to twenty minutes before twelve, and had stopped there; and – stranger stil – Stefano's watch had done the very same. Now tell me, signor, do you believe that there is any meaning in this, or do you think, as Stefano persists in thinking, that it was all a dream?"

"What is your own conclusion, Battisto?"

"My conclusion, signor, is that some harm has happened to poor Christien on the glacier, and that his spirit came to me last night."

"Battisto, he shall have help if living, or rescue for his poor corpse if dead; for I, too, believe that all is not well."

And with this, my brother told him briefly what had occurred to himself in the night; despatched messengers for the three best guides in Lauterbrunnen; and prepared ropes, ice-hatchets, alpenstocks, and all such matters necessary for a glacier expedition. Hasten as he would, however, it was nearly mid-day before the party started.

Arriving in about half an hour at a place called Stechelberg, they left the char, in which they had travelled so far, at a chalet, and ascended a steep path in full view of the Breithorn glacier, which rose up to the left, like a battlemented wall of solid ice. The way now lay for some time among pastures and pine-forests. Then they came to a little colony of chalets, called Steinberg, where they filled their water-bottles, got their ropes in readiness, and prepared for the Tschlingel glacier. A few minutes more, and they were on the ice.

At this point, the guides called a halt, and consulted together. One was for striking across the lower glacier towards the left, and reaching the upper glacier by the rocks which bound it on the south. The other two preferred the north, or right side; and this my brother finally took. The sun was now pouring down with almost tropical intensity, and the surface of the ice, which was broken into long treacherous fissures, smooth as glass and blue as the summer sky, was both difficult and dangerous. Silently and cautiously, they went, tied together at intervals of about three yards each: with two guides in front, and the third bringing up the rear. Turning presently to the right, they found themselves at the foot of a steep rock, some forty feet in height, up which they must climb to reach the upper glacier. The only way in which Battisto or my brother could hope to do this, was by the help of a rope steadied from below and above. Two of the guides accordingly clambered up the face of the crag by notches in the surface, and one remained below. The rope was then let down, and my brother prepared to go first. As he planted his foot in the first notch, a smothered cry from Battisto arrested him.

"Santa Maria! Signor! Look yonder!"

My brother looked, and there (he ever afterwards declared), as surely as there is a heaven above us all, he saw Christien Baumann standing in the full sunlight, not a hundred yards distant! Almost in the same moment that my brother recognised him, he was gone. He neither faded, nor sank down, nor moved away; but was simply gone, as if he had never been. Pale as death, Battisto fell upon his knees, and covered his face with his hands. My brother, awe-stricken and speechless, leaned against the rock, and felt that the object of his journey was but too fatally accomplished. As for the guides, they could not con-ceive what had happened.

"Did you see nothing?" asked my brother and Battisto, both together.

But the men had seen nothing, and the one who had remained below, said, "What should I see but the ice and the sun?"

To this my brother made no other reply than by announcing his intention to have a certain crevasse, from which he had not once removed his eyes since he saw the figure standing on the brink, thoroughly explored before he went a step farther; whereupon the two men came down from the top of the crag, resumed the ropes, and followed my brother, incredulously. At the narrow end of the fissure, he paused, and drove his alpenstock firmly into the ice. It was an unusually long crevasse – at first a mere crack, but widening gradually as it went, and reaching down to unknown depths of dark deep blue, fringed with long pendent icicles, like diamond stalactites. Before they had followed the course of this crevasse for more than ten minutes, the youngest of the guides uttered a hasty exclamation.

"I see something!" cried he. "Something dark, wedged in the teeth of the crevasse, a great way down!"

They all saw it: a mere indistinguishable mass, almost closed over by the ice-walls at their feet. My brother offered a hundred francs to the man who would go down and bring it up. They all hesitated.

"We don't know what it is," said one.

"Perhaps it is only a dead chamois," suggested another.

Their apathy enraged him.

"It is no chamois," he said, angrily. "It is the body of Christien Baumann, native of Kandersteg. And, by Heaven, if you are all too cowardly to make the attempt, I will go down myself!"

The youngest guide threw off his hat and coat, tied a rope about his waist, and took a hatchet in his hand.

"I will go, monsieur," said he; and without another word, suffered himself to be lowered in. My brother turned away. A sickening anxiety came upon him, and presently he heard the dull echo of the hatchet far down in the ice. Then there was a call for another rope, and then – the men all drew aside in silence, and my brother saw the youngest guide standing once more beside the chasm, flushed and trembling, with the body of Christien lying at his feet.

Poor Christien! They made a rough bier with their ropes and alpenstocks, and carried him, with great difficulty, back to Steinberg. There, they got additional help as far as Stechelberg, where they laid him in the char, and so brought him on to Lauterbrunnen. The next day, my brother made it his sad business to precede the body to Kandersteg, and prepare his friends for its arrival. To this day, though all these things happened thirty years ago, he cannot bear to recal Marie's despair, or all the mourning that he innocently brought upon that peaceful valley. Poor Marie has been dead this many a year; and when my brother last passed through the Kander Thal on his way to the Ghemmi, he saw her grave, beside the grave of Christien Baumann, in the village burial-ground.

This is my brother's Ghost Story.

The chairman now announced that the clock declared the teetotum spun out, and that the meeting was dissolved. Yet even then, the young fisherman could not refrain from once more asking his question. This occasioned the Gentlemen King Arthurs, as they got on their hats and great coats, evidently to regard him as a young fisherman who was touched in his head, and some of them even cherished the idea that the captain was his keeper.

As no man dared to awake the mighty Parvis, it was resolved that a heavy member of the society should fall against him as it were by accident, and immediately withdraw to a safe distance. The experiment was so happily accomplished, that Mr. Parvis started to his feet on the best terms with himself, as a light sleeper whose wits never left him, and who could always be broad awake on occasion. Quite an airy jocundity sat upon this respectable man in consequence. And he rallied the briskest member of the fraternity on being "a sleepy-head," with an amount of humour previously supposed to be quite incompatible with his responsible circumstances in life.

Gradually, the society departed into the cold night, and the captain and his young companion were left alone. The captain had so refreshed himself by shaking hands with everybody to an amazing extent, that he was in no hurry to go to bed.

"Tomorrow morning," said the captain, "we must find out the lawyer and the clergyman here; they are the people to consult on our business. And I'll be up and out early, and asking questions of everybody I see; thereby propagating at least one of the Institutions of my native country."

As the captain was slapping his leg, the landlord appeared with two small candlesticks.

"Your room," said he, "is at the top of the house. An excellent bed, but you'll hear the wind."

"I've heerd it afore," replied the captain. "Come and make a passage with me, and you shall hear it."

"It's considered to blow, here," said the landlord.

"Weather gets its young strength here," replied the captain; "goes into training for the Atlantic Ocean. Yours are little winds just beginning to feel their way and crawl. Make a voyage with me, and I'll show you a grown-up one out on business. But you haven't told my friend where he lies."

"It's the room at the head of the stairs, before you take the second staircase through the wall," returned the landlord. "You can't mistake it. It's a double-bedded room, because there's no other."

"The room where the seafaring man is?" said the captain.

"The room where the seafaring man is."

"I hope he mayn't finish telling his story in his sleep, remarked the captain. "Shall *I* turn into the room where the seafaring man is, Alfred?"

"No, Captain Jorgan, why should you? There would be little fear of his waking me, even if he told his whole story out."

"He's in the bed nearest the door," said the landlord. "I've been in to look at him, once, and he's sound enough. Good night, gentlemen."

The captain immediately shook hands with the landlord in quite an enthusiastic manner, and having performed that national ceremony, as if he had had no opportunity of performing it for a long time, accompanied his young friend up-stairs.

"Something tells me," said the captain as they went, "that Miss Kitty Tregarthen's marriage ain't put off for long, and that we shall light on what we want."

"I hope so. When, do you think?"

"Wa'al, I couldn't just say when, but soon. Here's your room," said the captain, softly opening the door and looking in; "and here's the berth of the seafaring man. I wonder what like he is. He breathes deep; don't he?"

"Sleeping like a child, to judge from the sound," said the young fisherman.

"Dreaming of home, maybe," returned the captain. "Can't see him. Sleeps a deal more wholesomely than Arson Parvis, but a'most as sound; don't he? Good night, fellow-traveller."

"Good night, Captain Jorgan, and many, many thanks!"

"I'll wait till I 'arn 'em, boy, afore I take 'em," returned the captain, clapping him cheerfully on the back. "Pleasant dreams of – you know who!"

When the young fisherman had closed the door, the captain waited a moment or two, listening for any stir on the part of the unknown seafaring man. But, none being audible, the captain pursued the way to his own chamber.

## Chapter IV
## The Seafaring Man

**WHO WAS THE** Seafaring Man? And what might he have to say for himself? He answers those questions in his own words:

I begin by mentioning what happened on my journey, northwards, from Falmouth in Cornwall, to Steepways in Devonshire. I have no occasion to say (being here) that it brought me last night to Lanrean. I had business in hand which was part very serious, and part (as I hoped) very joyful – and this business, you will please to remember, was the cause of my journey.

After landing at Falmouth, I travelled on foot: because of the expense of riding, and because I had anxieties heavy on my mind, and walking was the best way I knew of to lighten them. The first two days of my journey the weather was fine and soft, the wind being mostly light airs from south, and south and by west. On the third day, I took a wrong turning, and had to fetch a long circuit to get right again. Towards evening, while I was still on the road, the wind shifted; and a sea-fog came rolling in on the land. I went on through, what I ask leave to call, the white darkness; keeping the sound of the sea on my left hand for a guide, and feeling those anxieties of mine before mentioned, pulling heavier and heavier at my mind, as the fog thickened and the wet trickled down my face.

It was still early in the evening, when I heard a dog bark, away in the distance, on the right-hand side of me. Following the sound as well as I could, and shouting to the dog, from time to time, to set him barking again, I stumbled up at last against the back of a house; and, hearing voices inside, groped my way round to the door, and knocked on it smartly with the flat of my hand.

The door was opened by a slip-slop young hussey in a torn gown; and the first inquiries I made of her discovered to me that the house was an inn.

Before I could ask more questions, the landlord opened the parlour door of the inn and came out. A clamour of voices, and a fine comforting smell of fire and grog and tobacco, came out, also, along with him.

"The taproom fire's out, says the landlord. "You don't think you would dry more comfortable, like, if you went to bed?" says he, looking hard at me.

"No," says I, looking hard at *him*; "I don't."

Before more words were spoken, a jolly voice hailed us from inside the parlour.

"What's the matter, landlord?" says the jolly voice. "Who is it?"

"A seafaring man, by the looks of him," says the landlord, turning round from me, and speaking into the parlour.

"Let's have the seafaring man in," says the voice. "Let's vote him free of the Club, for this night only."

A lot of other voices thereupon said, "Hear! hear!" in a solemn manner, as if it was church service. After which there was a hammering, as if it was a trunk-maker's shop. After which the landlord took me by the arm; gave me a push into the parlour: and there I was, free of the Club.

The change from the fog outside to the warm room and the shining candles so completely dazed me, that I stood blinking at the company more like an owl than a man. Upon which the company again said, "Hear! hear!" Upon which I returned for answer, "Hear! hear!" – considering those words to mean, in the Club's language, something similar to "How-d'ye-do." The landlord then took me to a round table by the fire, where I got my supper, together with the information that my bedroom, when I wanted it, was number four, up-stairs.

I noticed before I fell to with my knife and fork that the room was full, and that the chairman at the top of the table was the man with the jolly voice, and was seemingly amusing the company by telling them a story. I paid more attention to my supper than to what he was saying; and all I can now report of it is, that his story-telling and my eating and drinking both came to an end together.

"Now," says the chairman, "I have told my story to start you all. Who comes next?" He took up a teetotum, and gave it a spin on the table. When it toppled over, it fell opposite me; upon which the chairman said, "It's your turn next. Order! order! I call on the seafaring man to tell the second story!" He finished the words off with a knock of his hammer; aud the Club (having nothing else to say, as I suppose) tried back, and once again sang out altogether, "Hear! hear!"

"I hope you will please to let me off," I said to the chairman, "for the reason that I have got no story to tell."

"No story to tell!" says he. "A sailor without a story! Who ever heard of such a thing? Nobody!"

"Nobody," says the Club, bursting out altogether at last with a new word, by way of a change.

I can't say I quite relished the chairman's talking of me as if I was before the mast. A man likes his true quality to be known, when he is publicly spoken to among a party of strangers. I made my true quality known to the chairman and company, in these words: "All men who follow the sea, gentlemen, are sailors," I said. "But there's degrees aboard ship as well as ashore. My rating, if you please, is the rating of a second mate."

"Ay, ay, surely?" says the chairman. "Where did you leave your ship?"

"At the bottom of the sea," I made answer – which was, I am sorry to say, only too true.

"What! you've been wrecked?" says he. "Tell us all about it. A shipwreck-story is just the sort of story we like. Silence there all down the table! – silence for the second mate!"

The Club, upon this, instead of keeping silence, broke out vehemently with another new word, and said, "Chair!" After which every man suddenly held his peace, and looked at me.

I did a very foolish thing. Without stopping to take counsel with myself, I started off at score, and did just what the chairman had bidden me. If they had waited the whole night long for it, I should never have told them the story they wanted from me at first, having all my life been a wretched bad hand at such matters – for the reason, as I take it, that a story is bound to be something which is not true. But when I found the company willing, on a sudden, to put up with nothing better than the account of my shipwreck (which is not a story at all), the unexpected luck of being let off with only telling the truth about myself, was too much of a temptation for me – so I up and told it.

I got on well enough with the storm, and the striking of the vessel, and the strange chance, afterwards, which proved to be the saving of my life – the assembly all listening (to my great surprise) as if they had never heard anything of the sort before. But, when the necessity came next for going further than this, and for telling them what had happened to me *after* the saving of my life – or, to put it plainer, for telling them what place I was cast away on, and what company I was cast away in – the words died straight off on my lips. For this reason – namely – that those particulars of my statement made up just that part of it which I couldn't, and durstn't, let out to strangers – no, not if every man among them had offered me a hundred pounds apiece, on the spot, to do it!

"Go on!" says the chairman. "What happened next? How did you get on shore?"

Feeling what a fool I had been to run myself headlong into a scrape, for want of thinking before I spoke, I now cast about discreetly in my mind for the best means of finishing off-hand without letting out a word to the company concerning those particulars before mentioned. I was some little time before seeing my way to this; keeping the chairman and company, all the while, waiting for an answer. The Club, losing patience in consequence, got from staring hard at me to drumming with their feet, and then to calling out lustily, "Go on! go on! Chair! Order!" – and such like. In the midst of this childish hubbub, I saw my way to what I considered to be rather a neat finish – and got on my legs to ease them all off with it handsomely.

"Hear! hear!" says the Club. "He's going on again at last."

"Gentlemen!" I made answer; "with your permission I will now conclude by wishing you all good night." Saying which words, I gave them a friendly nod, to make things pleasant – and walked straight to the door. It's hardly to be believed – though nevertheless quite true – that these curious men all howled and groaned at me directly, as if I had done them some grievous injury. Thinking I would try to pacify them with their own favourite catch-word, I said, "Hear! hear!" as civilly as might be, whereupon, they all returned for answer, "Oh! oh!" I never belonged to a Club of any kind, myself; and, after what I saw of *that* Club, I don't care if I never do.

My bedroom, when I found my way up to it, was large and airy enough, but not over-clean. There were two beds in it, not over-clean either. Both being empty, I had my choice. One was near the window, and one near the door. I thought the bed near the door looked a trifle the sweetest of the two; and took it.

After falling asleep, it was the grey of the morning before I woke. When I had fairly opened my eyes and shook up my memory into telling me where I was, I made two discoveries. First, that the room was a deal colder in the new morning, than it had been over-night. Second, that the other bed near the window had got some one sleeping in it. Not that I could see the man from where I lay; but I heard his breathing, plain enough. He must have come up into the room, of course, after I had fallen asleep and he had tumbled himself quietly into bed without disturbing me. There was nothing wonderful in that; and nothing wonderful in the landlord letting the empty bed if he could find a customer for it. I turned, and tried to go to sleep again; but I was out of sorts out of sorts so badly, that even the breathing of the man in the other bed fretted and worried me. After tumbling and tossing for a quarter of an hour or more, I got up for a change; and walked softly in my stockings, to the window, to look at the morning.

The heavens were brightening into daylight, and the mists were blowing off, past the window, like puffs of smoke. When I got even with the second bed, I stopped to look at the man in it. He lay, sound asleep, turned towards the window; and the end of the counterpane was drawn up over the lower half of his face. Something struck me, on a sudden, in his hair, and his forehead; and, though not an inquisitive man by nature, I stretched out my hand to the end of the counterpane, in spite of myself.

I uncovered his face softly; and there, in the morning light, I saw my brother, Alfred Raybrock.

What I ought to have done, or what other men might have done in my place, I don't know. What I really did, was to drop back a step – to steady myself, with my hand, on the sill of the window and to stand so, looking at him. Three years ago, I had said good-by to my wife, to my little child, to my old mother, and to brother Alfred here, asleep under my eyes. For all those three years, no news from me had reached them – and the underwriters, as I knew, must have long since reported that the ship I sailed in was lost, and that all hands on board had perished. My heart was heavy when I thought of my kindred at home, and of the weary time they must have waited and sorrowed before they gave me up for dead. Twice I reached out my hand, to wake Alfred, and to ask him about my wife and my child; and twice I drew it back again, in fear of what might happen if he saw me, standing by his bed-head in the grey morning, like Hugh Raybrock risen up from the grave.

I drew my hand back the second time, and waited a minute. In that minute he woke. I had not moved, or spoken a word, or touched him – I had only looked at him longingly. If such things could be, I should say it was my looking that woke him. His eyes, when they opened under mine, passed on a sudden from fast asleep to broad awake. They first settled on my face with a startled look which passed directly. He lifted himself on his elbow, and opened his lips to speak, but never said a word. His eyes strained and strained into mine; and his face turned all over of a ghastly white. "Alfred!" I said, "don't you know me?" There seemed to be a deadly terror pent up in him, and I thought my voice might set it free. I took fast hold of him by the hands, and spoke again. "Alfred!" I said—

Oh, sirs! where can a man like me find words to tell all that was said and all that was thought between us two brothers? Please to pardon my not saying more of it than I say here. We sat down together, side by side. The poor lad burst out crying – and got vent that way. I kept my hold of his hands, and waited a bit before I spoke to him again. I think I was worst off, now, of the two – no tears came to help *me* – I haven't got my brother's quickness, any way; and my troubles have roughened and hardened me, outside. But, God knows, I felt it keenly; all the more keenly, maybe, because I was slow to show it.

After a little, I put the questions to him which I had been longing to ask, from the time when I first saw his face on the pillow. Had they all given me up at home, for dead (I asked)? Yes; after long, long hoping, one by one they had given me up – my wife (God bless her!) last of all. I meant to ask next if my wife was alive and well; but, try as I might, I could only say "Margaret?" – and look hard in my brother's face. He knew what I meant. Yes (he said), she was living; she was at home; she was in her widow's weeds – poor soul! her widow's weeds! I got on better with my next question about the child. Was it born alive? Yes. Boy or girl? Girl. And living now; and much grown? Living, surely, and grown – poor little thing, what a question to ask! – grown of course, in three years! And mother? Well, mother was a trifle fallen away, and more silent within herself than she used to be – fretting at times; fretting (like my wife) on nights when the sea rose, and the windows shook and shivered in the wind. Thereupon, my brother and I waited a bit again – I with my questions, and he with his answers and while we waited, I thanked God, inwardly, with all my heart and soul, for bringing me back, living, to wife and kindred, while wife and kindred were living too.

My brother dried the tears off his face; and looked at me a little. Then he turned aside suddenly, as if he remembered something; and stole his hand in a hurry, under the pillow of his bed. Nothing came out from below the pillow but his black neck-handkerchief, which he now unfolded slowly, looking at me, all the while, with something strange in his face that I couldn't make out.

"What are you doing?" I asked him. "What are you looking at me like that for?"

Instead of making answer, he took a crumpled morsel of paper out of his neck-handkerchief, opened it carefully, and held it to the light to let me see what it was. Lord in Heaven! – my own writing – the morsel of paper I had committed, long, long since, to the mercy of the deep. Thousands and thousands of miles away, I had trusted that Message to the waters – and here it was now, in my brother's hands! A chilly fear came over me at the seeing it again. Scrap of paper as it was, it looked to my eyes like the ghost of my own past self, gone home before me invisibly over the great wastes of the sea.

My brother pointed down solemnly to the writing.

"Hugh," he said, "were you in your right mind when you wrote those words?"

"Tell me, first," I made answer, "how and when the Message came to you. I can't quiet myself fit to talk till I know that."

He told me how the paper had come to hand – also, how his good friend, the captain, having promised to help him, was then under the same roof with our two selves. But there he stopped. It was not till later in the day that I heard of what had happened (through this dreadful doubt about the money) in the matter of his sweetheart and his marriage.

The knowledge that the Message had reached him by mortal means – on the word of a seaman, I half doubted it when I first set eyes on the paper! – eased me in my mind; and I now did my best to quiet Alfred, in my turn. I told him that I was in my right senses, though sorely troubled, when my hand had written those words. Also, that where the writing was rubbed out, I could tell him for his necessary guidance and mine, what once stood in the empty places. Also, that I knew no more what the real truth might be than he did, till inquiry was made, and the slander on father's good name was dragged boldly into daylight to show itself for what it was worth. Lastly, that all the voyage home, there was one hope and one determination uppermost in my mind – the hope, that I might get safe to England, and find my wife and kindred alive to take me back among them again – the determination, that I would put the doubt about father's five hundred pound to the proof, if ever my feet touched English land once more.

"Come out with me now, Alfred," I said, after winding up as above; "and let me tell you in the quiet of the morning how that Message came to be written and committed to the sea."

We went down stairs softly, and let ourselves out without disturbing any one. The sun was just rising when we left the village and took our way slowly over the cliffs. As soon as the sea began to open on us, I returned to that true story of mine which I had left but half told, the night before – and, this time, I went through with it to the end.

I shipped, as you may remember (were my first words to Alfred), in a second mate's berth, on board the Peruvian, nine hundred tons' burden. We carried an assorted cargo, and we were bound, round the Horn, to Truxillo and Guayaquil, on the western coast of South America. From this last port – namely, Guayaquil – we were to go back to Truxillo, and there to take in another cargo for the return voyage. Those were all the instructions communicated to me when I signed articles with the owners, in London city, three years ago.

After we had been, I think, a week at sea, I heard from the first mate – who had himself heard it from the captain – that the supercargo we were taking with us, on the outward voyage, was to be left at Truxillo, and that another supercargo (also connected with our firm, and latterly employed by them as their foreign agent) was to ship with us at that port, for the voyage home. His name on the captain's instructions was, Mr. Lawrence Clissold. None of us had ever set eyes on him to our knowledge, and none of us knew more about him than what I have told you here.

We had a wonderful voyage out – especially round the Horn. I never before saw such fair weather in that infernal latitude, and I never expect to see the like again. We followed our instructions to the letter; discharging our cargo in fine condition, and returning to Truxillo to load again as directed. At this place, I was so unfortunate as to be seized with the fever of the country, which laid me on my back, while we were in harbour; and which only let me return to my duty after we had been ten days at sea, on the voyage home again. For this reason, the first morning when I was able to get on deck, was also the first time of my setting eyes on our new supercargo, Mr. Lawrence Clissold.

I found him to be a long, lean, wiry man, with some complaint in his eyes which forced him to wear spectacles of blue glass. His age appeared to be fifty-six, or thereabouts; but he might well have been more. There was not above a handful of grey hair, altogether, on his bald head – and, as for the wrinkles at the corners of his eyes and the sides of his mouth, if he could have had a pound apiece in his pocket for every one of them, he might have retired from business from that time forth. Judging by certain signs in his face, and by a suspicious morning-tremble in his hands, I set him down, in my own mind (rightly enough, as it afterwards turned out), for a drinker. In one word, I didn't like the looks of the new supercargo – and, on the first day when I got on deck, I found that he had reasons of his own for paying me back in my own coin, and not liking *my* looks, either.

"I've been asking the captain about you," were his first words to me in return for my civilly wishing him good morning. "Your name's Raybrock, I hear. Are you any relation to the late Hugh Raybrock, of Barnstaple, Devonshire?"

"Rather a near relation," I made answer. "I am the late Hugh Raybrock's eldest son."

There was no telling how his eyes looked, because they were hidden by his blue spectacles – but I saw him wince at the mouth, when I gave him that reply.

"Your father ended by failing in business, didn't he?" was the next question the supercargo put to me.

"Who told you he failed?" I asked, sharply enough.

"Oh! I heard it," says Mr. Lawrence Clissold, both looking and speaking as if he was glad to have heard it, and he hoped it was true.

"Whoever told you my father failed in business, told you a lie," I said. "His business fell off towards the last years of his life – I don't deny it. But every creditor he had was honestly paid at his death, without so much as touching the provision left for his widow and children. Please to mention that, next time you hear it reported that my father failed in business."

Mr. Clissold grinned to himself – and I lost my temper.

"I'll tell you what," I said to him, "I don't like your laughing to yourself, when I ask you to do justice to my father's memory – and, what is more, I didn't like the way you mentioned that report of his failing in business, just now. You looked as if you hoped it was true."

"Perhaps I did," says Mr. Clissold, coolly. "Shall I tell you why? When I was a young man, I was unlucky enough to owe your father some money. He was a merciless creditor; and he threatened me with a prison if the debt remained unpaid on the day when it was due. I have never forgotten that circumstance; and I should certainly not have been sorry if your father's creditors had given him a lesson in forbearance, by treating him as harshly as he once treated me."

"My father had a right to ask for his own," I broke out. "If you owed him the money and didn't pay it—"

"I never told you I didn't pay it," says Mr. Clissold, as coolly as ever.

"Well, if you did pay it," I put in, "then, you didn't go to prison – and you have no cause of complaint now. My father wronged nobody; and I won't believe he ever wronged *you*. He was a just man in all his dealings; and whoever tells me to the contrary—!"

"That will do," says Mr. Clissold, backing away to the cabin stairs. "You seem to have not quite got over your fever yet. I'll leave you to air yourself in the sea-breezes, Mr. Second Mate; and I'll receive your excuses when you are cool enough to make them."

"It is a son's business to defend his father's character," I answered; "and, cool or hot, I'll leave the ship sooner than ask your pardon for doing my duty!"

"You *will* leave the ship," says the supercargo, quietly going down into the cabin. "You will leave at the next port, if I have any interest with the captain."

That was how Mr. Clissold and I scraped acquaintance on the first day when we met together! And as we began, so we went on to the end. But, though he persecuted me in almost every other way, he did not anger me again about father's affairs: he seemed to have dropped talking of them at once and for ever. On my side I nevertheless bore in mind what he had said to me, and determined, if I got home safe, to go to the lawyer at Barnstaple who keeps father's old books and letters for us, and see what information they might give on the subject of Mr. Lawrence Clissold. I, myself, had never heard his name mentioned at home – father (as you know, Alfred) being always close about business-matters, and mother never troubling him with idle questions about his affairs. But it was likely enough that he and Mr. Clissold might have been concerned in money-matters, in past years, and that Mr. Clissold might have tried to cheat him, and failed. I rather hoped it might prove to be so – for the truth is, the supercargo provoked me past all endurance; and I hated him as heartily as he hated me.

All this while the ship was making such a speedy voyage down the coast, that we began to think we were carrying back with us the fine weather we had brought out. But, on nearing Cape Horn, the signs and tokens appeared which told us that our run of luck was at an end. Down went the barometer, lower and lower; and up got the wind, in the northerly quarter, higher and higher. This happened towards nightfall – and at daybreak next day, we found ourselves forced to lay-to. It blew all that day and all that night; towards noon the next day, it lulled a little, and we made sail again, But at sunset, the heavens grew blacker than ever; and the wind returned upon us with double and treble fury. The Peruvian was a fine stout roomy ship, but the unhandiest vessel at laying-to I ever sailed in. After taking tons of water on board and losing our best boat, we had nothing left for it but to turn tail, and scud for our lives. For the next three days and nights we ran before the wind. The gale moderated more than once in that time; but there was such a sea on, that we durstn't heave the ship to. From the beginning of the gale none of us officers had a chance of taking any observations. We only knew that the wind was driving us as hard as we could go in a southerly direction, and that we were by this time hundreds of miles out of the ordinary course of ships in doubling the Cape.

On the third night – or rather, I should say, early on the fourth morning I went below, dead beat, to get a little rest, leaving the vessel in charge of the captain and the first mate. The night was then pitch-black – it was raining, hailing, and sleeting, all at once and the Peruvian was wallowing in the frightful seas, as if she meant to roll the masts out of her. I tumbled into bed the instant my wet oilskins were off my back, and slept as only a man can who lays himself down dead beat.

I was woke – how long afterwards I don't know – by being pitched clean out of my berth on to the cabin floor; and, at the same moment, I heard the crash of the ship's timbers, forward, which told me it was all over with us.

Though bruised and shaken by my fall, I was on deck directly. Before I had taken two steps forward, the Peruvian forged ahead on the send of the sea, swung round a little, and struck heavily at the bows for the second time. The shrouds of the foremast cracked one after another, like pistol-shots; and the mast went overboard. I next felt our people go tearing past me, in the black darkness, to the lee-side of the vessel; and I knew that, in their last extremity, they were taking to the boats. I say I *felt* them go past me, because the roaring of the sea and the howling of the wind deafened me, on deck, as completely as the darkness blinded me. I myself no more believed the boats would live in the sea, than I believed the ship would hold together on the reef – but, as the rest were running the risk, I made up my mind to run it with them.

But before I followed the crew to leeward, I went below again for a minute – not to save money or clothes, for, with death staring me in the face, neither were of any account, now – but to get my little writing-case which mother had given me at parting. A curl of Margaret's hair was in the pocket inside it, with all the letters she had sent me when I had been away on other voyages. If I saved anything I was resolved to save this and – if I died, I would die with it about me.

My locker was jammed with the wrenching of the ship, and had to be broken open. I was, maybe, longer over this job than I myself supposed. At any rate, when I got on deck again with my case in my breast, it was useless calling, and useless groping about. The largest of the two boats, when I felt for it, was gone; and every soul on board was beyond a doubt gone with her.

Before I had time to think, I was thrown off my feet, by another sea coming on board, and a great heave of the vessel, which drove her farther over the reef, and canted the after-part of her up like the roof of a house. In that position the stern stuck, wedged fast into the rocks beneath, while the fore-part of the ship was all to pieces and down under water. If the after-part kept the place it was now jammed in, till daylight, there might be a chance – but if the sea wrenched it out from between the rocks, there was an end of me. After straining my eyes to discover if there was land beyond the reef, and seeing nothing but the flash of the breakers, like white fire in the darkness, I crawled below again to the shelter of the cabin stairs, and waited for death or daylight.

As the morning hours wore on, the weather moderated again; and the after-part of the vessel, though shaken often, was not shaken out of its place. A little before dawn, the winds and the waves, though fierce enough still, allowed me, at last, to hear something besides themselves. What I did hear, crouched up in my dark Corner, was a heavy thumping and grinding, every now and then, against the side of the ship to windward. Day broke soon afterwards; and, when I climbed to the deck, I clawed my way up to windward first, to see what the noise was caused by.

My first look over the bulwark showed me that it was caused by the boat which my unfortunate brother-officers and the crew had launched and gone away in when the ship struck. The boat was bottom upwards, thumping against the ship's side on the lift of the sea. I wanted no second look at it to tell me that every mother's son of them was drowned.

The main and mizen masts still stood. I got into the mizen rigging, to look out next to leeward – and there, in the blessed daylight, I saw a low, green, rocky little island, lying away beyond the reef, barely a mile distant from the ship! My life began to look of some small value to me again, when I saw land. I got higher up in the rigging to note how the current set, and where there might be a passage through the reef. The ship had driven over the rocks through the worst of the surf, and the sea between myself and the island, though angry and broken in places, was not too high for a lost man like me to venture on – provided I could launch the last, and smallest, boat still left in the vessel. I noted carefully the likeliest-looking channel for trying the experiment, and then got down on deck again to see what I could do, first of all, with the boat.

At the moment when my feet touched the deck, I heard a dull knocking and banging just under them, in the region of the cabin. When the sound first reached my ears, I got such a shock of surprise that I could neither move nor speak. It had never yet crossed my mind that a single soul was left in the vessel besides myself – but now, there was something in the knocking noise which started the hope in me that I was not alone. I shook myself up, and got down below directly.

The noise came from inside one of the sleeping berths, on the far side of the main cabin; the door of which was jammed, no doubt, just as my locker had been jammed, by the wrenching of the ship. "Who's there?" I called out. A faint, muffled kind of voice answered something through the air-grating in the upper part of the door. I got up on the overthrown cabin furniture; and, looking in through the trelliswork of the grating, found myself face to face with the blue spectacles of Mr. Lawrence Clissold, looking out!

God forgive me for thinking it – but there was not a man in the vessel I wouldn't sooner have found alive in her than Mr. Clissold! Of all that ship's company, we two, who were least friendly together, were the only two saved.

I had a better chance of breaking out the jammed door from the main cabin, than he had from the berth inside; and in less than five minutes he was set free. I had smelt spirits already through the air-grating – and now, when he and I stood face to face, I saw what the smell meant. There was an open case of spirits by the bedside—two of the bottles out of it were lying broken on the floor and Mr. Clissold was drunk.

"What's the matter with the ship?" says he, looking fierce, and speaking thick.

"You shall see for yourself," says I. With which words I took hold of him, and pulled him after me up the cabin stairs. I reckoned on the sight that would meet him, when he first looked over the deck, to sober his drunken brains – and I reckoned right: he fell on his knees, stock-still and speechless as if he was turned to stone.

I lashed him up safe to the cabin rail, and left it to the air to bring him round. He had, likely enough, been drinking in the sleeping berth for days together – for none of us, as I now remembered, had seen him since the gale set in – and even if had had sense enough to try to get out, or to call for help, when the ship struck, he would not have made himself heard in the noise and confusion of that awful time. But for the lull in the weather, I should not have heard him myself, when he attempted to get free in the morning. Enemy of mine as he was, he had a pair of arms – and he was worth untold gold, in my situation, for that reason. With the help I could make him give me, there was no doubt now about launching the boat. In half an hour I had the means ready for trying the experiment; and Mr. Clissold was sober enough to see that his life depended on his doing what I told him.

The sky looked angry still – there was no opening anywhere – and the clouds were slowly banking up again to windward. The supercargo knew what I meant when I pointed that way, and worked with a will when I gave him the word. I had previously stowed away in the boat such stores of meat, biscuit, and fresh water as I could readily lay hands on; together with a compass, a lantern, a few candles, and some boxes of matches in my pocket, to kindle light and fire with. At the last moment, I thought of a gun and some powder and shot. The powder and shot I found, and an old flint pocket-pistol in the captain's cabin – with which, for fear of wasting precious time, I was forced to be content. The pistol lay on the top of the medicine-chest – and I took that also, finding it handy, and not knowing but what it might be of use. Having made these preparations, we launched the boat, down the steep of the deck, into the water over the forward part of the ship which was sunk. I took the oars, ordering Mr. Clissold to sit still in the stern sheets – and pulled for the island.

It was neck or nothing with us more than once, before we were two hundred yards from the ship. Luckily, the supercargo was used to boats; and muddled as he still was, he had sense enough to sit quiet. We found our way into the smooth channel which I had noted from the mizen rigging – after which, it was easy enough to get ashore.

We landed on a little sandy creek. From the time of our leaving the ship, the supercargo had not spoken a word to me, nor I to him. I now told him to lend a hand in getting the stores out of the boat, and in helping me to carry them to the first sheltered, place we could find in shore on the island. He shook himself up with a sulky look at me, and did as I had bidden him. We found a little dip or dell in the ground, after getting up the low sides of the island, which was sheltered to windward – and here I left him to stow away the stores, while I walked farther on, to survey the place.

According to the hasty judgment I formed at the time, the island was not a mile across, and not much more than three miles round. I noted nothing in the way of food but a few wild roots and vegetables, growing in ragged patches amidst the thick scrub which covered the place. There was not a tree on it anywhere; nor any living creatures; nor any signs of fresh water that I could see. Standing on the highest ground, I looked about anxiously for other islands that might be inhabited; there were none visible – at least none in the hazy state of the heavens that morning. When I fairly discovered what a desert the place was; when I remembered how far it lay out of the track of ships; and when I thought of the small store of provisions which we had brought with us, the doubt lest we might only have changed the chance of death by drowning for the chance of death by starvation was so strong in me, that I determined to go back to the boat, with the desperate notion of making another trip to the vessel for water and food. I say desperate, because the clouds to windward were banking up blacker and higher every minute, the wind was freshening already, and there was every sign of the storm coming on again wilder and fiercer than ever.

Mr. Clissold, when I passed him on my; way back to the beach, had got the stores pretty tidy, covered with the tarpaulin which I had thrown over them in the bottom of the boat. Just as I looked down at him in the hollow, I saw him take a bottle of spirits out of the pocket of his pilot-coat. He must have stowed the bottle away there, as I suppose, while I was breaking open the door of his berth. "You'll be drowned, and I shall have double allowance to live upon here," was all he said to me, when he heard I was going back to the ship. "Yes! and die, in your turn, when you've got through it," says I, going away to the boat. It's shocking to think of now – but we couldn't be civil to each other, even on the first day when we were wrecked together!

Having previously stripped to my trousers, in case of accident, I now pulled out. On getting from the channel into the broken water again, I looked over my shoulder to windward, and saw that I was too late. It was coming! – the ship was hidden already in the horrible haze of it. I got the boat's head round to pull back – and I did pull back, just inside the opening in the reef which made the mouth of the channel – when the storm came down on me like death and judgment. The boat filled in an instant; and I was tossed head over heels into the water. The sea, which burst into raging surf upon the rocks on either side, rushed in one great roller up the deep channel between them, and took me with it. If the undertow, afterwards, had lasted for half a minute, I should have been carried into the white water, and lost. But a second roller followed the first, almost on the instant, and swept me right up on the beach. I had just strength enough to dig my arms and legs well into the wet sand; and though I was taken back with the backward shift of it, I was not taken into deep water again. Before the third roller came, I was out of its reach, and was down in a sort of swoon, on the dry sand.

When I got back to the hollow, in shore, where I had left my clothes under shelter with the stores, I found Mr. Clissold snugly crouched up, in the driest place, with the tarpaulin to cover him. "Oh!" says he, in a state of great surprise, "you're not drowned?" "No," says I; "you won't get your double allowance, after all." "How much shall I get?" says he, rousing up and looking anxious. "Your fair half share of what is here," I answered him. "And how long will that last me?" says he. "The food, if you have sense enough to eke it out with what you may find in this miserable place, barely three weeks," says I; "and the water (if you ever drink any) about a fortnight." At hearing that, he took the bottle out of his pocket again, and put it to his lips. "I'm cold to the bones," says I, frowning at him for a drop. "And I'm warm to the marrow," says he, chuckling, and handing me the bottle empty. I pitched it away at once – or the temptation to break it over his head might have been too much for me – I pitched it away, and looked into the medicine-chest, to see if there was a drop of peppermint, or anything comforting of that sort, inside. Only three physic bottles were left in it, all three being neatly tied over with oilskin. One of them held a strong white liquor, smelling like hartshorn. The other two were filled with stuff in powder, having the names in printed gibberish, pasted outside. On looking a little closer, I found, under some broken divisions of the chest, a small flask covered with wicker-work. "Ginger-Brandy" was written with pen and ink on the wicker-work, and the flask was full! I think that blessed discovery saved me from shivering myself to pieces. After a pull at the flask which made a new man of me, I put it away in my inside breast-pocket; Mr. Clissold watching me with greedy eyes, but saying nothing.

All this while, the rain was rushing, the wind roaring, and the sea crashing, as if Noah's Flood had come again. I sat close against the supercargo, because he was in the driest place; and pulled my fair share of the tarpaulin away from him, whether he liked it or not. He by no means liked it; being in that sort of half-drunken, half-sober state (after finishing his bottle), in which a man's temper is most easily upset by trifles. The upset of *his* temper showed itself in the way of small aggravations – of which I took no notice, till he suddenly bethought himself of angering me by going back again to that dispute about father, which had bred ill-blood between us, on the day when we first saw each other. If he had been a younger man, I am afraid I should have stopped him by a punch on the head. As it was, considering his age and the shame of this quarrelling betwixt us when we were both cast away together, I only warned him that I *might* punch his head, if he went on. It did just as well – and I'm glad now to think that it did.

We were huddled so close together, that when he coiled himself up to sleep (with a growl), and when he did go to sleep (with a grunt), he growled and grunted into my ear. His rest, like the rest of all the regular drunkards I have ever met with, was broken. He ground his teeth, and talked in his sleep. Among the words he mumbled to himself, I heard as plain as could be father's name. This vexed, but did not surprise me, seeing that he had been talking of father before he dropped off. But when I made out next, among his mutterings and mumblings, the words "five hundred pound," spoken over and over again, with father's name, now before, now after, now mixed in along with them, I got curious, and listened for more. My listening (and, serve me right, you will say) came to nothing: he certainly talked on, but I couldn't make out a word more that he said.

When he woke up, I told him plainly he had been talking in his sleep – and mightily taken aback he looked when he first heard it. "What about?" says he. I made answer, "My father, and five hundred pound; and how do you come to couple them together, I should like to know?" "I couldn't have coupled them," says he, in a great hurry—" what do I know about it? I don't believe a man like your father ever had such a sum of money as that, in all his life." "Don't you?" says I, feeling the aggravation of him, in spite of myself; "I can just tell you my father had such a sum when he was no older a man than I am – and saved it – and left it for a provision, in his will, to my mother, who has got it now – and, I say again, how came a stranger like you to bo talking of it in your sleep?" At hearing this, he went about on the other tack directly. "Was that all your father left, after his debts were paid?" says he. "Are you very curious to know?" says I. He took no notice – he only persisted with his question. "Was it just five hundred pound, no more and no less?" says he. "Suppose it was," says I; "what then?" "Oh, nothing?" says he, and turns sharp round from me, and chuckles to himself. "You're drunk!" says I. "Yes," says he; "that's it – stick to that – I'm drunk" – and he chuckles again. Try as I might, and threaten as I might, not another word on the matter of the five hundred pound could I get from him. I bore it well in mind, though, for all that – it being one of my slow ways, not easily to forget anything that has once surprised me, and not to give up returning to it over and over again, as time and occasion may serve for the purpose.

The hours wore on, and the storm raged on. We had our half rations of food, when hunger took us (I being much the hungrier of the two); and slept, and grumbled, and quarrelled the weary time out somehow. Towards dusk the wind lessened; and, when I got up, out of the hollow to look out, there was a faint watery break in the western heavens. At times, through the watches of the long night, the stars showed in patches for a little while, through the rents that opened and closed by fits in the black sky. When I fell asleep towards the dawning, the wind had fallen to a moan, though the sea, slower to go down, sounded as loud as ever. From what I could make of the weather, the storm had, by that time, as good as blown itself out.

I had been wise enough (knowing who was near me) to lay myself down, whenever I slept, on the side of me which was next to the flask of ginger-brandy, stowed away in my breast-pocket. When I woke at sunrise, it was the supercargo's hand that roused me up, trying to steal my flask while I was asleep. I rolled him over headlong among the stores – out of which I had the humanity to pull him again, with my own hands.

"I'll tell you what," says I, "if us two keep company any longer, we shan't get on smoothly together. You're the oldest man – and you stop here, where we know there is shelter. We will divide the stores fairly, and I'll go and shift for myself at the other end of the island. Do you agree to that?"

"Yes," says he; "and the sooner the better."

I left him for a minute, and went away to look out on the reef that had wrecked us. The splinters of the Peruvian, scattered broadcast over the beach, or tossing up and down darkly, far out in the white surf, were all that remained to tell of the ship. I don't deny that my heart sank, when I looked at the place where she struck, and saw nothing before me but sea and sky.

But what was the use of standing and looking? It was a deal better to rouse myself by doing something. I returned to Mr. Clissold – and then and there divided the stores into two equal parts, including everything down to the matches in my pocket. Of these parts I gave him first choice. I also left him the whole of the tarpaulin to himself – keeping in my own possession the medicine-chest, and the pistol; which last I loaded with powder and shot, in case any sea-birds might fly within reach. When the division was made, and when I had moved my part out of his way and out of his sight, I thought it uncivil to bear malice any longer, now that we had agreed to separate. We were cast away on a desert island, and we had death, as well as I could see, within about three weeks' hail of us – but that was no reason for not making things reasonably pleasant as long as we could. I was some time (in consequence of my natural slowness where matters of seafaring duty don't happen to be concerned) before I came to this conclusion. When I did come to it, I acted on it.

"Shake hands, before parting," I said, suiting the action to the word.

"No!" says he; "I don't like you."

"Please yourself," says I – and so we parted.

Turning my back on the west, which was his territory according to agreement, I walked away towards the south-east, where the sides of the island rose highest. Here I found a sort of half rift, half cavern, in the rocky banks, which looked as likely a place as any other – and to this refuge I moved my share of the stores. I thatched it over as well as I could with scrub, and heaped up some loose stones at the mouth of it. At home in England, I should have been ashamed to put my dog in such a place – but when a man believes his days to be numbered, he is not over-particular about his lodgings, and I was not over-particular about mine.

When my work was done, the heavens were fair, the sun was shining, and it was long past noon. I went up again to the high ground, to see what I could make out in the new clearness of the air. North, east, and west there nothing but sea and sky – but, south, I now saw land. It was high, and looked to be a matter of seven or eight miles off. Island, or not, it must have been of a good size for me to see it as I did. Known or not known to mariners, it was certainly big enough to have living creatures on it – animals or men, or both. If I had not lost the boat in my second attempt to reach the vessel, we might have easily got to it. But situated as we were now, with no wood to make a boat of but the scattered splinters from the ship, and with no tools to use even that much, there might just as well have been no land in sight at all, so far as we were concerned. The poor hope of a ship coming our road, was still the only hope left. To give us all the little chance we might get that way, I now looked about on the beach for the longest morsel of a wrecked spar that I could find; planted it on the high ground; and rigged up to it the one shirt I had on my back for a signal. While coming and going on this job, I noted with great joy that rain water enough lay in the hollows of the rocks above the sea line, to save our small store of fresh water for a week at least. Thinking it only fair to the supercargo to let him know what I had found out, I went to his territories, after setting up the morsel of a spar, and discreetly shouted my news down to him without showing myself. "Keep to your own side!" was all the thanks I got for this piece of civility. I went back to my own side immediately, and crawled into my little cavern, quite content to be alone. On that first night, strange as it seems now, I once or twice nearly caught myself feeling happy at the thought of being rid of Mr. Lawrence Clissold.

According to my calculations – which were made by tying a fresh knot every morning in a piece of marline – we two men were just a week, each on his own side of the island, without seeing or communicating, anyhow, with one another. The first half of the week, I had enough to do with cudgelling my brains for a means of helping ourselves, to keep my mind steady.

I thought first of picking up all the longest bits of spars that had been cast ashore, lashing them together with ropes twisted out of the long grass on the island, and trusting to raft-navigation to get to that high land away in the south. But when I looked among the spars, there were not half a dozen of them left whole enough for the purpose. And even if there had been more, the short allowance of food would not have given me time sufficient, or strength sufficient, to gather the grass, to twist it into ropes, and to lash a raft together big enough and strong enough for us two men. There was nothing to be done, but to give up this notion – and I gave it up. The next chance I thought of was to keep a fire burning on the shore every night, with the wood of the wreck, in case vessels at sea might notice it, on one side – or the people of the high land in the south (if the distance was not too great) might notice it, on the other. There was sense in this notion, and it could be turned to account the moment the wood was dry enough to burn. The wood got dry enough before the week was out. Whether it was the end of the stormy season in those latitudes, or whether it was only the shifting of the wind to the west, I don't know – but now, day after day, the heavens were clear and the sun shone scorching hot. The scrub on the island (which was of no great account) dried up – but the fresh water in the hollows of the rocks (which was, on the other hand, a serious business) dried up too. Troubles seldom come alone; and on the day when I made this discovery, I also found out that I had calculated wrong about the food. Eke it out as I might, with scurvy grass and roots, there would not be above eight days more of it left when the first week was past and, as for the fresh water, half a pint a day, unless more rain fell, would leave me at the end of my store, as nearly as I could guess, about the same time.

This was a bad look-out – but I don't think the prospect of it upset me in my mind, so much as the having nothing to do. Except for the gathering of the wood, and the lighting of the signal-fire, every night, I had no work at all, towards the end of the week, to keep me steady. I checked myself in thinking much about home, for fear of losing heart, and not holding out to the last, as became a man. For the same reasons I likewise kept my mind from raising hopes of help in me which were not likely to come true. What else was there to think about? Nothing but the man on the other side of the island – and be hanged to him!

I thought about those words I heard him say in his sleep; I thought about how he was getting on by himself; how he liked nothing but water to drink, and little enough of that; how he was eking out his food; whether he slept much or not; whether he saw the smoke of my fire at night, or not; whether he held up better or worse than I did; whether he would be glad to see me, if I went to him to make it up; whether he or I would die first; whether if it was me, he would do for me, what I would have done for him – namely, bury him, with the last strength I had left. All these things, and lots more, kept coming and going in my mind, till I could stand it no longer. On the morning of the eighth day, I roused up to go to his territories, feeling it would do me good to see him and hear him, even if we quarrelled again the instant we set eyes on each other.

I climbed up to the grassy ground – and, when I got there, what should I see but the supercargo himself, coming to *my* territories, and wandering up and down in the scrub through not knowing where to find them!

It almost knocked me over, when we met, the man was changed so. He looked eighty years old; the little flesh he had on his miserable face hung baggy; his blue spectacles had dropped down on his nose, and his eyes showed over them wild and red-rimmed; his lips were black, his legs staggered under him. He came up to me with his eyes all of a glare, and put both his hands on my breast, just over the pocket in which I kept that flask of ginger-brandy which he had tried to steal from me.

"Have you got any of it left?" says he, in a whisper.

"About two mouthfuls," says I.

"Give us one of them, for God's sake," says he.

Giving him one of those mouthfuls was just about equal to giving him a day of my life. In the case of a man I liked, I would not have thought twice about giving it. In the case of Mr. Clissold, I did think twice. I would have been a better Christian, if I could – but just then, I couldn't.

He thought I was going to say, No. His eyes got cunning directly. He reached his hands to my shoulders, and whispered these words in my ear: "I'll tell you what I know about the five hundred pound, if you'll give me a drop."

I determined to give it to him, and pulled out the flask. I took his hand, and poured the drop into the hollow of it, and held it for a moment.

"Tell me first," I said, "and drink afterwards."

He looked all round him, as if he thought there were people on the island to hear us. "Hush!" he said; "let's whisper about it." The next question and answer that passed between us, was louder than before on my side, and softer than ever on his. This was the question: "What do you know about the five hundred pound?"

And this was the answer: "It's *Stolen Money!*"

My hand dropped away from his, as if he had shot me. He instantly fastened on the drop of liquor in the hollow of his hand, like a hungry wild beast on a bone, and then looked up for more. Something in my face (God knows what) seemed suddenly to frighten him out of his life. Before I could stir a step, or get a word out, down he dropped on his knees, whining and whimpering in the high grass at my feet.

"Don't kill me!" says he; "I'm dying – I'll think of my poor soul. I'll repent while there's time—"

Beginning in that way, he maundered awfully, grovelling down in the grass; asking me every other minute for "a drop more, and a drop more;" and talking as if he thought we were both in England. Out of his wanderings, his beseechings for another drop, and his miserable beggar's-petitions for his "poor soul," I gathered together these word – the same which I wrote down on the morsel of paper, and of which nine parts out of ten are now rubbed off!

The first I made out – though not the first he said – was that some one, whom he spoke of as "the old man," was alive; and "Lanrean" was the place he lived in. I was to go there, and ask, among the old men, for "Tregarthen—"

(At the mention by me of the name of Tregarthen, my brother, to my great surprise, stopped me with a start; made me say the name over more than once; and then, for the first time, told me of the trouble about his sweet heart and his marriage. We waited a little to talk that matter over; after which, I went on again with my story, in these words:)

Well, as I made out from Clissold's wanderings, I was to go to Lanrean, to ask among the old men for Tregarthen, and to say to Tregarthen, "Clissold was the man. Clissold bore no malice: Clissold repented like a Christian, for the sake of his poor soul." No! I was to say something else to Tregarthen. I was to say, "Look among the books; look at the leaf you know of, and see for yourself it's not the right leaf to be there." No! I was to say something else to Tregarthen. I was to say, "The right leaf is hidden, not burnt. Clissold had time for everything else, but no time to burn that leaf. Tregarthen came in when he had got the candle lit to burn it. There was just time to let it drop from under his hand into the great crack In the desk, and then he was ordered abroad by the House, and there was no chance of doing more." No! I was to say none of these things to Tregarthen. Only this, instead: "Look in Clissold's Desk – and, if you blame anybody, blame miser Raybrock for driving him to it." And, oh, another drop – for the Lord's sake, give him another drop!

So he went on, over and over again, till I found voice enough to speak, and stop him.

"Get up, and go!" I said to the miserable wretch. "Get back to your own side of the island, or I may do you a mischief, in spite of my own self."

"Give me the other drop, and I will" – was all the answer I could get from him.

I threw him the flask. He pounced upon it with a howl. I turned my back—for I could look at him no longer – and climbed down again to my cavern on the beach.

I sat down alone on the sand, and tried to quiet myself fit to think about what I had heard. That father could ever have wilfully done anything unbecoming his character as an honest man, was what I wouldn't believe, in the first place. And that the wretched brute I had just parted from was in his right senses, was what I wouldn't believe, in the second place. What I had myself seen of drinkers, at sea and ashore, helped me to understand the condition into which he had fallen. I knew that when a man who has been a drunkard for years, is suddenly cut off his drink, he drops to pieces like, body and mind, for the want of it. I had also heard ship-doctors talk, by some name of their own, of a drink-madness, which we ignorant men call the Horrors. And I made it out, easy enough, that I had seen the supercargo in the first of these conditions; and that if we both lived long enough without help coming to us, I might soon see him in the second. But when I tried to get farther, and settle how much of what I had heard was wanderings and how much truth, and what it meant if any of it was truth, my slowness got in my way again; and where a quicker man might have made up his mind in an hour or two, I was all day, in sore distress, making up mine. The upshot of what I settled with myself was, in two words, this: Having mother's writing-case handy about me, I determined first to set down for my own self's reminder, all that I had heard. Second, to clear the matter up if ever I got back to England alive; and, if wrong had been done to that old man, or to anybody else, in father's name (without father's knowledge), to make restoration for his sake.

All that day I neither saw nor heard more of the supercargo. I passed a miserable night of it, after writing my memorandum, fighting with my loneliness and my own thoughts. The remembrance of those words in father's will, saying that the five hundred pound was money which he had once run a risk with, kept putting into my mind suspicions I was ashamed of. When daylight came, I almost felt as if I was going to have the Horrors too, and got up to walk them off, if possible, in the morning air.

I kept on the northern side of the island, walking backwards and forwards for an hour or more. Then I returned to my cavern; and the first thing I saw, on getting near it, was other footsteps than mine marked on the sand. I suspected at once that the supercargo had been lurking about watching me, instead of going back to his own side; and that, in my absence, he had been at his thieving tricks again.

The stores were what I looked at first. The food he had not touched; but the water he had either drunk or wasted – there was not half a pint of it left. The medicine-chest was open, and the bottle with the hartshorn was gone. When I looked next for the pistol, which I had loaded with powder and shot for the chance of bird-shooting that never came, the pistol was gone too. After making this last discovery, there was but one thing to be done – namely – to find out where he was, and to take the pistol away from him.

I set off to search first on the western side. It was a beautiful clear, calm, sunshiny morning; and as I crossed the island, looking out on my left hand and my right, I stopped on a sudden, with my heart in my mouth, as the saying is. Something caught my eye, far out at sea, in the north-west. I looked again – and there, as true as the heavens above me, I saw a ship, with the sunlight on her topsails, hull down, on the water-line in the offing!

All thought of the errand I was bent on, went out of my mind in an instant. I ran as fast as my weak legs would carry me to the northern beach; gathered up the broken wood which was still lying there plentifully, and, with the help of the dry scrub, lit the largest fire I had made yet. This was the only signal it was in my power to make that there were men on the island. The fire, in the bright daylight, would never be visible to the ship; but the smoke curling up from it, in the clear sky, might be seen, if they had a look-out at the mast-head.

While I was still feeding the fire, and so wrapped up in doing it, that I had neither eyes nor ears for anything else, I heard the supercargo's voice on a sudden at my back. He had stolen on me along the sand. When I faced him, he was swinging his arms about in the air, and saying to himself over and over again, "I see the ship! I see the ship!"

After a little, he came close up to me. By the look of him, he had been drinking the hartshorn, and it had strung him up a bit, body and mind, for the time. He kept his right hand behind him, as if he was hiding something. I suspected that "something" to be the pistol I was in search of.

"Will the ship come here?" says he.

"Yes, if they see the smoke," says I, keeping my eye on him.

He waited a bit, frowning suspiciously, and looking hard at me all the time.

"What did I say to you yesterday?" he asked.

"What I have got written down here," I made answer, smacking my hand over the writing-case in my breast-pocket; "and what I mean to put to the proof, if the ship sees us and we get back to England."

He whipped his right hand round from behind him, like lightning; and snapped the pistol at me. It missed fire. I wrenched it from him in a moment, and was just within one hair's breadth of knocking him on the head with the butt-end, afterwards. I lifted my hand – then thought better, and dropped it again.

"No," says I, fixing my eyes on him steadily; "I'll wait till the ship finds us."

He slunk away from me; and, as he slunk, looked hard into the fire. He stopped a minute so, thinking to himself – then he looked back at me again, with some mad mischief in him, that twinkled through his blue spectacles, and grinned on his dry black lips.

"The ship shall never find *you*" he said. With which words, he turned himself about towards his own side of the island, and left me.

He only meant that saying to be a threat – but, bird of ill-omen that he was, it turned out as good as a prophecy! All my hard work with the fire proved work in vain; all hope was quenched in me, long before the embers I had set light to were burnt out. Whether the smoke was seen or not from the vessel, is more than I can tell. I only know that she filled away on the other tack, not ten minutes after the supercargo left me. In less than an hour's time the last glimpse of the bright topsails had vanished out of view.

I went back to my cavern – which was now likelier than ever to be my grave as well. In that hot climate, with all the moisture on the island dried up, with not quite so much as a tumbler-full of fresh water left, with my strength wasted by living on half-rations of food two days more at most would see me out. It was hard enough for a man at my age, with all that I had left at home to make life precious, to die such a death as was now before me. It was harder still to have the sting of death sharpened – as I felt it, then – by what had just happened between the supercargo and myself. There was no hope, now, that his wanderings, the day before, had more falsehood than truth in them. The secret he had let out was plainly true enough and serious enough to have scared him into attempting my life, rather than let me keep possession of it, when there was a chance of the ship rescuing us. That secret had father's good name mixed up with it – and here was I, instead of clearing the villanous darkness from off of it, carrying it with me, black as ever, into my grave.

It was out of the horror I felt at doing that, and out of the yearning of my heart towards you, Alfred, when I thought of it, that the notion came to comfort me of writing the Message at the top of the paper, and of committing it in the bottle to the sea. Drowning men, they say, catch at straws – and the straw of comfort I caught at was the one chance in ten thousand, that the Message might float till it was picked up, and that it might reach you. My mind might, or might not, have been failing me, by this time – but it is true, either way, that I did feel comforted when I had emptied one of the two bottles left in the medicine-chest, had put the paper inside, had tied the stopper carefully over with the oilskin, and had laid the whole by in my pocket, ready, when I felt my time coming, to drop into the sea. I was rid of the secret, I thought to myself; and, if it pleased God, I was rid of it, Alfred, to *you*.

The day waned; and the sun set, all cloudless and golden, in a dead calm. There was not a ripple anywhere on the long oily heaving of the sea. Before night came I strengthened myself with a better meal than usual, as to food – for where was the use of keeping meat and biscuit when I had not water enough to last along with them? When the stars came out and the moon rose, I gathered the wood together and lit the signal-fire, according to custom, on the beach outside my cavern. I had no hope from it but the fire was company to me: the looking into it quieted my thoughts, and the crackling of it was a relief in the silence. I don't know why it was, but the breathless stillness of that night had something awful in it, and went near to frightening me.

The moon got high in the heavens, and the light of her lay all in a flood on the sand before me, on the rocks that jutted out from it, and on the calm sea beyond. I was thinking of Margaret – wondering if the moon was shining on our little bay at Steepways, and if she was looking at it too – when I saw a man's shadow steal over the white of the sand. He was lurking near me again! In a minute, he came into view. The moonshine glinted on his blue spectacles, and glimmered on his bald head. He stooped as he passed by the rocks and looked about for a loose stone: he found a large one, and came straight with it on tiptoe, up to the fire. I showed myself to him on a sudden, in the red of the flame, with the pistol in my hand. He dropped the stone, and shrank back, at the sight of it. When he was close to the sea, he stopped, and screamed out at me, "The ship's coming! The ship's coming! The ship shall never find *you*!" That notion of the ship, and that other notion of killing me before help came to us, seemed never to have left him. When he turned, and went back by the way he had come, he was still shouting out those same words. For a quarter of an hour or more, I heard him, till the silence swallowed up his ravings, and led me back again to my thoughts of home.

Those thoughts kept with me, till the moon was on the wane. It was darker now, and stiller than ever. I had not fed the signal-fire for half an hour or more, and had roused myself up, at the mouth of the cavern, to do it, when I saw the dying gleams of moonshine over the sea on either side of me change colour, and turn red. Black shadows, as from low-flying clouds, swept after each other over the deepening redness. The air grew hot – a sound came nearer and nearer, from above me and behind me, like the rush of wind and the roar of water, both together, and both far off. I ran out on to the sand, and looked back. The inland was on fire!

On fire at the point of it opposite to me – on fire in one great sheet of flame that stretched right across the island, and bore down on me steadily before the light westerly wind which was blowing at the time. Only one hand could have kindled that terrible flame – the hand of the lost wretch who had left me, with the mad threat on his lips and the murderous notion of burning me out of my refuge, working in his crazy brain. On his side of the island (where the fire had begun), the dry grass and scrub grew all round the little hollow in the earth which I had left to him for his place of refuge. If he had had a thousand lives to lose, he would have lost that thousand already!

Having nothing to feed on but the dry scrub, the flame swept forward with such a frightful swiftness, that I had barely time, after mastering my own scattered senses, to turn back into the cavern to get my last drink of water and my last mouthful of food, before I heard the fiery scorch crackling over the thatched-roof which my own hands had raised. I ran across the beach to the spur of rock which jutted out into the sea, and there crouched down on the farthest edge I could reach to. There was nothing for the fire to lay hold of between me aud the top of the island-bank. I was far enough away to be out of the lick of the flames, and low enough down to get air under the sweep of the smoke. You may well wonder why, with death by starvation threatening me close at hand, I should have schemed and struggled as I did, to save myself from a quicker death by suffocation in the smoke. I can only answer to that, that I wonder too – but so it was.

The flames eat their way to the edge of the bank, and lapped over it as if they longed to lick me up. The heat scorched nearer than I had thought, and the smoke poured lower and thicker. I lay down sick and weak on the rock, with my face close over the calm cool water. When I ventured to lift myself up again, the top of the island was of a ruby red, the smoke rose slowly in little streams, and the air above was quivering with the heat. While I looked at it, I felt a kind of surging and singing in my head, and a deadly faintness and coldness crept all over me. I took the bottle that held the Message from my pocket, and dropped it into the sea – then crawled a little way back over the rocks, and fell forward on them before I could get as far as the sand. The last I remember was trying to say my prayers – losing the words – losing my sight – losing the sense of where I was – losing everything.

The day was breaking again, when I was roused up by feeling rough hands on me. Naked savages – some on the rocks, some in the water, some in two long canoes – were clamouring and crowding about on all sides. They bound me, and took me off at once to one of the canoes. The other kept company – and both were paddled back to that high land which I had seen in the south. Death had passed me by once more – and Captivity had come in its place.

The story of my life among the savages, having no concern with the matter now in hand, may be passed by here in few words. They had seen the fire on the island; and paddling over to reconnoitre, had found me. Not one of them had ever set eyes on a white man before. I was taken away to be shown about among them for a curiosity. When they were tired of showing me, they spared my life, finding my knowledge and general handiness as a civilised man useful to them in various ways. I lost all count of time in my captivity – and can only guess now that it lasted more than one year and less than two. I made two attempts to escape, each time in a canoe, and was balked in both. Nobody at home in England would ever, as I believe, have seen me again, if an outward-bound vessel had not touched at the little desert island for fresh water. Finding none there, she came on to the territory of the savages (which was an island too). When they took me on board, I looked little better than a savage myself, and could hardly talk my own language. By the help of the kindness shown to me, I was right again by the time we spoke the first ship homeward-bound. To that vessel I was transferred; and, in her, I worked my passage back to Falmouth.

## Chapter V
## The Restitution

**CAPTAIN JORGAN,** up and out betimes, had put the whole village of Lanrean under an amicable cross-examination, and was returning to the King Arthur's Arms to breakfast, none the wiser for his trouble, when he beheld the young fisherman advancing to meet him, accompanied by a stranger. A glance at this stranger, assured the captain that he could be no other than the Seafaring Man; and the captain was about to hail him as a fellow-craftsman, when the two stood still and silent before the captain, and the captain stood still silent, and wondering before them.

"Why, what's this!" cried the captain, when at last he broke the silence. "You two are alike. You two are much alike! What's this!"

Not a word was answered on the other side, until after the seafaring brother had got hold of the captain's right hand, and the fisherman brother had got hold of the captain's left hand; and if ever the captain had had his fill of handshaking, from his birth to that hour, he had it then. And presently up and spoke the two brothers, one at a time, two at a time, two dozen at a time for the bewilderment into which they plunged the captain, until he gradually had Hugh Raybrock's deliverance made clear to him, and also unravelled the fact that the person referred to in the half-obliterated paper, was Tregarthen himself.

"Formerly, dear Captain Jorgan," said Alfred, "of Lanrean, you recollect? Kitty and her father came to live at Steepways, after Hugh shipped on his last voyage."

"Ay, ay!" cried the captain, fetching a breath. "*Now* you have me in tow. Then your brother here, don't know his sister-in-law that is to be, so much as by name?"

"Never saw her; never heard of her!"

"Ay, ay, ay!" cried the captain. "Why, then we every one go back together – paper, writer, and all – and take Tregarthen into the secret we kept from him?"

"Surely," said Alfred, "we can't help it now. We must go through with our duty."

"Not a doubt," returned the captain. "Give me an arm apiece, and let us set this ship-shape."

So, walking up and down in the shrill wind on the wild moor, while the neglected breakfast cooled within, the captain and the brothers settled their course of action.

It was, that they should all proceed by the quickest means they could secure, to Barnstaple, and there look over the father's books and papers in the lawyer's keeping: as Hugh had proposed to himself to do, if ever he reached home. That, enlightened or unenlightened, they should then return to Steepways and go straight to Mr.Tregarthen, and tell him all they knew, and see what came of it, and act accordingly. Lastly, that when they got there, they should enter the village with all precautions against Hugh's being recognised by any chance; and that to the captain should be consigned the task of preparing his wife and mother for his restoration to this life.

"For, you see," quoth Captain Jorgan, touching the last head, "it requires caution any way; great joys being as dangerous as great griefs – if not more dangerous, as being more uncommon (and therefore less provided against) in this round world of ours. And besides, I should like to free my name with the ladies, and take you home again at your brightest and luckiest; so don't let's throw away a chance of success."

The captain was highly lauded by the brothers for his kind interest and foresight.

"And now, stop!" said the captain, coming to a stand-still, and looking from one brother to the other, with quite a new rigging of wrinkles about each eye; "you are of opinion," to the elder, "that you are ra'ather slow?"

"I assure you I am very slow," said the honest Hugh.

"Wa'al," replied the captain, "I assure *you* that to the best of my belief I am ra'ather smart. Now, a slow man ain't good at quick business; is he?"

That was clear to both.

"You," said the captain, turning to the younger brother, "are a little in love; ain't you?"

"Not a little, Captain Jorgan."

"Much or little, you're sort preoccupied; ain't you?"

It was impossible to be denied.

"And a sort preoccupied man, ain't good at quick business; is he? said the captain. Equally clear on all sides.

"Now," said the captain, "I ain't in love myself, and I've made many a smart run across the ocean, and I should like to carry on and go ahead with this affair of yours and make a run slick through it. Shall I try? Will you hand it over to me?"

They were both delighted to do so, and thanked him heartily.

"Good," said the captain, taking out his watch. "This is half-past eight A.M., Friday morning. I'll jot that down, and we'll compute how many hours we've been out, when we run into your mother's post-office. There! The entry's made, and now we go ahead."

They went ahead so well, that before the Barnstaple lawyer's office was open next morning, the captain was sitting whistling on the step of the door, waiting for the clerk to come down the street with his key and open it. But, instead of the clerk, there came the master: with whom the captain fraternised on the spot, to an extent that utterly confounded him.

As he personally knew both Hugh and Alfred, there was no difficulty in obtaining immediate access to such of the father's papers as were in his keeping. These were chiefly old letters and cash accounts: from which the captain, with a shrewdness and despatch that left the lawyer far behind, established with perfect clearness, by noon, the following particulars.

That, one Lawrence Clissold had borrowed of the deceased, at a time when he was a thriving young tradesman in the town of Barnstaple, the sum of five hundred pounds. That, he had borrowed it, on the written statement that it was to be laid out in furtherance of a speculation, which he expected would raise him to independence: he being, at the time of writing that letter, no more than a clerk in the house of Dringworth Brothers, America-square, London. That, the money was borrowed for a stipulated period; but that when the term was out, the aforesaid speculation had failed, and Clissold was without means of repayment. That, hereupon, he had written to his creditor, in no very persuasive terms, vaguely requesting further time. That, the creditor had refused this concession, declaring that he could not afford delay. That, Clissold then paid the debt, accompanying the remittance of the money, with an angry letter, describing it as having been advanced by a relative to save him from ruin. That, in acknowledging the receipt, Raybrock had cautioned Clissold to seek to borrow money of him no more, as he would never so risk money again.

Before the lawyer, the captain said never a word in reference to these discoveries. But when the papers had been put back in their box, and he and his two companions were well out of the office, his right leg suffered for it, and he said:

"So far, this run's begun with a fair wind and a prosperous – for don't you see that all this agrees with that dutiful trust in his father, maintained by the slow member of the Raybrock family?"

Whether the brothers had seen it before or no, they saw it now. Not that the captain gave them much time to contemplate the state of things at their ease, for he instantly whipped them into a chaise again, and bore them off to Steepways. Although the afternoon was but just beginning to decline when they reached it, and it was broad daylight, still they had no difficulty, by dint of muffling the returned sailor up, and ascending the village rather than descending it, in reaching Tregarthen's cottage unobserved. Kitty was not visible, and they surprised Tregarthen sitting writing in the small bay-window of his little room.

"Sir, said the captain, instantly shaking hands with him, pen and all, "I'm glad to see you, sir. How do you do, sir? I told you you'd think better of me by-and-by, and I congratulate you on going to do it."

Here, the captain's eye fell on Tom Pettifer Ho, engaged in preparing some cookery at the fire.

"That crittur," said the captain, smiting his leg, "is a born steward, and never ought to have been in any other way of life. Stop where you are, Tom, and make yourself useful. Now, Tregarthen, I'm agoing to try a chair."

Accordingly, the captain drew one close to him, and went on:

"This loving member of the Raybrock family you know, sir. This slow member of the same family, you don't know, sir. Wa'al, these two are brothers – fact! Hugh's come to life again, and here he stands. Now, see here, my friend! You don't want to be told that he was cast away, but you do want to be told (for there's a purpose in it) that he was cast away with another man. That man, by name, was Lawrence Clissold."

At the mention of this name, Tregarthen started and changed colour. "What's the matter?" said the captain.

"He was a fellow-clerk of mine, thirty – five-and-thirty – years ago."

"True," said the captain, immediately catching at the clue: "Dringworth Brothers, America-square, London City."

The other started again, nodded, and said, That was the House."

"Now," pursued the captain, "between those two men cast away, there arose a mystery concerning the round sum of five hundred pound."

Again Tregarthen started and changed colour. Again the captain said, "What's the matter?"

As Tregarthen only answered, "Please to go on," the captain recounted, very tersely and plainly, the nature of Clissold's wanderings on the barren island, as he had condensed them
in his mind from the seafaring man. Tregarthen became greatly agitated during this recital, and at length exclaimed:

"Clissold was the man who ruined me! I have suspected it for many a long year, and now I know it."

"And how," said the captain, drawing his chair still closer to Tregarthen, and clapping his hand upon his shoulder, "how may you know it?"

"When we were fellow-clerks," replied Tregarthen, "in that London House, it was one of my duties to enter daily in a certain book, an account of the sums received that day by the firm, and afterwards paid into the banker's. One memorable day – a Wednesday, the black day of my life – among the sums I so entered, was one of five hundred pounds."

"I begin to make it out," said the captain. Yes?"

"It was one of Clissold's duties to copy from this entry, a memorandum of the sums which the clerk employed to go to the banker's paid in there. It was my duty to hand the money to Clissold; it was Clissold's to hand it to the clerk, with that memorandum of his writing. On that Wednesday, I entered a sum of five hundred pounds received.

I handed that sum, as I handed the other sums in the day's entry, to Clissold. I was absolutely certain of it at the time; I have been absolutely certain of it ever since. A sum of five hundred pounds was afterwards found by the House to have been that day wanting from the bag, from Clissold's memorandum, and from the entries in my book. Clissold, being questioned, stood upon his perfect clearness in the matter, and emphatically declared that he asked no better than to be tested by 'Tregarthen's book.' My book was examined, and the entry of five hundred pounds was not there."

"How not there," said the captain, "when you made it yourself?"

Tregarthen continued:

"I was then questioned. Had I made the entry? Certainly I had. The House produced my book, and it was not there. I could not deny my book; I could not deny my writing. I knew there must be forgery by some one; but the writing was wonderfully like mine, and I could impeach no one if the House could not. I was required to pay the money back. I did so, and I left the House, almost broken-hearted, rather than remain there – even if I could have done so – with a dark shadow of suspicion always on me. I returned to my native place, Lanrean, and remained there, clerk to a mine, until I was appointed to my little post here."

"I well remember," said the captain, "that I told you that if you had had no experience of ill-judgments on deceiving appearances, you were a lucky man. You were hurt at that, and I see why. I'm sorry."

"Thus it is," said Tregarthen. "Of my own innocence, I have of course been sure; it has been at once my comfort, and my trial. Of Clissold I have always had suspicions almost amounting to certainty, but they have never been confirmed until now. For my daughter's sake and for my own, I have carried this subject in my own heart, as the only secret of my life, and have long believed that it would die with me."

"Wa'al, my good sir," said the captain, cordially, "the present question is, and will be long, I hope, concerning living, and not dying. Now, here are our two honest friends, the loving Raybrock and the slow. Here they stand, agreed on one point, on which I'd back 'em round the world, and right across it from north to south, and then again from east to west, and through it, from your deepest Cornish mine to China. It is, that they will never use this same so-often-mentioned sum of money, and that restitution of it must be made to you. These two, the loving member and the slow, for the sake of the right and of their father's memory, will have it ready for you tomorrow. Take it, and ease their minds and mine, and end a most unfort'nate transaction."

Tregarthen took the captain by the hand, and gave his hand to each of the young men, but positively and finally answered, No. He said, they trusted to his word, and he was glad of it, and at rest in his mind – but there was no proof, and the money must remain as it was. All were very earnest over this; and earnestness in men, when they are right and true, is so impressive, that Mr. Pettifer deserted his cookery and looked on quite moved.

"And so," said the captain, "so we come – as that lawyer-crittur over yonder where we were this morning, might – to mere proof; do we? We must have it; must we? How? From this Clissold's wanderings, and from what you say, it ain't hard to make out that there was a neat forgery of your writing committed by the too smart Rowdy that was grease and ashes when I made his acquaintance, and a substitution of a forged leaf in your book for a real and true leaf torn out. Now, was that real and true leaf then and there destroyed? No – for says he, in his drunken way, he slipped it into a crack in his own desk, because you came into the office before there was time to burn it – and could never get back to it arterwards. Wait a bit. Where is that desk now? Do you consider it likely to be in America-square, London City?"

Tregarthen shook his head.

"The House has not, for years, transacted business in that place. I have heard of it and read of it, as removed, enlarged, every way altered. Things alter so fast in these times."

"You think so," returned the captain, with compassion; "but you should come over and see *me*, afore you talk about *that*. Wa'al, now. This desk, this paper this paper, this desk," said the captain, ruminating and walking about, and looking, in his uneasy abstraction, into Mr. Pettifer's hat on a table, among other things. "This desk, this paper – this paper, this desk," the captain continued, musing and roaming about the room, "I'd give—"

However, he gave nothing, but took up his steward's hat instead, and stood looking into it, as if he had just come into Church. After that

be roamed again, and again said, "This desk, belonging to this House of Dringworth Brothers, America-square, London City—"

Mr. Pettifer, still strangely moved and now more moved than before, cut the captain off as he backed across the room, aud bespake him thus:

"Captain Jorgan, I have been wishful to engage your attention, but I couldn't do it. I am unwilling to interrupt, Captain Jorgan, but I must do it. *I* know something about that House."

The captain stood stock-still, and looked at him – with his (Mr. Pettifer's) hat under his arm.

"You're aware," pursued his steward, "that I was once in the broking business, Captain Jorgan?"

"I was aware," said the captain, "that you had failed in that calling and in half the businesses going, Tom."

"Not quite so, Captain Jorgan; but I failed in the broking business. I was partners with my brother, sir. There was a sale of old office furniture at Dringworth Brothers when the House was moved from America-square, and me and my brother made what we call in the trade a Deal there, sir. And I'll make bold to say, sir, that the only thing I ever had from my brother, or from any relation – for my relations have mostly taken property from me, instead of giving me any – was an old desk we bought at that same sale, with a crack in it. My brother wouldn't have given me even that, when we broke partnership, if it had been worth anything."

"Where is that desk now?" said the captain.

"Well, Captain Jorgan," replied the steward, "I couldn't say for certain where it is now; but when I saw it last – which was last time we were outward-bound – it was at a very nice lady's at Wapping, along with a little chest of mine which was detained for a small matter of a bill owing."

The captain, instead of paying that rapt attention to his steward which was rendered by the other three persons present, went to Church again, in respect of the steward's hat. And a most especially agitated and memorable face the captain produced from it, after a short pause.

"Now, Tom," said the captain, "I spoke to you, when we first came here, respecting your constitutional weakness on the subject of sunstroke?"

"You did, sir."

"Will my slow friend," said the captain, "lend me his arm, or I shall sink right back'ards into this blessed steward's cookery? – Now, Tom," pursued the captain, when the required assistance was given, "on your oath as a steward, didn't you take that desk to pieces to make a better one of it, and put it together fresh – or something of the kind?"

"On my oath I did, sir," replied the steward.

"And by the blessing of Heaven, my friends, one and all," cried the captain, radiant with joy— "of the Heaven that put it into this Tom Pettifer's head to take so much care of his head against the bright sun – he lined his hat with the original leaf in Tregarthen's writing – and here it is!"

With that, the captain, to the utter destruction of Mr. Pettifer's favourite hat, produced the book-leaf, very much worn, but still legible, and gave both his legs such tremendous slaps, that they were heard far off in the bay, and never accounted for.

"A quarter-past five P.M.," said the captain, pulling out his watch, "and that's thirty-three hours and a quarter in all, and a pritty run!"

How they were all overpowered with delight and triumph; how the money was restored, then and there to Tregarthen; how Tregarthen, then and there, gave it all to his daughter; how the captain undertook to go to Dringworth Brothers and re-establish the reputation of their forgotten old clerk; how Kitty came in, and was nearly torn to pieces, and the marriage was reappointed; needs not to be told. Nor, how she and the young fisherman went home to the post-office to prepare the way for the captain's coming, by declaring him to be the mightiest of men who had made all their fortunes – and then dutifully withdrew together, in order that he might have the domestic coast entirely to himself. How he availed himself of it, is all that remains to tell.

Deeply delighted with his trust, and putting his heart into it, he raised the latch of the post-office parlour where Mrs. Raybrock and the young widow sat, and said:

"May I come in?"

"Sure you may, Captain Jorgan!" replied the old lady. "And good reason you have to be free of the house, though you have not been too well used in it, by some who ought to have known better. I ask your pardon."

"No you don't, ma'am," said the captain, "for I won't let you. Wa'al to be sure! By this time he had taken a chair on the hearth between them. "Never felt such an evil spirit in the whole course of my life! There! I tell you! I could a'most have cut my own connexion – Like the dealer in my country, away West, who when he had let himself be outdone in a bargain, said to himself, 'Now I tell you what! I'll never speak to you again.' And he never did, but joined a settlement of oysters, and translated the multiplication-table into their language. Which is a fact that can be proved, if you doubt it, mention it to any oyster you come across, and see if he'll have the face to contradict it."

He took the child from her mother's lap, and set it on his knee.

"Not a bit afraid of me now, yon see. Knows I am fond of small people. I have a child, and she's a girl, and I sing to her sometimes."

"What do you sing?" asked Margaret.

"Not a long song, my dear.

*Silas Jorgan*
*Played the organ.*

That's about all. And sometimes I tell her stories. Stories of sailors supposed to be lost, and recovered after all hope was abandoned." Here the captain musingly went back to his song:

*"Silas Jorgan*
*Played the organ,"*

—repeating it with his eyes on the fire, as he softly danced the child on his knee. For, he felt that Margaret had stopped working.

"Yes," said the captain, still looking at the fire. "I make up stories and tell 'em to that child. Stories of shipwreck on desert islands and long delay in getting back to civilised lands. It is to stories the like of that, mostly, that

*Silas Jorgan*
*Plays the organ."*

There was no light in the room but the light of the fire; for, the shades of night were on the village, and the stars had begun to peep out of the sky one by one, as the houses of the village peeped out from among the foliage when the night departed. The captain felt that Margaret's eyes were upon him, and thought it discreetest to keep his own eyes on the fire.

"Yes; I make 'em up," said the captain. "I make up stories of brothers brought together by the good providence of GOD. Of sons brought back to mothers – husbands brought back to wives – fathers raised from the deep, for little children like herself."

Margaret's touch was on his arm, and he could not choose but look round now. Next moment her hand moved imploringly to his breast, and she was on her knees before him: supporting the mother, who was also kneeling.

"What's the matter?" said the captain. "What's the matter?

*Silas Jorgan*
*Played the—"*

Their looks and tears were too much for him, and he could not finish the song, short as it was.

"Mistress Margaret, you have borne ill fortune well. Could you bear good fortune equally well, if it was to come?"

"I hope so. I thankfully and humbly and earnestly hope so!"

"Wa'al, my dear," said the captain, "p'raps it has come. He's – don't be frightened – shall I say the word?"

"Alive?"

"Yes!"

The thanks they fervently addressed to Heaven were again too much for the captain, who openly took out his handkerchief and dried his eyes.

"He's no further off," resumed the captain, "than my country. Indeed, he's no further off than his own native country. To tell you the truth, he's no further off than Falmouth. Indeed, I doubt if he's quite so fur. Indeed, if you was sure you could bear it nicely, and I was to do no more than whistle for him—"

The captain's trust was discharged. A rush came, and they were all together again.

This was a fine opportunity for Tom Pettifer to appear with a tumbler of cold water, and he presently appeared with it, and administered it to the ladies: at the same time soothing them, and composing their dresses, exactly as if they had been passengers crossing the Channel. The extent to which the captain slapped his legs, when Mr. Pettifer acquitted himself of this act of stewardship, could have been thoroughly appreciated by no one but himself: inasmuch as he must have slapped them black and blue, and they must have smarted tremendously.

He couldn't stay for the wedding; having a few appointments to keep, at the irreconcilable distance of about four thousand miles. So, next morning, all the village cheered him up to the level ground above, and there he shook hands with a complete Census of its population, and invited the whole, without exception, to come and stay several months with him at Salem, Mass., U.S. And there, as he stood on the spot where he had seen that little golden picture of love and parting, and from which he could that morning contemplate another golden picture with a vista of golden years in it, little Kitty put her arms around his neck, and kissed him on both his bronzed cheeks, and laid her pretty face upon his storm-beaten breast, in sight of all: ashamed to have called such a noble captain names. And there, the captain waved his hat over his head three final times; and there, he was last seen, going away accompanied by Tom Pettifer Ho, and carrying his hands in his pockets. And there, before that ground was softened with the fallen leaves of three more summers, a rosy little boy took his first unsteady run to a fair young mother's breast, and the name of that infant fisherman, was Jorgan Raybrock.

**If you enjoyed this, you might also like...**
The Chimes, see page 337
A Christmas Carol, see page 30

# The Magic Fishbone

**THERE WAS ONCE** a King, and he had a Queen; and he was the manliest of his sex, and she was the loveliest of hers. The King was, in his private profession, Under Government. The Queen's father had been a medical man out of town.

They had nineteen children, and were always having more. Seventeen of these children took care of the baby; and Alicia, the eldest, took care of them all. Their ages varied from seven years to seven months.

Let us now resume our story.

One day the King was going to the office, when he stopped at the fishmonger's to buy a pound and a half of salmon not too near the tail, which the Queen (who was a careful housekeeper) had requested him to send home. Mr Pickles, the fishmonger, said, "Certainly, sir, is there any other article, Good-morning."

The King went on towards the office in a melancholy mood, for quarter day was such a long way off, and several of the dear children were growing out of their clothes. He had not proceeded far, when Mr Pickles's errand-boy came running after him, and said, "Sir, you didn't notice the old lady in our shop."

"What old lady?" enquired the King. "I saw none."

Now, the King had not seen any old lady, because this old lady had been invisible to him, though visible to Mr Pickles's boy. Probably because he messed and splashed the water about to that degree, and flopped the pairs of soles down in that violent manner, that, if she had not been visible to him, he would have spoilt her clothes.

Just then the old lady came trotting up. She was dressed in shot-silk of the richest quality, smelling of dried lavender.

"King Watkins the First, I believe?" said the old lady.

"Watkins," replied the King, "is my name."

"Papa, if I am not mistaken, of the beautiful Princess Alicia?" said the old lady.

"And of eighteen other darlings," replied the King.

"Listen. You are going to the office," said the old lady.

It instantly flashed upon the King that she must be a Fairy, or how could she know that?

"You are right," said the old lady, answering his thoughts, "I am the Good Fairy Grandmarina. Attend. When you return home to dinner, politely invite the Princess Alicia to have some of the salmon you bought just now."

"It may disagree with her," said the King.

The old lady became so very angry at this absurd idea, that the King was quite alarmed, and humbly begged her pardon.

"We hear a great deal too much about this thing disagreeing, and that thing disagreeing," said the old lady, with the greatest contempt it was possible to express. "Don't be greedy. I think you want it all yourself."

The King hung his head under this reproof, and said he wouldn't talk about things disagreeing, any more.

"Be good, then," said the Fairy Grandmarina, "and don't! When the beautiful Princess Alicia consents to partake of the salmon – as I think she will – you will find she will leave a fish-bone on her plate. Tell her to dry it, and to rub it, and to polish it till it shines like mother-of-pearl, and to take care of it as a present from me."

"Is that all?" asked the King.

"Don't be impatient, sir," returned the Fairy Grandmarina, scolding him severely. "Don't catch people short, before they have done speaking. Just the way with you grown-up persons. You are always doing it."

The King again hung his head, and said he wouldn't do so any more.

"Be good then," said the Fairy Grandmarina, "and don't! Tell the Princess Alicia, with my love, that the fish-bone is a magic present which can only be used once; but that it will bring her, that once, whatever she wishes for, provided she wishes for it at the right time. That is the message. Take care of it."

The King was beginning, "Might I ask the reason—?" when the Fairy became absolutely furious.

"*Will* you be good, sir?" she exclaimed, stamping her foot on the ground. "The reason for this, and the reason for that, indeed! You are always wanting the reason. No reason. There! Hoity toity me! I am sick of your grown-up reasons."

The King was extremely frightened by the old lady's flying into such a passion, and said he was very sorry to have offended her, and he wouldn't ask for reasons any more.

"Be good then," said the old lady, "and don't!"

With those words, Grandmarina vanished, and the King went on and on and on, till he came to the office. There he wrote and wrote and wrote, till it was time to go home again. Then he politely invited the Princess Alicia, as the Fairy had directed him, to partake of the salmon. And when she had enjoyed it very much, he saw the fish-bone on her plate, as the Fairy had told him he would, and he delivered the Fairy's message, and the Princess Alicia took care to dry the bone, and to rub it, and to polish it till it shone like mother-of-pearl.

And so when the Queen was going to get up in the morning, she said, "O, dear me, dear me; my head, my head!" and then she fainted away.

The Princess Alicia, who happened to be looking in at the chamber-door, asking about breakfast, was very much alarmed when she saw her Royal Mamma in this state, and she rang the bell for Peggy, which was the name of the Lord Chamberlain. But remembering where the smelling-bottle was, she climbed on a chair and got it, and after that she climbed on another chair by the bedside and held the smelling-bottle to the Queen's nose, and after that she jumped down and got some water, and after that she jumped up again and wetted the Queen's forehead, and, in short, when the Lord Chamberlain came in, that dear old woman said to the little Princess, "What a Trot you are! I couldn't have done it better myself!"

But that was not the worst of the good Queen's illness. O, no! She was very ill indeed, for a long time. The Princess Alicia kept the seventeen young Princes and Princesses quiet, and dressed and undressed and danced the baby, and made the kettle boil, and heated the soup, and swept the hearth, and poured out the medicine, and nursed the Queen, and did all that ever she could, and was as busy busy busy, as busy could be. For there were not many servants at that Palace, for three reasons; because the King was short of money, because a rise in his office never seemed to come, and because quarter day was so far off that it looked almost as far off and as little as one of the stars.

But on the morning when the Queen fainted away, where was the magic fish-bone? Why, there it was in the Princess Alicia's pocket. She had almost taken it out to bring the Queen to life again, when she put it back, and looked for the smelling-bottle.

After the Queen had come out of her swoon that morning, and was dozing, the Princess Alicia hurried up-stairs to tell a most particular secret to a most particularly confidential friend of hers, who was a Duchess. People did suppose her to be a Doll; but she was really a Duchess, though nobody knew it except the Princess.

This most particular secret was a secret about the magic fish-bone, the history of which was well known to the Duchess, because the Princess told her everything. The Princess kneeled down by the bed on which the Duchess was lying, full-dressed and wide awake, and whispered the secret to her. The Duchess smiled and nodded. People might have supposed that she never smiled and nodded, but she often did, though nobody knew it except the Princess.

Then the Princess Alicia hurried downstairs again, to keep watch in the Queen's room. She often kept watch by herself in the Queen's room; but every evening, while the illness lasted, she sat there watching with the King. And every evening the King sat looking at her with a cross look, wondering why she never brought out the magic fish-bone. As often as she noticed this, she ran up-stairs, whispered the secret to the Duchess over again, and said to the Duchess besides, "They think we children never have a reason or a meaning!" And the Duchess, though the most fashionable Duchess that ever was heard of, winked her eye.

"Alicia," said the King, one evening when she wished him Good Night.

"Yes, Papa."

"What is become of the magic fish-bone?"

"In my pocket, Papa."

"I thought you had lost it?"

"O, no, Papa."

"Or forgotten it?"

"No, indeed, Papa."

And so another time the dreadful little snapping pug-dog next door made a rush at one of the young Princes as he stood on the steps coming home from school, and terrified him out of his wits and he put his hand through a pane of glass, and bled bled bled. When the seventeen other young Princes and Princesses saw him bleed bleed bleed, they were terrified out of their wits too, and screamed themselves black in their seventeen faces all at once. But the Princess Alicia put her hands over all their seventeen mouths, one after another, and persuaded them to be quiet because of the sick Queen. And then she put the wounded Prince's hand in a basin of fresh cold water, while they stared with their twice seventeen are thirty-four put down four and carry three eyes, and then she looked in the hand for bits of glass, and there were fortunately no bits of glass there. And then she said to two chubby-legged Princes who were sturdy though small, "Bring me in the Royal rag-bag; I must snip and stitch and cut and contrive." So those two young Princes tugged at the Royal rag-bag and lugged it in, and the Princess Alicia sat down on the floor with a large pair of scissors and a needle and thread, and snipped and stitched and cut and contrived, and made a bandage and put it on, and it fitted beautifully, and so when it was all done she saw the King her Papa looking on by the door.

"Alicia."

"Yes, Papa."

"What have you been doing?"

"Snipping stitching cutting and contriving, Papa."

"Where is the magic fish-bone?"

"In my pocket, Papa."

"I thought you had lost it?"

"O, no, Papa."

"Or forgotten it?"

"No, indeed, Papa."

After that, she ran up-stairs to the Duchess and told her what had passed, and told her the secret over again, and the Duchess shook her flaxen curls and laughed with her rosy lips.

Well! and so another time the baby fell under the grate. The seventeen young Princes and Princesses were used to it, for they were almost always falling under the grate or down the stairs, but the baby was not used to it yet, and it gave him a swelled face and a black eye. The way the poor little darling came to tumble was, that he slid out of the Princess Alicia's lap just as she was sitting in a great coarse apron that quite smothered her, in front of the kitchen-fire, beginning to peel the turnips for the broth for dinner; and the way she came to be doing that was, that the King's cook had run away that morning with her own true love who was a very tall but very tipsy soldier. Then, the seventeen young Princes and Princesses, who cried at everything that happened, cried and roared. But the Princess Alicia (who couldn't help crying a little herself) quietly called to them to be still, on account of not throwing back the Queen up-stairs, who was fast getting well, and said, "Hold your tongues, you wicked little monkeys, every one of you, while I examine baby!" Then she examined baby, and found that he hadn't broken anything, and she held cold iron to his poor dear eye, and smoothed his poor dear face, and he presently fell asleep in her arms. Then, she said to the seventeen Princes and Princesses, "I am afraid to lay him down yet, lest he should wake and feel pain, be good, and you shall all be cooks." They jumped for joy when they heard that, and began making themselves cooks' caps out of old newspapers. So to one she gave the salt-box, and to one she gave the barley, and to one she gave the herbs, and to one she gave the turnips, and to one she gave the carrots, and to one she gave the onions, and to one she gave the spice-box, till they were all cooks, and all running about at work, she sitting in the middle smothered in the great coarse apron, nursing baby. By and by the broth was done, and the baby woke up smiling like an angel, and was trusted to the sedatest Princess to hold, while the other Princes and Princesses were squeezed into a far-off corner to look at the Princess Alicia turning out the saucepan-full of broth, for fear (as they were always getting into trouble) they should get splashed and scalded. When the broth came tumbling out, steaming beautifully, and smelling like a nosegay good to eat, they clapped their hands. That made the baby clap his hands; and that, and his looking as if he had a comic toothache, made all the Princes and Princesses laugh. So the Princess Alicia said, "Laugh and be good, and after dinner we will make him a nest on the floor in a corner, and he shall sit in his nest and see a dance of eighteen cooks." That delighted the young Princes and Princesses, and they ate up all the broth, and washed up all the plates and dishes, and cleared away, and pushed the table into a corner, and then they in their cooks' caps, and the Princess Alicia in the smothering coarse apron that belonged to the cook that had run away with her own true love that was the very tall but very tipsy soldier, danced a dance of eighteen cooks before the angelic baby, who forgot his swelled face and his black eye, and crowed with joy.

And so then, once more the Princess Alicia saw King Watkins the First, her father, standing in the doorway looking on, and he said: "What have you been doing, Alicia?"

"Cooking and contriving, Papa."

"What else have you been doing, Alicia?"

"Keeping the children light-hearted, Papa."

"Where is the magic fish-bone, Alicia?"

"In my pocket, Papa."

"I thought you had lost it?"

"O, no, Papa."

"Or forgotten it?"

"No, indeed, Papa."

The King then sighed so heavily, and seemed so low-spirited, and sat down so miserably, leaning his head upon his hand, and his elbow upon the kitchen table pushed away in the corner, that the seventeen Princes and Princesses crept softly out of the kitchen, and left him alone with the Princess Alicia and the angelic baby.

"What is the matter, Papa?"

"I am dreadfully poor, my child."

"Have you no money at all, Papa?"

"None my child."

"Is there no way left of getting any, Papa?"

"No way," said the King. "I have tried very hard, and I have tried all ways."

When she heard those last words, the Princess Alicia began to put her hand into the pocket where she kept the magic fish-bone.

"Papa," said she, "when we have tried very hard, and tried all ways, we must have done our very very best?"

"No doubt, Alicia."

"When we have done our very very best, Papa, and that is not enough, then I think the right time must have come for asking help of others." This was the very secret connected with the magic fish-bone, which she had found out for herself from the good fairy Grandmarina's words, and which she had so often whispered to her beautiful and fashionable friend the Duchess.

So she took out of her pocket the magic fish-bone that had been dried and rubbed and polished till it shone like mother-of-pearl; and she gave it one little kiss and wished it was quarter day. And immediately it *was* quarter day; and the King's quarter's salary came rattling down the chimney, and bounced into the middle of the floor.

But this was not half of what happened, no not a quarter, for immediately afterwards the good fairy Grandmarina came riding in, in a carriage and four (Peacocks), with Mr Pickles's boy up behind, dressed in silver and gold, with a cocked hat, powdered hair, pink silk stockings, a jewelled cane, and a nosegay. Down jumped Mr Pickles's boy with his cocked hat in his hand and wonderfully polite (being entirely changed by enchantment), and handed Grandmarina out, and there she stood in her rich shot silk smelling of dried lavender, fanning herself with a sparkling fan.

"Alicia, my dear," said this charming old Fairy, "how do you do, I hope I see you pretty well, give me a kiss."

The Princess Alicia embraced her, and then Grandmarina turned to the King, and said rather sharply:—"Are you good?"

The King said he hoped so.

"I suppose you know the reason, *now*, why my god-Daughter here," kissing the Princess again, "did not apply to the fish-bone sooner?" said the Fairy.

The King made her a shy bow.

"Ah! but you didn't *then*!" said the Fairy.

The King made her a shyer bow.

"Any more reasons to ask for?" said the Fairy.

The King said no, and he was very sorry.

"Be good then," said the Fairy, "and live happy ever afterwards."

Then, Grandmarina waved her fan, and the Queen came in most splendidly dressed, and the seventeen young Princes and Princesses, no longer grown out of their clothes, came in newly fitted out from top to toe, with tucks in everything to admit of its being let out. After that, the Fairy tapped the Princess Alicia with her fan, and the smothering coarse apron flew away, and she appeared exquisitely dressed, like a little Bride, with a wreath of orange-flowers and a silver veil. After that, the kitchen dresser changed of itself into a wardrobe, made of beautiful woods and gold and looking glass, which was full of dresses of all sorts, all for her and all exactly fitting her. After that, the angelic baby came in, running alone, with his face and eye not a bit the worse but much the better. Then, Grandmarina begged to be introduced to the Duchess, and, when the Duchess was brought down many compliments passed between them.

A little whispering took place between the Fairy and the Duchess, and then the Fairy said out loud, "Yes. I thought she would have told you." Grandmarina then turned to the King and Queen, and said, "We are going in search of Prince Certainpersonio. The pleasure of your company is requested at church in half an hour precisely." So she and the Princess Alicia got into the carriage, and Mr Pickles's boy handed in the Duchess who sat by herself on the opposite seat, and then Mr Pickles's boy put up the steps and got up behind, and the Peacocks flew away with their tails spread.

Prince Certainpersonio was sitting by himself, eating barley-sugar and waiting to be ninety. When he saw the Peacocks followed by the carriage, coming in at the window, it immediately occurred to him that something uncommon was going to happen.

"Prince," said Grandmarina, "I bring you your Bride."

The moment the Fairy said those words, Prince Certainpersonio's face left off being stickey, and his jacket and corduroys changed to peach-bloom velvet, and his hair curled, and a cap and feather flew in like a bird and settled on his head. He got into the carriage by the Fairy's invitation, and there he renewed his acquaintance with the Duchess, whom he had seen before.

In the church were the Prince's relations and friends, and the Princess Alicia's relations and friends, and the seventeen Princes and Princesses, and the baby, and a crowd of the neighbours. The marriage was beautiful beyond expression. The Duchess was bridesmaid, and beheld the ceremony from the pulpit where she was supported by the cushion of the desk.

Grandmarina gave a magnificent wedding feast afterwards, in which there was everything and more to eat, and everything and more to drink. The wedding cake was delicately ornamented with white satin ribbons, frosted silver and white lilies, and was forty-two yards round.

When Grandmarina had drunk her love to the young couple, and Prince Certainpersonio had made a speech, and everybody had cried Hip hip hip hurrah!

Grandmarina announced to the King and Queen that in future there would be eight quarter days in every year, except in leap year, when there would be ten. She then turned to Certainpersonio and Alicia, and said, "My dears, you will have thirty-five children, and they will all be good and beautiful. Seventeen of your children will be boys, and eighteen will be girls. The hair of the whole of your children will curl naturally. They will never have the measles, and will have recovered from the whooping-cough before being born."

On hearing such good news, everybody cried out "Hip hip hip hurrah!" again.

"It only remains," said Grandmarina in conclusion, "to make an end of the fish-bone."

So she took it from the hand of the Princess Alicia, and it instantly flew down the throat of the dreadful little snapping pug-dog next door and choked him, and he expired in convulsions.

**If you enjoyed this, you might also like...**
A Child's Dream of a Star, see page 386
The Queer Chair, see page 321

# Biographies

**Charles Dickens**

Charles Dickens was born in 1812 in Portsmouth, though he spent much of his life in Kent and London. A prolific writer, Dickens kept up a career in journalism as well as writing short stories and novels, with much of his work being serialised before being published as books. He gave a view of contemporary England with a strong sense of realism, yet instilled his stories with a sense of charm, fantastic characters and humour like no other.

**Dr. Emily Bell**
*Foreword: Charles Dickens Supernatural Short Stories*
Dr. Emily Bell is a Dickens expert, editor and biographer. She was the first Communications Committee Chair of the international Dickens Society, and has published on Dickens, life writing and commemoration. Dr. Bell edited *Dickens after Dickens* for White Rose University Press, a volume of new research analysing Dickens's legacy in unconventional forms. She is a member of the board of the *Oxford Dickens* series, and is currently editing Dickens's later short fiction for this series. Dr. Bell also acts as editor for the Dickens Letters Project, and has a new biography of Dickens forthcoming.

**Wilkie Collins**

William Wilkie Collins (1824–1889) was a novelist and playwright who enjoyed a close friendship with Charles Dickens. He was the first English author of crime fiction to achieve both critical and commercial success, and his technique of describing events through multiple witness testimonies proved highly effective. *The Woman in White*, first published in 1860 is one of two novels for which Collins is best remembered; the other is *The Moonstone*, which appeared eight years later.

**Elizabeth Gaskell**

Elizabeth Gaskell (1810–65) was born in London and is widely known for her biography of her friend Charlotte Brontë. In a family of eight children, only Elizabeth and her brother John survived past childhood. Her mother's early death caused her to be raised by her aunt in Knutsford, Cheshire, a place that inspired her to later write her most famous work, *Cranford*. Tragedy struck again when Gaskell's only son died, and it was then that she began to write. All the misfortune in her life led her to write her many gothic and horror tales.

**Adelaide Anne Procter**

Adelaide Anne Procter (1825–64) was an English poet and philanthropist. Her short life ended due to tuberculosis at the age of 38, but her life was very well lived. Her poems were first published in magazines when she was a teenager and later published in book form. Adelaide was heavily involved in feminist politics, protecting women and the homeless and her writing was often about these subjects. She was incredibly popular throughout her career, and was Queen Victoria's favourite poet.

## George Augustus Sala

An author and journalist, George Augustus Sala (1828–95) wrote primarily for *Illustrated London News* as well as *The Daily Telegraph* at a later date, for which he became most famous. His writing became synonymous with the newspaper and was known for being egotistical, pompous and written to provoke reaction. George met Charles Dickens in 1851 who took a shine to his writing and published several of his short stories and articles in *All the Year Round* and *Household Words*.

## Hesba Stretton

Hesba Stretton, the pen name of Sarah Smith (1832–1911), was an English children's writer. She grew up in the literary world, as the daughter of a bookseller in Shropshire, and was largely self-educated. Her career took off with the publication of *Jessica's First Prayer*, first published in book form in 1867. It was to become hugely popular, selling at least a million and a half copies by 1900, and paved the way for many novels about the homelessness of children.

# Sources

## Ghostly Tales

**The Ghosts of the Mail**
Originally Published in *The Pickwick Papers*, Chapman & Hall, 1837

**The Lawyer and the Ghost**
Originally Published in *The Pickwick Papers*, Chapman & Hall, 1837

**The Baron of Grogzwig**
Originally Published in *The Life and Adventures of Nicholas Nickleby*, Chapman & Hall, 1839

**A Christmas Carol**
Originally Published by Chapman & Hall, 1843

**The Haunted Man and the Ghost's Bargain**
Originally Published by Bradbury & Evans, 1848

**To Be Read at Dusk**
Originally Published in *The Keepsake*, 1852

**A Christmas Tree**
Originally Published in *Household Words,* 1858

**Mr. Testator's Visitation**
Originally Published in *The Uncommercial Traveller*, 1859

**The Haunted House**
Originally Published in *All the Year Round*, 1859

**Four Stories**
Originally Published in *All the Year Round*, 1861

**The Portrait Painter's Story**
Originally Published as 'Mr. H.'s Own Narrative' in *All the Year Round*, 1861

**The Trial for Murder**
Originally Published in *Three Ghost Stories*, 1867

**The Signal-Man**
Originally Published in *Three Ghost Stories*, 1867

**The Ghost in the Bride's Chamber**
Originally Published in *The Lazy Tour of Two Idle Apprentices*, 1905

## Murder & Revenge

**A Madman's Manuscript**
Originally Published in *The Pickwick Papers*, Chapman & Hall, 1837

**The Convict's Return**
Originally Published in *The Pickwick Papers*, Chapman & Hall, 1837

**The Old Man's Tale About the Queer Client**
Originally Published in *The Pickwick Papers*, Chapman & Hall, 1837

**The Mother's Eyes**
Originally Published in *The Old Curiosity Shop and Other Tales*, Chapman & Hall, 1841

**Well-Authenticated Rappings**
Originally Published in *Household Words*, 1858

**Captain Murderer and the Devil's Bargain**
Originally Published in *All the Year Round*, 1860

## Fantasy & Adventure

**The True Legend of Prince Bladud**
Originally Published in *The Pickwick Papers*, Chapman & Hall, 1837

**The Queer Chair**
Originally Published in *The Pickwick Papers*, Chapman & Hall, 1837

**The Story of the Goblins Who Stole a Sexton**
Originally Published in *The Pickwick Papers*, Chapman & Hall, 1837

**The Chimes**
Originally Published by Chapman & Hall, 1844

**A Child's Dream of a Star**
Originally Published in *Household Words*, 1850

**A Message from the Sea**
Originally Published in *All the Year Round*, 1860

**The Magic Fishbone**
Originally Published in *All the Year Round*, 1868